SOJOURNER

SOJOURNER

VICTOR OF TUCSON ‡ BOOK EIGHT

PLUM PARROT

Podium

Cover design by J Caleb Design

ISBN: 978-1-0394-5558-0

Published in 2025 by Podium Publishing
www.podiumentertainment.com

Podium

SOJOURNER

1

NIGHTMARE MANIFESTATION

Victor and Ranish Dar sat together on a low, freshly oiled wooden pier that extended from the grounds of his mentor's house into the placid deep blue waters of a lake. Sojourn's atmosphere was thin, though the dense Energy of the small world served to make life comfortable for the people living there. The overall effect, however, was that the stars were almost always visible, especially away from the city. It also made the water look dark and almost like a mirror of the star-filled firmament overhead. The lake was beautiful, and the soft breeze tickling his bare chest as he dried off put Victor at ease as he dangled his feet over the edge.

"Enjoying the view?" Dar asked, his bright gaze aimed at the brilliant expanse of stars above.

"How could I not? When I heard the guide say Sojourn was a 'city world,' I'd thought countryside homes and lakes were out of the question."

"Well, it's a small world, and much of it is taken up by the city. People want to be where the action is, so the vast majority of the populace lives in, around, and above its streets."

"Like the, uh, Arcanum where we met?" Victor pictured the floating spires on their stony rune-etched platforms.

"Exactly. It doesn't hurt that grounds such as mine are prohibitively expensive. Those of us who own the lakes, forests, and valleys would charge a dear price for the city to expand."

"But no one owns the sky," Victor said, connecting the dots. "That's why the Arcanum is floating above the city?"

"Perhaps, though it's likely that the first towers were simply put up as a show of power." Dar shrugged and leaned back, basking in the sunlight. "I received word from my driver; your friend is en route."

"Lam? That's great." A knot of tension Victor hadn't acknowledged melted away. Thanks to the way he'd dominated the challenge dungeon, he knew his friends weren't exactly safe around the city. He sighed, closing his eyes, enjoying how the cool water lapped on his shins with the gentle waves stirred by the breeze. "I share Far Scribe books with Edeya and Valla, so when they finish their dungeons, I'll pick them up."

"Providing you're available, aye, that's a good enough idea."

"You think I might not be?" Victor opened one eye and regarded his stone-fleshed host.

"I have tasks and training for you. The city may reach out with one of their demands." He shrugged, both of his blazing eyes still closed. "The future is fickle; don't make too many plans, especially about trivialities. If you're busy, I'll see your friends home safely."

"Fair enough." Victor started to relax again.

"Speaking of tasks, there's the matter of the Fae girl."

"Sora. Right." Victor had been dreading the topic ever since Dar had mentioned it on the coach ride from the city. He didn't like thinking about his time as the Aspect of Terror, let alone looking at the aftermath.

"She'll likely have a fit and regress when she sees you. Well, perhaps not. In your current form, you don't resemble the one who terrorized her. You can make yourself smaller, yes?"

Victor nodded. He was naturally close to Dar's size, closing in on ten feet, and with just the two of them on the pier, it felt perfectly natural. Still, he'd recently improved his Alter Self spell and knew he could bring himself down to a much less intimidating stature if he wanted to. "Yeah. You think I should be smaller when I see her?"

"I do. I'm also quite interested in that spell. I noticed a curious lack of its mention in your journal."

"Yeah . . ." Victor didn't know how to proceed. Dar was easily one of the top five most powerful people he'd ever known, and he didn't want to offend him by lying or holding back information, but he also didn't want to betray Tes's trust. Now that he'd visited Sojourn and learned about some of the power scales of people in the universe, he couldn't help wondering how she'd stack up. She hadn't ever mentioned "iron ranks" or "tests of steel," let alone the "lustrous veil" that lay beyond. He knew those were terms coined by the old masters of Sojourn, but surely other civilizations had names for the same stages. Or did they?

Tes came from a world of dragons, a place where elder magic reigned and the System held no sway. Perhaps things were different in that case. How would Tes compare to Dar? Victor had only seen her true form in a couple of illusory glimpses, but he'd felt her aura, or at least the part of it she'd let loose to make a point. What's more, she'd been altering herself down to the size of a petite human. If Victor changed himself so much, his Core would be a fraction of itself, yet Tes had been starting from the size and shape of a dragon! Even so reduced, she'd been immensely powerful.

"My innocent question seems to have set your mind's gears spinning." Dar chuckled.

"I'm trying to think of a way to explain to you, without offending you, that a very powerful being taught me how to do that magic and made me promise not to spread that knowledge."

"And you fear angering this being?" Dar's stony brow lifted over one eye.

"I . . . fear what it would do to my spirit if I betrayed her trust."

"Ah! Don't lose sleep over it. We've years of study and work ahead of us. Perhaps one day you'll introduce me to this friend of yours, or perhaps you'll realize the secret isn't something you need to fear sharing. It's possible I know more about it than you think." Dar winked at him, and then, with a grunt, he stood, water streaming off his stone legs. Victor shook his head; he kept thinking of Dar's flesh as stone, but he knew it wasn't. It moved and felt like flesh. "Come, it's time you faced your handiwork."

Victor swallowed a groan as it tried to escape his lips, and hopped up, nodding. He summoned a clean pair of pants and a comfortable loose linen shirt. Dar gestured to the house. "I'll meet you on the deck if you want to change."

"Thanks." Victor watched his retreating back, then he quickly slipped out of his damp homemade shorts; he'd cut the legs off a pair of torn pants. He pulled on his dry clothes, shrugged into Lifedrinker's harness, and then, still barefoot, made his way up the long, steep flight of sandstone steps to the house. It was situated on a hill, but the slope was severe enough that Victor couldn't see the house until he stepped onto the upper landing. The back of the residence was set with windows that opened onto a broad wooden deck that overlooked the lake, and Dar stood near one of the big glass doors, waiting for him.

It was a beautiful, well-appointed home, but it wasn't ostentatious. It had a few large living spaces—a dining room, two parlors, a library, and half a dozen or so bedrooms. Everything was open and bright, and Victor had the distinct impression that it was designed as a place for Dar to relax. Victor liked the whitewashed brick exterior walls and the tarnished copper roof; it looked as if it belonged to the rocky, hilly landscape. Soft-spoken servants, all wearing the same uniform of pale blue shirts over tan pants, could be seen here and there, cleaning, cooking, and basically waiting on Dar's every whim.

In the few hours Victor had been at the house, he'd seen at least four different servants, but they all looked related—green skin, yellow eyes, and pointy ears. He was curious whether they worked for a company or directly for Dar, and why they all looked so similar. The topic hadn't come up yet, so he pushed the thoughts aside as he stepped across the deck and followed Dar through the giant-sized glass door into one of the home's parlors.

"The Fae girl is in one of the bedrooms. My steward restrained her for her safety." He didn't elaborate, but Victor could read between the lines. Whatever his alter ego had infected her with might drive her to harm herself. "I'm going to explain what you must do, but then I'll leave you to it. My presence seemed to alarm her."

"Oh, you checked on her already?"

"Yes, while you were swimming, I took a look." They were standing in a hallway now, and Dar nodded toward one of the closed wooden doors. "Fear not; these doors and rooms are enchanted against prying ears. When I examined her, I could see the infection you caused, and while it would be devastating if left unchecked, it's nothing a strong Spirit Caster with the proper affinity couldn't remedy." He inclined his head toward Victor. "It should be trivial for the original caster to rectify."

"Didn't you say the other guy . . . what was his name? I wanna say Eleanor . . ."

"Elandor. Yes, his mentor came to me distraught, but I'll be surprised if he hasn't paid someone to fix the lad by now. I'll check on it before I send you there."

"I thought you were going to give me a choice." Victor's objection was half-hearted. He and Dar both knew he'd do it.

As if to illustrate that point, Dar ignored his words. "When you look with your inner eye upon the girl beyond yonder door, you'll see that your fear-attuned Energy has manifested into a sort of pseudo-spirit and is assaulting her on two fronts. It attacks her Core on this plane, and on the spirit plane, it attacks her very spirit. It's powered by your will, so it shouldn't be difficult to command it to return home. Pull that Energy out of her, and, if you must, spirit walk to claim any that resists."

"Seems easy enough." Victor scratched the back of his neck, wondering if he'd missed something.

Dar was quick to drop the other shoe: "There will be a small challenge involved. Your fear manifestation has been corrupting her Energy, attuning it to fear, making it something you could cultivate if you wanted. You may find it difficult to resist the urge to drain her dry, which would kill her just as surely as if you opened one of her veins."

"Shit. Is that going to mess up her Core?"

Dar clapped him on the shoulder. "Not permanently. Once you remove the influencing corruption, her Core will slowly cleanse itself. You have a powerful will. Use it. Silence your urges and command your Energy to return. This is an excellent chance for you to practice—a safe exercise; if she dies, none will come looking for her."

"What the fuck, Dar?" Victor looked at his new mentor with sudden anger flaring behind his eyes.

Dar scowled at him and shrugged. "I'm simply trying to put your mind at ease. This woman has no family or sponsor in Sojourn. Her homeworld is distant, as are her kin, and none know that I brought her here." His big hand was still on Victor's shoulder. It was heavy, but none of his aura leaked out, and though his face was scowling, Victor didn't feel any anger. Was the man testing him? Was he making light of Sora's life to see how Victor would act?

"I'm not going to kill her." Victor turned to the door and took a step, part of him bracing, wondering if Dar would tighten his grip and stop him, but the giant let his hand drop. Victor stopped before the door, concentrated, and cast Alter Self, shrinking himself back to his old human proportions—just a fit, broad-shouldered man of about six feet. Without looking back, he opened the door and stepped through.

The first thing he noticed was the stench. It smelled like sweat and piss and fear. Idly, he wondered when he'd begun to be able to smell that scent. Had he always? "No," he whispered as his eyes caught up with his nose, and he took in the scene. The curtains were mostly closed, allowing only a sliver of light into the spacious suite. Closed doors on the left and right led away to other rooms, but there, in the main chamber, the space was dominated by a big four-poster bed draped with gauzy pale blue curtains. A table, bookcase, and several comfortable chairs filled the rest of the space.

Victor stepped onto a plush dark carpet and moved toward the bed, noting the shadowed, veiled figure writhing there. He could hear ragged breaths, whispered words, and the soft clink of chains. Victor reached up a hand to Lifedrinker's haft, seeking some comfort as his nerves suddenly turned to ice. He'd seen countless horrors, from monsters to evil men to the terrible aftermath on a battlefield, but this was something different. Sora wasn't a monster. She wasn't a dead soldier. She was a person twisted by the dark side of Victor's spirit, made ill and mad by the force of his will.

Lifedrinker's haft was warm, and he felt strength radiating from her. Suddenly, he felt ashamed. Who was he to hide from his own handiwork? Did he answer to his fear, or did it answer to him? Growling, Victor summoned a torrent of inspiration-attuned Energy and cast Inspiration of the Quinametzin. As his eyes flared with the white-gold Energy, the shadows fell back, driven away by the clarity of his mind. He strode forward, and in three long steps, he was at Sora's bedside, throwing aside the gauzy curtains. She lay there, wrists and ankles bound by padded silver chains to the bedposts.

Sora's eyes were wild, wide open, and bloodshot. Her gray, nearly white hair was a sweat-matted mess, and he could see the sheets around her were drenched—sweat or urine or both, Victor wasn't sure. It smelled like both. She wore the same clothes she'd had on in the dungeon, though someone had removed her leather armor, leaving her in a soft, earth-toned, close-fitting vest over stained tan pants. Her lips were pale and cracked with dehydration, her cheeks devoid of color, and when she briefly focused on him, a whisper croaked in her throat, but Victor couldn't make out the words.

"Shit, *chica*," Victor sighed, reaching down to grasp her wrist. She tried to pull away, but Victor's fingers were like iron bands, his arm an immovable force. Still, he held her gently and willed his inspiration to extend, to include her. "Come on, focus on me. You're okay. Whatever you're seeing or feeling—it's not real." She continued to writhe, her knees going up and down, her hips shifting left and right, her head flopping about on the pillow. It seemed as though she was trying to get something off herself. "Goddamn it," he hissed. "If I'd known this was so bad, I wouldn't have been swimming like an asshole while you were suffering. Fucking Dar should have said something."

Victor's frown deepened, and he closed his eyes, turning his gaze inward, starting with his Core and pathways as he always did to open his inner eye. He quickly let his gaze travel out of himself, and that's when he saw and felt the rich, roiling storm of fear-attuned Energy raging at the center of Sora's being. Despite himself, something in Victor felt excited, like a wolf eyeing a wounded rabbit. It would be so easy to pull that Energy out of her, to add it to his Core, swelling it, pushing it toward another advancement.

Victor looked at the temptation abstractly, almost as if he were outside his body, watching himself figuratively salivate over the feast his corruption had created for him. He squashed that feeling, crushing it into nothing with his will, and then he turned back to Sora and traced the corruption away from her Core into her pathways. He could see his Energy there—almost like an echo of one of his spirit companions, he recognized the shape of his spirit. Dar's description was apt; his spell had created a pseudo-spirit entity that was carrying out his Aspect of Terror's will.

With a surge of focused will, Victor walled off Sora's Core and pulled the corruption, dragging it through her pathways and into his, through the connection where he held her wrist. It resisted at first, hungry to complete its task, but once it felt his touch and tasted the familiar grounds of his pathways, it practically charged toward his Core. It rejoined the glowing ball of purple-black Energy from whence it had spawned. When nothing more came out of Sora, Victor stared for a long time at her Core, watching to see if it would begin to recover, to drive away the corrupted, fear-attuned Energy.

If Dar hadn't warned him, Victor might have tried to help, to siphon away some of that tainted Energy, but he knew better. Her Core needed time to cleanse itself and generate new, properly attuned Energy. If he pulled all of that tainted Energy out, she would die. "Did I get it all?" he asked softly, not expecting an answer. Sora's writhing had ceased, and she lay with closed eyes, still pale and slick with sweat but quiet. Victor kept hold of her wrist, then sat on the side of the bed, shifting her slightly to make more room. He needed to see how things looked on the spirit plane.

He wasn't worried about his body; he was in Dar's home, and there wasn't any way anyone would get to him to cause harm without the powerful Spirit Caster knowing. Additionally, if Dar wanted to harm him, he didn't need Victor to be on the spirit plane to do so. He closed his eyes, built the pattern for Spirit Walk, and flooded it with Energy. When he looked around, the house was gone, and he was sitting on a large flat stone overlooking the twilight landscape of Sojourn.

Before he could take in the vista, marveling at the changes between the world's spirit plane version and that on the material plane, he noticed the coiled, black-feathered serpent on the stone beside him. It was both alien and familiar, and Victor knew it was the manifestation of the pseudo-spirit his Aspect of Terror had created to infect Sora. It watched him through hooded eyes, black with vertical red pupils. As he regarded it, the serpent's tongue flicked out and seemed to lap up some misty white Energy that coalesced in the air before it.

"Is that Sora's spirit?" he growled. The serpent unwound and slithered toward him, but Victor didn't flinch. It was probably four feet long, with weird glossy black feathers adorning its scales that invited his touch as it slithered into his lap, slowly sliding up along his chest, resting against him as if it were coming home. Part of Victor wanted to recoil, but part of him recognized the serpent as part of himself. Its weight was comfortable, its chilly aura a perfect echo to the resonance of his fear-attuned Energy. "Okay, *hombre*. You're done. Leave her alone now and come home."

The serpent's head was on his shoulder, and it lifted further still, bringing its face close to his and looking him in the eyes. Its dark tongue flickered out again, and then it simply burst into a cloud of purple-black smoke. Unlike natural smoke, though, it didn't waft away. Rather, it settled on Victor and sank into him, and regardless of his wants or desires, he felt a massive influx of fear-attuned Energy. Victor grunted in surprise as his Core swelled, stretching to bursting and then compressed with a soul-jarring pulse of Energy.

*****Congratulations! Your Core has advanced: Advanced 9.*****

"Shit," Victor muttered, then he cut the Energy feeding his Spirit Walk spell. As the material world slammed into his senses, he jerked his head, looking at Sora, hoping she was all right. To his relief, some color tinted her cheeks, and her eyes were closed as she breathed deep, steady breaths. He reasoned that the serpent had been the spiritual manifestation of his spell and had been slowly feeding on the corrupted Energy from Sora's Core, siphoning it like a leech.

Using his inner eye, he looked at her Core again and saw it was still roiling with fear-attuned Energy, but that at its center, a tiny pearl of pale shimmering Energy slowly grew. Victor was reasonably sure that as her Core recovered, it would slowly push out the corrupted Energy, and she'd be okay. "Are you in there, Sora?" He squeezed her wrist, still cool to the touch, but then, everyone's skin felt cool to Victor's hot hands.

Her eyelids fluttered, and she took a slow, wheezy breath. It took a few seconds, but her gray eyes finally focused on him. She licked her cracked lips and croaked, "Victor?"

"Hey!" Victor summoned a copper water bottle from one of his rings and handed it to her. "Drink that."

"What . . ." Her eyes widened, and something flickered behind her irises like a shadow, and she shuddered. She squeezed them shut, took the bottle, gulped several mouthfuls, then handed it back. "I'm embarrassed to say that I feel terrified right now. My Energy feels wrong, and I keep having flashes of . . . nightmares. Has my Core been poisoned?"

"Sort of. I removed the infection; it'll recover. You'll probably feel much better if you can sleep until tomorrow."

"You removed it? Why?"

"I caused it! I guess I tore you with my talons or something; it's all a blur to me. I mean, whenever I wear that aspect, things are unclear afterward."

She closed her eyes, and he could tell she relived some painful memories. When they opened again, he could see she had more questions, but she looked around, taking in the gauzy curtains around the bed and the dim room beyond. "Where am I?"

"At my, uh, mentor's house. He had you picked up when he saw you didn't have anyone looking after you."

Sora glanced at his hand, where it held her wrist, then up into his eyes. "Weren't you taller before?" Before he could answer, she asked, "You're not angry?" Her eyes pooled with tears.

"Seriously? I thought you were going to be pissed at me. I mean, you just went through a day of hell."

"It's . . . I don't remember it all." Her voice was quiet and soft, and he could see her eyes getting heavy. Whether she remembered it or not, Victor's nightmare manifestation had done a number on her. He found himself feeling more than a little responsible for her. Learning that she had no mentor or family in the city and that one of Dar's people had found her alone and taken her without any objection—it all felt a little sad.

He recognized the feeling as different than guilt; they'd been fighting, and she'd known the risks. He wasn't guilty. He supposed he just empathized with her. Even he, the only Earthling in this part of the universe, had a support group here in Sojourn. How bad would it feel not only to lose but to find yourself alone afterward?

"All right." Victor shook his head, standing. "Time for you to get some rest. We can talk more tomorrow." His musings loosened his tongue, and he added, "Hey, you know what?"

"What?" He couldn't help noticing how she turned her hand up, her fingers stretching toward his.

Victor took a step back, but he smiled and said, "I guess we're more than just dungeon friends."

2

AN EARNEST APPEAL

Lam sighed and stood, stretching as she took another deep breath of fresh lake air. She'd been relaxing on the little sandy, gravel-strewn beach outside the entrance to the Grotto, reluctant to leave in case Edeya and Darren found something was wrong and came out prematurely. She'd hardly noticed the hours ticking by as she lazily soaked in the sun and listened to the water lapping against the stony shore.

She wasn't the only one who'd been enjoying the day; ten or so others, even a couple with a child, had been picnicking on the sand. It was strange to think that children could be playing just a stone's throw from the entrance to a dungeon. It said a lot about how tame and regulated Sojourn was.

"Guess they're not coming out early." She sighed, brushing the sand off her butt. With just a touch of obsessiveness, she pulled out the Far Scribe book she shared with Edeya and flipped to the last page, ensuring she hadn't missed a message. The last note was still the same: *We're in. Everything's fine—write to you before we camp for the night.* Lam couldn't argue with that, so she tucked the book away and started following the path out of the narrow lakeside gorge. The cave entrance and the beach were at one end, while the access road and public transportation were at the other.

Looking up, squinting into the setting sun, Lam was tempted to flutter her wings and fly to the top, but she saw other flight-gifted folks soaring by occasionally, and she wasn't sure of the etiquette of it all. If she were honest, she might admit that she didn't want to flutter around while people soared past—Ghelli flight was best used for flitting between branches, not gliding through canyons. She'd met a few who were fast and could fly great distances, but they had other, more advanced bloodlines. Lam's race was listed simply as "Ghelli," and when she'd pushed it into an advanced class, her wings had grown, and she had gotten faster, but nothing like how Valla could fly.

"A strange tangent," she muttered, shaking her head. Was she already talking to herself? "I'm not that lonely!" She blushed a little when a pair of youngsters hurried past her, eyeing her strangely as they went. Sighing, she inwardly admitted she was indeed lonely and, on top of that, worried. It was quite normal for her to find odd topics to think about to keep from obsessing over Edeya. To her, it seemed mad to send her into a dungeon after all that she'd been through, but everyone disagreed. Victor was the only one who'd been partially on her side, but only because he worried too much. In a way, his agreement had helped Lam to take a second look at herself and realize she was being just as bad.

Ultimately, it hadn't been anyone's decision but Edeya's. Well, she supposed, Edeya's and Darren's. They were both adults, and they both wanted to go in. "That was that." She sighed, rounding, she was reasonably sure, the last bend before she'd climb a slight slope to the cluster of carts and temporary storefronts. Apparently, many trailheads started at the same point, and people came out this way for recreation, nature walks, and access to not only the Grotto but several other low-level dungeons. The city rented space near the road to merchants—food vendors, general suppliers, alchemists, and even taxidermists who would buy pelts and monster trophies.

As she crested the rise and saw more and more people, Lam took in the eager faces and the bouncing steps and felt a little jealous. What would she have given to grow up in a place like this? What would she have given to have parents who supported her, whom she didn't have to flee to seek a life of fortune, selling her early years to the Empire and its Legion? The thought brought her round full circle to Darren and Edeya, and she nodded, a little pride swelling her chest. If she couldn't have it, then they would. She couldn't have it, could she? A far-fetched idea began to tickle the back of her mind.

"Excuse me, miss," a tremulous voice called from a nearby open-backed wagon. Lam paused and turned toward it, her hand opening, ready to summon her hammer from her ring. A girl, maybe seven years old, looking very much like a little red-skinned Shadeni with red, almost pink irises, looked back at her. She was sitting at the back of the wagon, her legs dangling, and beside her was a box of polished stones.

Lam was curious about seeing a Shadeni there, so she stepped toward the wagon, looking for an adult that might belong to the girl. When she didn't see anyone, she said, "Did you call me?"

"Yes, miss. Are you from Fanwath?" She had a sweet, singsong voice, and Lam smiled at her, nodding.

"How'd you know?"

"My da has friends who look like you."

"Your father?"

"Aye, miss. He works in Lord Warin-dak's household." That statement made everything fall into place. Of course, the Ridonne would bring servants over with them.

"And you, sweetling? What are you doing here?"

"My da drops me off some mornings so I can sell some little enchantments. Luck stones." She smiled with pride, exposing her pointy canines as she gestured to the case of polished rocks.

"Luck stones, hmm?" Lam looked again at the sun moving toward the western horizon. "And you've been here all day? By yourself?"

"Aye, miss. My da will pick me up when he's done for the day in the lord's kennels."

Lam stepped closer, peering at the colorful, smooth stones. "What do they do?"

"Well, miss, I'm a Spirit Caster like my granny, at least that's what my da told me. I was born here in Sojourn, so I've never met her. I have an affinity for luck, and I put a bit of my spirit into these stones while I polish them. If you have one of my stones in your pocket, you'll find things looking up for you!"

Lam narrowed her eyes and looked more closely at the little girl. She didn't seem to be lying. She reached for one of the stones. "May I?"

"Please!"

"Hmm." Lam hefted the little smooth stone. It was striated with shades of orange and gray, but she felt some warmth emanating, just a hint of Energy. "Luck, you say?"

"That's right, miss."

Lam idly rubbed the stone with her thumb, enjoying the sensation. "What's your name?"

"Dalla, miss." She ducked her head subserviently.

"Well, Dalla, I know a very strong Spirit Caster, and he's going to be thrilled to learn about you. Would you mind if I bought a few of your stones?"

"A few?" Her reserved formality faded as her bright eyes widened.

"Oh, aye. I can't buy one for just one of my friends. Let's see. I need . . ." Lam counted on her fingers as she silently recited the names of her friends. "Six of them."

"I sell 'em for three beads each, miss. Is that all right?"

"Oh, sure. Pick me out your best six, and I'll get your payment." While she fished out one of her sacks of Energy beads, Lam couldn't help thinking of the strange coincidence. She'd run into Warin-dak himself just the other night, and now she'd come across one of his servants' children? Was this an elaborate ruse? The stones were harmless, and she couldn't deny the positive nature of the Energy within them. Victor would likely know more—

"Ahem, would you be the Lady Lam?" a stodgy voice behind her asked. Lam whirled, once again ready to summon her hammer, Victor's warning fresh in her mind. She relaxed immediately when she saw a small elderly man with wrinkled green skin and bright white hair. He wore a coachman's livery—a tall black hat, black jacket, and a striped gray and blue shirt tucked into black pants.

She nodded. "That's right."

"I'm one of Lord Dar's coachmen."

"Dar? Oh! Ranish Dar?"

The man nodded, the folds of skin on his neck piling up into four distinct layers. "Yes, my lady. Your companion, Victor, has requested you join him at Lord Dar's lake house."

"Really? My, how things change! Back home, it was I sending coaches around for Victor." Lam sighed, shaking her head, then turned back to the little girl. She carefully counted out eighteen beads into her cupped hands, then added three more and offered her a wink. "Those are for you, just in case your father's counting your profits."

"Thank you so much, mi—" She caught herself, looked at Dar's driver, and quickly said, "My lady."

"Sweet girl, you can call me Lam. I hope we meet again."

"Me too!" Dalla said, quickly looking down. Lam knew if her skin weren't so red, she'd see her cheeks flush with color. She laughed and reached out to tousle the girl's thick black hair.

"Did you pick me six good ones?"

"Aye! The best!" She scooped up a little pile of the stones she'd gathered by her knee. "They're all good, but this one"—she held up a gray, silver-flecked flat stone, about twice the size of Lam's thumbnail—"is very lucky." She smiled again, her sharp white teeth flashing. Lam nodded and took the stones into her palm.

"Then I'll keep that one with me."

"Thank you again, Lady, um, Lam." Again, the little girl ducked her head, and Lam's heart almost burst. Did she want a child so badly? She sighed, gently tousled her hair again, then turned back to the driver.

"Well? Shouldn't you show me Lord Dar's sigil or something?"

"Of course, my lady." The driver opened his black jacket, displaying a complicated pattern on his vest's left breast. It meant nothing to Lam, but from what she'd gathered about Dar and the city of Sojourn, it would be suicide for someone to go around pretending to be a member of his household. She nodded and gestured down the row of carts, wagons, and stands.

"Lead the way."

He pivoted on his heel and began striding toward a hovering, brass-colored metallic conveyance shaped vaguely like a coach—one with no need for wheels or a tongue to tether animals. The inside was spacious, decorated in plush burgundy velour fabric and buttery smooth leather. Lam was the only occupant; the coachman closed her in and entered a different compartment. She sighed, leaning back in one of the soft couches, and opened the perfectly tooled little cabinets, curious about what a man like Ranish Dar stocked in his coach.

As her stomach flipped, indicating the vehicle had lurched into motion, she found a collection of liquors and crystal tumblers. Lam smiled as her mouth began to salivate at the idea of a strong drink; she'd been too stressed lately. Didn't she deserve to let go a little? Edeya was "safe" in the dungeon; none of Victor's enemies could reach her there. Lam nodded to herself and poured a quarter glass of a rich, caramel-colored liquor into it. The smell wafting from the glass reminded her of decadent spices and brown sugar. The first sip altered that opinion as she coughed, wondering if her breath had turned to fire.

The second sip went down easier, and Lam was certain the liquor was her new favorite by the third. She wasn't sure how long the ride took because, as the tension left her body and the warm buzz of the alcohol brought a silly smile to her face, she began to doze. Of course, her half-waking thoughts were focused on Edeya. She saw her smile and heard her laugh. She watched her shouting, her face fiercely determined as she worked to be just as tough as Victor and the other deep delvers. The coach vibrated slightly, startling her awake, and Lam chuckled as she tried to snatch at the dream, adding it to her waking memories. When was the last time she'd thought of the mine? What a strange life!

"We've arrived, Lady Lam," the coachman said, standing just outside the open door. Lam yawned and stretched, then, graceful as a cat, slid out of the coach and onto the pink and tan cobbles of a walkway leading to a charming little estate with a tarnished copper roof and whitewashed stone walls. In the distance, she could see a long narrow landlocked lake, its waters so dark and reflective that they looked like a mirror to the dark, starlit sky.

"Lovely," she said, smiling.

"Yes, my lady. Lord Dar is proud of this property. He and your friend await within." He gestured toward the house.

"Excellent." Lam nodded to him, fished out a handful of Energy beads, and held them out. He accepted them with a smile, and Lam winked, breezing past. At least that was common ground between Fanwath and Sojourn—the servant class was eager for a few extra beads. Or, she supposed, he may have been humoring her. Perhaps she'd just gravely insulted him. The idea made her laugh, and she enjoyed her sudden good mood. A green-skinned bald man with sharply pointed ears stood near the front door and pulled it wide as she approached.

"Welcome, Lady Lam. The Lord and his guest are on the rear deck. Shall I guide you?"

"Just point the way, good man." As he did so, she paused on the threshold and gave him a closer look, peering into his yellow irises. "Tell me, what's the hour?"

"Just past seven."

"Ah, not so bad. I had such a restful ride in Dar's coach." Lam stretched again, then asked, "Does your culture see gratuities favorably?"

"Gratuities are always welcome, my lady."

"Ah, that's a relief." She smiled and handed him a few Energy beads. "Thank you for your candor." She followed his directions, walking through the foyer, past a small library, a well-appointed parlor, and then into another living area with great crystal-clear windows open to a deck and the picturesque starlit lake beyond. She saw Dar and Victor right away, standing near the far railing, each holding a glass, talking animatedly. Other green-skinned servants bustled about, nodding deferentially to her as she passed. She stepped onto the smooth polished decking and said, "Lovely place you have here, Lord Dar."

The two men stopped talking, and Victor smiled brightly, his eyes twinkling in the starlight. Dar's eyes were blazing like tiny suns, per usual, but he offered her a smile and gestured for her to approach. They were both gigantic, making her feel small—an absurd notion considering she was a foot taller than an average Ghelli. Still, as she approached, she had to crane her neck to continue looking them in the eye. "Welcome to my lake house, Lam. Victor's told me a bit about you today; I understand you've a few lovely properties of your own."

"I have some nice homes and recently have gained some beautiful acreage, but this is something quite different. Standing here, with the lake below us and the night sky above, it almost feels like we're soaring through the stars!"

"Aye! That was my thought when I chose this spot to build. I rather enjoy your description. I may use that to impress the next guest I invite out this way." Dar gestured toward one of the servants and said, "Bring Lady Lam a glass of the forty-year Rovahl."

"You're going to like it, Lam," Victor said, grinning, and Lam realized his cheeks were flushed; was the giant idiot drunk? She supposed if anyone had liquor that could get the titan buzzed, it would be Dar.

"Your young protégés are safely ensconced in their dungeon?" Dar asked, leaning on an elbow, likely putting a tremendous strain on the railing, as he tried to lower himself more to Lam's level.

"Well, I'm not sure that's the right word." She didn't know what she'd call Edeya, and to avoid having to think about it too much, she turned the topic to a target closer to hand. "One time, I might have tried to call Victor that, but he quickly outpaced my grasp."

"I know a very abbreviated version of Victor's history. He mentioned the mine and your role in his escape. I understand you must have been walking a fine line, trying not to anger the lords and ladies you served while attempting to retain some semblance of morality."

"I . . ." Lam sighed, and it was her turn to feel flushed. How did the topic get around to this? "I'm not really proud of that time, Lord Dar. Things changed when I met Victor and took Edeya under my wing. I used to do anything possible to improve my lot, to gather wealth and power. I sought a place among the nobility, too blinded by my ambition, my desire to reach a place of respect among them, to see that there were other ways to surpass them. I'm happy to say that, rather than pay homage to their gatekeepers, I joined with Victor, and we made our own gate."

"You disagree with the notion of nobility?" Dar asked, and Lam wondered if she'd just put her foot in her mouth.

"The notion of it?" She glanced at Victor and saw that he wasn't really drunk by the clever gleam in his eyes. He nodded, and Lam pressed on. "I have a problem with nobility as it pertains to people being born into positions of power. I'm far more impressed by those who earn their power."

"Hard to argue with that." Dar nodded. He gestured to her right, and Lam turned to see one of his servants holding a tray out to her, a tumbler like Victor's, but smaller, at its center. She lifted the chilled crystal and smelled the amber liquor within. It reminded her quite a lot of the alcohol she'd helped herself to in Dar's coach. A sip confirmed it was the same stuff, and her smile widened as her tastebuds woke up.

"Excellent stuff, Lord Dar."

"It's one of my favorites. Well, Lam, tell me, what will you do with yourself for the next few days?"

"Honestly? I had an idea, Lord Dar. I know Victor's going to be learning from you for the next, um, few years." She knew she was making an understatement; Victor had agreed to ten years of servitude, though honestly, it didn't exactly look as if Dar intended to make him work in a quarry.

Victor shifted, perhaps uncomfortable with the reminder. Lam smiled and fluttered her wings, sending motes of golden Energy sparkling down behind her. She watched as both men's eyes followed the motion, distracted as people always were by the display. She fished her hand into the pocket where she'd stowed Dalla's stone and gently rubbed it with her thumb. Grinning, she continued, "Dar, might I bargain for your help?" She purposefully left off his honorific.

"Hmm?" He looked into her bright emerald eyes. "I didn't expect this. Should I sober up before I hear your proposal?"

"I would think a great man such as you could match wits with a lowly soldier like me, no matter the drink involved!" Again, she fluttered her wings and leaned closer, resting one of her hands on the railing between Dar and Victor.

"What's this got to do with me serving Dar, Lam?" Victor's tone proved her right; she was making him nervous.

"Well, if you're going to be in Sojourn for years, and Edeya's going to be here learning and challenging dungeons and . . . other things, I don't see me running back to Fanwath to live."

Dar took a big sip from his very large tumbler of alcohol. "Go on."

"Well, when you saved Edeya, and she lost all those levels, you mentioned something I found very intriguing. You said something to the effect that there were powerful people who paid greatly for opportunities to have a second run at gaining their levels and classes, that they sought out master Spirit Casters to perform something very much like what Edeya went through."

"This is true." Dar nodded.

"Lam—" Victor started to say.

Lam put her hand on Victor's wrist, startled by how hot his flesh felt. She licked her lips, swallowed, and in a rush asked the question, uttering the idea she'd barely realized she'd formed in the back of her mind. "Well, what would it take for me to get you to do that to me? What favor or price could I pay to get you to wash away my accumulated Energy and bring me closer to Edeya's level?"

3

DINNERTIME

As Lam uttered her request, Victor felt his eyebrows shoot up, and even Dar grew quiet, staring with his blazing eyes into Lam's. Was she serious? Victor couldn't imagine the Lam he knew giving away most of her levels and power. He found his brain scrambling for explanations. Was it all about Edeya? Was she going through some kind of identity crisis? He knew Kethelket had saved her from Catalina; had that near-death experience made her reconsider her strength, seeing weakness where once she'd seen power?

While his tongue was tied with too many questions to choose from, Dar simply said, "Why?"

Lam smiled, perhaps taking the lack of an instant refusal as a good sign. Victor saw her thumb moving, rubbing against her palm or something small she clutched there. She looked up, her eyes filling with moisture as she gathered her thoughts. "Many reasons," she finally said.

"I'd like to hear them before considering your request." Dar's voice was softer than Victor had ever heard; there was no grating of boulders for Lam, but rather the soft susurration of gravel washed along stone by a gentle stream.

"To begin with, there's the obvious," Lam said, wiping her eyes and smiling. "I love Edeya, and I want to be close to her. It could take years for her to approach my level. Meanwhile, I'll find it hard to advance, knowing I'd continue to leave her behind. Valla and Lesh invited me to their dungeon dive; part of me wanted to go, but another part hated the idea of gaining another level while I'm already nearly forty ahead of Edeya."

"How do you love her? As a mother? An older sibling? In such a role, being more powerful is natural, it's . . ."

"Not like that," Lam said, smiling and, to Victor's horror, blushing. What had become of the stoic champion he'd so idolized? *Blushing*?

"Ah." Dar nodded. "What else?"

"I had a base-tier class until twenty. I've only had an advanced class since. I was preoccupied with fast levels and gaining wealth; I took classes with those short-sighted goals in mind. I'd like another chance to make those selections, to earn more powerful options."

As Dar nodded, she continued, "More than anything, I crave the experience of adventuring with friends and learning for the sake of it. I never had friends or companions when I was at a low level. I joined the Legion, and everything was competitive; everyone was scheming. The few friends I made died or moved on, constantly transferred. I didn't see my first dungeon until I was Tier Three, and that wasn't a fun experience, though I did make a valuable ally." She looked at Victor and smiled. "Polo."

"Ah," Victor said, nodding as he finally found his voice. "Is this really something people do, Dar?"

Dar leaned back on the railing, causing the wood to creak ominously, though he seemed unbothered by the sound. "Very few, for obvious reasons. First, it takes a great leap of faith to relinquish decades' worth of growth for the chance at a second run. Few people consider their lot so bad that it's worthwhile. I had an heir to an imperial throne from a world called Rikahl as a supplicant because he'd failed to earn the class all of his forefathers had held. He gave away eighty-nine levels. I wonder how he did on his second attempt . . ." Dar rubbed his chin, shrugging. "Well, no matter. The second reason is that only a few Spirit Casters on a handful of worlds know how to perform the ritual. Yes, and I suppose there's a third factor: cost."

Victor sighed, knowing Lam had nothing Ranish Dar needed. He could only think of one thing that might pique the Spirit Master's interest, and there wasn't any way he was giving that up, not unless it meant saving someone's life—the ivid royal jelly. Lam, apparently, didn't share his pessimism. "I'm not one to be scared away by high costs, Ranish." Victor almost snorted, hearing Lam use Dar's first name. Had he heard anyone call him Ranish?

"No. No, Lady Lam, I'd be inclined to believe that statement. You've quite a determined look in your eye. In fact, you remind me of my young protégé here. It's no wonder you took to each other when he was naught but a slave."

Lam looked at Victor, and when their eyes locked, Victor couldn't help smiling. He remembered the first time he saw her back in the mines, how he'd been utterly struck dumb by her beauty and power. The memory made him consider what she was asking of Dar in a different light; she was fearless. When she saw something she wanted, she took it. If she couldn't, she changed her life around that goal until she could. He nodded, deciding to take up her cause. "You should do it, Dar. Earning Lam as an ally is worth it—she has a spine of solid steel."

"Is that what you're offering, Lady? An alliance? A favor owed?" Something about Dar's tone and the way his eyes blazed gave the words a lot more weight than their simple nature warranted. Dar was a man who might be thousands of years old; he had the patience to make long, long bargains.

Lam seemed to understand the weight of his words, too. She locked her emerald eyes on Dar's blazing ones, and her green irises sparkled with the reflected light. They stared at each other for several long seconds, and then she nodded. "If that's what you're asking, then that's what I'll pay."

Dar straightened up, and Victor imagined the railing breathed a sigh of relief. Dar gestured for Lam to sit down around a small outdoor firepit one of his servants was stoking. The chairs arranged around it were of various sizes. Some were just right for Victor or Dar, but several were perfect for people of Lam's stature. Once they'd all taken a seat and were comfortably looking at one another over the faintly crackling fire, the master Spirit Caster said, "I'd like to explain a few things to you before we continue this negotiation."

"I'm all ears, sir," Lam said, suddenly more deferential.

"Ensure you pay attention, Victor. This may become one of your first lessons." Victor was already quite piqued, but the idea that Dar might teach him how to do the apparently secret ritual really got his attention. He nodded and leaned forward as Dar continued speaking. "Lam, you need to know that there's some risk involved. What you ask for is known as a type of resurrection. We'll have to take your spirit from your body, leaving behind a tiny shard that I'll cleave from the whole. Once that's done, the ritual, which I won't explain at this time, will require the greater part of your spirit to pass through a crucible, testing it and burning away your Energy to protect it in the process. Your spirit, newly reforged, will be reunited with the tiny shard in your body, bringing you back to life with a stronger spirit and broader karmic ties. You'll have a new chance at all the things for which you yearn."

Lam's eyes were wide, and she leaned forward, hanging on every word of Dar's. As he finished, she nodded and fervently whispered, "Yes."

"However!" Dar held up a thick, stony finger, wagging it back and forth. "The crucible must be designed with precision, providing the perfect resistance to your spirit's passage. If I miscalculate, or if your will is too weak, you may not make it. You may fade from this plane of existence, lost to wander the spirit plane until such a time that you gather the Energy to breach the veil and begin the journey meant for all once-living spirits."

"Do you think you can do it?"

"Oh, aye, I think so. I've been wrong about important things before, however. Bear that in mind." Dar looked at Lam and seemed to like what he saw. He nodded and said, "Dinner then. We'll toast to our bargain, Lam."

"Truly? You'll do it?"

"I'm here in Sojourn to recover and amuse myself between tribulations. Victor has already proven his value in that regard, but I wouldn't mind seeing what you do with yourself if given a second run. I'll hold you to your word, however, Lam. There's no escaping an oath to a master of the spirit."

Lam launched herself out of her chair, and her wings veritably blazed with golden motes, showering the deck in a carpet of bouncing, sparkling Energy as she fell to her knees before Dar, grasping one of his great stony hands in her slender, tanned, well-scarred fingers. "Thank you, Lord Dar. Thank you!"

He nodded, suddenly sober. "You thank me now, Lady Lam, but someday you may find yourself cursing my name." When Lam's expression didn't waver, he nodded and said, "Victor and I can perform the ritual. I have plans for him in two days, but if you're ready, we will do it tomorrow."

Victor was almost startled by the use of his name. "You have plans for me . . ."

"I'm ready!" Lam said earnestly, cutting him off.

"Tomorrow, then. Victor, this will be a good lesson for you, and the day after, a good friend of mine, Lo'ro the Grim, will help you start work on a cultivation chamber."

Victor heard him, and he nodded, but his mind had drifted back to Dar's words to Lam. Someday she may curse his name? Was he trying to say that the payment he took, whatever favor he collected, would be unbearable? He didn't doubt that Dar could collect what he wanted; he'd keep tabs on Lam, and she'd never be able to outstrip his power before he came calling. Half his mind wanted to warn Lam off, to discourage her from bargaining with the man; wasn't one of them under his yoke enough? The other half thought about how he'd feel. If someone tried to talk him out of doing whatever he could to be closer to Valla or acted as if he was too weak or stupid to enter into a bargain . . . Victor shook his head at the thought—enough to say he'd be pissed.

"Why not you?" he asked, suddenly snapping back to the current topic.

"What, boy?" Dar's chuckle sounded dangerously like a growl. "I use up a precious favor to have one of the most powerful men in Sojourn spend his equally precious time helping you earn the heart of your cultivation chamber, and you dare to imply that I . . ."

Victor held up both hands in surrender. "No, no! I didn't mean it like that. I just meant, is there something your friend can do that's, I don't know, like, a specialty?"

"Yes. He can pierce the veil in the spirit plane and open a gateway for you. With Lo'ro's aid, you'll find spirits twisted into manifestations of your affinities. You'll need to capture and bring them back to add to your chamber."

Victor's mind painted wild images for him at those words. He'd seen Belikot trying to pierce the veil, pulling spirits through to inhabit his undead armies. It didn't surprise him that Dar's friend could easily do what Belikot had been working for years to accomplish, but it also gave him pause. "I've seen tormented spirits brought through the veil before. They weren't happy to be enslaved . . ."

"I'll leave the finer explanations to Lo'ro, but you won't deal with intact, mindful spirits. You're going to be looking for spirits who have been twisted beyond rationality by their obsession with certain darker emotions. Can you guess which ones I mean?"

Victor didn't have to think very hard. "Fear and rage."

"In one try!" Dar chuckled, snapping his fingers with a loud *crack*. He turned back to Lam, still kneeling on the floor before him. Her eyes had gone distant as she either listened to their side conversation or, Victor guessed, thought about what she'd just agreed to. "Dinner?" Dar raised one side of his stony brow.

"Yes!" Lam jumped up, her wings fluttering to make the move look magical. Victor laughed and also stood. He was hungry and all too willing to push his darker contemplations aside. He'd had a hell of a few months—years, even—and he was pretty damn sure Dar wasn't going to be easy on him, so he planned to grab any chance he could to enjoy life. If Lam wanted to be happy right now, if she wanted to celebrate, then Victor wouldn't throw shadows on the occasion.

"All right," he said, "I'm fuckin' starved!"

Darren lifted his boot from the cold water onto the stone and smiled, realizing his feet had survived the passage without getting wet. "These are damn good boots," he whispered. Edeya had already scolded him several times for being too loud.

"Victor appreciates good footwear." She laughed, making herself a hypocrite. She visibly winced as her high-pitched voice echoed down the partially submerged passage. "Sorry," she whispered.

"Do you think anything's down there?" Darren pointed to the opening they'd spied upon rounding the bend. So far, they hadn't encountered anything other than cold damp tunnels, stony caves, and lots and lots of lichen, moss, and probably mold. Darren wasn't great with identifying fungi and the like, but it seemed like all sorts of things were growing in the grotto.

"I've never heard of a dungeon without monsters and traps, so yeah, be ready," Edeya whispered, shifting her grip on her spear. "Make your light a little brighter." Since he had no other abilities to use his Energy on, he was in charge of providing the light. He pushed a little more Energy into the little faintly buzzing orb of red electricity floating above his head, and the sparks intensified, losing some of their red tint and shedding a lot more light in the dark tunnel.

The walls lost some of their gloomy shadows, and the lichen and fungi brightened, displaying a remarkable array of colors.

"Oh, nice," Edeya whispered. "It's not as red when you brighten it."

Darren nodded, feeling proud of his light for some stupid reason. He chuckled, gripped his staff, and gestured toward the tunnel opening. "Shall we?"

"We shall!" Edeya grinned, and he saw her spear blade start to rime over with a thin layer of frost. He'd learned she had a water affinity, which allowed her to deliver extra cold-based damage with each strike. She said she had other, more potent spells but that she'd have to wait to use them until her level increased and she gained more attribute points and, consequently, more Energy. She stalked toward the opening. His light reflected off the shimmersteel rings on the back of her vest, and Darren pressed his palm to his own chest, reminding himself he had armor on. He didn't know if he was terrified or excited, but his hands felt shaky, and his breaths were quick and shallow.

"Okay, Darren," he mouthed, not really vocalizing, "get it together. It's a newbie dungeon. Edeya's a good fighter. We got this." Just then, Edeya stepped through the opening and froze. When he caught up to her, she pointed, and Darren followed the gesture, taking in the enormous cavern. It was wide but had a low ceiling, covered with more moss or whatever the green, orange, yellow, and white fuzzy stuff was. Water dripped from a dozen shallow points into pools, and about halfway across the expansive space, Darren saw some honest-to-God frogmen lazing about, in and around a large pool of water.

"Frogmen?" he whispered an inch from Edeya's ear.

She flinched and brushed at her ear, and he could see she wanted to scold him, but she regained her composure and nodded. "Never seen 'em before, but they look amphibian. See the clubs?"

Darren nodded, eyeing the big polished yellowed bones some of them clutched. He scanned the cavern, trying to get a count, and came up with five. He whispered as much: "I see five."

Edeya nodded. "Same."

"Is there a chance they're friendly?"

Edeya slapped a hand over her mouth, stifling a snort of laughter. "Friendly frog people? In a dungeon?"

"I guess that was dumb." Darren sighed. "What's the plan?"

"Let's channel our inner Victor," Edeya said, grinning wickedly.

"Uh—" Darren pictured Victor smashing his tanks, charging headlong into ordnance that would've turned an average person to paste. "There are five!"

"I'm Level Seven! C'mon, Dare! Get my back!" Before he could object further, she turned and charged, spear gripped tightly in both hands. Darren stood dumbfounded for a moment, watching as she fluttered her blue, dazzling wings like a dragonfly, turning a hop into a twenty-foot leap, clearing one of the pools of water. She came down, stabbing her spear into one of the lounging frogmen.

Darren's eyes widened as he saw the freezing Energy stored in her spear rush out into the little humanoid's flesh, freezing a significant portion of its torso. It croaked and thrashed weakly, and then the other frogmen jumped into action, clamoring in a cacophony of alarm. Their croaks echoed in a dozen different tones throughout the cavern.

"Shit!" Darren said, realizing he was still standing there. He lifted his quarterstaff over his head and charged, skirting the pool of water Edeya had flown over, aiming for her right flank. Meanwhile, she began to dash and fly about, dodging the frogmen's retaliation and delivering punishing blows with her spear. It was clear to Darren, for the first time, that she really did know a thing or two about fighting. The frogmen might be a mottled green with yellow spots, but their blood splashed bright red as Edeya laid about with her wicked, enchanted ivory spear.

Darren arrived in time to crack his staff into a frogman's skull, shocking himself with the decisive blow. Victor had promised the staff was enchanted to increase its bludgeoning damage, and Darren was inclined to believe him after hearing the crunch of bone. Considering how Edeya was thrashing the frogmen, Darren realized there had to be more than the five they'd counted. It was hectic in the melee, but he swore he counted more than five still up and about, warbling, croaking, and flailing with their primitive weapons. Darren used his quarterstaff's reach and his superior height to keep them at bay, delivering jabs and overhead chops whenever possible.

"Good job, Dare! Keep 'em busy!" Edeya shouted, and a spray of something hot hit him on the back of the neck. He spun to see she'd impaled a frogman holding a sharpened bone that might have managed to stab him in the ass if not for her intervention. "Don't stare at the dead ones! Look behind you!" Darren whirled, swinging his staff in a wide arc out of reflex. The length of heavy, polished wood cracked another frogman in the side of the head and carried through to drive back another two.

Just as he began to fear they'd be overwhelmed, the handful of frogmen left standing began to try to flee, and Edeya pursued them, stabbing them in their backs. She was relentless and fast, using her wings in bursts, streaking forward on showers of blue Energy motes to drive her spear home over and over. Darren knew he couldn't keep up, so he watched her flitting around the cavern, finishing them one by one.

He was leaning on his staff, amused by the show and proud of their victory, when he heard a wet *thwap, thwap*, and turned to see an enormous toad, probably two hundred pounds of warty green-brown flesh, crawling out of the pool behind him. It opened its wide mouth, bulged out its huge yellow eyes, and croaked a challenge.

"Ah, shit," Darren said, lifting his staff, holding it sideways before himself as Lesh had told him to do when he needed to defend. "Edeya!" he called. Then the frog flicked out its big pink tongue. It was faster than Darren's eye could follow as it streaked out and slapped against his armored chest. "Ha!" he chortled when it didn't even hurt. Then, as it began to tug him forward, he realized it wasn't trying to hurt him. It was trying to eat him.

4

GROTTO TALK

Darren panicked. His first instinct was to pull back, but the damn toad was twice his weight, and its tongue, well, it had to have some sort of magical effect because it wouldn't loosen its sticky grip. When he found himself losing the tug-of-war, he slammed his staff into the rubbery pink flesh, hoping to knock it loose, but only managed to get it caught in the sticky slime coating its surface. "Son of a bitch!" Darren yelled, a note of hysteria tinging his voice. He bunched his legs and, with everything he could muster, leaped backward. He was awarded for his efforts; the tongue ripped free from his armored vest, but he also lost his grip on the staff.

Darren scrambled backward, his hands scraping over the damp, stony cavern floor, his feet scrabbling for purchase as the toad struggled with the eight-foot length of hardwood it had inadvertently pulled into its maw. Suddenly, motes of blue Energy showered Darren as Edeya flitted over his head, streaking toward the monstrous amphibian, spear out like a lance.

She drove it straight into the soft cream-colored flesh under the monster's mouth, punching the frost-coated silvery blade all the way through until it poked out the back of its neck, up near the base of its skull. Frosty rime spread from the devastating puncture wound, and the toad flopped onto its belly, legs splayed, red and yellow fluids gushing from its burbling lips.

Darren was on his feet in an instant, pumping his fist. "Nice one!"

"Good job keeping it busy, Dare!" Edeya laughed, jerking her spear free. She scanned the cavern, ensuring nothing else would jump out at them. Then her eyes lit up, and she said, "Are you ready?"

"For?" Darren looked around, trying to see what was coming.

She pointed to the first cluster of frogmen she'd fought, and he saw tiny orbs of golden Energy gathering in the air above them. "Your first Energy infusion!"

"Ah!" Of course, he'd heard tales of the System awarding battle victors some of the Energy from their defeated foes. He looked back to Edeya, and sure enough, there were now a few fat blobs of Energy drifting up from the dead toad. They gathered in two clumps, one a bit larger than the other, and as he watched, they streaked toward them, one directly to Edeya and one to him. The other motes of Energy around the cavern had done something similar, so both adventurers were struck by several thin streams of Energy at once.

"Holy cow!" Darren said, inadvertently using one of his father's favorite exclamations as the Energy poured into him. It wasn't like anything he'd ever felt—shudders and chills wracked his body as he tried to wrap his mind around the physical euphoria that almost felt orgasmic. He swore he saw stars and flashes of rainbow light, and when it ended, there was a message before his eyes—faintly transparent white letters on an opaque gray background:

*****Congratulations! You have achieved Level 2 Base Human. You have 5 attribute points to allocate.*****

"It's true," he breathed, finally experiencing what so many of his colleagues back in First Landing had tried to explain to him. He looked at Edeya and saw her smiling at him, her big gold-flecked blue eyes bright in her lean, angular face. She looked vibrant and alive, far more than he'd ever seen her. "Did you level, too?"

"Nope, but I reckon I'm close. You're Two now?"

"Yes." Darren leaned over, bracing his hands on his knees, still feeling woozy from the burst of Energy. A few seconds later, he saw the butt of his staff thump into the stone before him and looked up to see Edeya grinning as she offered him his weapon.

"Gonna allocate your points?"

Darren smiled and took the staff, standing up to lean on it instead of his knees. "I guess I should. Lesh says I should focus on will and vitality."

Edeya nodded, rubbing her chin. "I agree, especially after knowing Victor. I bet you wouldn't guess his main attribute."

"Uh, *strength*?" He said it as though only an idiot would think otherwise.

"Wrong—will."

"Seriously?"

"Yep. But he cheats; somehow, he can use his spirit magic to add some of his will to his physical attributes. So, in a way, you're right." She thumped him on the shoulder. "How'd your master tell you to do it?"

Darren sighed and chuckled. "I know you're trying to get a rise out of me. Lesh isn't my 'master.' Anyway, he said to put five into vitality at Level Two, then five into will at Level Three, and alternate like that until Ten. He thinks it will result in me getting some class options that will complement my affinities at Level Ten."

Edeya frowned. "He wants you to try to become some kind of spell flinger? No, no, I suppose not. He'd have you take intelligence and some dexterity, too. Lesh is a strange one, but he knows a lot. I guess do what he says."

Darren shrugged. "I suppose it'd be foolish not to take advice from someone with so much experience."

"Still, even if you wanted to be some kind of lightning master, you're going to need dexterity, too—weaving complicated spell patterns isn't easy. I guess at Level Ten, depending on what kind of class you get, you can cross that bridge."

"Yep." Darren had already made up his mind that he'd follow Lesh's advice. So, as Edeya surveyed the cavern, he opened his status sheet and added all five of his new points into vitality. Back in Sojourn, when he'd imagined this moment, he'd wondered what it would be like to boost his vitality by five full points, nearly doubling his starting amount. He was a little disappointed by the reality. Thanks to the Energy infusion, he already felt fantastic, so he hardly noticed anything more—some general well-being, maybe, but it was impossible to tell if it was all in his head. Nevertheless, he looked at his status sheet with pride.

Status			
Name:	Darren Whitehorse		
Race:	Human: Base 1		
Class:	-		
Level:	2		
Core:	Wildarc Class: Base 1		
Energy Affinity:	Lightning 8, Chaos 7.4, Unattuned 6.1	Energy:	97/97
Strength:	6	Vitality:	12
Dexterity:	5	Agility:	5
Intelligence:	9	Will:	3
Points Available:	0		
Titles & Feats:	-		
Skills:			
System Language Integration		Not Upgradeable	
Wildarc Cultivation Drill		Basic	
Spells:			
Arclight Wisp		Basic	

"All done?" Edeya asked, and Darren realized she was staring at him again.

"Yep!" He looked around, wrinkling his nose at all the bloody, slumped figures of dead frogmen. "No treasure?" He'd heard things about dungeons. Shouldn't there be a chest or something?

Edeya shrugged. "Not that I could see, but maybe this dungeon doesn't award special chests, or maybe it does, but only after we find a boss or something."

"What did your book say?"

"There are definitely reports of special awards and System-generated loot. I just don't know where exactly. This dungeon changes its layout and monsters regularly."

Darren nodded, scanning the periphery of the cavern. "I don't see an exit . . ."

"Lucky for us, I have a water affinity. I can feel the extent of these little pools with my Core sight. I think that one near the wall over there is a passage."

"Core sight? Oh, like your inner eye? What you see your Energy with?"

"Yes. C'mon!" She fluttered her wings and sort of hop-glided toward the pool she'd mentioned. Darren trudged after her. She was already slipping into the water when he caught up. "Ugh! It's *cold*!" She visibly shivered.

"We're really getting in there? What if more frogs . . ."

"It's just a short swim under this cavern wall. I'll go first and try to spy out any trouble." She must have noticed his perplexed expression because she added, "It's not deep! You can walk on the bottom and just duck when you slip under here." She splashed the water near the wall, and Darren saw a curtain of mossy growth sway with the current. "Put your staff in your storage pouch."

Darren nodded and did so, then sat at the edge of the pool, sliding into the water, clothes and all, just as Edeya had done. Meanwhile, with a ripple of the chilly water, she ducked into the passage and disappeared. His light still hovered above, illuminating the scene, but Darren keenly felt her absence. The water wasn't cold enough to take his breath away, but it wasn't comfortable, so he hurried toward the wall, hoping to follow Edeya and quickly be out of it. He'd just gotten there and was lifting the curtain of slimy growth to peer into the darkness when she came back into view, her nose and eyes barely above the water.

"It's clear, come on." She winked, then turned and went back into the darkness. Darren followed, relieved to feel the smooth, unobstructed nature of the stone under his feet. After a few steps into the narrow watery tunnel, the ceiling dipped, and he had to hold his breath for a few steps, but then his light revealed the water lapping above him, and he poked his head up into another cavern, this one much smaller.

Edeya sat on the edge, watching him as he approached. "Good job, Dare!" Her pleasant enthusiasm brought a smile to his lips, and he nodded, pulling his long damp hair back from his face and wringing it with his hands as he stood up in the shallower end of the pool.

"Should we put on dry clothes?"

"You're wearing the clothes you bought in Sojourn, right?"

"Yeah . . ." He, Edeya, and Lam had gone shopping in preparation for the dungeon dive.

"They'll dry on their own."

"Oh! I knew they'd self-repair and clean; I guess it makes sense they'd dry faster."

"Yep." She turned and pointed toward a waterlogged door in the little cavern, revealed by the glow of his floating light. "Look—a door. Want to take a minute for a snack before we continue?"

Darren hopped out of the pool beside her, noted some nice flat stones between the pool and the door, and shrugged. "Yeah. This seems a good spot."

Edeya nodded and picked one of the natural benches to sit on. As Darren sat beside her, he rethought that assessment; the stones were worn smooth in the center as if they'd been used for just that purpose many, many times. "You think the frogmen used these as seats?"

"Maybe. It's a dungeon, so there's no telling what's natural and what the System designed. I have no idea how all that works. Does the System take things from the worlds it governs and place them into its dungeons? Does it just create copies of things it has seen? I wish I knew."

Darren nodded and fished a sandwich out of his storage pouch. "Yeah. I wish the System would speak to us. I have so many questions." Edeya nodded, chewing on a piece of bright yellow fruit. She looked vibrant and full of eager excitement. Darren couldn't help blurting, "You look fantastic. I can't believe you're the same person that we guided to Sojourn . . ." He trailed off, realizing he might be treading on a sensitive topic.

"Don't worry, Dare. I don't really remember that whole ordeal. When I first woke up, I could remember little flashes of it, almost like how you remember a nightmare. Now, though, it's like looking into thick fog—I know something's there, but I can't remember what it is for the life of me."

"You don't remember what that . . . um, Death Caster, right?"

Edeya nodded and sank her teeth into the fruit with a loud *crunch*. "Right, Death Caster," she mumbled around her large bite.

"You don't remember what she did?"

She chewed and swallowed and said, "I remember her wrapping me up in her creepy mist, and then . . ." Edeya closed her eyes, and her brows furrowed, but she shook her head. "And then it's all fog."

"Well, I'm glad you're okay. I know I never knew you before, but I heard plenty from Lam."

Edeya's eyes twinkled. "She spoke about me?"

"Oh yes! I could tell she was desperate to see you recover. Um, are you two related?"

"*What?*" Edeya almost choked on her bite.

"Oh, um, well, you're both Ghelli, right? And I saw how worried she was; I just sort of assumed she was . . ."

"We're not related!" Edeya laughed. "She loves me, though." As her cheeks flushed, the picture cleared up in Darren's mind.

"Ah, I'm an idiot." He chuckled and chewed his food for a moment, then added, "I should have realized."

"We're not, like, sexual or anything. She's told me how much she loves me, and I definitely love her too, but we're just . . . close for now. I'm younger than she is, and, yeah, we just want to be close." Edeya shrugged and grinned at him. "Ghelli are different about that sort of thing, Dare. We share spiritual connections a little more tangibly than some other species. Lam was suffering so much when I first met her! She didn't really know it, but when I got hurt, and Victor left me with her, she started caring for me, and through that, we built a connection." She held her hand over her heart. "In here"—she moved her fingers to her forehead—"and here. She realized how empty her life had become—she'd separated herself from the people she once loved, and Dare, Ghelli don't do well alone."

"Oh? Why was she alone?" Darren felt his neck heat up and winced. "Am I overstepping with that?"

Edeya laughed. "The old Lam might have beaten you up for asking, but I think she'd happily share her story with you. It's her story, but I'll just tell you the abbreviated version. Anyway, it's not complicated: She wanted to adventure, and her family didn't want her to leave home. She ran away, joined the Legion, and then spent her time pursuing wealth and power. When she met me, I was, well, I was sort of a slave, and she was in charge of me."

"What?" Darren's mouth fell open. "She was a slave master?"

"Not . . . exactly. She worked for the mine as a mercenary, leading crews of diggers deeper and deeper, but while the miners worked, she was exploring, looking for artifacts and monsters to kill. So, I guess the diggers, like me and Victor, would have been down there with or without her. Oh," Edeya laughed, shaking her head, "I'm being silly—she knew working for the mine was wrong. She's sorry for it now. If it matters to you, she helped Victor and his friend Thayla escape, and then she took me under her wing and left the mine's employ."

"So, she was out for herself down there? Using the mining company as a means to explore and gain wealth?" Darren shrugged. "Sometimes, we have to work within a corrupt system. I know all too well how one compromise can lead to another and another." He sighed and took the last bite of his sandwich, chewing as he thought. After a while, when Edeya was done eating and sat there sipping from her water flask, he said, "I'm glad you both found someone who makes you a better person. I mean, I'm assuming Lam's good for you in some way, yeah?"

"Oh yes, Dare!" Edeya laughed. "She inspires me! You don't know what a strong person she is—impossibly brave, loyal to a fault, and Roots protect the fool who harms someone she loves!" She laughed, clearly savoring a private memory. Darren brushed the crumbs off his surprisingly dry pants, then summoned his water bottle and took a long drink. While he was screwing the cap on, Edeya said, "Ready to find our next encounter?"

Darren stood, summoned his quarterstaff, and said, "Yep. Let's get another level!"

"That's the spirit!" Suddenly, Edeya's spear was in her hands, and she turned to the door.

When Darren saw her spear start to frost over with ice, he asked, "Do you think I'll learn any spells before I gain my class at Level Ten?"

"Hmm?" Edeya paused and turned back to him. "Yeah, I bet you will. Honestly, I bet I could teach you the spell that lets me put ice Energy into my spear now that you're level two with a little more Energy. I bet we could alter it to make it simpler. Part of the pattern turns my water affinity to ice; if we took that out and you used your lightning-attuned Energy instead of water . . ." She shrugged. "I bet it could work."

"Really? I can learn spells from patterns?"

"Yes! When you learned your light spell, we taught you how to channel Energy into the air through your pathways. Once the System saw you do it, you gained the spell, right? Now, you can see the pattern in your pathway when you cast the spell."

"Right . . ." Darren nodded, squinting his eyes, trying to guess where she was going.

"So, if I drew you the pattern for my Frost Touch spell, you could build it in your pathways with lightning Energy from your Core. That would, in essence, cast the spell. The System would recognize what you did, and you'd gain the spell knowledge. At least, that's how I've learned a couple of spells. Most of the ones I learned came from levels in a particular class, though."

"Is it a complicated pattern? Would it be hard?"

"There's no way I could write out one of my Tier Two spells, not until I boost my dexterity and intelligence from some levels, but Frost Touch is pretty darn simple." Edeya frowned and looked at the closed door. "Want to try it? It shouldn't take too much time."

"I have some paper!" Darren said, mentally digging through his pouch.

Edeya laughed and proceeded to drag one of the heavier stones in the room in front of the door. "Let's make sure we're not interrupted. I think this will be worthwhile; the dungeon will go faster if you're doing some lightning damage!"

5

HORSEPLAY

The following day, Victor rose with the dawn and walked, barefoot and shirtless, out to the deck to greet the warm light of the sun. The house was quiet, and one of the servants looked up from dusting and polishing the furniture and told him that Dar was already gone, seeing to one errand or another, and wouldn't be back until noon. It wasn't a surprise, really; Dar had impressed on Victor his lack of a need for sleep. Victor had meant to ask him if it was some quirk of his species or a result of his advanced level, but their conversation had moved quickly away from the topic, and it hadn't come up again.

"Next time," he sighed, stretching, yawning, and wondering if his idea to take a quick morning swim was still a good one or if he should get some breakfast—something smelled delicious.

A soft, sleepy voice startled him by speaking up from one of the lounge chairs. "Up with the sun, mighty berserker?" Victor took a few steps forward to better see the speaker's face and confirmed what his ears had already told him: Sora was up and about.

"Feeling better?"

"Much!" She yawned and stretched. The blanket she'd obviously brought out from her room slipped down over her shoulders, exposing the gossamer thin garment she'd been sleeping in. Victor smiled and looked away; he couldn't be sure, but he was starting to suspect she was coming on to him. She wouldn't be the first, not since he'd helped lead an army to victory in the Free Marches and become something of a celebrity back home. Once people learned about and saw Valla, though, they tended to back off.

"Been out here long?"

"I woke in the early hours, and Lord Dar suggested some fresh air. He said the sunrise might help my day start on the right foot."

"He spoke to you?" Victor leaned on the railing, still looking out at the water, watching as its dark, mysterious depths took on the orange glow of the sunrise.

"Yes, he looked in on me before he left. Quite a nice mentor you have, if frightening."

"I wouldn't really know. We only met a few days before the dungeon."

She didn't respond for a moment, and when she did, she changed the subject. "Look at the sky—see how it streaks with color? It's the only time this world reminds me of home. I'm used to a sky that's blue as an agate and stars that know they're only supposed to reveal themselves at night!"

"Yeah," Victor grunted. "Same."

"Not much of a talker, are you? Even in the dungeon, you were rather reticent with your words."

"Eh, sometimes I talk too much. I'm trying to learn to listen and choose my words more carefully." Victor shifted to lean on one elbow so he could look back at her. Her hair looked more silver than gray in the sunlight, and her cheeks were flushed with vibrant color; she looked fully recovered. He said as much. "I'm glad what I did to you in the dungeon didn't cause any permanent harm."

"No. I'm well, and that ordeal feels like a bad dream. It grows fainter by the minute." She had to squint, looking at him with the sun in the background. "Did you mean what you said yesterday?"

"Hmm?"

"About us being friends?"

"Yeah, sure." Victor smiled. "I'm new in town. It's good to make friends, right?"

"Even after my betrayal?" Something flickered behind her eyes, and she narrowed them. "Can you tell me about the others? Did any of them die or . . ."

"Your friends? The ones you ditched me for?" Victor grinned, enjoying watching her expression reflect the emotions playing out: concern, shame, irritation, embarrassment. He didn't see any fear, though, and that made him happy. "Nah, they're all okay. Even the nature guy; I guess his people paid someone Dar knew to remove his affliction."

"Affliction?" She looked confused, and Victor realized she probably didn't have a clue about any of the fights he'd gotten into in that dark cavern.

"Yeah. He had the same problem as you."

"Ah." She nodded and once again pulled her blanket up to her chin. He wondered if he saw a shudder run through her or if she'd just felt a bit of a chill on her nearly bare shoulders. "When you say the others are all fine, do you mean you didn't eliminate them?"

"Nah, I did. All but that Death Caster. What was her name?"

"Arona. She defeated you?"

"No, no." Victor chuckled and moved to sit in the lounge chair next to her. "We got kicked out before she and I fought. There was a . . . problem with the dungeon. Anyway, she's fine and doesn't seem to hold a grudge. I can't say the same about the others 'cause I haven't spoken to any of 'em."

"Well, the only one I know well is Brontes, and he won't hold a grudge, not after I tell him you helped me recover."

"Yeah, I was going to ask you about that. Dar said you didn't have any family or sponsor here, but you seemed pretty friendly with Cam and seemed familiar with quite a few of the others. How's that?"

"We're all of a similar rank, so we run into each other often in the dungeons around the city. There are also plenty of friendly competitions and social gatherings." She shrugged and smiled. "I'd have to be a real recluse to avoid making a few acquaintances here."

"Dar thinks some of the people I knocked out will want revenge. He thinks they might go after my friends."

Sora frowned and turned onto her side, looking more directly at Victor. "You have some friends here? Any family or"—she smiled slyly—"anyone important?"

Victor chuckled, nodding. "Someone very important, yeah, but she's not the one I'm worried about. I have a couple of low-level friends who are much more vulnerable."

Sora's frown turned into a wistful smile as she turned onto her back, breaking eye contact. "Well, I hope I get to meet this lady of yours. I'm sure some of the rich folk around here will be throwing parties to celebrate this or that. I'm surprised you haven't been inundated with invitations."

"Her name's Valla, and I'm sure she'll enjoy meeting you. Right now, she and another friend are in one of the city dungeons. As for invitations, I mean, it's been less than a day. Dar will let me know." He sniffed the air, his stomach rumbling at the scent of pork and fresh bread. "Are you hungry?"

"I am, but I should get going." She stood, her blanket still clutched tightly around her, suddenly a good deal more demure.

"Why the rush?"

"My neighbors are probably worried, and I should write to my family. I . . ." She shrugged. "I just want to be home and take some time to decompress. I lost five levels in that dungeon, which will have repercussions on my finances."

"Really? Your finances?"

"Yes. I have a fund at Voyage Trust, but my family may cut me off when news of my . . . setback reaches my homeworld."

Victor blinked, his mind dumbfounded by the idea of interplanetary banks and trust funds. As everything slowly settled into place, he nodded. "That's how you paid for the exception for your dimensional quiver and bought your entry into the dungeon?"

"Yes. I make a decent living adventuring around the city, but not enough to run with the crowd in the challenge dungeon." She shrugged. "So, I'm off to plead my case with my family and to try to avoid getting called home."

Victor nodded but then remembered something he'd meant to ask her. "Hey, hold on. Before you go—any chance you might sell that cloak you got in there?"

"The set piece?" She wrinkled her brow. "You didn't seem impressed by it in the dungeon . . ." Understanding dawned in her eyes. "You got more pieces?"

"Yeah, I've got four."

"Well, I could try to take advantage of you, but you'd learn fairly quickly that people sell those blank set pieces at auction fairly often. I bet you could get a cloak like mine for twenty or thirty thousand beads . . ."

"I'll give you thirty." Victor figured he could shop around for another piece and maybe save some money, but thirty thousand beads wasn't a lot to him anymore, and he sort of felt sorry for Sora, seeing as she was about to beg her family for money.

"Sold!" She laughed. "That'll cover my rent for a few months. Maybe by then, I'll be back in my family's good graces." She held out her hand, and the silky, dark gray garment appeared, draped over it. "You know, the set bonuses aren't cheap, and the best ones require you to provide magical materials."

"Oh yeah? Well, that's all right; it'll give me something to work for." Victor fished around in his dwindling Energy bead supply until he found a sack with nearly the right amount in it. He summoned it out of the storage ring and handed it over. "There might be a few hundred more or less in there."

"That's fine. I know we'll be seeing each other." She grinned mischievously and added, "That cloak smells like my perfume; don't let your lady get the wrong idea." Before Victor could think of a witty reply, she shuffled, wrapped in her blanket, into the house, and he heard her asking one of the servants about a ride back to the city. Her words got the better of him, and he lifted the cloak to his nose, giving it a good sniff. She hadn't been lying—a distinct floral scent lingered.

"No big deal," he muttered, sending the garment into the storage ring with the other set pieces. He was eager to go to the Sojourn City Stone to see what the deal was with the set bonuses, but he wasn't sure when he'd get the chance. Dar and he were supposed to help Lam with her ritual that afternoon, and the next day, apparently, he was going to be taking a field trip with Dar's Death Caster buddy. He almost reached up to grab Lifedrinker's haft for comfort, but he'd left her in his bedroom, which reminded him of his original intent for coming out to the deck dressed in nothing but his comfortable, loose-fitting linen pants: He'd meant to go for a swim.

He turned back toward the lake and took the steps, two at a time, down to the pier. He dove, sending his pants into his storage ring as he flew through the air and plunged into the water. It was chillier than he remembered it from the previous afternoon, and it instantly invigorated him.

Victor swam for quite a while, laughing and diving, endlessly entertained by his body's capabilities. He could hold his breath for minutes and minutes, and his Quinametzin eyes could pick out the flicker of shiny scales on fish and the long, colorful drifts of strange aquatic plant life dozens of yards beneath him.

After a time, he surfaced to find Lam sitting on the pier, her feet dangling into the water. She laughed when he burst out of the water in a shower of bubbles and spray, leaning back to avoid the worst of it. "It's cold, you big thunderak!"

Victor was anything but cold after swimming for a while, and he laughed with her, wiping his nose and face. "You should swim and warm yourself up!"

She shook her head. "I don't have lava for blood."

"Neither do I." He laughed again. "I don't think!" He brought back his hand, acting as if he was about to splash her, and Lam squealed, leaning further onto the pier.

"Don't!" she shrieked.

"Did I find the great Lam's weakness? Brought low by a bit of slightly chilly water?"

Still smiling, Lam sat up, kicking one foot out to send a splash his way. "Stop it now, or I'm going to tell Valla." Her mention of Valla made Victor wonder how she and Lesh were doing in their dungeon, which made him remember why Lam wasn't with them. His smile fell away as he regarded the emerald-eyed Ghelli. She looked happier and more youthful than he'd seen her in a long time.

"You look like a weight's been lifted," he said, treading a few yards from her, glad the water was dark because he was naked as the day he'd been born.

"I feel so good, Victor. I slept last night more than I have in months. I just woke!" She squinted toward the sun. "It must be midmorning, and I'm usually up at dawn."

"That's great. Edeya's gonna freak out when you tell her you can go in the next dungeon with her." He chuckled, adding, "And Darren."

Lam *tsked*. "Oh, be a little easier on that poor man. He's trying very hard to impress you and Lesh, you know."

"Yeah, I know. My first impression of him has been hard to shake, but I gotta give him credit. I thought he'd be begging to go home long before now. I'm pretty surprised he agreed to go on a dungeon dive at Level One."

Lam nodded, leaning so her neck and upper chest were exposed to the morning sun. "It doesn't hurt that Edeya basically told him he was coming. She's been good for him."

"She can be persuasive." Victor chuckled.

"Roots! I remember thinking you and she would get in trouble back in the mine, flirting the way you did!"

"What the hell?" Victor's jaw fell open. "We weren't flirting!"

"Oh, please, Victor. You might have a stoic, brooding face most of the time, but when you're talking to a pretty girl, you sure light up. Edeya got a lot of laughs out of you."

"I was mostly trying to cheer *her* up, if I recall correctly . . ." Victor tried to shrug in the water, letting his arguments fall away. Why did he care? "Truth is, that time isn't so clear in my mind. I think I was a little too stressed to build good memories."

"Understandable. Let's put it behind us, hmm?" She gestured expansively at the lake and the horizon beyond. "We're starting a new chapter."

"You're starting *over*!" Victor couldn't resist sending a small splash her way, darkening the fabric of her rolled-up pants.

"Brat!" Suddenly, her wings began to flutter, throwing off motes of golden Energy, and she launched off the deck toward him. Victor was too surprised to put up much of a fight as she landed on his shoulders, pushing down on his head, trying to dunk him under the water. He took a breath and went down but didn't stop there. Snatching one of her ankles, he dove further still, completely submerging her. He was amazed to see her wings continue to function underwater, spreading their golden light in the dark water as they buzzed, exposing his nakedness. In a panic, he dove further down and summoned some underwear to pull on before reengaging. That began an hour of horseplay that left them both starved and ready for a good brunch.

Dar's ubiquitous serving folk delivered platters of savory meats, fresh bread, and fruit on the deck while he and Lam let the sun and soft breeze dry them off. They were mid-meal when the Spirit Master returned, arriving on the back of a misty flying serpent with glowering yellow and green eyes. Victor was sure the serpent was a spirit companion because as soon as Dar leaped off its back, landing on the decking, wringing forth creaks and groans from the sturdy wood, the creature dispersed like smoke in the breeze.

"You look well, children," he observed in his booming voice, sitting on the opposite side of the table.

"Children?" Lam asked, arching an eyebrow.

"Well, to me, surely so. It's been a very long time since I was your age, dear Lam." He glanced over the table and picked up a fat greasy sausage. He tucked it into his mouth, chewed twice, and swallowed it. "I'm glad you're eating a hearty breakfast. This ritual will take a lot out of us all. Did you enjoy the lake?"

"Yeah," Victor said, spreading jam on a slice of fresh, dark, buttery bread. "I'm damn jealous, to be honest. My little house . . ." He thought about the many complaints he might utter about his townhome and decided to keep it simple. "Doesn't have a nice lake out the back door."

Dar snorted and leaned back. "Ha! Someday, Victor."

"He has millions of acres with beachfront property back home, though," Lam said, nudging Victor's shin with her toes under the table.

"Yeah . . ." Victor shrugged.

"Perhaps in a month or two, you can visit and check on things, hmm?" Dar said, surprising them both.

"Really?" Victor asked, pausing his food shoveling.

"Why not? After reading through your journal, I've begun to devise some training for you in the near future, which may involve that world." As Victor and Lam both opened their mouths, he held up a hand. "I won't say more because I'm still thinking about it, and there may be better opportunities I haven't considered. For now, just know that I'll certainly allow you to visit and check on your properties sometime relatively soon." As Victor nodded, taking a large bite, Dar continued, "I suppose you may have wondered where I went this morning?"

"I did!" Lam nodded, and Victor grunted his agreement.

"Lam's ritual required a few ingredients I didn't have handy here at the lake house, so I took a morning flight out to the Arcanum. The weather was beautiful, but then it usually is in Sojourn." He sighed, closing his dark eyelids, instantly extinguishing the fiery orbs of his eyes, and Victor wondered what he was thinking about. After a moment, though, he inhaled deeply, opened his eyes, and said, "Are you ready, Lam? The perfect time is nearly upon us."

"So soon?" Lam gulped her last bite of food and pushed her plate away. "Um, yes! Yes, I'm ready, Lord Dar."

"Very well." He pushed himself up from the table and gestured to the house. "Come, you two. We'll perform the ritual in the cellars."

For some reason, Victor was nervous, and when he glanced at Lam, he knew why. What if Dar made a mistake? What if his mistake was trusting Victor to help with the ritual? What if they did something wrong and Lam didn't make it through? What if they miscalculated and her Core was destroyed, or she was reduced to a shadow of herself? Could something like that happen?

Dar must have seen the concern on his face because he clapped his shoulder with one of his boulder-like hands and said, "This is going to be an important lesson for you, Victor." He nodded to Lam. "Yes, there's much at stake, but all the best things come with risk." He smiled, exposing his glittering, diamond-like teeth. "You know, I really am a great teacher, aren't I, Lam? Did you hear that drop of wisdom?"

"I did, Lord Dar. Victor is fortunate!" She grinned and winked at him, and Victor sighed.

"Is this what the next few decades will be like? Maybe I should piss off the council some more so I can get thrown in jail or something."

Dar nodded, squeezing his shoulder. "You jest, but that was certainly on the table at that inquest. Why, it was a much closer thing than I let on! It's better that you avoid the dungeon beneath the council building, lad."

"Do you mean dungeon as in . . ."

"As in filled with monsters and traps. Many a dangerous Energy user has been banished into that particular pocket dimension, never to return." While Victor stewed on that, Dar led the way into the house and then through the kitchens to a stairwell situated at the rear of the pantry. It was a spiral, metal affair that led straight down into darkness. "Come now, we've work to do. There's a natural cave down here that will be just right; its echo on the spirit plane has the perfect resonance." With that, he started down, his bulk causing the stairs to creak with each step. Lam looked at Victor, raised her eyebrow, and then shrugged, following. Victor set his face in a determined mask and began his descent.

6

SPIRIT RITUAL

"You see," Dar said, gesturing around the damp, dome-shaped cave, "the space offers excellent resonance. Not as perfect as something constructed for the purpose, but very good, nonetheless."

Victor didn't know exactly what Dar meant by resonance or even "the purpose," but he tried to fill in the blanks and sound as if he had a clue: "You mentioned something about the spirit plane?"

"Correct. Tell me, Victor, when you spirit walk from within a city, how many buildings do you see on the spirit plane?"

"Usually none."

"Exactly!" Dar gently ushered Lam toward the center of the cave. "Take a seat there on that smooth section of stone. Assume a cultivation pose and try to tune out our conversation; you should be working to still your mind and prepare for a difficult ordeal."

"Oh." Lam looked around the cave, illuminated by a bright white globe of Energy that Dar had summoned. She suddenly looked less than enthusiastic, and Victor couldn't blame her; this was a massive leap of faith she was taking. Nevertheless, she steeled herself and moved to sit where Dar had indicated.

"So, Victor," Dar asked, "if a building doesn't exist on the spirit plane, can we use it to focus Energy, creating our crucible for Lam's spirit?"

"No, but I've seen structures on the spirit plane. Would it be possible to—"

"Build something more precise than a cave beneath my home? Certainly! Though it would take years to force the essence of such a structure to bleed into that realm. This natural space is perfectly fine, and I think Lam would rather not wait."

"You're right, sir," Lam grunted as she sat and assumed a lotus position on the smooth stone.

"Stand close, Victor," Dar said, "and listen to what I say. I'll be using some spells you've not learned, but this will be a good learning experience, nonetheless.

Your primary role in this ritual will be to supply large amounts of Energy as I construct the crucible."

"All right." Victor moved closer to the large stony man. Dar wore one of his signature pajama-like sets of silken clothing. They were the color of habañero peppers and looked very comfortable as he gracefully sat before Lam, his large frame dwarfing hers.

"Listen, Lam; part of this ritual involves me separating a part of your spirit to keep safe and secure in your body. It will be the anchor that pulls the rest of your spirit home through the crucible Victor and I will construct around it."

"I see." Lam licked her lips and nodded, her eyes darting to Victor and then back to Dar. Victor wanted to sit beside her, to put his arm over her shoulders and protect her. He banished the impulse, knowing there was a lot more to Lam than her current nervousness. She was a walking incarnation of determination; if she wanted to succeed, she would.

"To that end, you'll need to slip into a cultivation trance, opening yourself to the Energy around us. That will help me access your spirit from the spirit plane."

"Is that all?"

"No, that's only the first step. While you're meditating upon your Energy, I need you to focus your thoughts on the part of yourself that's most stubborn, most willful, and most defiant. Using your focus, I'll be able to carve that aspect away, and it will be that shard, with heavy, deep roots, that I'll leave anchored in your body."

"How do I focus on that?"

Surprising himself, Victor answered, "Think about all the times you've been denied and all the times you've risen up to take what people said you couldn't have. Think about when you fled home. Think about how you rose in the Legion despite captains who tried to keep you down. Think about how you used the Greatbone Mining Consortium to gather wealth and power, taking a noble title when the old nobility tried to keep you under their boots. Think about—"

"I think I have it, Victor. Thank you." Lam's eyes shimmered with unspent tears as she smiled at him. Maybe she didn't think he'd paid attention to all those things, but he had.

"Good." Dar nodded and then motioned for Victor to sit beside him. "We'll spirit walk now, Lam. When you've done what I instructed, we'll know it."

"Should I summon my coyotes to watch us?" Victor asked.

Dar shook his head. "My guardian aspect will watch over us, apprentice. Save your Energy, for I'll use every drop."

Victor nodded and sat down, forming a triangle with Dar and Lam. He felt a small surge of Dar's Energy and knew the master had sent his spirit onto the spirit plane. Before following him, Victor looked at Lam and said, "I know you can do this."

"I know, Victor. Thank you for your confidence and for being here with me. If something goes wrong, please tell—"

"Nothing's going to go wrong!" Victor growled.

"Please tell Edeya I loved her, and don't let her know what I was doing when I died."

"Damn it, Lam!" It was one thing for her to contemplate failure, but now, if the worst happened, she wanted him to lie to Edeya.

"Please?"

Though he didn't like to admit there was a chance she'd fail, he forced himself to contemplate it and be serious. He took her hand, pressing her calloused, narrow palm with his thick, equally calloused thumb. "You don't want to carry that kind of burden out of this world, Lam. Don't leave Edeya here with a lie, and don't make me be the one to deliver it. This isn't the sort of secret that would make her life easier. You're not doing this only for her, and she needs to know this side of you, the side that's willing to risk everything for a better shot."

Again, her eyes filled with tears, and she pressed her lips together, clearly stifling some emotion as she slowly nodded. "Okay, Victor. You tell her, then. Tell her I loved her with everything in me."

"I will, but stop this line of thought. Focus on what Dar told you. You aren't going to fail this. Your spirit is fucking strong, *hermana*."

She took a deep breath, squared her shoulders, and nodded, pulling her hand free and resting it atop her knee. "Okay. Go. I'm sure your mentor wonders what you're doing."

Victor nodded, closed his eyes, formed the pattern for Spirit Walk, and cast it. When he opened them, he sat in the spirit plane's strange echo of the cave. Weird wisps of Energy flitted about in the dark, glowing with faint lavender light and turning the cave into a mysterious, magical place. Dar's spirit-self paced about, carving runes into the stone floor with a rod of solid, peach-colored Energy. "You had words with her?" the man rumbled.

"Yeah. She had some doubts, and I tried to get her focused on success." Victor stood as Dar grunted his acknowledgment.

"Last-minute nerves are common in any high-stakes endeavor." He gestured with his weird glowing orange rod. "This is a manifestation of my Energy. I use it to impart my will upon this tiny piece of the spirit plane. These runes will hold our Energy, funneling it into a pattern that will test Lam's spirit, forcing it to shed Energy to pass through, stripping it down to her most essential, most vital essence. I could try to explain each rune as I work, but they all will require a lesson, and each lesson could take hours. We don't want to turn this ritual into a weeklong affair."

"Will I ever learn them?" Victor asked, moving to peer down at one of the runes with its swirls and jagged lines. They reminded him of something he couldn't quite put his finger on.

"Of course. You'll learn some of them as I teach you rituals, and I'll also give you a text to study." Dar moved and began carving another of his magical glyphs into the stone, and Victor decided it was a good time to voice a concern he'd only partially acknowledged himself.

"I'm not sure I'll be in my current townhome for long, and it sounds like this cultivation chamber is a big project. Shouldn't I wait until I have a better, more permanent place?"

"It can be moved. It's a large task, but as you gain more power and wealth, you'll want to do so in any case." He looked up from his task, made eye contact with Victor, and nodded. "You'll want to create a chamber in a portable room, something you can take with you from world to world on adventures and journeys." He sighed and turned back to the glyph he was carving. "Such a portable space, capable of holding the Energy of strong cultivation treasures, is not something an iron ranker will likely come across. Not unless he's fabulously rich and can have his family purchase it for him at auction."

Victor narrowed his eyes and absently reached for his neck, but the vault wasn't present on the spirit plane. "I . . ."

Dar snorted. "Have a fabulously wealthy mentor who will absolutely not spoil you to such a degree."

"I was going to say I might have something like that already."

"Doubtful. Still, if you think I'm wrong, we can look at what you have to evaluate the possibility."

Victor nodded, dropping the subject; he didn't want to show Dar the vault until he'd hidden the ivid royal jelly somewhere else first. He trusted Dar, to a degree, but had no idea how an old monster like him would react to such a treasure. On many levels, Dar and his peers believed that might made right, and he very well might see Victor's possession of such a treasure as a mere formality.

He bided his time and watched Dar work and, after a while, began to notice a shimmer of pale yellow mist at the center of the circle of runes. When he stepped toward it, he had an overwhelming sensation of being close to Lam. He could smell her faintly musky, cloying perfume mixed with her sweat. He could hear her laugh, her battle cry, and her desperate pleas for Edeya to wake. He could see her bright emerald eyes, the glitter of her wings, and the shimmer of golden Energy around her war hammer. He could feel her hard, muscular arms squeezing around his ribs. All those things combined into "Lam," yet when he took a step back, all he saw was the misty yellow blur in the air.

"She's opening herself well. You're feeling her spirit, yes?"

"Ah!" Victor nodded, suddenly understanding. "Yeah, I can definitely feel her."

"Another fifteen or twenty minutes, and I'll have the circle prepared. Then we'll begin charging the runes." He gestured with his free hand. "Come. Watch me closely. Even if you don't understand the runes, you'll benefit from the experience."

Victor did as he was told, following Dar as he moved about the circle, seemingly at random, tracing one glowing glyph after another into the stone cavern floor. Meanwhile, Lam's spirit became more and more palpable as she opened herself to the spirit plane. While watching, Victor asked, "Is everyone open to the spirit plane when they cultivate?"

"To some degree, aye, though Lam's in a place where the barrier between planes is very thin, partly because of the nature of this cave, but mostly because you and I are currently spirit walking here, our spirits have pierced the veil, and they hold the doorway open for our return."

"Veil? Like the veil to the land of the dead?"

"No, a more generic sense of the word. There are many veils separating the various planes, universes, and realities. The veil to the land of the dead is far more commonly mentioned, primarily thanks to Death Casters and their fascination with it."

"But—" Victor couldn't help but fish for answers to questions that had plagued him ever since he'd learned about Belikot and his death-attuned magic. "What is that place? If the spirit plane is where spirits wander, what's through the veil? The one the Death Casters are obsessed with? I mean, I met Old Mother on the spirit plane, and she had no intention of going—"

"It's complicated, Victor. Our spirits are influenced by our lives and our beliefs. When your Old Mother died, she believed she would wander far as a spirit and start a new life. Her belief strengthened her will, and she made it so. Some people have no such conviction, and they'll wander the spirit plane for a while until their inertia fades, their lingering personality disperses, and they succumb to the pull of one of the places beyond the veil. There, they may wallow and wander for millennia or even eons before something happens to spark their desire to begin anew. Alternatively, some force, some god or equally powerful entity, pulls them out, and they make their way into another material plane to begin a new life."

"So, what you believe affects what happens to your spirit?"

"Exactly so. For that reason, I'm convinced there are many heavens and many hells created from the combined force of will of millions of spirits believing one thing or another. Not everyone is lucky enough to be a Spirit Caster, walking around without their body long before they die, learning the universe's secrets before their time. Your Old Mother has likely already wandered far and chosen a wonderous place to begin anew."

"So the place your friend, Master Lo'ro"—Victor tried to show the proper respect—"is taking me is through that veil, but will he know where we are when we step through?"

"Oh, he'll have his theories. It could be some version of a hell or limbo, but it won't be a nice place; you're looking for tormented vestiges of intelligence. It may seem cruel, but you're likely doing those spirits a service, bringing them forth and exposing them to repeated contact with your will. It may shorten their torment by thousands of years." Dar stood, and his glowing wand of Energy disappeared. He brushed his hands off, looked around the circle, and nodded. "Done. We'll charge these sigils with Energy, strategically intermixing our harsher affinities with our more encouraging ones. We must test Lam's spirit, but we must be careful to ensure she makes it through."

"Are you going to split off a shard to keep safe in her body?"

"Only when we're ready to begin will I pull her spirit through, entrapping it in this circle. Then we'll return to the material plane with her shard and coax the rest of her home through this crucible." He clasped Victor's wrist in his massive, surprisingly soft hand and pulled him toward the edge of the circle. "When I tell you to channel a certain Energy, do so; I'll guide it into the sigil."

"Okay." Victor nodded. "Ready."

"Fear," Dar said. Victor pulled a ribbon of the dark, purple-black Energy out of his Core and sent it through his pathways into Dar's hand, where it gripped his wrist. Dar grunted his approval, knelt, and touched a sigil with his other hand. It flared with the dark Energy. "Good!" He moved his hand to a nearby sigil and said, "Rage." Victor switched his pull, driving some of his red, angry Energy into Dar's hand, and a second later, the sigil flared with crimson fire. So it went on for nearly an hour. Dar led him around the circle, lighting most of the runes with fear or rage, but occasionally, he'd ask for glory or inspiration.

When Dar finally released his wrist, he said, "Rest now. I'll charge the rest." Victor saw that he'd only helped charge about half the runes. He nodded and sat down near the misty essence of Lam's spirit, watching as the giant pajama-clad man nimbly stepped around the circle, effortlessly charging each rune with taps of his bare toes. Some flared with golden, sparkling Energy, others with orange light that reminded Victor of Dar's rune carving rod, and still others were populated with cold gray Energy that filled Victor's heart with dread if he looked too long upon it.

"Stand," Dar said, startling Victor out of his ruminations. He blinked, wondering where he'd gone; he'd lost himself looking into those cold gray runes. "Watch now as I reach through this aperture into Lam's Core and pull forth her spirit." He didn't wait for Victor to acknowledge his words. He just did exactly what he said he'd do; he pushed his thick black hand into the misty golden Energy hanging at the center of the circle. He seemed to concentrate for a couple of seconds, then he pulled his hand back, gripping the ethereal, translucent shape of Lam's spirit by the wrist.

She was naked, with wild hair and blazing wings, and she looked furious. Her eyes scanned the cave, but they didn't seem to see Victor or Dar. Victor averted his gaze, somehow feeling dirty looking at Lam's nakedness, wishing he could banish that glimpse of her breasts from his mind. "She won't be aware of us. Her senses on this plane are wanting. This is her defiant aspect, the tough, willful piece of her that you helped her to focus upon. When we return to the material plane, I'll bring this part of her with us, but the bulk of her spirit will be left behind."

"Why can't I see the rest of her spirit?"

"Well, because this aspect is overbearing—when I pull it home, what's left will look similar, though likely less . . . angry." Dar chuckled, watching Lam's spirit crouch, hands out, ready to claw anything that challenged her. Victor had never seen such a fierce expression on her face, not even when he'd watched her fight.

"Are you sure she doesn't need that part of her to fight through the crucible?"

"She may, but it's better to have her strongest aspect in her body, clinging tightly to her flesh, forcing the rest of her to come home." Dar clapped Victor on the shoulder. "I know you're worried, but trust me, boy. I know what I'm doing. Let's return now." This time, rather than lead the way, Dar watched Victor until he nodded and severed his connection to Spirit Walk.

When he returned to the dim, natural cave, he found Lam slumped over, staring at the stone floor, drool running down her chin. As he reached out to wipe the saliva from her face and gently push her mouth closed, Dar moved, grunting. He was back in his body, and he reached out to touch Lam's forehead. A flash of golden Energy told Victor the Spirit Master had put the defiant fragment of Lam's spirit back inside. Her eyes sparkled momentarily, but then she slipped back into catatonia.

"Now, Victor, you will take her left hand, and I'll take her right. Together, we'll urge her spirit fragment to call the rest of her spirit home. We'll lend her Energy for the fight, and her spirit will push its way through the crucible we constructed. When it breaks free and comes home, Lam will be whole but greatly reduced in Energy potential."

Victor nodded, almost feeling as though he'd done something wrong, as if he was guilty of something, as he took Lam's hand. Was this a mistake? Should he have talked Lam out of this? Between himself and Dar, they'd put a hell of a lot of Energy into that "crucible." What if Lam couldn't make it? What if they had taken away too much of her defiance in the spirit shard they'd left in her body? "C'mon, *hermana*," he growled, gripping her thin, limp hand. "I'm not letting you get lost. Come on! Time to come home."

7

LAM

Lam sat in her tent, just a small canvas thing with a woolen blanket on the floor and her pack for a pillow. She could hear the others outside, talking, laughing, and carrying on about the women from Ardvale Falls, a small hamlet the cohort had marched through earlier that day. She frowned, pulled her polishing kit from her storage ring, and got to work on her boots. Lieutenant Vas had given her two demerits earlier for the scuffs on the leather.

She grimaced in anger and embarrassment at the memory. Of course, she knew the boots needed polish, but they'd been marching for days, and there were plenty of soldiers with boots in far worse condition. "Why do we even have to do this? How much would it cost for a few enchantments to keep this leather looking nice?" She angrily smeared the red-brown polish into the leather. She knew the answer all too well; the same reason they had to carry packs when most everyone had dimensional containers—character.

Hadn't Captain Trov-dak gone on and on about it when she'd addressed the recruit cohort? A soldier who cares for their gear appreciates their gear. A soldier who carries their equipment on their back knows the worth of that equipment. She'd heard similar things from her father when she was young. He wouldn't buy her a book about Evi ap'Sheni, the Blue Deep assassin, but he let her work for a week in the family store to earn the money herself. What had his lesson been? If she earned it, she'd appreciate it. Her father would have fit right in with the Legion.

"Ah, Father, I didn't think I'd miss you so soon." She sighed, setting the boot down to dry before buffing. Had she really run away? The thought came to her out of nowhere. Had she really broken her father's heart and abandoned the family business? For what? To play at swords and spears with a bunch of crude, loud, sex-starved adolescents?

As if to punctuate the thought, she heard Fol guffaw and shout, "Ancestors be true! She was asking for it!"

Lam bit her lip, wanting to shout something equally rude in defense of the unnamed woman, but knew better than to stir that hornet's nest. She picked up her tin of polish, spitting a little too vehemently into it. She worked the saliva around with her rag until she had a good amount of dark, oily stain to smear on the second boot. She was just setting the finished product beside the other to dry when she heard footsteps outside her tent. "Recruit Lam!" It was Sergeant Gonda. Lam felt her stomach start to churn with butterflies at the sound of his voice. The huge Vodkin never had a pleasant word on his tongue.

She quickly leaned forward and threw the tent flap wide. "Yes, sir?"

"Get your boots on and walk with me." He didn't wait; he just turned and started lumbering away. Lam jerked her boots onto her feet, wishing she'd had time to buff the polish. The damp leather would attract dust and dirt, and she'd have to start over. She scrambled after Gonda, and the men sitting around the cookpot—members of her own squad—laughed as she almost tripped over her long gangly legs; she'd grown a lot in the last few years and was still awkward with her body. She caught up to the sergeant and walked a pace behind and to his left as he trudged down the central row of the cohort's encampment.

"Recruit Lam, I'm going to have a talk with you that I reserve for a few individuals from every enlistment cohort."

"Yes, sir." Lam had a feeling this was a bad thing, and she didn't know what a proper response was, so she went with the old standby.

"I can see you're struggling to fit in. I reviewed your enlistment interview, and I think it might be wise to reconsider your decision. The Legion isn't the place for a runaway Ghelli. It's something of a miracle you've been here for more than a month and haven't gotten seriously injured, killed, or worse, ravaged by one of the men."

Lam's mouth fell open at the sergeant's words. She wasn't sure if she should be thankful that he was concerned or angry that he expected so little from her. "Thank you for your concern, Sergeant—"

"I'm not concerned about you, recruit!" he barked, cutting her off. "I don't want to lose good men dealing with a tribunal when you bring forth accusations!" He stopped, turned, and regarded her, frowning through the yellowed tusks that hung over his furry chin. "I'm giving you a choice: discharge with no dishonor or transfer to the Beneset Steppes Garrison. You've got until first duty to make a decision."

"B-Beneset Steppes, sir?" She'd heard of the place, the great plains north of the Empire, where raiders and roving bands of primitive monster tribes were a constant threat.

"That's right. Do the smart thing, young lady. Go home." His dark eyes narrowed, and he shook his head slightly. "I hope you can see I'm trying to help you." With that, he turned and stomped away, his heavy, enormous boots thudding on the freshly raked dirt. He called over his shoulder, "Dismissed."

As despair gripped her heart, Lam listlessly walked back to her tent. She barely lifted her feet, no longer able to muster any concern for the dirt caking the damp leather of her boots. When she reached her squad's cookfire, most of them were sitting around eating. No one offered her anything from the pot. No one called out, asking if things were all right. She was sure she heard whispers and snickers, though. They were always teasing her—she was too light. Her bones were hollow. Why would a pretty girl with fragile wings want to wear the Legion uniform? It didn't help that she was the only female on the squad. It didn't help that she'd never seen another Ghelli in the cohort.

She slumped down onto her woolen blanket and closed the flap of her tent. What had she been thinking? She dug through her thin, tarnished storage ring and pulled out the Far Scribe book she shared with her parents. She'd written one note in it, the night she ran away, trying to explain herself, trying to convey her need for adventure and accomplishment. They'd never responded, and a glance confirmed it was still true. Lam knew her mother would have, but there was no way her father would allow it. His pride was too wounded, and in their family, his word was law. Lam was quite sure, as far as he was concerned, she was dead.

If she went home at that moment, if she returned, wings tucked low in shame, begging for forgiveness, he'd let her stay. He'd punish her for years, though, and her miserable, simple existence from before would be twice as bad. Still, wasn't Sergeant Gonda right? She *wasn't* fitting in. She'd never felt so alone as she did in that moment.

When she'd fled home, at least she'd had her dreams and hopes to sustain her. At least she'd carried some pride in her chest, thinking of the famous Ghelli heroes she'd read so many tales about. But the Legion hadn't been what she'd expected. They had more than enough conscripts and volunteers; a tall scrawny Ghelli wasn't of much value. Gonda had proven that by offering her a discharge, a release from her oath.

She lay in bed, listening to the murmured conversations and laughter around her, wallowing in her despair. It was palpable, that hopelessness. She could feel it settling over her like a blanket, and her mind listlessly cast about for some way out. If the Legion didn't want her, why would she stay? At least her mother would be happy to see her. At least she had some friends back in Twilight Home. What would they say? She hadn't said goodbye to a single person. They'd resent her for that. They'd mock her when she wasn't listening.

Pools of tears overflowed from her eyes, soaking into her hair as they ran from the corners. She lay still, shivering, almost physically ill from the sadness overwhelming her, and the only thought that seemed to give her any comfort was a whisper of cold air tickling her ears and threatening to constrict her throat with its icy promise: "Just give up." She was lying still, contemplating those three words, wondering the best course of action to make them a reality, when they came for her.

A shadow fell over the tan material of her tent, and Lam wondered what it was; had someone moved one of the watch lamps? But then her tent rustled and collapsed on her, and a heavy hand pressed the material against her face, gagging her as other strong hands grabbed her ankles and wrists. She thrashed, but it was as they'd said; she was skinny and weak compared to the Shadeni and Ardeni recruits, and there had to be at least three of them holding her down, pinning her under the collapsed tent. She tried to scream, tried to think of a spell she could employ, but panic washed over her as the first heavy blow crunched into her unprotected stomach.

She jerked and pulled but couldn't move, and the punch knocked the wind from her lungs. Lam tried to scream, but the heavy hand pressing her head into the ground just jammed more of the tent's fabric between her teeth as she opened her jaws. More blows rained down. Whoever was behind them, whoever was delivering the beating, knew better than to break any bones. They knew better than to use any weapons that might leave a distinctive mark. Big, heavy impacts rocked her, smashing into her stomach, her chest, her thighs, even her groin, and Lam couldn't manage to pull in a breath, let alone formulate any sort of defense.

As a different sort of blackness closed in on her vision, as her panicked mind began to shut down, the pain of the impacts seemed to fade, and she felt herself pulling inward, away from the torment of her body, hiding in the depths of her mind with a memory that seemed strange and out of place. She saw a man, big and brooding, with short dark hair and golden, honey-brown eyes. He had a strong, sharp nose, and somehow he looked at her and nodded, his eyes full of fiery anger. "What are you doing, sister? You're not someone who gives up. Eat the pain. Eat the despair. Chew it up and turn it into rage. This won't kill you. You're tougher than that!"

Lam's mouth, pressed so hard that her lips split and she could taste the blood seeping through the tent's fabric, tried to form a single word, and she didn't know where it came from. "Victor," she mumbled, but only she could have understood the sound as distinct from the grunts and whimpers she'd been making. She didn't know who he was but wondered if the Roots were talking to her. Had they sent her an ancestor to stir her spirit? Chew up the pain? Chew up the despair? Turn it into rage? Suddenly, something snapped in her mind, and she saw her plight from a new perspective.

Why *shouldn't* she be angry? Why *wasn't* she? Her parents shouldn't have disowned her. That wasn't *her* fault. She'd written them a letter. She'd promised to remember her kin when she found fame and fortune! Why hadn't they believed in her? Why had her father disowned her rather than honoring her desire and boasting about his daughter's bravery? Were his own ends so crucial that he'd treat his only child as a means of achieving them?

Why were none of her squadmates looking out for her? Why were they picking on her for being weaker? Shouldn't they protect and nurture her strength? Wouldn't she be stronger with them by her side and at her back? Why was the dirty, rot-infested command structure condoning her release, threatening her with a dangerous post on the edge of nowhere, to get her to leave? Wouldn't the Legion do better if they found her strengths and brought those forth? Was any of that her fault? Was it her fault she had big dreams but no training? Was it her fault she'd grown tall and thin but hadn't had the chance to build muscle to fill out her frame?

As she endured the beating and ran through the litany of wrongs done to her, Lam noticed something strange—the blows, though just as heavy, just as measured, weren't bothering her anymore. She was breathing through her nose as she tensed her abdomen, absorbing the hits. A fierce, bloody smile spread beneath the crushing grip of her assailant, and she felt something else—an angry, smoldering heat at the center of her chest. They wanted to beat her into submission, but she wouldn't submit. She'd take the beating. She'd take the pain, the despair, the loneliness, and she'd chew it up.

When the punches and kicks or whatever they were raining down on her finally stopped, and the hand pulled away from her face, Lam lay still. As several booted feet walked away into the night, she breathed deeply through her nose and cataloged the pain, letting her mind mentally take stock of the aches. They hadn't broken any ribs. They hadn't even hit her in the face. Her stomach ached. Her thighs and groin were swollen with contusions, and she knew she'd struggle to stand, let alone march, in the morning, but again, nothing was broken.

Her wrists were sore from where they'd been squeezed through the tent's fabric, but she slowly lifted her arms, wincing at the sharp pains in her elbows and shoulders. She brought her hands to her chest, tenderly pressing on her breasts and sternum, wincing with the agony of bruised, aching flesh and bone. She had a minor healing potion in her storage ring, and she was tempted to drink it down, but another part of her, the angry part, sitting in the warm glow of the fiery rage deep in her core, wanted them to see the evidence of their crime in the morning. She wanted them to see what they'd done, and she wanted them to realize it hadn't worked.

She closed her eyes and, still lying under the fabric of her collapsed tent, tried to make herself sleep. She pictured the Beneset Steppes, and suddenly, the idea of being sent there didn't seem so bad. Maybe the men and women garrisoned near the frontier would be different. Maybe they'd recognize her potential and treat her as a fellow soldier despite her inexperience. Something about the idea felt right. She wasn't sure if it was the anger destroying her sadness and despair, but she suddenly felt she *wanted* to go there. Like the next step in her journey lay in that direction. It almost felt as if the person she was supposed to be would be waiting for her if she just started down that path.

When the horns blew the morning wake-up call, announcing the first duty, Lam opened her eyes to see that the fabric of her tent was no longer black with night. She could make out faint gray light through its coarse material. With winces and shuddering gasps of pain, she wormed her way out of it. When she emerged on hands and knees, she could hear others moving around the circle of her squad's tents. She could hear whispers and curses, but none came over. No one asked what was wrong. It wasn't a surprise, but it still stung knowing they'd either been aware or active participants in the beating. Lam bit down on that sadness. She chewed it up and found that warm glow of anger.

When she struggled to her feet, barefoot in the dirt, her boots tangled in the tent behind her, she leaned over and coughed until a long string of bloody drool hung from her lips. She wiped the bloody saliva with the back of her hand, smearing it across her chin, and looked around the camp with bloodshot, furious eyes. Not one of her squadmates would meet her gaze. "Cowards," she grunted, then leaned forward and spat another wad of bloody phlegm.

She'd just turned to try to dig her boots, blanket, and pack out of her tent when heavy footsteps crunched on the gravel-strewn dirt behind her. She heard her squadmates clamber to their feet and get quiet, so she knew it was the sergeant. He stopped behind her and cleared his throat, so Lam turned and offered him a salute, slower than was appropriate but faster than she could move without pain.

"Recruit," he grunted. He eyed her up and down but didn't ask about her bruised and bloodied condition. Lam wasn't surprised. "Have you made your decision? We have a supply wagon leaving for Gelica in a few hours."

Lam narrowed her white-blonde eyebrows and trained her bloodshot, bright green eyes on his, staring at him for several long seconds. When he blinked, she said, "I'll go to the Beneset Steppes, sir. Thank you for the opportunity."

"I believe she's doing well," Dar grunted, distracting Victor from his worry.

"What's it like for her?" he asked, glancing away from Lam's still, pale face to his mentor.

"The crucible will use memories from her mind to test her. It may change some minor details, but the overall goal of the ritual is to create an intelligent enchantment that will attempt to break her spirit in various ways. It's up to her to retain her focus and find her way back to herself. If she succumbs, well, she won't."

"Damn it," Victor groaned, hating the idea that he couldn't help her more than just holding her hand and urging her to "be strong" and "keep fighting." He'd been doing so for what felt like an hour already. "If it seems like she isn't going to make it, can we stop this? Yeah, I know I should've asked that before we started."

"If she fails, we may be able to rescue a vestige of her spirit, but it might be less cruel to simply free the shard in her body, allowing her to pass on." Dar's tone was final, and Victor stewed on that for a minute. He was distracted from his concern again when Dar chuckled and said, "She surprises me!"

"How?" Not for the first time, Victor was annoyed by Dar's ability to see so much more than he could.

"I wove your rage into many of the crucible's trials, thinking it would be another barrier, but she seems to be using it more often as a lever to break out of my other traps—despair and fear, mostly. Take heart in that, boy. With glory, inspiration, and hope mixed in, I believe she'll find the breadcrumbs she needs to return to herself."

"Fuck yeah, *hermana*," Victor said, squeezing Lam's slender hand again, willing his words to reach her. "You got this. Show them what you're made of! Show them all!"

8

FIGHTING SPIRIT

Darren grinned with glee as his quarterstaff impacted the mudman's stiff, clay-like flesh. It wasn't the impact of hardwood against clay—that was nothing special. It was the discharge of crackling red electricity that coursed through the little creature, sparking out of its eyeholes and sending steam into the air, that did the real damage. The mudman collapsed, utterly devoid of the animating force that had driven it up to that point. Edeya's frosty spear was equally effective, and though they both had to reapply the damage-boosting effects to their weapons every few hits, they were making short work of the swarm of little creatures as they emerged from the brackish muddy water.

He'd learned the spell, just as Edeya had predicted, using her spell pattern. When he'd completed it in his pathways, the System had awarded him a boost of Energy and a congratulatory message, informing him that he'd unlocked a spell called Shocking Arms at the "basic" level. At first, Darren had thought he'd created a spell that would only affect his "arms," but Edeya had quickly corrected his interpretation—by arms, the System meant weapons.

With his far more effective staff, they'd cleared another two chambers of frogmen, and now they were exploring a new area and battling their second wave of "mudmen," as Darren had creatively named the four-foot-tall, bipedal people who seemed to be entirely constructed of animated mud and clay. He whipped his staff around, pounding another mudman on top of the head, allowing the volatile lightning housed in the weapon to do its work.

He'd already gained two more levels, and though he hadn't allocated any stat points in strength or agility, he felt he was far more competent already, probably because the System had awarded him with basic staff mastery. That had been an experience that he'd never forget—it felt like warm liquid coursing over the contours of his brain as sudden understanding and weird, phantom memories filled his consciousness.

Out of nowhere, he realized he understood how to hold the staff properly, how to position his feet, and what muscles to tense when he blocked or swung the weapon. He knew about different guard positions, different attacks, how to follow through, and how to recover from overextension. He could, quite literally, fill a book with all the things he suddenly knew.

He laughed as he zapped another mudman and then recast Shocking Arms, recharging the staff as he whirled to check on Edeya. She was standing over a mound of mud and clay, grinning back at him. "Nice one, Edeya!"

"Dare! I think you killed more than me that time!" she crowed, scanning the wide, low-ceilinged cave for further threats. The only thing of note that Darren could see was a low muddy passage on the far side leading into darkness. "I think we're done with that fight; here comes the Energy." He followed her gaze, saw the golden motes forming around the piles of mud, and braced himself. A few minutes later, as they both shook off their euphoria, he read the System messages:

*****Congratulations! You have achieved Level 5 Base Human. You have 5 attribute points to allocate.*****

"Level!" he said, grinning at his partner. She nodded, smiling, her face flushed with the rush of Energy.

"Me too, Dare," she said with a happy trill in her voice. "One more level, and I'll get my class back."

"You're Nine?"

"Yep!" She glanced at the dark tunnel and then back at him. "Take a break? Or keep going? Maybe there's a boss nearby."

"Let me spend my attribute points, then I'm ready." Darren quickly pulled up his status page and put all five of his points into will—the second time he'd done so. He looked at his page with pride:

Status			
Name:	Darren Whitehorse		
Race:	Human: Base 1		
Class:	-		
Level:	5		
Core:	Wildarc Class: Base 1		
Energy Affinity:	Lightning 8, Chaos 7.4, Unattuned 6.1	Energy:	113/113
Strength:	6	Vitality:	17

Dexterity:	5	Agility:	5
Intelligence:	9	Will:	13
Points Available:	0		
Titles & Feats:	-		
Skills:			
System Language Integration			Not Upgradeable
Wildarc Cultivation Drill			Basic
Staff Mastery			Basic
Spells:			
Arclight Wisp			Basic
Shocking Arms			Basic

"My Energy went up a little, just like the last time I put my points into will."

Edeya nodded. "Yep, intelligence will make it go up even more. Will gives you some, but it mostly effects how fast you regenerate your Energy."

"How are you allocating your points? If you don't mind me asking."

"I want to try for a more magic-focused class. Unlike you, I was already Level Seven after, well, after that rotten witch took my spirit. When I leveled back in the day, I was trying to survive, so I put most of my points into vitality and agility. This time around, I'm going to put more points into will and intelligence. At Eight, I put my points into intelligence, and this time, I'm putting all five into will. I hope it changes things for me at Level Ten."

"Um." Darren leaned on his staff, looking at the tall, slender young woman. "Do you mind me asking what your first class was?"

"I don't mind, Dare!" She smiled and continued, "When I reached Level Ten the first time, I still lived with my family in the Blue Deep." She saw Darren's narrowed eyes and added, "That's a huge forest in the southern part of the Empire. I spent my free time exploring and scrounging for small game, so no one was surprised when my first class was Hunter." She sighed, shrugged, and said, "It's a basic class."

Darren nodded and asked, "Do you think you'll have different choices now?"

"Victor seems to think so. He thinks all my life experiences, all the skills and spells I've learned, my racial advancement, my fights, and even what I went through when Catalina stole my spirit will lead to the System offering me very different choices."

"Does Victor know?" Darren knew better than to underestimate Victor by then, but still, the giant warrior hadn't been away from Earth all that long.

"He's learned a lot, but I think his master, that big stone monster of a man, told him that."

"Ah, yeah. You told me about him. Or I heard you and Lam talking about him . . . can't remember." Darren straightened up and pointed his staff, still faintly sparking with red-tinged electricity, toward the distant tunnel. "Shall we?"

"All right, Dare. Let's do this!" Edeya shifted her spear so the tip was forward as she stalked along the muddy path toward the opening. As he usually did, Darren kept pace a few steps behind, and as they walked, he refreshed his Shocking Arms spell. It drained away fifty Energy points, but he regenerated five or so every few seconds. He supposed if he had more spells to cast, his small pool of Energy could become a problem, but as it was, he never had trouble keeping the staff charged up.

His light spell would eat up a little bit of Energy, but Edeya was currently shedding light on the scene with a soft blue orb that floated over her head. It was the same shade as the motes in her wings, but, like his spell, it turned more white than blue if she made it brighter. Darren watched the shadows retreat into the tunnel as she approached. She glanced back once, and he nodded, so she went in. He followed her but only took a few steps into the opening when he found her crouched low, unmoving. She looked back at him and held a finger to her lips.

Darren crouched and looked over Edeya's shoulder, immediately seeing what had alerted her. A flickering orange glow illuminated a large cave ahead. A big shadow slowly swayed on the far wall as though something moved in front of the source of the light. He leaned close to Edeya's ear and whispered, "Gonna scout?" She usually wanted to be the first to approach a new space, especially if there was evidence of enemies.

She kept her eyes on the cave opening but whispered, "We both will. Follow my movements."

Tension gripped Darren's heart like a vise, but he nodded, excited by her show of confidence. Edeya crept toward the tunnel mouth, hunched low, spear pointing forward, and carefully stepping on the smooth, hard, clay-like surfaces, avoiding the little pools of muddy water. Darren mimicked her movements and, despite his nerves, managed to avoid messing up. In just a few steps, they were both lurking near the opening and peering into the big firelit cave.

That was the source of the light, a fire. It burned in a low depression on the muddy floor, and Darren could see the fuel source nearby—piles of dry compact bricks of something like moss. It burned with orange, nearly smokeless flames and gave off quite a lot of heat; Darren could feel it from almost twenty yards away. Two large figures tended the fire, and Darren's hands tightened on his staff as he got a good look at them.

One was enormously rotund, sitting on the hard dry clay in the basin, occasionally tossing bricks of fuel into the flames. It was a mudman, but different; it wore a headdress of beads that glimmered like dull jewels in the firelight, and though it made the same sort of warbling grunts as the other mudmen, Darren thought he could detect syllables and intelligent intonations in the sounds. The other figure moved back and forth, shaking a large bone-yellow staff above its head as it paced, lifting its high bony knees with each step; it wasn't a mudman. The weirdly dancing figure looked like a skeleton coated in mud with too little of the clay-like substance to cover its bones completely.

Edeya backed up a couple of steps, and Darren moved with her. Then she motioned for him to lean close, whispering, "I'm sure those are bosses. It could get pretty tough with just the two of us. What do you think?"

"I, um, well, I think we've beaten up all the minions really easily. We should try this!"

"That's the spirit, Dare!" Edeya grinned fiercely. "Which one do you want to take? I think the big mudman is a healer."

"So." Darren licked his lips, thinking. "So, I think you should kill the healer. We should take him out fast! I'll try to keep the big muddy skeleton busy."

Edeya squinted her eyes, clearly playing the fight out in her head, before nodding. "Good plan. I'll try to sneak close to hit him before he sees us. I'll go right, you go left. If the skeleton sees you, try to get noisy so the big guy looks your way, too."

"So I'm the bait?" Darren chuckled, shaking his head. "Sounds like a good plan!"

"Okay, let's do this!" Edeya gripped her spear and crept back to the opening. She gave Darren one more look, confirming his readiness, and then she slipped into the cavern, hugging the right wall. Darren stepped in, moving to the left. There wasn't much to hide him in the room, not even any shadows, thanks to the bright fire, but he still crept low, moving slowly, hoping that if he didn't make any sudden movement, he might get close before they noticed him.

Somehow, Edeya didn't suffer the same problem; even though nothing was between her and the fire pit, she seemed to find shadows to slink through along the base of the wall. Seeing that, Darren realized her idea was perfect; him going the opposite direction would give her the ideal opportunity to pounce once the bosses noticed him. He'd only covered about ten yards before they did, or more accurately, before the mud skeleton did.

It lifted its bone staff and whirled to face him, eyes like candle flames flickering from the dark depressions under its brow. It warbled a weird, coughing curse, and the ground under Darren's feet instantly lost its firmness; he felt his feet sinking into cold mud as tendrils of ropy slime began to wrap around his ankles. "Oof!" he cried as he nearly fell onto his face, which likely would have sealed his fate. He caught himself on his staff, though, then lifted it to swipe down at the gross, black, muddy tendrils.

If his magical electricity had behaved like natural electricity, he would surely have electrocuted himself as the red sparks *zapped* into the tentacles wrapping around his ankles. Fortunately, just as he could grip the staff without discomfort, the electricity washed over him without any ill effect. As the tentacles of slimy mud burst apart, he jammed the butt of his staff into the soft ground and, using it for balance, yanked his feet free, one at a time, clambering onto firmer clay. He regained his footing just in time to receive a wicked side-swiping blow from the mud skeleton's ivory staff.

The length of hard polished bone caught him in the shoulder, and as a testament to the monster's strength, it knocked him off his feet and sent him sprawling. He slid sideways onto the semidry clay, thankfully not into the liquid section he'd just escaped. Darren could hear the monster begin to utter another mumbled spell, and he desperately scrambled to his hands and knees, favoring his numb left arm.

He glanced to the other side of the cavern where he'd last seen Edeya, but he didn't catch sight of her. Then he felt the ground loosen under his hands and, in a panic, drove forward with his feet. He exploded like back in high school when he'd practiced football drills, trying to please his dad by signing up for a sport he'd had no interest in. Still, the instinct was in him, and maybe he had his old sadistic coach to thank. He caught the skeleton in its midriff with his right shoulder and, despite their size difference, knocked it sprawling.

Darren fell with the boss, getting tangled in its mud-covered bony legs, but he'd kept his grip on his staff. He thrashed the length of lightning-charged wood left and right, batting away the muddy skeleton's grasping hands and thrilling at the sight of sparks dancing along those bones. He fought like a madman, driving forward grimly as he repeatedly battered the monster with his staff. Even when the enchantment faded and no more electricity aided his blows, the staff delivered noticeable damage, blasting mud away and cracking bones.

Darren couldn't believe it when he knelt in a pile of broken bones and dried-up clay. He'd won! He'd killed a boss! Somewhere in his frenzied, half-startled mind, Darren thanked Victor for the enchanted weapon. The sound of high-pitched grunts and repeated *thunk* sounds of something sharp impacting something wet startled him, and he looked toward the fire where the other boss had been.

He laughed and breathed a sigh of relief when he saw Edeya standing upon its enormous torso, repeatedly jamming her spear in and out of the soft muddy clay. Each blow sent tendrils of frost into the monster's body, and each time she drew the spear out and jabbed it in again, hunks of frozen clay broke off the boss's body. "I think it's dead!" he called after he'd gathered his breath.

"Better be! I've stabbed it twenty times!" she growled.

Darren stood up, wincing and rubbing his sore shoulder. He saw the ivory staff buried in the bones and mud and picked it up before walking over to Edeya, a staff in each hand. "Did that guy even get an attack off?"

"He was about to blast you with something when I buried my spear in his back." She breathed heavily, leaning on her spear still jutting out of the muddy corpse. "Nice job, by the way, Dare!"

"You too, Dey." He'd never used the nickname before the dungeon, but with her calling him "Dare" constantly, he'd decided it was fair game. She smiled and gave him an appraising look.

"Seems like you made a real mess of yourself. Are you hurt?"

"Just my shoulder. That guy was *strong*!"

"Need a healing potion?"

"Nah, I don't think so. We're about to get some Energy." Darren gestured with the staff in his left hand to the glowing motes of bright gold Energy gathering on the mound of mud.

"Whew! Thank the Roots! I was afraid this guy wasn't really dead. That's why I kept stabbing him." She sat down on the clay of the monster's corpse and then slid down to stand before Darren. "Get ready; I think it's a lot." She wasn't wrong. A moment later, a torrent of Energy, much larger than the ones Darren had felt before, surged into him, and he was lost in the euphoric bliss of it.

When he came back to himself, he was sitting on his butt before the corpse and the bonfire, and his shoulder pain was completely gone. Blinking, he squinted at the System message:

*****Congratulations! You have achieved Level 6 Base Human. You have 5 attribute points to allocate.*****

"Another level," he said, looking around, wondering if Edeya had gotten one too. He saw her sitting a few feet away, staring into space.

"Me too," she muttered, clearly very distracted.

"New options?" he pressed.

"Oh, Roots, Darren! It's amazing! I have two epic choices and three advanced!"

* * *

Victor lost track of the hours as he sat there holding Lam's hand, gently encouraging her, constantly sending a thin tendril of Energy into her through that connection. Dar never told him to start doing so, but he never told him to stop. If it was cheating, he didn't care; he'd do anything he could to ensure Lam's spirit came through. Dar hadn't spoken in a long time, and Victor noticed he didn't always hold Lam's hand. Sometimes he'd let it drop, and sometimes he'd pick it up, and Victor wondered what the master could see that told him when it was time to do so.

After he began to think it would never end, Dar surprised him when he cleared his throat, making a sound like gravel sliding down a concrete embankment, and rumbled, "She's nearly through, Victor. This is a good time to learn. Just as you gaze upon your own aura, spread your inner eye's awareness and watch her break through. Do it now!"

Victor felt the urgency in the command, and he immediately turned his gaze inward. Then he expanded his awareness from his Core, seeing his pathways and his dark, roiling aura. He stretched his awareness further still, then he saw what Dar meant. Could he have been watching this the whole time? He silently cursed the stoic Spirit Master for not telling him sooner.

From his inner eye's vantage, he could see his Core, his aura around it, and then, beside him, the wall of his mentor's aura, impossible to focus upon. However, between that deathly barrier and his own aura, he saw a split in the darkness, a breach between this world and that of the spirit plane, and when he peered closely at it, he could catch glimpses of Lam's spirit as it fought to claw through that aperture. "Come on, Lam!" he urged, not yelling but whispering forcefully. "Come on! You're almost there. Fight for it!"

He saw her face, different than when he'd stood with her naked, determined spirit on the spirit plane, and different from her physical self. She had bright, determined eyes, her brows drawn down in a sharp V, and teeth bared in a grimace. There was something primal and visceral about her. She pulled and tugged, squeezing first one shoulder, then another through the rip, and Victor couldn't help comparing the imagery to that of a birth, though Lam's spirit was clawing her way out; there was no midwife there to deliver her.

Suddenly, it was over; she'd overcome whatever resistance held her back, and she streaked like a ghostly light out of the aperture. As the glow of her spirit faded, Victor assumed she'd made it back into her body, so he turned his attention away from his inner eye and looked upon her still form with his physical eyes. He squeezed her hand and felt an answering twitch. There was a warmth in her flesh that hadn't been present before. "She made it," he breathed.

"Aye, lad. She did, indeed, no small thanks to you. I believe you profoundly touched her spirit; there will be lasting effects." Dar's hand clapped his shoulder and gave it a comradely squeeze. "You're a loyal, big-hearted friend, and she's lucky to have you."

"What do you mean?" Victor asked, looking into the giant's blazing white-hot eyes. "I mean about lasting effects?"

"I think you altered her affinities. Her Core. Can't you see it? Can't you feel it? I believe a new Spirit Caster was born this day."

9

IRONHEART

"Really?" Victor's eyes widened as he looked down at Lam's sleeping form. "You think I did that?"

Dar nodded, his blazing eyes staring intently into Victor's. "Aye. You and she. You fed her a near-constant stream of spirit Energy, but she was the one who embraced it, turning it to her purpose of pushing forward. I saw what you were doing and contemplated stopping you, but I was intrigued. I've done this ritual a dozen times over the years, and never has a subject made such use of the Energy I provided. I think—no, I know it has to do with your existing bond. She trusts you on an innate level. Despite the memory haze woven by the crucible, she recognized your spirit. Yes, this was quite an interesting turn of events, one upon which I'll need to meditate."

Victor stared at Lam, and though her body shouldn't have changed at all, he couldn't help but think she looked younger. Perhaps it was just that she was sleeping; all the worry lines she usually carried were gone, her face serene. "What level will she be?"

"Close to base, but perhaps still first tier. I tried to calculate the crucible to bring her just beneath her first class selection, but it's a tricky thing. Your aid may have also reduced the cost of her own Energy."

"Can you see her Core? Her affinities?"

"Aye, lad. I see a blazing red-gold Core of courage-attuned Energy. Did you feed her mostly rage and inspiration?"

"Yeah. Glory, too, but the others come more naturally to me; I've had them longer."

"She took what you offered and ran with it. She must have had some latent affinity for courage, in any case. Yes, I believe that's what happened. I wonder what else we might help her unlock as she progresses." Dar stood and gestured down at Lam's sleeping form. "Carry her. We'll put her to bed; then you should also turn in. Your day with Lo'ro begins in seven hours."

"Shit! The whole day is gone?"

"Yes. She fought long and hard and will sleep a long while."

Victor nodded, stooping to lift Lam. He followed Dar out of the natural caves beneath his cellar and then up the steps into his kitchens. When they stood in the open sitting area bordered by the big glass windows that provided a clear view of the deck and lake, Dar turned to him. "I have much to contemplate, and I think I'd like some time alone. Lo'ro will fetch you in the morning, sometime after dawn. Be sure to show him the proper respect and learn well the lesson he will teach. When you return, I'll be here."

"What about Lam?" Victor shifted the sleeping woman in his arms. "She's going to be confused about her Core, don't you think? Will I have time to speak to her in the morning?"

Dar scowled, his eyes flaring slightly, but he paused momentarily before responding, and Victor wondered if he'd been about to snap at him. Was the master tired? Irritable? "You heard my words, yes? Lo'ro will come sometime after dawn. Don't sleep in, and you'll have time to speak with your friend." Without another word, he strode out the open door to the deck, and Victor watched as his flying spirit mount appeared out of a cloud of bright sparkling Energy. It was probably thirty feet long and coiled around Dar like a great serpent until the giant straddled its luminescent back just behind its broad head. Then he streaked away, flying out over the lake on wisps of golden Energy.

"All right." Victor shook his head and walked toward the bedrooms. He deposited Lam on her bed, pulled off her boots, threw a soft quilted blanket over her, and then left, crossing the hall to his own room. Lifedrinker was where he'd left her, leaning against the wall beside the bed's headboard. He lifted and rested her on his lap. "Hey, *chica*. Tomorrow, we have to spend time with a Death Caster and go into some freaky places. Are you ready?"

"Always!" the axe sang into his mind. *"Every moment I don't dwell on my memories, I'm praying to enter battle in your hands!"*

"Heh," he chuckled, "I love how eager you are." Victor kicked off his boots, shrugged off his shirt, and lay down atop his blankets; the air was warm, and he liked the night breeze drifting in through his window. He cradled his axe and, as he tried to sleep, murmured, "Tell me about one of your memories. Tell me about the wolves that used to play in the vale where you grew."

"I have another memory I'd share! You know about the tree where my living wood was born, but have I told you of the time when I wandered the dark, deep depths, a being of fire and hunger?"

"What? No—"

"These memories are newly awakened! When I feasted on your recent foes, my increased Energy helped me to dig them from the depths of my dormant mind. Before

I was a spirit, set loose to wander and find a home in the metal you now cradle, I was a primal being living deep beneath the surface of the world, content to gather the violent, primitive Energies from which worlds and stars are birthed. My existence was simple, and I knew but two things: hunger and a need for growth. I had kin, but we weren't close. Something happened to me, but it's not clear to me. Something released my spirit from my physical form, and somehow, I clung to the silver vein from which my blade was forged."

"Was it just silver before you joined with it? Is that what made it Heart Silver?"

"I know not. With each answer, I find three new questions. The more I unravel my past, the more I realize I'm not a simple being born from a tree or a vein of metal. I'm both and more. You awakened me, Victor. Your Energy and spirit impacted mine. As you help me feast upon the Energy of your foes, my being solidifies, and I become more and, at the same time, less like I once was. It confuses me. Am I still me?"

"We all change, *chica*. I'm not the same person I once was, and it's my connections to you, Valla, and all the others I spend time with that make me different. I know I'm oversimplifying things, but, well, as you remember more about yourself and change, do you want something different?"

"No! My heart yearns for battle and always to be in your hand."

"Good, 'cause that's what I want. If something changes, just talk to me. We can work it out."

"Before you sleep, will you share your spirit with me?" When Victor had been ejected from the challenge dungeon, the System had canceled his spells, including his Imbue Spirit, which he, more often than not, cast on Lifedrinker.

"Yeah," he yawned, "of course I will." He concentrated and sent a fragment of his spirit, imbued with inspiration-attuned Energy, into the axe. As she hummed softly, clearly pleased, Victor closed his eyes and drifted into sleep. He had wild dreams about wolves and magma flows, fiery volcanos, and fleeing game. When he woke, it was to a gentle tap at his door, and he sprang up with unnatural alertness, Lifedrinker already lifted high in his right fist.

The tap sounded again, and a soft, faint voice called, "Sir, your companion, Lady Lam, requests your presence."

"Coming," Victor grunted, sliding to the edge of the bed and pulling on his boots. He quickly emptied his bladder in the attached bathroom, then hurried into the hallway where one of Dar's servants waited. The demure green-skinned woman ducked her head and hurried toward the sitting room adjoining the outside deck. Victor could see the sun had barely risen, which he hoped meant he had some time before Lo'ro came calling. Lam sat at one of the couches sipping a large glass of peach-colored juice, and when she saw Victor, her eyes brightened.

"Victor!"

"How do you feel?" he asked, hurrying over.

Before she could reply, the servant hastily asked, "Can I bring you some fresh juice and breakfast?"

"Bring him the same as I ordered." Lam gestured to her glass, and Victor smiled, seeing some of her old aura of command asserting itself.

"As you say." The woman bowed and shuffled toward the kitchen. Victor still had many questions about Dar's strange household staff, but he never seemed to think to ask when the moment was right.

"To answer your question, Victor, I'm well, but very, very, Roots-be-damned confused."

"I take it you noticed your Core has changed?"

"Ha! What an understatement! I woke to about twenty-five System messages. Most of my spells have been wiped from my mind! 'Incompatible with your current affinity,' the System said!"

Victor chuckled, well aware of the limitations of spirit-attuned Energy. "You wanted a fresh start, right? Don't worry, you're going to learn new, badass abilities."

"Am I? Courage—it sounds wonderful, but Victor, all my life, I've learned to look down on Spirit Casters!"

"That's because of Ridonne propaganda. Do you think I'm weak?"

"Roots, no!" she cried. "I don't remember what I went through, not every detail, but I feel such deep gratitude to you, Victor. I know you were in here," she laid her palm over her heart, "helping me. So, will you help me choose my first class?"

"You're Level Ten?"

"Yes! I think I was brought down to something like twelve, but then the System removed my Leaf Warden class, saying it wasn't 'compatible with . . .'"

"Your current affinities." Victor laughed. "So, it dumped you down to Ten? I bet it loved stealing that Energy away."

"I get the feeling the System isn't exactly approving of the ritual Dar performed. Or, I don't know; maybe that's just my bias."

"No, I think you're right." Victor sat beside her. "The System wants us to be stronger so we can harvest more Energy, and it can siphon off its percentage. You dropped all those levels, bleeding that Energy off into the universe. That's, well, that's kind of a gamble. If you don't regain the levels, you're a smaller, weaker Energy battery in the System's eyes."

Lam narrowed her eyes, slowly nodding. "I see what you're getting at. When I go fight Tier One monsters, the System's going to get a lot smaller cut than if I went into a Tier Six dungeon with Valla and Lesh."

"Right." Victor looked Lam over, smiling as he did so. "You look good. The ritual didn't mess you up, at least."

"Mess me up?"

"I mean your head. You seem upbeat."

"I told you; it's all a blur. I think that's by design, yes?" When Victor nodded, though he was just guessing, she continued, "I'm a little disturbed about the loss of my Core and its levels, but it was just a Pearl Class Core, and those are so basic—I had no affinities. All of my spells were cast with pure unattuned Energy. It was easy to level, and I'd learned some strong abilities, but I'm trying to keep an open mind, hoping this new Spirit Class Core will have greater potential."

"I'm sure that's the case!" Victor nodded, taking a tall glass of juice as the servant returned and handed it to him.

"Your food will be out shortly," she said, ducking away.

"Hey, hang on a sec." Victor looked at the woman, at her pointy ears, yellow eyes, and smooth green skin. "Are you all related? You and the other staff?"

"Indeed, sir. Lord Dar liberated our world, and now he offers employment to my people. It's a great honor to work in one of his homes."

"He liberated your world?" Lam asked, raising an eyebrow.

"Yes, ma'am. A great demon conquered Wanxue many centuries ago. My people were slaves, bred for service and entertainment. Lord Dar visited our world in his travels and helped us to rise up, throwing off the yoke of our oppressor."

"How long ago was that?" Victor asked, curious to hear a little of Dar's side history.

"We celebrated the two hundredth anniversary of our liberation just a few years ago." She bowed low and took a step back. "May I please be excused? My shift ends, and my daughter awaits."

"Oh, of course!" Lam eyed Victor with wide eyes. As the servant shuffled out, she said, "Imagine that! How old is your master?"

"Not my *master*!" Victor growled, then shrugged. "Yeah, thousands of years old, I think. He hints at it sometimes. When he takes a 'vacation,' it lasts ten years. He acts like that's the blink of an eye. Speaking of Dar, he was excited about your Core, I think."

"Truly?"

"Yeah. You know, I don't have a courage affinity. He thinks I helped you form your Core because I sent a lot of rage and inspiration into you; those two can be woven into courage."

"There are spirit affinity weaves?" Lam grabbed his wrist in excitement.

"Oh yeah. Also, you probably have more affinities; we just need to help you find them."

"Find them? I can add more?" Lam's voice had grown shrill with excitement.

"Yes!" Victor laughed. "When I first came to the mine, my only affinity was rage, but my Core was broken. I figured out how to rebuild it with a second affinity—inspiration. You know what?" Victor's eyes widened, and he returned Lam's grip, squeezing her much more slender fingers.

"What?"

"You were a big part of that! You inspired me so much when you first flew into the mine and beat the shit out of those little beetle monsters. I focused on that feeling, and that's how I figured out I had an affinity for inspiration!"

Lam sighed happily and leaned back on the couch, throwing her arms behind her head and smiling broadly. "Imagine that! It seems lifetimes ago! Young, skinny Victor, fighting bravely against a horde of beetles!" She laughed, shaking her head. "Well, I won't be flying to your rescue anytime soon."

"Ha. Well, you can rescue Edeya and Darren instead."

"Speaking of which!" She leaned forward again. "Help me choose my class, though I think I've already made up my mind."

"Okay. What are the options?" Victor could smell their breakfast by then, and his stomach gurgled in anticipation.

"I won't bore you with the basic ones, but here are the two I'm struggling with: Ironheart Sentinel and Valor Striker. They're both advanced!"

"Oh, shit! Now you're making me jealous! I can see they're both based on your courage affinity, but how are they different?"

"Ironheart Sentinel gives will, vitality, and unassigned attribute points at every level, and it says members of that class 'emphasize endurance and resilience, drawing on their unyielding hearts to withstand enemy assaults and defend their comrades.' The other one sounds more offensive. It gives strength, agility, and dexterity and says, 'These warriors specialize in bold attacks, often turning the tide of battle with their fearless assaults.' What do you think?"

"I mean, they both sound great. Personally, I'm partial to will as an attribute, and the Ironheart Sentinel also gives you some unassigned points. That would make up my mind. It sounds a lot more defensive, but you could pump those unassigned points into strength and agility. Who knows what you'll get at Twenty?"

Lam's smile had grown broader as Victor spoke, and she nodded along with him. "I'm in agreement!" She got quiet, and her eyes unfocused, so Victor sat back and waited while she went through the process.

Two members of Dar's staff brought steaming platters of food, some plates, silverware, and a basket of fresh buttered bread. He began tucking into the food and was chewing a large mouthful of eggs when Lam turned to him and grinned. "I'm a Level Ten Ironheart Sentinel! I gained a spell called

Daunting Roar. It 'boldens the hearts of my allies and strikes fear into those of my foes.' Ha!"

"Badass!" Victor covered his mouth so she didn't see his half-chewed eggs. "Hey! I need to teach you how to cultivate. It's different from normal Energy."

"Oh?" She unfocused her eyes for a moment, then in an alarmed tone added, "Oh! I don't have a cultivation drill!"

Victor chuckled, shaking his head. "Relax, I'll teach you. I bet we can bug Dar for some pointers, too. I mean, I'm not sure how involved he'll be with you, but anything he teaches me, I'll pass on. I have a feeling, though . . ." Victor trailed off, remembering how distracted Dar had been after Lam's spirit had made its way home. "I think he's pretty interested in you."

"Really?" Lam leaned back again, contemplating, and Victor reloaded his plate from the platter.

"Better eat something before I get it all," he said around a bite of fresh, soft, buttery bread.

"Hey! I'm only Level Ten now. I *need* this food! You're just a pig!" Lam commenced to load her plate, but before she started eating, she grew serious and gave him a look. "Victor, what are we going to do about our lands back home?"

While he chewed, Victor thought it over. Not a lot had changed for him in that regard. Yes, he owed Dar some service as an apprentice, but he'd never intended to live full-time on Fanwath. Lam's entire world and her future plans had been upended by, first, Edeya's situation and then her own decision to "resurrect." He swallowed and shrugged. "You're going to have to find an outstanding governor. You can visit as much as you like, or, I guess, as much as you can afford to, but I think, just like Edeya, you're better off in Sojourn for now."

Lam folded a piece of bacon into her mouth, licking the grease from her fingers, and nodded. "I suppose that's right. I just have to face the facts; my priorities have changed. Speaking of Edeya . . ." She summoned a Far Scribe book from her ring and began leafing through it. "Roots!"

"What?"

"They're out of the dungeon! Edeya got to Ten and wants our help choosing her class. They want to know where we are."

At that moment, one of Dar's servants stepped into the room. "Victor, sir?"

"Yes?"

"Master Lo'ro calls. His coachman awaits at the front door."

10

DEATH CASTER

"Ah, damn," Victor said, standing. "I guess I gotta go, Lam."

She nodded, shifting to the edge of the couch as though she'd get up, too. "Should I stay here? Should I send for Edeya and Darren?"

Victor looked at the servant who'd come to summon him. "Excuse me, but is there a coach available to pick up some friends of ours?"

"Master Dar left Mr. Qwor at your disposal. He can fetch your friends." Victor had heard the name a time or two. Qwor was one of Dar's drivers.

"Can you send him to speak to Lam? She can give him directions."

"I'll do better," Lam said, standing. "I'll ride along with him. Where will I find Mr. Qwor?"

"At the carriage house. I'll guide you, milady."

"All right. See you later, Lam." Victor wanted to get moving before he inadvertently upset Lo'ro; he had no idea how touchy the master Death Caster might be.

Lam and the servant walked with him toward the door, and the one-time Imperial Captain said, "Keep an eye on your Far Scribe book! We'll keep you updated on any developments. Speaking of Far Scribe books, have you heard from Valla or Lesh?"

Victor shook his head, frowning. "Not since they entered their dungeon. I'm not too surprised, though; it's supposedly pretty challenging. I'm sure she'll send me an update sometime today." With those words, Victor stepped through the lake house's front door and saw Lo'ro's coach.

So did Lam, and she exclaimed, "Roots, Victor! Be careful," as she took in the weird, spectral carriage. It was a sleek, dark wood and metallic shape—it reminded Victor of some kind of luxury car from the 1940s, but larger. It glowed an unearthly silver-blue and had a faintly translucent quality. As he approached, Victor saw that it hovered over the cobbles on two discs of pulsing blue light, and he could feel the air being displaced by tangible waves of force.

It had four doors like a sedan, but the rear ones were overlarge, and one of them opened as he stepped up to the strange vehicle.

"Get in, prodigy. We've a task to complete, and I'd prefer not to spend the whole day at it." The voice that came out was rough but loud and clear, and Victor felt the words spur him to action. He nodded and slid through the opening, finding himself in a spacious compartment that reminded him more of a parlor in an old manor than the inside of a vehicle. Two luxurious blue couches faced each other over a plush black carpet. Dark wood paneling lined the walls, and matching wooden tables sat at the ends of the sofas. A man clad in a dark gray suit with a fancy round hat and short silk-lined cape gestured for Victor to sit across from him.

He was clearly undead; the pale skin, black eyes, and rictus grin gave it away, but his eyes shone with amusement as he took Victor in. Seeing that, Victor reflected on the other undead creatures he'd met. Had any of them ever smiled or laughed? If so, he couldn't remember it, not unless you counted Hector's mean-spirited, mocking laughs as Victor had gotten trapped in the volcano's caldera. He sat on the sofa across from Lo'ro. "Thank you for picking me up."

"Oh! He has *manners*, too! I wouldn't have guessed from the way you thrashed those mewling pups in the dungeon." The coach lurched, and Victor felt a sinking sensation in his stomach, indicating they were moving upward and quickly. "We'll travel to my research tower, and from there, I'll guide you through the veil. Don't worry; I made it sound like this would be a difficult job when I spoke to your master, but it won't be so bad. We'll be done by lunchtime." He chuckled and cleared his throat. "For those of us who eat lunch."

"I'm still not totally clear on what we're going to—" Victor started to fish for details about their task, and Lo'ro chuckled, waving a hand.

"I'll take you through the veil into a plane of suffering and woe, a place reserved for those spirits obsessed with darker emotions, overwhelmed by them, and lost to their pitiless embrace. You'll capture one or two of them and bring them back to this plane of existence so that your master can teach you to cultivate from them."

"Yeah, he kind of said that, but, like, why?"

"Why?" Lo'ro lifted a hairless brow. "You surprise me! I know you're not a dolt, so I must assume you understood my words when I said that you can cultivate from them. That means you must question the act of cultivating itself. Hmm, do you have another way to strengthen your Core?"

Victor had not meant that, but now that Lo'ro asked, he found himself looking down, not willing to share his secret about consuming the hearts of his foes. "I have other ways to cultivate," he said, trying to deflect. "I create constructs of my emotions, pure, essential memories of rage or fear, for instance, and reflect on them. Doing that, I slowly create Energy to add to and build my Energy pool."

The deflection didn't fool Lo'ro. "Ah, the lad has a secret!" His dusty words faded into a soft chuckle as he shook his head. "Keep it, young prodigy. You and I both know that, yes, you can cultivate a spirit Core through reflection and meditation, focusing on the powerful emotions your memories can harbor. We also both know that it will only get you so far. You must seek sources of Energy outside yourself if you want to master your cultivation. I can tell from the strength blazing in that inferno of roiling emotions you call a Core that you've broken through at least a couple of tiers, so you must have something more that you're not sharing with me. Something to do with that Breath Core, perhaps?"

Victor looked up sharply, narrowing his eyes, hoping that if he looked defensive about his Breath Core, it might deflect from his real secret. It seemed to work, because Lo'ro chuckled and waved it off. "Worry not. I have my interests when it comes to Spirit Casters, but such a strange application is too novel, too bloodline-specific to be of much use to me and mine."

"Bloodline-specific?" Now, it was Victor's turn to show interest.

"Not just anyone can grow a Breath Core! Draconic species, elemental beings, and just a handful of elder races with the right constitution, I'd say. Still, I wonder how you did it. How'd you get that second Core to take root in there, hmm?"

For the second time in just a few minutes and from a completely different angle, Lo'ro began to pry at the edges of Victor's biggest secret. How pissed would Dar be if he told this guy about his ability to consume hearts for his own gain? He had no idea, of course. The master Spirit Caster hadn't told him not to mention it, but somehow Victor knew he shouldn't. "It's a long story," he grunted, closing his eyes and leaning back on the couch. He decided it was better to be a little churlish than to spill his guts. He snorted as he thought of the word. Churlish—he must have gotten that one from Borrius.

Lo'ro rasped a soft chuckle, and when he spoke, Victor realized he'd made the right decision. "Keep your secrets, then, lad. I'm sure my old friend warned you about trading information freely among our kind. It's not as though he didn't pay dearly for what I will teach you today."

They rode in silence for several minutes before Victor said, "Dar was trying to explain the realms beyond the 'veil' to me. He said something along the lines of how spirits are influenced by their lives, by what they believe, when it comes to what happens to them after they pass beyond the spirit plane. Am I understanding that correctly?"

"Indeed. Consider the tortured spirits we'll be seeking today—they lived lives obsessed with negative emotion to the point that it overcame their personality, their desires, and their dreams. When they died, they embodied that emotion. Passing through the veil, they find themselves drawn to kindred spirits. Their combined will and influence carved out a piece of the universe, a plane for them to haunt and wallow in their misery. Dar mentioned fear and rage and, as luck would have it, I've found a plane on which many such spirits roam."

"What about my other affinities? Glory or inspiration?" Victor figured the Death Caster, being a peer of Dar's, would at least know his affinities, so he didn't bother trying to hide them.

"Ah, think, Victor!" Lo'ro squinted his eyes once again in genuine amusement. It was plain for Victor to see that he enjoyed teaching. "What will you be doing with these spirits?"

"Cultivating from them, right? So, I'll be drawing the rage and fear out of them—"

"Correct!" He stared at Victor, waiting for him to make the next connection.

"So, if I found a spirit with an excess of glory . . ." Victor trailed off, trying to imagine it. He snapped his fingers. "It wouldn't be right. Draining a positive or even partially positive affinity would be wrong."

"Yes! Now, many cultivators wouldn't care. If you wanted to be evil, though—why, you could capture a living soul who exhibits great glory or inspiration and cultivate from them, far easier than finding such a being on one of the many planes of existence beyond our own. Your master believes in karmic bonds, debts, and merits, however. What we do today will be a net positive in his eyes. Can you imagine how?"

"I guess, when I take these souls consumed by anger and fear back to my cultivation chamber and siphon away those negative emotions, over time, I'll be helping them?"

"Exactly so, lad! You'll be doing your part to help those spirits move on from the folly of their previous lives. If you believe Dar's preaching, the spirits we seek have built up a tremendous karmic debt. Using them for cultivation will help them pay it off, allowing them to move on to a new existence."

"I get it. So I'll need to find different sources of Energy for glory and inspiration."

"Yes, I'm afraid I'll not be helping with that. Your master will have plans within plans, however."

As the coach lurched, and Victor felt as if he were riding in an elevator going down, he asked, "Have you known him long?"

"Oh, yes. We've been friends and foes for more years than I care to count."

"Enemies?"

"Certainly, though only for brief spats. Overall, we see eye to eye." The coach shuddered to a stop, and he stood, walking toward the polished wooden door.

"We've arrived." When Victor followed him out, he found they were atop one of the many spires of the Arcanum where he'd first met Dar. This particular tower was black as coal and just as flat and nonreflective. Victor could only see the top fourth or so, looming above the dock where Lo'ro's coach had settled, but it fit any preconceived notions he might have had about a Death Caster's lair. Victor turned, scanning the dozens of spires within view, wondering if the one Dar used was in sight.

"Looking for your master's tower?"

"Yeah. Just curious . . ."

"It's that way." Lo'ro pointed into the thin clouds toward an angular, pointed spire. "Past that tower a ways. I can't see it from here at the moment, but if the sun's just right and the clouds cooperate, sometimes I catch a glimpse." He moved to the big black metal door. "Come."

Victor grunted in agreement and started after him, following the Death Caster through dark hallways, down winding iron stairs, and into a vaulted black marble chamber about the size of a half-court basketball gym. Victor thought of it in that light because of the rows of tiered benches on either side of the smooth black stone floor. The ceiling was vaulted, and strange, foggy, pale blue lights hung from the black stone arches holding the ceiling aloft.

"Don't mind the extra seating; my students will not be attending us. Still, this room has wonderful resonance with the spirit plane, and I've already created a breach through the veil on the other side. Make yourself comfortable." He gestured to the smooth stone floor. Victor nodded and sat down cross-legged in the center of the room. Lo'ro moved to sit before him and said, "First, the bulk of my debt to Dar will be paid in the form of a spell pattern."

"Oh?" Victor hadn't expected to learn a new spell.

"That's right. I discovered this technique through many years of research and have only taught it to two of my apprentices. Well, and Dar, of course. The only reason he's having me help you is because I did the same for him when he built his latest cultivation chamber. Still, this is valuable knowledge, Victor."

"Um, thank you, Master Lo'ro." Victor suddenly felt the need to show more respect. There was no denying the man before him was powerful, and knowing that, it didn't rankle his Quinametzin pride to be a little subservient.

"Study this," Lo'ro wheezed, producing a paper-thin sheet of silvery metal stamped with the pattern for a complex spell. He set it on the floor between them, and Victor leaned forward, eyeing the intricate whorls mixed with sharp angles; it was a spell unlike any he'd ever learned, but nothing near as complicated as the Alter Self spell he'd learned from Tes.

While he stared at it, Lo'ro continued to speak. "I will supply two vessels in which you will capture the wayward geists."

"Geists?"

"A term I use to describe spirits consumed by emotion." Victor was smart enough, even when he was just a kid from Tucson, to recognize a word from Earth. He was also smart enough to know the System was probably choosing that word to fit whatever term Lo'ro used. Whenever he thought about the System and its strangely powerful language integration skill, he found himself falling down rabbit holes of contradictory evidence, so he forcefully turned his mind away from it. He instead continued staring at the pattern, trying to memorize its many shapes.

Meanwhile, Lo'ro had produced two polished bones, densely inscribed with runes. He glanced at them, noting the harsh angles of the runes, far different from those the System used on its many artifacts. One of the bones looked like a femur, and the other was curved and thin, like a rib. Victor wondered if they came from people or animals, but he didn't really want to know. "These took my apprentices many hours to prepare properly; understand that, and be aware that I will not teach you how to replicate them."

"Okay." Victor didn't know what else to say; did Lo'ro expect him to argue? To beg for the knowledge? If he ever wanted to learn how to make vessels that could hold spirits, he doubted Lo'ro was the only person with such knowledge; even Belikot back on Fanwath had been able to do it.

"Now, once you've learned that pattern, we'll step onto the spirit plane where my window through the veil awaits. I'll guide you to the unquiet geists, but it will be up to you to choose the right ones and capture them. Even though I've given you the spell to do it, you'll have to overpower their will, so it's important that you don't choose spirits that are too powerful. It's also important not to find one too weak; what good would that be for cultivation?"

"No, I guess that wouldn't be much good," Victor grunted, only half listening as he studied the pattern.

"I've promised Dar that I'd show you this much and guide you, but I've no obligation to protect you from your own folly. Attempt to bind the wrong spirit, and it could overwhelm your will and follow your tether back to your body." That got Victor's attention, and he looked up and frowned.

"They could take over my body?"

"There will be geists in the realm I lead you to who are far more powerful than you. I'll protect us from their attention, but should you attempt to capture one, there's not much I can do to keep them at bay." Lo'ro reached up and took his fancy round hat off, sending it into a dimensional container.

Victor noted his wispy white hair, and a stray thought came unbidden to his lips. "Do all Death Casters become undead?"

"Ha! Not easily daunted, are you?" Lo'ro shook his head, chuckling that raspy laugh. "Not all, Victor, though the paths to power through death-attuned Energy almost all lead to that road in one way or another. It's difficult to walk the balance between life and death without the perspective undeath provides." He gestured to the pattern in Victor's hand. "Well? Are you ready? You needn't memorize it perfectly; I'll create a circle of relative calm where you can concentrate on your first casting."

"Oh, in that case, yeah, I'm ready." Victor nodded. He wasn't scared off by Lo'ro's warnings. If it was a matter of will, he was more than qualified. It sounded like he just had to avoid being stupid and trying to bite off more than he could chew. On the heels of that thought, another came to him, and he asked, "Will it be difficult to tell how powerful the geists are? Will I be able to gauge their strength?"

"Excellent question! You will have two jobs while I maintain our calm oasis—identify the geists with the proper affinity for you to cultivate, and then determine if you can overpower them with your will. Some will be obvious, but others not so much, and it is those that you must target; pick something too weak, and it will be a waste of our time, but pick something too strong, and . . ." He trailed off, opening his hands as he shrugged.

"Right." Victor chuckled, then he summoned his coyotes using inspiration-attuned Energy. They sprang out of white-gold clouds of Energy, yipping and whining as they paced around the two men. Their nails clicked on the marble, and one paused to lick Victor's neck. "Good boy," he laughed, unslinging Lifedrinker and laying her across his knees. "I'm ready."

Lo'ro wore an amused expression, his black eyes gleaming from beneath his pale, bony brow. He watched the coyotes for several long seconds, then nodded. "Wise to have your companions guard you, though this room is quite secure. Nevertheless, I won't hold it against you." He lifted the two bones and nodded to Victor. "When you're ready."

"Here we go," Victor whispered, mostly to himself, as he formed the pattern for Spirit Walk. The world shifted, and he became aware of the spirit plane; he felt a baleful blast of death-attuned Energy and leaped to his feet, shielding his eyes from the brilliant, icy-blue rip in the fabric of reality that hung in the air before him. Lo'ro's tear in the veil reminded him of Belikot's half-formed one, though the Energy wafting off it was a thousand times more potent. Moreover, it reminded Victor of Hector's veil star. As dark thoughts and memories crowded for attention in his mind, he looked to the Death Caster, only to find a nightmare standing where Lo'ro had been sitting.

11

LOADED PROPOSITION

Darren sat on the bench, carefully nibbling the edges of the pastry, trying to savor the softer, sweeter, cream-filled portion at the center. Edeya had no such intention—she wolfed hers down in two big bites, groaning in pleasure as the hot fresh dough melted in her mouth. "Now it's gone," Darren teased, taking another small bite.

"Worth it!" She licked her fingers. "How can you even enjoy such tiny bites?" They were waiting for Lam in the small park at the entrance to the network of trails leading to a few different dungeons, including the Grotto. When it had taken Lam nearly an hour to respond to their first message, saying they were out, Edeya had insisted on waiting for word, just in case she was already in the park, en route, or elsewhere. It turned out to be a good idea; the older Ghelli was on her way to escort them to one of Victor's mentor's homes.

"You think Lam will agree with you about your class choice?"

Edeya shrugged, wiping her fingers on her pants. "I hope so, but I'm willing to consider the other option." She'd narrowed her decision down to the two "epic" options she'd been offered, refusing to consider any of the "advanced" ones. Darren had to admit that the class she preferred sounded decidedly fierce—Nimbus Reaver. Moreover, it seemed to focus on her strengths: her water affinity, weapon skill, and ability to fly. The other option was called a Cerulean Gale Summoner, and Edeya thought it was more of a caster class. Both epic options mentioned her "Cobalt Wing" bloodline as being critical in their unlocking.

"Whatever your choice, it seems like you're on a much different path than when you first gained levels." Darren tried to be encouraging, but there must have been a hint of concern in his tone because Edeya looked at him more closely with those big glittering blue eyes of hers.

"Something bothering you?"

"Oh, um, no." Darren forced a smile. "I think I'm just a little worried about my first choice. I haven't exactly been training my whole life for this sort of thing like you have. I also don't have a fancy bloodline or—"

"Oh hush, Dare! You're going to be fine. You have an amazing Core and powerful affinities. I bet you get at least an advanced option."

"I hope you're—" He cut his words short as he saw a slender, very human-looking young woman leaning close, slowly inching toward the two of them. She had pale skin and rosy cheeks, and she kept pursing her thin pink lips in half-formed words as though she wanted to say something but feared interrupting. Darren pondered her, wondering if she was, in fact, human; her hair was a nondescript black, her eyes pale brown, and he didn't see any wings or horns or other things that might set her apart. "Um, hello?"

"Oh, dear! Excuse me! I didn't mean to intrude, but I saw you two leaving the Grotto and meant to approach you. I got a bit turned around on the path and only just now stumbled upon you." She had a melodic voice and spoke with a funny quirk, stressing the first syllable of seemingly random words.

Edeya regarded her coolly, her wings fluttering as she turned on the bench to face her more fully. "What can we help you with?"

"Um . . ." The girl—Darren didn't think she could be much older than twenty—held her hand to her chest, gently touching the blue gem hanging from a loose silver necklace. "I'm Trin, Trin Volpuré, and I'm seeking Tier One adventurers to fill out my party."

"Sorry." Edeya waved her hand dismissively. "We're good."

"Hang on, Edeya," Darren said, feeling a little sorry for the girl. She looked positively crestfallen as she turned away.

"Oh, fine," Edeya sighed. "We'll listen to what you have to say, but we're a strong duo and not really looking for a party right now. We have our own friends we need to catch up to."

"Is that so?" Trin took another step closer, standing so she faced both Darren and Edeya. "Well, you should know that a strong party makes leveling all the faster! Additionally, the reason I'm trying to form a party, rather than soloing as I have been, is that my father acquired a pass for First Clash Coliseum—I've heard of people gaining five levels into the second tier from a run through there. Of course, they likely went in at Level Nineteen; that's the level limit for the place."

"Really?" Edeya shifted her gaze from the willowy woman to Darren. "I just hit Ten, and Darren's only Six. I think you should keep looking."

"But you seemed so upbeat after exiting the Grotto; it seemed you had an easy time of it . . ." She trailed off, stepping back and looking Darren up and down.

"I mean, it was kind of a walk in the park, to be honest." Darren wasn't sure if he was trying to impress the girl or save face after Edeya outed him as a Tier Zero neophyte.

"I myself am Level Fourteen, but we have two weeks! Surely you can gain the first tier by then—Darren, is it?"

"Right, Darren." He held out a hand, a reflex from his recent years as a politician and a businessman before that. Trin regarded it for a moment with narrowed eyes, then clasped it. Her fingers were strong and warm, making him feel much more comfortable about her.

"Look, you only just met us, found out we're kinda low-level, and you're still pushing? Don't you have some friends you could ask?" Edeya sounded suspicious, but Darren couldn't really blame her; she made a good point.

"I have friends," Trin replied, nodding, "but we compete more than we help one another. I've been a bit on the outs with some of them ever since they formed a party without me and completed Dagger's Wharf. The truth is that my best friend is now Tier Two and won't give me the time of day. I'm desperate to help her hone her humility!"

"We're waiting for a ride, so listening won't hurt." Darren nudged Edeya's knee. "Tell us about this First Clash Coliseum."

Trin grinned, and suddenly she was holding a canvas camp stool. She set it down so she could sit and face the two of them as she spoke. "It's a dungeon set up like a series of arenas! You enter directly into the first arena, fight a wave of monsters, and then the boss. If you win, the door opens, and you progress to the next arena. It's supposed to be amazing! The crowds are populated by dungeon-dwelling denizens, and I've heard stories about them throwing coins and trinkets into the arena if they like your performance. Each arena offers a unique treasure, and there's even a title awarded to those who finish the whole coliseum."

"A title?" Darren frowned at Edeya.

She shrugged. "It's a special System award that usually gives you a feat."

"That's right!" Trin said. "There are reports of several different titles being awarded in this dungeon."

"And you have to be Tier One to go in?" Edeya clarified.

Trin smiled, and Darren noted a small gap between her front teeth. "Correct."

Edeya sighed, shaking her head. She glanced at Darren, clearly annoyed that she was the only one being critical. "Look, it sounds great. I won't deny that, but don't you think it's odd to come up to a couple of random strangers and ask them to do this with you?"

Trin nodded, but her smile didn't falter. "It would be strange, but I haven't been completely forthright with you. To me, you aren't random."

Edeya lifted an eyebrow. "Go on."

"My older brother, Arcus, was in the recent challenge dungeon. A man—I believe it was your friend or patron or father—I don't know—beat my brother. It was the happiest moment of my life!"

Edeya turned red and almost choked. "Victor is not my father!" She laughed, slapping Darren on the knee.

Darren grinned along with her at the idea; as far as he had surmised, Victor was quite a bit younger than he was. Still, he tried to defuse Edeya's sudden hysteria. "He's kind of a patron, though."

Trin smiled along with Edeya's laughter. She didn't seem insulted as she shrugged. "Whatever he is to you, I am forever in his debt. He took my prideful brother down a few notches and lightened the shadow in which I live."

Edeya finally relented, breathing deeply, smiling as she slapped Darren's knee again. "Well, that's neat, but how do you know who we are?"

Trin leaned closer and spoke softly. "My family is wealthy, and I have many employees at my disposal. When your, um, patron, Victor, beat Arcus, I immediately had my head of security research him. I was desperate to know more about the man who humiliated my brother in the first few minutes of the challenge. I'm sorry for the intrusion, but when I learned he had family or close friends who were near my level, it just felt like fate. You see, my father only gave me this dungeon pass because Arcus lost."

Darren leaned back, folding his arms over his chest. He didn't love the sound of the whole thing. It felt like scheming, and he was trying to get away from that sort of business. Edeya gave him a questioning look, and he said, "I don't like the idea of you using us as pawns to get at your brother. We don't know enough about the politics in this city to get involved in something like that."

"Pawns? Not at all! I want to be strong! I want to make allies of people who are themselves allied with the great Victor! Surely you'd be boon companions; I wasn't lying when I said you seemed relaxed and unharrowed by your time in the Grotto. Not everyone comes out of there so chipper."

She sighed and twisted her hands before her, looking deeply into Darren's eyes. "My brother has eclipsed my life. My entire existence is a mere amusement for my father, an excuse to spend money on pretty necklaces or dresses while he devotes all of his real resources toward building Arcus and my other siblings up to their tests of steel. When your patron thrashed him, it was an eye-opening experience in my household. Only minutes after Arcus was rescued, my father gave me this dungeon pass, and I believe it's a test; he wants to see what I can do with it."

Darren opened his mouth to respond, but then Edeya pointed and jumped up. "Lam's here!" She turned to Trin and said, "It's an interesting proposal. Is there some way we can get ahold of you?"

"Of course!" She, too, stood and produced a small gold-leafed card, a bit larger than a modern business card. "My calling card." Edeya took it, turning it front to back, a puzzled twist to her lips as her upturned nose twitched. Trin quickly added, "Simply channel some Energy into it, and we'll be able to communicate for a few moments."

"Sounds good. Nice to meet you, Trin. Let's go, Dare!" Edeya practically skipped toward Lam and the waiting coach, her wings veritably showering the cobbles with sapphire motes of Energy.

Darren started after her, but Trin took his wrist, tugging until he looked back into her eyes. "It was very nice to meet you, Darren. I hope you'll consider my offer."

"Yeah." He smiled, rather enjoying her gentle touch. "Of course we will."

"I mean, even if your friend is uninterested, I hope you'll still consider it. Here." She handed him a calling card just like she'd given Edeya.

"Dare! Come on!" Edeya called, and he glanced back to see both of the Ghelli ladies waving at him to hurry.

"I gotta—"

"Yes, I'm sorry to delay you." Trin released his wrist, and Darren smiled at her once more before hurrying away. He was interested, and he thought Edeya probably was too. Still, the whole family politics aspect was a little off-putting, and he thought it would be wise to talk to Lesh about things first. He chuckled at the idea; the old Darren wouldn't have trusted anyone's opinion over his own.

"Maybe I really am changing," he muttered, smiling as he approached Lam.

"Are you ready?" Lam asked, grinning very brightly. "You two will love the house where Victor's mentor has us staying. I'm not sure how long we'll be allowed to stay, but we'll enjoy it while we can." She opened the coach door. "Come on, I have some rather big news for you, Dey-dey."

"Really? Well, wait until you hear about my new class options!"

Lam smiled and winked at Darren. "I'm breathless with anticipation!"

Lo'ro the Grim had a terrifying countenance on the spirit plane. His form had stretched to match Victor's, standing nearly ten feet tall, but his arms and legs were long and skeletal beneath his tattered, layered black robes. His face, though, was a thing of nightmares—great black hollows in which white, haunting flames flickered, sharp cheekbones, pulling free of the paper-thin gray flesh that struggled to contain his skeletal maw with its worm-filled jagged teeth, and a forked tongue that slithered along his rotten lips like a black, two-headed worm.

He coughed at great length as Victor stood to his full height, Lifedrinker humming in his hands, yearning to cleave the monstrosity before him. After a moment, Lo'ro gathered himself and said, "My aspect here reflects my Core more than I'd like; I've mastered some facets of the spirit plane, but it's never been a comfortable place for me. Come, I'll tune the aperture to the realm we seek, and we can step free of this vile place."

Victor squeezed Lifedrinker, reining her in; Lo'ro might be a disgusting Death Caster on the spirit plane, but that didn't make him weak. He nodded and watched as the master of death chanted an ancient-sounding limerick in a language the System didn't translate, and then the blazing blue rend in space flared with black smoke and took on a gray hue. "Now!" Lo'ro cried, and he led the way, stepping into the light. Victor figured he was too committed to back out, so he followed him. It felt like his body flash froze as he passed through, and when he took stock of his surroundings, his spirit form's teeth were chattering.

His eyes were immediately drawn to Lo'ro, who once again looked like his physical self, back on the material plane. The realm they stood in was a featureless gray plane, and Lo'ro's faintly translucent body bled black smoke into the gray air. Victor looked down at himself and saw that his usual form prevailed on this plane, too, though he was limned with faint white light that wisped away into foggy smoke. "What's with the smoke?"

"Our Cores bleed Energy to keep us solid in this place. Fear not. You're strong enough to last a good long while. Ware, now, while I craft a circle." Lo'ro summoned a long, thin black rod and began to trace it on the weird gray ground. The white-gray light of the aperture through which they'd traveled illuminated their surroundings for nearly fifty yards in every direction, and Victor slowly turned in a circle, wondering what the denizens of that place might look like.

Lo'ro drew a circle and then began etching runes within it while Victor watched their surroundings. He didn't have to wait long before he saw his first geist. It floated in the air, a being of red light that twitched and flickered, occasionally giving Victor glimpses of its features—a skeletal hand, a yawning, silently screaming mouth, wide horror-filled eyes, and strands of wispy, ragged hair. The creature drifted past them, never coming close, and as it moved beyond the light of the aperture, it faded from sight. "How do I tell which geists share my affinities?"

Lo'ro grunted as he scrawled another glowing white rune into the gray silty soil. "You'll feel it. Don't worry; they'll start to crowd around after I finish my circle; it will bait them close while keeping them at bay."

Victor stooped to touch the ground, noting it felt a lot like the wet sand near the lake back in the Free Marches. "What is this stuff?"

"No idea. The primal roots of the universe? The spirits who've carved this dimension out aren't concerned with scenery—this is a place to wallow in misery and hate." Lo'ro straightened, and his rod disappeared. "Done! Get that spell ready." Victor nodded, lifting the silvery sheet. He glanced at it, studying it while they waited. He was confident he could build the pattern in his pathways.

Proving that the Death Caster knew what he was talking about, a few geists drifted out of the grayness. They weren't all red like the first one Victor had seen; some were sickly green, others shades of gray and black, and still others in varying intensities of red, from pale, nearly pink, to deep bloody crimson. "Do the colors indicate an affinity?"

"Perhaps," Lo'ro chuckled. "Use your inner eye."

The geists began to drift toward them, hissing and moaning, their features obscured by the wisps of smoky steam drifting off their forms. Victor could catch glimpses, though, their faces flickering with expressions of fury and pain, agony and terror. He closed his eyes and looked in on his Core, expanding his view outside himself, and then he saw what Lo'ro meant—the various geists were like flames burning Energy. Victor immediately recognized some with fear and rage attunements; the Energy was too familiar to miss.

He began to understand what Lo'ro had meant about the geists varying in strength. Some of those flames flickered like candles, some burned bright like torches, and still others were like geysers of fire, difficult to look upon. Victor wondered if he could dominate such a spirit. He was concentrating on the red, rage-attuned geists, trying to choose a target for his first spell, when he heard a soft, sibilant whisper enter his mind: *"I sense a kindred fear in your heart, bright one."*

Victor looked toward the source of the sound—how he could tell, he didn't know—and saw a dark purple-black flame, a powerful, overbearing one that roared up from the ground like a pillar of billowing black smoke. He stopped looking with his inner eye and saw the geist, a willowy, spectral woman sheathed in misty black and purple steam. The steam parted long enough for him to catch a glimpse of her horror-filled expression, wide eyes, yawning mouth. It flickered, and he swore she smiled, suddenly serene. It only lasted an instant before awful fear returned, clouding her eyes and twisting her face.

The voice came into his mind again: *"Take me! Take me with you, and I'll whisper secrets your master could only dream of."* Victor frowned, wondering if she meant Lo'ro. Surely that was the case; there wasn't any way the geist could know about Ranish Dar. The idea that this spirit could communicate bothered him. Lo'ro had suggested that the spirits or geists, as he called them, were driven mindless by their past lives, their overcultivation of fear or rage, or whatever other negative emotional affinity they'd taken in.

He looked at the Death Caster and saw his dark eyes on him, watching intently. Victor cleared his throat. "Should they be able to speak to me?"

"What?" Lo'ro chuckled, shaking his head. "Are you daftly trying to communicate with them? They're mindless! Choose one and try the spell, lad; I've plans for the rest of my day."

"Your master knows little. Take me! I won't fight!" The voice came to him again, and Victor switched back to his inner eye, studying the powerful, dark pillar of midnight purple Energy. The geist was strong; if it was overwhelmed by fear, how could it talk to him? Why would he be foolish enough to listen? Again, she spoke into his mind: *"Secrets! Bind me; take me from here! Help me!"*

If the thing hadn't said those last two words, if it hadn't asked for help, Victor might have ignored it. He might have chosen caution for once in his life and picked a fear-attuned geist with a much smaller presence. How could he ignore the pleas of any being able to think and form words in a place like that, however? The smart thing would be to back away, not risk this thing trying to trick him, trying to overpower him, or trying to follow his spirit tether back to his physical form.

Regardless of what was smart, his Quinametzin pride wouldn't let him back down. Not from a challenge and not from a plea for help. That was one factor. The other was that Lo'ro didn't even know it was possible for a geist to communicate; how could Victor ignore such a development? How could he pretend it didn't happen and leave it behind? Carefully weaving a thick rope of bright, glory-attuned Energy, he built the pattern for the spell Lo'ro had given him, and, focusing on the purple-black geist, he cast it.

12

UNQUIET ANCESTORS

As Victor meticulously completed the intricate pattern, the spell snapped into place, and a surge of Energy was drawn from his Core. Despite crafting the spell with glory-attuned Energy, a choice he instinctively believed would be most effective in subduing the will of a fear-attuned geist, the spell drew from all of his affinities, blending his various Energy types as it materialized. He could feel it flowing out of the pathway apertures in his hands, manifesting in the air. Mighty spectral chains burst forth, their clanking links resonating eerily as if the sound had to ascend from a profound abyss.

The black, fear-drenched geist jerked back at their touch, thrashing, but Victor could feel the tugs, and they weren't strong. It was almost as though the spirit was putting on a show, making it look as if she was resisting while in reality she welcomed the embrace of the bindings. He could feel the spell working, binding her Energy and seeking a place to cage it. He glanced at Lo'ro and saw the Death Caster watching intently, a mad gleam in his eye, and the rune-inscribed rib bone held ready.

"That's it, lad. You've captured a formidable one—with such ease! I'm astounded! Now, direct the chains to this vessel." Victor obeyed, exerting his will through the Energy-forged chains, guiding them toward the bone. The geist silently writhed and screamed, but he encountered little resistance as the radiant, spectral chains plunged into the bone and began to retract, drawing her in. Victor observed, pondering the enigma he had become a part of; he could perceive with his inner eye that the geist was potent, yet he barely had to exert himself to guide the chains into the bone. Was the ruse just meant to fool Lo'ro, or was he also being duped in some greater scheme?

As if reading his mind, the voice came into his head again, *"Thank you for taking me! The bindings on this cage will keep me silent, but if you hold it, we can speak again. I will await your call, fear-brother!"* With that, the chains lurched, yanking her spectral form into the bone with a final baleful red flash of the many jagged, harsh runes.

"Well done! You made quick work of that one! Do you require rest before attempting the second?"

Victor took a deep breath and let it out slowly, glancing at the System messages he'd previously ignored:

*****Congratulations! You've learned a new spell: Greater Spirit Binding, Advanced.*****

*****Greater Spirit Binding, Advanced: You have learned to bind a bodiless spirit using spirit-attuned Energy. Once bound, you can draw it into a properly prepared vessel. This spell pits the potency of your Energy combined with your will against that of the spirit, though the greater nature of this spell offers a force multiplier in your favor. Failure to control the target spirit will give it access to your spirit's vessel. Energy Cost: 10,000. Cooldown: minimal.*****

Victor's eyes widened when he saw the spell was at the "advanced" stage—not something he'd complain about. "I should be good for another," he grunted, noting he'd already gained back a quarter of the Energy the first spell had required. His high will attribute was proving to be quite a boon when it came to Energy regeneration. A thought occurred to him, and he asked, "The spell description specifies spirit-attuned Energy. Are you also a Spirit Caster?"

Lo'ro nodded, his thin lips pulling back in a sly smile. "I have some small talent, a specialized Core that harbors death and spirit Energies. I only tell you that much because it's not much of a secret, and I'm sure your master would explain it if you asked him."

"Ah, right. I actually know someone with something similar, though she's let her death affinity atrophy." Victor was thinking of Thayla, but what he didn't mention was that he was responsible for her affinity with courage-attuned spirit Energy.

"Intriguing, but not overly so; half a Death Caster's dealings are with the dead, and many of those are bodiless. It pays to learn a thing or two about the spirit. Still, it's not the same as you Spirit Casters. I don't delve into the deep secrets of my soul, seeking to harness the power of my psyche, my virtues, vices, and traumas. Ha! No, lad, I cultivate a particular brand of attuned Energy, and I do it from an external source. Now, you *must* be ready! Find your second geist, and we can be on our way, my debt to Ranish Dar paid in full."

Victor watched as the Death Caster shifted the rib bone to his other hand and held the long, rune-inscribed femur ready. He changed his view to that of his inner eye and surveyed the geists crowding the circle Lo'ro had drawn. He recognized a familiar heat, a similar smoldering anger in some of the geists. They were universally red-toned, though the darker, deeper, crimson-wreathed ones resonated most with his rage-attuned Energy. He narrowed his target down to a choice between two. Both had a clear rage signature, though one was significantly brighter than the other.

Victor studied the baleful spirit, watching with his inner eye as the fury roiled out of it in a towering flame that eclipsed the lights of the nearby geists. He could feel the furnace of that rage, taste the bitter hate that lingered along the edges of it. Was it too much for him? Could he master such a geist? He had no idea how hard it would be, thanks to the fear geist coming along willingly. The other geist that seemed a match for his affinity was half its size but still significant. Should he settle? Victor snorted, drawing a quizzical glare from Lo'ro, but he ignored the Death Caster.

He'd snorted at his inner dialogue because he knew the question was basically rhetorical by now. It felt as if he was a slave to his Quinametzin ego; if he saw a challenge, he felt he had to take it. Perhaps that was a challenge in itself. Was he in charge here, or was the blood coursing through his veins? Victor changed the focus of his gaze to the smaller yet still potent-seeming rage geist. There was no reason his pride had to push him away from doing something smart. Hadn't he already risked enough by binding that powerful fear geist?

He formed the pattern for Greater Spirit Binding and grinned savagely as the spectral chains burst into being, immediately lashing around the smaller rage geist. From there, things became less amusing as the spirit thrashed and jerked, and this time, Victor felt it. His connection to the chains was palpable, a coil of Energy connected directly to his own spirit, and the creature's first wild, bucking pulls against the chains almost yanked Victor out of the circle. He wrapped his hands around the spectral links and pulled, but it did little. He was being drawn, one shuddering inch at a time, toward Lo'ro's carefully drawn lines.

"Don't pull with your hands, boy! Use your will as you did with the fear geist! What's gotten into you? The rage?"

Victor growled and, switching to his inner eye, focused on the flaming, flaring light of the geist. He bore down on it with all of his prodigious intent, willing it forward, willing it to calm, to settle, and accept its fate. "You're mine now!" Victor snarled, something rising in him, something ancient that knew what it meant to subjugate another's will. Victor didn't like it, but he needed it; he was still losing the tug of war.

As his will surged and his blood grew hot, he could hear Lo'ro chortling as the spirit bent to his demands, slowly, painfully, growing still and drifting toward the bone in the Death Caster's hand. Baleful hate and fury boiled off the geist as it crossed the circle, pulled in by the chains, but by then, it had grown sullen and quiet, and the chains sank into the bone, dragging it along with them.

As the opposition to his will faded, so too did the specter of Victor's bloodline. Was it an ancestor rearing his or her head? Had one of them come through the veil to help him, or was it just a dormant, remnant personality trait buried in his Quinametzin bloodline? He growled, annoyed to have one more thing to watch out for as he continued to grow in power.

Lo'ro interrupted his musings. "I was impressed! That must have been a feisty geist!" He chortled again, then added, "Still, that wave of intent nearly had *me* wanting to crawl into that bone! Ha! Your master will be pleased to hear of it. Now, let's be gone from this realm. Step through the aperture and then end your Spirit Walk."

Victor only scowled, his mind too crowded with dark thoughts to find amusement in the Death Caster's words. He stepped through the rip in the veil, and the frigid cold of the death-attuned Energy did much to cool his frustration. By the time he'd ended his Spirit Walk and found himself sitting among his coyotes, his mood had begun to lift. He let his coyotes lick his face while he waited for Lo'ro's return. Victor dismissed the pack when the Death Caster stirred, sending them home to the spirit plane.

He was slinging Lifedrinker onto his back When Lo'ro opened his eyes and stood, producing a polished ivory case with a silk-lined interior. He gently placed the two rune-inscribed bones into the case, closed it, and handed it over to Victor. "Don't store that in your cheap dimensional containers."

Victor tucked the case against his side, holding it tight with his left hand and elbow. He nodded. "I won't."

"Any idea where your master's run off to?"

"None. He said he had to contemplate some things or something along those lines."

"So introspective, you Spirit Casters!" Lo'ro chuckled again, then beckoned Victor to follow him. "I'll deliver you back to his lake house. You've done me a favor by completing this task so quickly. You might be interested in knowing why I wanted to finish it so quickly." He looked back at Victor, raising one of his hairless eyebrows.

Victor nodded and quickly said, "Yes, sure."

"Recall, if you will, the young lady who nearly completed the challenge dungeon while you tussled around in that great cave."

"Arona?"

"Correct! Her master is Vesavo Bonewhisper, and we're rather friendly rivals. I'm trying to steal her from him." He began climbing the metal stairs that would take them to his tower's dock, and Victor followed, puzzling over his words.

"Steal her?"

"As an apprentice. She's too smart for Vesavo, and he's a cruel master. Well, so am I, but less so, I think." He laughed, that dry raspy laugh of his, and Victor found himself scowling further. If he had Chantico's strength, he might burn the man on the spot to make the world a brighter place. He stopped in his tracks as the thought ran through his mind. Chantico? It took a second for it to click; she was the ancestor who'd gifted him with her fire when he faced the reaver army. He hadn't thought of her name in months, yet he'd just named her like she was as familiar as a friend or cousin.

Lo'ro continued speaking, but when he realized he'd moved ahead of Victor, he paused and looked back. "Something amiss?"

"I'm . . . not quite myself," Victor admitted.

"Ah! Not too surprising, considering the realm you just spent time in. Come now. Let's get you into the coach; you'll be feeling yourself in no time."

Victor grunted and began climbing the stairs again. "Right, sorry about that. What were you saying about Arona?"

"Yes! I'm attending a ball of sorts next week. Vesavo will be there, and I intend to steal his heart with my latest creation. He'll lose his mind when he sees her! He'll simply have to have her, and I intend to bargain for his apprentice." They reached the landing, and he pushed open the heavy metal door, exposing them to the chilly gusts of the heights. Victor stepped out, inhaling the fresh air deeply and sighing in relief to feel the sun on his face. Something about the Death Caster's tower had definitely been rubbing him the wrong way.

As Lo'ro pulled the door closed with a heavy *clang*, Victor looked at the pale, skeletal man. "Your latest creation is a woman?"

"In a sense! She's not done yet, which is why I'm eager to get back to work today. She'll be a construct of flesh and blood, animated by my magic and infused with spirit fragments. It was quite the puzzle to find enough complementing shards, ones that harmonize and strengthen one another. It's been a labor of love for decades." He led the way along the docking spire toward the coach as he continued. "You see, I take more pleasure in the process than the final product, but Vesavo won't be able to say the same; I've crafted her to resemble his first love, a woman we both knew as young men."

Victor thought the whole thing sounded macabre and, frankly, disgusting, and the only thing he could manage to feel other than that was sympathy for Arona. He grunted in a way that he hoped Lo'ro might interpret as him being impressed, then he climbed into the coach, walking over to sit on the sofa where he'd ridden before. He closed his eyes and rubbed them with his thumbs, feeling a headache in the back of his skull, something he hadn't experienced in a very long time.

"That rip in the veil was deep, lad. I have incredible torrents of death-attuned Energy feeding it from my tower. Your exposure to that, and also your spirit's travel beyond the veil—I'm sure, for someone with a sensitive Spirit Core, it threw things out of balance. You'll be fine after a bit more time out in the sun. Dar's lake house is just what the doctor ordered." He paused and added, "Do you have a way to communicate with your ancestors?"

"Um . . ." Victor was surprised by the question and wasn't quite sure how to answer. "I guess sometimes I talk to them. I don't know if they hear. Oh! I can also send them gifts."

"Do so again soon. It may be that they sensed you beyond the veil, which may make them unquiet." Lo'ro sounded sincerely concerned about him, and Victor forced himself to dial back some of the disdain or perhaps just dislike he was feeling for the man. Yes, his magic was creepy, and Victor wasn't on board with it, but he had just taught him a spell and helped him gather two powerful sources for cultivation. Not only that, but he seemed pleasant enough, though Victor would have bet money his joviality was a side effect of doing a favor for Ranish Dar.

He nodded and forced a smile, then closed his eyes, letting his mind wander, thinking about the sun—visualizing its orange-red reflection on Dar's lake. Soon, the image wavered in his mind's eye, and he pictured himself on the ziggurat's steps, the great sky-metal altar behind him, the sun glowing orange-red overtop the thick, hazy jungle canopy. It felt glorious on his face and chest, soaking into his muscles, blood, and bones. He savored it, pulling the potent Energy into his pathways, letting it run through its cycles . . .

"Dead Gods! Wake up, lad!" Victor felt a viselike, frigid grip on his shoulder, jostling him, and he opened his eyes, bleary with disorientation. He smelled smoke, and when he jerked fully awake, leaping to his feet, he saw that Lo'ro's couch was blackened and smoking, and he himself was wreathed in red flames.

"What the fuck?" he grunted, slapping himself, but the flames were cool to the touch and hadn't burned him or his clothes. Still, the couch . . .

"What the fuck, indeed!" Lo'ro laughed. He still gripped Victor's shoulder, and Victor could see his sleeve was scorched, but his hand was unharmed. "Channeling spirit flames through the spirit plane, if I'm not mistaken. You were dreaming?"

"Yeah. Shit, I'm sorry, Lo'ro!" Victor looked down at the couch, relieved to see the fire flickering and fading away from his body. "I was . . . I was one of my ancestors, I think."

"They're worried about you. It seems one of them made a connection, in any case. That should put them at ease. Still, if you have something worth giving them, I'd do so. Your connection to the realms beyond ours is profound; I don't think Dar quite realizes how much so. Is this something you want me to keep between us?"

Victor opened his mouth to respond but paused, weighing the words. Was Lo'ro offering to help him keep a secret from Dar? Was it a trap? Surely the Death Caster valued Dar's friendship more than whatever he had with Victor. Victor sighed and shook his head. It didn't matter; he had no reason to hide his connection to his ancestors from Dar. "It's nothing I'm trying to hide. Thanks for your concern, though. Can I pay for that couch?"

"It's nothing. The damage will be repaired in an hour's time, and I'll have this carriage cleaned; it was due in any case. Luckily, we're just now arriving, and you can get some fresh air and water—things I'm told the living much prefer to an undead lord's crypt-like accommodations!" He laughed, and Victor found it easier to forget his earlier disgust.

Victor held up the ivory case containing the two bound geists, trying to shake off the strange thoughts, feelings, and apparently manifestations that had been plaguing him. "Thank you for all of your help today, Master Lo'ro."

"It was my pleasure. Never doubt I got something out of this little endeavor. I do have a small proposal for you, though, my young friend. How would you like to earn a favor of your own?"

Victor paused by the door, eager to be gone from that strange coach but also intrigued. Lo'ro was a powerhouse; having him in his debt wouldn't go amiss. "I'm listening."

"The ball I mentioned—I'd appreciate it if you attended. I'm certain I can convince Vesavo to make the trade, but Arona might be unwilling; she's grown used to his tutelage and might find the prospect of a new master daunting. If she saw you there as my guest, I might mention that your master and I are rather close and that there may be opportunities for joint training ventures sometime soon. I believe she'll be intrigued. Well, if I were honest, I might say that anyone who witnessed the events in the Vault of Valor would be."

"You want me to help you convince her to switch, um, masters?" Victor hated the word and hated how Dar was constantly being labeled as his master, but it seemed very ingrained in the culture of Sojourn and likely most worlds with powerful cultivators.

"Exactly so! As I said, I'd owe you a favor."

"Um, can I bring a guest?" Victor was missing Valla and figured she might enjoy a party.

"Certainly! Never fear; I'll arrange things with Dar. It's settled, then?" He pulled the door to the coach open, and Victor felt the sun on his face like air to suffocating lungs.

"Sure. I can do that." Victor smiled, respectfully nodded one more time, and then ducked out of the coach and into the bright sunshine. It was glorious. Lo'ro waved and closed the door, and then his ghostly carriage silently streaked away in a hazy cloud of gray spectral smoke. Victor squinted down the drive toward the front of the house, but before he walked toward the door, he fished the Far Scribe book he shared with Valla from his ring and flipped to the last page. He was suddenly desperate for some word from her. To his relief, a new message awaited him:

Victor,

All is well, though we are exhausted and drained. More battles await us after our rest, and I'm on watch. Lesh already snores nearby. I'll share more news when we're out, but for now, I'll give you this good news: We've each gained two levels!

I love you,

Valla

Victor smiled and closed the book. He'd write her a response once he was sitting in the sun with a big glass of something fresh and still full of life, something like orange juice. He clutched the ivory box and started for the house, wondering when Dar would make his next appearance.

13

PERSONAL TIME

When Victor entered Dar's lake house, it was quiet, and the servant who opened the door for him said, "Your guests are down at the lake, swimming, I believe."

He nodded, smiling at the woman. He tried to look her in the eyes while he spoke, but she kept looking down, and he didn't want to press the issue; he couldn't tell if she was trying to be respectful or if it was some cultural thing. "I'll join them soon." He gestured with the smooth ivory case. "I'll stop by my quarters first. Any word from Dar?"

"Lord Dar has indicated that he'll be here for dinner. He does not expect you to join him. I'm sure he'll communicate his expectations. Do you share a Far Scribe boo—"

"Shit!" Victor slapped his head, interrupting her. "I do. I better check it. Thanks!" He hurried to the rooms Dar had given him to use and closed the door. He sat at the suite's study desk, pulled out the Far Scribe book Dar had given him, and flipped past the several dozen pages he'd written in already. On the furthest script-covered page, he found a short note from Dar:

Victor,

Lo'ro has indicated to me that you were successful. He has reported that the experience was hard on you and that your connection to the plane of spirits and your ancestors is particularly sensitive. Given your history, I should have anticipated that. Do not be alarmed; when you stepped through the rip in the veil, no doubt your ancestors sensed it and grew concerned. If they weren't trying to guide you to join them, they certainly, at least, wanted to know where you had gone. Perhaps they sought to aid you. In any case, their unrest will ease knowing you are back among the living.

Take the next few days for yourself. See to your prizes from the competition, consume that monster's heart—I see no reason to delay that process. I've made the decision to allow you and your guests to stay at my lake house until such time that you've built up your fortune and can afford a home more suitable to your stature. At first, I thought it was too much, that I'd spoil you, but I believe the natural environment is vital to your spiritual development. That said, if you need funds, sell your home in the city.

To avoid my ire, check this book each day at sunrise and sunset for my instructions. When we next meet, I'll guide you to a proper location in the caves beneath the lake where we can begin the construction of your cultivation chamber.

Congratulations on your success,

Ranish Dar

Victor read the text twice, feeling strangely comforted by the Spirit Master's words and concern. He looked around the room and smiled; it was a damn sight nicer than the one he and Valla had claimed in his townhome. She was going to love it at the lake house. "How the hell did he find all that out so fast? Lo'ro *just* left!" He chuckled at his muttered words. He supposed he could assume the two masters had some way of communicating that he didn't understand. Maybe Lo'ro spoke to Dar while Victor had dozed, having his ancestor's dream. "Before I burned up the couch!" He laughed.

He reached up to his chest, feeling the vault pendant under his shirt. He supposed Dar's idea of building his cultivation chamber in a cave was smart for now. Victor liked having the vault with him, storing his treasures and secrets, apparently keeping them safe even from people as powerful as Lo'ro and Dar. Nodding with purpose, he left the room, still clutching the ivory box, and made his way out onto the deck. Before he descended the stairs to the pier, where he could hear laughter and splashing, he took his necklace off and opened his vault on a clear section of the deck.

The tiny metallic ball rapidly expanded with clicks and gouts of steam. The deck groaned a little under the weight, but Victor figured Dar had built it to accommodate people of his stature. How much would a dinner party of giants weigh? He chuckled at the image that conjured and opened the vault, stepping inside. His ivid royal jelly, wrapped in the ivid silk, still sat in a satchel against the wall, and Victor set the ivory box containing his two trapped geists down a few feet away from it. That done, he stepped out, closed the heavy vault door, and twisted the key until it began to shrink again.

One of Dar's household staff had approached, a look of concern on his face, but he relaxed and offered a quick nod as Victor bent to pick up the pendant, hanging it over his neck. "Just had to put something away."

"Of course, sir." He gestured toward the stairs leading down to the lake. "Would you like us to prepare refreshments?"

"Yeah, that would be great." When the man nodded and turned back to the house, Victor started down the steps. As he walked, he pulled off his shirt, sending it into the ring where he kept most of his clothes. The sun and lake air felt terrific against his skin, and he let it soak in while he took in the sight below.

Lam and Edeya sat at the end of the pier, wearing garments that looked more like underwear than swimsuits. Their wings were spread wide, fluttering in the warm breeze while they dipped their feet in the water. A splash drew Victor's eyes out to the lake, and he saw Darren floating on his back, his long black hair splayed out in the water behind him like a fan. They were certainly enjoying the setting.

None of them had noticed him yet, and an evil grin spread on Victor's lips as he silently sat on the steps and reached down to send his boots, socks, and pants into his dimensional ring. He stood, wearing just his boxer-like underpants. With an effort of will, he clamped down on his aura, ensuring none of it leaked out, and like a hulking musclebound barbarian sneaking up on a foe, he stalked down to the pier. He crept over its twenty-five-yard length until he was just a few feet behind the two women. He then bunched his thighs and leaped over them, cannonballing into the water.

Screams and curses greeted his ears when he surfaced, and Victor laughed, shaking his head and wiping the water off his face. He looked up with glee, observing the chaos he'd caused. Lam was on her feet, a hammer much smaller than the one she usually used in her right hand. Edeya was hovering in the air behind her, her ivory spear in her hands. Her wings hummed and shed thousands of motes of blue-tinted Energy, and both women scowled, dripping water onto the drenched decking. "What?" he asked with mock innocence.

"Victor!" Edeya screamed, diving toward him, swinging the spear like a club, intending to clobber him. Lam chuckled, shook her head, and sent her hammer back into her ring. Of course, Victor knew more about horseplay in a pool than Edeya was prepared to handle. He snatched the spear haft as she swung it close, and with just a fraction of his titanic strength, he used it to launch her toward the center of the lake.

Edeya howled, her wings humming with effort to correct her flight. She almost succeeded, righting herself and slowing her descent, but not quite enough; she splashed into the water a dozen yards beyond where Darren floated. Victor laughed and reached the spear toward Lam so the other woman could take it and lay it on the pier.

"She's going to be angry!" Lam said, shaking her head.

"Nah," Victor chuckled. "She enjoyed that. See?" He was right; Edeya's wings buzzed and splashed, and then she shot out of the water, streaking back toward the pier. He wasn't sure, but he thought she was flying faster than she used to.

"Bully!" she cried as she settled onto the pier, then plopped down again beside Lam. Victor flopped onto his back in the water, letting his momentum carry him a little farther away from them.

When he surfaced, he chuckled. "I'm going shopping soon; I'll buy you all some swimsuits." He stared up into the hazy sky, amazed by how many stars he could still see, even in the middle of the day.

"What?" Edeya asked, but then Lam laughed, and Victor heard her whisper. "He thinks our impromptu swimming garments are too immodest!"

"Well," he said, trying not to sound like a prude, "I mean, when they got wet, I could see through 'em."

"Creep!" Edeya howled, and when he smiled her way, he saw she and Lam were both shrugging into loose-fitting shirts.

"He's not a creep," Lam said, lifting an arm over Edeya's shoulders. "He's just a man. He didn't have to say anything."

"I know," Edeya sighed. "You know he and I like to tease. Don't fret. Besides, when I tell Valla . . ."

"Hey!" Victor splashed a wave of water her way. "Don't make me pull you down to the bottom!" She kicked water back at him, and when he finished laughing, he said, "So? What did you think of Lam's news?" Victor heard splashing behind him and turned to see Darren slowly swimming back toward the dock. He had a smooth way of moving in the water as though he'd done a lot of swimming in his life.

Meanwhile, Edeya gushed, "It's amazing! We're going to level together! Can you think of anything more wonderful?" Victor had expected her to be a little upset with Lam, considering the risks involved in the process. When he peered at the older woman, she narrowed her eyes and ever so slightly shook her head. That clarified things: Lam had omitted some of the facts. Victor figured she'd give Edeya the details as time passed and the younger woman grew more and more comfortable with the idea.

He considered Edeya's question and shook his head. "No, I really can't. I want to do the same with Valla; I wish circumstances allowed us to do more together."

Lam looked at Edeya and sighed. "I keep trying to tell her that I wanted a second go at leveling, at classes, skills, and rewards. It's not all about you, Deydey." Victor could see Edeya wasn't buying it.

"Of course, of course." She grinned, eyes twinkling. Then she gasped and turned to face Victor. "You gave her a Spirit Core! And we both have new classes!"

Victor knew what she wanted, so he asked, "Well? Tell me about your class, then."

"I'm a Nimbus Reaver, and as soon as I chose it, I gained a skill! Improved flight!"

"I *thought* you seemed faster. Nice one, Edeya. Nimbus Reaver, huh? Sounds tough." He nodded in approval. "You can still use the spear?" He'd given her one of the finer, though not overly heavy and powerful, spears that had belonged to

Karnice, the onetime champion of Coloss. He knew the question wasn't necessary; hadn't he just flung her with that same spear? But he knew she wanted to talk about the class, so he thought it was a good opening.

"Yes! It's a class that will take advantage of my water affinity while nourishing my bloodline development and combat abilities."

"Should go nicely with Lam's new class, too." Victor nodded and turned to look at Darren, who'd been treading water nearby for a while. "Getting close to Ten, Darren?"

He nodded. "Level Six, but close to Seven, I think."

"Cool. Nice job, man." Victor wanted to go for a swim, but he figured he should share some of his news. "Dar gave me permission to live here, and he explicitly said me and my 'guests,' so I think I'll head into town and pick up our belongings from the villa. I think I might sell it."

"Really?" Edeya squealed, and Victor saw her grasp Lam's hand, squeezing it tightly.

"Yeah, he thinks it'll be good for my development." Victor shrugged. "Speaking of development, Lam, I have a few spell patterns I should teach you."

"You'd do that?"

Her surprise caught Victor off guard. He nodded and shrugged. "Of course I will."

"Well." Lam squinted down at him between the fingers of her hand, fighting to make eye contact in the bright glare of the sun's reflection. "I really appreciate that, Victor. We're talking about heading into another dungeon soon. If Lesh and Valla get out in the next day or two, do you think Dar would be okay with us having a dinner party here? Edeya and I want to cook for you."

Victor grinned at the idea. "He said I could live here with my guests, so there's no way he'd say we can't have a dinner party. Besides, who knows how many houses that guy has? I'll write it into the Far Scribe book when I make my report tonight."

"Yay!" Edeya said, throwing an arm around Lam's neck and squeezing her close. "We want to invite someone for you to meet. She asked us to join her party to go into a kind of exclusive dungeon, and we want your opinion about her."

Lam held up a hand. "That's Edeya's idea. I haven't met this girl."

"It's fine with me. Maybe I could invite a friend, too." Victor was thinking of Sora. He flopped back and kicked his legs, moving farther into the water. "I'm heading to town in an hour or so, if any of you want to come. For now, I'm going to try to swim across the lake." With that, he turned and struck out, swimming over the surface, face down, marveling at how good it felt to exert himself in the cool water with the sun on his back.

While he swam and considered the idea of hosting a dinner party, he pictured a few other potential guests. Would Drobna, the turtle-like berserker, want to come? Victor thought it would be fun to chat with him about the things they had in common. He grinned as he imagined inviting Cam, too, just to put him on the spot to see how he acted toward Sora. Would he hold a grudge? Then there was the giant armor-plated warrior and his wife—they'd be fun to talk to, wouldn't they?

When he realized he was thinking of inviting the people he'd thrashed in the dungeon, Victor rolled onto his back and laughed. Was he so eager for some drama? Was he trying to stir shit up, or was he trying to clear the air? He liked to think it was the latter.

He stopped halfway into the lake, not because he was tired but because it was taking too long. He didn't want the whole afternoon to slip away while he swam. When he returned, the others were already on the deck, comfortably dressed and enjoying a light lunch. Victor's stomach rumbled, but he knew it was just habit; he felt amazing after the swim and knew the rich ambient Energy on Sojourn was doing plenty to nourish his body. Still, he sat down with the others and ate a plate of cold meats, each marinated or cured with different seasonings and spices.

The meats were rolled and skewered with toothpicks, along with complementing cold, crisp vegetables, and he wished he had some kind of guide to explain what each of them was. "This is so good," he mumbled around a mouthful. "Valla would love this."

"Lesh wouldn't." Darren laughed. "He'd take a tray, pull out all the toothpicks, and then eat the meat in one or two bites."

Victor laughed and raised an eyebrow at the guy. He was a damn sight different from the suit-wearing politician from First Landing that he'd been. He wore a loose button-up linen shirt, the collar hanging wide, over soft-looking gray slacks. His feet were bare, and his long black hair hung loose over his shoulders. The guy looked like a lounging movie star. "You're looking better, Darren. Just a few levels, and you already seem more . . . solid, I guess."

"Dare was great in the dungeon, Victor!" Edeya said, licking her fingers after a bite.

"Yeah?"

"Yep. I was worried he'd be, you know, maybe a little hesitant, I guess, but he was positively brave. He fended off a toad boss that was twice his size!"

"Dare, huh?" Victor nodded. "I like it. Well, good job." Victor stood and walked toward the house, pausing on his way to clap Darren on the shoulder. He was careful not to knock him out of his seat, and he could see the man's smile broaden at the gesture. "Anyone going with me?"

"I will," Lam said. "I want to shop for new hammers and a shield. I'm going to try to be a front line for these two." She looked at Victor. "Will that be all right? Are you going to a weapon shop?"

"Better—I'm gonna check out the auction house. Sora mentioned it to me while I was in the dungeon. I'm pretty sure we can find you what you need." Victor planned to try to trade one of the five set-piece items he had for a pair of pants in the set; he was tired of his pants getting shredded all the time. He also had his prizes from the campaign back on Fanwath to look into—the magma attunement gem and the lava king hide. "After that, I want to speak to my realtor and stop by the house."

Edeya gestured a toothpick toward Darren. "I'm going to help him cultivate."

Victor nodded. "When you get to Level Ten, Darren, if that staff isn't going to be ideal, I have a shitload of other weapons. We'll make sure you're ready for the next dungeon."

"Thank you!" Darren stood, and it looked as though he was about to bow, but he just nodded respectfully. "I wish there was a way to level without going into a dungeon. Wouldn't it be great if I were Ten before then?"

"A level or two from cultivating and learning spells isn't unheard of," Lam said, "but four levels in just a day or three won't be likely."

"Speaking of spells," Edeya said, leaping up. "Victor, will you see if you can find any cheap lower-level spell patterns for water or lightning affinities? I mean, chaos, too, but that sounds scary, so . . ."

"Uh," Darren said, holding up a hand, "don't go out of your way or anything . . ."

"Relax." Victor chuckled. "I'll check the auction house."

Lam gestured to the door. "Come on, Victor. Before our shopping list grows any more. You can talk to me about courage affinity spells while we ride in the coach."

Victor shrugged and waved at Edeya as he followed Lam through the door. It was nice to have friends around him, but he missed Valla. While he followed Lam to the coach house, he thought about the gargantuopod heart in his dimensional ring. Should he eat it that night? He had Dar's blessing but didn't want to get knocked out for days. What if Valla came home and he missed her? He didn't think that was all that likely—he'd eaten a few potent hearts, and none of them had knocked him out for all that long, unlike the bloodline evolution treasures he'd consumed.

"Yeah," he said, though all he got from Lam was a puzzled look. He winked at her, adding, "I'm going to have a busy night."

14

UPGRADES

"So," Victor said as Dar's coach pulled away, sending his stomach sinking as it lurched into the sky, "Edeya seems happy."

"She is! Thanks, Victor, for not mentioning the risks of the ritual. I'll let her warm up to the idea and put a little distance between us and what I did before I give her those details."

"Yeah, I figured." Victor smiled and leaned back, enjoying the comfortable ride; like Dar's other coach, this one had plenty of room for him at his normal stature. "So you need a new hammer?"

"My current favorite requires a good deal more strength than I can muster. Oh! Speaking of equipment, though, I got you something." She produced a small flat circular stone and handed it over. Victor took it, feeling a slight warmth and a tiny tingle of Energy. It felt good.

"What's this?"

"I met a girl by the path to the lower-level dungeons. She claimed to have a luck affinity and sold these stones for extra money. Do you think it's real? I already gave one to Edeya and Darren."

"There's definitely something in here." Victor narrowed his eyes. "Luck, huh? Is that a spirit affinity?"

"You're asking me?" Lam laughed but nodded and added, "She said it was. I liked the way it felt, and I think mine already brought me some luck. I was rubbing it when I asked Dar to help me."

Victor chuckled. "Well, thanks, Lam. I won't turn down a bit of luck." He tucked the little stone into a pocket. "How about I give you a spell to study? From what I've been able to figure out, it's a courage affinity's version of Berserk. I don't use it much, so I only have it at the basic level, but I bet it gets better and better as you improve it."

Lam leaned close and gripped his wrist in her much smaller hands. "That would be amazing!"

Victor smiled and produced a sheet of paper and one of the magical quills he'd picked up while browsing curio shops. "I have this pattern memorized and could probably draw it blindfolded." As he began to trace the lines, he continued, "It's called Heroic Heart. The basic level of the spell will give you immunity to fear effects and make it hard for anyone to affect your mind with spells that might confuse or even control you. Your will is important, of course, but the spell gives you a massive boost to any resistance you put up."

"That sounds incredible!"

"Yeah, this is the basic pattern I used to create most of my most potent spells; I just try it with different affinities as I gain them. My first was Berserk, then I gained my inspiration affinity and learned to weave that with rage to create courage-attuned Energy. That's how I figured this one out."

"So, mixing other spirit affinities can create a different one?"

"Yep! It's not just mixing, though." Victor finished the pattern with a flourish. He had to admit that his higher dexterity and intelligence were really starting to show in his control of the pen; his lines were straight, his curves perfectly formed, and his artistic flair matched what he imagined in his mind. He'd added shading and contours without even thinking about it. He handed the sheet to Lam. "When you combine different spirit Energies, you have to use the right weave, which takes some guidance to learn the first few times. I'll help you, but first, we need to find a second affinity for you."

Lam took the pattern almost reverently, and her eyes widened as she studied it. "This is so different from the other spell patterns I've learned. It resonates with me somehow!"

"It's meant to use the Energy in your Core, which is now a reflection of your spirit. I bet that's a lot different than learning spells for generic Energy." Lam only nodded, her eyes glued on the pattern. "I have a few other spells I should teach you before you go getting into fights. When we get back to the house, I'll write 'em out for you, okay?"

Lam nodded, blinking her eyes and laughing, looking away from him. "I've been so stupidly emotional ever since the ritual. Thank you, Victor."

"Hey, don't worry about it. If you think you're emotional now, wait until I show you what cultivating is all about as a Spirit Caster." Victor chuckled ruefully. "Be thankful your first affinity isn't rage." He left it at that, and Lam was too engrossed in the spell pattern to dig further into his meaning, so Victor sat back and enjoyed the rest of the short ride into the city.

Their first stop was the Sojourn Auction House, something he'd heard Cam and Sora talking about during their initial meandering trip through the ruins toward the stairs of the competitive dungeon. When they arrived and the coachman opened the door, Victor looked at him and asked, "Mr. Qwor, should we find another ride back to the lake house?"

"No, sir. My latest instructions are to serve as your coachman until Lord Dar instructs me otherwise. I'll remain in the vicinity. If I'm forced to move the coach while I wait, simply tap your signet ring three times, and I'll locate you."

Victor looked down at his ring and frowned. "It can do that?"

"Oh, yes. Three taps for your coach, two to summon a servant in the house. It has other functions, but I'm sure Lord Dar has given you those details."

"Not exactly." Victor shrugged, adding it to the list of things to write to Dar about that evening. He nodded to the driver, then turned, joining Lam near the steps leading up to the auction house. "Quite a building." She only nodded, staring up at the massive blue-crystal rectangular edifice that soared into the sky before them. The crystalline walls were dark blue at the base, in the shadows of the other towers of Sojourn, but grew progressively lighter as they gained altitude and were exposed to more and more light. Near the top, high in the sky, the building blended with the sky to become almost invisible.

"Incredible," Lam said, finally gathering herself and looking to Victor to lead the way.

"Right. I'm not sure how this place works. Like, I wonder if there's always an auction going on or if there's some kind of listing. Let's go in and check things out."

Quite a crowd walked by at the street level, and a constant stream of people climbed the steps to and from the building. Victor had also noticed entrances in the clouds on the crystalline walkways of the elite. "Popular place," he remarked, nodding to Lam and starting up. When they entered the open archways in the crystal walls, the ambient temperature dropped a few degrees, and the lighting reflected the blue of the structure. It wasn't a deep, off-putting color but a calming tint that fell on the pale gray marble floors.

Beings of gas and light operated hundreds of kiosks in the big, open hall. They were members of the same alien species Victor had seen in other official capacities around the city. He'd heard Dar mention their species name when they'd had to go to the "inquest" after his dungeon run, but Victor had already filed it away somewhere too difficult to retrieve. He picked a kiosk without a queue and approached, smiling toward the floating, pulsing ball of yellow light.

"Greetings, Sojourner. I am V-eleven. Are you here to access the auction listings?" The creature spoke directly into his mind, or so it seemed, but Lam's body language indicated she'd heard the voice, too.

"I'd like to learn more about it. Is it difficult to put something up for sale? When are the auctions held?"

"Ah, my apologies," the smooth, genderless voice replied. "When I saw the signet of Ranish Dar upon your finger, I assumed you were more familiar with Sojourn. This auction house is, essentially, a large, never-ending silent auction. You can access the items listed for sale using a menu on your city tablet. I'll gladly take any items you'd like to list on the auction and store them in this building. I'm sorry to say that we cannot list items that aren't in the custody of the Sojourn Auction House."

"Oh, that's even better than I'd hoped." Victor looked at Lam, raising an eyebrow, wanting to ensure she'd heard everything the helpful being had said. She nodded.

V-eleven pulsed, and Victor felt as though it exuded pleasure at his words. "If you would like, I'm happy to help you search through the listings. Is there anything you're interested in finding?"

"Yeah, we have a few things. Can we start with this?" Victor fished his Cloak of Sojourn out of his storage ring and set it on the counter. "It's really nice, and I like it, but I've never been a guy to wear a cape or a cloak, and, honestly, I never get cold. I was hoping to sell or trade it for some pants in the set."

"Direct trades aren't offered through the auction house. However, we can list this item. Similar items have an average list-to-sale time of four days, rounded up. I can see nine different 'pant' variations of items for this set. Would you like me to elaborate?"

"Are the pants different?"

"There are seven cloth variations and two leather. My database indicates that materials, regardless of their starting variety, can be altered by purchasing set upgrades at the Sojourn City Stone."

Lam helped Victor move things along. "What are the prices?"

V-eleven pulsed and said, "The cloth variations range in price from fifteen thousand Energy beads to twenty-seven thousand. The leather variations are twenty and twenty-four thousand."

"What about this cloak? How much can I expect?"

"Seven others are listed for an average price of eighteen thousand beads."

Victor nodded. If he'd known there were so many set pieces in the auction house, he wouldn't have bothered Sora for the cloak. He shrugged and said, "List it for me, will you? Put it up for seventeen thousand. Also, I'll buy the leather pants for twenty k." Almost before he finished his sentence, the cloak disappeared, clearly snatched away to some dimensional container, perhaps the building itself.

V-eleven pulsed again and said, "I've listed the cloak with a twenty-thousand-bead buyout and a one-month auction period with a minimum bid of ten thousand beads. If that's not acceptable, I can change those terms."

Victor thought about that, having never really dealt with an auction house of any kind. It sounded as though anyone could bid as little as ten thousand beads, and if no one else bid, they'd get the item in a month. However, if anyone bid twenty thousand beads, they'd get the item immediately, just as he would for the pants. "Is someone likely to get it for the minimum bid?"

"Minimum bids for such items have a sub-one-percent chance of success on items in the Sojourn City set."

"Okay, I'm fine with those terms."

V-eleven pulsed several times, then said, "I'm sorry, but unless you'd like to open a credit account with the auction house, I'll need to collect payment for the pants before taking them off the listing."

"No problem." Victor dug around in his bag, frowning at his dwindling hoard of Energy beads, and pulled out a large sack of them.

"May I?" the pulsing light asked.

"Yeah, sure." Victor watched as the sack shrank in on itself, the proper number of beads pulled away by some magic. A couple of seconds later, a pair of fine, supple chocolate-colored leather pants appeared on the counter. Victor collected the remainder of his beads and the pants, sending them into storage. "Thanks. I have a few more things to shop for, but talk to my friend here first. This is Lam, and I believe she's in the market for a war hammer."

He listened while V-eleven helped Lam narrow down the thousands of options, settling on a hammer that could be wielded one-handed by someone of her current strength while also providing two magical combat bonuses—reverberating impacts and a paired ring that allowed her to recall it, if thrown, at the expense of Energy from her Core. Victor liked that idea and wondered if there was any way to add such functionality to Lifedrinker. He almost felt he should be able to talk to her about it and, as he'd been doing a lot lately, added it to his list of things to do. Lam also purchased a sturdy round shield, and it was Victor's turn again.

He spent more time than he wanted to, if he were honest, trying to find spell books or just single spell patterns for Edeya and Darren. There were a lot of possibilities, but spell patterns weren't so blithely traded away, it seemed, and there were a lot of restrictions on some of the cheaper ones—exacting affinity requirements, Class prerequisites, attribute prerequisites, and even disclaimers of potential harm if used "incorrectly."

In the end, Victor decided to try to buy some well-known stable offensive spells for each of them. He almost bought a Lightning Strike spell for Darren but stopped when he considered the sheer foolishness of spending nearly forty thousand Energy beads on a spell that Valla could probably teach him. So he asked for any chaos-attuned spells, and that's when he had a much more difficult decision to make. Only one chaos-attuned spell was available in the entire auction house, and it was selling for ninety-five thousand Energy beads.

"Fractured Reality?" he asked, frowning.

V-eleven pulsed rapidly and said, "The listing describes the spell as 'causing distortions and illusions that disorient and confuse enemies in a targeted area.' It's listed as rare."

"I'll buy it," Lam offered. Victor opened his mouth to argue, but Lam pressed, "No, really. I'm going to be spending time in dungeons with him, and I can afford it. Let me get this one. You buy one for Edeya."

Victor thought about it and nodded. He didn't know how much money Lam had squirreled away, but he knew it was probably more than he did. "Okay, cool. In that case, V-eleven, I'll buy the Frozen Aura spell you told me about." It was a spell that would persist as long as Edeya fed it Energy and was supposed to slow enemies she engaged in melee range, at least at the basic level; it might become even more effective if she could rank it up. He handed over another thirty-three thousand beads, and Lam paid for Darren's spell.

"Where now, Victor?" she asked as they stepped away from the kiosk.

"We're near the building that houses the System Stone. Let's go there next; I want to check out what I can do with this armor set I've got." She nodded, and Victor led the way. When they passed by the coach, he let Mr. Qwor know where they were going, and the driver said he'd be waiting outside.

Victor enjoyed watching Lam's reaction walking around downtown, especially when they stepped into the hall where he'd claimed his prize from the dungeon. Her mouth fell agape, and she marveled at Sojourn's enormous, massively upgraded System Stone. "Imagine the millions of beads they've put into that!" Her neck craned back as she sought the highest point of the stone with her eyes.

"More like billions, I'm pretty sure." The hall was busier than when he'd come there with Dar. Hundreds of people milled about and moved to and fro, and lines of citizens led up to each side of the stone, waiting for their turn. Victor led the way up to the shortest queue on the far side of the stone, and they waited for their opportunity to interact with it.

They made small talk about Spirit Cores, Energy weaves, spell patterns, and how Victor had learned what he knew. He found it sort of cathartic to talk about Gorz and Old Mother. He spent half an hour or more talking about the old Shadeni and how she'd reminded Victor of his own grandmother. When he finally got around to mentioning Khul Bach, though, he felt a surge of guilt and hastily changed the subject; he didn't want to think about how annoyed the sleeping Degh spirit would be when he finally got around to filling him in on everything that had happened in Sojourn.

When it was his turn to approach the stone at last, Lam accompanied him up to the dark surface with its hundreds of drifting golden runes. He navigated a simplified menu offered to the public until he came to a section titled **EXCLUSIVE SYSTEM-GRANTED EQUIPMENT SETS**. He selected it and found five options:

IRON RANKED, FIVE-PIECE ARMOR SET
IRON RANKED, TWO-PIECE WEAPON AND ARMOR SET
IRON RANKED, THREE-PIECE ARMOR SET
IRON RANKED, THREE-PIECE JEWELRY SET
LUSTROUS SET

"Huh," Victor said, a little surprised that there were several different sets. Only one option said "five-piece," so he figured that was the one. He selected it, and a prompt appeared:

Please remove the set piece items from storage and place them before the stone.

Victor did as prompted, pulling out the helmet, belt, gauntlet, boots, and pants and setting them on the smooth marble floor next to the stone. Another System message appeared on the weird floating display that apparently only he could see:

This five-piece armor set can be upgraded with Energy-rich materials and enchantments prior to choosing set bonuses. If you wish to do so, place the materials before the stone.

Victor thought about it for a moment, then dug through his rings until he found the "legendary-tier magma-attunement gem" and the "master-artisan-grade hide of a lava king" he'd won during the conquest of the Untamed Marches. He set the heavy, incredibly dense, red smoldering gem on the ground beside the thick roll of supple, deep crimson, mottled leather. Another message appeared:

Analyzing.

"Can it use those treasures?" Lam asked, finally unable to maintain her silent observation.

Victor grinned at her. "I'm about to find out." He watched the word pulse for several seconds, then another message appeared.

Lava King Hide is of sufficient Energy density and size to imbue all five items as follows:

Helm of Sojourn. Infused with the resilience of the Lava King: immunity to fire damage, enhanced density, and rapid damage regeneration.

Belt of Sojourn. Infused with the volatile Energy of the Lava King: once-daily activation to boost the wearer's agility and dexterity. Partially infused with the resilience of the Lava King: immunity to fire damage and rapid damage regeneration.

Gauntlet of Sojourn. Infused with the resilience of the Lava King: immunity to fire damage, enhanced density, and rapid damage regeneration.

Boots of Sojourn. Infused with the swiftness of the Lava King: permanent movement speed boost to the wearer. Partially infused with the resilience of the Lava King: immunity to fire damage and rapid damage regeneration.

Greaves of Sojourn. Infused with the stability of the Lava King: enhanced stability and balance for the wearer, regardless of terrain. Partially infused with the resilience of the Lava King: immunity to fire damage and rapid damage regeneration.

Magma Attunement Gem is of sufficient Energy density to imbue one of two items. Please make a choice:

1. **Helm of Sojourn: Flame Control. Channel Energy of any type into this helmet to gain the ability to manipulate and control any existing flames.**
2. **Gauntlet of Sojourn: Magma Lash. Channel Energy of any type into this gauntlet to create a whip of stable magma, usable as a melee weapon capable of extending to strike even distant enemies.**

Once you have made your decision, these items will be imbued, then you may select and purchase the Sojourn set bonuses.

"Holy shit," Victor laughed. "I'm about to get some massive upgrades, Lam, but let me run some options by you. I could use a second opinion."

15

A NEED FOR FUNDS

As he eagerly explained his choices to Lam, Victor's eyes gleamed with anticipation. He glanced over his shoulder at the line of people waiting, his annoyance at the rush fading into the background. This was a moment of significance for him, and he saw no reason to feel guilty about utilizing a service the city provided. He reasoned that the city must benefit from the transaction, and if it took him a few minutes, that was just the way it had to be.

"I've heard you say that you wish you had a weapon to use when Lifedrinker isn't handy," Lam said, rubbing her chin thoughtfully. "The ability to control flames is nice, but what if there aren't any?"

"I guess I could make some." Victor chuckled, thumping his chest.

"Ah! That's a good point. Still, a lash that can stretch to hit 'distant' targets might be just the thing you need. I've seen you fight. You're a terror up close, but you *do* have to get close."

Victor nodded, smiling at her a little sheepishly. "I *wanted* the whip, so I'm glad you're not convincing me otherwise. One time, I channeled one of my ancestor's powers, and she gave me a magical whip to use. God, it was incredible. I'm not saying this will be the same, but the idea that I might recapture that feeling even just a little . . ." He shrugged, trailing off, as Lam reached up to squeeze the meaty part of his shoulder.

"Do it, then!"

Victor turned to the stone and selected the second option, choosing to put the power of the magma attunement gem into the gauntlet. Suddenly, a new message appeared:

Imbuing items with selected treasures in 5 seconds. To cancel, select the option now.

Victor didn't cancel it, and he watched the items lying at his feet, wondering what the process would look like. As he mentally counted out five seconds, a shimmering cloud of gray and yellow fog erupted around the items. He heard crackles and pops and felt a wash of potent System Energy, and then the cloud dissipated, and he saw the objects had changed drastically.

"Roots!" Lam breathed, suitably impressed. Victor grinned, studying the set. The gauntlet and helmet had changed the most; they weren't leather any longer but seemed to be made from a lustrous deep red, almost black metal. Was that because they'd gotten the full "resilience of the Lava King"? More than their material, they'd changed in form. The helmet looked like a scowling monstrous reptile's head.

"It's almost like a dragon's head. Even more than a wyrm." He could only say that with any authority because he'd seen Tes's draconic form. It looked as if his face would peer out between the metallic fangs that stood out from the draconic snout. The beast's angry eyes would be on his forehead, and the long black horns would sweep back from there. It was an intimidating countenance. The gauntlet was similar in style, made of the same dark red metal, and would sheathe his entire arm up to the elbow in reticulated scale plates. Spikes protruded from the knuckles, and he could see it was, like the helmet, lined with supple red leather.

The pants, belt, and boots retained their original leather material but underwent a transformation in appearance, mirroring the deep red-black hue of the metal components. The leather now appeared sleek and supple, as if infused with the essence of the lava king's hide. Each piece was meticulously tooled with intricate patterns and adorned with small gleaming studs that caught the light with a faint, fiery shimmer.

"Fancy," Lam said without a hint of sarcasm.

"It's not done," Victor said, studying the System display:

Treasure imbuement complete. Sojourn five-piece set enchantments are available. Note: This set may be imbued with up to three Class A enchantments, two Class B enchantments, one Class C enchantment, and one Class D enchantment. Prices are based on material imbuement and enchantment value. Options are dependent on material imbuement. Set bonuses do not have to be purchased at this time and can be purchased separately at different times. Set bonuses cannot be removed or changed.

Class A:

1. **Resizing Enchantment: 5,000 standard Energy beads**
2. **Self-cleaning & Repairing Enchantment: 5,000 standard Energy beads**
3. **Enchantment Toggle, Disguise Armor as Clothing: 25,000 standard Energy beads**
4. **Feather Fall Enchantment: 40,000 standard Energy beads**
5. **Water Breathing Enchantment: 55,000 standard Energy beads**

Class B:

6. Ten Percent Bonus to a Physical Attribute. Choose one:

- **Strength: 50,000 standard Energy beads**
- **Vitality: 75,000 standard Energy beads**
- **Dexterity: 50,000 standard Energy beads**
- **Agility: 50,000 standard Energy beads**

7. Fifteen Percent Resistance to a Damage Type. Choose one:

- **Fire: 5,000 standard Energy beads**
- **Cold: 500,000 standard Energy beads**
- **Electricity: 25,000 standard Energy beads**
- **Poison: 25,000 standard Energy beads**
- **Acid: 25,000 standard Energy beads**
- **Slashing: 10,000 standard Energy beads**
- **Piercing: 15,000 standard Energy beads**
- **Crushing: 20,000 standard Energy beads**

8. Ten Percent Enhanced Damage Type. Choose one:

- **Fire: 5,000 standard Energy beads**
- **Cold: 500,000 standard Energy beads**
- **Electricity: 25,000 standard Energy beads**
- **Poison: 25,000 standard Energy beads**
- **Acid: 25,000 standard Energy beads**
- **Physical: 25,000 standard Energy beads**

9. Enchantment Toggle, Reflective Shielding: 90,000 standard Energy beads

10. Enchantment Toggle, Fire Aura: 125,000 standard Energy beads

11. Minor Regeneration Enchantment: 150,000 standard Energy beads

Class C:

12. Enhanced Mass Enchantment: 150,000 standard Energy beads

13. Lava Blast Enchantment: 250,000 standard Energy beads

Class D:

14. Lava Domain Enchantment Toggle: 1,000,000 standard Energy beads

15. Roar of the Lava King Enchantment: 1,250,000 standard Energy beads

16. Flight of the Lava King Enchantment Toggle: 1,500,000 standard Energy beads

"Shit," Victor sighed, looking at the overwhelming list. He glanced over his shoulder at the queue of citizens waiting for him to finish and shrugged, offering a quick apologetic wave. He pulled out a notebook and pen, and as quickly as he could, he scribbled down all of the options. "I'm going to need to think about this and probably raise some funds to get what I want. As usual, the System doesn't give enough details for me to feel confident, but maybe Dar will have an opinion."

Lam watched him writing, nodding. "Lots of options. I bet the enchantment 'toggles' require a certain amount of Energy to activate. Otherwise, I bet low-tier rich folk would load up these sets with the most expensive options."

"Yeah," Victor muttered, finishing his work. "Though a lot of these are clearly tuned to the hide of the lava king I put in there. I wonder how rare that shit was? What the hell even is a lava king? Judging by the helmet, it's related to dragons." He chuckled, amused and a little chagrined by his impulsive decision to put the hide into the mix. He picked up all the items, stowed them away, then turned away from the stone. "I'll come back."

He and Lam walked down the steps, and Victor winked at the lady who'd been waiting to go next as he passed. "You're up." To his surprise, she smiled pleasantly, reaching up to preen her black feathery plume of "hair," blinking her overlarge avian eyes at him while smiling coyly. She clearly wasn't a full avian, she didn't have a beak or wings, and Victor idly wondered if she was some mix of species or a different type of person entirely. It seemed as though he saw a new kind of person everywhere he looked, and he despaired at the idea of ever getting them all straight. He'd struggled in Coloss with only a handful of different species.

"C'mon, flirt." Lam pulled his arm, guiding him to the exit. "You're going to sell the house, right? Seems you need some funds."

Victor nodded, and that's what they did. First, they visited the realtor who'd helped him find the place, and then, with her guidance, he put it back on the market, asking pretty much the same price he'd paid, which was just a bit more than 800,000 beads. Even if he got his asking price, he'd still be sitting at less than a million beads, and he could already predict he'd want to spend at least twice that much on his armor enchantments.

As he and Lam rode in the coach, heading to the house, intent on cleaning out the personal items they'd all left behind, he occupied himself thinking about the armor options. He felt that the three class A enchantments were going to be ones of necessity. He needed his armor to be able to resize, and he wanted it to be able to clean and mend itself, even though the lava king hide seemed to have given it regeneration capabilities. Finally, he really liked the idea that he could make it look like regular clothing; it would be a game changer for social activities.

Of course, the feather-falling and water-breathing enchantments seemed great, too. How much did he need those, though? He could already fall from enormous heights without getting hurt, and when was the last time he'd needed to breathe underwater? It sounded cool, but he could already hold his breath a ridiculous amount of time, and if he ever needed more, couldn't he buy a potion or item for that?

The hard choices started with the class B options. He could only pick two, and he liked them all. Should he boost an attribute? Ten percent of his maximum was a *big* boost. Still, he liked the idea of buying two damage boosts—fire and physical. He grinned at the thought but then shook his head. Maybe a ten percent strength boost would outperform a ten percent physical damage bonus. Considering his enormous strength when Berserk, he had to admit the choice wasn't a clear-cut one.

Then there was the class C choice—enhanced mass or lava blast? What did "enhanced mass" even mean? Was it like his old Kethian Juggernaut helm? Would all of his armor impart extra density to him? If so, that might be better than being able to "blast lava," but again, Victor didn't know. How big was the blast? How often could he do it? Did it drain a lot of Energy? The System loved to be vague, and he hoped Ranish Dar would have some insight, especially when he considered the class D options.

Of course, the Flight of the Lava King was immediately tempting. How great would it be to fly like Valla? What if it wasn't like that, though? What if it just gave him short, hovering spurts of flight? It would help if he had any idea what a real lava king could do. The roar was the least interesting option to him. He already did plenty of roaring. A lava domain, however? Would that change his surroundings? Would it give him boosts, thanks to his class? "Too many damn questions," he muttered.

"Dwelling on your armor?"

"Yeah. Hey, after the house, let's visit an enchanter I know. I've got a few questions for her. Her shop's not far away."

Lam shrugged. "Sure. I've got nothing else to do, and so far, these errands have been very interesting. I'd like to look into alternate means of travel back to Fanwath. There's got to be a cheaper way than paying the System at the World Hall."

"Yeah. Should I ask Dar about it? He might point me in the right direction, but he might just tell me to figure it out. If we have that dinner party, though, maybe one of our 'friends' will have some ideas."

"Oof! Thanks for reminding me! Let's see if there's a stationery shop nearby." She produced one of the crystal guide tablets and began flipping through it.

"You're cooking? Or should we look for a caterer?"

She poked his knee. "I'm cooking! I told you that."

"Right." Victor smiled and relaxed, waiting for the coach to arrive. When they reached his house, he spent a few minutes going through each room, collecting furniture, art, and odds and ends into his storage rings. His bedroom took longer because he tried to carefully separate Valla's things from his so he could hand them over more easily. When he was done, he went out to the courtyard and collected his travel home, clipping it onto his belt.

While he waited for Lam to go through the grounds one more time, ensuring he didn't miss anything, he looked at his wrist and the bracer where Khul Bach's gemstone sat. He really needed to talk to him and fill him in on everything that was going on. While he thought about it, he considered the gauntlet from the Sojourn set; it would go on the same arm. "I guess I could put you into the vault," he said, idly tapping the pink gem. "Probably safer in there, anyway." He liked the idea, though it did make him worry he'd go even longer between his visits to the Degh spirit.

Footsteps crunched on the gravel walkway leading into the garden, and Lam appeared, carrying a copper sculpture of roses that Valla had purchased. "Don't want to forget this."

"Shit, right." Victor reached out and claimed the item into his storage ring. "Thanks, Lam."

She winked at him, and smiling, they left the house. Victor looked back at it and contemplated the wrought iron gate. He wondered if he should be upset about selling the house, but nothing stirred in his chest. He decided he hadn't spent enough time at the house to feel anything—it hadn't become "home" to him yet. Lam caught him looking back and reached up to grip his shoulder.

"Sad you didn't keep it longer?"

"Nah, the opposite. Maybe I should feel something, but I don't. I guess I didn't spend enough time here." While he spoke, he pictured the night before the competition dungeon. He remembered walking through the little courtyard to the gate, looking back to see Valla in the doorway to the house—"Ah! There it is," he said as a little pang of nostalgia hit him. "Just had to add Valla to the picture."

"Home is where the heart is. Just picture her at the lake house waiting for you."

Victor laughed and nodded. "Yep, that'll do it. C'mon." He turned down the sidewalk and began walking, but he waved at Mr. Qwor and called, "We're going to a nearby Artificer's shop." The driver nodded and got into the coach. Victor was fairly sure he'd be waiting outside Tria's shop when they finished.

Ten minutes later, he opened Tria's shop door and guided Lam inside. When he saw the yellow-feathered avian woman at her counter, he waved. "Tria. How's it going?"

She made her strange trilling, cooing pleasure sound and said, "Hello, sir! Welcome back. I'm quite well, thank you."

Victor grinned as he approached the counter. "You forgot my name, didn't you?" It felt wonderful to be on the other side of that problem for a change.

"I . . ." she sputtered, tilting her head to the side. "I apologize, but your name escapes me! It's something distinctly violent-sounding, if I'm not mistaken. That's right! It starts with a *vvvv* sound." She drew out the consonant as if she were revving a motor. "I *should* know it! I saw you battling in the Iron Challenge! Another patron bought me a round when I said I knew you. Oh, drat! Put me out of my misery! What is it?"

"His name's Victor, and I'm Lam. I'm pleased to meet you, ma'am." Lam grinned and took the avian woman's softly feathered hand.

"Too easy, Lam," Victor sighed. "I could have tortured her a bit longer, don't you think?" He chuckled and leaned on the counter, causing it to creak ominously. "Anyway, I promised I'd bring you more business, and here I am. Do you know anything about the Sojourn item sets?"

"Bah! Of course! They're stealing a lot of my business with those damn things."

"Really?" Lam asked, raising an eyebrow.

Tria clicked her tongue and shook her head. "Oh, not really. All of us Artificers like to complain, but not enough people are completing those sets for it to impact us much. What's your question, big fellow?"

"Well, one of the enchantments you can purchase for those items is to have the armor 'disguised' as clothing. Do you know anything about that?"

"Of course! It's not so much a disguise as it is a kind of altered state. Each armor piece is imbued with a dimensional space. The space is very limited, and it can only contain the item in question or the alternate version of the item, which, in this case, is a piece of clothing. If you had a breastplate, for instance, it might share a dimensional space with a fine shirt. As you toggle the enchantment, they will swap places."

"So, I won't actually be armored unless the armor is showing?"

"Correct."

"But it's instant? The change?"

"Yes, quick as a thought."

"Do you know how to do that enchantment?" Victor brought out his wyrmscale vest and laid it on the counter. The scales rasped against one another, and the weight of the vest was palpable in the way it *thunked* onto the wood. "I mean, to something like this?"

Tria sucked in her breath, causing it to whistle through her beak as she leaned close, gently tracing her fingers over the wyrm scales. "So fine! So perfectly cured, cut, treated, and imbued! A true master crafted this! What wonderful scales! A truly ancient wyrm, if I'm not mistaken."

"Yeah. He was a big son of a . . ." Victor trailed off, for once recognizing his cursing might not be appropriate.

"These scales are imbued with something exceedingly potent! It hurts my Artificer's sight to peer at them! The blood of something mighty, something well into the lustrous veil. Was it given freely? Did you slay such a creature?"

"It was a gift," Victor said, smiling. Some bittersweet memories of Tes ran through his mind at the memory. Did she know where he was? She had his blood, after all. What would he say to her now? How much had he changed since he'd last seen her? Would she be proud? Disappointed?

"This armor is beyond me. I could add the enchantment you asked about, however. The materials won't mind the extra weight of such a simple working." She looked up from her study of the armor and blinked her big round eyes at him. "You'll need to provide the alternate clothing item, and it will take me a few hours."

"And the price?"

"A few thousand beads. Nothing much. It's basically the same as crafting a simple dimensional container. Oh!" She held up a finger. "If I were you, I'd buy an enchanted shirt! One that can change its style and color. Then, when you switch to it, you can make it fit your outfit!"

Lam laughed and elbowed Victor in the ribs. "She's smart. You know, I've been wanting to buy some new clothes." She turned to Tria. "Is there a tailor with such items nearby?"

16

WORTHY FIGHTS

It was well into the evening before Victor and Lam returned to Dar's lake house. Victor hadn't intended to be out so late, but they'd spent hours at a tailor Tria had recommended. Victor had been focused on buying a single good shirt that could change its color with a gentle nudge of Energy into a stitched rune pattern, but Lam had spent a lot more time shopping, buying half a dozen garments. Victor would be hard-pressed to describe any of them; he'd gotten his shirt and then waited outside, watching the people of Sojourn while she shopped.

After she was done, they'd stopped by Tria's shop again so Victor could give her the shirt and his wyrm-scale armor to enchant, which she promised to have ready first thing in the morning. Victor was a little leery about leaving the armor, not because he worried Tria would steal it, but because it bore special meaning to him. It was priceless because Tes had crafted it for him, and she'd literally put her blood into it. He resolved to wake up at dawn and wait outside for Tria's shop to open in the morning.

Of course, they hadn't been done even after dropping off Victor's armor. Lam, brimming with excitement about the upcoming dinner party, had wanted to buy some fancy stationery for their invitations. This led to a lively discussion about how they had no idea how to address or deliver them. When Lam mentioned the problem to Mr. Qwor upon their arrival at the house, the coach driver had the answer. Apparently, Dar's staff at the lake house was managed by a man named Mr. Ruln, who acted as the household steward. Mr. Qwor said Mr. Ruln would "be happy to see the invitations delivered."

Walking down the cobbled path from the coach house to the front door, Victor's curiosity was piqued. "I wonder if I've met Mr. Ruln. I need to start paying attention to people's names," he mused aloud.

"It's not like they go around introducing themselves," Lam replied, nodding toward the servant, who was standing ready to open the door for them as they approached. When they reached the stoop, she said, "Excuse me, will you please let Mr. Ruln know that I'd like to speak to him when he has a minute?"

"Of course, ma'am." He turned to Victor and added, "Sir, your other guests await you in the central parlor."

"Thanks." Victor nodded and stepped into the home, leading the way back to the large sitting area that adjoined the outside deck. Darren and Edeya sat together on one of the couches, both reading. Edeya's nose was buried in a thick, leather-bound tome, and Darren was flipping through one of the crystal guidebook tablets.

Darren didn't notice them and spoke almost idly as they approached. "Yeah, I'm not finding anything on that dungeon Trin mentioned. Either it's too exclusive to be in the guidebook, or she was making the whole thing up."

"Mrs. Woy said there was a lot about Sojourn you won't find in that guidebook." Edeya sighed, idly rubbing at something on her chin. She glanced toward Darren, caught sight of Lam and Victor standing there, and leaped to her feet. "You're back!'

"Hey." Victor walked over as Lam hurried to sit beside Edeya. "Who's Mrs. Woy?"

"One of your, um, mentor's staff. She made us dinner."

"We missed dinner?" Lam's voice rose in a near whine. Victor chuckled, shaking his head. Though he felt he could eat, he wasn't hungry. How would he feel if he were only Level Ten with a fraction of the Energy coursing through his body's cells, though?

"I'm sure they'll fix you something," he started to say, but Edeya was already producing plates of steaming food from her storage ring, arranging them on the coffee table in front of the couch.

"I saved you plenty."

Lam grabbed a hot buttered roll and started eating. Victor chuckled and shook his head. "I'm going to go to my room and eat something else." Everyone, even Darren, stopped what they were doing and looked at him strangely. He shrugged. "I've got a monster's heart I want to consume, and the damn thing is massive."

Darren blanched a little and looked at Edeya. "I thought you were teasing me."

"I *told* you!"

"Anyway," Victor groaned, starting for the hallway leading to the bedrooms, "I'm going to write a note to Valla, too. I've got an early start tomorrow, so good night."

"Night!" Edeya chirped.

Lam cleared her throat, wiped her mouth with the back of her hand, and said, "I know you want to retire, Victor, but when can we talk about more spell patterns?"

"Ah, shit." Victor paused near the hallway. "Tomorrow, when I return from picking up my armor. Promise. Oh!" He fished through his storage ring for the spell pattern he'd purchased for Edeya. "This is for you." He tossed it to her and winked. "Lam has one for Darren."

"Thank you!" Edeya cried, snatching the rolled-up parchment from the air.

Lam met his eyes and gave him a quick nod. "See you tomorrow, then, Victor. Thank you for everything." She didn't wait for a reply, turning to watch as Edeya scrambled to unwind the scroll.

Victor watched them for a moment, then left. He was halfway down the hallway when his excellent Quinametzin ears picked up Darren's hushed whisper. "Is he angry?"

"No, dummy," Edeya laughed. "I think he's probably missing Valla."

Victor sighed and went into his room, locking the door behind him. Edeya was right on target. He felt as though it had been months, not just a bit less than a week, since he'd seen Valla, and he was missing her. He sat on the side of the bed and opened the Far Scribe book he shared with her. Nothing had been added since her last short message earlier that morning. He looked over the words again, frowning, wondering if there was something to them other than their face value.

She said all was well, but they were exhausted, and more battles awaited after their rest. That was normal, wasn't it? They were in a dungeon, after all. She said Lesh was snoring, so things couldn't be that dire. He shook his head, forcing himself to stop worrying, to stop imagining nightmare scenarios that weren't at all likely. Instead, he drew a line and wrote a message:

I miss you, Valla. I hate that we aren't together, and I hope you'll be home soon. I hate the circumstances that keep us apart, but on the other hand, this time away makes me appreciate you more. It makes me realize how damn lucky I am. Let's do something together, just the two of us, when you're back. I'll be waiting for you.

Victor paused, tapping the pen on his chin while he thought, imagining Dar or the Sojourn city council sending him to complete some quest or task before he got to wrap Valla in his arms again. Grinning fiercely, he added:

If someone tries to stop me from welcoming you home, I'm going to fight them. I don't care. I really don't.

I love you,

Victor

He put the book away, then stood up, moving to a large open section between his door and the foot of his bed. He almost summoned the gargantuopod heart from his storage bag but stopped, thinking things over. What if something crazy happened? What if he started bursting with flames like when he'd eaten the wyrm's heart? He doubted that would happen, but *something* might. Did he want to risk Dar's house? His decision made, he walked into the hallway, but rather than turning right and going back the way he'd come, he walked the other way.

There was a small library at the end of the hall, just before the big double doors leading to Dar's suite. He headed that way because the library also opened onto a small deck connected via a wooden walkway to the main one. Victor hoped to make his way down to the lake without being noticed; he didn't want to explain his actions or risk getting waylaid by a side conversation. A few minutes later, having succeeded in avoiding everyone except for a single member of the house staff tidying the main deck, he padded down the steps to the long starlit pier.

The lake was placid and beautiful at night, as it usually was. Its dark, deep waters reflected the stars, making Victor feel as if he were standing on a wooden platform floating in space. He moved to the very end of the pier and stripped off most of his clothes. The air was a little chilly, but Victor was always warm, and he figured it would be nice to jump into the water when he was done with his task.

He took a deep breath and cast Iron Berserk; there was no way he was going to try to consume the gargantuopod heart without the size boost of the spell. As the power of rage-attuned Energy flooded his body, tinting his vision with crimson, he stood there basking in the furnace of his heart, the cool night air a profound contrast to the heat radiating from his flesh. He reached into the storage pouch hanging from his belt and summoned out the enormous, still-bloody heart. It steamed in the night air, and the hot blood dripping from the great severed arteries sizzled on the decking, splashing onto his bare toes.

Even standing twenty feet tall, with hands the size of serving platters, the heart was enormous. Eating such a great organ would take time and effort, but Victor's mouth salivated at the idea. Another reason he wanted to be in his full titanic form was that more than his size changed with the transformation. Instincts that were becoming ordinary for him in his usual state were far more profound in his rage-engorged body; he *hungered* for the flesh of the organ in his mighty hands. He yearned to bite into it. He wanted to taste that hot blood and chew the tough flesh. He yearned to swallow it and let his body sift through it for the secrets of his fallen foe's strength.

Grinning madly, he gave in to his instincts and took a massive bite, his great Quinametzin teeth slicing the powerful flesh with ease. After that first coppery, tangy bite, there was no stopping him. He lost himself to the feast, gorging himself, bite after bite. He could feel the Energy buried in the meat of the heart in his stomach, churning and gathering. Despite the size of the organ, despite the need to take bloody bite after bloody bite, he never felt full, never felt like stopping. He couldn't have if he'd wanted to—the gathering Energy was like the pleasure of a scratched itch, and each bite brought the metaphorical fingernails closer to the perfect spot.

Even when he swallowed the last morsel, he lifted his hands and licked the bloody remnants from his palms and wrists. As he did so, he felt the ball of Energy in his gut begin to expand like a slow-motion explosion. It spread through his body, a wave of ecstasy that ignited the dense, potent molecules that made up his Quinametzin anatomy. A tiny voice in his mind wondered at that; if he hadn't been so thoroughly Quinametzin, if he'd failed to advance his titanic race so far, would the heart have affected him differently? Would it have burned his flesh rather than refined it?

The tiny voice was banished as the wave of Energy reached his mind and all thoughts were blown from his consciousness. Victor arched his back, and while the pulsing Energy of his mighty, vanquished foe coursed through him, he roared his triumph to the stars.

Lam was licking sticky honey from her fingers, and a member of the kitchen staff was taking away dirty plates, when Darren looked up from his tablet and pointed to the windows facing the deck and the lake beyond. "Is it getting brighter out there?"

Lam stood and turned, looking over the back of the couch to where he'd pointed. Sure enough, a bright glow was starting to illuminate the darkness, and it seemed to be coming from the lake. She looked at Edeya, who'd stood to look with her. "You don't think anyone would attack Dar's home, do you?"

"I hope not! That's definitely Energy, though!" Edeya spun toward the hallway leading to the bedrooms. "We should get Victor."

The servant—Mrs. Woy, Lam had learned—cleared her throat and said, "Nothing to be alarmed about. Lord Dar warned the staff to stay inside; he and his student are working on something by the lake."

"Dar's here?" Lam asked, noting the brightness was still growing. It almost looked like a false sunrise.

"Yes, Lord Dar arrived at dinner time but has been in his quarters. His warning came just moments ago. At his bidding, I was just about to advise you all to stay inside."

Lam nodded to the woman and then walked around the couch to press her forehead against the glass. That's when the ground trembled and a roar shook the night, rattling the glass and vibrating the curios in their cabinets.

"What the hell?" Darren cried, scrambling off the couch and ducking down with a wide stance as though an earthquake was imminent.

"Is that—?" Edeya asked with wide eyes, her voice hushed.

"Victor." Lam nodded. The roar was deep and animalistic, like something from the mouth of a great monster, but it had a certain familiar note that brought back memories of battlefields back on Fanwath. She'd seen and heard Victor roar into the night in triumph too many times not to recognize his voice, even though it was louder and deeper than ever.

"That's Victor?" Darren hissed. He hurried closer to the two of them and then, surprising them both, nodded. "I'm not surprised, I suppose. I heard him screaming like that when he destroyed my war machines in First Landing. Well, not quite like that, but he was farther away . . ." As his words trailed off, so did the roaring, and the light began to dim. "What was he yelling about? Is he angry? Is he battling something?"

In the sudden stillness and absence of light, Lam shook her head, chuckling. "No, that sounded more like victory to me. He must have liked the heart."

When Victor came back to himself, he was floating on his back in the lake, a good fifty yards from the pier. He was immediately aware of two things—one, he had some System messages clouding his vision, and two, he felt amazing. Grinning, wanting to laugh at his circumstances, he quickly read through the notifications:

*****Congratulations! You have advanced your Quinametzin Bloodline: Epic 2.*****

*****Congratulations! You have earned a new Feat: Behemoth's Regeneration.*****

*****Behemoth's Regeneration: You have gained the uncanny resilience of a behemoth. Given enough time, your flesh will recover from even the most grievous wounds. This ability will complement and magnify similar benefits gained from other sources.*****

Victor, for once, was stupefied, unable to say anything, even "huh" or "cool." He just stretched out on his back, floating in the cool water, staring up at the stars, and smiling in wonder. He knew all about regeneration; his berserking abilities granted it to him, at least a limited form of rapid healing. This felt different, however. It sounded as though he could regenerate all the time now, and it might extend beyond rapid healing. It might be genuine regeneration—like, he might be able to grow back limbs.

A tiny part of him, some remnant from his old human-boy self that had grown up in Tucson, was freaked out. It felt as if he was moving further and further away from that seed of himself. He wasn't just a human with "titan blood" anymore. He was entirely Quinametzin. He'd accepted that. Now, though, he'd absorbed some part of that giant *pinché* monster from the dungeon. Was he straying away from his bloodline? Was he less Quinametzin now?

That couldn't be, could it? Hadn't the heart also boosted his Quinametzin bloodline? After all, the whole reason he could steal the gargantuopod's ability was *because* he was Quinametzin. His further thoughts were interrupted by a deep, rumbling voice.

"Something troubling you, lad?" Dar asked.

Victor straightened, switching from a back float to water-treading, and turned toward the pier. Dar sat there, his bulky, dark form like a hulking shadow with blazing eyes. "Hello, sir. I didn't realize you were here."

"A dozen creatures like the one you ripped that heart from could have approached unnoticed during the din you stirred up." He chuckled and moved away from his original question, letting Victor off the hook at least momentarily. "I've been eager to watch you go through that process. My eyes see much; would you like to hear my thoughts?"

Victor nodded, knowing the man could see him clearly despite the dark. Even so, he added words to the gesture: "I would."

"Your bloodline is incredibly potent. You know this, of course, but I don't think you quite understand the scope. The ability to gain strength from your foes—that ritual you just completed—is something I've never seen before, not on that scale. I saw your body harness the Energy of that gargantuopod. You ripped it apart on a cellular level, subsuming some essential part of it—some piece of its bloodline. More than that, a piece of the creature's spirit lingered in that dead heart! How that's possible, I'm not sure. It must have something to do with you taking it from the corpse; it must be part of the ritual whether you realize it or not."

"Ritual?" Victor frowned. "I don't do any kind of ritual—"

"Ha! Says the man who rips the hot hearts from his foes and eats them bloody and raw. It's a ritual whether you label it so or not." Dar waved a hand in the air. "That's not important, in any case. I could do the same thing but wouldn't gain what you do. All I'd get is a raw, rather under-seasoned meal. Well? What did you gain? Shall I guess?"

"I don't mind telling you—"

"Some advancement to your bloodline? Some Energy for your Core? Or something more? That was quite a flare of Energy that tore through your body."

"My bloodline advanced, and maybe my Core got some Energy, but it didn't advance. I, uh, gained a new feat, though."

Dar leaned forward, and his eyes flared brighter. "Is that common? What feat?"

"It's not all that common, though I *have* gained something unique from most of the more powerful hearts I've eaten."

"And this one?"

Victor tried to shrug, which was not a natural movement while treading water, and said, "I gained regeneration." The Spirit Master grew quiet and leaned back, staring at the stars.

"Dead Gods, lad. This changes things. Such an ability . . ." He let his voice trail off, and Victor floated for a few moments while Dar stared at the stars. "There are those who would do terrible, terrible things to gain that ability. We must keep the nature of your ability a secret. It would be one thing if all you gained from a heart was some Energy—a bit of a cheat on cultivation. Absorbing aspects of other bloodlines, though—wars have been fought for less."

Victor stared at the man who was meant to be his mentor and couldn't help the dark thoughts that nibbled at his mind. Could he trust him? Was he, even now, trying to plot a way to steal Victor's bloodline? If the Warlord of Coloss knew a way to do so, surely the great powers of Sojourn knew of methods. Dar chuckled, a deep grating sound like wet stones sliding against each other. "Relax, Victor. I take my role as your mentor very seriously. It weighs on me. Knowing your secret, protecting it and you, will do much for my karmic balance sheet."

"I'd feel better if you, you know, *wanted* to."

"Ha! Of course I do! Fear not, lad. Having a desire to build karma in my favor only helps me tune out the dark whispers everyone hears occasionally. My waking mind is set on teaching you, fostering your spirit, and building you into a true conqueror."

"Conqueror?"

Dar leaned forward and growled, his voice carrying sharply over the still water, "Of course! Did you not come to me with such desires? I recall tales of a warlord who needed slaying, an undead world that needed to feel the fire of your wrath, and a certain history of righting injustices. Do those things no longer appeal to the rage burning in your heart?"

Victor felt chills on his spine and a growl building in his chest as he answered, through a throat thick with emotion, "Yes!"

"Good. It's clear to me that your ancestors were a potent people, and I'm not surprised they moved beyond this realm. You should be proud to carry their bloodline, proud to remind this universe of who they were. If hearts can advance your power so, then you should claim more. We need to pick some worthy fights for you."

17

ECHOES OF INSECURITY

When Victor woke up, he had a message from Valla in the Far Scribe book:

Victor,

We failed the boss fight but escaped without serious injury. We're resting at an inn near the entrance. We'll return to the house after breakfast.

"Shit," Victor grunted, sliding out of bed and pulling on his clothes. A glance at the window told him it was still early; the sky had yet to brighten with sunrise. He summoned a pen and wrote a quick reply:

Valla,

We're all staying at Dar's lake house. I'm coming to pick you up. Wait there!

That done, Victor went into the kitchen and asked the staff, the only people already awake, if one of them could wake Mr. Qwor to let him know he wanted to leave even earlier than planned. When a young woman nodded and hurried away, Victor went outside and stood by the cobbled drive, waiting. The coachman was quick to arrive, and Victor had a feeling he was an early riser because he was dressed sharply in his uniform, looking alert when he pulled the levitating vehicle around.

"Good morning, sir."

"Hey, Mr. Qwor. Sorry to change things up, but I just found out some friends are out of a dungeon and need picking up. Do you know about a dungeon called 'Desperation Gap?' They're waiting at an inn near the entrance."

"Of course, sir. It's southwest of the city near the Opal Sea. I'll have you there in an hour."

So Victor climbed into the coach, wrote Valla another message saying he'd be there in an hour, and then leaned back in the cushions, comfortable and relaxed, knowing he'd soon be with her again.

The Opal Sea wasn't as big as the lake on Dar's property. Victor looked out the window to watch as they approached, and that was his first thought. Not only was it smaller, but the shoreline was rocky, barren, and lined with hundreds of piers, all crowded with fishing boats of varying sizes. The sight gave Victor a new perspective on Dar's power and influence. Clearly, this "sea" wasn't privately owned and was in high demand for fishing, if nothing else. How much would the working-class folk of Sojourn love to gain access to the beautiful, clear, fish-filled waters on Dar's vacation property?

The inn at the mouth of a narrow canyon where the Desperation Gap dungeon was situated was a five-story asymmetrical building that looked as if only the force of Energy-fueled enchantments was keeping it upright. Victor stepped out of the coach amid a busy little market square. They'd flown over many homes, and it was evident that this area near the Opal Sea was sort of a smaller town center away from the larger city.

Victor wondered if it was still considered part of Sojourn, which made him wonder just how things on the "city world" were structured. The world and city were called Sojourn, but was every other community part of that? Were they all ruled by the same council of powerful beings?

He'd reduced his size to that of the majority of the local populace—something close to an average human—so he didn't have to duck when he stepped into the tavern on the inn's ground floor. Valla had yet to respond to his messages, but he hoped she and Lesh would be waiting there.

When he pushed open the door, still clad in regular clothes but with Lifedrinker on his back, it looked to him as if the inn was still waking up and that breakfast was being served. The space was noisy and crowded, and Victor had to stand there for several seconds before anyone gave him any notice. He didn't care, though; he was scanning the crowded tables for Lesh's hulking form or Valla's silvery wings.

To his relief, he spotted them in the front, in a far corner by a window, and when he started toward them, Lesh caught sight of him first and stood up, knocking his chair back with a clatter. "Lord Victor!" he roared, which got Valla's attention, whose back was to him. She shifted to look his way, and Victor almost fell over when he saw her face. She had a bandage over her left eye, and above and beneath it, on her forehead and cheek, was a deep, fresh scar that stood out, red and swollen, on her beautiful silvery-blue flesh.

Victor rushed to her, indiscriminately shoving people, chairs and all, out of his way. He hadn't realized he was doing it, but by the time he stood before her, he'd released his size-altering spell and easily lifted her into an embrace, gently cradling her head onto his shoulder as he held her. "*Pobrecita!* What happened?"

Valla squirmed in his embrace, and he heard her muffled reply, "Victor! Put me down!" He did as she asked, gently lowering her, oblivious to the outraged clamoring of the customers he'd left in his wake. He had eyes and ears only for Valla.

As for her, all she could see was Victor, his giant form looming before her. She sighed and reached out to take his left hand with both of hers. "I knew you were going to overreact! I got hurt; that's the whole story. Nothing more to say. It's a risk that comes with the territory—"

"*Fuck*, Valla!" Victor reached toward her bandage, but then he was jostled, and a heavy hand gripped his biceps, pulling with enough strength to turn him.

A deep, guttural voice growled, "You owe me a gods-damned breakfast, you great oaf!"

Victor released Valla and whirled, rage rushing into pathways primed by his shock at seeing Valla wounded. His vision turned red, and he laid eyes on the man accosting him and . . . fought to get himself under control. The man was old and gray with a bent, hunched back, but judging by the size of his forearm and powerful grip, Victor knew he was someone who'd worked hard his whole, very long life. More sobering than that was the mess he saw behind the old fellow. In his haste to get to Valla, Victor had overturned several chairs, sent a few folks sprawling, and even upended an entire table.

"Shit," he said, his eyes widening. "I'm sorry about that. I, uh, saw my—"

"He saw me, sir," Valla said, stepping around to get a look at what Victor had done. "He saw me and my injury and lost all sense. We'll pay for the damages, of course."

The old man released Victor's arm and nodded. "Shoulda guessed. Well, I've lost my head a time or two for a pretty face." He nodded and turned, stooping with a grunt to lift his table upright.

"Help him!" Valla hissed, and Victor, his rage utterly washed away by his embarrassment, cast Alter Self again, reducing his size so he could more nimbly help pick up the mess he'd created. He was still worried about Valla, but the initial instinctual need to get to her had been banished by shame, especially as he watched her, injured as she was, helping to clean up. When the innkeeper came around to see what the fuss was about, she was the one who handed him a pouch full of beads and said that she wanted to buy everyone's meal.

Lesh, too large to help efficiently, sat back down and continued to eat while he watched. When all was righted, Valla urged Victor to sit at the table. She gave him a long look, staring into his eyes with her single unbandaged one. Victor tried not to stare at her bandage, forcing himself to peer into her silvery-turquoise iris. "I know this looks bad, and I know how upset you are, but I will recover. My eye was damaged beyond a healing potion, but a regeneration mixture will probably restore it. I have one, a treasure from the war, but Lesh and I also won racial advancement elixirs, and my hope is that the process will mend my eye."

"You did?" Victor glanced at Lesh and saw the big dragonkin grinning a toothy reptilian smile.

"Aye, Lord Victor. We gained three levels, too, and a great many minor treasures. We got far, much farther than the guidebook said we would as a duo."

"The truth is, we went too far!" Valla chuckled. "We should have stopped before the boss encounter."

"You got to the boss?"

Valla shook her head. "Only of the section we were in. The dungeon is strange; it's not arranged in levels but rather like a long beach along a stony cliff. There are inlets and coves, caves, and beached ships—all swarming with scaly, water-breathing men and women. Some are small and come in great numbers, while others are huge and monstrous and fight alone, too savage for even their own kind to approach. It was one such that seemed to be the 'boss' of the area we were exploring, and it was he who took my eye and forced us to retreat."

Victor found his vision clouding with red again, and he clenched his fists until his knuckles noisily popped. Valla grabbed his hand. "Stop it! Stop acting like I'm a doll you have to protect. I'm an adventurer, Victor." He could hear real frustration in her voice, which more than anything allowed him to push the rage out of his pathways. While Lesh continued to feed his bottomless hunger and Valla looked away, perhaps trying to think of the right thing to say, Victor struggled with his conflicting emotions.

Part of him wanted to tell Valla it wasn't worth it. What was she trying to prove? He loved her and didn't care if she was as powerful as he was. Didn't she understand that? She didn't have to go into dungeons and push her limits; he wouldn't leave her. Their relationship was based on more than that. Of course, Victor wasn't stupid, not if he really tried to think through a problem, and he knew that saying those words would only infuriate her. He knew they weren't fair. If he didn't think Valla had anything to prove, then what was he doing? How was it fair for him to constantly push himself if he didn't want her to do the same?

Worse than the hypocrisy of his feelings was the knowledge that he had another objection that would only hurt and alienate Valla if she ever knew he harbored it: He didn't think she would be able to catch him, so what was the point of risking her life? It was a shameful thing to admit to himself, but Victor knew he wasn't normal. He'd thrashed not one but several Tier Nine combatants in the challenge dungeon. He sparred with Valla frequently—she wasn't a match for those folks.

Victor knew that if he wanted to challenge himself, he'd be doing things that she couldn't participate in, whether she was level Sixty or One Hundred. Would things be different if they both broke through the "iron ranks"? Would it be different once they'd passed their "test of steel"? He wanted to hope so, but that would also mean that other people at that level would be a risk to him and, by that virtue, a risk to Valla. Would they be safer at that tier of power, or would they simply have more dangerous enemies? After all, the only thing keeping Victor safe from the masters of Sojourn was their self-imposed code of conduct—the rules and laws of the city world.

Would that even matter if he didn't have Dar's backing? He supposed the city's laws stood for something, even to those without an influential mentor. While he sat there, lost in thought about his self-centered ambition and desire to keep Valla safe, he must have worn a look that betrayed his disgust, because she eventually said, "I've upset you." Before he could deny it, she scowled further and pushed back her chair. "Amazing. I'm the one who should be irritated, but you've somehow made me feel like I've done something wrong!"

"No, I—" His objection died on his lips as she walked stiffly past him to the door and out.

"Deep thoughts?" Lesh rumbled, wiping his toothy maw with a napkin.

"Unpleasant ones."

"Valla grows powerful, Victor. She has more than one solution for the eye."

"It's not the eye. It's . . . I guess it's my own insecurity. She's trying so damn hard to catch up to me, or, if not that, at least keep up. What will she do if she can't? She's not a housewife, Lesh." As he said the words, his real fear clicked into place, and sudden understanding dawned on him. The root of all of his angst wasn't that he feared leaving Valla behind or that he was already too far ahead; it was more that he was afraid she'd figure it out and realize she couldn't catch up. Would she be willing to live a life in his shadow? Before Lesh could respond, he said, "Don't repeat that."

"No, I wouldn't. You speak to me from the heart and seek advice; how could I even consider betraying that trust?" He made a face, and Victor wondered if he'd alienated yet another person. Lesh didn't storm off, though. He took a moment to consider and then said, "Why do you worry about something you can't control? You are what you are. Valla is what she is. You both love each other, and, at least for the moment, you're together. Enjoy that."

Victor knew Lesh had a strange perspective on love. He'd given up his life with his actual wife to follow Victor. Thinking about that and realizing they were talking about personal things, he voiced a question that had been on his mind since he'd learned about the man's wife. "Will your wife wait for you? Are you planning to return to her someday?"

"Yassa is my *mate*. I suppose it's similar to a wife in your culture, but . . . it has some nuances. She will wait for a time, but if I tarry too long, she will seek another." Lesh's words were matter-of-fact, but Victor could feel some emotion behind them.

"I mean, do you hope to get back to her?"

"Ah, Victor, I know you mean well, but this is a topic I've settled my mind about. I'd rather not dwell on what *may* have been or what *may* be; I've set my course for different shores. Fate's winds move me now."

The dragonkin's mild rebuke stung more than it should have. Victor realized he'd been harboring some hope for wisdom or advice to see him through this hopefully minor conflict with Valla. As he had the thought, he wondered if the conflict was really with Valla or with himself. Sighing, feeling as though nothing had been resolved, he pushed his chair back and stood. "I better go after her."

"I'll be right behind. I need to visit the toilets." Lesh stood and lumbered toward the back of the restaurant, and Victor silently wished the plumbing luck. He went outside to find Valla sitting on the edge of the wooden boardwalk that lined the row of buildings. Her feet dangled toward the cobbled street, and she held her wings slightly open to make it easier to sit down. When Victor hopped down to the cobbles and turned to face her, she scowled and pointedly looked to the side.

"That mad? Won't even look at me?" A corner of her mouth quirked up, and he knew he had her on the ropes. "Come on! I'm sorry I reacted that way." He reached out to take her chin and turned her face toward him. "Let me see that cut. I bet you look tough as hell." To his surprise, her cheeks flushed, and she looked away again. "Are you being shy?"

"Stop it, Victor!" She slapped his hand, and he sighed, turning his hand so his palm was facing up.

"Well, take my hand at least. I'll walk you to the coach." She relented at that and put her hand in his, and he pulled, making it easy for her to slide to the edge of the boardwalk and hop to her feet. "You're going to like Dar's lake house."

"How long will we stay there?"

Victor paused, looking back at the inn. "Let's wait a minute so Lesh can follow us. The coach is over there." He pointed to the oval, black-lacquered vehicle, where it floated a few feet over the cobbles on the other side of the square. "Dar said that we can stay at the lake house until I've got enough money to buy a house that, uh, 'suits my station' or something like that."

To his further surprise, Valla sighed and shook her head. "I like our little townhome. It's cozy, and it, well, it's ours—" She was looking up at him while she spoke, and Victor's guilt must have been apparent, because she cut off her words and took a step away, turning to look at him more directly with her single eye. "Why do you look like that? Did something happen to our house?"

"I . . ." Victor had that feeling he'd had too many times in his life when he realized he'd been stupid, and it seemed so obvious after the fact that he couldn't quite believe the extent of his mind's betrayal. Of course, he should have spoken to Valla before emptying the house and putting it up for sale. They'd picked the place together. They'd moved in together. What would it say about his opinion of her that he'd just undone all of that without so much as asking her what she thought?

"Is that the coach, Lord Victor?" Lesh asked, once again being overly formal for some damn reason. Victor nodded, his mind still on Valla and how hurt she looked. He hadn't even told her what he'd done, but she was more than clever and could read his face like a book. She slipped her hand from his and walked with Lesh to the coach. Victor followed, trying to think of a way to smooth things over. Nothing brilliant came to him. When he climbed into the vehicle's spacious interior, he wasn't surprised to find Valla sitting in one of the bucket seats rather than the longer benches, so he sat alone.

"I have to go to an enchanter's shop to get my armor. Should I take you two home first?"

Valla nodded. "Yes, please."

Frowning, almost scowling, Victor slid open the little window to the driver's compartment. "Back to the lake house first, Mr. Qwor." After a few minutes of silence, Victor looked at Lesh. "Tell me about the dungeon."

"Ah, my pleasure," the big man rumbled, and Victor tried to relax, sitting back in the cushions, listening to Lesh recount their experience, describing the dungeon, the denizens, and the fights. Every so often, Victor would glance at Valla, but she refused to meet his gaze, and he decided the best thing he could do was give her some space. There wasn't always a quick fix, some magical combination of words, that would end a fight, and he figured he just had to give her some time to cool off.

If their differences had been just about the house and his unilateral decision to sell it, he wouldn't have felt so troubled as he sat there listening to the dragonkin. His earlier thoughts, though, his admission to fearing Valla would grow tired of being in his shadow, weighed heavily on him. He wondered if she also suspected there was more to the anger she felt. He wondered if she was sitting there drawing her own conclusions, finding rifts where before she'd thought things were smooth.

He hated how he felt. He hated that Valla was upset with him. He hated that he hadn't said or done the right thing when he'd seen her injury, and rather than make things better for her, he seemed to have made them worse. He tried to listen to Lesh, nodding along and acting impressed at the right moments, but he was only half-present as he replayed one conversation after another, trying to think of the right things to say. When he failed, he finally closed his eyes and leaned back, hoping he was right and that a bit of time was all it would take.

18

TRUST AND PARANOIA

Victor was heartened when Valla looked at him and smiled as she exited the coach at the lake house. Even so, he found his tongue sluggish when he tried to think of the right words. The moment passed, and she stepped away from the coach, briskly walking toward the waiting staff member by the front doors. Lesh clapped his shoulder on his way out. "You don't mind if I rest? I'd go with you if you need someone to watch—"

Victor waved him off. "Nah, it's nothing. I just need to run a couple of errands." He watched the dragonkin turn to close the coach's door, then signaled Mr. Qwor to leave. Once he was flying toward town again, alone in the coach, Victor sighed and leaned back. Feeling Lifedrinker press into his back reminded him that he wasn't really alone. He smiled at the idea and almost reached up to pull the axe free of her harness but stopped himself—he wanted his mind clear, and he knew Lifedrinker would just take his side in any sort of conflict. She was wonderful for her fierce loyalty, but she didn't give impartial advice.

He rode in silence, and though he tried to think about Valla and their issues, his mind wouldn't stay focused, and he thought about other things. His thoughts often wandered toward Coloss and their time in that strange, savage city. Victor wondered about the Warlord and how far beyond Level One Hundred he'd reached. Had he completed his "test of steel"? Had he honed his class to the point where he'd entered his "lustrous veil"?

He knew the Warlord wouldn't call those stages of progression those names; they were unique to Sojourn and the worlds under its influence, but he imagined the process was the same no matter what someone called it. Remembering his fight with Karnice, Victor wondered how small the Warlord kept his little club of enlightened people. Karnice had been a common iron ranker, somewhere in the eighth tier. Were the Warlord's "war captains" beyond the iron ranks? Were they "steel seekers," or were they beyond that point?

Victor remembered feeling War Captain Black's aura and his power. He remembered bowing to it, knowing the man far outstripped him, but he'd changed a lot since then. Still, the man had been stronger than Karnice; there wasn't any doubt of that in Victor's mind. "So, maybe I'll have to deal with some people beyond the iron ranks." He nodded to himself. Then, realizing what he'd said, he wondered what had made him contemplate returning to Zaafor. He had to admit that maybe he was looking for a way to get away from things, to give himself something else to focus on.

When the coach arrived, and Victor stepped out to collect his armor from Tria, he resolved to meet with Khul Bach when he returned to the lake house. Considering all he'd learned since coming to Sojourn, he and the Degh spirit had much to discuss. Tria didn't fail to deliver on her promise; his wyrm-scale vest was in perfect condition, and the new enchantment worked flawlessly.

When he put the vest on and trickled a little Energy into the new rune, he felt a flicker of Energy over his skin, and then he was wearing the shirt he'd purchased the day before. The shirt was made of a blend of fabric that breathed like cotton and hung luxuriously like silk. The fabric was dyed a rich gray-black, but Victor knew he could make it match just about any color he could imagine with a simple focus of his will and touch of Energy.

"This is great, Tria."

"Well, the shirt is lovely, but I didn't make it."

"No, I mean the enchantment. It's nice to walk around in comfort, knowing I can have my armor on in an instant."

"Yes. Invaluable for a man of action, I'm sure." She made a funny chirping sound after her words, and Victor wondered if she was laughing at him.

With a wave and a promise to return soon, he left and had Mr. Qwor take him back to the Sojourn City Hall, where the System Stone stood. He didn't want to empty his pockets by purchasing any of the massively expensive set bonuses for his new armor, but he figured he'd buy the class A enchantments so he could wear the new armor in comfort. He especially wanted to equip the gauntlet so he'd have the option of using the magma whip if he got into a fight.

Either the early hour proved fruitful or his luck was better that morning, because not a single person stood in line when he arrived. He went straight to the stone and selected the three class A bonuses he wanted: the resizing enchantment, the self-cleaning and self-repairing enchantment, and, of course, the enchantment to disguise the armor as clothing. Altogether, it cost him thirty-five thousand standard beads, which he paid for using some of those he'd won in the challenge dungeon.

When he returned to the coach, Victor took a minute to put the armor on, switching Khul Bach's bracer to his right arm until he had a chance to stow it in his vault. The armor was comfortable, and even the dense metallic gauntlet and helmet felt as if they were made for his body, flexing and moving easily when he twisted and turned his wrist and neck. Still, he activated the disguise runes and was pleased to find that everything morphed into clothing that wouldn't be out of place among the finely dressed individuals he'd seen around Sojourn.

The red leather pants seemed to take a cue from the shirt he wore, becoming dark, narrow-legged slacks of fine material and craftsmanship. The boots changed from heavy, combat-oriented adventuring boots to fine polished leather ones, easily the most comfortable Victor had ever worn. The belt went from a girdle-like piece of heavy "lava king" hide to a supple leather strap that matched his boots. Even the bracer and helmet changed to something far more comfortable—soft leather bands that looked almost stylish on his wrist and around his forehead. Looking closely, he saw that they were stitched with angular designs in a faintly metallic thread.

Pleased, Victor closed his eyes and tried to relax during the short flight back to the lake house. Upon arrival, he walked through the house and onto the deck, looking for any sign of Valla and their friends. Following sounds of splashes and laughter, he looked down the steps to the pier, where he saw Edeya, Lam, and Darren playing some convoluted game of keep-away with Lesh. Darren leaped out of the water, something bright red clutched in his hand, and Victor could hear the breathless, almost panicked nature of his laughter as Lesh erupted like a damned crocodile, roaring as he gave chase. Edeya's high-pitched cackle was too much, and Victor turned away before he jumped down there and joined the fun.

Of course, he wanted to, but he wondered where Valla was, and he'd also made a promise to himself to meet with Khul Bach before he found another excuse to put it off. So he returned to the house and proceeded down the hall to his bedroom. He found Valla inside, sound asleep under the covers, her left eye still covered by a thick white bandage. He knew she didn't need the bandage, that she was just hiding the damaged eye, either because she was self-conscious or because it was unpleasant to look at. He wanted to pull it aside, wanted to see what some *pinché* monster had done to her face, but he knew it would add to her list of grievances with him.

Victor quietly passed through the room into the adjoining study. It was a relatively large space with a big round table and chairs at the center, a large desk on the left-hand wall in front of a window, and built-in bookcases lining the right-hand wall. Victor carefully paced across the room and determined that if he removed the table and chairs, he should be able to open the vault.

Rather than drag the furniture around, moving it to the other room, he just pulled the table and chairs into one of his storage rings; he didn't think Dar would mind as long as he put them back when he moved out of the house. He closed the study door, then, on the big woven carpet, he twisted the key in the marble-sized vault, and he watched as it hissed with steam, slowly expanding to fill most of the empty space in the room.

Victor opened the door and removed the key; he would be inside for a while and hated the idea that someone might lock him in. Inside the vault, he regarded the ivid royal jelly and the ivory box containing the geists. He worried that Ranish Dar, or anyone, really, might step into the vault while he was in there talking to Khul Bach, so he contemplated the door and noticed a keyhole on the inside. "Huh." He inserted the key, ensuring it fit. He pulled the door shut and then turned the key until it clicked. He was reasonably sure the keyhole hadn't been present before. Was that because the key had been on the outside?

He wondered if he could keep turning the key, shrinking the vault down with him inside it, but the idea sent shivers down his spine, and he refused to try it. Instead, he took a step back and sat down in the middle of the spherical chamber. He removed the bracer he'd made to hold the seventeen Ancestor Stone shards and touched the only occupied slot. After a moment to clear his head, Victor sent Energy into it, summoning the crystal's weird, white-gray, angular landscape.

"You've changed much, student of mine," Khul Bach rumbled, suddenly sitting a few feet away, his countenance creased in its usual glower. He sat with his legs folded before him, his big scarred knuckles resting on the ground at his sides.

"Hello, Khul Bach. I've changed a bit and learned a lot. Have you been doing well?"

"You know how things go for me—time passes, and I hardly notice. How long has it been? A year? Twenty? More?"

"Nah, not all that long. Less than a year."

"Yet you have a gravity about you that speaks of great advancements. Tell me, then, lad, what have you been about?"

Victor nodded, and, slowly at first, but then, in a rush of words, he told the old spirit about the Free Marches and all about his mistakes and triumphs in the war. He told the giant about First Landing and how he'd smashed the human-made constructs before traveling to Sojourn. The giant grew quiet and very attentive when he described the power of the great masters of the city and then about his journey to the ivid hive world. When he mentioned Ranish Dar and his bargain with the master Spirit Caster, Victor thought he saw a flicker of something odd on the giant's face—doubt? Fear? Worry? He supposed any of those reactions would be reasonable.

"So," the giant said, resting one elbow on a knee and placing his chin in his palm. He looked almost depressed.

"So?"

"So. You've no need for me and my backward ways."

"Oh, come on!" Victor chuckled. "You're still old as hell; you'll always have things to teach me."

"My age?" the giant roared. "Of all my qualities, you choose my age as my saving grace?"

"Khul Bach! Come on, I still plan to talk to you regularly, and yes, I intend to fulfill my promise to you. I'm going to free your people from the Warlord."

The Degh spirit nodded, somewhat mollified, and lifted his chin out of his palm. Sitting up, his backbone rigid, he said, "You're stronger, but I still think Thoargh will beat you. He was strong when the Degh were yet whole."

"I know I'm not ready yet. Well, no, I don't, but I'm not planning to go back soon. I have a lot to learn here. Khul Bach, do you know about what happens after Level One Hundred?"

"Aye. Endless, slow cultivation. Years spent in meditation to eke out a bit more Energy at glacial paces. A rare level here and there that seems a hollow echo of those in the lower tiers."

"You don't know anything about something that might be described as a 'test of steel'? A custom class that you need to improve and refine?"

"I know people who reach Level One Hundred are given a new choice of class based on their earlier experiences. I don't recall anything about refining and improving that class. Victor, very few Degh reached such a level, and few lingered on Zaafor; most are in the Ancestor Stone."

"Well, there's more to the process of advancing after Level One Hundred, Khul Bach. I don't know the secrets yet; I've only heard hints, but I'm going to learn them before I go back to Zaafor. The Warlord might know the secrets; he might have advanced past his 'test of steel,' or whatever he called it. He might not, however. He seemed pretty damn frustrated with his progression . . ." Victor trailed off, letting the implications of his words speak for themselves.

Khul Bach nodded. "You should pass that milestone before you return."

"Yeah, maybe. I'll see what Ranish Dar thinks. Is that all right with you? Are you doing okay?"

"I'm fine, lad. I've languished for millennia. My people await, but another year or twenty won't change much. No, I'd rather you were ready and met with success than attempt to take on Thoargh ill-prepared and fail."

Victor nodded. "I have another question for you. Have you ever heard of the idea that some people who become obsessed with or overwhelmed by a negative affinity like rage or fear might carry that Energy with them into the spirit plane when they die? That they might go through the veil with it, driven mad, wandering in a kind of purgatory with their delusion?"

"The lure of a strong emotion is powerful. You should know this. Haven't you tasted the power of fear? Of rage? Imagine you succumbed to the call of your fear and never gave it up. Imagine you feasted on the emotion to the exclusion of all else. Now, imagine doing that for hundreds or thousands of years. What would be left of Victor when you died? Your spirit would be twisted and shunned. I've seen it. I've seen Degh who lost themselves to greed or envy, to vengeance or lust. Their spirits were pushed away from the Ancestor Stone and driven through the veil. Such poison couldn't be allowed to fester among us."

Victor folded his arms and frowned. "Ranish Dar sent me with a Death Caster through the veil. He had me capture two such spirits. One full of rage and the other with fear. He wants me to use them for cultivation, to gather their attuned Energy."

Khul Bach frowned, rubbing his prodigious jawline with a thick thumb. "It may be my ignorance speaking, but that sounds like a dark dealing to me, Victor. Use caution."

"He says that we're helping the spirits by pulling their rage and fear off, helping them to recover faster than if we'd let nature take its course."

"An optimistic outlook. I won't pretend to know as much as this man, this Ranish Dar, who has lived for thousands of years and reached pinnacles of power unheard of on Zaafor. No, learn what you can, but please be cautious, Victor. You are a gifted warrior. A man with potent blood and deep potential. It wouldn't be the first time, nor even the millionth, that a powerful man promised great knowledge to a protégé who had something he coveted. Perhaps my caution is misplaced, and your new mentor is so far beyond you that anything he may gain from your abuse would be too small, too trifling, to warrant such betrayal, but . . ." It was Khul Bach's turn to let his words die out, leaving Victor ruminating on them.

"All right. I appreciate the advice, Khul Bach. I'll try to keep a clear head and not get overwhelmed by the wonders I see." Victor chuckled, trying to lighten the mood a little.

"Do that, and keep working on your skills and spells. How many have you lifted into the epic tier?"

Victor sighed, wishing he'd said goodbye just a little quicker. "Only two. My Iron Berserk and Inspiration of the Quinametzin."

"What? All this time? All this advancement in power, and you've neglected your Sovereign Will?" The giant Degh spirit leaned forward, his eyes boring into Victor's.

"No! I haven't neglected it. I use the damn skill all the time, but it won't move past advanced."

Khul Bach stared into his eyes for several seconds but finally relented, nodding with a grunt. "I see you speak the truth. Well? Ask your new master for insight. There must be a way to push it forward, and push it forward you must; it's a central, defining skill of yours. Don't let it languish." Victor nodded, opening his mouth to reply, but Khul Bach waved him off. "I must rest and think on all that you've revealed. Come again soon, Victor."

Victor felt Khul Bach's push and relented, pulling his Energy back into himself and slipping out of the domain of the Ancestor Stone shard. He looked around the curved, rune-inscribed walls of his vault and let his eyes drift toward the ivid royal jelly. The fact that he was hiding it in there said a lot; he clearly didn't fully trust Ranish Dar. Was there something to Khul Bach's warning? He sighed and stood. Moving over to the satchel, he slipped the bracer with the Ancestor Stone shard inside next to the silk-wrapped jelly, then he stooped to pick up the ivory box containing the geists. Dar would want to see them when he helped set up Victor's "cultivation chamber," and he didn't want to have to awkwardly try to sneak them out of the vault, exposing the jelly.

He turned the key counterclockwise until it clicked, pushed the door open, and stepped out. He was still alone in the study. Victor locked up the vault, and when he had it shrunk again and hanging from around his neck, tucked under his shirt, he breathed a sigh of relief, letting go of some stress he hadn't even been aware of. Was he being paranoid? He didn't think so. He didn't know what the royal jelly would do, but he knew it was powerful, the most potent stuff he'd ever laid eyes on. Dar might be a good man who wanted to do right by him, but Victor didn't see any reason to tempt his good nature.

When he opened the study door and walked into the bedroom, he tried to move silently, but he saw the light streaming through the window reflected in Valla's eye as she peered at him from her nest of blankets. "Hey," he said softly, almost a whisper. She didn't reply, but she pulled the blankets down, revealing her naked chest, and then gently patted the sheet beside her. Victor wasn't stupid enough to question such an invitation.

19

THE PULL OF GLORY

Some time later, Victor lay on his back, one arm behind his head on the pillow and the other outstretched, cradling Valla. She lay on her side, looking at him, and after several minutes of silence, reached over and began to trace little circles on his chest. Her fingertip felt cool to his hot Quinametzin flesh, and he loved it. While he luxuriated in the attention, Valla softly asked, "You know why I was upset, why I'm *still* upset, right?"

Victor inhaled deeply through his nose. "I guess 'cause I was impulsive and didn't ask you about selling the house."

"You guess?" The finger stopped moving, pressing into his breastbone.

"No, Valla, I know. I also know that's not the only thing that got you pissed at me. I shouldn't have freaked out in the restaurant when I saw you. I shouldn't have, but—" Victor turned slightly so he could look down into her good eye. "I worry about a lot of things, and I'm not good at explaining what I'm feeling."

"So try. Just tell me what was going through your mind." Her finger started moving, gently tracing the outline of his pectoral muscle.

"If I say it, you're going to think I'm an even bigger asshole. It's a feeling I'm not proud of."

"Whatever kind of asshole you are, however big you are," she chuckled, "I still love you. So?"

Victor's mind raced, and he wondered if he should be honest. It wasn't that he wanted to hide his feelings from Valla, but in this case, he honestly thought his feelings made him seem like a prick. "Even if I know my thoughts make me seem, I don't know, conceited? Full of myself? Insecure?" Valla's thumb joined her finger, and she squeezed his skin between the two—a clear threat of a wicked incoming pinch. "Easy! Easy," he laughed. "Let me gather my thoughts."

"Just say what you're feeling. Don't spend time twisting words to hide the truth!"

"Really? Well, get ready to be pissed again." Victor took a deep breath, then began letting his thoughts fall out of his mouth in a rush. "When you were telling me how you got hurt, I couldn't stop thinking about how I wished I'd been there, that I could have killed that *pinché* boss. Of course, that made me think about how you and Lesh were just about my level, so why was I so sure? I *am* sure, though, which makes me sound like a conceited asshole, but shit, Valla, I've beaten several Tier Eights and Nines *at once*."

Valla was quiet, and she released his flesh and started to withdraw her hand, so Victor rushed to try to explain. "It's not that I was sitting there thinking you guys are weak or anything. I was worrying about how you might not be able to catch up to me. Ever. It's not just about levels, it's about . . . shit, I don't know. My bloodline? My class? The goddamn freakish synergy of everything that makes me into some kind of monster. What if you get tired of trying? What if you decide it's not worth it? What if we grow further and further apart? I hated being away from you for just a few days, but honestly, it looks like there's more time apart than together in our future."

"Oh, Victor," Valla sighed, flopping over onto her back with a huff and a faintly metallic rustle of feathers. "Do you think I only want to gain levels and strength to 'catch up' to you?" The blunt question drove home the point so clearly that Victor, as usual, felt like an idiot.

"No. I guess not. But even so, Valla, what about"—he reached out and gently touched the scar on her forehead, just above her bandage—"the rest of it? What about me getting pulled into more and more situations where you'd be at risk if you were with me? What about me, during my downtime, sitting around missing you 'cause you're doing your thing?"

"Well, what did Lesh tell you?"

The question seemed to come out of left field, surprising Victor and putting him even more off balance. "Huh?"

"You sat at the table for a while after I walked out. My hearing's not as good as yours, but I heard your voices. What did you tell him?" Something told Victor she'd heard much more than she was letting on. She'd been sitting right outside the window, after all. Was that why she'd made the peace overture after her nap? Had she heard him stumble upon the truth of his self-centered concern?

"Well, he basically told me that I should be happy for the time I have. I should be happy for what I can grasp and stop trying to control what I can't." He sighed. "I don't remember the exact words."

"So?" Valla turned toward him again, reaching to gently scrape her nails through the rough, short stubble on his jawline. "Aren't you happier having grasped this moment?"

"Yeah. Of course. I don't like feeling like you're angry or that I've messed things up. I just also wish I could count on some stability in our future together—"

"Victor!" She spoke sharply, but her lips and eyes smiled as she leaned closer, pressing her forehead against his. "The only way that will happen is if we both decide we're content with what we have, if we both stop going out and risking ourselves. We'd have to decide we don't need more levels, more knowledge, or more strength. We'd have to admit that we're okay with a huge portion of the population being stronger than us and having power *over* us. Even if we returned to Fanwath, we'd need to worry about the next threat that might come through a gateway. Could you do that?"

His voice was quiet and a little thick with emotion when he eventually responded, "No."

Valla smiled and leaned close, kissing him softly. "I have to confess that I was feeling a similar way. It's why I got upset about the house. For a tiny moment, when we first moved in there, I could picture a life with you, making a home together. I'm not saying we won't do that. I'm not saying it's impossible, but I think when I realized you sold the house, I recognized the fantasy for what it was. So, let's do our best. Let's find ways to improve while spending as much time together as possible. Let's try not to be irritated with each other and spoil our precious time with fights."

"All right." He moved his hand to the side of her face, gently stroking her cheek with his thumb. "You know, it's not sold yet. I could tell the realtor to stop trying—"

"No. You made the right decision. A home isn't the right place to tie up our money right now. Besides, if we want to spend time in a place that's truly ours, we can visit home." Victor smiled at the words; having a place to think of as home was nice, and the Free Marches fit nicely. She grasped his hand, halting his gentle exploration of her injury. "Don't worry about the scar. I'll consume the racial advancement elixir I earned in the dungeon. If it's not enough to repair my eye, I'll use the regeneration tonic I saved."

"I'm not worried. I don't give a shit how many scars you have!" Victor growled, his voice gaining some volume and a bit of a rumble. "You're the most beautiful woman in the universe. Any scars you get only make things a little fairer for the other goddesses out there."

That brought a giggle burbling out of Valla's throat, and she bounded atop him, her wings spreading wide. "Did you just call me a goddess?"

"Obviously—" Victor started to say, but then a knock at the door interrupted his further efforts to earn her good favor. "What?" he barked, more harshly than he intended.

A muffled voice came through the door, "Victor, sir, Lord Dar would meet with you. He awaits you in the library."

"Shit," Victor sighed. "I hope I'm not in trouble. I wrote in the damn Far Scribe book like he asked—"

"Go!" Valla rolled to the side and nimbly off the bed. She padded, barefoot and naked, toward the bathroom. "I'll be here. I'm going to consume the racial advancement! Check on me later."

"I will." Victor sat up on the side of the bed and quickly began pulling on his hastily discarded clothing.

He thought she was gone, out of sight in the bathroom, but after a few seconds, she spoke up from the doorway, her voice very sweet and almost a little plaintive: "I love you, Victor."

He jerked his head up to lock eyes with her and immediately replied, "I love you, too." She smiled at that and pulled the door closed, and then Victor finished getting dressed and hurried out.

When he stepped into the brightly lit library, shielding his eyes from the sun reflecting off the lake shining through the enormous floor-to-ceiling windows, he found Ranish Dar sitting at one of the study tables, thumbing through a text so thick that it would have put his *abuela*'s old-school dictionary to shame.

"Thank you for hurrying, Victor. I hope I didn't interrupt your nap."

Victor tried to hear sarcasm or wry humor in the man's deep, grating voice, but the words felt sincere. "No, I was awake." He strode over to the table and gestured to the empty seat across from Dar. "Should I sit down?"

"Yes, by all means." Dar closed the thick book with a *thud* and turned his smoldering eyes toward him, watching Victor take a seat. "You've made yourself small again?" He chuckled, clearly finding Victor's human-sized form in his oversized chair amusing.

"Well, I was with Valla," Victor mumbled, reaching into his Core to cut the connection to the Alter Self spell. As he surged in size, filling the chair out and putting himself eye to eye with Ranish Dar, he shrugged. "It makes things easier."

"Yes." Dar rubbed his stony chin. "No doubt it does." He leaned back, causing the dense hardwood chair to creak. "I read your reports in the Far Scribe book. I appreciate you asking if I mind you and your friends hosting a gathering here, but as I told you before, I want you to consider this your home for now. I generally don't entertain, so you needn't worry about my schedule. Once I get you started on some rigorous practice routines, I will return to the tower and give you some space."

"Oh. Well, thanks." Victor smiled, knowing Lam and Edeya would be pleased.

"I've been thinking about your ritual. The heart, I mean. We spoke only briefly after you consumed it, but I was serious about finding you some worthy opponents, enemies whose hearts might be worth claiming. I believe I've stumbled upon a solution in the most unlikely of places—a letter from one of my grandchildren."

"Your, um, grandchildren?"

"Have I not mentioned that I'm old, Victor? Some might say ancient." He chuckled. "When a man conquers worlds, a few dozen children here and there are to be expected." He looked hard at Victor, and his stony brows lifted in amusement. "Unless his heart is claimed, perhaps. Love? I've had love, Victor, but centuries tend to pull even the most desperate lovers apart."

Victor was silent, contemplating Dar's words. Was it a coincidence? It felt strange to be hearing about love and centuries "pulling people apart" directly after the discussion he'd just had with Valla. Was Dar teasing him? Offering him advice in a strange, roundabout manner?

Despite Victor's preoccupation, Dar continued speaking. "When I was younger, I conquered a kingdom in a world called Ruhn. I lived there for quite some time and built up a rather extended family before my yearnings for knowledge, adventure, and power called me away. My wife was gone, and my children had either left to seek their own glory or had become elderly due to their lack of ambition. I didn't feel compelled to stay."

That got Victor's attention, and he pushed away his unquiet thoughts and tried to pay attention to the master Spirit Caster. Dar noticed his renewed focus and smiled as he continued, "These days on Ruhn, you can find many high-tier individuals in the iron ranks and even a few hundred working through their tests of steel. However, only a very few have entered their lustrous veil. According to my granddaughter's letter, ten such individuals watch over the world, and they are, to put it simply, hands-off."

"Yeah?" Victor liked the sound of that, but probably only because he was still an "iron ranker." He didn't enjoy having hundreds or even thousands of people at Dar's power level hanging around, reminding him of his insignificance.

"Yes. Ruhn is, in effect, ruled by an empire of which the kingdoms, like the one I left to my descendants, are member states. The kingdoms are often vying for power and influence. The most influential will occasionally force a war of succession, changing the empire's rulership. I've lost touch with the world and my children's children, but this letter surprised me recently. Well, it was recent to me—something like four years ago. It was after our discussion last night, following your ritual, that I was reminded of my granddaughter's plight."

"Her plight?" Victor was trying to keep track of Dar's rambling tale and how it might impact him. He'd yet to figure that part out.

"Yes, the point of her letter—my kingdom, well, hers now, is beset by hostile neighbors who've been putting tremendous strain on her economy and infrastructure. She fears they'll soon challenge her and lay claim to her lands, destroying my descendants' legacy." Dar spoke matter-of-factly, betraying no emotion at all, and his uncaring demeanor brought storm clouds to Victor's narrowed eyes.

"She wanted your help? Four *years* ago?" He couldn't keep the snarl out of his words.

"That's right." Dar nodded, drumming his fingers on the table, ignoring Victor's evident judgment. "At the time, I contemplated a walk back to Ruhn, but that would throw me into conflict with the ten veil walkers of that world. No, someone of my stature could not aid her. So, I set the letter aside with plans to find a solution, and now I have!"

"But . . ." Victor started to object, wanting to chastise his "master" for taking so long to help his descendants, but something else had caught his attention. "What do you mean you were thinking about a 'walk' back to Ruhn?" He quickly followed up with, "And what's a veil walker?"

"Ah, that's right." Dar looked at him with an even expression, and Victor got the distinct impression that he was pitying him. "I let slip my mind your lack of formal education. Fear not; I'll spend some months giving you lessons before I send you on your way."

"Send me—"

"But, to answer your questions." Dar held up a finger, interrupting Victor. "When I 'walk' somewhere distant, I use the spirit plane. Yet another lesson I must add to your long list of study topics."

"You can—"

Dar brandished his finger again. "Veil walker is a general term for those who've completed their test of steel and moved into their lustrous veil." He paused for a moment, letting his words sink in. "Now, to the point: I told you we need to find you more hearts from worthy foes. On Ruhn, wars are decided by battles between two kingdoms' champions. The fools pressuring my distant granddaughter won't be worthy hearts for you, but after you've vanquished them, you will champion my granddaughter as she begins a war of succession. You and she will conquer Ruhn."

"*Seriously*? When? How long will that take? Why wo—"

Dar held up a hand. "Victor! Such panic from a titan? Calm yourself and think. There are more than a hundred kingdoms on Ruhn. Of those, twenty-two are formidable and will have champions that will truly test your mettle. When you face the seven great houses, you will earn hearts that will make the one from the behemoth seem a mere snack! Of course, those champions will likely all be steel seekers, so you'll have your work cut out for you."

Victor opened his mouth to reply, but Dar pressed on. "There are several ways to gain raw power for a standard cultivator—vanquish foes for their Energy, cultivate Energy from other sources, and improve one's species or bloodline. You have *another* method that does all three and *more*!"

Dar's passion broke through to Victor, and he nodded, his eyes narrowing as he scowled in determination. Dar was right. He gained a lot of Energy from every heart he consumed, sometimes improved his bloodline, and often gained traits from his enemies. Even his Breath Core had come from eating a heart. "Are the fights always to the death?"

"Always. It's meant to deter conflict."

"So I have to win a hundred duels?"

"Once the war of succession has begun, other kingdoms will likely seize the opportunity to remove enemies, claim weaker neighbors, or even unite in mutual defense. Many may kneel to my granddaughter, accepting her claim."

Victor's scowl deepened. He wanted to have an idea of what he was up against. "How many? Will I have to win fifty? Twenty?"

"There's no telling. The last champion to lead a claimant to the imperial throne won sixty-four duels."

Victor shook his head, baffled by the strange custom. "So that's all it takes? One champion kills another, and they lose their kingdom?"

"Not quite. Wars of succession are much more complicated. You'll be dealing with shifting alliances, resource management, and political intrigue. A kingdom is not required to accept a duel, and should they refuse, my granddaughter will need to coerce them. That's what has been happening to her. Her hostile neighbors have been putting pressure on her in myriad ways—cutting off food supplies, severing communication with the greater empire, destroying resources, assassinating members of her court, and even kidnapping civilians."

"How do you know she hasn't fallen?"

"Because I used a treasure to scry her this morning. Her current champion yet lives. She's close to breaking, but her neighbors feel no hurry; they slowly bleed her of resources and know she'll be forced to accept the challenge eventually. A year or ten is nothing for people who count their lives in centuries."

Victor sighed and reached up to run his fingers through his short, stiff hair as though he could stimulate his brain by pulling on it. "You said her neighbors are weaklings. Now you say they count their lives in centuries."

"Few people push much past the middle of the iron ranks. Why would they? They feel not the pull of glory! The competition for resources becomes deadly, the grind of cultivation becomes an all-consuming obsession, and the pace of progress becomes glacial." He snorted softly, amused by some private thought, as he eyed Victor knowingly. "For most. Nevertheless, reaching level thirty or fifty greatly extends a natural life, yes? So, most people in worlds like Ruhn will gain levels while it is easy or entertaining and then fall back into rather mundane lives, enjoying the gains they've accumulated for hundreds or thousands of years."

Victor slowly nodded, lowering his hands to the arms of his chair as he thought about that. His perception of the worlds he'd visited was badly skewed; he was always seeking to advance, so he encountered other people on that path, whether it be in arenas, on monster hunts, in wars, or even in dungeons. Still, he encountered seemingly mundane people daily—servants, officials, merchants, and countless people on the street about whom he knew nothing. Suddenly, Valla's point that he and she would need to agree that they were content before having real quality time together took on a new light.

The truth was, Dar was out of touch. Victor knew that it wasn't just people who no longer found gaining levels "easy or entertaining" who stopped. He knew that life wasn't fair and that on many worlds, maybe most of them, the people with power actively worked to keep others from acquiring it. All he had to do was remember the Wagon Wheel and the Greatbone Mine to cement that point in his mind.

He turned his attention back to the topic of their meeting. "So your granddaughter needs to force the other kingdoms to accept her challenges before I'll need to fight?"

"That's right. She may need your help with some of her strategies, but, for the most part, you'll remain in her court, training and making yourself available for duels. If a kingdom bends the knee to her rather than having their champion duel you, you'll receive a portion of the tribute they pay—a tariff for your formidable intimidation value. I'll instruct my granddaughter to demand growth items as payment for your services."

"How long?"

"Before I send you? Two to six months, I'd say. There's the matter of your education—etiquette, the laws of succession on Ruhn, and some general knowledge about advancement. More than that, I want to get you started on methods of training that you can practice while away."

"And my companions?" Victor already felt he knew the answer before Dar shook his head.

"They must remain here. I will extend my hospitality to each of them; I know their safety is important to you, and I won't have you distracted with worry. Besides, I rather like Lam, and I'm eager to see how she advances. I can see you formulating an objection, especially with regard to your lady love, but Victor, she will languish on Ruhn. There aren't easily accessible dungeons, and once it begins, the war will turn the countryside perilous with lurking assassins and saboteurs. She'd have to stay at court and watch as you grew ever more powerful, winning duel after duel. No, I think it best you leave her here with your dragon-blood friend."

Victor felt that earlier dread, that cold hard grip on his heart, slide back into place. Had he somehow felt this coming? Had he known Dar would be sending him places for God knows how long? He must have suspected it on some subconscious level. "Shouldn't she have the option?"

"Yes. Talk to her. Explain that Ruhn is four jumps away via a System Stone and that when I help you make the journey, you'll use the spirit plane—a method unavailable to anyone without a sufficiently sturdy Spirit Core." Dar pushed his chair back and stood. "Go now. I have things to arrange." He scowled at Victor, but the slight tilt of an eyebrow made it clear he wasn't really upset. "Primary among them, I must negotiate with the Sojourn Council in an attempt to release you from your debt of three tasks."

"So that I can leave?"

"Exactly. Now, enjoy some time with your friends. Come dawn, we will build your cultivation chamber and begin your training in earnest."

20

MAKING PLANS

When Victor returned to his room, he found Valla lying on the carpet beside the bed, dressed in loose silken pajamas. She was clearly unconscious, her body slowly emitting wispy vapors of golden Energy. She'd consumed her "racial elixir," and Victor had a feeling she'd be out for a while. It wasn't a particularly potent treasure, according to Lesh, but even a single racial rank could take time, and no one knew that better than Victor. Even so, he sat on the edge of the bed and watched her for a while, taking the moment of quiet to unpack everything Dar had told him.

Victor was torn. On the one hand, he was drawn to the idea of aiding a struggling nation, especially one led by the descendants of Ranish Dar. On the other, the thought of facing off against the champions of numerous enemy nations, particularly the more formidable ones who had honed their skills for centuries, was daunting. He pondered Dar's words and how he'd described these champions as "steel seekers," indicating they were beyond Level One Hundred and had crafted custom classes with the System's aid.

From what Victor had gathered, a person's test of steel could span years or even centuries. Some individuals were "steelbound" and never transitioned into their lustrous veil, whatever that entailed—Victor was growing increasingly frustrated by the enigmatic secrecy surrounding that particular stage of advancement. The crux of the matter was that Victor knew he'd be pitted against champions who'd honed their skills for far longer than he'd even been alive. It was one thing to face off against some iron rankers outside his level range, but did Dar genuinely believe it was prudent to match him against adversaries so much more powerful?

If Dar's reasoning was simple confidence in his strength, Victor supposed he found it encouraging, but after listening to Dar talk about his granddaughter and the kingdom he'd left behind, almost as if they were a footnote in the long history of his life, Victor wasn't so sure Dar cared if he won the duels. As far as he knew, Dar was just throwing him out there as a long shot; if he survived, great, but if he didn't, some other distraction would surely already be in place by the time Victor died.

Regardless, Victor knew he was going. Dar had baited the trap well, speaking of glory and spinning the tale in a way that had Victor envisioning himself standing up for a smaller nation and turning the tables, helping the underdog to rise against its oppressors. It didn't hurt that he'd be fighting out of his weight class, something Victor found he truly enjoyed. The prizes of potent hearts, growth items, and tribute from the conquered nations were certainly enticing, too. Victor liked the idea of leaning into his rare ability to gain power from his vanquished foes and was glad Dar was encouraging it. He liked fighting and eating hearts a lot more than he enjoyed cultivating for long, slow hours.

Looking at Valla, he was reminded of his other reservations; he'd be leaving her behind. Even if she wanted to spend the exorbitant price to purchase four different System teleports, he wouldn't want her to come. Dar had said it perfectly: She'd languish while he gained more strength. Wouldn't it be better if she stayed in Sojourn with Lesh and continued to utilize the more accessible leveling opportunities? Maybe she'd get lucky, find more racial advancements and other rare boosts, and surprise him by gaining ground.

"How long?" he whispered. How long would he be gone? He didn't know, but he couldn't imagine a succession war was easily or quickly wrapped up. Sighing, Victor reached down and took Valla's hand, speaking softly as though she might hear him, "If it takes a long time, though, and I'm winning enough duels, I could pay for you to visit." He could imagine winning "wars" for a kingdom would bring a fair amount of riches.

Besides, wasn't he going to learn how to walk through the spirit plane, not just as a spirit, but bringing his body along for the ride? It sounded as though Dar felt he'd have to help him, but maybe while Victor was on Ruhn, training and gaining more power, he'd master the skill himself. Perhaps he'd be able to visit Valla! He sighed and stood. A lot remained to be seen, but he needed to keep hopeful, or he'd let himself spiral into a foul, despondent mood again. He left his room and went looking for Lam; he wanted to give her the good news.

He wasn't surprised to find her and Edeya on the deck, lying in the afternoon sun. "Hey, ladies."

"Victor!" Edeya sat up, grinning, and Lam opened her eyes, peeking through her fingers to avoid the direct sun.

"I have good news, Lam. Master Dar"—Victor grinned, using the honorific; he only did it because he knew Dar was home and he was trying to earn some points with the man—"says you can host your party. Any idea when?"

Lam nodded, also sitting up to look up at him more easily. He stood a few paces from their lounge chairs and shifted to the side to put himself in front of the sun. Lam smiled as she lowered her hand, safe in his large shadow. "At the end of the week—four days. I want to make sure everyone has time to respond."

"That means I have your party this weekend, and then I have to go to some other damn party for Lo'ro next week."

"Don't forget about the Ridonne's party!" Edeya added cheerfully.

"What?" Victor's scowl at the mention of the word "Ridonne" was automatic.

"You didn't tell him?" Edeya eyed Lam.

"It never came up. Besides, we never agreed to go." Lam held out her hand, and a small piece of stiff, creamy paper appeared on her palm. It looked almost like a business card. "This is Chal-dak's calling card. We ran into him while watching you in the challenge dungeon. He invited us to attend a 'victory' party for his brother, Warin-dak. He was sure he'd win." Lam shrugged and flicked the card his way. Victor snatched it out of the air and frowned.

"Not really looking to make nice with the Ridonne."

Lam shrugged. "Tear it up if you want. If you change your mind and decide to go, we'll come along." She smiled and lay back, flopping her arm over her eyes. Lazily, she said, "He might have changed his plans when his brother got beaten by that Death Caster. He hasn't exactly reached out to us."

Victor lifted an eyebrow. "Arona beat him?"

"Yes, according to Lesh." Lam yawned, and Victor could see she was trying to check out of the conversation.

"Thanks for the spell, Victor," Edeya said. "The Frozen Aura. It's perfect for me when I'm engaging with my spear or when enemies are flanking me."

"You like it?" Victor gave her a good look. She was wearing a new swimsuit Lam had purchased when they were in town, and he had a hard time reconciling her appearance with the skinny, dirty, tough-looking girl he'd met in the mines. She looked so clean, happy, and healthy that it brought a big stupid grin to his face.

"Of course I do. Don't worry, though; as soon as I find something worthwhile, I'll pay you back."

"Hey! Friends don't expect to be paid back. Remember that." He shaded his eyes and looked around, gazing at the lake over the deck railing. "Where are the boys?"

"Lesh is sunning down by the water. I'm sure his 'fosterling' is with him." Edeya giggled. Victor nodded, his grin only growing wider as he started down the steps. Sure enough, he saw Lesh's big dark form lying on the pier. Darren was out in the water. When he reached the bottom of the stairs, and his boots echoed hollowly on the planks, Darren looked up from where he floated and waved.

"Hey, Darren." His voice brought a stir to Lesh's slumbering bulk, and the big dragonkin, naked other than a pair of knee-length leather trousers, pushed himself into a sitting position to regard him.

"Lord Victor," he rumbled. "How goes it?"

"Good, Lesh, but I need to talk to you."

"I'm at your disposal. Shall we go inside?"

Victor stretched, pressing his hands into his lower back as he looked out over the water. "Nah, this is good. Let's talk here." With that, he sat on the pier and began pulling his boots off.

Darren floated, watching Victor sit beside Lesh, both men dropping their feet into the water. They were giants, and Darren felt tiny in their shadows, treading water beneath them. While he contemplated getting out, Victor said, "I have to speak to you about what Dar has planned for me."

Lesh rumbled his acknowledgment, then looked at Darren. "Should I send my fosterling to train?"

Victor looked at Darren and locked eyes with him for a moment. It was intimidating, and Darren shuddered to think what it would be like to stare into those bright golden hawkish eyes if Victor let his aura loose. "No," he said, scratching the rough stubble on his jaw. "You can hang out here, Darren, but don't repeat any of this until I've had a chance to speak with Valla. It may be a day or two."

The flush of pride that swelled his chest would have been embarrassing if he hadn't been so damned happy to be included in the men's private talk. Darren nodded eagerly. "Of course! I won't repeat a word."

Victor nodded and turned to Lesh. "Well, Dar is going to send me to a world that's four jumps away from here. He wants me to help his distant granddaughter conquer an empire and, along with it, her entire world."

"That sounds a worthy cause!" Lesh nodded, smashing a heavy scaled fist into his palm. "When shall we be ready?"

Victor sighed and kicked his foot through the water. "That's the thing, Lesh. The fighting between kingdoms in that world is kind of strange. Wars are settled by dueling champions. If you came, you'd be bored watching me fight one duel after another."

"Ah. It becomes clear. You are releasing me from your service." Lesh sounded so despondent that Darren wanted to swim over to him and offer a comforting word, but Victor laughed and put his arm over the hulking warrior's shoulders, jostling him.

"No, Lesh! Not unless you want to be free, and then I'll let you go, though it would be painful. I have other plans for you if you'll stick around. I want you to stay in Sojourn and continue running dungeons with Valla. I need you to keep an eye on the others, too. Listen, man, I've sparred with you a lot; you're a match for most of those *pendejos* I fought in the dungeon. If you keep up the training and keep winning treasures from the dungeons, you'll be one of the strongest iron rankers in Sojourn. You and Valla, both."

"And your master?" Lesh looked around the lake pointedly. Darren knew what he was thinking; he obviously loved the water and the sun.

"He wants you all to stay here. He says it's important I'm not distracted with worry, and he wants to extend his hospitality to each of you. Darren, Edeya, and Lam can continue adventuring together, too."

Lesh nodded and grunted, "Yes."

Victor held out a hand. "You'll stay? You'll watch Valla's back?"

"I will." Lesh took his hand with a meaty *thwap*, and the two squeezed each other's palms. Darren watched, inwardly amused but also a little awed at the bulge of their muscles, the gravity of those grips. "How long until you leave?"

"Leaving in less than six months. I think Dar's eager to get me out there. That's the other thing I wanted to talk to you about. I'm going to bug Dar for information about Breath Cores. If he doesn't know anything, I'm sure he can come up with a book or point me at another master who might owe him a favor. He wants me to have something to study while I'm there, so I think he'll be generous with his help. Anyway, whatever I learn, whatever knowledge I get ahold of, I'll pass it on to you. I even have a means to copy books."

"I would be in your debt!" Lesh started to bow his head, but Victor laughed and pushed his shoulder.

"Cut that shit out, *hermano*! I'm the one who owes you! So, Dar will go over my training schedule with me tomorrow. I'll make sure there's at least an hour set aside for sparring every day. You and me, brother. We'll go at it hard until I leave, all right?"

"Yes!" Lesh's voice was full of swelling pride and eagerness. Darren could see he'd been yearning for some attention from Victor, and he had to admit, he knew how that felt. It was nice when someone you admired took notice of you. It was nice when they included you in their plans. He'd felt the same from Lesh. He felt something similar from Edeya and Lam, too—he was thrilled to learn they'd have the older, more experienced woman with them the next time they went out. He was *more* thrilled to learn they still wanted him to come along now that the women had each other.

He floated there, listening to Victor and Lesh make plans, and then, as it seemed their conversation was coming to a close, Lesh turned to him. "We'll surprise Lord Victor with our gains while he's gone, won't we, fosterling?"

Darren quickly straightened up and nodded. "Yes! We'll bring pride to your house, Victor!"

Lesh rumbled his approval, and Darren could see the amusement in Victor's eyes as he nodded and held up his thumb. "Good, Darren. Kick some ass out there. I want to see you gain some inches, so find a racial advancement, huh?"

"Will that make me taller?" Darren couldn't keep the excitement out of his tone.

Lesh laughed and nodded. "Almost everyone gains some height on their first few advancements; it's your body reaching the potential you were born with. If you can unlock a bloodline, things could change even more; you might grow smaller, or you might become much larger." He elbowed Victor, eliciting a laugh, then added, "Or you might stay the same."

Darren nodded, grinning at the small joke, and then a thought came to his mind. "Victor, are you worried about the duels? For Dar's granddaughter?"

"Worried? Not too much. I guess quite a few of the champions are well over Level One Hundred, though, so that'll be interesting. Hopefully, I'll make some gains before I fight them." Darren wasn't sure why he'd asked, but he thought Victor might appreciate it. He was always concerned about everyone else, but Darren rarely saw anyone worrying about Victor. Even Valla treated him like a rock, at least in public.

"Dar must be pleased," Darren said. "I'm sure he's worried about his family."

Victor chuckled and shook his head. "Maybe, but I'm not too sure. I don't think he's returned to that world for hundreds of years—maybe thousands. I don't know if he's ever met this woman, and I'm not even sure how many generations removed she is from him. Anyway, it doesn't matter. It'll be a good experience for me, and I'm glad I have a purpose—I'm not just fighting to fight." He laughed and elbowed Lesh. "Not that that would stop me."

"Well, I think it's commendable. Imagine it, Victor!" Darren stretched his arm up to the sky, the atmosphere so thin you could see the stars clearly, even in the afternoon sunlight. "One of those stars could be the one where you're going. The world you will conquer could be floating out there before our eyes."

Victor and Lesh both leaned their heads back, staring up, following Darren's gaze, and for perhaps the first time in his life, Darren felt he was being respected. He'd had people show him respect before, but it wasn't because they respected him. Usually, it was because they feared whatever office or position he held. If not that, they were simply respecting his station's status, whether at a political event, in court, or in the board room. None of them really respected *him*, however.

Victor and Lesh were different. There sat two men who were so beyond him that they could literally squash him like a bug. Yet, rather than dismiss him, they included him in their conversation. They listened to his words, and they demonstrated expectations of him. That was genuine respect, given, not earned, but still far better than the false respect, which was all he'd ever felt.

For the first time, as they spoke with him, Darren didn't feel like an imposter. He felt as though he belonged, and confident that he'd continue to earn his place among these people. With a broad smile, he said, "Elder Lesh, would it be all right if I seek out my party members? I think we should do some training."

Lesh nodded, grinning at Darren toothily. "Go, fosterling. I'm pleased by your ambition. Master Dar has a sparring court on the far side of the house. Go through the front door, turn right, and follow the cobbled path through the citrus grove."

As Darren swam to the pier and pulled himself up, Victor raised an eyebrow. "Seriously? I didn't even know that."

Lesh nodded. "I scouted the grounds before swimming this morning."

"Shit, man," Victor groaned, rubbing a hand through his hair. "I'm going to have to get my shit together. It's going to suck not having you to rely on, *hermano*."

Darren smiled, listening to Lesh rumble a reply, placating Victor. He hurried up the steps, still in the swimming trunks Lam had given him. When he burst onto the deck, he saw the two Ghelli lounging in the sun, both with their eyes closed. He suddenly wished the water was closer; they were perfect splashing targets. "Hey!" he shouted, clapping his hands. "Dey-dey and Lammy!" He laughed as he said Lam's new nickname, already anticipating the beating she would give him.

Edeya's eyes sprang open, and she leaped up, her wings buzzing. "What? Is something wrong?"

Lam lazily opened her eyes. "He's laughing, *Dey-dey*. I doubt anything's wrong."

Darren growled and clapped his hands again. "Something *is* wrong, lazy bones! I'm not Level Ten yet. Come on, let's go spar!"

21

RENEWED FOCUS

"Have you seen a cultivation chamber before, Victor?" Dar asked, looking around the small cave. He'd brought Victor down beneath his lake house again, not far from where they'd performed Lam's ritual.

"Yeah. The Warlord in Coloss had one. He let me and Valla use it for a little while before I figured out he was going to try to steal my bloodline."

Dar nodded. Victor had given him most of the details of his adventures on Zaafor, back when he'd written in the Far Scribe journal and recently when they'd spoken about his ability to claim power from the hearts of his defeated foes. "From what I've surmised about this 'Warlord,' I think it's safe to say that he's steelbound. His frustrations sound like those of a man who hasn't been able to break through."

"Does that mean I might be able to take him?"

"Perhaps, but I think caution is advisable. Someone who's been steelbound for centuries, especially a man holding sway over an entire planet, may have gained enormous power, even though he never broke into his lustrous veil."

Victor sighed as he watched Dar slowly unpacking materials from a dimensional sack he'd carried down, grasped in his thick, stony fist. At the moment, he was making stacks of plate-sized, slightly concave stones that looked almost as if they could be used for paving a garden. He held the sack, and it took no effort to summon the objects out, or Victor would have asked to help unload the supplies. He would have, that is, if his mind weren't fixated on something Dar had said. "I'm starting to get frustrated with the constant mentions of the 'test of steel' and the 'lustrous veil' when I really don't understand them," Victor told him. "Is it such a mystery? Can't you tell me what to expect?"

"You know more than you think," Dar said. "When you reach Level One Hundred, what will happen?"

"I'll have to choose a new class?"

"You'll have to *create* a new class." Dar looked at Victor and moved his shoulders in a gesture he had come to recognize as his best attempt at a shrug. "There's a reason it seems mysterious; the process differs from person to person. Once you create your class, you'll need to continue gaining levels, using a portion of the Energy to improve the class—another 'mysterious' process in that, as you may guess, it isn't the same for any two individuals. If you think that's frustrating, understand that things only worsen. Your breakthrough will likely take you by surprise, and when it happens, you'll slip into your 'lustrous veil' and face new, unique roads to advancement."

"Why 'lustrous veil?' I mean, the term sounds—"

"Frilly? Overly poetic? Think of it this way: In the iron ranks, you're building up your foundation, your core of strength. During the test of steel, you're refining all of that iron into something stronger, sharper. The lustrous veil is named so for two reasons: You're adding the shine to your steel, and your process is hidden, obscured in the mystery of your individualism. No two people will hone their steel to a mirrored, lustrous shine in the same way."

Victor sighed, realizing he wasn't going to get much help. Dar continued to look at him and chuckled. "You think you're the first iron ranker who felt frustrated by this? Listen, Victor, I won't tell you what to do in your test of steel for a simple reason—if you try to repeat what worked for me, you're likely to set yourself back. Things might *seem* to be working, and you may advance partially over the course of years or decades, only to find that the foundation you built with my guidance won't work for you. There's no surer way to become steelbound."

"So, it's something I need to figure out myself."

"Not entirely. I'll guide you as you move from stage to stage, which should help you gain an advantage over this insular Warlord enemy of yours. He's done himself no favors by keeping to his world, refusing to learn from the greater universe."

"I still don't get it, though." Victor chuckled at himself, shaking his head. "I mean, I don't think I'm stupid, but can you tell me how it's different after Level One Hundred? I get that the System will help me build a new class, but so what? I choose the class I like, and then I gain levels; what's *different*?"

Dar set down his sack and turned to face him, a broad smile exposing his teeth. "I see what's got you confused. You don't *pick* a class and move on. You have to build your class. Up to now, you've been given a class by the System. You have no idea how that works, how it molds the Energy into your body with each level. At Level One Hundred, you're going to have to do things the way our ancestors did before the System arrived. You'll understand why you need that foundation when you enter your veil. As for the System, it won't give you much help. It'll start you on the first stage of creating your class, and after that, you'll only hear from it when you succeed in forming and refining it."

Victor nodded, feeling his frustration slipping away. "I think I'm starting to see the picture more clearly." He wondered if the Warlord had even finished building his class. If the System only got him started and he had no idea what was expected, being the only person on Zaafor to reach that stage . . . Victor shook his head; it wasn't worth speculating. He'd find out when he faced the man.

"Good. Now, let's talk about cultivation. There's a reason the Warlord had a cultivation chamber. A person's advancement has three interlocking restrictions. One, you must build up Energy in your physical form. The System measures that in 'levels.' Two, you must strengthen your Core, building it, compacting it, and expanding it. The System measures that in Core ranks. Finally, you must also improve your body with racial advancements. If you don't, two things will happen. Do you know what they are?"

"I know I can't gain levels past a certain point if I don't advance my race."

"Exactly! How can you advance in levels, enhancing your physical aspect with Energy, if your body cannot contain that Energy without being destroyed? The second?"

"I'm guessing it has something to do with advancing my Core?"

"That's right! Just as you can't gain levels beyond the limits of your body, your Core cannot outstrip your physical form, else it, too, could destroy you with the Energy it contains."

"So, the Warlord?"

"Yes, the Warlord—he likely spends much of his time cultivating because he's grown too powerful for his world. The Energy he takes from slaying the beasts or people on Zaafor likely doesn't impact him much. You'll learn that if you push your Core, reaching the limit of your racial tier, then you can use the excess cultivated Energy to advance your level. Again, you can only do that until you reach the peak of your body's capabilities. With an 'epic' race or bloodline, that peak is well over Level Two Hundred."

"So, if he has an epic racial tier, he could be Level Two Hundred or more?"

"Yes, and likely with a Core in the epic tier as well. Do you see how, even steelbound, he could be formidable? Even so, it's not as dire as it may seem. Levels gained while steelbound are far less impactful than levels gained in the iron ranks."

"Are all people who've entered their 'lustrous veil' that high level?"

"Some. Some might break through early and quickly. I know a woman who was only Level One Hundred and Eight when she broke through."

"So the Warlord could be stronger for staying steelbound for so long?"

Dar barked a quick laugh, shaking his head. "No, lad. He'll be stronger than any iron ranker and some other steelbound folks, but anyone in their veil will have glimpsed true power. They'll have abilities that he simply cannot fathom or counter."

Victor nodded, reaching up to scratch the back of his head. Was Tes in her lustrous veil or whatever name the dragons had for that stage of advancement? He had to think she was; she'd been utterly fearless when facing the Warlord. Was her "elder magic" a clue to the test of steel? Was it what masters in their lustrous veil used? He hoped her early lesson in the pre-System magic would aid him when the time came, and he resolved to practice with it and try to learn new applications for it as he'd done with the spell to summon his spirit totems.

"Was the Warlord's cultivation chamber a spherical chamber?" Dar asked, interrupting his thoughts. Victor looked up to see his mentor was once again piling what looked like building materials on the cave floor.

"Yeah, it was. He had a platform suspended in the center so a person could sit in the middle of the chamber."

"Mmhmm. I imagine he had many treasures in there, considering he's lord over the entire planet. I've done something similar in a world or three. I don't think you quite understand how wondrous your ability to build up your Core via the heart ritual is. Your tale of running through the wastes of Zaafor, eating the hearts of great spiders and minor wyrms, each time flooding your Core with Energy . . . Honestly, Victor, I wonder if we waste our time with this chamber. It might be wiser to simply send you into dungeons to rip the hearts from every monster you encounter."

Victor looked at him, not sure what to say. If he were honest, he'd be just as happy to do what Dar suggested; the act of cultivation was sometimes cathartic, but frequently, for him, it dredged up painful memories as he forced himself to relive and work out what made him so angry and fearful.

Dar saved him from a reply by saying, "No. Cultivation isn't only about building Energy, not for a Spirit Caster. You must inure yourself to the Energies with which you toil. In any case, we won't try to match the Warlord's chamber with your first one—a flat floor, curved walls, and a domed ceiling will suffice." He grunted as he shifted a large stack of lumber. "I sent Drema to collect these building supplies, and she did you some favors. She had the timbers cut to the exact lengths I specified and purchased brackets to join them. You'll have an easy time of it."

Victor surveyed the stacks of stone, the bags of mortar, the large metal buckets, the sacks of nails, and the piles of wood. "What am I building?"

Dar smiled, produced a large roll of parchment, and unfurled it, holding it out to Victor. It was densely inscribed with the detailed plans for a domed, stone-lined room. Victor could see the blueprints for a wooden framework and instructions for building it down to the individual nails. The next stage showed where to place each octagonal, plate-sized stone, with precise instructions for mortaring them into place. "Huh. I thought there'd be more magic involved."

"Sometimes it's good to do things with your hands, Victor." Dar nodded and moved toward the tunnel leading back to his house. "While you construct the chamber, I'll procure the other cultivation items you'll need. Normally, I'd send you on quests to gain each one, but we're a bit pressed for time. Speaking of which." He pulled a golden watch from the pocket of his bright orange, silken pants and studied it. "I also need to stop by the council building. They're making a decision about releasing you from your debt."

"You think they'll let me off?"

"I have my enemies on the council, but I'm hopeful that a bit of wealth and a favor owed will move things our way. The truth of the matter is that they cannot stop me from sending you away, though it could make your return problematic if we disregard their decision."

Victor wanted to tell him to forget it, that he'd do the three tasks, but he knew Dar didn't want the Sojourn Council to interrupt his training or delay his departure. Nevertheless, he hated that his debt to the master Spirit Caster was mounting by the day. Thinking of debts, he frowned, looking at the building supplies. "Are these magical materials?"

"The tiles, aye. They're a dense material, resistant to the passage of Energy and further enchanted to reflect it. Don't fret; they're cheap in the greater scheme of things. It's the cultivation sources that are going to cost me."

"Nothing I can do?"

"Nay. Again, don't worry; the service you will provide to my neglected descendants on Ruhn will be worth the meager investments I make in you. Let's see here." He paused by the tunnel opening and gave Victor a long look. "You've got fear and rage, so I need inspiration, glory, and magma, yes? Nothing else you're keeping secret?"

Victor looked up from his study of the blueprint and narrowed his eyes at Dar. "You expect me to believe you can't see my different affinities?"

Dar smiled and shrugged. "I believe you have a secret or two you've yet to entrust to me." When Victor's eyes widened, he held up a stony hand and said, "No matter. I trust you've told me what's important. We're all entitled to a closely held secret or three. Build this chamber, and we'll speak again tonight."

As his mentor turned to leave, Victor said, "Dar, wait. Um, I promised Lesh I'd try to get a regular practice schedule planned out. He's a good sparring partner, and I also was wondering if there was anything you could tell me about Breath Cores—"

"One thing at a time, Victor. Finish this construction, then spar with your friend. Tomorrow, we'll add your treasures to this chamber, and then we'll talk about your schedule. And yes, I have a few things I can tell you about Breath Cores; it will be part of your training. Now, I'm off." With that, he turned and almost seemed to flicker out of sight as he employed some skill or spell to whisk himself away.

Victor straightened the blueprint in his hands and looked over the steps Dar had outlined for him. Had he written this out? It wasn't exactly something only a master Spirit Caster would know; basically, Victor was going to do some wood framing and then build up an interior stone façade. The whole thing made him think of corny movies where a martial arts master would make the student do sweeping or carry stones, driving the student crazy with frustration. Then the master would laugh and explain how the chore movements *were* the martial arts techniques.

Victor chuckled as he began hammering nails into the pre-cut wooden frame pieces. The blueprints said to start with the base, so that's what he did, using metal brackets to connect each length of wood as he placed them around the edge of the cavern. Dar must have measured the space because the framework filled it as much as possible while maintaining a roughly circular shape. In reality, it would have sixteen sides, with each face aiming directly at the center of the space.

His hands were nimble and strong, and Victor no longer grew tired from manual labor, at least nothing he'd been able to throw at himself. Perhaps if he went to a world rich in Energy and had to dig or mine dense, powerful ore, he'd find that exhausting. He didn't know. As it was, he had the frame built in less than an hour. Fifteen minutes later, he'd nailed up all the backer boards for the stone façade. He set to work mixing the mortar, and when it felt thick enough to spread, he used the trowel Dar had given him to begin mounting the bottom row of eight-sided concave stone tiles.

While he worked, Victor's mind wandered. He thought about the dinner parties he had lined up and began to warm up to the idea of meeting and speaking with some of the people he'd fought in the dungeon. He felt it was the right thing to do, inviting those folks. Even the ones who'd talked trash in the dungeon might be totally different in a social setting. He'd known wrestlers like that. Shouldn't he work to mend fences and build peaceful relations before leaving his friends here? Lam had said she would invite them, so he didn't feel he had to do anything more. If some showed up, great, and if none did, so be it.

Thinking of parties reminded him of Fanwath and the people he'd left there. Wouldn't it be nice to visit? Wouldn't it be fun to invite them to see Dar's lake house and experience Sojourn? Deyni would be in heaven! He wished he could afford a permanent portal like the ones connecting the cities of Fanwath.

Something told him such a gateway between worlds would require an order of magnitude more power and know-how. Even setting that aside, though, he knew some people could open temporary gateways between worlds. He wanted to learn that kind of power. Would the ability to walk through the spirit plane be similar? How hard would it be to bring people? Dar acted as though it wasn't trivial.

The instructions on the blueprint were to trickle Energy into each stone after setting it, and when Victor did so, they grew solid and unmoving, the mortar beneath completely cured. The ability to instantly set the tiles made for easy and quick work, and despite the chamber being a good fifteen feet in diameter, he rapidly built up the stone façade. Seeing the chamber take shape around him was gratifying work. Victor was relaxed, and his mind gradually stopped worrying at all the things going on in his life, and he lost himself to the work, utterly zoning out.

When he finished, he was almost disappointed that he was done. He'd enjoyed the honest labor, seeing the room taking shape and feeling a little accomplishment as each stone tile fit snugly into place. He thought those feelings said a lot about what was going on with his life. He was trying to control too much. He was racking his brain trying to understand love, trying to keep track of too many, sometimes conflicting, goals. He needed to take Lesh's advice and focus on what he could control, grasp the joys within reach, and make the best of the hand he'd been dealt.

Building the enclosure perfectly—and it was perfect—had been an excellent example of that. He felt better having done it, having let his mind rest, and having focused wholly on the task. It was an introduction to what he needed to do for the next few months. He needed to give himself over to his training. When he wasn't training, he needed to make the most of his time with Valla. He needed to let go of the many worries that gnawed at the fabric of his sanity. "Yeah," he said, stooping to pick up the tools and leftover building supplies, stuffing them into the dimensional sack Dar had left behind, "that feels good."

22

PROMISES

When he emerged from the underground, it was only an hour or so after noon, and Victor found Lesh more than eager to get some sparring done. They made their way to the area Lesh had dubbed Dar's sparring ground, only for Victor to question the designation; to him, it felt more like a fancy courtyard meant for entertaining. Stone columns lined the space, and off to one side was a covered area that looked like an outdoor kitchen. Still, Victor couldn't argue that the sandy center of the space made for a perfect place to do some fighting, especially considering how everything about Dar's home was giant-sized.

They worked out like usual, falling into old routines. Victor used Inspiration of the Quinametzin, giving them both a little more insight into their training, and neither of the two used any Energy abilities, at least not at first. Victor wore his armor, wanting to see how Belagog, Lesh's cudgel, fared against the set pieces and their lava king materials. A few glancing blows got past his guard now and then, and the leather held up fine, though it wasn't adept at stopping bludgeoning damage. The helmet and heavy gauntlet were another matter; the dense material easily rebuffed the blows.

About an hour into their practice, after a particularly violent exchange, Victor backed off and said, "I want to try my new weapon."

"A new weapon?" Lesh eyed Lifedrinker resting on Victor's shoulder.

"Yeah. I enchanted this gauntlet with the, um, magma attunement gem that I won from the conquest chest."

"Ah! What will it do? Punch with fire damage?" Lesh readied Belagog, holding the great metallic cudgel in a two-handed grip before himself.

"Actually," Victor said, channeling some Energy into the gauntlet, "it's supposed to be a whip." As the Energy fed the hungry runes along the back of the gauntlet where the metal wrapped around his wrist, hot, dripping liquid fire began to drizzle from his palm into the sand, cooling with sizzling pops into beads of porous stone. Victor pushed more Energy into the gauntlet, increasing the steady flow from his Core. The trickle of liquid fire turned into a stream that partially solidified into a flaming, smoking coil of magical magma that hung down from his gauntleted hand into the sand, where it sizzled and smoked.

"You wish to strike me with *that*?" Lesh backed up, eyes narrow, shaking his head. "I've the blood of dragons in my veins, but fire can still harm me!"

"Yeah, I, uh, guess I need some practice with it before I can promise not to do any real damage. Can you hold Belagog out? Let me see how hard it is to control."

"Aye. Some fire won't hurt this lad." Lesh chuckled, his voice deep and rumbling, as he extended the long metal cudgel before him. Victor nodded and jerked his left hand back over his shoulder and then forward, whipping out his "magma lash" a little awkwardly. His much improved dexterity and agility made him more adept than he had any right to be on his first attempt at such a feat, but the whip of smoking, glowing lava still missed the cudgel. It snaked out and snapped in the air beneath it, cracking like a gunshot, spraying sizzling magma onto the sandy ground.

"Oho!" Lesh crowed, enjoying the show. "That would sting!"

Victor grinned, pleased by the savage crack and spray of magma. He pulled his wrist back, swinging the lash of magma around behind him with a *whoosh*. He tried again, adjusting his wrist movement slightly, and this time, the lash snapped around the cudgel, coiling with a splash of magma and billowing black smoke as it fought to transfer its fiery heat to Lesh's weapon. The cudgel was made of nigh-indestructible stuff, though, and Lesh laughed as he pulled against the lash, trying to unbalance Victor. Victor grinned, jerking his fist against Lesh's pull, and the two came to a stalemate.

"Not bad!" Victor panted as he and Lesh continued to strain. "The lash is durable; we're putting a lot of strain on it!"

"Aye! It's made of your Energy. I bet you can learn to guide and control it more than any physical whip; use your will!" Lesh grunted as he spoke, still straining to pull Victor off balance. What he said made sense, and Victor reached out with his will, urging the lash of magma to uncoil so he could pull it back. To his amazement, it worked.

"That is badass!" he howled as the lash snapped in the air beside him, moving as much with the force of his will as the motion of his wrist. He turned and jogged to the far end of the sandy ground and then, still targeting Lesh's cudgel, some thirty yards distant, whipped the magma lash forward, guiding the fiery tendril with his will. He howled with delight when it stretched out and struck home, snapping its distant, smoldering end around the weapon. "You're a genius, Lesh!"

After that, Victor spent another hour with Lesh as a willing participant, learning the ins and outs of his new weapon. He quickly realized that his first somewhat ranged attack was near the extent of the whip's reach—something close to thirty or thirty-five yards. He learned that he could nudge the whip with his will, making minute targeting adjustments, and direct it to either coil around a target or lash it with devastating results based on how he flicked his wrist.

Belagog was a good test subject, but Victor wanted to see how something less durable would hold up, so he destroyed several pieces of furniture he'd stored in one of his dimensional rings. The whip blasted them to fiery splinters in just a few strokes. By the time they called it a day, he felt good about the new weapon but knew it would require a lot of training to use effectively in conjunction with Lifedrinker in an actual combat situation.

As they walked along the path leading back to the house, Lesh said, "I will use my racial advancement elixir now, so I will likely be out for a while."

Victor nodded. "This is a good time. Valla's still out, and I'm gonna be training with Dar. When you wake up, I'll hopefully have something to share with you about Breath Cores. I know you're eager to improve yours."

"I am, though I always thought it was dependent upon improving my bloodline. I hope there's something more—"

Victor looked at him with raised eyebrows and interrupted, "I mean, you know how to cultivate Energy into it, right?"

"Into my Breath Core? When I cultivate Energy, it enters my pathways, which lead to my Energy Core—"

"Holy shit! Seriously, Lesh? But, like, you come from a world full of *dragonkin*!" The truth of the matter was that Victor had only recently learned to cultivate with his Breath Core, and that had been out of necessity, trapped in the caldera of a volcano by Hector. Still, once he'd made the breakthrough, he thought it must have been something obvious to people *born* with one.

Lesh stopped in his tracks and looked at Victor with a scowl, though whether he was angry at Victor or irritated in general wasn't clear. "Not all of us have a Breath Core. We sometimes gain one when advancing our race, but it's not a guarantee, and my people are . . . combative. Having scales"—he held out one of his arms, clenching his fist so the faintly glossy black scales along his forearm flexed—"is a mark of power and dominance, a Breath Core even more so. I was rising quickly in the esteem of my people, but those above me, those with the ability to send forth plumes of destructive breath"—he narrowed his eyes at Victor, reaching out to tap a long, thick claw into his chest—"like you, don't share their knowledge. It's something that must be discovered."

Victor stared at him, sudden comprehension dawning on him, all of his conversations with Lesh taking on a new light. "I'm such a self-centered dumbass."

"Self-centered?" Lesh let his claw slide off Victor's scaled vest, his hand falling to his side.

"Yeah, Lesh. I listened to you ask to follow me. I listened to you say you turned against the damned *System* when you saw me breathe my ancestor's fire, but I never fucking sat down with you and asked what that meant. I thought you were . . . I don't know, weird! God! I'm so sorry, man. Listen, when you get done with your racial advancement, we're going to sit down, and I'll teach you how to cultivate your Breath Core. I need to find a source for mine, and while I'm at it, I'll find one for yours. I'll go shopping tomorrow after Dar gives me my cultivation lesson. Deal?"

"A source?"

"I need something that gives off magma-attuned Energy. I can use fire, but it's not as effective—turns out magma has the rage of a volcano mixed into it. Your breath affinity is acid, yeah?"

"Yes!" Lesh leaned forward, speaking forcefully, and Victor could see the excitement in his eyes.

"All right, *hermano*! When you wake up, we're going to get to work. Promise." He held out a fist, and Lesh smashed his rough knuckles into it, nodding with a wide grin, exposing the many pointy teeth along his short, snout-like mouth.

"Yes, brother!"

With that, the two continued walking toward the house, but Victor felt a certain warmth of camaraderie that hadn't been there before. He *had* been preoccupied with all of his own problems and had been taking Lesh for granted. It was good that he'd acknowledged it, and he meant to make things up to the man before he left Sojourn. They parted ways in the hallway, Lesh turning to enter the bedroom Dar's staff had assigned him.

When Victor returned to his room, Valla was still out, but the cloud of Energy-filled steam that had gathered around her was much thinner, and he didn't see any new vapors rising from her body. He leaned close, studying her face, and he was relieved to see the scar above and below her bandage was much fainter, just a thin, dark silver line in her pale flesh, almost more like a tattoo than a scar.

He was tempted to peel the bandage aside and look at her eye but knew it would irritate her if she were awake, and doing it while she slept felt wrong. Her skin felt cool, and she breathed peacefully, almost as if she was simply sleeping. He leaned down and kissed her forehead before going into the bathroom to clean up. Part of him hoped the gesture would wake her, but another part was pleased to see her resting so deeply.

The bathrooms in Dar's house were marvels of magical ingenuity, especially the showers. The one in Victor's room was a sunken, tiled enclosure with a row of windows high in the wall, beneath which half a dozen lush ferns grew in a planter. When he stepped into the basin, some enchantment he couldn't see caused miniature storm clouds to form near the ceiling, and then, accompanied by the rumble of distant-sounding thunder, they began to shed gentle warm rain.

It was difficult not to overindulge; Victor lost himself as he stood in the refreshing rain, occasionally breaking from his reverie to soap off a body part, scrub his hair, or carefully scrape a razor-sharp blade over his soapy stubble. There didn't seem to be any sort of time or Energy limitation on the shower, at least not one he'd yet run into. By the time he got out and the storm cloud dissipated, he was pretty sure he'd spent nearly two hours in there.

He donned his wyrm-scale vest and new armor in its clothing form, first holding it up to his nose to ensure everything was still smelling fresh. "It's damn nice never having to do laundry." He chuckled, stepping out of the bathroom.

"Finally!" Valla said, sleepily stretching on the bed.

"Hey! You were out cold when I went in there."

She smiled, and Victor's gaze was drawn to her eye, devoid of its previous bandage. He stepped close and grinned when he saw her tracking him with both eyes. When he leaned close, the only sign of her earlier injury was a very faint line of silver in her teal iris. "Looks all better!"

"I haven't looked in a mirror, but I can see fine." She pulled him close, squeezing him in a tight hug. "I was more worried than I let on. It was the worst injury I've ever had. Before Lesh poured a healing potion over the wound . . ." She trailed off, and Victor hugged her again.

"Hey, it's all right. How many ranks did you get?"

"Just one. My bloodline is advanced six now."

"Well, that's pretty great that your eye basically regrew with just one racial rank."

"How did—did you look?" She pushed him back, narrowing her eyebrows.

"No, I was just assuming, Valla. I mean, you wouldn't let me see it, so I figured it was bad." He chuckled and backed away from her. "You never said anything about my new clothes. Check this out." He trickled some Energy into the runes on his armor, and suddenly, he was clad in his dark crimson and black wyrm-scale vest, his glowering lava king helm, the deep red metallic gauntlet, and the rest of his thick red leather armor.

"Ancestors!" Valla said, leaning back and clapping. "Fierce! Is that helmet supposed to look like a dragon?"

"Nah, I think it's what a lava king looks like." He shrugged. "Maybe they're related—you know, like wyrms." Victor made a slow turn, giving her a view of every angle, then sent Energy into the disguise runes, swapping the armor out for his clothing again. "Pretty cool, huh?"

"Lava king? Isn't that the hide you won for the campaign?" She reached out to feel his shirt. "But what about your armor? How are you changing it so quickly?"

He chuckled, then spent a few minutes explaining the set pieces and how he'd added his treasures from the Free Marches. When he told her about the matching enchantment he'd gotten on his wyrm-scale vest, she interrupted with a gasp, "Victor! That's so helpful! I want it, too!"

"No problem! I'll introduce you to Tria." Victor sat beside her and held her hand. "Hey, you remember how Dar wanted to talk to me before you drank that elixir?"

"Yes. Was it bad?"

"Depends on how you look at it." Victor inhaled deeply. "I guess there's not an easy way to say this."

"Just tell me, Victor." She squeezed his hand. "Are you going away?"

He looked at her for a long minute, shifting sideways to stare into her eyes. "You're pretty damn smart, you know that?" When she didn't reply, he sighed and told her, haltingly at first, then in a rush of words, about Dar's distant granddaughter and the plight of her kingdom. She tried to interject midway through, saying she'd come with him, but she slowly began to nod when he got to the part about fighting duels and not actual wars.

"You want me to stay here."

"I don't *want* you to. I think it'll be smarter, though. You can continue to dungeon delve and train with Lesh. There are other things in the city, too—nonlethal tournaments, even some weird sports, according to Mr. Qwor."

"Sports?"

"Yeah, games for prizes. They have rules about Energy usage, I guess, and they vary in terms of physical conflict, but I think they might be worth looking into. The point I'm getting at is that there's a lot for you to do here. There's a shitload of ways you can advance. If you came with me, the best thing you could hope for would be sparring with me or other people in the granddaughter's household. The world will be at war, and the only open part of it will be the champion duels. Everything else is going to be fucking cloak and dagger bullshit—kidnappings, assassinations, sabotage, you name it."

Valla frowned, thinking things over for a few moments before replying, "You'll have dozens of duels, maybe more? Against people who are all likely at a higher level than you. You'll make huge gains, maybe not early on, but when you face the stronger champions. You're afraid I'll fall further behind if I come along with nothing much to do but watch your duels? Does that about sum it up?"

"I'm going to earn hearts, Valla—hearts and tribute for my victories. I'll make gains in many ways, not just Energy from my kills. Don't you think it would be better if you and Lesh were here, earning treasure, gaining levels, and improving your bloodlines?"

"Of course, logically." She chuckled and stood up, summoning some clothes from her storage ring. She began to change out of her pajamas as she continued speaking. "I suppose things will be easier for me if I'm not there to watch you fight champions who are beyond Level One Hundred. I understood that correctly, yes? Dar says many of the champions are steel seekers?"

"Yeah." Victor looked at the floor as he answered, his voice low and resigned, expecting Valla to start another argument.

"Well, I'd rather not witness that. Fine, I'll stay here with Lesh, but you must promise to write to me daily in the Far Scribe book. You have to promise you'll visit me if you earn lots of tribute and have some time between duels." She'd pulled on a knee-length, pale gray skirt and a breezy white blouse, tying its tails in a knot at her waist. "For now, though, let's go see this lake you were going on about to Lesh in the coach. I went straight to bed when we arrived, and I'd like to get a little sun before it sets."

Victor looked at her, perhaps a little hungrily. "I do, Valla. I promise. Have I told you I love you lately?"

"Not enough." She stood on her tiptoes to kiss him quickly before darting toward the door, her wings rustling with faint metallic tinkles. Victor gave chase, and soon, she was giggling in near hysterics as the two exploded through the open door and onto the deck. Victor was right on her heels when she spread her wings and, with a *crack*, snapped them down, launching herself over the rail and into the air. She soared out over the lake, and Victor laughed, too amazed by her grace to be bothered by her cheating escape.

23

THE COUNCIL'S RESPONSE

When Victor woke the next day, he saw that the sun had yet to rise, which was good because he was supposed to meet Dar in his new cultivation chamber at dawn. He concentrated, reactivating Sovereign Will, which had a tendency to drop while he slept, and pushed his bonuses into dexterity and agility. With his already nimble body boosted, he practiced his stealthy movements, sliding out of the bed and creeping toward the door.

He only paused to pick up Lifedrinker and the ivory case containing his captured geists before carefully pulling the door open, inch by inch, until he could slip through. He was certain he hadn't made any more noise than a feather falling onto grass, but Valla still rolled over and mumbled, "See you for lunch."

He chuckled. "See you." Then he slipped out and, standing in the dim, quiet hallway, got dressed. "That was pointless," he muttered, imagining one of the staff coming upon him half-naked outside his room. With a grin and a shake of his head, he hurried to the kitchens, pausing to use the bathroom, where he cleaned his teeth and splashed water on his face. That done, he descended into the tunnels beneath the house. They were wide, well-lit, and sized for a giant, so it wasn't an unpleasant walk to his cultivation cave.

Victor arrived before Dar, which had been his main goal for not lying in bed, waiting for the sun to brighten the sky outside his window. Smiling at his small victory, he sat in the center of the chamber and set the box before him. He hadn't opened it, let alone touched the bones since Lo'ro had dropped him off at the house, and he was a little nervous. He'd thought long and hard about the bone where the fear-attuned geist dwelled, wondering if he should mention how it spoke to him. Would Dar be angry? Would he destroy the spirit and force Victor to find another, less . . . conscious one?

He didn't know, and part of him wanted to speak to the spirit again to see what it thought and discover the "secrets" it had promised before Dar arrived. Another part recognized the danger of it and couldn't see a real downside to asking his mentor. He was trusting the master Spirit Caster with a lot, more than anyone outside of Valla or Tes—it felt like the right move would be to ask him for advice on the matter. So he sat there, staring at the box, trying to clear his mind, until he heard the faint scuffs of Dar's bare feet on the stone.

"Ah, apprentice," he said, as though he was surprised to see him sitting there. Victor wasn't buying it—he was pretty sure Dar could feel every presence, down to the smallest rodent, on his property. "Eager to renew your studies into cultivation?" He stepped out of the oval opening in Victor's stonework and surveyed the chamber before sitting across from him. The two giant men made the chamber feel small even as they sat on the floor, legs crossed. When their eyes met, and Dar's smoldering orbs peered into Victor's mind and soul, he said, "I can feel a question burning your tongue."

"It's more like a confession."

Dar's stony brow lifted. "Oh?"

Victor bit the bullet and decided to get straight to the point. "Yeah. When I went through the veil with Master Lo'ro, I deceived him."

Dar's brow fell, his eyes narrowed, and Victor felt the tiniest fragment of the man's aura pressing against him. Even that brief touch felt like a mountain grinding against his spirit, vast and possessing a gravity that defied common adjectives. "Yet you intend to speak plainly and expose the deception to me. I am placated." No hint of the weight remained, and Victor breathed out the breath he'd been holding.

"That's right. When we were collecting the geists, trapping them in the bones,"—Victor gestured to the ivory case between them—"I managed to capture a powerful fear-attuned spirit. Lo'ro was impressed, but the truth is, the spirit came willingly. There was no battle of wills. The spirit spoke to me, told me not to reveal that fact, and that she would share 'secrets' with me if I took her out of that place with me."

Dar looked at the case. "And has 'she' spoken to you since?"

"No. I haven't touched the bone."

"Well, you're both an idiot and wise, it seems." When Victor opened his mouth, unsure if he should object to the label or just apologize, Dar held up a thick stony finger and continued, "An idiot for risking your mind and spirit by pulling this geist into the containment vessel, wise for not trifling with the thing before first speaking to me." He turned the box so the clasp faced him and opened it. His eyes brightened momentarily as he stared at the two bones, then he snatched the rib bone out, holding it before him.

Suddenly, Victor felt a flare of potent, brilliant Energy, and though he wasn't the focus, he felt the edge of Dar's formidable will. He stood beside a mighty river as it carved a canyon from the stony ground. His mind filled with the image, unable to resist visualizing the metaphor, watching as waters deeper than an ocean and broader than most continents dug through a Jupiter-sized planet of solid rock. The water broke it up, transforming the world as it went, sending life-giving tendrils through the stone, enabling trees and grass and . . .

The feeling abruptly ended, and Victor opened his eyes, his mind once again his own. He saw Dar before him, holding the bone in his palm as half a dozen new runes etched themselves into it, glowing with brilliant white Energy. "This enchantment will harmlessly prevent the spirit from interacting with you. I'm quite impressed by the being lurking within this vessel, Victor. You're not ready to deal with such as she, however. You'll need to advance your will; I'd say you're about halfway there. When you can easily wipe these runes free with your own Energy, then it will be safe for you to commune with the spirit who dwells within." He set the bone back in the case.

"Thank you, Dar. Did she plan to harm me?"

"She's a being utterly consumed and twisted by fear. Her intentions are less than lucid. She's ancient, even to me, but her potency in death is a fraction of what it might have been in life. Still, she wouldn't reveal her so-called secrets, even in the face of my wrath. I might have wrung them from her, but she has entered a contract with you. I could feel the karmic ties. Fragile though they are, I won't be the one who severs them; the repercussions may be far-reaching."

"A contract?"

"Did you not agree to bring her forth in exchange for her secrets?"

"Yeah—"

"Victor, you're no longer a boy with no weight in the universe. As your power grows, so do the impacts of your actions. Everything you say, especially where emotions are involved, bears weight—everything you *do*, even more so." He held out his hand and wriggled it in the air. "Someone like you, someone with an intense, potent spirit, sends ripples through the ether with every meaningful act. Making deals with desperate, powerful spirits is not something the universe takes lightly. There are beings even I cannot grasp who take notice of such things."

"Gods?"

Dar shifted his boulder-sized shoulders in an attempt at a shrug. "Perhaps. There are people on myriad worlds who would see me and name me a god. Am I? I think not. I've visited a thousand worlds, and my travel has taught me that I've only scratched the surface. There are many *millions* of planets in the System-controlled part of the universe. I've talked to scholars who speculate that the System is relatively new, that there are more worlds outside its control than within. There are beings out there with the mystery and power to be considered godlike to even the likes of me. Knowing that, knowing how little I know, who am I to say what a god is and whether they exist?"

Everything Dar said made Victor think of Tes, and he asked, "Have you ever been to one? I mean, a world that resisted the System?"

"Aye. The Fae don't traffic with the System, and I've visited a world controlled by them. It's a lengthy tale, but I'll say this: I stood before the Winter Queen and felt insignificant. I finished my business and haven't looked back in centuries." Dar sighed and pulled a small ring off his pinky. He held it in the palm of his hand, and Victor leaned close to look at it. "Enough philosophizing. I have gifts for you."

The ring looked as though it was made of polished gray stone, though he saw a vein of silvery metal running through it. It was pretty and lustrous, and when Victor squinted, he could see that it gave off a tiny amount of light against Dar's black stony flesh. "Nice," he said, waiting for further explanation.

"It *is* nice." Dar chuckled. "It's a dimensional container, though far finer than any of those you wear. This container has limited space, but it can contain objects of power, such as these bones and the other cultivation items I've acquired for you." Dar moved his hand over the ring and suddenly held a perfectly round orb. It looked like the glass part of a snow globe, but inside, Victor could see the swirls and sparkles of bright golden Energy that could only be glory. He knew he was right when his Core flared in response.

"Glory." His voice was barely a whisper.

"Aye." Dar set the orb on the dark blue, silky padding inside the case, next to the two bones. He waved his hand over the ring again, producing another orb, this one full of bright, misty, white-gold Energy that Victor immediately knew was inspiration-attuned. Dar set it in the case, then, from the ring, produced a third—this one roiling with a heart of molten magma, white-hot in spots and cooling toward somber orange-red in others.

After he'd set it in the case, Dar touched the two bones and said, "These captured spirits are more potent than these hearts, but—"

"Hearts?"

"Ah." Dar clicked his tongue and shook his head briefly. "When a cultivator enters their lustrous veil, they become capable of creating these Energy hearts using a process similar to the creation of Energy beads. This heart"—he tapped the glory-attuned globe—"is a hundred thousand times more potent than a glory-attuned Energy bead you might create."

"That's worth a hundred thousand beads?"

"Ha. No, lad, as flat currency, Energy hearts are useless—the System will not accept them at its City Stones. I'm not sure why, but people speculate that it doesn't want to destroy its economy for the vast majority of Energy users. Still, they can be used in trades; creating one is a lengthy, tedious process, and they can be valuable for someone who might need a particular Energy type."

He waved his hand dismissively. "Let's not get distracted by trivia. These three hearts will serve as potent cultivation sources for you until you reach your test of steel. After that, you'll need to find sources with more depth."

"The bones will last longer?"

Dar snorted. "Yes. That's like asking if your spirit is more potent than a single Energy bead."

"Are they hard to get?" Victor could see the crease in Dar's brow as his questions began to irritate him, so he hurried to explain, "I'm just asking because I feel a, well, a duty to my friend, Lesh. He followed me here, hoping that I would help him advance, and I'm leaving him behind to go to your granddaughter's world. I wanted to give him something he could use to cultivate his Breath Core."

Dar frowned, but seemed more contemplative than angry. "An acid attunement?"

"Yeah—"

"I'll acquire one for him. However, that will be the last gift I will freely give to your comrades. I've already offered my home—"

"No, no. I understand, Dar. If you think it's within my means, I'll gladly get Lesh a source for cultivation. He doesn't have to have an Energy heart."

Dar rubbed his chin and nodded. "Actually, there is a way for you to accomplish just that. Yes, that would be better than creating more debt between you or your companions and me. I was saving this news until after I'd taught you your new cultivation technique, but I suppose it's something we can discuss now. Yes, perhaps that's best—we'll speak, I'll teach you the technique, and then I can leave you to practice."

"News?" Victor didn't like Dar's almost ominous tone.

His mentor shifted, pressing one fist into the stone floor and leaning into it, bringing himself closer to Victor as he replied, "I told you I have some enemies on the council, yes?"

"Yeah." The question told Victor precisely what this was about; the council wasn't going to let him off when it came to the three "tasks" he was supposed to perform.

"Well, that faction has made matters a touch difficult for us. Rather than accepting my generous offer to pay the Energy debt in full, restoring the city's coffers after the repair of the training dungeon, they've countered with an offer of their own." He paused, ensuring he had Victor's attention, then continued, "They've agreed that if I pay for the repairs, they'll release you from two tasks. They claim the remaining task was already decided upon and that losing you would greatly increase the risk of death for the others involved."

"Others?"

"Aye. Two others. Do you recall me mentioning a prison dungeon beneath the Sojourn City Council?"

"I do." Victor nodded, his mind racing with the implications of the question.

"Well, it's called the Iron Prison because it's meant to contain iron rankers—nothing higher. It was specifically purchased from the System with that restriction, and there's no altering that. The council cannot send anyone over Level One Hundred into that place."

"So?"

"So, the council has sent quite a few powerful iron rankers into it over the years. Unfortunately, evidence has surfaced indicating that one such individual was unjustly imprisoned, and they want him extracted. The System provides an interface for the dungeon, allowing the council to see who still lives in the dungeon, and they assure me that this man, Rasso Hine, has not been slain."

Victor groaned and put his elbows on his knees, resting his chin in his palms. "Why am I the only one who can do this? That's what you're about to tell me, right?"

Dar chuckled, the sound deep and coarse. "I asked the same. There are restrictions on dungeon entry—one person per hour. In the last few weeks, as they've attempted to retrieve Hine, each emissary has been killed within minutes. Apparently, they've lost half a dozen promising iron rankers."

"And this guy, Rasso Hine, is worth all those lives?"

Dar nodded, his eyes dimming from their usual hot glow. "The council believes the information he holds is that valuable, aye. I tend to agree with them after hearing the details of the case." Before Victor could ask, he held up the hand he wasn't leaning on, forestalling his question. "I cannot share those details."

Victor wanted to growl in frustration, but he settled for narrowing his eyes in a half scowl. "If I have to go in alone, what's the deal with the two others you mentioned?"

"One is a Death Caster. You know her—Arona Moonshadow, the one from the challenge dungeon who outsmarted you." Victor wanted to object, but he'd reflected plenty on that dungeon challenge and had to agree—he hadn't exactly acted cleverly. Dar continued, "They want her to accompany you because she's one of the top Death Casters still in the iron ranks, and the dungeon is death-attuned. The other is Arcus Volpuré, another friend of yours from the challenge dungeon."

"Why is that name so familiar? I mean, I feel like I've heard it since the dungeon."

"He's an incredibly powerful Elementalist, and his master is Lord Roil, one of the consuls. There's little love lost between Roil and me, if you'll recall the inquest. He claims to want Arcus to accompany you and Arona because his fire magic will be a potent aid, but I suspect he intends to betray and kill you."

"Lord Roil was the guy in the black robes hiding his face with smoke, right?"

"Aye, though the smoke is a part of him, not a disguise; he's partially taken the aspect of an elemental."

Victor thought about that, about how powerful Dar was and about how he walked on eggshells around Roil. Was this the sort of enemy he wanted? "So, they want me to go in first and clear the entrance so the other two can come in safely." Victor smiled grimly as Dar nodded. "Then we're supposed to find this dude, Rasso, and get him out? How's that work?"

"You'll be given an attuned recall item that will function on yourself and one other. Arona and Arcus will also have such an item. Because they're attuned, no one else can use them to escape." Dar shifted to his other fist, pressing it into the stone floor as he leaned the other way.

"And Arcus? Am I going to get in trouble if I kill that asshole?"

"As long as you don't start the conflict, I can shield you from Roil's temper. I believe you can count on the Moonshadow girl to be a neutral party. I know her master, Vesavo Bonewhisper, quite well. He's a cruel man but honest. We've been aligned politically in the past, and I know he has no love for Roil."

Victor groaned again, dreading the answer to his next question. "When?"

Dar nodded, grinning widely. "The day after your dinner party. They wanted quicker action, but I explained that you were hosting an event at my house and that several of their pupils were invited, including Arona and Arcus."

"Ah, shit. That's where I heard that name. Lam was talking about him or . . . was it his sister?" Victor shook his head. "Whatever. So, I have a few days before I get sent into a meat grinder?"

"That's right. Rasso has been in the dungeon for more than a decade—a few more days shouldn't hurt. I thought to argue about this task, to claim it was unjust and that it was a clear conspiracy to rid me of a promising protégé, but then I thought about you and how you tend to rise to challenges. I've decided to treat this as an opportunity in disguise. I managed to squeeze some additional promises out of the council. If you succeed in this task, there will be additional compensation."

Victor grinned, matching his mentor's expression. "That's where you think I can get Lesh's cultivation item."

"Precisely. I won't be very surprised if you also gain some valuable treasures from the dungeon. Some of the criminals still lurking within are sure to have amassed rewards from the denizens, and they'll also be worth significant Energy infusions."

"I can kill the prisoners?"

"I would hope so; they'll surely try to kill you! No soft men or women could survive in that vile place. It will be a good challenge." Dar chuckled and straightened up. "Now, let's talk about cultivation. First," he stood and scooped up Victor's cultivation items, "place the items around you in a loose circle. Because you've built your chamber to contain and gather Energy, you can put them near the wall. As they emit Energy, the tiles will contain and condense it. Moreover, as you cycle the Energy—in a way I will teach you—the shape of this chamber will help you focus it on yourself."

"Shouldn't I have built a door to cover the tunnel opening?"

"In an ideal world, yes, a sealed cultivation chamber is best. You'll only be here a few months, though, and this is not your primary means of advancement, so I cut a few corners. The chamber will still contain most of the Energy emitted from your treasures."

"Oh, will I leave them here?"

"While you're here on Sojourn, yes! That way, the Energy will gather while you're gone, making your next cultivation session more fruitful." As Dar spoke, Victor nodded along, but all the while, he couldn't help but imagine how his "vault" container would make a perfect cultivation chamber. Victor tried to pay attention to Dar's lesson, picturing the flows of Energy and how he was supposed to weave them together as he drew them into his pathways. He told Victor it would be challenging to weave more than two differently-attuned Energies as he cultivated, but practice would make it easier. He was confident that Victor could eventually pull all five, including the magma he'd send into his Breath Core.

The problem was that Victor felt distracted. Just as he'd been learning to let go of the things he couldn't control, Dar had thrown another at him. He was literally going to step into a trap that had killed a "handful" of promising iron rankers ahead of him. Was Dar that confident in him, or did he simply not value Victor as more than an amusement? It was the same question he'd had about the duels on his Ruhn—did Dar really think he could win against people well above Level One Hundred?

"You're not listening, Victor," Dar growled. "I have men and women scheming and killing for an hour of my time, and you sit there daydreaming while I explain the fundamentals of cultivation?" His eyes had taken on the dangerous gleam Victor had only seen a couple of times, and it brought his mind back into focus.

"Sorry, Lord Dar. I keep thinking about the trap waiting for me as I step into that prison."

Dar nodded and sat down in front of him again. "This is why I think you must continue to cultivate, despite your ability to strengthen your Core through the consumption of hearts. When you cultivate, Victor, you must face all facets of your Spirit Core. You must confront your fear, your rage, your glory, and even your inspiration to understand how they rule your spirit. You must master them. The fear, though, that's the biggest challenge for you. You mask it well, usually using your rage, but it runs amok in your mind." He reached out and—almost gently—punched Victor's knee. "Come, pay attention. Using this new drill, you'll learn to master your fear."

24

CORE CONSOLIDATION

Victor sat before Dar, waiting for his next words. His master's face was relaxed, the fire in his eyes simmering low, but he knew, like coals, they were ready to ignite with the faintest breath of oxygen. So he waited patiently, not willing to provide that fuel. The Spirit Master had just spent nearly two hours describing the method of gathering Energy from his various sources—how to weave the different aspects together and pull them into his Core. Victor had been about to make his first try at it, when Dar had said, "I must study your Core." And then he'd apparently begun to do so, staring at Victor unblinking for nearly another hour.

Finally, just as Victor was starting to fear Dar had fallen asleep with his eyes open, the man's stony countenance shifted, his eyes moving to lock onto Victor's. The master took a deep breath and slowly exhaled. "The cultivation method I just described isn't going to work. Not yet. The entire point of cultivating for you, rather than growing your Core, is to learn to harmonize your affinities and embrace every aspect of your spirit whilst tempering the more destructive aspects through the lens of the more positive. Your Core, however, is in disarray. I see what you've done. I believe I even understand why you did it. It's simply not ideal. No," he chuckled, "not even an approximation of ideal."

"What I've done?"

"In the development of your Core. It makes a kind of sense; I can see how you've tried to create counterbalances between your various affinities—inspiration against rage, glory against fear, a sort of light versus dark side in your spirit, pushing and pulling against each other. The problem is that your affinities aren't equal, and even if they were—a near impossibility—they contend with each other rather than building upon each other."

"Well, it's not like I had a teacher. Not really." Victor's mind flitted to Gorz and then Old Mother—both had provided guidance, but neither had ever talked to him about the actual structure of his Core. Not even Khul Bach had broached the topic.

"I know. I can see the logic in your efforts. Energy tends to compress into a sphere; it's the easiest way to build up the density and then break it through into the next stage. As you gained more affinities, you naturally assumed you should have more spheres of Energy. It's not a terrible thing, but there's a much better, more elegant design that I want to teach you. It's better because it will shore up the less volatile aspects of your spirit, using your stronger affinities to compress them.

"You see, Victor, considering this formation, I'm somewhat astounded by the strength of your spirit and Core. You've essentially split your Core into four smaller ones. Rather than compounding them, using the weight of each affinity to compress the ones beneath it, your cultivation has revolved around building each one individually, pushing them to a breaking point before advancing the level of your Core. I'm not sure you'd ever break through into epic tier with this structure.

"The design I'll teach you will combine the weight—the gravity—of each affinity, creating a single Core that will be far denser and stronger than these four individual ones. Moreover, it will take your most valuable aspect and put it closer to your spirit while keeping the others, the ones that tend to overwhelm your spirit, at a bit of a distance."

"My most valuable aspect?" Victor guessed Dar would confirm his suspicion that his rage was the most valuable part of his Core, but he was surprised by the master's response.

"Your inspiration, lad. It's quite a rare affinity and one that any Spirit Caster would be wise to cultivate if they could. In fact, I suspect that affinity is responsible for much of your uncanny success and strength. You may feel you're 'lucky' for learning a rare, treasured ability like Sovereign Will, or that your hard work is what led you to the Paragon of the Axe, and to some degree, you'd be right, but I believe your easily inspired nature has been a large influence in your growth. Thank the old gods that you've had some positive influences in your recent development."

When Dar said the last bit, Victor saw a parade of faces run through his mind's eye: Yrella and Vullu from the Wagon Wheel, Lam in the mines, Old Mother, Thayla, Tellen, Tes, and even his enemies, like the Warlord and his subordinates. He did take inspiration from many sources—there was no denying it. "So, even though it's not my strongest affinity?"

Dar chuckled, clicking his tongue and shaking his head in admiration. "Aye, you lean toward the others more, but your affinity to inspiration is by no means weak. All of your affinities are absurdly strong."

Victor nodded. He didn't want to argue. His rage had, without a doubt, kept him alive in many desperate situations, but he *liked* his inspiration more. If Dar thought he should bring that closer to his spirit, whatever that meant, then he wouldn't argue. "What do I do?"

"This will not be easy, especially with your Core sitting on the cusp of epic. If I recall correctly, you told me it is ranked Advanced Nine, yes?"

Victor nodded but looked at the Energy and Core section of his status again to be certain:

Breath Core:	Elder Class: Improved 3		
Core:	Spirit Class: Advanced 9		
Breath Core Affinity:	Magma: 9	Breath Core Energy:	2200/2200
Energy Affinity:	Fear 9.4, Rage 9.1, Glory 8.6, Inspiration 7.4, Unattuned 3.1	Energy:	25407/25407

"I believe this new formation will push you over into epic. Such tension will make the reshaping process incredibly difficult. I'm pleased you've worked so hard to cultivate your will because you'll need it." He paused, then snapped his fingers. "Didn't you mention a natural treasure from the challenge dungeon? Something for breakthroughs?"

"Oh." Victor nodded, mentally sifting through his dimensional containers. "I did, yes. Something like a berry, but bigger." He found it and summoned the fruit onto his palm.

Dar peered closely at the plump blue apple-sized fruit, reading the label. "Perfect! An urd berry—useful for a difficult breakthrough!"

"Should I eat it?" Victor's mouth was already filling with saliva at just a hint of the fruit's fragrance.

"Patience! First, I must describe the process. You'll need to focus on your Core space, and using the strength of your will, you'll need to arrange the four orbs of your affinities into a stack, with inspiration at the bottom, then glory, then rage, and finally, at the top, fear."

"I thought I wanted inspiration at the top?"

"No! Patience, whelp!" Dar growled, and his eyes flared momentarily. "This will be a tremendous battle for your will, so listen carefully lest you hobble yourself with a lopsided, mangled Core!" He glared for a moment, ensuring Victor would remain quiet and pay attention, then said, "Once you've created the stack, as I said, the real battle will begin. You will use part of your will to hold the stack in place while stretching the orb of your glory-attuned Energy into a ring, encircling your inspiration-attuned Energy.

"If you do it correctly, you'll feel it snap into place, and you'll no longer have to exert your will to hold the glory around your inspiration. After that's done, you'll repeat the process with rage, stretching it to encircle your glory. The ring will be larger but narrower, as it has to stretch further. Finally, you'll complete the process with your fear-attuned Energy, pulling it into a ring that encompasses the others."

Before Victor could ask the half dozen questions burning to escape his mouth, Dar continued, "Each ring will be an order of magnitude harder to shape. The resistance will increase, but so, too, will the compression as it snaps into place. This is what will push your Core toward the next tier—the different affinities working with each other instead of against each other as they're currently arrayed. I think you'll be able to complete the first ring without the fruit, so save it. When you begin to shape the rage ring, that will be the time to consume it."

Victor nodded, visualizing what Dar described. He could picture it, the inspiration at the center, still a compact, glowing sphere, with each of the other affinities wrapped around it in layers. "Um, how will this bring inspiration 'closer to my spirit'? I mean, aren't they all still in my Core?"

Dar nodded, leaning back to look down his nose at Victor. "A good question. This is an advanced topic, but one you should contemplate as you approach your test of steel and beyond. Your spirit is tied to your physical form through a pathway, not unlike your Energy pathways. This pathway breaches the veil between planes at the very center of your Core. With inspiration there, every other affinity must pass through it before it can touch your spirit. Moreover, the outermost affinity, fear, will also need to pass through rage and glory."

Victor's eyes widened with understanding. "So, right now, all of my affinities can touch my spirit equally?"

"They could if you had equal affinities. As it is, your rage and fear get through more often. This new Core structure will change you, Victor. You may not notice it right away, but you will start to experience your rage and fear to a lesser degree. What makes it through to your spirit will be colored by your glory and inspiration.

"This was the entire point of the cultivation drill I've taught you—how to filter the fear and rage-attuned Energy through your other affinities, primarily your inspiration. It will grant you a greater measure of control over those powerful emotions. They'll still be a part of you, still powerful, especially when turned outward into the structure of a spell, but they'll influence you less."

"Will it mean my Volcanic Rage won't make me lose control?" Victor had high hopes of holding on to that spell's tremendous power while keeping his Iron Berserk's rationality.

"No. That spell has an effect that you embrace when you cast it. Its destructive design is incredibly potent, but it opens your pathways wide to accept the rage in both your Cores. It will take improving the spell and strengthening your will to accomplish greater control. What reshaping your Core will do, Victor, is allow you to begin thinking in your day-to-day life without the constant, unfiltered influence of your fear and rage."

"What if all I had was rage or fear? Is that what happened to the geist I captured?"

Dar nodded, glancing to his left where he'd placed the rib bone. "I'm sure that was part of her problem, aye. She likely cultivated fear to the exclusion of all else. You can imagine how that would shape a spirit, especially if she were allowed to run amok, unchallenged by someone stronger in her world." Before Victor could ask another question, the giant smoothly stood and, looking down at Victor, said, "I've spoken enough today—more than I have all at once in years. You know what to do."

Victor's heart began to hammer in embarrassing panic, and he pushed it down, his pride refusing to allow it to show on his face. Of course, he'd wanted Dar to stick around to watch his progress, perhaps even help somehow, but the way he'd been dismissed rankled something inside him, and he just nodded. "Thanks, Lord Dar."

He didn't doubt that Dar could read him like an open book, but the master Spirit Caster didn't let on. "I'll know when you're finished. We'll talk more after that." As he strode from the room, Victor almost called after him to ask that he let Valla know he'd miss lunch but changed his mind; she'd figure it out, and he didn't want to sound so needy to the gruff, powerful man.

Frowning, gritting his teeth in angst, he turned his gaze inward and tried to control his racing thoughts. He took several deep, calming breaths, and then, staring at the four orbs of his Core, he gathered his will, contemplating the method of his attack. He decided to try to move his inspiration-attuned Energy first, pushing it closer to the other three orbs. Countless times, Victor had pulled Energy out of the orbs in his Core. Similarly, he'd gathered and pushed Energy into them more times than he could count, but he'd never tried to move one of those densely packed globes of thick, pulsing Energy.

When he began to exert the pressure of his will against the sphere of inspiration-attuned Energy, he felt it start to deform, bulging with the pressure, but then it stopped, and nothing more happened. Victor doubled down, pushing harder. He scowled in concentration and effort and bore down.

Slowly at first, then with more and more momentum, he pushed it where he wanted it, near the center of his Core space, and definitely out of the original, almost circular pattern his four orbs had once maintained.

Nodding with satisfaction, Victor repeated the process, moving his glory-attuned orb atop the inspiration. It shifted more easily, perhaps because he'd started with a vicious jab of his will rather than a slow ramp-up. Wanting to maintain his momentum, Victor buckled down and drove his will against his rage orb, growling with the effort as beads of sweat emerged all over his scalp, running in rivulets down his forehead. Like a boulder breaking free of the stony soil, the red glowing orb began to move, and Victor pushed with everything he had, driving it up and over to the top of the stack.

His initial placement of the inspiration orb was paying off; he'd arranged his three orbs so the empty spot near the top was close to his orb of fear-attuned Energy—he'd guessed it would be the hardest to move. His fear—Victor snorted at the thought—proved well-founded. The dark purple-black orb, pulsing with slow dread-filled beats, resisted his will for several long strenuous minutes. Victor felt his ire rising but pushed it back, clearing his mind; rage might make him feel better, but it wouldn't help his concentration, and it would almost certainly undermine his will.

He took a massive breath, filling his lungs to bursting, then bore down, concentrating on what he intended, bending that orb, that part of himself, to his resolute desire for it to *move*. If the rage orb had been a boulder, Victor's fear moved like a glacier—a mountain—slowly, painfully, with tremendous gravity, sliding into position. "*Chingado*," he hissed, brushing the rivulets of sweat off his face, shaking his head, and sending a fine mist of perspiration around the chamber. "That was the easy part?"

Victor stretched and breathed, trying to recharge his reserves as he realized he'd only just begun the task Dar had set before him. When he settled down and turned his gaze inward again, he was dismayed to see that his inspiration and glory-attuned orbs had begun to slide out of formation, pulled up around the rage by the fear-attuned orb. Victor cursed and forced them back into place, holding them still with his will. It was clear that outside of the semicircular, lopsided "balance" he'd managed to push his Core into, the fear was trying to take the central position. It was trying to pull the other orbs into a sort of orbit.

Once again, Victor took a deep breath, and pushing all thoughts from his mind, he willed his glory-attuned Energy to begin stretching out. He pulled the largest tendril of Energy out of it that he could control, stretching it around the inspiration-attuned orb. The tendril kept trying to fly free, to drift through his Core space, back toward the orb of glory-attuned Energy. Victor held it firm, wrapping it down and around the inspiration orb and then up and back into itself.

Once he'd created that loop, things became a little easier—even though the Energy flowed back into the glory orb, his will held it firm around the inspiration orb, so it flowed like a river with a fat bulge at the top. From there, Victor used his will to manipulate strand after strand, flattening the orb as he built up one loop after another. When he could no longer see any evidence of the glory orb, and he had just a dozen thick strands of glory looping the inspiration orb, he pressed them together, squeezing, *willing* them all to combine.

When the strands of glory-attuned Energy combined into one thick rope, it snapped into place—a bright golden glittering ring around his white-gold, misty orb of inspiration. "Fuck yes!" he howled, pumping his fist. Victor felt as if he'd just defeated a state champion and proven his legitimate claim to the title. He allowed himself a few minutes to relax and study his Core, basking in the pride of accomplishment.

What Dar hadn't told him was that it wasn't a two-dimensional ring. In that space, things had depth, and Victor felt more like he was looking at a multilayered sun, somehow able to perceive it in a cross section. He saw how the glory-attuned Energy hugged the inspiration-attuned Energy, how they interacted with each other, the wisps interlocking, clasping, *pulling* on each other. What he saw was no stack; it was a bond, and Victor couldn't imagine the force of will it would take to undo what he'd done. The orbs of fear and rage, while heavy and dense, looked far less vibrant, less *vital*. Had he really had such an inferior Core all this time?

With renewed excitement, Victor picked up the fruit. He chuckled at his reluctance to call it a berry just because it was the size of an apple. In his massive hand, it looked enough like a berry. Maybe the world where it grew was populated by giants. "Or titans," he chuckled, plucking the stem and plopping the whole thing into his mouth. It was the most delicious thing he could remember tasting. It tickled his tastebuds—tangy and sweet, but more than that, it burst with uncountable flavors, one rolling into the next as the juice washed over the flesh of his mouth, down his throat, and into his stomach.

Victor's eyes were closed, but each new flavor, from vanilla to honey to cloves to citrus to a thousand others, seemed to send bursts of colorful light into his mind. He felt inspired but a thousandfold more than he ever had with his inspiration spells. Everything felt possible. No, Victor decided, not possible—trivial.

He laughed as he considered his earlier struggles, and he turned to his rage-attuned orb of Energy and pulled a thin strand from it, looping his new Inspiration and Glory Core. It was easy, of course, to manipulate a single thread like that, and he kept pulling, looping it again and again around the Core. The thread wanted to go back into his rage orb, but it was nothing to keep it away. It was so easy that he started moving it faster, looping around the edge of the glory-attuned Energy.

It wasn't hard to keep the thread, now in a hundred loops, bunched up. All it took was a slight pressure from his will while he continued to pull. A hundred loops became two hundred became five hundred, and then, to his delight, he no longer found any rage-attuned Energy to pull. Victor had stretched his entire supply of rage into a long, looping thread around his Core. With a forceful exertion of his will, he pressed the loops together, and with a jolt like a thunderbolt to his heart, the rage snapped into place.

He now had a dark red, vibrant band of hot angry Energy that slowly bled into the band of glory-attuned Energy, turning from hot red to orange to yellow to white-gold as it seeped toward the center of his Core. Victor wanted to celebrate, wanted to study the beauty of his new Core—the sturdy, dense, powerful nature of it—but he was still riding high on the fruit he'd eaten and didn't want to lose his momentum.

Just as he'd done with the rage, he began to stretch his fear-attuned Energy around his new Core. He thought it would be more challenging, that there would be some hidden difficulty, but despite the density of that fear-attuned orb, his other three affinities, working together, had far more gravity. It was almost effortless at this point to pull his fear out in a ribbon, wrapping it again and again, faster and faster, around his Core. When he'd stretched it to the limit, utterly diminishing the orb, he squeezed, and with a burst of blinding, soul-wrenching Energy, it snapped into place. Victor's new, fully realized Core began to pulse like a neutron star, and System messages danced across his vision.

*****Congratulations! You have advanced your Core: Epic 1.*****

*****Congratulations! You have constructed a unified, multilayered Core. Your total Energy reflects the potential of any of your affinities.*****

Grinning from ear to ear, Victor pulled up his Energy stats again:

Breath Core:	Elder Class: Improved 3		
Core:	Spirit Class: Epic 1		
Breath Core Affinity:	Magma: 9	Breath Core Energy:	2200/2200
Energy Affinity:	Fear 9.4, Rage 9.1, Glory 8.6, Inspiration 7.4, Unattuned 3.1	Energy:	30507/30507

"Ha!" Victor slapped his hands together in celebration, the crack of his thick palms echoing in the chamber. His Energy pool had jumped by more than five thousand, and if he understood what he was reading, he was reasonably sure he could now use his entire pool of Energy to fuel a particular affinity. For instance, if he wanted to, he could burn all his Energy for Berserk. It would make managing his Energy during combat a hundred times easier.

A deep, rough voice rumbled behind him, "I felt that five miles away. I am pleased, apprentice. If they thought you a monster before, wait until they feel the pressure of an epic-tier Core behind your aura."

Victor grinned fiercely, his white teeth shining in the dim chamber as he turned to regard Dar. "They?"

"Your foolish enemies. Come. You've been at this for hours and deserve to celebrate; we'll join your friends for dinner."

25

PARTY

Victor stood in his shower, washing away the sweat of a hard day's practice. He was a little late for Lam's party but figured he had some time before people—Lam and Valla, mostly—began to get irritated with him. He and Lesh had been sparring for hours, and he was a mess. The dragonkin had put him through a rough one, eager to demonstrate his scales' new resilience and the strength and agility he'd gained from his bloodline upgrade.

Victor chuckled at the thought, turning his face toward the mini rainclouds, washing the soap out of his hair. With his eyes squeezed shut, he turned his gaze inward and marveled proudly at his new Core. Once he'd started using the cultivation technique that Dar taught him, the bands of glory, rage, and fear-attuned Energy had begun to rotate around his compact central sphere of inspiration. The gleaming, sparkling band of glory-attuned Energy moved quickly, while the overarching ring of smoky purple-black fear moved more ponderously. Rage was somewhere in between.

It amazed Victor to no end, watching the interplay between his different affinities. He could see the slow trickle of fear, rage, and glory toward the center, but he saw how they changed as they passed through each layer. Dar hadn't been lying; his Energy fed his spirit, and now none of his rage or fear got through unaltered by his other affinities. He wasn't sure if it was a result of his Core's redesign or if he was just experiencing some sort of placebo effect, but Victor had felt great the last couple of days. His mood had been good, his outlook positive, and it seemed as if he was getting more out of everything he did.

Smiling at the idea, Victor got out of the shower, intent on being amicable at the party. He was a little apprehensive; there was the chance that some hard feelings might come up. After all, he'd been fighting no-holds-barred against many of Lam's guests not too long ago. Still, the challenge dungeon had been a competition, and he hoped some grudges could be forgiven after some pleasant conversation, drinks, and food.

He dressed in the clothing version of his armor, choosing a midnight blue shade for his shirt. The other pieces, his pants, boots, belt, bracelet, and headband, all shifted to a deep black that complemented the choice. "Nice," he grunted, looking at himself in the mirror. The headband took a little getting used to, but it was supple leather, tooled with silvery thread, and according to Valla, it gave him an almost regal appearance.

As he left the bathroom, he glanced at Lifedrinker leaning beside the bed and thought about wearing her. He decided it was a little much, considering it was "his" home. Still, he didn't trust all the people Lam was inviting, so he summoned his coyotes and left them in the room to keep watch. They yipped and cried a little, but when he expressed his intentions, they curled up as though they were sheltering for the night on his bed. Grinning, Victor walked out and nearly bumped into Sora.

"Oof," he said, falling back against his door, "almost ran you over."

She looked up at him, smiling. "Victor! I was just wandering a little, trying to avoid Cam."

"Yeah? Cam's here?" Victor got a little frustrated looking down his nose at her, so he cast Alter Self, reducing his height to something more like seven feet.

"So weird that you can do that! What an interesting ability!" She giggled and sipped her drink; from the flush of her cheeks, he didn't think it was her first. She looked lovely, Victor couldn't deny—a slim-fitting dress that didn't cover much of her lithe, tan figure. Her grayish hair was curled and shone vibrantly, almost like silver, and she had a mischievous twinkle in her big bright eyes.

"So, you're hiding from Cam?"

She nodded, brushing a droplet of condensation from her drink off her chin. "He's going to deny everything I told you about his betrayal. Be warned."

"Well, come on. I'll shield you from his wrath," Victor said, feeling too smooth for his own taste, and turned down the hallway. "I should get to the party before Valla kicks my ass."

"I get to meet her? The mysterious woman that holds the leash of a mighty titan?"

Victor sighed and chuckled. He had no doubt that there were plenty of rumors around Sojourn about him and, of course, anyone connected to him. "You'll meet her, all right." He could hear music, surprisingly modern Earth-like music, with instruments playing that reminded him of synthesizers, drums, and even guitars. It was mellow, nothing like rock and roll, but definitely not the jaunty medieval stuff he'd gotten used to on Fanwath. "Is that local music?"

"Strista brought a minstrel box, a good one, loaded with music from dozens of nearby worlds."

"Strista . . ." Victor ran the name through his mind. "The avian woman with the whip? Her master is a consul, right?"

"Yes, Master Yon." As she answered, Victor stepped out of the hallway into the main parlor of Dar's house and was a little surprised by the size of the crowd. There had to be more than thirty people in the room, and he could see, through the floor-to-ceiling windows, an equal or greater number out on the deck. "Damn, Lam," he breathed, scanning the space, seeing some familiar faces but many he didn't recognize.

Sora leaned close, speaking low, "Quite a showing. I don't think any invites went unanswered. Can you blame them all? Everyone in the city is *still* talking about the thrashings you handed out in the Vault of Valor. Then there's the venue—Ranish Dar's lake home! He's never had a gathering here. Many masters are feeling irritated that their apprentices were invited here before they were."

Victor nodded absently, still trying to spot Valla while avoiding locking eyes with any of the dozens of people already staring his way. He saw a glimpse of silvery, teal wings out on the deck and started moving that way, only to have an enormous figure, someone he first thought was Dar because of his colorful, loose clothing, step into his path. "Oho! There she is, and there's the man of the hour!" Victor looked up into Brontes's brutish face and couldn't help smiling at the giant's crooked-toothed grin. He also couldn't help noticing how Sora inched closer to him, practically pressing her side against his as Brontes stuck out a meaty hand.

"Brontes!" Victor clasped the meaty palm. "I'm glad to see you didn't bring your club."

"Oh, Ballsmasher?" He laughed. "I have him resting in a pool of hot clay back home, still recovering from your axe's wicked edge!" His grip felt like a sandpaper-wrapped ham hock, and as he squeezed, Brontes frowned, his brow wrinkling in confusion. "Shit! Have I gone mad, or have you shrunk?"

"Careful, Brontes," Sora sighed.

Victor chose to ignore the question and pulled his hand back. "Nice to see you, big guy. Wanna do some sparring sometime soon? I have a friend I want you to meet."

"Do you jest?" Brontes boomed. "Of course!" He gestured expansively and enthusiastically, and Victor felt very glad Dar's home had been built with giants in mind.

"Cool, well, let's talk some more in a bit. I need to go ask the hostess if she needs any help."

"Cool?" Brontes frowned, then grinned. "I like it. You were right, Sora, he's not half bad!" Victor just smiled and pushed by the big man, only to be accosted by another group of people, all avian, one of whom was Strista Kono, the hawk-featured lady with the whip he'd knocked out by charging and smashing her through a dozen trees. The two avians flanking her both looked decidedly feminine and clung to her arms as though she were a flotation device keeping them above water.

"Victor!" she trilled, her voice surprisingly melodic. He could hear Brontes talking to Sora behind him—it was hard *not* to hear the giant—so Victor took another step closer to Strista and her entourage.

"Hello, Strista."

"You remembered my name?" Her golden eyes widened, and though her beak couldn't smile, he recognized the pleased-sounding clicks she made in her throat; he'd learned them from Tria, his yellow-feathered, avian Artificer friend. "Victor, can I speak to you alone for just a moment?" She leaned close. "Before Arcus finds us?" She glanced at her friends—dates?—and said, "Mingle! Shoo! I'll be back in a moment." Then, before Victor could even reply to her request, she grabbed his wrist in surprisingly strong fingers and tugged him toward the hallway leading to the kitchen.

"Strista!" He pulled against her grip, and it was only when his pull didn't slow her that he had to take into consideration that this woman might be stronger than he was at that moment. He wasn't channeling Sovereign Will into his strength, he wasn't Berserk, and worst of all, he'd hobbled himself with Alter Self, reducing his attribute maximums by close to thirty percent. As far as he knew, Strista was Tier Eight, and he had no idea how much she'd built up her strength attribute. She pulled him around the corner and then let go, turning to face him.

"I'm so sorry about that. I know it was rude. I know you could have gone mad and thrown me around like a child, so thank you for holding back. I wanted to grab you before you became too busy with all the fawning people in that room and before Arcus realized I was here. You see, Victor, I believe he means you harm! In fact, I know he does! He tried to involve me."

Victor sighed. Dar had already told him that Arcus Volpuré would probably try to kill him before they were clear of the Iron Prison. He was Lord Roil's protégé, and Lord Roil and Dar had plenty of history. He smiled at her and shrugged. "I know."

"You do?" Her throat clicked awkwardly as she clutched her hands together. "That's embarrassing. I seem to have betrayed a friend for naught."

"Eh, relax. I appreciate the heads-up, but yeah, I figure he'll pull something while we're in the prison. You've heard about that, I suppose?"

Strista nodded, her throat clicking rapidly. "Yes! Arcus has been *crowing* nonstop about the mission to rescue Rasso Hine. He anticipates great rewards and, of course, a chance to avenge his pride against you. I'm glad you're aware. He told me that Arona will also be a part of the mission, yes? Be wary of her. I don't know her well, but Arcus does, and he speaks about her as though she's an ally."

Victor nodded absently, certain he heard Valla's voice, slightly raised, saying his name. He turned back toward the hallway and nodded that way. "Hey, thanks again, Strista. You're all right. I gotta get back in there; I think I heard my name."

She nodded but deftly snatched his wrist again, saying, "Please don't mention my warning to anyone. I don't want Arcus to turn his schemes against me. He's already furious that I backed out of his plan to 'avenge' himself. How ridiculous! We all went into that dungeon knowing the risks, and he's the one who struck first! I've seen the full battle review in the *Daily*!"

"The, uh, *Daily*?"

"The *Sojourn Daily*? It's the biggest newspaper in the city . . ." She trailed off, giving him a chance to interject, so Victor did.

"Ah, right. Of course." He nodded and jerked his head back toward the parlor. "I'm heading back. Have a good time, all right?"

"Thank you. I see a restroom down the hall. I think I'll use that before I rejoin the party."

Victor grunted in acknowledgment, already walking away. He supposed he should be more grateful to her, but what more could he do than say thank you? He wouldn't tell Arcus or anyone else that she'd tried to warn him, so it wasn't like she'd get in any trouble. When he stepped into the parlor, he saw several people angling his way, but he refused to make eye contact and hurried toward the door to the deck. He could see Valla standing out there speaking to a man in a bright red robe with a high collar that obscured his head. If he were the kind of guy to say things like "speak of the devil," he might have uttered those words.

Feeling just a hint of agitation, despite the buzz of conversation, music, and general good humor around him, Victor shoved his way out, muttering, "Excuse me," as he nudged people aside. When he stood a bit behind and to the right of the man in red, he grinned at Valla as she shifted her eyes to meet his gaze. He felt his anxiety plummet as he listened to her.

". . . several different instructors over the years, but haven't yet met anyone who practiced that particular style."

The man nodded, or at least Victor thought he did; he could only see the top of his head over his high collar. His voice was smooth and cultured as he replied, "Ah, well, as I said, my father's man-at-arms is a master, and I'm sure he'd be interested to see how your style might differ."

Valla smiled and nodded to Victor. "Arcus, this is Victor. I believe you've met."

Arcus whirled, his silken robe's hem flaring out expansively at the movement, and turned to face Victor in surprise. He wasn't wreathed in flame as he had been at the start of the challenge dungeon, but his eyes glowed like smoldering coals beneath his dark brows as he smiled and bowed shallowly—really more of a respectful nod. Victor shifted closer to Valla while the man said, "I'm pleased to meet you outside of a contest, Victor. I hope there aren't any hard feelings?"

Victor grinned, perhaps a little savagely. "Why would there be? You might have struck first, but I believe I hit back harder. We're all good in my book."

Arcus had thin lips, and they became even more so as he pressed them together in a smile that his eyes didn't reflect. No, his eyes spoke more of murder than pleasantries. "You certainly are a sturdy fellow, no doubt about that. I underestimated you to my folly. Safe to say, I won't make that mistake again." He glanced to Victor's left and right, and Victor saw what had gotten his attention; they'd drawn a small crowd. Arcus turned to Valla. "I can see why the council has chosen your man for such a dangerous job."

Victor felt a growl starting to take shape deep in his chest. The little asshole was trying to get Valla upset. He'd told her about the Iron Prison, of course, but as he was wont to do, he'd downplayed the danger. She, of course, wasn't one to be easily manipulated, however. "Oh, Arcus!" She laughed. "It may seem dangerous to you, but that's only because you've only just met Victor. He'll be fine." She moved close to Victor and grabbed his arm, leaning against him. "Won't you, my sweet?"

"Yeah," he chuckled, kissing her forehead, "of course."

"You're not worried?" Arcus pressed. "The council has lost five iron rankers trying to make a foothold in that place!" The muttered conversations on the deck told Victor they had done more than draw a small crowd; everyone was listening. He was about to spout some bravado to try to change the topic and prevent Arcus from actually getting to Valla, but then another voice spoke up, raspy and low—Arona.

"Haven't you read the reports of the fights after you were eliminated, Arcus? I think Victor will be fine." The Death Caster stepped up to Victor's left as she spoke, and he glanced at her; she looked similar to the other times he'd seen her—black lips, dark eyes, and sharp teeth. He quickly shifted his gaze back to Arcus when he saw that she wore a very slinky black dress that exposed a lot of pale flesh rather than her usual layered black robes. Valla's hands tightened on his biceps.

Arcus chuckled, waving a hand dismissively. "Right, yes. I suppose if they couldn't get one of the top-ranked bulwarks in the city to clear the entrance, someone like Victor will have to suffice."

"I'm a top-ranked bulwark. Number two in the city. Thank your fiery gods that Victor will be going in there." The new speaker had a deep, rumbling voice. Victor peered at him, only to see it was a man he didn't recognize, easily eight feet tall but leaner than Brontes, with a rigidly straight posture. He was dressed in a fine suit layered in different shades of purple, and his face was classically handsome with a square jaw, straight nose, and lips that curled in a pleasant smile. "That man is the sturdiest, hardest-hitting bastard I've ever crossed blades with."

Finally, it clicked for Victor, and he realized it was the man who'd been encased in plate armor. He glanced at the woman by his side to confirm—she didn't have her crossbow, but there was no doubt she was the one he'd eliminated—his wife. Victor smiled at her and asked, "How's your bow?"

"She's fine, sir. Thank you for your honorable mercy." She let go of the man's arm and bowed, and the tall man stepped closer, reaching out a hand.

"Victor, you have my thanks as well."

Victor took the hand and squeezed, nodding and smiling, pleased that most of the people he'd fought seemed to be good sports about their losses. He racked his brain, trying to remember the giant warrior's name, but it wouldn't come to him. Finally, he sighed and shrugged helplessly. "I'd introduce you to Valla, but I'm an idiot when it comes to names."

Valla let go of his arm and reached out a hand to the woman, who smiled. "I'm Lyla Rose, and this big fellow is Dovalion Boarheart."

It seemed that Arcus didn't like being left out. He shouldered closer, bumping Arona, and asked, "Boarheart, why didn't you accept the council's offer?"

"Because I've lost enough this decade. I'll be spending my time grinding away at the Dread Spire for the next few years."

"*We* will be," Lyla corrected, clasping Dovalion's hand with hers.

Arona, done being patient, shifted to lock eyes with Victor. "Don't let Arcus discourage you, Victor. If you can hold the entrance until the portal opens again, I'll help you subdue that dungeon. I'd go first, but the council thinks that prisoners are lying in wait, killing the council representatives, not the undead inhabitants of the dungeon." She frowned, and Victor felt some cold Energy wafting off her as she struggled to contain some emotion—anger? Irritation? She sighed. "I wanted to go in first. My bone thralls are made for such a situation, but Master Vesavo refused to allow it."

Arcus started talking then about how he'd handle it if he were "allowed" to go in first. Victor didn't buy it; he knew damn well that Arcus and his master hoped that Victor would die when he stepped into the dungeon. Then they could drop the whole charade. Maybe he was being paranoid, but he doubted there was any real reason to get Rasso Hine out of the dungeon. As that thought occurred to him, he waited for Arona to finish saying something about monsters respawning in a dungeon and asked, "What's the deal with this Rasso Hine guy, anyway? They're risking all these lives to get one man out?"

"Justice!" Arcus cried. "We cannot allow the council to punish an innocent man!"

"It's more than that," Arona added. "My master thinks Hine knows something about the half-finished invasion circle that Consul Rexa found and destroyed last month." The conversations around them had picked back up, but a new hush descended at Arona's raspy declaration.

"Imagine that!" Arcus scoffed. "Who would think to invade Sojourn? We've nearly a thousand veil walkers in the city at any given time."

"The circle was real," Strista said. Victor hadn't seen her approach, but she stepped forward on the other side of Valla. "My master saw it with his own eyes. I saw him sketching it from memory later that day."

"Consul Yon?" Again, Arcus scoffed. "You know what the other consuls call him, yes?"

Arona nudged him with her elbow. "Don't be rude."

"Arcus is brave," Strista said, irritated clicking sounds coming from deep in her throat, "when he has Lord Roil's robes to hide behind."

Victor saw Arcus's face tinting toward crimson and could even feel some heat emanating from the man, so he stepped forward and cleared his throat. "Let's keep it cool, huh? This is a party. Strista, I liked the music I heard earlier; it had a different kind of beat—a little faster. Can you play it again? On your device, I mean? Valla, where's Lam? I wanted something to eat, and the table was picked over when I passed by. Also, damn, but I'm thirsty! Anyone else want a drink?"

His interjections seemed to have done the trick. Glowering but visibly restraining himself, Arcus turned to speak more quietly with a young woman who looked as if she might be his sister. Victor frowned at that thought—hadn't Edeya said something about his sister? Everyone else started speaking at once about drinks, snacks, the view, the fabulous setting, or Strista's music. Valla pulled his arm, and he turned to see her pointing out Lam, who was waving her hands, speaking to some of Dar's house staff. Victor chuckled and walked over; it would be a long night, but he was already having fun. He hoped he'd run into the turtle guy, Drobna.

26

GIRD YOURSELF

Victor ate some kind of sweet, smoky meat on a skewer as he listened to Lam, Darren, and Edeya talk to Arcus and his little sister. He and Valla sat on a cushioned bench, their backs against the deck railing, as Arcus spoke, waving a hand for emphasis. Victor had done a lot of mingling, even spent some time comparing notes on Berserk with Drobna, and now things were winding down a little. It had been a surprisingly relaxing night; Arcus hadn't stirred up any further arguments, and in fact, Victor had hardly seen him, as the Pyromancer spent time with others, rarely in the same conversation.

"I, um, was going to bring that up," Darren said, answering Arcus's pointed question about his class. "I'm still only Level Eight."

The fire mage snorted. "If you're going to enter the First Clash Coliseum, you'll want a class."

"They have a week, brother dear. Well, nearly so. In any case, don't be dismissive! It's not like I have groupmates lining up at our door." The familial resemblance between the two was striking; their eyes and noses mirrored each other, and they spoke with a certain refined air that Victor found grating from Arcus but almost endearing from Trin. He supposed he was biased.

Lam cleared her throat. "Speaking of the 'coliseum,' can you tell us why it's not in the guidebook?"

"Of course," Arcus chuckled. "The dungeon is on my family's estate and not open to the public."

Edeya looked at Trin. "You said your father 'acquired a pass' for the dungeon—"

She was cut off by a burst of laughter from Arcus as he shoved Trin's shoulder. "Trying to be coy? Trying to downplay your—"

"*Our* family's wealth? Yes, I was! It's embarrassing. I'm sorry, Edeya. My father controls access to the dungeon, so the 'pass' was a fabrication of sorts. The true part of my tale is that he never lets me go into the place; it only opens a few times a month, and he sells the slots for favors and influence with the council."

Victor lost track of Edeya's response because Arona approached and leaned close to whisper, "Victor, might we speak in private for a moment?"

"Um—" Victor glanced at Valla, but she shrugged and stood up, giving his shoulder a gentle squeeze on the way.

"I'm going to check on the kitchen staff. I'll find you again soon."

Arona stepped back, lowering her head in a respectful nod. Victor couldn't help smiling at how Valla squared her shoulders and looked down her nose at the Death Caster as she brushed past.

He stood. "Come on, let's take a walk." They meandered through the little conversation groups, following the deck along the back of the house, past the library, and then onto a cobbled path that led into Dar's gardens. The same path would eventually open up to the area where he and Lesh liked to spar. Once the music and conversation were a muted background hum, Arona quickened her step to walk beside him.

"I know I spoke confidently about the little quest the council is sending us on, but I hope you understand how dangerous your part in this will be."

Victor sniffed deeply of the night blooms, enjoying a faint citrus tang that tickled his nose. He shrugged. "I need to do this to be free of them. You know about my punishment for damaging the dungeon."

"I know. I hope you realize that anyone with a brain recognizes that there's a faction on the council trying to get to Dar through you."

"Well, he used me pretty well to strike blows of his own, didn't he? I have a feeling he made a fortune betting on me, and let's not forget that many people, such as Arcus, are significantly weaker today than before going into that dungeon." Victor shrugged, peering up at the bright stars. "I guess I'm just trying to say I don't blame people like Roil for trying to abuse the situation."

"You seem . . . different." Arona chuckled, even her laugh raspy and low. "I'd imagined you to be fuming over this whole situation."

"I've had some clarity over the last couple of days. My rage is still there, trust me, but with Dar's guidance, I'm learning to use it more like a tool than a road I must walk upon."

"An interesting analogy. It doesn't bother you that the council has lost five representatives trying to gain a foothold in the dungeon?"

"There's a part of me, Arona, that truly enjoys challenges. I love to fight, and more so when people are around to see me win. I mean, honestly, if people thought I'd be discouraged because some others failed before me, they don't know me very well. Valla knows that. It was funny listening to Arcus trying to rile her up; she knows me better than I know myself. I told her what we were doing, but I didn't mention the people dying before me. Still, do you think she didn't suspect something like that?" He barked a short, genuine laugh. "She's probably relieved to hear what's really going on."

Arona's small smile didn't waver, and in the starlight, her teeth shone in the dark void of her black-painted lips. "You think she was imagining something worse?"

"Yeah, considering the trouble I've gotten up to in the past, I wouldn't be surprised."

Arona's voice grew even quieter as she said, "She's beautiful. I've never seen anyone like her."

Victor stopped and turned to look at her, listening to the night sounds—chirps, clicks, and even the warbling song of a nocturnal bird. He took a deep breath and nodded—how could he deny it? "Yeah, she is. Was there something else you wanted to say? Were you just hoping to warn me about the danger we'd be facing tomorrow?"

"I wanted to be sure you were aware of the politics at play. Some masters keep their students in the dark. Lord Roil and Master Dar have fought wars against each other—not only politically, here on Sojourn, but with armies on other worlds. Arcus is one of Roil's students, and he lost much favor by being eliminated from the Vault of Valor so quickly. He will be looking to save face and regain his master's favor. He may try something underhanded."

Victor grinned and reached out, resting a hand on Arona's bare shoulder. He supposed it was a little forward, but he wanted to convey his confidence and didn't think words were enough. Her flesh was icy to his hot flesh, and she shuddered slightly at the touch. "You're the third person to give me that warning. If he surprises me, then I'm a fool who deserves it. Do me a favor, though, will you?"

"I will." She nodded, a little too eagerly, if Victor were being honest.

"Be the first to follow me through. I'll have that entrance safe for you."

Again, she nodded. "I will!"

"Perfect, then." Victor removed his hand and smiled, turning back to the house. "Let's get another drink, then I'm going to try to talk Valla into a swim. Care to join us?"

Victor sat beside Dar in the Spirit Master's favorite coach, the black lacquered one that made Victor think of a steampunk batmobile. It was hurtling through the air toward the Council Spire, where he was meant to descend to the Iron Prison and put his life on the line—again—to establish a foothold in the place. Dar was quiet, contemplative, perhaps, and Victor was reminded of Arona's words the night before. He cleared his throat and risked irritating the giant stone-faced man. "I heard you've been at war with Roil for a long time."

"Didn't I tell you as much?" the giant rumbled.

"Well, I mean, you said you two had differences, but at the party, someone said you'd actually had armies battling each other on other worlds."

"Aye, that's a fact. We've fought over some of the same territory. It's not uncommon, Victor. As new worlds are added to Sojourn's registry, one with resources or cultures worthy of notice occasionally strikes the fancy of more than one of us old masters." Apparently, he was done with the subject because he asked, "Tell me of your cultivation. Any insights into your next breakthrough? I would suspect you'd tell me if your drill had reached the epic tier."

"Nope, still advanced, even using what you taught me. I can tell it's more effective than my old method, and it's a hell of a lot easier on my mind. I just don't know why it's still considered advanced."

"Because, like your old one, it *is* an advanced method. It simply has more potential for growth. Never fear, the improvement will come, and when you see what you've been doing wrong, you'll likely think yourself a dolt for not realizing it sooner."

"Heh. I'll take your word for it."

"You mentioned the party. How was it? I'm told you had quite a showing—more than eighty guests, according to Mr. Ruln. I'm pleased that no fights broke out."

"It was surprisingly fun. Something like ten of the people I fought in the dungeon showed up, and they were all pretty cool, even Cam and Arcus. Arcus tried to start a little shit at the beginning, but he got over it after a few drinks. I still don't like the guy, but he behaved all right. I also set up a few new sparring partners—Drobna, Brontes, Dovalion, and Sora—assuming I survive the dungeon today."

"You'll survive, but you may be in longer than a day. I believe there's some time dilation involved." Victor opened his mouth to ask what he meant, but Dar must have read his mind. "It won't be a major effect, but if I'm not mistaken, each day in that dungeon is closer to a week of standard System time."

"Is that on purpose?"

"Time dilation affects many dungeons, especially naturally formed ones, but it seems the System always adds the effect to level-locked dungeons to one degree or another. Didn't you notice how your time in the Vault of Valor seemed shorter than the time that passed outside?"

Victor's eyes opened wide. "Yeah. Shit! That makes sense! I thought I was only in there for about a day!"

Dar chuckled, nodding. "I'll be sure to inform your friends so they don't worry." He shifted, looking directly into Victor's eyes. "Let's talk about worst-case scenarios."

"You mean for the dungeon or my friends if I die?"

"The dungeon, boy!" Dar chuckled, shaking his head. "There's a good chance that someone has set up an Energy void on the other side of the transport portal, meaning if you step through, you may not be able to use your Energy abilities; anything you expend from your Core will be depleted, pulled away by the formation."

"Mmm." Victor nodded, scratching his chin. "Sounds bad." He pointedly remembered his time in the caldera, suffering from Hector's trap.

"The problem with such a formation is that it will only draw Energy you expend. Your Sovereign Will ability will function fine, and other abilities not dependent on an Energy expenditure will also work—Titanic Leap, for instance."

"And my axe." Victor, out of habit, reached up to stroke Lifedrinker's haft.

Let us slay your foolish foes! she cried into his mind, her voice thick with the lust for battle.

"Precisely. I saw a list of the iron rankers who were slain attempting to accomplish this task, and three of the five were mages. They died quickly—each in under two minutes. Another was an assassin variant. No doubt he believed he could sneak past or use his incredible speed to bypass the trap, but he died in just under five minutes. However, one fellow lasted nearly twenty minutes—a bulwark-type with a legendary shield. I'd seen him in a few gladiatorial events, and he was impressive."

"So, he was the most sturdy without spending Energy?"

"Just so." Dar nodded. "You are both sturdy and deadly, with or without Energy."

"Not so much if I can't berserk."

"Is that so?" Dar produced an obsidian blade engraved with smoldering orange runes and, faster than even Victor's Quinametzin eyes could follow, slashed it through the meat of Victor's forearm.

"Fuck!" Victor hissed, slapping his hand over the deep cut as blood began to swell out. Dar deftly slapped his hand away, his stony fingers impossible to resist, and stared at the cut. Victor followed his gaze and watched as his flesh stitched back together in just a few seconds.

"A fine cut, easily healed, but it illustrates the point. You're a hard man to kill. Use that axe of yours, use that strength and vitality, and bully your way out of their trap. Once you're clear of whatever formation they've set up, you can use your other abilities and lay waste to them."

Victor rubbed the blood into his arm, trying to smear it into nothing. "What will the formation look like?"

Dar nodded. "A good question. Look for a pattern of runes on the floor or pillars or totems or flags. If the magic prevents you from passing through, turn your axe against the formation. It will be sturdy and may resist your blade, but Lifedrinker and you are strong. If you can get her edge to pierce the formation, she can siphon the Energy. Have you imparted your spirit unto her?"

"Yes."

"What aspect?"

"Inspiration." Victor snatched Lifedrinker from her harness and held her on his knees so Dar could see the white-gold gleam that limned her shiny metal head.

"Not a bad choice, but for this, give her rage. She must be her most ferocious, with a blade that can melt stone."

Victor nodded, and then he quietly said, "*Chica*, I'm going to pull back this spirit, but then I'll give you another piece, the part of me that's always pissed off. Can you handle it?"

I yearn for it!

Victor chuckled, almost nervously, and then canceled his Imbue Spirit spell. Lifedrinker lost her white-gold aura, but as soon as it was gone, he cast the spell again, fueling it with rage-attuned Energy. A deep crimson light that smoldered almost like fire began to limn the axe, and he felt her eagerness for battle redouble—she vibrated and practically pulled away from him, desperate to strike *something*. Victor carefully lifted the axe over his shoulder and let his harness snatch her tight. "She's ready."

"And your Sovereign Will?"

"Already on strength and vitality."

Dar nodded. "Even if you don't break free, if Montes Foh can last twenty minutes, you can last an hour."

Victor grunted his acknowledgment, leaned back, and tried to relax; the coach would arrive in just a few minutes. He'd probably be nervous or worried if he thought about things too much, but he didn't like to do that. Before a match or, in this case, a fight, he simply wanted to think about how he'd perform. It calmed him to visualize his movements, to picture foes taken down or cleaved in half. He liked to think about his axe work—his stances, cuts, blocks, combinations, and counters. If he couldn't use his spells in this fight, it just meant he'd get to concentrate more on his fighting style. Frankly, that sounded fun to him.

It wasn't long before the coach settled with a gentle bump, and Dar threw the doors open, leaping out with a ground-shaking thud. Victor followed suit; he was just as large as his mentor, and the two of them easily cleared the crowds on the bustling sidewalk outside the city council's tower. They made their way inside, past the enormous System Stone, and then onto an elevator made of crystal that, rather than ascending as Victor thought it would, dropped down beneath the ground floor and beyond, descending rapidly for several seconds.

When the elevator lurched to a stop, Victor followed Dar out into a polished gray-and-white marble corridor wide enough for a city bus to drive through. It led toward an equally large pair of wide open double doors. As they approached, Victor's boots clicking on the stone, he saw a huddle of robed individuals in the room beyond. When Dar led the way into the chamber, the figures looked toward them, and Victor recognized several of the consuls he'd met at his "inquest."

As he glanced around the spacious, domed chamber, taking in the murals—torture scenes, body-strewn battlefields, and a depiction of what could only be described as hell—he saw Arona and Arcus standing to the side of the otherwise empty chamber, chatting. Dar nodded toward them. "Wait over there. We'll open the portal soon."

Victor walked over, and, to his surprise, Arcus inclined his head in a nod of greeting. "A pleasure to see you made it, Victor."

Victor offered him a half-smile. "Arcus." He shifted his gaze to Arona, noting she was back in her dark robes with the deep cowl. "Arona." He gestured to the macabre murals. "Lovely space."

Arona breathed a soft chuckle, then rasped, "This is the antechamber to a prison dungeon. You wanted flowers and angelic beings? Would you like a statue of your lady love, Valla, here?"

Victor felt some heat in his chest, felt the rage trying to slide out of his Core into his pathways, but he willed it down. Arona's lips turned up in a smile, and he could see she was being playful, perhaps even trying to pay Valla a compliment with the "angelic beings" line. He shrugged. "If it were the last thing I'd see before getting dumped into a death-attuned dungeon? Hell yes!"

Arona's smile widened, exposing her sharp canines. It looked as if she'd say something more, but then Arcus ran his gaze up and down Victor's figure. "I see you're back to your gigantic size. No armor?"

"I'll put it on before I go in." Victor was, in fact, wearing the clothing versions of his armor; he'd been tempted to wear his old dragon-steel belt instead of the new Sojourn-set belt, but the old one was starting to lose its value; opponents at his level, especially casters like Arcus, could unleash enormous torrents of Energy in their attacks, and the belt only absorbed a small fraction. His new one could boost his agility and dexterity in a pinch, and was pretty much immune to damage.

"Nervous?" Arcus asked, his head craning back inside his high, sharp collar to see Victor's face better.

Victor stepped back to make it easier on the much shorter pair. "I don't generally feel nervous before a fight, bud. I'm a little anxious, I guess, but that's just because I'd rather fight than stand around talking about it." Arona stifled a raspy laugh at his words, turning away and feigning a cough, and Arcus stiffened. Victor grinned and turned toward the gaggle of older men and women standing at the chamber's center. "Think they'll let me get things started soon?"

As if his words had been prophetic, Victor felt a surge of chilly, death-attuned magic, and then, with the howl of a thousand tormented souls, a swirling portal formed at the center of the chamber, casting the space in malevolent cold blue light. Lord Roil's unmistakable cowled figure stepped out of the group of consuls and masters and called out, "Victor, the time is nigh. Gird yourself."

27

FOOTHOLD

At Lord Roil's words, Victor nodded and channeled a little Energy into his armor, instantly armoring himself in crimson and black scales, thick red leather hide, and dense, deep-red gleaming metal. Victor found the helmet strangely comfortable, and something about the enchantment allowed him an unobstructed view from within the lava king's fanged maw. Arona lifted an appreciative eyebrow, and Arcus nodded, a slow smile spreading on his face. The expression surprised Victor, but not as much as the Pyromancer's words.

"Impressive. I begin to wonder if I should have made some wagers on your success." Genuine levity tinged the man's voice.

Victor smirked. His voice reverberated, slightly amplified by the nature of the helm, as he said, "I hope you didn't bet against me. You've lost enough thanks to me, don't you think?"

Arcus shrugged and again surprised him: "Nothing I hadn't signed up for. Best hurry over; I see Lord Roil's vapors quickening—an expression of impatience I'm all too familiar with."

"Right. See you soon." Victor nodded to Arona.

She smiled, exposing her sharp canines, and shrugged. "Not soon enough. An hour for you, seven for us out here. I'll be ready."

With nothing to add, Victor turned and stomped toward the group of older, far more powerful men and women standing near the brightly glowing portal. His boots thudded on the marble, and he flexed his gauntleted left hand, eager to put his new lava lash to work. The thought brought a question to his mind, and as he approached, he asked, "If they've set up an Energy void, will it not drain my Core? If not, why can't I use abilities that stay within my body? Or this?" He channeled some Energy into the gauntlet, and the molten lash handle filled his hand, the coil sizzling and popping, dripping hissing magma onto the marble as it extended to hang from his hand.

Dar opened his mouth to reply, but another consul, one Victor hadn't met, stepped forward. She was a tall, slender woman wearing silken blue robes. As she spoke, she pulled her cowl back, revealing a beautiful elven face with odd white-furred fox ears jutting up through her pale blonde hair. Her voice rang out, melodic and chime-like. "Only an Energy trap properly attuned to your affinities can pull the Energy from your Core. However, a general void trap will drain any Energy that so much as touches one of the pathways outside your Core. You must resist the temptation to activate any abilities or spells, lest you diminish yourself for naught."

"Thank you, Lady Rexa," Dar rumbled. Then he turned his gaze on Victor and more loudly said, "Understand? Capture the foothold as we discussed, Victor." Victor nodded and turned to the portal, but then he realized several consuls had stepped forward with packages. Again, Dar spoke: "We'll equip you with a few minor treasures to help ensure your victory. I'll start." He held out a small, brightly glowing golden pill-like capsule in his hand. "If, for some reason, your Core becomes drained, swallow this. It will partially replenish you."

Victor smiled, recognizing a waft of glory coming off the little treasure. He took it in his palm and then tucked it into one of the many near-invisible pockets on his new armored pants. To his surprise, Yon, the avian consul and master of Strista, stepped forward with a brace of five vials, each filled to the cork stopper with thick red liquid. "Regenerative healing draughts. Some of my best work. I give you these with the understanding that this undertaking will benefit all of Sojourn and is far beyond the scope of the three tasks you owe this council."

Victor was sure he heard Lord Roil hiss at those words, but when he glanced at the man, all he saw was impassive smoke inside his heavy cowl. Victor slung the brace of vials crosswise over his shoulder so the five potions were on his chest and easily accessible. Yon spoke again. "The crystal containers are exceedingly sturdy."

"Awesome," Victor grunted, taking a moment to pull Lifedrinker from her harness while he was at it. He started to step toward the portal but realized one more consul was holding a package out to him. It was the grandmotherly woman from the inquest, the one with solid black eyes. He'd almost overlooked her, for unlike most of the other consuls, she wasn't nearing giant-sized proportions. Rather, she was probably around five feet tall with a stooped back. She shakily stretched up her arm, and Victor accepted the heavy billiard-ball-sized orb she proffered. It was cold and metallic and inscribed with hundreds of tiny, neat runes. He could feel the Energy pulsing at its dense core.

"A bomb!" she cackled. "Were I you, I'd throw it at the first fool I saw once I emerged from the portal!"

Victor grinned, hefting the ball in his gauntleted hand. "Hell yeah! Thanks . . ."

"Kreshta Griss." She mock-curtseyed, and it looked as if she might fall as she grinned lopsidedly and cackled.

Victor arched an eyebrow, then looked around at the old masters and, with the helmet adding extra resonance to his voice, boomed, "Anything else?"

Dar clapped him on the shoulder. "Only one more thing, Victor." He held out a small many-colored marble. "This recall token will bring you and one other out of that place. Attune it to yourself so another cannot use it in your stead." Victor did as he asked, sending a trickle of Energy into the tiny glass ball. Then he tucked it away in his "good" dimensional ring, along with his cultivation treasures. "Excellent. Don't rely on that recall token in an emergency. Due to the nature of this prison dungeon, you'll need to channel Energy into it for several minutes before it will activate."

Victor nodded, then clapped his mentor on the shoulder. "See you soon." Hefting Lifedrinker in his hands, he stepped toward the portal. When he stood before the blue, swirling rip in reality, he turned and ran his gaze over the room one more time. Arona and Arcus stood to the side, both looking pensive. Dar didn't flinch from his gaze, and the steady blaze of his eyes gave Victor confidence. Roil's smoky cowl was useless when it came to reading his intentions or thoughts, so Victor shifted his gaze over the rest of the consuls. Some smiled and nodded. Some looked disturbed—guilt, perhaps? More than half refused to meet his gaze.

Victor couldn't stomach the idea that so many of them wouldn't even look him in the eyes or acknowledge him before he stepped through. He hefted Lifedrinker overhead, staring hard at each of the consuls. They might be more powerful than he, they might be able to squash him if they wanted to, but he was damned if he'd go into this death trap without them even looking at him. He released his aura, letting it fall around him like a lead blanket. Of course, none of the old masters flinched, but he got a couple more to look his way.

Victor grinned and lifted his head to the sky. Shouting as loudly as he could, with the magical amplification of his helm, he screamed, "Ancestors! I go to bring you *glory*!" The final word was deafening, echoing strangely in the domed chamber. Seeing that his cry had gotten everyone's attention, Victor smiled savagely, turned, and leaped into the portal. Cold washed over him, but the passage was brief, and when he emerged, he was struck by the sudden change of his environs.

He'd jumped into the portal, so he came out mid-leap, and, as he descended toward a bone-strewn stone platform, he took in the scenery. He wasn't in a cave or a network of tunnels as he'd always pictured "dungeons" in his mind. A night sky hung overhead, devoid of stars but illuminated by a gibbous gray moon. A landscape of broken ruins lay around him, low walls and small crumbling buildings in the foreground and taller, more whole structures farther away.

The portal was bright and blue, and before it snapped closed, Victor saw that the platform he was falling toward was surrounded by a dozen stone totems carved with brightly flaring runes. He'd just noticed the skulking, shadowy outlines of watching individuals, more than a handful, when the portal snapped shut with an ear-popping collapse of air, and the world was thrown into momentary darkness.

It was only momentary because a bright white globe of Energy flared to life, and a man in ragged gray robes stepped forward, just on the far side of the stone platform. The light was above his hood, casting his face in deep shadow, but his voice rang out stridently, "What's this, then? Another lackey of the council come to feed the grinder?"

Victor didn't respond, ignoring the *pendejo* as he turned in a slow circle, allowing his eyes to adjust. He could feel the emptiness around him and knew that Dar's theory had been correct; there was no Energy in the space contained by the totems. He could feel their tug, and it brought to mind Hector's trap in the volcano's caldera, only weaker and less tailored to Victor's affinities. He could see the other figures moving closer to the circle, watching him. Most wore tattered clothing, but a few had armor on—mismatched chainmail, leather, and a few pieces of plate. One giant man with the head of a bull held a shield and a spiked mace.

Nodding as he counted the seven different foes, Victor finally turned back to the speaker. "What's the deal? You guys just camping here hoping for easy kills?" Victor stepped toward the man and the platform's edge, wondering when they'd attack, but the fellow just shifted to his left, keeping Victor in view as he approached the totem. Lifedrinker was vibrating hungrily in his right hand, but he kept her low, her smoldering edge hanging below his knee. He still held the "bomb" in his left gauntlet, unsure of its best target. Should he toss it at the man? Should he try to blow up the totem?

"Look at the gear on this one," the man said, chuckling. "Ronkerz will appreciate the armor, no doubt."

Victor smirked, then lifted Lifedrinker toward the edge of the circle. She pressed against something invisible—a barrier created by the totems, no doubt. If he tried to throw the bomb, he didn't think it would go well for him. "Who's that? Your master?" Just then, a sizzling *zwap* echoed behind him, and a bolt of hot lightning slammed into his back. It hurt—well, stung was probably a better word for it—and Victor took a step forward, bumping into the barrier. He grunted in annoyance, then turned around to see one of the others, a tall, thin man lowering a smoking iron rod. He wore a crooked, mad grin as he began to cackle.

"We have no master here, fool. In this realm, every man is free!"

Victor chuckled at the irony of that statement. "Free? You're in a prison, dipshit." A twang sounded, and Victor shifted, lifting his left arm so the incoming projectile bounced off his heavy bracer. "Speaking of dipshits, are any of you guys Rasso Hine?" As he'd figured they would, his words brought forth a torrent of attacks. The mage with the smoking rod fired another lightning bolt, which Victor ate, knowing he couldn't dodge it. He ducked his shoulder into another arrow, and then a huge fireball streaked through the air, cast by a woman standing on a pile of broken gray stones. Victor smiled as the orb of screaming flames came, ignoring it to deflect a hurled boulder with his bracer.

As the fireball exploded at his feet, great orange flames burst out, black smoke billowed upward, and Victor's mad smile spread in the almost pleasant heat. The attack obscured him, and he took that moment to turn and try Lifedrinker against the nearby totem. He grunted as he swung her, putting his muscle and bulk behind it, and she struck home, carving a thin groove in the rock in a shower of sparks. Victor grinned. It wouldn't be easy, but he could do it; he could break their formation.

When the flames and black smoke cleared, and the attackers saw he was still standing, largely unscathed, he could feel them gathering Energy for another, perhaps more intense, round of attacks. "Don't you think you should maybe try talking? You guys so sure killing me is the right move?"

This time, one of the people behind him spoke, responding in a deep, hoarse voice that had Victor imagining him living a life in a smoky factory, shouting constantly at his coworkers. "Unless you've come to take us out of this fucking hell, then you can die like the rest!"

Victor sighed, lifted Lifedrinker, and with a grunt, hacked her into the totem again. He aimed for the same spot, and she bit into her previous groove, chiseling it out just a little deeper than before. He figured if they left him alone, he'd cut through enough of the totem to break it in half within thirty or forty chops. He felt the attacks coming before he saw them, then he was bombarded by fire, electricity, arrows, stones, knives, crossbow bolts, and even something that felt like a splash of acid.

He tried to dodge around, rolling, jumping, and waving his gauntlet at any projectiles he saw in time. He kept his chin tucked, allowing his helmet to receive the attacks that might have hit his face through the open maw of the lava king's snarling countenance. When the wave of attacks let up, he wasn't hurt all that badly. A few bolts and arrows protruded from his arms, and one very large, nearly spear-sized arrow had pierced the tough hide of his greaves and stood proudly from his left thigh. His armor smoked and ticked as it rapidly repaired itself, but overall, he felt okay.

Holding the bomb in one hand and Lifedrinker in the other, he couldn't very easily pull the bolts and arrows out of his flesh. As more arrows and other projectiles flew toward him, Victor looked in frustration at the totem he'd been attacking. During his dodging, he'd ended up near the center of the platform, and the totem was a good ten yards from him. Shrugging, he tossed the bomb at it. A crossbow bolt, fired by a skilled or very lucky marksman, hit him in the armpit as he launched the bomb, burying itself a good eight inches into his flesh.

"Fucker!" Victor roared, and then the bomb went off. If his wits hadn't been blown from his mind, he might have reflected that he should have considered the word "bomb" more literally. The billiard-ball-sized orb didn't explode like a grenade but more like a pile of dynamite. A white flash blinded Victor, a roar like a collapsing mountain deafened him, and a shockwave like a tsunami slapped him back to crash into the stone totem opposite the one he'd thrown the bomb at.

He smashed into the column of solid rock, carried by the wave of fire and pressure from the bomb. The forces ground him against the stone until the formation burst, and he was blown through. Blinded, deafened, stunned, and flopping brokenly, Victor tumbled head over heels into one of his attackers, knocking him aside like a bowling pin. If he hadn't been knocked senseless, he would have cried out at his broken, twisted limbs. He would have gasped in pain, struggling for air as his ribs collapsed.

All he knew, though, was silence, darkness, and a vague sense of movement as he bounced and slid over the stone. Later, he'd reflect on whether he was unconscious or simply deprived of senses by the blast. Had the damage to his body been so severe that it overwhelmed his nerves? Whatever the cause of his initial numbness, it soon faded. His nerves began to wake up, and agony washed over him like a hot blanket. He still couldn't see or hear, but he could feel the strange, grating pain of his bones slowly, inexorably shifting, straightening, and knitting back together. His Behemoth's Regeneration wouldn't let him lie broken for long.

Victor couldn't see it, but the effects of the bomb and his body shattering the formation were farther reaching than he knew. When the orb exploded, it sent a tremendous wave of fiery Energy out that gathered against the invisible barrier of the formation. It took nearly a full second for the first totem to fracture and for Victor to smash through the other. In that second, enormous forces gathered against the barrier, and when it failed, they washed outward in a tidal wave of fire.

His ears began to heal, and the silence gave way to ringing. Then the ringing faded, and he heard the moans, woeful screams, and angry shouts of the others. Despite his own agony, Victor felt a smile tugging at his lips. He was lying in a crumpled ball, a pile of stone blocks covering much of his body—a broken stone wall he'd crashed through. He still couldn't see, but he heard more and more as each second ticked by.

"The fool killed himself," the deep, hoarse voice said.

"*Himself*? Look at Forkan! He nearly killed us all," panted a woman, her voice strained with pain.

"Check him!" the man who'd first spoken, the one with the orb of light, shouted. He sounded distant; had he been knocked farther in the other direction from the blast? Victor almost laughed but managed to keep his thoughts inside his head—*Pendejo! That crazy old bruja gave you a bomb, and you set it off inside the trap!* The thought was quickly followed by another: Had she tried to kill him? Didn't she say to throw it right away?

He felt a new pang of agony as a huge stone was shifted off his leg. They were uncovering him, and his body had yet to heal. He could feel his bones knitting with agonizing slowness, and Victor decided he'd had enough. He turned his gaze inward to his pulsing, Energy-filled Core and tugged out a rope of thick Energy, channeling it into the pattern for Iron Berserk. His body exploded with increased mass, his bones straightening with audible *pops* and *cracks* as they grew. Victor choked out a sound that was half roar, half scream as his muscles expanded, and he lurched to his feet, shrugging off the tons of stone.

"He lives!" the hoarse voice cried.

Victor felt the fiery warmth of rage in his eyes, and his vision rapidly returned to him as they healed. Darkness was replaced by smoke and the crimson haze of his fury. He began to hear more clearly—the crackling of flames, the clink of tumbling stones, muttered curses, sobs, and angry shouts. He laughed as he flexed his mended muscles, his torn flesh rapidly smoothing over. He'd come up from the broken pile of stone hunched, leaning over, still in pain, but when he straightened, stiffly at first, then more smoothly, he realized he still clutched Lifedrinker—it would take a lot more than a bomb and some shattered bones to knock her from his grasp.

The giant bull-headed man with the shield didn't waste time. He immediately charged Victor, but he wasn't a giant any longer. To Victor, he might as well have been a child. He grabbed the Minotaur's—he figured that was as good a name as any—shield, jerked it aside, and hacked Lifedrinker down, cutting halfway through his muscle-bound, fur-covered neck. Victor's laughter intensified as hot blood sprayed his face.

He threw the dying man aside and scanned the blasted landscape through crimson-tinted eyes. He saw one charred corpse and another half-burned woman rolling and moaning in agony. He saw two men lying stunned and another loading a massive bow with an equally enormous arrow. He saw the cocky speaker, the one who'd called him a boot licker, and Victor zeroed in on him.

He held out his left hand and sent Energy into it. An angry orange-and-red coil of magma unwound from his gauntlet, and Victor snapped it back and forward with a terrible *crack*, wrapping it around the archer's neck. At the same time, he cast Energy Charge, targeting the first man—the speaker. As he streaked forward in a cloud of howling, shrieking, purple-black shadows, his whip pulled on the poor archer's neck ferociously, burning deep through his flesh to his spine and then ripping his head clean off. Meanwhile, he slammed into the criminals' spokesperson, with Lifedrinker leading the charge.

The man wasn't weak; Victor would give him that much. He wasn't weak, but he wasn't a match for an enraged titan. Victor's Energy exploded out of his Core, tore through his pathways, and surged around him, protecting him from the impact. The man, too, managed to raise a shield of shimmering purple Energy that matched him . . . for a moment. Victor's Energy kept coming, but the shield cracked and shattered, and the prisoner flew back to crumple wetly against a broken stone wall.

Victor whirled, a mad grin on his face, his teeth white but washed in blood, his eyes ablaze with fiery rage. "Well? Who's next?"

28

LAY OF THE LAND

Victor sat on a large stone block and, groaning and cursing, worked to dig the crossbow bolt out of his armpit. A dozen bloody, broken bolts and arrows already lay at his feet. He'd finally run out of enemies to kill—they'd kept coming in twos and threes out of the ruins, seeking to capitalize on his "weakness" after he'd killed the original crew of ambushers. Those latecomers had soon learned the folly of their ways. Victor chuckled at the thought, glancing around the clearing at the many corpses and pieces of corpses. A few had escaped sans a limb or two.

One thing bothered him: The System had yet to send him any Energy, and he'd been done fighting for nearly five minutes. Did that mean other attackers still lurked nearby? As the bolt finally slid free, following the widened channel he'd made with his knife, Victor grunted in relief, dropping the bloody shaft. He stood and shouted, "If anyone else is waiting for a fight, let's get this shit done. If not, then get the hell out of here!" His Iron Berserk had worn off, but his voice still boomed from his giant-sized chest.

He heard some scrabbling, some sliding stones, and rapid footfalls, but nobody showed themselves, and the noises grew more and more distant. Had he just frightened off some would-be attackers? He looked around at the corpses. Some were large—giant-sized as he'd come to consider his usual form—whereas others were more human in proportion. None had been close to his titan form. None had been much of a challenge for him, either, not once he'd gotten out of the formation trap.

He supposed it wasn't quite a fair comparison; these people had been stripped of everything before being sent into the prison. None had much in the way of armor or magical items, and few had any weapons that were worth mentioning. He wondered about that—hadn't they slain a few fully geared iron rankers ahead of his arrival? He remembered the loudmouth saying something about giving his armor to someone named Ronkerz. Was there a hierarchy in the prison dungeon? Was there a caste system for divvying out loot gained from the monsters that spawned within? If so, these folks hadn't been high on the pecking order.

Victor was approaching the "Minotaur" to look at his gear when he noticed rainbow-hued Energy beginning to coalesce around the body. He grinned, looking around to see a similar glow around the other bodies in the clearing. "Here we go," he said, eagerly twisting his hands on Lifedrinker's haft. A few moments later, an enormous surge of Energy hit him. The influx instantly healed his puncture wound, mending deep tissues that were slower to regenerate than simple flesh. More than that, it filled him to bursting, knocking him senseless as his mind drifted into the ether.

Almost immediately, he felt a familiar presence. It was Golgothaz, the Master of the Axe, who'd put his mark on Victor's chest. He came near, and Victor felt his approval, though the master said nothing. When Victor tried to speak, he found no voice in his throat. Soon, the weighty presence faded, and Victor's vision returned to normal. Once again, he stood in the blasted ruins of the death-attuned dungeon, the glowering gray moon high overhead. A System message marred his vision, and he read it quickly.

*****Congratulations! You have achieved Level 66 Herald of the Mountain's Wrath and gained 12 strength, 17 vitality, and 12 will.*****

"Good," he grunted, slowly turning, ensuring no one was sneaking up, ready to take advantage of his distraction. The ruins were quiet, though, so he turned back to the Minotaur corpse. His spiked mace seemed to be rough black iron, and his shield wasn't anything much better. Victor stooped and turned the corpse over, hoping that he'd find something worth looting on the inmate's corpse; after all, he'd come into this dungeon hoping the denizens had managed to pry some treasures from the deeper, more powerful monsters. The man's clothes were ragged, stinking leather.

Victor stood. "Shit," he growled. Not only were the inmates devoid of decent gear, but he'd expected to gain more than one level. He'd killed close to twenty attackers, and though they hadn't felt particularly strong, they were "iron rankers." Surely some of them were higher level than he was. If not, how had they managed to kill five strong individuals before him? Was it just due to the trap?

One thought tickled the back of his mind, and examining it, he saw that he'd been ready to compare his gains from this battle against those awarded by the System in the challenge dungeon. The situations were too different, he decided. The System's awarded Energy in the Vault of Valor had been a portion of that taken from high-ranking, living cultivators—enough to account for ten levels. Looking around at the broken bodies of his foes, he began to understand just how little the System typically granted for slaying someone.

Victor spat, rubbing his hands together irritably. He'd touched something damp on the Minotaur's fur, and when he looked at the smear, he saw that his hands were covered in ash and blood. He dug a water bottle from one of his containers, poured some over his palm, then rubbed his hands together before drying them on a self-cleaning towel—he had half a dozen in one of his rings.

He scanned the quiet ruins, wishing he'd marked the time when he'd arrived. He looked at his watch for the second time since the fighting ended and saw he'd wasted another twelve minutes. "Twelve minutes and what? Five minutes of fighting . . . Nah, longer than that with all those guys slinking in after the first group. So maybe twenty-something minutes so far? Gotta hold for forty more?"

"Who you talking to, mister?" a youthful voice asked behind him. Victor whirled to see a lean, impish young man sitting atop a nearby broken wall, his bare feet kicking up and down as he stared. He had empty hands and wore nothing but brown sackcloth pants and a rough-spun green shirt. Victor relaxed his stance and lowered Lifedrinker. The kid had a pleasant face, smudged with grime as it was. Under a mop of sandy-brown hair, he had wide green eyes, a sharp narrow nose, and a pleasant smile.

"Myself," he grunted.

"Oh! I do that, too. Not many friendly folks to talk to around here, but the Enclave's better."

"Enclave?" Victor frowned at the kid. "Aren't you a little young to be in a prison like this?"

The young man smiled and shrugged. Even atop the wall, he had to look up to meet Victor's gaze. "Well, it's not a prison to me. I was born here."

"Seriously?" Victor shifted Lifedrinker onto his shoulder, holding on to her haft with one hand. He supposed he should have gotten more details about the place from Dar or the council. How many iron rankers had they sent in there over the years? How big was it? If a man and woman managed to survive inside the "prison" for a while and one thing led to another, he supposed it wasn't so far-fetched to think some kids might be born. In a dungeon, though? Who would want to raise a family in a death-attuned dungeon? "Are there many kids here?"

"I'm not a kid, sir! I'm not strong enough to fight the spawns, but I know how to get around 'em. I'm allowed out of the Enclave, unlike the children. To answer your question, there are lots of 'em." He held up his hands and started turning his fingers down one by one as his face twisted in concentration. "Seventeen in the Enclave, and I don't know how many in Rumble Town."

"Rumble Town?"

He nodded eagerly. "Yeah, where Ronkerz rules."

"There's a *town* here? How big is this place?"

"*Big!*" The kid laughed. "It keeps growing, too. A gap opened in the southern range last year, and my own father found a new valley!"

Victor scratched his head and turned in a slow circle, surveying the carnage he'd wrought. "You know these guys?"

"*Me*? No sir! Those are Ronkerz's people. They attack anyone from the Enclave who comes this far north; that's why I was hiding." He rubbed his chin, adding a new spot of soot. "Well, they'd probably capture me 'cause I'm young and only Tier Two. My da' says they'd put me to work in the mine till I was tough enough to fight the spawns."

"Tier Two, huh?" The conversation had taken on a surreal feel to Victor. He was struggling to believe he was chatting with a random kid in the middle of a dungeon after fighting off nearly twenty criminal inmates. "You know a guy named Rasso Hine?"

"Um . . ." The boy—Victor couldn't help thinking of him as such—continued to fidget, kicking his feet up and down, while he contemplated. "I think it sounds familiar, but there's a lot of folks at the Enclave. My da' knows all their names."

"How many people are in this place, kid?"

"I dunno. Hundreds? Maybe more! I've never been to Rumble Town or Vasso Cavern. My dad's gonna be mad I came up this way, but he'll be happy to hear you thrashed a bunch of Rumblers."

"You should be more careful." Victor sighed. "You saw me kill all these people, and you still thought it would be smart to talk to me?"

"They're bad folks. I heard you try to talk to 'em." He lifted his too-large shirt, pulled a crude water skin from his belt, and held it over his mouth, wringing it tight in his fists to get a few drops to fall onto his tongue. "Wish I knew where safe water was around here."

Victor tossed him the bottle he'd used to wash his hands. "Here. I've got plenty." It was true. He had cases of water bottles and a dozen kegs of weak wine. He had juices, liquor, beer, and mead. He'd go for years before running out of fluids, not to mention his body didn't really need to drink much at all—a perk of advancing his bloodline into the epic tier and having a body steeped in Energy.

"You've got one of them, uh, di-dimension bag things?" the boy asked as he wriggled the cork from the glass.

"Dimensional container, yeah. Some people call them spatial containers. I think it depends on where you're from." Victor glanced back to the charred stone dais upon which he'd arrived. "Listen, I've got some friends coming in the next hour or two. When they get here, you wanna earn a few beads or food or whatever? You can guide us to the Enclave."

"That would be great, but you'll have to pass by the Gate Warden before they let you into the Enclave. He'll probably just ask you some questions; Duke Brosia will be happy to have a real fighter join us!"

"Duke Brosia?" Victor chuckled and shook his head. "Never mind. What's your name, anyway, kid?"

"Tyn." He hopped off the wall and approached Victor. He couldn't have been more than five and a half feet tall, and Victor doubted he weighed a hundred pounds. Still, he moved with vibrancy and stuck his hand out proudly for Victor to shake. Victor nodded and squeezed the slender appendage. "My first companion should be here pretty soon. You think Ronkerz is going to send more people to attack me?"

"Probably, but the ones who ran will have to get back to him first. It's a good stretch of ground between here and Rumble Town, with lots of spawns in the way. It'll probably take half a day for any of his Big Ones to come out here."

Victor sighed, scratching his hair at yet another new term. "And they are?"

"Big Ones? They're his . . . well, they're his head smashers, his bone breakers, his troublemakers. They're the ones who keep other folks from coming into his territory. My da' says one of 'em killed a whole party of folks from the Enclave 'cause they were farming a spawn in a valley that Ronkerz claimed. That happened when I was six, which was eight *years* ago. We ain't had any big fights with 'em since, seeing as Duke Brosia put strict rules on where the Enclavers can wander—south."

Victor snorted, shuffling over to the flat stone where he'd been sitting earlier. He kicked aside the arrows and bolts he'd pulled out of himself and sat down. "But you're here, and this is north of the Enclave, yeah?"

"Well, I'm not supposed to be here, but I can hide and sneak better than most. I got my Tier Two class a while back and, along with it, a pretty good skill. Even so, my da' will get mad if he knows I came this far, so can you tell him you met me closer to the Enclave?"

Victor grunted, pulling some dried smoked meat out of his ring. "I barely know you, kid. Don't ask me to lie for you."

Tyn moved closer, squatting to sit on a smaller stone near Victor's seat. "Well, can you at least not mention it?"

Victor shrugged. "I won't bring it up." Sitting there, amid the carnage of his earlier battle, he reflected on how it wasn't such a healthy place for a youngster to hang out, so he gathered a thread of Energy and shaped it into Honor the Spirits. The spell flickered out of his outstretched hand, a tendril of wispy, flickering white flames that jumped from corpse to corpse, flaring brightly as it touched each one. The bodies burned away, reduced to ethereal smoke that vanished, transitioning away from the material plane and into the realm of spirits.

Victor must have been frowning as he sat, watching the corpses disappear, because the boy asked, "Are you angry?"

"Hmm?" Victor shifted to look at the kid. He ripped the hunk of dried meat in half and offered it to him. "Nah, just thinking about how I didn't put on much of a show for my ancestors. These guys weren't worthy enemies. The only thing they had going for them was the trap they'd set up."

Tyn took the meat and immediately stuffed it into his mouth, biting off a large hunk. The work of chewing the dense, dry meat kept him quiet for a while, and Victor brooded some more. He didn't like the idea that kids were being born and raised inside of a prison dungeon. The whole thing was a stark contrast to the elegance and beauty of Sojourn. The city seemed so evolved and advanced, yet this prison was disgusting on many levels. Victor could understand banishing iron rankers who caused trouble or committed heinous crimes, but something about this situation didn't sit right with him.

Sending hundreds or thousands of criminals into the same free-for-all wasn't justice—there was no way every prisoner was equal in terms of raw strength, so that meant the stronger ones were going to have more power inside. They would suffer less than the ones who couldn't stand up for themselves. Did they all deserve a fate like that? Even if you could argue that they did, Victor would be damned if he'd hear anyone say the children born inside deserved that fate. Tyn looked like he was starved half to death, which was bad enough, but the kid clearly didn't have much going for him, even if he could get enough to eat.

"You said there are a lot of kids in the Enclave?"

"Oh, sure! Like I said, I'm a man, but I've got a younger sister, and she's got many classmates at the school."

"There's a school?"

"Yessir. Lady Breeze runs it."

"Lady Breeze?"

"The most beautiful woman in the world, sir." Tyn grinned while he stuffed another wad of dried meat into his mouth. "You should meet her, but be warned: I'm going to marry her!"

"Oh yeah?" Victor chuckled as he leaned back, watching the stone circle, waiting for the portal while listening for any signs of approaching inmates. Tyn grew quiet as he ate and drank, and Victor lost himself in half-baked plans to help the children in this weird pocket-world. He had no idea what he could do; he had the ability to rescue precisely one other person. He supposed he could argue their case with the council when he got out, but beyond that, he felt his hands were tied.

His frustrated musings were interrupted by the flare of blue light and the weird wailing sounds of the portal, and then Arona appeared, stepping out of the swirling blue disc of Energy. She whirled, her polished bone staff held out defensively, and when she saw Victor sitting on the stone watching her, she relaxed and stepped closer as the portal snapped shut with an audible *pop*. "You did it," she said by way of greeting.

"Yeah. Almost killed myself with that old lady's bomb, but it broke the formation."

"Old lady . . . Kreshta Griss? She gave you a 'bomb'?" She looked around at the blasted area around the dais. "You set it off inside the formation with you?" Her raspy voice was incredulous as she shook her head. Victor simply nodded with a half smile. "Who's this, then?" She looked at Tyn with a raised eyebrow.

"I'm Tyn, milady!" He hopped up and bowed sloppily, dragging both hands through the dusty gravel near his feet.

Victor stood and gestured at the kid. "I guess the inmates are building towns and having families. Tyn's going to show us to one of the towns, and hopefully Rasso will be there. If not, maybe someone will know where to look."

"Children . . ." Arona looked Tyn up and down, her slender fingers tapping the polished bone of her staff. "How interesting." She turned in a slow circle, her brows creasing as she observed the strange world with its black sky and oddly close moon. "The death-attuned Energy is strange here—too thin. I wonder if perhaps the many cultivators are causing a shift in the ambient Energy. The dungeon was created with death-attuned Energy, but that was thousands of years ago, and they've sent many cultivators into it since."

"How many?" Victor asked. "The kid doesn't know."

"They've been sending a few dozen a year into this place since it was opened. I always assumed that most criminals banished here would have short, violent lives dealing with the dungeon's denizens—it's supposedly Tier Nine. If they're cooperating and having children, though . . ." Again, she trailed off, probably, like Victor, trying to imagine growing up *inside* a dungeon.

"They don't all cooperate. I had to kill a dozen or so people who were lurking outside the trap. They mentioned a guy named Ronkerz, and Tyn says he runs a town called . . ." Victor looked at the boy. "What's it called, again?"

"Rumble Town, sir."

"Ronkerz Gatebreaker is a legendary figure in Sojourn," Arona rasped, and Victor felt a small surge of cold Energy waft off her staff as she gripped it and looked around nervously. "He led an insurrection, trying to overthrow the council two thousand years ago. He breached the Spire and killed four council guardians—all steel seekers. The story goes that Ronkerz was only Tier Eight!"

"Great," Victor said, shifting Lifedrinker on his shoulder and turning to look out over the dead landscape. "And he's had two thousand years to get stronger."

"Closer to three hundred—remember the time dilation." Arona pulled a handful of tiny bones from her robe and scattered them around her feet. "We should get moving. I'd rather not run into him."

Victor nodded, distracted, thinking about Ronkerz. The story of an iron ranker killing some guards in their "test of steel" was acutely interesting to him, considering Dar's expectations for him when he went to Ruhn to help his granddaughter. In all honesty, Victor felt a wave of relief hearing about Ronkerz's exploits—if he could do it, then it was possible. Maybe Dar's confidence in him wasn't so unusual. When he saw Arona's five bone guardians spring up from the stony soil, it brought him back to reality, and he gestured to the stone dais. "We gotta wait for Arcus."

"Do we?" Arona rasped. "You know he can't be trusted. Wouldn't it be wiser to leave him to his own devices?"

Victor chuckled and poked one of the weird blue-fire-eyed skeletons with Lifedrinker's blunt axe-head. It stumbled back in a clatter and hissed at him like an angry cat. "Arona, no offense, but I hardly know you. We've had a few good conversations, and I'll hand it to you: You were honest when you spoke at the inquest. I appreciate that, but I think I'll wait for Arcus so I can keep you *both* where I can see you."

29

A SLIGHT DETOUR

Arona wasn't exactly what Victor would consider a socially adept person, but after he'd basically told her he didn't trust her, she became decidedly standoffish. She brooded by herself on the northern edge of the clearing with her five skeletal servants standing watch in a wide circle while Victor and Tyn continued to chat, sitting on flat stones and snacking while they waited for Arcus. Victor checked his watch regularly, and after some time had passed, he called out, "Just a few more minutes," hoping to get Arona to perk up a little. She ignored him, staring into the ruins, leaning on her ivory staff.

"Is she angry with you?" Tyn whispered.

"She's a Death Caster, kid. Who knows?" Victor chuckled and handed him a slice of buttered pumpkin bread. At some point, he'd decided to do what he could to put some meat on Tyn's bones. He watched him wolf the treat down, enjoying the expression of bliss on the youngster's face.

After he swallowed a huge mouthful, Tyn cleared his throat and jerked his thumb at his chest. "I'm not a kid."

Victor nodded solemnly. "Right." He couldn't stop glancing at Arona's pale, glowering face as she stared into the dark sky. After another couple of minutes, he sighed, standing. "Wait here." He gave Tyn's shoulder a friendly slap, careful not to knock him over, and walked over to the Death Caster. "Hey, was I too blunt earlier?"

She snorted and turned slightly, making it hard to see into her eyes. "About not trusting me?"

"Do I know you, Arona? I mean, really? Give me a chance to—"

"Please put the matter out of your mind, Victor. It's fine." She still wouldn't look at him, and Victor could hear her bone guardians clattering as they moved. Were they agitated? Could they sense their master's mood? Staring at the side of her face, seeing the partial scowl and hearing the stiffness in her voice, Victor recognized a kindred outcast. He'd been in her shoes a hundred times with his cousins and their friends. He knew what it was like to act unbothered when something was eating at him. He'd gotten over it with friends from school, and obviously his friends in this new life, but those memories still stung.

He reached into his Core and pulled out a thread of inspiration, casting Globe of Insight. It had a more subtle effect than Inspiration of the Quinametzin, but he could explain it by saying, "This dim landscape is getting to me."

Arona glanced up at the glowing ball of white-gold Energy, and he saw some of the creases around her eyes fade as her glowering countenance relaxed. "A pleasant glow."

Victor nodded, watching her, and then, as he'd hoped, some inspiration struck him. "Hey, you're worried I won't ever trust you, huh? You're thinking about those friends of yours you abandoned in the challenge dungeon."

"I didn't—" She cut her protest short, clenching her fist around her staff until her pale fingers turned white. After a moment, with Victor staring at her the whole time, she sighed and seemed to collapse inward. "I did. I left them to fight you so that I could win the competition. My *master* was *proud*." She practically spat the last sentence.

"Well, I'm not thinking about that. I just, well, I've got a bad history with Death Casters. I guess that's a kind of prejudice, but I can't help being wary."

She turned to face him, her dark eyes wide and earnest. "You *should* be wary. Death-attuned Energy wears on a person's spirit. It eats away at qualities people generally view as virtuous—honesty, kindness, honor, empathy. I'm Tier Nine, Victor, but I'm young—a prodigy, some say. I haven't lived with this *cursed* Energy for centuries like most at my level. I tell you this with an open heart; do not trust a Death Caster, *especially* my master!"

Victor's mouth hung open in surprise. He'd expected her to deny being bothered or to shrug off his concerns and tell him she was different. He certainly hadn't expected that emotional outburst. He cleared his throat and tried to think of the proper response, but she was already turning, already stomping away, and he decided to give her some space. He shifted to look away, staring into the distant ruins as he contemplated. Softly, he whispered, "Shit, *chica*, I guess I hit a nerve."

Lifedrinker vibrated against his shoulder, and he knew exactly what she was thinking: It didn't matter to her what kind of Energy his enemies used—she was ready to fight. He was saved from further introspection when the portal howled to life in a flare of bright blue Energy. Seconds later, Arcus walked through in his bright red robes, a two-foot metallic rod in each of his hands. One was red and radiated heat. The other was dark iron and seemed to absorb the light around it.

"Well done, Victor! The council is pleased." Before Victor could respond, Arcus whirled to face Tyn and lifted his red rod. It began to glow with white-hot flames, and Victor realized he was about to blast the kid.

"Chill out!" he roared. "That's my friend!"

Arcus looked at him with a cocked eyebrow, his eyes ablaze. When Victor returned his gaze, glowering, the Pyromancer shrugged and lowered his rod. "Who's this, then?"

"I'm Tyn, sir!" The kid jumped up and surprised Victor by approaching Arcus with an outstretched hand. Victor stared, trying to decide if Tyn was too stupid to understand the danger he'd been in or if he was just so used to being in danger that it hadn't registered.

Victor cleared his throat. "Arcus, did you know people were having kids in here? Did you know there are *towns* in this dungeon?"

Arcus stared down his long straight nose at Tyn, then, surprising Victor, took his hand. He shook his head slowly. "I had no idea. How strange! You were born here, young man?"

"Yes, sir." He nodded eagerly, the unruly mop of hair atop his head bobbing back and forth.

"Come," Arona said, and her skeletons emerged from the nearby ruins, *click-clacking* over the stony ground as they took up positions around the four living beings. "We should get moving before Ronkerz sends another group of attackers."

"Ronkerz? He's still alive?" Arcus waved his red rod in the air, and Victor felt a surge of Energy. A flash of flames and sparks erupted above Arcus's head, and then a fiery bird appeared, shrieked, and flapped its wings, flying high into the dark sky. Victor watched as the magical creature continued to rise and then leveled off, gliding in a wide circle around them. "I'll be able to keep an eye out with my flame kestrel."

"Come on," Victor said, following Arona and her bony guardians. "I'll fill you in while we walk. Lead the way, Tyn."

They hiked through the ruins for a while, moving ever "south." At first, Victor wasn't sure how Tyn could determine their direction, but when he asked, Tyn pointed to the moon. In all the time Victor had been there, he hadn't noticed it moving, but he could see how it hung in a particular half of the sky. If that was constant, he supposed it would be easy enough to mark direction using it as a guide.

As they walked, he filled Arcus in on the situation in the dungeon and was surprised to find the fire mage ready to agree with him about the abhorrent nature of the place. "That's not right!" he shouted after Victor told him about the schoolchildren in the Enclave.

"Do you think all the consuls and old masters know about this?" Victor asked, only to receive a derisive snort from Arona. He scowled at her. "Stupid question?"

It was Arcus who answered, "I'm sure they do. There's a reason they're called 'old masters' in Sojourn, you know. Not one of them is less than a thousand years old. I'm sure the tribulations of some wretches born of criminals in one of their dungeons don't precisely *impact* their day-to-day plans."

"Your tongue is awfully free when you know Lord Roil can't hear you," Arona rasped, and Victor thought he caught her trying to send him a look. What the look meant, he couldn't say.

"Ah yes, I forgot I'm with the ever-worshipful Arona Moonshadow. I'm sorry if I cast any unintended aspersion your master's way." Arcus mock-bowed, and Arona quickened her pace, moving ahead.

Victor was about to change the subject when Arcus held up a hand and shouted, "Stop!" Everyone froze, and he said, "A palpable fog roils this way from the east. I see figures within."

"Death wind!" Tyn cried. He broke into a run, heading the way they'd been going but at an angle, toward the west. Arona waved her staff, and one of her bone constructs leaped after the boy, quickly catching him and wrapping its bony arms around him. They tumbled to the ground, and Tyn cried, "Let me go! We'll die!"

"We'll not." Arona's voice was firm as she turned to the east and asked, "How far, Arcus?"

"Half a minute." Arcus sounded almost bored.

Victor looked at the sky where Arcus's fiery bird still circled, then he cast Banner of the Champion, and the world was instantly bathed in the golden, fiery light of his bloody sun.

"Old gods!" Arcus whooped. "Let's hope this 'death wind' brings us a challenge!" Suddenly, he was wreathed in fire, a man-shaped torch with a blazing, fiery brand in one hand and a shaft of pure darkness in the other.

"Quiet, oafs!" Arona hissed. "Let me dispel it lest we become embroiled in a cataclysmic battle that will draw denizens for miles." She drew a long line in the dirt with the end of her staff and then began rapidly scrawling runes along its length. By the time she finished, stepping back from her line, Victor saw a wave of mist barreling over the broken rocky hills and ruined buildings. It looked almost like a tsunami, but rather than water, it roiled with dark shadows, spirit-like wisps, flashes of ghostly light, and ever-changing glimpses of horror-filled, rictus-bound faces.

Arona slammed the butt of her staff into the ground on the near side of her rune-inscribed line, and suddenly a wall of blue shimmering Energy sprang into being, soaring for dozens of feet into the air. Victor felt a surge of Energy pour out of the Death Caster, and the barrier widened, stretching north and south for hundreds of feet. The 'death wind' slammed into the barrier, and with the wailing roar of a ghost-filled hurricane, it burst apart into blue-gray smoke that rose upward and faded into nothing.

The process wasn't instant, and the noise was such that Victor wanted to cover his ears, but he held Lifedrinker ready. He and Arcus stood shoulder to shoulder, staring at the barrier as it tore the death wind to bits, reducing it to blue-tinged steam, inch by inch. When it was over, the silence was so profound that Victor had to speak to ensure he wasn't deaf. "That was pretty damn wild! Nice one, Arona!"

"Was that a creature?" Arcus's flames dimmed as he slowly came to grips with the realization that he wouldn't have to burn anything.

"A pack of unquiet spirits, bound together by the thin nature of the veil in this place. I've never seen one that large." Arona slumped against her staff, and Victor could see the circles under her eyes had grown. She looked exhausted.

"You," Tyn said, kicking his legs and scrabbling away from the skeleton as it released him. "You destroyed it! I've never seen that! Even da' has to hide from those winds." He rushed toward Arona, and at first, Victor thought he was going to hug her, but he ran past her, leaping her runic line in the dirt. He rushed to and fro, scanning the ground. "Lady Breeze says they can drop Energy orbs!"

Arona twitched her staff, and her five guardians clattered into the area where the wave of spirits had been, flipping over rocks, running up and down the hillsides, and clambering over and through the ruins. Her raspy voice was even more ragged than usual as she said, "If so, my servants will find it."

Victor stepped over to her, and though she tried to avoid his gaze, he persisted until she looked at him. "You okay? That was bigger than you thought it would be, huh?"

"I need rest or, if the boy is right, an Energy orb."

"Why doesn't the System simply award Energy for slaying the thing?" Arcus asked, moving closer.

Arona sighed, shaking her head. "It's not exactly a monster. More a force of nature common to death-attuned environs."

"Would fire have an effect?" Arcus held up his red rod, still ticking with heat.

"Perhaps." She squeezed her eyes closed for a second, then inclined her head to Arcus. "Well, yes, I'm sure it would. If we meet another and I cannot handle it, I'll call for your flames."

Victor was feeling particularly useless, wondering how he'd handle a "death wind." Would Lifedrinker have any effect? He supposed if worse came to worst, he'd go berserk and breathe magma into it. He was about to say as much when Tyn cried, "Here! Here! Great Lady!"

They all looked to see that the boy had scrambled atop a high wall and was standing, pointing at his feet where a lustrous glow illuminated his rough brown pants. "You found one?" Arona perked up when she saw the light and gestured with her staff. One of her skeletons, humanoid like the others but with extra-long arms ending in hooked claws, bounded over and pulled itself atop the wall, nearly knocking the boy off. "Careful, fool thing!" Arona growled. "Sorry, Tyn. Don't fall!"

Arona's skeletal helper lifted out a brightly glowing object and dropped down in a clatter of bones. As Tyn more carefully descended, the skeleton loped over to Arona, holding an orb of swirling rainbow Energy cradled between two long claws. Arcus stepped forward and said, "Transferable? Usually, they're consumed on touch!"

Arona smiled, her canines brightly reflecting the light from the orb. "This isn't a System award. It's . . . I suppose it's a type of natural treasure."

Victor didn't want to look like an idiot, so he didn't speak up. He was fairly sure he knew what the orb was. He'd gotten one in a chest from the dungeon when he'd escaped the Greatbone Mine. The one he'd received had glowed with golden Energy, and when he'd touched it, it gave him a level. To clarify without sounding too ignorant, he asked, "Will it give a full level?"

"I think so," Arona said, making him feel a little better—they didn't know for sure, either. "This would sell for a handsome price to someone of our tier." Victor could see she spoke mainly to Arcus but included him in the glance she threw their way.

Arcus was clearly struggling with his words, trying to think of a reason why he should be able to claim the orb or at least a partial stake. Victor decided to earn some points with the Death Caster and spoke his feelings plainly: "You did all the work. Keep it."

Arcus sputtered, "She only did all the work because she told us to stand down! I could have summoned an inferno upon that *death wind*." He spat the name derisively.

"Well, you didn't." Victor shrugged. "Don't worry; I'm sure we'll have plenty of opportunities to earn our own prizes."

"So unconcerned, hmm? So easy for you to be the generous one—you, who didn't lose any *cursed* Energy to the System's greedy clutches." Arcus's smooth veneer had cracked, and Victor was only slightly surprised at how quickly it had occurred.

"You want this so badly?" Arona rasped, gesturing at the orb still in her skeletal pawn's clutches.

"Of *course*! Don't act like you aren't thrilled. That, there, represents a year's hard labor for you or me at our tier!"

"Seriously?" Victor raised an eyebrow, looking from Arcus to Arona. "A year for a level?"

"You're not—" Arona started to say, but Arcus spoke over her.

"That's right! When you're Tier Nine, you'll see. Things come *slowly*!"

"Probably depends on what you do, yeah? Didn't you gain any levels in the challenge dungeon, Arona?"

She nodded. "I did—one."

Again, Victor shrugged. "Well, there you go."

"Listen to this rube! Victor, just because you stumbled ass-first into a challenge dungeon doesn't mean the competition runs all the time. There's great risk involved. Take me—rather than gaining a level, I lost *ten*!" He practically screamed the last word, and Victor saw flames dancing in his eyes. He was well and truly losing his grip on the relaxed, friendly façade he'd been putting forth.

Victor sighed and glanced down at Tyn, watching the back and forth with wide eyes. "How far to the Enclave, Tyn?"

"Maybe an hour if we're careful and avoid the spawns."

"Forget that." Victor grinned at the kid and ruffled his mop of sandy-brown hair. "Lead me through all the spawns; let's kill some shit on the way, and maybe Arcus can find a treasure." He snorted, turned his back on the casters, and stomped southward.

"Victor," Arona called, her voice hoarse as she raised it. "What of the orb?"

He waved dismissively with his free hand. "Do what you want." He only took a dozen steps before Tyn jogged past him, angling for a row of low hills with scraggly, dead-looking trees on their slopes.

"Victor, sir!" he panted, turning to walk backward while he spoke. "There's a lich-wyrm in those hills. We all give it a wide berth when we hunt and scavenge. I bet you could find a trinket or two in its lair!"

Victor laughed and turned to look back at Arona and Arcus. They were walking behind him, though separated by a good ten feet. Arona's skeletons were ranging out, establishing their usual marching perimeter. He couldn't see the orb, but he could tell by Arcus's scowl that Arona had kept it. "Did you hear that, Arcus?"

The Pyromancer quickened his steps, and though his eyes still burned with angry fire, he spoke almost pleasantly when he caught up. "What's that? The boy said something of note?"

Victor nodded. "There's a lich-wyrm ahead. I don't know exactly what that is, but I know what a wyrm is and what a lich is. Sounds like it might be a decent challenge. Sounds like it might drop a treasure or two. What do you say? Shall we make a slight detour?"

30

LICH-WYRM

Victor looked up the scree-covered slope to the dark cave entrance. It opened into the side of the hill, some hundred yards from where he and the others stood. He and the others were watching one of Arona's skeletons, the one with the long hook-clawed arms, scrabble upward. They stood in a narrow valley between two rows of low hills. The environment was largely barren, with only stunted trees here and there, devoid of leaves.

While they stared, hardly moving, Victor looked at Tyn, who stood on his toes, clearly ready to run for his hiding spot. They'd found him a place around the hillside near a pile of boulders where he could watch whatever battle unfolded from relative safety. "Hey, what the hell do you all eat around here? Does anything grow?"

Arona looked at him and shushed, but Tyn whispered, "Gardens, sir! There are folks who can treat the soil with earth magic and—"

"Hush!" Arona said, clapping a slender pale hand over Tyn's soot-stained face. "Grasper sees something."

"Grasper?" Victor whispered.

"My minion." Arona gestured toward the bony creature who'd, at that moment, begun crawling into the cave opening.

Victor frowned, watching the skeleton slink into the darkness. He contemplated calling forth his coyotes and sending them up to get a look, but it seemed Arona had much clearer communication with her minions. She claimed to see through their eyes. He glanced at Arcus, whose fiery bird still circled a thousand feet in the air, and began to wonder if he shouldn't try to add a new totem to his repertoire. He couldn't help thinking a flying one would be nice—either as a scout like Arcus's bird or a mount like the creature he'd seen Ranish Dar riding.

His mind wandered down paths of elder magic and his last experience on the spirit plane when he'd claimed Guapo. Should he tell Dar about those strange, powerful beings who'd visited him? How would they match up to Dar in power?

Could his new mentor protect him from those two who'd seemed intent on finding him again once he'd 'ripened'? It was hard to say because they'd only given him a glimpse of their power, and he'd changed a lot since then. His musings were interrupted when the ground lurched under his feet, and a great *whump* of stale air, dust, and debris was thrown from the cave mouth.

"What the—" he started to ask but was cut off as Arona cried out.

"It comes! Grasper is no more!"

Victor held Lifedrinker in both hands and watched the cave entrance, rapidly building the pattern for Iron Berserk in his pathways. Arcus had a similar idea—Victor could feel the waves of heat radiating from him as he wreathed himself in fire and began to float above the ground. Arona had drawn forth a large black silver-rune-inscribed bone and set it on the ground at her feet. "Buy me a minute or two," she rasped to no one in particular. Victor shrugged, cast Iron Berserk, then bunched his massive legs and leaped up the hill toward the cave opening.

Lifedrinker had grown significantly as she'd evolved, but she was still more of a hatchet than a battle-axe when he gripped her in his titanic fist. He held her outstretched in one hand as he flew through the air and grinned savagely when a target for his wrath emerged from the cave. The lich-wyrm was much as he'd imagined—a great slithering creature of desiccated flesh and bone, wreathed in cold blue mist.

Victor had battled an ancient wyrm on Zaafor, so he'd been expecting something massive. This creature wasn't half the size of that great beast. How could it be with such a lair? The wyrm he'd helped to kill on Zaafor wouldn't have begun to fit in that cave opening. Still, this monster was probably a hundred feet long, with a body as wide around as a horse's belly. Its fangs were like sabers, and it moved far more quickly than Victor had expected—it had shot out of the cave and glided down the slope before his leap ended, and he crashed onto the stony ground outside the cave.

The lich-wyrm was driving toward Arona, likely angered by her minion and tracing it to the source. As a pillar of flames erupted from the ground, flipping the monster onto its side and sending it careening down the slope, Victor didn't hesitate and cast Energy Charge, fueling it with glory-attuned Energy. He streaked over the broken ground, gliding over the stones and broken trees like a comet of sparkling golden Energy. As the bony serpent fought to right itself, he crashed into its side with a violent concussion. His impact shattered bones, and misty blue Energy erupted from the point of impact as the lich-wyrm flopped over in a tumble to the base of the hill.

His spell had protected him, as usual, but it had also stopped his momentum at the point of impact. As the dust and mist cleared, he saw the serpent-shaped skeleton shift, righting itself, as its broken bones rapidly regrew, filling in the damage Victor had done. He was preparing another attack, bunching his legs to leap down the hill, when the sky darkened, and a swirling maelstrom of fire appeared over the valley. Victor paused to watch as a handful of tumbling boulders alight with flames and trailing black smoke emerged from the cloud, falling like meteors toward the monster.

Victor knew all too well how much that spell hurt. He glanced back at Arona as he waited for the flaming boulders to do their damage, unwilling to dive into the fray only to be blasted back by the concussion. Arona was standing, arms wide, sheathed in a scirocco of blue Energy as her black bone stretched and multiplied, taking the form of a gargantuan four-legged skeleton. It reminded Victor of museum exhibitions—displays of predatory dinosaurs. The thing, composed of black bones and claws, looked like a cross between a Tyrannosaurus rex and an elephant. It had four legs ending in scythe-like claws, a body fifteen feet high at the shoulders, and a head like an enormous crocodile.

The ground shook, and a roar like a series of bombs going off brought Victor's eyes back around to the destruction wrought by Arcus's spell. The lich-wyrm had been obscured by dust, smoke, and fire. Even so, he saw the blue glow of its Energy and caught glimpses of long yellowed bones moving about in the destruction—it wasn't dead. That was all he needed to know; he charged down the hill into the lingering flames and choking smoke, and when he ran up against the thrashing monster, furiously working to repair its shattered bones, he went to work with Lifedrinker.

As he fought, beams of fire lanced through the black smoke, scorching the monster, and then Victor was joined by Arona's skeletal monstrosity as it trampled down the hill and smashed into the bony wyrm, flipping it over. Victor laughed and summoned his magma lash, whipping it back and forth, wrapping it around bones, and yanking them out of the monster as the fire burned the creature's desiccated scales to ash. Lifedrinker split through bone after bone, and when she met the ancient armored hide of the monster, she tore it like paper.

Not once did the wyrm manage to land a bite with its great gnashing maw; Victor was too fast, and the thing simply had too many targets to choose from. One moment, Victor would think he had to dodge as the head snapped backward on its serpentine spine, only to have Arona's skeletal monster get in the way, shrugging off the attack with its iron-like bones. Many times, the lich-wyrm tried to summon great torrents of death-attuned Energy, only to have Arona siphon it away or Arcus break its concentration with a ball of explosive fire.

The melee was furious, but before long, Victor noted that the bones were slower to reknit and that some ribs he hacked out remained separate, inert, and no longer part of the monstrous undead being. He finished things by fighting his way up to the wyrm's thrashing head and planting Lifedrinker in the center of its skull with a thunderous *crack*. She screamed her fury and dug deep into the bone, jerking and pulling until he let go and let her do her thing. With a Titanic Leap, he launched himself up the hillside to land with an earthshaking *thud* beside Arona. As she staggered, he laughed and watched the lich-wyrm's death throes.

Arcus continued to pepper the monster with lancing beams of fire and an occasional ball of exploding flames, but it was over already, Victor could tell. Something like a hundred of the monster's rib bones were broken or missing, and the blue glow of its Energy had faded. It hardly moved as each explosion rocked it, and most damning of all was Lifedrinker's proud haft sticking up from the skull while rivulets of deep blue Energy coursed through the bone into her brightly gleaming metal.

"Your axe feeds," Arona noted.

"Yeah," he rumbled, still titan-sized. "Don't worry, she doesn't take anything from the Energy awarded by the System."

"I know. My Brutus is similar." She pointed to the tremendous black-boned monstrosity as it took bite after bite out of the wyrm's spine.

"He gets stronger?"

"Yes. He gains power from the foes we defeat together." She pointed to Arcus standing on the hillside opposite them, still firing spells into the dying monster. "Does he think to win a bigger stake in the kill? Can't he see it's over?"

Victor shrugged. "I think he just likes blowing shit up."

She rasped a soft chuckle, nodding. "In truth, I believe any one of us could have killed this monster. Isn't it odd that the boy said everyone avoids this 'spawn'? I know for a fact the council has sent many dozens of Tier Seven and higher iron rankers into this prison. Of course, many of the prisoners are lower, and of course, they're all sent in with no possessions, but I would think . . ." She trailed off, but Victor knew what she was thinking. It was strange that there weren't high-level groups of inmates regularly killing creatures like this lich.

"Speaking of prisoners and what you know of the inmates, do you think the council knows about the kids in here? Do they know generations of people have been born in this place? If they can tell that Rasso Hine is alive, can't they see these other folks in here somehow?"

Arona frowned, and her raspy voice was almost a whisper when she said, "I don't know, Victor. None but veil walkers have ever been on the council, and they don't share the secrets of their power with the rest of us. Or, if they do, they don't announce their confidants. My master certainly doesn't tell me things like that. Perhaps Roil has told Arcus more."

Victor nodded, watching as Arcus engulfed himself in flames and began to float their way. "You still think he's gonna try to screw me over?" She didn't answer him, and Victor turned away from the dying monster to regard her. Her jaw was clenched, and he could see her dark eyes drifting from one distant object to another, avoiding his gaze. He sighed, understanding what was going through her mind: Why would he care what she thought if he didn't trust her? He turned and looked up the hill to the pile of boulders where Tyn had taken cover. "Come out, Tyn."

As the kid scrambled from behind the outcropping and began sliding down the slope toward them, Arcus landed nearby. "It dies," he announced, as though they'd all been waiting for his pronouncement.

Victor chuckled and canceled his Iron Berserk, and as he resumed his natural size, he started sliding down toward the dying creature, aiming for the head, where Lifedrinker still throbbed, pulling Energy into herself. Before he'd gotten to the floor of the gully, the monster gave up its struggles, and gigantic orbs of rainbow-hued Energy began to bubble up around it, taking shape into three distinct streams. Victor stood still, waiting for his infusion, and when it hit, he was ready.

The reward was significant, and he knew it moved him well toward the next level, but still, it wasn't as much as he received from defeating the ambush at the dungeon entrance. By the time he settled back down to the ground and the waves of euphoria began to fade, he'd been joined by Tyn, who hadn't received anything from the kill. Victor looked up the hillside to see Arona and Arcus sitting on the slope, both looking dazed. "I don't think they're used to infusions that size," he said.

"That was a lot of Energy, Sir Victor." Tyn bounced over to the inert skull of the monstrous lich-wyrm and tapped on a yard-long fang. "If you reclaim your axe, could you cut me one of these fangs?"

Victor chuckled and stepped over to the kid. He grasped ahold of the fang and gave it a jerk, cracking it out of the brittle jawbone. "Here you go." Once Tyn took the mighty tooth, a look of wonder in his eyes, Victor reached up and wriggled Lifedrinker back and forth until she slipped free of the skull. "Have a good drink?" he asked, slinging her back into her harness. She didn't answer with words, but he felt a wave of satisfaction from her.

A weird grinding clatter caught his attention, and he looked toward the sound only to see Arona's bone monster collapsing into hundreds of smaller bones that rolled over the stony ground to collect in a clump. It shivered and vibrated until it had condensed into the singular black rune-covered bone from which she'd summoned the creature. "We should check out the monster's lair, sir!" Tyn cried, already struggling to climb up the steep slope. Victor nodded and stooped to pick up Arona's bone.

"Don't!" she cried, halfway down the hillside on her way, no doubt, to collect the bone herself. Victor held it up to show he meant no harm, striding toward her. It was dense and heavy like lead, and the cold that radiated from it was almost uncomfortable, but it didn't bother his Quinametzin flesh much. She snatched it quickly when he held it out to her, and then it disappeared into one of her containers.

"Isn't it conscious?"

"Of course!" she hissed, clearly flustered that he'd had her treasured item in his grasp. Victor shrugged and started climbing toward the cave. He'd asked because he still thought of dimensional containers as unsafe for conscious beings, but he wasn't surprised that Arona could afford a higher quality one that allowed for it. When he reached the opening, he found it brightly illuminated by fiery orbs and saw Arcus digging through the bones and debris strewn about.

Tyn was climbing ever deeper, scrabbling over rocks and kicking piles of small bones, and Victor decided to let him and Arcus dig around. He didn't necessarily trust any of these people, but he had a feeling the kid would cry out if they found anything. He stood in the opening and turned, folding his arms over his chest, surveying the strange, dark landscape of the pocket world. From the cave mouth, he could see quite a ways, and judging by the moon, he was facing "north."

Beyond the hills and the ruins where he'd come into the dungeon, it looked as if some dark, massive mountains climbed toward the sky in the extreme distance. He was surprised to see a faint yellow glow in the side of one of those distant peaks, and squinting against the gloom, he was reasonably sure they were either hundreds of little fires or perhaps the lights of a town. "Rumble Town, maybe," he mused.

"I think you're right," Arona rasped, startling him. Somehow, she'd approached and stood at the cave entrance with him.

Victor exhaled in irritation, reaching behind himself to press his hands into his lower back as he stretched. "Why do I feel like we're wasting our time going to this 'Enclave'? Something in my gut's telling me that Rasso Hine is up there, on that mountain."

"I'll see what I can learn." Arona reached into her dark robes and pulled out a clear pale-blue crystal. With a surge of cold Energy, she threw it out of the cave mouth into the air, and it burst into a misty cloud. With a despondent wail, the cloud coalesced into an ethereal ghost-like thing that rapidly surged through the air to the north, fading from sight in seconds.

"Shit," Victor grunted. "Didn't know you could do that."

"There's much you don't know, berserker." The words were a dig—a bit of ribbing, maybe—but her soft raspy voice and the finality of her tone made them sound more like a confession. Victor looked at her, the moonlight making her pale face even paler than usual, but her dark eyes were focused on the black night sky, and she didn't engage his gaze. Before he could question her further, Tyn whooped from deeper in the cave.

"A chest!" his youthful voice cried. Victor couldn't help grinning, wishing he could share his prediction-come-true with a friend. He turned to look and saw a flare of fiery magic as Arcus summoned a disc of floating, flaming Energy.

"He'll bring it forth," Arona said. "I've delved into many a dungeon with that man-child. That disc is something he uses to carry burdens." Victor nodded, suddenly feeling he was missing out when it came to utility spells. He wondered if he could convince his bear to drag a chest out of a cave for him. A few minutes later, sure enough, Arcus and Tyn came marching out of the cave with a large iron-bound chest atop Arcus's magical floating table of fiery Energy.

When Victor stepped close, holding out a hand, curious as to why it wasn't burning the chest, he found the flames to be only warm, not even hot enough to burn paper. Arcus waved his red rod, and the disc lowered to the stone floor and sputtered out, leaving its burden behind. It was big—large enough to hold Tyn if he wanted to curl up inside. Victor reached for the clasp but paused, looking at the others. "Can I open it?"

"It's safe," Arcus said. "I disrupted the trap runes." His words, once again, reminded Victor of his ignorance, but he shrugged and opened the heavy lid, exposing a pile of glittering treasures, one of which was a brightly glowing rainbow-hued orb just like the one Arona had gotten from the death wind. He heard Arcus's intake of breath and Arona's shifting feet, so Victor stepped back, afraid spells were about to start flying.

"Relax, you two," he growled. "Let's take stock of all the treasure before we worry about who gets that orb."

31

FRIENDS OR FOES

Arcus locked eyes with Victor and nodded. "Agreed. Let us evaluate the rest of this treasure before settling the matter of the orb."

"Of course." Arona took a step back and gestured at the big iron-bound chest. "This orb is part of a treasure, likely generated by the System. If touched, it may be absorbed, so let's use caution."

Victor nodded, but part of him was thinking he should just grab the orb. If Arcus wanted to fight about it, maybe it was better to get it over with. It would be an easy way to push things to a head. Of course, it would make him the aggressor, and he'd lose any moral high ground he might currently enjoy. As it was, all he had were rumors of Arcus's impending betrayal. So far, the man had been occasionally acerbic, and his personality wasn't exactly Victor's cup of tea, but he hadn't done anything to warrant outright hostility.

"Victor," Arcus said, startling him out of his musings of betrayal. "Do you object to me taking out the other items in the chest? I won't touch the orb."

Victor shrugged and glanced at Arona. Her dark eyes were focused on the chest, and her face was impassive. "Why are you asking me?"

Arcus smiled and tapped the heavy wood of the chest with his dark metal rod. "I've adventured with Arona. She knows I won't attempt any subterfuge."

"It's true," Arona rasped. "Arcus may have character flaws, but he's no thief."

Victor grunted in assent; he figured it was easy for a guy whose family was considered wealthy in a city full of rich demigods to resist the temptation of thievery. The Pyromancer leaned over the chest and lifted out a glittering, jewel-studded golden crown. It was a massive, gaudy thing, and Victor found himself hoping it wasn't anything great because he couldn't see himself wearing it. "Mundane treasure," Arcus announced. "I'd estimate its value at two hundred thousand standard beads." He set it on the ground before the chest.

Arcus reached back into the chest and took out a broadsword. It was about a yard long with a wide double-edged blade of shimmering, opalescent gray-black metal. It would be a short sword to Victor, and he doubted his hand would be comfortable on the human-sized, narrow hilt. Still, the metal looked amazing, and he could sense the quality of the weapon without even touching it. Arcus cleared his throat, narrowing his eyes. "A Rhovarian broadsword crafted from sableglow steel."

"Does it live?" Arona asked, leaning close.

"There is no conscious spirit within this blade." Arcus hefted it, a thoughtful expression behind his eyes, then added, "It's well made, but I'd say the materials are worth more than the sword itself. I'd wager it would garner more than a million standard beads at auction." He set the sword down beside the crown.

Victor heard a grunt of consternation and turned to see Tyn leaning forward, hesitantly lifting a hand. "What is it, Tyn?"

"What's an auction?"

Arona answered before Victor could think of an easy explanation. "A way for large numbers of people to express interest in an item. They make offers, and the one who 'bids' the most wins the item."

"Ah!" Tyn nodded eagerly.

Arcus chuckled, then took another item from the chest. It was a dark blue crystal ring. "A ring of Crystal Protection—two charges." He set the ring beside the crown, and when he looked up, he must have seen Victor's expression, because he added, "It will create a shell around the wearer made of dense crystal. The shell lasts a few seconds and absorbs significant damage."

Victor nodded. "Thanks."

Arcus reached back into the chest and withdrew a black leather-bound tome. It wasn't very large, about five by seven inches, and it contained, Victor figured, around fifty pages. Arcus frowned, opening the top cover and peering at the first page. He leafed through the following few pages and then shrugged. "It doesn't offer any information when I attempt a bond, and I don't recognize these runes." To Victor's slight vexation, he passed it to Arona. "Any idea?"

She, too, flipped through the pages and shrugged. "My master has some tomes and scrolls with runes of this style on the binding. He's never taught me from any of them, and I certainly don't know what they mean. It may be precious, or it may be junk."

"Can I see it?" Victor held out his hand, and Arona passed the book to him with a raised eyebrow. Victor knew what they were thinking; it wasn't a secret that he was a berserking brute in combat. He didn't often do things that exhibited much finesse, and it was probably becoming common knowledge that he was relatively uneducated compared to the other "prodigies" around Sojourn. With that in mind, he fought to keep a straight face when he thumbed through the pages and immediately recognized the runes and patterns as elder magic.

The book contained a spell, or at least some of the building blocks of a spell, written in elder magic. Why would the System award it? Was it because the dungeon was Tier Nine? Was it meant to help people prepare for their test of steel? It wasn't the first time Victor had postulated that the "test of steel" and "lustrous veil" had something to do with learning to use Energy without the System's training wheels. He shrugged and set the book down next to the crown. "Anything else?"

Arcus reached into the chest, and Victor could hear the *clink* of metals rubbing against each other as he ran his hand around the bottom. "Nothing but gems, precious metal coins, and some attuned Energy beads. I'd estimate another million in total value."

Victor sighed and stretched his neck, wringing forth some pops, trying to look impatient as he said, "Well, listen, nothing here looks all that great, and, as you said, a full level from an Energy orb is worth an awful lot for people at our level." Inwardly, he laughed as he said "our level." If Arona and Arcus knew he was twenty or thirty levels beneath them, he could only imagine the apoplectic reaction his performance in the challenge dungeon would have elicited.

"I . . ." Arona paused and looked at Victor, then shrugged. "I think it's more valuable to Arcus and me. I don't know your level, Victor, but my master indicated that you had a ways to go to reach Tier Nine."

"Yes, I must concur with Arona, Victor. You're aware of the exponential increase in the Energy requirement for levels, yes? As I'm sure you know, the curve becomes very steep around Tier Seven. Do you know, though, that going from level Ninety to Ninety-One is nearly thirty times that of Seventy to Seventy-One?"

Victor, in fact, did *not* know that, but it made a lot of sense; he'd gained his first few levels almost effortlessly and had gone through entire tiers in a matter of weeks. Things were definitely slower in the sixties, and hearing Arcus, it sounded as if it would only get a lot worse. It also explained why Arona and Arcus had been so excited about an Energy orb they didn't have to use immediately. What if she could save that orb until she hit level Ninety-Nine? It might save her years of work. Still, he didn't want them to know how little he knew. He nodded and shrugged. "Yeah, but it's still worth a lot to me."

Arcus's mouth fell open, and he looked a little flustered, as though he was trying to explain to a child why he didn't need a grown-up's dress shoes. Arona stepped in with, "What if we give you your pick of two of the other items?"

"And the loose coins and treasure," Arcus added.

Victor rubbed his chin, trying to make it look like a hard sell. In truth, he wanted that book. "If I take all that, it doesn't leave much for you or Arona if you don't get that Energy orb."

"It's fine." Arcus shrugged. "We'll settle the matter by chance, and the loser will have to accept the smaller award. If you recuse yourself from the claim on the orb, it increases our chances significantly."

Victor looked at Arona. "You're okay with that?"

"Yes. We've settled disputes like this before."

Victor nodded, then reached down and picked up the sword. He didn't plan to start training with swords, but he liked the idea of having a piece of metal worth a million beads. He tucked it away in a storage ring and then picked up the book, quickly storing it as well.

"Interesting," Arona said, her rough voice only a hoarse whisper.

Arcus nodded. "Indeed."

Victor shrugged. "What? It might be valuable, and I'm not interested in that crown or ring."

"No matter." Arcus pointed to the chest. "Victor, will you kindly pick a coin and show both sides to us?" Victor did as he asked and picked up a large golden coin. One side displayed a tower and the other a blooming flower. "Now, Arona will call tower or flower when you flip it."

Arona grinned. "I get to call?"

Arcus just clenched his jaw and focused on Victor's hand. "Do it."

Victor shrugged and flipped the coin. As it spun in the air, Arona said, "Flower." Victor caught the coin and slapped it down on the palm of his gauntlet. Sure enough, the flower was showing.

"Gods *damn* it!" Arcus growled, stomping away from them, out of the cave, and onto the slope where he sat on a flat rock in a huff.

Arona sighed but didn't offer to give up the prize. She reached into the chest, and as soon as her finger touched the orb, she exploded with multicolored light, blazing like an incandescent bulb. She groaned and fell to her knees, slowly rocking back and forth as she processed the enormous Energy infusion. Victor shrugged and touched the chest, sending it and all the coins and gems into his storage container. "Watch her," he said to Tyn, then he picked up the crown and crystal ring and walked over to Arcus.

He held them out. "Here you go."

The man sighed bitterly and quickly touched each item, sending them into a storage device. "She's a greedy bitch."

Victor sat down on a nearby rock. "Eh, can you blame her? She's Tier Nine, so those two orbs she got were worth a shitload."

"Of course! I *know* that! I would have done the same, but it doesn't lessen the sting."

Victor could hear the pain in the words, and he almost felt a little sorry for the man. Arcus seemed young, but Victor knew a person's looks were deceptive after they'd gained twenty or thirty levels. "Things haven't exactly gone your way lately, huh?"

Arcus snorted. "As you well know. I don't deal with failure well, Victor. You might be amused to know I contemplated vengeance against you after that challenge dungeon." When Victor raised an eyebrow, he waved a hand dismissively. "I soon gave up the notion. I wish I could say I'd found some honor to stiffen my backbone, but it was Roil who spoke sense to me. He made me watch recording crystals of your battles with the other entrants and reminded me that my first strike against you was better than any attack I'd get off in a formal duel, considering I caught you by surprise. No, I'm afraid I had to eat my pride and accept that my loss wasn't due to anyone's failing but my own."

Victor grunted, thinking. How was he supposed to respond to that? The Pyromancer had just admitted to everything he'd suspected. Should he just accept that he'd buried the hatchet? He didn't like that idea. No, he knew that Roil hated Dar and that Arcus found lies easy on his tongue. Victor let some rage seep into his pathways, and when he spoke, he allowed some palpable menace to tinge his voice. "I appreciate your words, Arcus, but if you think I'm going to be put at ease by some platitudes, think again. I'm glad you watched my performance in the challenge dungeon, but know this: However harsh I seemed when I fought in there, I was holding back."

The sound of stones clattering as they slid down the hillside saved Arcus from having to reply. Both men looked up to see Arona and Tyn approaching. Arona may have been trying to avoid gloating, but her lips were curved upward, her face was full of vibrancy, and her step was vigorous. "I guess that was a lot of Energy, huh?"

"If I could quantify it . . ." Arona trailed off, staring into the dark sky. "No, I don't think I can. Yes, 'a lot' will suffice." She gestured to the north. "I have news. My ghostly scout has caught whispers of Rasso Hine. I believe he is, indeed, in that town we glimpsed to the north."

"Rumble Town?" Tyn asked, his voice rising with dismay. "But we're close to the Enclave, and I—"

"Listen, Tyn," Victor said, reaching to clasp the boy's slender shoulder. "I want you to get home. We're going to handle our business here, but I promise you, I will make sure that something's changed about this place. There's no reason for families to be trapped in here." When Tyn just stared at him with wide eyes, Victor glanced at Arona and Arcus, wondering if they'd add anything. They stared back at him, and Victor felt a growl in his chest as he said, "Yeah. I don't know how, but those old bastards are going to change things. If they're so goddamn powerful, they ought to be able to think of something better than this."

"I agree," Arcus said, standing. "I'll certainly support your report, Victor."

Victor caught Arona's narrowed eyes and the slight shake of her head as the other man spoke. Still, she cleared her throat, reached out to grasp Tyn's slight hand, and hoarsely whispered, "There's a woman on the council, a good, kind, powerful woman who doesn't abide the suffering of children. We'll speak to her."

Arcus snorted. "Rexa won't speak to the likes of you."

Arona's reply was more a hiss than a whisper. "She'll speak to Victor." A chill ran down Victor's spine as she said his name, and he felt the power behind her voice. She leaned close to Tyn's face. "Get home, boy. Stay safe. Tell your father that things will be changing for the better and to avoid trouble."

Tyn took a step back and looked up at Victor, who grinned, nodded, and held out his massive fist. "Punch it." Tyn smiled, exposing teeth with many prominent gaps as he punched his small knuckles into Victor's. "Right. Let's go." Victor turned and started up the hill, setting a brutal pace for the shorter legs of his companions. When he reached the top, he looked down the slope to see Tyn's small wiry frame jogging up the gully, back the way they'd come.

Arcus and Arona stopped to look back with him, and Arcus cleared his throat. "I hope you're right about Rexa. Sometimes she acts like mortal concerns are beneath her."

"She won't abide this situation."

Victor turned and started hiking again. "She can influence the others?"

Arcus nodded. "Oh, yes. Especially considering many others are always on her side of things—your master, Lord Yon, Kreshta Griss, and Lord Venryn. Never mind the hundreds of veil walkers not currently serving as consuls who consider her a friend."

"But not my master or the other undead." Arona practically sighed as she spoke, and Victor could hear the disappointed longing in her words.

"Why?"

"She's a Summer Fae. Well, not full-blooded, but very close. She's been to the Faewild and served on the Summer Court." Arona shrugged. "The Summer Fae see undead and Death Casters in general as antithetical to all they hold dear."

Victor looked at Arona as she spoke; the sadness in her voice was impossible to miss, but it was hard to see any emotion in her dark eyes. He didn't want to get personal with her, not really, especially with Arcus part of the conversation, but he couldn't stop himself from asking, "Are you? Undead, I mean? I knew you were a Death Caster, but . . ." He trailed off, allowing her to assume his intention.

"I'm . . . in between. It's hard to explain, Victor. Suffice it to say that in her eyes, I am. Given time, I will be, so why argue the fine point?"

"Oh, poor Arona," Arcus scoffed. "Here we go again. Victor, you've no idea how many times I've listened to her get drunk around a campfire and lament her fate." He shoved Arona's shoulder and continued, "Weren't you and Valeska scheming to escape Sojourn and your masters last Frost's Day? Didn't you betray her in the Vault of Valor?"

"Valeska—" Victor started, about to say he remembered that name, but Arona cut him off.

"Eat corpse bowels, Arcus!" She quickened her pace, and Victor sighed, looking down at the Elementalist.

"That wasn't too cool, dude."

"What?" Arcus asked. "To speak the truth? She's fickle, that one. She makes promises to that boy, but if killing the children in this place would somehow advance her or her master's power, she'd do it." Arcus shook his head, gathered some phlegm, and spat. "I'll take the lead. We should avoid more monster spawns so we can be done with this damned place. Follow me, or my bird if you can't see me." He gestured to the fiery bird of prey circling high in the sky. Before Victor could agree, Arcus burst into flames and began to jog, quickly outpacing Arona. When he reached a steep grade in the hill, he leaped off and glided to the next slope.

When Victor caught up to Arona, she pointed to Arcus's fiery form, already climbing the next hill. "He often does that in a dungeon, especially wide-open ones like this."

"It must be hard growing up in a clique like that. I was going to say I remember Valeska; she was that tall strong woman with the two hatchets, right?"

"Yes. Thorn and Bloom are her axes. She hasn't spoken to me since the contest, but I heard from a mutual friend that she nearly went wild with despair when she thought she'd lost Thorn; the axe was stuck in your back when the System rescued her. Then you stabbed it into Brontes, and when the System rescued him, the axe came along. She was overjoyed. I'm surprised she wasn't at your party."

"Well . . ." Victor trailed off. He could think of a few reasons the woman might not want to come, starting with the fact that she'd broken dozens of bones during their fight. He shrugged, though, and tried to keep things positive. "Maybe we'll be able to spar or something. I'm glad she got her axe back, too. I wasn't exactly thinking clearly during that fight."

"No," Arona chuckled. "My master made me watch the battle, much as Arcus's did. I'd say you were anything but analytical during that fight, though your battle instincts are incredible."

Victor ignored the veiled compliment. "So, you don't like your master much, huh?"

"Well, I told you not to trust him for a reason."

Victor frowned, thinking, and then remembered what Dar's friend, Lo'ro, had told him—how he meant to steal Arona away from Vesavo Bonewhisper. "How do you feel about Lo'ro?"

"Lo'ro the Grim?" Arona shuddered. "He's a different sort of horrible."

"Damn."

"Why do you ask?"

Victor didn't want to make enemies by running his mouth about things that might have been said in confidence, so he tried to skirt around the subject. "He's a friend of Ranish Dar's, I guess." Before she could follow up for more detail, he changed the subject: "You think your friends are really pissed? Don't you think they understand what you were trying to do?"

"Brontes doesn't hold a grudge, but Valeska and Elandor refuse to speak to me. It's of little importance. My loyalty is to my master, and I did what he expected me to do." She didn't say more, and Victor didn't want to press. She sounded depressed, and he knew it was a lot deeper than her recent betrayal in the challenge dungeon. She spoke scornfully of Death Casters and the undead. She spoke longingly of people like Rexa, the Summer Fae. She was trapped by the Energy in her Core, and Victor wished he could help her.

Of course, he had some ideas. Thayla had gained a death-attuned Core in the dungeon attached to Greatbone Mine, and he'd helped her to alter it, giving her a courage affinity. Hadn't he done something similar for Lam? Could he help Arona escape the influence of her Core's attunement? Could he do something like that without becoming public enemy number one to all the Death Casters in Sojourn? Should he? For all he knew, she was just manipulating him. Victor was aware of his blind spot when it came to pretty women in need.

He snorted, drawing a glance from her, but shook his head and looked away. The truth was that it wasn't just women. Didn't he want to help Tyn, too? He liked to think he enjoyed helping people in need—underdogs, for lack of a better term. He nodded, liking the sound of that. It fit; wasn't he planning to return to Zaafor to help the Degh? Talk about underdogs! He just had to decide: Was Arona an underdog in need of help, trapped by her affinity and master, or was she just manipulating him? If so, why?

He glanced from Arona's dark-shrouded form to Arcus's distant fiery one on the next hilltop. They were both dangerous. They both wanted something, but Victor wasn't sure what or how far they'd each go to attain it. He knew he could take Arcus in a fight, but what about Arona? What if she was just trying to lull him into complacency? What if she and Arcus were aligned against him? He hated the paranoia twisting his thoughts but couldn't help it. There were too many factions and too many different motivations to consider. He wished he had an ally he could trust in that place, but without one, he simply determined to do what Arcus suggested: finish and get the hell out.

32

LIGHTNING AND CHAOS

"Well?" Lam asked, wiping the toad blood from her cobalt-blue hammer head with a well-soiled rag. They'd all just recovered from their Energy infusions after the "boss" toad battle, and she wanted to know if Darren had hit Level Ten. He grinned at her, then at Edeya, who sat, eyes glazed, staring at System messages of her own. He'd hoped to have both of their attention, but Lam wasn't going to wait. She stepped closer to him and prodded his shoulder with her boot, almost knocking him off the flat rock.

"Okay, okay!" He laughed and held up his fist triumphantly. "Level Ten! And, according to the messages in front of my eyes, I'm ready to choose my class."

"Excellent! That was faster than I feared! Spend your points before you look at your class options. I don't know if it makes a difference, but I'm superstitious."

Again, Darren glanced at Edeya, but she was still distracted, so he nodded to Lam and put his latest five points into vitality. That done, he studied his new attributes:

<table>
<tr><td>Name:</td><td colspan="4">Darren Whitehorse</td></tr>
<tr><td>Race:</td><td colspan="4">Human: Base 1</td></tr>
<tr><td>Class:</td><td colspan="4">-</td></tr>
<tr><td>Level:</td><td colspan="4">10</td></tr>
<tr><td>Core:</td><td colspan="4">Wildarc Class: Base 1</td></tr>
<tr><td>Energy Affinity:</td><td colspan="2">Lightning 8, Chaos 7.4, Unattuned 6.1</td><td>Energy:</td><td>140/140</td></tr>
<tr><td>Strength:</td><td>6</td><td>Vitality:</td><td colspan="2">32</td></tr>
<tr><td>Dexterity:</td><td>5</td><td>Agility:</td><td colspan="2">5</td></tr>
<tr><td>Intelligence:</td><td>9</td><td>Will:</td><td colspan="2">28</td></tr>
</table>

"Not too bad." He nodded to himself.

"Getting some big numbers, Dare?" Edeya asked, finally done staring off into space. "Sorry," she added, throwing him a wink with one of her big blue eyes. "I made Level Twelve."

"Ugh!" Lam laughed. "Slow down! I'm still only Eleven."

"Why did I gain four levels in the time you gained two, Edeya?" Darren knew more Energy was required as levels increased, but he thought the two women would simply receive a larger share of the rewards.

Before Edeya could answer, Lam spoke. "A few factors. For one, affinity affects how much Energy impacts you as the System awards it. Also, contributions during a battle can change your share. The main thing, though, is that levels get slower and slower the higher you climb. We'll all get to Tier Three pretty fast, but then the requirements start to really get steep." She nudged him with her boot again. "Well? Tell us about your options!"

"Shouldn't we get out of here first?" Edeya asked, fruitlessly trying to wipe some greenish-brown sludge off her hands.

"Darren?" Lam asked, hoisting her shield and raising an eyebrow. "Can you wait until we're out, so Miss Edeya doesn't have to suffer this muck any longer?"

Darren nodded and stood. "Let's get out. I'd prefer some fresh air to think." He hopped up and, feeling fresh and invigorated after their Energy infusion, followed Lam back through the winding corridors, sunken wet passages, and rooms filled with dead frogmen. Edeya and Lam chatted away; things were certainly different with Lam along for the dungeon crawl.

The two Ghelli had a hundred topics to talk about, and though Darren wasn't usually involved in any of them, the two women made a point to include him—most of the time. At that moment, the women were talking about someone named Sergeant Fath, laughing about how he used to carry his shield atop his head while marching. Of course, Darren could infer why it came up; Lam was constantly stowing and pulling her shield from her storage ring.

"Lam," he asked as they approached the dungeon's exit, "why didn't your friend, Sergeant Fath, use a storage device?"

Edeya laughed and answered for the older Ghelli, "Because Fath was an indentured soldier for the Greatbone Mine. He wasn't much higher on the pecking order than me and Victor."

Lam shrugged her agreement, then they all stepped through the portal, emerging in the quiet, damp cave where Sojourn City caretakers stood nearby, monitoring the portal entrance. "Out early?" asked a thin woman with pale lavender skin, massive black eyes, and half a dozen finger-length tentacles constantly wriggling under her large proboscis. "Is anyone hurt?"

"We're fine," Edeya announced. "Thank you. We're done with our slot."

"Much appreciated." The woman bowed, pressing her slender four-fingered hands together at chest level.

Lam sketched a quick bow, then led the way out of the cave. "Let's get a carriage back to the lake house, and you can go over your classes with us while we travel."

Darren nodded, and they hurried their way back to the small outdoor market at the entrance to the park. They'd found that most of the coaches, or "carriages" as some people called them, were much slower than the ones powerful individuals like Dar owned. When they'd hired one to pick them up at the lake house and deliver them to the grotto, the flight had taken over an hour. While they might be slower, there were plenty to choose from, and it wasn't long before they'd flagged down a strange copper bird-shaped coach with an open-air seating arrangement on its back.

At first, Lam had wanted to wait for a different vehicle, afraid the wind would be too distracting for Darren to concentrate on his class offerings, but the coachman, a small beetle-like fellow with a bright yellow shell, had insisted that his coach was enchanted to shield the passengers from the elements. So in short order, they were soaring into the wind, comfortable on a wide cushioned bench, with Darren somehow in the middle. The bird's metallic wings clanked and squeaked with each Energy-fueled flap, but the ride was smooth as could be.

"All right, Dare." Edeya scooted closer to him on the bench. "Let's hear 'em!"

"Okay, um, give me a minute. I have to find the right screen . . ." Darren opened his status sheet, and just as the System had told him he would, he saw a blinking round button that said, "Level Ten Class Selection." He "touched" the button by gesturing toward it with his finger, and then a list appeared, filling the strange transparent gray System screen with white text:

Class selection option 1: Elemental Attendant, Basic. Control and wield Energy compatible with your elemental affinity. Your primary focus is on harnessing elemental energy to perform attacks and defenses. Class attributes: Will, Intelligence, and Vitality.

Class selection option 2: Arcane Battler, Basic. Use arcane and physical abilities in combat to gain an edge over your opponents. Master the balance between magic and martial prowess to become a versatile combatant. Class attributes: Strength, Will, and Vitality.

Class selection option 3: Chaos Sorcerer, Advanced. Prerequisites: Chaos affinity plus any Elemental affinity. Embrace the chaotic energies of the universe to perform powerful and unpredictable spells. Your ability to manipulate chaos combined with your elemental mastery allows you to bend reality to your will and create mayhem on the battlefield. Class attributes: Intelligence, Dexterity, Will, and Vitality.

Class selection option 4: Arc Reaver, Advanced. Prerequisites: Lightning affinity. Channel your mastery of lightning into both magical and physical attacks. You become a fearsome warrior who can strike with the speed and ferocity of an electrical storm, combining martial prowess with lightning Energy. Class attributes: Will, Vitality, Strength, and Agility.

Darren smiled and blew out a slow whistle. "Well, I didn't get any epic options, but I got some really neat-sounding ones." He only mentioned "epic" options because of Edeya's class. "I mean, honestly, all four of my options seem really good, even the basic ones."

Edeya groaned and punched him in the shoulder, bringing a giggle burbling out of Lam. "So? *Tell* us!"

Darren chuckled and nodded, then spent about five minutes describing his options to his two companions. Lam rubbed her chin and then, demonstrating her wisdom, asked, "Do you have any questions about those or the idea of classes in general?"

Darren nodded, his question already primed before she'd asked. "Yeah, I'd like to know, if the System is going to offer me an advanced class, why does it keep the basic ones in there? Who would choose basic over advanced?"

"There are several reasons. My first time around, I skipped over an advanced class twice to keep my basic one. I did it for two reasons: I liked my basic class's focus, and I knew I'd level faster. Each tier adds to the Energy requirement of your levels. That's another reason I only gained two levels in the dungeon today while you gained four—I have an advanced class, and the Energy the System requires to give me a level is higher than your 'base' levels. When I was young and first gaining levels, I was concerned with gaining power quickly. That's not quite so important to me now." Darren didn't miss the sly smile Lam shared with Edeya.

"So, if I want fast levels, I should take one of the basic classes?"

"Come on, Dare! You want Lesh to whip your hide?" Edeya gave his shoulder another playful punch, and he nodded.

"Yeah. You're right. It wouldn't be fitting for a member of his household to take an easy solution." He thought for a minute, then asked, "Why does it list attributes at the end? Won't I get to assign them where I want?"

"Nope." Edeya shook her head. "Not with those classes. Sometimes the System offers classes with 'unbound' attribute points, but you didn't get one."

"Looks like the, um, Arc Reaver class will give me more physical attributes."

"Yes, it sounds like a melee fighter class. Does it interest you?" Lam shifted to look at him more squarely, and Darren felt a little flustered under the scrutiny of those beautiful emerald eyes. Both she and Edeya had such big, clear eyes that it was difficult for him to focus on anything else when he looked into them.

"Ye-yeah." He nodded eagerly, shifting his gaze to glance over the side of the mechanical bird's passenger compartment. He almost swooned from vertigo when the thing banked, and he got a good look at the tiny trees below them. He looked back to Lam, cleared his throat, and said, "I thought it sounded tough, like something Victor would approve of."

"Are you trying to impress Victor or trying to pick what's right for you, Dare?" Edeya asked, nudging him with her elbow until he looked her way.

"Well, I want what's best for me, of course. And, well, the *other* advanced class mentions both of my affinities. Do you think it's a better fit?"

"I think—" Edeya started to say, but Lam reached across Darren to slap her knee.

"Darren, why don't you tell us what *you* think."

Darren looked from one woman to the other and gathered his thoughts. Slowly at first, then with more confidence, he began to vocalize thoughts that had only been half formed up to that point: "Edeya is fast and deadly with her spear. You, Lam, are strong and durable and also fight in melee range. I know the two of you will have spells that do a lot of damage when we gain more levels, but I think our team would benefit more from me learning to use magic as much as possible. I think the Arc Reaver class would suit me well, but the Chaos Sorcerer class is even more ideal, especially as it focuses on magic-using attributes. If I'm understanding things correctly, intelligence, will, and dexterity are all needed for advanced magic abilities, right?"

Lam nodded. "That's accurate. Of course, it's nice to have some improved physical attributes, even if you are a spell caster, but you'll be gaining vitality, too. As for strength and agility, those may come with future class evolutions, or you can always shore them up with enchantments."

"I just hope that chaos affinity isn't too . . . chaotic." Edeya laughed.

Darren nodded. He'd yet to use the new spell Lam had acquired for him. Lesh had promised to let him test it with him in a "safe" manner, but the opportunity hadn't presented itself so far. "I wonder . . . lightning is my strongest affinity. Maybe I should just focus on it. I mean, what if chaos spells are too unpredictable or something?"

"Is that why his lightning is red?" Edeya asked, ever quick to leap down tangents. "Does the chaos in his Core change it? I've only seen Elementalists casting lightning spells that looked, well, natural."

"I've seen red lightning," Lam said, and her voice grew hushed as her gaze went distant. "You wouldn't remember, Edeya, because it was the night Catalina betrayed us. Hector . . ." She trailed off.

"Tell us!" Darren urged, eager to hear anything that might reveal more about his seemingly uncommon mix of affinities.

Lam sighed heavily and shrugged. "When Hector flew down from the mountain on his undead dragon, he threw bolts of red lightning. We know he was a Death Caster, but he could have had other affinities. In any case, he was powerful. Victor fought him more closely. Maybe he could tell you something."

"Right, well, who knows when he's coming out of that prison dungeon? I'll talk to Lesh about the class choices, but I'm pretty settled on the Chaos Sorcerer." Darren leaned back and tried to enjoy the view. His two companions grew quiet, the mood soured by Lam's reminiscence of Hector, Catalina, and their army's near-pyrrhic victory over the ambushing undead. The flying mechanical bird proved faster than their earlier carriage, and they arrived back at the lake house much more quickly than Darren had anticipated.

Lam paid the coachman, and then they went their separate ways—Edeya and Lam to unwind and Darren to seek out Lesh. Darren cornered one of Dar's house staff and asked where he might find Lesh. The young woman squinted her angular yellow eyes, smiled, and looked down submissively as she pointed toward the deck. If Darren hadn't thought it too wild a notion, he might have thought she was being shy and that a bit of color had tinged her pale green cheeks. As the thought struck him, he grinned and turned back to her. "I'm sorry, but what's your name? I'm embarrassed that I've waited so long to ask."

She continued to gaze toward Darren's feet as she wrung her hands. "I'm Wensa, sir."

"Well, please call me Darren. I'm nobody special. I'm only here"—Darren gestured to the beautifully appointed parlor—"because of the people I know."

"Thank you, Darren." Her voice had a lilting quality that sounded almost melodic, and Darren found himself grinning stupidly as he savored the sound. After a moment, the silence became awkward, and he cleared his throat and gestured toward the deck.

"I'll go find Elder Lesh. Thanks again." She ducked her head again, and Darren quickly hurried out the door, suddenly flustered by his brazen behavior—it wasn't like him. How many pretty women had he admired in his life and never approached? Too many to count, he decided. Lesh wasn't on the deck, so he stepped to the railing and peered down at the lake. Sure enough, his mentor's giant scaly form was stretched out on the pier, soaking in the afternoon sun.

Darren hurried down the steps, and as his footfalls echoed hollowly on the pier, Lesh lifted his fang-lined snout to peer lazily at him. "Fosterling. Your pride swells your aura."

"I hit Level Ten, Elder Lesh!"

"And you've chosen a class?"

"I have a preference, but I wanted your advice."

Lesh grunted and used one of his thick arms to push himself into a sitting position. Darren could feel the heat radiating off his black scales. How long had he been lying there? "Well, tell me, then."

Darren nodded and sat down before his mentor, crossing his legs before himself. He took a few minutes to review his four options and, as Lesh yawned and stretched, said, "I won't take a basic class because it seems like a weakling's decision. I'm not trying to find the easiest route to level. If I had an option higher than advanced, I'd take that, too." Lesh grunted, nodding, and Darren forged ahead. "I think the class that seems tailored to both of my affinities is the one I should take. Not only will I, hopefully, learn some chaos spells, but I'll be able to support my friends with a caster's abilities."

Lesh cleared his throat, summoned a bottle of pale green liquid, and took a long pull. Darren could smell the eye-watering alcohol vapors as Lesh exhaled a sigh of pleasure. "Good logic, but let me ensure you understand something: All sorts of folks can gain 'caster's abilities,' as you label them. Victor can do things with Energy that would make many pure 'casters' jealous. Of course, someone who specializes in intelligence and will and takes classes focused on ranged spells and support abilities will generally be better at spell casting, but don't assume a man in heavy armor and carrying a massive weapon won't be a dangerous Energy user."

"Understood."

"Other than that small flaw in your logic, I agree with your decision. Taking a class meant to take advantage of both of your affinities now will open better options for you at Level Twenty. Don't be concerned with your strength and agility. You're young, and your future options may well shore them up a bit. If not, we'll find natural treasures to improve you physically, at least to the point where you won't suffer from the imbalance."

Darren's ears had begun to whoosh with the rush of blood in his excitement as Lesh signaled his agreement—he was about to take his first class! "I can take it?"

Lesh chuckled and took another swig of liquor. When he belched, the mist that wafted away from his snout was green, and Darren took a step back as a hint of chlorine tickled his nose. "Yes. I'm glad you sought my advice, but this decision is yours."

Darren didn't need to hear more than that. He opened his status page, selected the class selection menu, and touched the option for Chaos Sorcerer.

*****Congratulations! You have gained your first Class: Chaos Sorcerer.*****

*****Congratulations! You have gained a Class skill: Sense Chaos, Basic.*****

*****Congratulations! You have gained a Class spell: Chaos Storm, Basic.*****

*****Sense Chaos, Basic: This ability allows you to discern the latent chaos**

Energy in a given area, thing, or being. Finding chaos is the first key to understanding it and allows for its cultivation.***

*****Chaos Storm, Basic: Calling on the nature of chaos and the power of elemental lightning, you create an area of tumultuous, chaotic Energy. The area's size depends on the Energy provided to the spell. Inside the Chaos Storm, any living being will be subject to random electrical discharges that can have the following effects: 1. Direct lightning-based damage, 2. Short, random teleportation, 3. Medium-duration stun, or 4. Temporary madness. This spell will not discern between friend and foe at the basic level. Energy Cost: Minimum 100, scalable. Cooldown: Medium.*****

33

RUMBLE TOWN

They don't seem threatening or particularly dangerous." Arcus was staring at the two men guarding the "gatehouse" of the town as he spoke, and Victor had to agree with him. One of the men was sitting on his butt, leaning back against the rough stone wall while idly tossing pebbles. The other sat on one of the stone blocks haphazardly scattered near the half-built structure. She was preoccupied with some dice, repeatedly tossing them on the flat rock beside her. Neither wore much in the way of armor, nor had they touched the spears leaned against the nearby wall.

It had taken Victor and his companions the better part of a day to make the trek through the ruins and hills, but as they approached the town, Arona had solidified her certainty that Rasso Hine was within; her scouting ghost had—according to her—seen a man being addressed as such. It gave Victor some comfort knowing that the day they'd spent in the dungeon would hopefully be the only one; he didn't want to be gone from Sojourn for weeks or months. "Already been away nearly seven days on the outside," he muttered.

"That's right, so let's get this over with." Arcus nudged Arona with his red metal rod. "They'd be fools to outright attack the three of us." He'd nudged Arona because she was the one who'd urged caution, saying they should observe the town for a while before approaching. Victor hadn't argued, but in this instance, he was inclined to agree with Arcus. Why not get things over with?

"If you want caution, Arona, let me approach the entrance. You and Arcus can back me up if shit goes sideways."

Arona had been crouching behind a stack of broken stone blocks, but she turned and arched a sharp black eyebrow at his words. "You trust us for such a duty?"

Victor chuckled as his earlier words came back to bite him. "Okay, don't rub it in. Just look me in the eyes and tell me if you'll have my back." He stared at her, and those black eyes widened slightly as she straightened up and stepped in front of him, never breaking eye contact.

"I will aid and support you if the denizens of yonder community seek to do you harm." She spoke gravely, her rough voice rasping the words as she carefully enunciated every syllable. Victor held her gaze for another few seconds, then nodded and turned to Arcus.

"You gonna betray me?"

He grinned, and one of his eyes blazed with inner flames. "Not today, Victor."

"Fair enough." Victor slid down the slope behind them into a small gully, then cleared his mind and summoned Guapo, using glory-attuned Energy. The mighty stallion burst from a pool of sparkling golden Energy and lifted his hooves in the air, whinnying loudly. Victor laughed, then swung onto the massive horse's back, letting him prance forward and back for a few steps. At first, Arona scowled at his display, but a corner of her mouth twitched upward as he continued to show off. Arcus snorted a short laugh and glanced through the stacks of broken stones.

"They're looking this way."

"Good; they'll see me coming in a second." Victor mentally urged Guapo forward, and the horse bounded out of the gully, rounding the small hill where Arcus and Arona still watched. Then he pounded down the slope toward the steep trail leading up to Rumble Town. They'd gotten a pretty good look at the place from their vantage. The town was situated in a natural cleft in the mountainside, forming a sort of canyon. Though a low, ramshackle wall had been built to block the entrance, it was easy to see the hundred or so buildings built up around the walls of the narrow box canyon.

The trail switchbacked up the mountainside and was probably half a mile long, so it only took Guapo a few minutes to thunder his way up to the clearing before the gate. By the time Victor arrived, the two guards had clambered to their feet and stood with spears held ready. Victor could feel their auras; they were weighty but nothing near as substantial as those of Arcus or Arona. Even setting aside the fact that their equipment was lackluster, Victor figured he could take them both if he had to.

"Halt!" the man bellowed, and Victor pulled Guapo up short. The stallion snorted sparks and danced, each of his hooves *thudding* like bass drums on the firm stony soil. Victor regarded the two guards from within his monstrous helm, and he could see their resolve weakening as they glanced toward each other for support.

The woman was covered with dirty orange hair, from her arms to her shoulders and even her face—the rest of her was hidden behind a dirty brown cloak and well-oiled stained leather armor. She had a round pink nose under big green eyes, and her mouth spread in a decidedly feline grin as she said, "Go get Ronkerz," to her companion. As he turned and slipped through the gate, she looked back at Victor, and he thought he caught the soft rumble of a purr in her voice as she asked, "New around here?"

"Yeah, that's accurate. The place is certainly a lot different from the dungeon I expected."

"Oh? Thought you'd find some tunnels and monsters and a bunch of old prisoner bones?" She lowered her spear, and Victor saw her nostrils twitch as she looked him up and down. "You're no prisoner, are you? Nobody gets sent into hell with a bunch of pretty armor and weapons. Are you one of them? One of the bastards who sent us here?"

Victor grinned as her purr turned into a snarl. "Nah, you ever heard of an iron ranker on the Sojourn City Council? I'm just an asshole who owes them a debt."

"Oh? That right? What kind of debt?" As she spoke, Victor couldn't help noticing how a crowd was gathering on the dirt road behind the gate. He frowned at that thought—why call it a gate? It was just two short walls of roughly stacked stone blocks that narrowed the canyon's entrance; no door was attached. Still, people were gathering on the other side—all sorts of people. He saw human-looking folks, Fae, avians, and beastkin. Some were the size of giants, and some were much smaller. All in all, there had to be a hundred people forming the crowd, and he could see signs of many more coming from the tumbledown structures of the town.

"I need to find someone and ask a few questions." Victor and the others had decided that announcing they needed to get Rasso Hine *out* of the dungeon wouldn't be wise, not to a bunch of inmates. If the denizens of the prison knew they could take someone out with them, things could get ugly fast. Seeing the number of inmates gathered at "Rumble Town" only reaffirmed Victor's conviction in that plan. Even if he and the others could win in an all-out mad free-for-all, he didn't relish the idea of slaughtering a bunch of starved, ill-kept inmates.

"Oh? That right? Someone like me?" The purr had reentered her voice.

"Maybe." Victor sent a little Energy into his armor-changing runes and smiled as his helmet and heavy armor converted to clothing. He gently patted Guapo's neck as he directed his grin to the cat-woman. "Are you the leader around here?"

She opened her mouth to reply, but a basso voice echoed from behind the wall, "That'd be me, stranger." As the words hit his ears, an aura fell over Victor that almost made him grimace. Guapo snorted and took a few sparking steps back, but Victor growled and pressed his knees into the stallion's sides, and he pranced forward, deliberately lifting each hoof in a showy act of defiance in the face of the heavy aura.

"I'm Victor," he called to the opening, wondering why he couldn't see the man with the deep echoing voice.

"I'm Ronkerz," the booming voice replied, and this time it was behind him. Guapo whirled with a whinny, lifting his front legs and snorting. Victor scowled when he laid eyes on the man who'd startled his mount. Ronkerz was a giant—a hulking, black-furred gorilla of a man. His arms were like tree trunks, and his knuckles, quite literally, dragged on the stone ground. He really *did* resemble a gorilla, with a few notable differences. His eyes were angular and shrewd and glowed with violet Energy. His mouth was more of a muzzle, with a long snout and big canines that made Victor think of a bull terrier more than a gorilla. Finally, he wore armor—thick steel-plated armor with gleaming needle-sharp spikes on the shoulders.

Victor slid off Guapo, gave his rump a slap, then sent the mount back to the spirit plane. As the glittering golden fog of the horse's departure faded, Victor stepped toward Ronkerz and held out a hand. "Good to meet you." It wasn't lost on Victor that Ronkerz didn't hold a weapon, nor did he assume the man needed one to inflict some damage—his fists looked like wrecking balls.

Ronkerz narrowed his shrewd-looking eyes and then took a lumbering step closer. He was probably about Victor's height but half again as broad. When he swung one of his long arms out and grasped Victor's hand, the power in that grip was apparent. It had been a while since Victor had trouble getting his fingers around a person's palm, but he grinned as he squeezed what he could and felt the other man's powerful fingers struggle to compress his flesh—even the little bones in his hands were made of the stuff of titans and wouldn't bend easily.

"So, you come seeking an inmate?" Ronkerz asked as he released his hold and let his knuckles fall to the ground.

"That's right. I guess he has some information that's important to the city's safety."

"And we should care?"

Victor shrugged. "My understanding is that the city maintains this dungeon. Not sure what would happen if the City Stone were destroyed—"

"Bah! Impossible!"

"Is it? Have you ever seen an invasion led by veil walkers? Sojourn's a ripe target for some of the darker corners of the universe." Again, Victor spoke from prepared talking points. It had been Arona's idea to play up the invasion angle. Even prisoners generally wanted to continue existing, and the idea that an invasion might lead to the dungeon's destruction was the only card they could think to play to get some cooperation from the inmates.

"Oh?" Ronkerz lifted one of his thick, powerful digits and scratched at the short black fur atop his head. "What about your friends lurking on yonder rock pile?"

Again, Victor shrugged. "We didn't know what to expect."

Ronkerz huffed a breath out his nostrils, and the dust on the ground stirred at the powerful exhalation. Something in Victor stirred, and he found himself wondering what it would be like to fight the man. He remembered what Arona had said about how Ronkerz had beaten four steel seekers when he was just a Tier Seven iron ranker. Something in Victor's chest began to swell with excitement as he imagined testing his strength against the formidable man.

Ronkerz must have seen something in his expression because he took a step back, and a deep, rich chuckle welled out of him. "Ha! Who did those fools send in here? You look like a dog eyeing a bitch in heat." He stepped closer, putting his fang-filled snout just inches from Victor's face. "If you want to test yourself, *boy*, stick around; I may give you the chance."

Once upon a time, having a man call him "boy" like that might have set Victor off. His rage surged in his Core, but it was easy enough to hold it there. With a slight twitch of his will, he expanded the fiery white-gold center of his Core and allowed a wave of inspiration to wash into his pathways. With a fierce grin, he nodded and thumped the thick metal plate on the side of Ronkerz's boulder-like shoulder. "I'd like that. In the meantime, would you mind if I called my companions closer? We could use a break. Been hiking through this damn dungeon for nearly a day, and that was after a bunch of scoundrels tried to ambush us at the entrance."

Ronkerz stared at him for several tense heartbeats, but then he, too, grinned, and it was quite a fierce expression on his animalistic face. "Call them over. We can bargain for what you need." Victor had been facing him throughout their entire conversation, but he was peripherally aware that a considerable crowd had formed on both sides of the gate and even atop the wall. Ronkerz turned and bellowed in a voice that echoed and reverberated through the narrow box canyon. "Get back to work! If I have a fight, you'll damn well *know it*!"

Victor didn't have to look to know that the denizens of Rumble Town knew who their boss was. He could hear their hurried steps as they scurried to do as he commanded, scattering into the canyon and the narrow streets and ramshackle buildings it contained. As they dispersed, Victor stepped closer to the trail leading down the slope and raised his arm, waving toward the hill where he knew Arona and Arcus lurked, watching. A few moments later, he and Ronkerz watched Arcus, red as a Christmas candle, and Arona, another shadow among many, walk down to the trail and climb toward the canyon entrance.

"Tell me who it is you seek," Ronkerz demanded as the two spell casters fell out of view on the steep trail.

"Rasso Hine."

Ronkerz hummed or growled—Victor wasn't sure—in his throat but didn't say more. He was content to wait; he'd done fairly well, in his opinion, but was eager to let Arona or Arcus do some talking, bargaining, or whatever it would take to get Ronkerz to hand over Hine. While they waited, Victor glanced back at the canyon and saw only the two gate guards remained, though a few people could be seen lingering near the dirt road that led into the center of the town. Without thinking, he let his thoughts escape his mouth: "Must be hard as hell to live in a place like this. Does the sun ever come out?"

"No sun in this world," Ronkerz rumbled. "No good soil. No game animals. Some fish and slugs can be found in the deeper caves. Some clever fools over the centuries have managed to bring in some seeds. Not on purpose, mind you; no one goes into prison thinking they'll need to farm. Still, there must be some council members who take pity on fools like us and have sent prisoners in with sacks of fruit and vegetables. With the right Energy, we can get some things to grow in this damned soil." As he spoke, Ronkerz's voice became more and more pleasant, less gruff, and if Victor closed his eyes, he couldn't make the smooth, well-enunciated words match up to the gorilla-like giant standing beside him.

Before he could respond with a comment or another question, Arcus came into view, sheathed in flames, floating along the trail. Victor snorted derisively; of *course* the man had to make a showy entrance. Arona, just a short distance behind him, had no such qualms. She grunted softly as she climbed the steep slope using her ivory staff as a walking stick. "Ronkerz," Victor said, gesturing to the two arrivals. "This is Arcus, and behind him is Arona."

Arcus settled to the ground, and his flames faded to a faint flicker that limned his shoulders as he bowed. "I've heard much about you. It may please you to know that your name still strikes fear into the hearts of the Sojourn elite."

Ronkerz snorted a huff of air, and the flames on Arcus's shoulders flickered and faded. Victor raised an eyebrow as he saw Arcus flinch back. Arona stepped forward and sketched a stiff formal bow. "Lord of Greatscarp, I greet you and offer you the regards of my master, Vesavo Bonewhisper."

"Vesavo still haunts those gaudy towers?" Ronkerz leaned close to Arona; she was tiny in his shadow—a thin, pale figure with a great hairy armor-clad monster looming over her. Even so, she didn't flinch as his big nostrils twitched, and he snuffed the air around her. "Yes, I remember that scent. *Interesting*."

The way he said "interesting" left Victor wondering at the layers that word contained. Was he simply interested in the fact that Arona was Vesavo's apprentice? Or was he concerned? Dismayed? Did it impact his plans? What were his plans? Victor could have wondered about a thousand similar questions but forced his mind to be quiet; he'd only learn by talking to the man and seeing what came. "Ronkerz has agreed to bargain with us," he said, hoping to get the ball rolling again.

"Indeed." Ronkerz turned and lifted one of his long, powerful arms, gesturing toward the town. "I'd invite you to a feast, but I doubt you'd enjoy our fare. Perhaps you have some rations you might share?"

Victor glanced at Arona and Arcus, hoping they'd answer, but they both looked preoccupied. Arcus looked as if he'd seen a ghost, and Arona was pensive, her eyes distant. "I've got food to spare, Ronkerz. Let's sit down and talk."

Ronkerz shifted, and his shrewd violet eyes regarded Victor. "I didn't expect you to be the leader." Victor opened his mouth to protest but stopped short as the bulky simian turned and lumbered toward the gate. What had he meant? Could he tell Victor wasn't as high level as the others? Did he think the "leader" would be one of the casters who hung back? Did he believe Victor didn't have leadership qualities? He almost laughed as his mind raced. He shook his head and pushed the disquiet down, reminding himself, once again, that clarity would come with time.

He followed Ronkerz past the gate guards and could hear Arona and Arcus walking behind him. They were still quiet, and he wondered if Ronkerz had dropped the full force of his aura on them. He wanted to question them, to speak softly about what they thought of the situation, but, giant as he was, that wasn't an option. He was a little annoyed at himself for revealing his actual size. If he'd reduced himself, he could have saved his full strength as a bargaining chip. Not only that, but he would have been able to walk more closely to Arona and Arcus and gauge their moods. It would surely draw too much attention if he made himself small now.

Victor contented himself by looking over his shoulder, down at the much smaller man and woman. He raised an eyebrow, and Arcus shrugged with something of a smirk on his face. Oddly, the haughty expression gave Victor some comfort; Arcus was still his pretentious self. Arona pressed her darkly stained lips together and gave him a firm nod. The look said plenty—she was ready to deal with whatever sort of bargain or trouble Ronkerz had in store.

Those thoughts made Victor think of an ambush, so he turned his attention to the town as they walked. The buildings were largely built from stone, with mud and clay used as mortar. The little wood he could find on roofs or shoring up leaning walls looked ancient and dry, and he wondered if it was scavenged from the lairs of the dungeon's monsters. He could picture the planks as part of ancient "ruins" where undead might spawn. None of the buildings were tall, and most were built against the canyon walls. Victor figured the citizens of Rumble Town gained a lot of square footage by carving caves out of the cliffsides.

They were about two hundred yards past the gate when he saw the first children. Dirty faces with wide eyes watched from corners and dark alleys between structures. They wore rags and looked half starved. Victor felt his rage stirring again. The whole place was *wrong*. He could understand banishing a powerful, dangerous figure like Ronkerz. Victor didn't know his story, but even if he had been in the right, he was a grown man who'd reaped the consequences of his own conflicts. You couldn't say the same for all of these children. There had to be a better solution.

Ronkerz led them to the end of the road, an open square where the dirt had been cleared away from the hard stone bedrock. It was probably fifty yards across, and all around it, the canyon walls were lined with rough buildings and shoddy ladders that led up to open caves. Hundreds of people lingered around. They stood in clusters near buildings, sat in cave mouths with their legs dangling, and lined the rough stone walls separating one rough building from another. They reminded Victor of an audience, and as he looked around the square, he understood why; they were standing in the center of an arena—a fighting pit. As the understanding struck him, a flash of insight lit up his eyes, and he glanced at Arona and Arcus and grinned. "*Rumble* Town."

34

BIG ONES

Ronkerz turned to face the three of them, and that's when the nature of their situation became clear to everyone, not just Victor—the giant simian had no intention of bargaining, at least not with words. To drive the point home, a line of hulking armored figures filed out of the centermost cave opening and took up positions in a semicircle behind Ronkerz. Victor felt his lips begin to stretch into a grin as he took their measure.

If he'd wondered why everyone he'd run into, save Ronkerz, had been dressed in rags and wielding low-quality weapons, the answer was becoming apparent. If Victor had to guess, he'd say that the denizens of Rumble Town paid for their relative safety by pooling their resources. They took their loot from monster spawns and their scavenged items and gave them to Ronkerz, who distributed the equipment to these men and women.

"These are my Big Ones," Ronkerz announced, spreading his arms in an impressively wide gesture. As he said "Big Ones," the thirteen men and women pounded their weapons in a reverberating *boom-boom*, smashing them on shields or onto the hard stone ground.

"Lord Ronkerz," Arcus said, looking left to right at the line of heavily armored, mostly gigantic warriors, "I must confess that the ambiance of this gathering has begun to evoke a rather unsettling premonition. I might go so far as to speculate that the atmosphere suggests an imminent display of hostility—"

"Hah!" Ronkerz barked a deep, rough laugh that sent spittle flecking over the short black hairs on his chin. "Hostility? We live in *hell*, boy!"

Arona tried another approach. "We're your *guests*. You invited us in."

"I invited you to bargain, and we've got only one way of doing that in Rumble Town—"

"Fighting," Victor interrupted. He sent a stream of Energy into the runes on his armor, and suddenly he was bedecked in his snarling draconic helm and armor. "Great. How's this work?" His voice echoed, enlarged by the magic in the lava king's maw. He didn't remember reaching for Lifedrinker, but she was in his right hand, her head aglow with glowering red Energy and her haft twitching with eagerness.

"Victor." Arona reached for his arm, but if she grabbed him, he didn't feel it; she was too small and his gauntlet too thick. He had eyes and ears only for Ronkerz. Ever since Arona had told him about how Ronkerz had wound up in the prison, something in him had wanted to fight the warrior. He wanted to test his mettle against a man who was—

"You think you can touch me, boy?" Ronkerz interrupted his rambling thoughts, leaning toward him with a curled lip. "I was chewing up steel seekers before I got put in here, and that was four centuries ago! You think I haven't found my own steel by now?"

"You're a veil walker?" Arona asked, her voice hushed. Victor glanced down at her and saw her eyes were wide and that she'd taken a step back. He was just turning back to Ronkerz when the giant blurred and, with a sickening wet pop, snatched ahold of Arcus's right arm and ripped it off at the shoulder. To Victor's amazement, the arm shimmered with bright blue light and then disappeared. Meanwhile, Arcus had fallen backward, stumbling for two steps before succumbing to gravity and falling onto his butt. Crimson blood pumped into the torn sleeve of his robe, sluicing onto the stone ground.

The crowd cheered, and the assembled Big Ones smashed their weapons again. *Boom-boom.* "Tried to leave the party early, boy?" Ronkerz rumbled a deep, mocking chuckle. "Drink a healing draught before you're too weak to entertain the people."

Victor felt his eagerness to fight evaporate. Ronkerz had ripped Arcus's arm off so fast that he hadn't been able to track it. Moreover, Arcus hadn't even been able to utter a spell to defend himself. In fact, Ronkerz had moved so quickly that he'd interrupted the recall spell, sending the recall charm and Arcus's severed arm out of the dungeon. How could someone that bulky and powerful move so damn *fast*? The Quinametzin pride that had been eager to test itself against the brute was suddenly nowhere to be found; it was almost enough to make Victor laugh.

"That was unkind," Arona said, and Victor noted she'd moved her staff into a defensive position. She wasn't planning to let Ronkerz rip her arms off. Arcus's face was ashen, and he hadn't moved to drink a potion. He seemed dumbstruck, utterly shocked by the horror of his ruined arm. Victor didn't want him to bleed out, especially if they were going to be fighting for their lives for Rumble Town's amusement, so he lifted one of the healing potions Master Yon had given him from his baldric and pulled the cork stopper. While Ronkerz watched, Victor leaned over and tilted the oily red liquid into Arcus's mouth.

The crowd's raucous cheer had died down, and Victor began to get the feeling that they were sort of playacting, responding as tradition dictated. The people, the Big Ones, even Ronkerz—they all behaved as if they were putting on a show, and he wondered how much of their lives in the bleak dungeon world was dedicated to strange ritual entertainment.

Arcus greedily slurped the potion down, and his color immediately improved. The blood sputtering from his shoulder ceased, and he gasped, taking a deep breath. He looked at Victor and nodded. "Thank you. I . . ." He frowned and looked at his shoulder. "I . . ." Victor followed his gaze to see something wriggling under the torn fabric of his robe. "I—ah! D-did, er, was that a regeneration p-pot—" Arcus's words broke off in a wail of surprise and disgust as a black, slippery tentacle began to probe its way out of his robe.

"What the *fuck*?" Victor stepped back as the tentacle continued to grow longer and thicker, stretching outward from Arcus's shoulder. It was lined on one side with tiny pink suckers but was otherwise jet-black. "Dude, Master Yon told me they were regenerative potions. He said they were his best work!"

"Yon? That shit-eating bird gave you those potions?" Arcus wailed, leaping to his feet. His new appendage waved about, out of control, and Arcus grimaced with a mixture of pain and disgust as he fought to get it under control. "One of his experiments, no doubt! Gods *damn* it!"

Halting at first, then with more and more volume and intensity, Ronkerz began to laugh. His great chest heaved with the sound as he roared, "Ha! Ha! *Ha!* Oh, Dead Gods, the beauty of it. Yes, young Pyromancer, rejoice, for now a part of your body reflects the dark stain on your soul."

Arcus whirled on the man, his eyes wild with frustration, pain, anger, and a dozen other emotions—Victor had no doubt. "What do you know of my soul, fiend?"

"Only what I can see, which is *much*." Ronkerz stared at Arcus for a couple of heavy seconds, but the Pyromancer had stopped scowling at him and was now preoccupied, staring intently at his new tentacle as he attempted to wrap its narrow end around his fallen black metallic rod. Ronkerz directed his gaze at Victor and Arona. "Well, are you three ready to hear my offer, or will we have more theatrics? Do either of you other fools wish to attempt to flee?"

Victor shrugged. "I'd rather keep my arms."

Arona watched Ronkerz warily as she rasped, "You have an offer?"

"I do!" he roared, lifting his arms wide again. His Big Ones bashed their weapons and shields, and the crowd cheered. The cacophony died down immediately when Ronkerz lowered his arms. "I'm sure you came here thinking to ply us with threats or a few trinkets or piteous scraps of food and liquor, hmm? Well, your fool masters should have warned you! They know I live! They fed the dungeon my *blood*, just as they took that vital force from every one of the people they sacrificed to live in this hell! The dungeon crystal would have told them I reached my test of steel more than three centuries ago. The dungeon crystal would have told them I broke through!"

Ronkerz stopped to pace back and forth before his Big Ones. Some were larger than he, physically, but his presence made them seem small. They didn't shrink back, however. They stood straight and tall, and Victor began to realize something—the denizens of Rumble Town didn't fear Ronkerz; they worshipped him. He was a god incarnate to them. Being a Big One, in close proximity to the great man, was an honor everyone lining the cliff walls, the rooftops, the dirt streets, and the cave openings aspired to.

Ronkerz continued his rant, "So, they sent you to your doom, or they had some sort of mad confidence in your ability to deceive someone an order of magnitude more powerful than yourselves. No, we won't take your pitiful offerings. You'll play our games, and if you prove worthy, we'll give you Rasso Hine. If you prove unworthy, we'll take everything you own and either kill you or add you to our ranks."

"Ronkerz, wait—" Arona started to say, but he whirled on her and growled.

"Just Ronkerz, now? No 'Lord of Greatscarp'? What happened to your pretty tongue, death sparrow?"

"I-I just want—"

"Irrelevant!" Ronkerz clapped his hands thunderously. "Let me introduce my thirteen Big Ones! My pride! After I honed my steel and breached my veil, I stopped hunting these lands and took on my first apprentice. That was two hundred years ago." Ronkerz stepped to the center and rested his hand on a tall avian woman's shoulder. She had a notched beak and dark, dirty-looking gray feathers, but her chainmail armor gleamed with power, and her curved saber rang like a crystal chime when she whipped it from its sheath. "Lira Stormclaw is that apprentice. Like most of my Big Ones, she's a steel seeker, but I think she's getting closer and closer. Aren't you, my pretty bird?"

"I am, Lord Ronkerz." Her voice was lyrical and breathy, and Victor could see the adoration in her big golden eyes as she stared at the great simian. Victor looked up and down the row of powerful warriors and wondered if the apish man was really going to introduce them all.

"Next to Lira is Gorruk the Crusher!" The crowd cheered, and Gorruk smashed his enormous gray hammer into his heavy spiked shield. Ronkerz continued down the line, and each name brought forth cheers and a display of power from the Big One. Victor, never great with names, sort of zoned out and tried to concentrate on which warriors seemed like they'd be a threat to him. The answer was simple: all of them.

Despite his mind's tendency to tune out details like names, some of them stood out—Zara Bloodmoon, an eight-foot, four-hundred-pound lupine woman with stark white fur and glowing crimson eyes, Thrak Ironfist, a man with hands and arms that were, literally, made of dark blue-black metal, and Ulgor the Brutal, a mountain of muscle that loomed half again as tall as Ronkerz. He was hunched with piles of veiny muscles stacked on his shoulders and back. His red bloodshot eyes peering from beneath his thick hairy brows looked decidedly insane.

After he finished, Ronkerz turned from the last of his Big Ones and regarded Victor, Arona, and Arcus. "Well? Are you suitably impressed?"

"Are—" Arcus started to speak, but his tentacle twitched violently, and he scowled and tried to grab it with his right hand, dropping his red scepter in the process. "Damn it!"

"Are?" Ronkerz glared his angular violet eyes at Arcus, then turned to regard Victor. "Will you speak for your distracted companion?"

"Um, I think he can speak." Victor stepped closer to Arcus and reached down to snatch his writhing tentacle arm in his fist. Thankfully, it wasn't slimy, but it certainly felt weird—pulsing and throbbing as it flexed, trying to move. "Pay attention, man! He's going to rip your other arm off."

Arcus scowled at him but nodded as the misbehaving appendage settled in Victor's firm grasp. "I say, Lord Ronkerz, am I right in my understanding that these fine warriors are all beyond the iron ranks? I don't understand how. Aren't only iron rankers allowed in this dungeon?"

"Allowed in, yes, fool. We all were iron ranked when we came to this hell." Ronkerz ambled closer to Victor and Arona, his right fist acting as a third leg as he leaned on it, pressing his massive knuckles into the stone. "By now, you must be putting things together, yes? I said we settle bargains by fighting here in Rumble Town, and then I introduced my Big Ones. What's in store for you? Hmm?"

"You want us to fight your champions," Arona rasped.

"*Big Ones!*" Ronkerz roared and, for the first time, unleashed his true aura. Arona fell to her knees, tears of blood streaming out of her obsidian eyes. Victor stumbled back, and the tiniest voice in the back of his mind, crying out from a dark corner where he kept his deepest fears, told him to run. He glanced left and right and caught sight of Arcus, lying flat on his back, eyes squeezed shut, struggling to writhe away from Ronkerz. Seeing him like that, wriggling like a worm, woke something in Victor and, almost like a palpable whisper tickling his ear with her hot breath, he swore he heard Chantico's voice again. *"Do not break, child of the Sun. You are made of sterner stuff than that one."*

He looked away from Arcus, squared his shoulders, and stepped into the pressure of Ronkerz's will. He heard the screams of countless foes, felt the anger of a dozen lifetimes lived in captivity, tasted the bitterness of defeat, the hatred of a righteous man condemned, and the killing intent built from a hundred thousand brutal massacres. He had no right to stand against that weight but did it anyway. With eyes quivering in their sockets, bloody with burst vessels, he stared into Ronkerz's violet gaze as sweat erupted from his pores and his body shook with adrenaline.

"Oh, they chose you well, didn't they, boy? Do they hate you so much?" Like a switch being flipped, the aura was gone, and Victor could hear his heaving breaths and the rushing of his blood. He could hear Arona's soft gasps and Arcus's sobs. "Well, as your Death Caster princess has surmised, you'll need to best one of my Big Ones. You'll each need to—one by one. No team fights, and no, you don't get to pick which ones you'll be matched against. Tonight, I'll allow you to feed my people. We'll have a feast, and come the morrow, Rumble Town will watch you do battle!" He raised his voice at the last pronouncement, and, once again, the townsfolk cheered, and the Big Ones slammed their weapons.

Ronkerz stepped closer and lifted one of his massive hands. "Agreed?"

Victor regarded the hand, then looked at Arcus, still flat on his back, and Arona, slowly, shakily, struggling to stand. "To the death?"

"Death, unless you yield, yes. Understand this, however: Should you yield, you will remain in this world with us. Don't get any ideas about using your recall charms—I'm watching."

Victor knew he couldn't argue. Ronkerz had already proved that he could kill them all easily. Just because he'd managed to remain on his feet while his aura was on display didn't mean Victor could fight under that strain. He had trouble following the man's movements *without* that pressure; he had no delusions of being able to stand against him in combat. Something about breaking through to the "lustrous veil" seemed to lift powerful Energy users into legitimate demigod status. Was that what Ronkerz had going for him here? Was he a god among mortals in the prison dungeon? As he began to judge the man, Victor reminded himself that Ronkerz wasn't there by choice.

He reached out and clasped the rough-fleshed hand, and Ronkerz squeezed firmly but didn't try to dominate him. When he released the grip, the veil walker grinned, exposing his lupine fangs, and then he *moved*. One second, he stood before them, and the next, he was standing in the mouth of a cave a hundred yards up the cliff face. He bellowed, his basso voice booming and echoing in the canyon, "Rumble Town! Tonight, you *feast*! Tomorrow, there will be *fights*!"

The cheering was thunderous, and despite everything, Victor found himself basking in it. He raised his arms and slowly turned in a circle, and the cheers intensified, bringing a fierce grin to his face. If he had to fight, then he'd give the Big Ones something to think about. He continued grinning as he tried to make eye contact with as many of them as he could. "Okay, *pendejos*," he said into the cacophony. "Which one of you suckers has to fight me? Don't everyone jump at once." His desire to intimidate them fell flat as most of the Big Ones roared and cheered, flailing their weapons in the air.

"Don't taunt them, fool!" Arcus hissed, and Victor looked to see he'd managed to get to his feet. Even so, Arcus looked terrible despite the healing elixir, or maybe *because* of it. Apparently, the tentacle was still struggling to move on its own, and Arcus was fighting to hold it still with his other hand, having stowed away both of his magical scepters. "Man, I'm sorry about that *pinché* tentacle. That asshole didn't tell me it would do that."

"I don't hold you to blame. I saw the bastard hand them to you before you stepped in. Besides, I was stupefied. I might have died had you not stepped in."

Arona moved beside Victor and coughed, clearing her throat before asking, "What are we supposed to do now?"

Victor looked around, noting how the Big Ones had all gone off to wherever people of their status spent their days. The townsfolk were moving again, no longer lining the "arena," as he'd come to think of the space. They were walking about, talking, carrying things—going about their usual business, he supposed. "I dunno. I have a lot of food, but I'm not sure I can feed hundreds of people. What about you two?"

Arcus ignored the question. "How, by the fate of all the elder gods, did that man enter his lustrous veil while trapped in this damned dungeon?"

"Hundreds of years of killing Tier Nine monsters, I suppose." Arona shrugged. "He was a prodigy before he was sent in here. I'm sure he made breakthroughs that some of our masters would kill to learn."

"They'll never let him out to ask. Think of the damage he could do!"

"Something tells me," Victor said, rubbing his chin, turning slowly to look around the strange scenery of Rumble Town, "that Ronkerz is kind of biding his time. I'm not so sure a dungeon meant for iron rankers can really hold a guy like him."

Arona and Arcus grew quiet at that, and then they, too, began to look around, evaluating the place in the light of Victor's words. It was Arona who spoke first. "He's building an army."

35

A TOAST BEFORE WE DIE

The hell are we supposed to do?" Victor asked after he and his two companions stood in the arena for several minutes, staring around, watching the people of Rumble Town go about their business.

Arcus, still restraining his new appendage with his remaining hand, shrugged. "I imagine they'll set something up for the feast and give us some instructions. I would hope . . ." He looked around with a sour expression, his once fiery eyes mere embers, glowing faintly in their dark hollows. "I'd almost rather they just made us fight now—nothing worse than stretching out your neck, waiting for the ponderous drop of the headsman's axe."

Arona leaned against her tall ivory staff and sighed. "I have foodstuffs, though they aren't exactly gourmet—barrels of spring water, some wheels of cheese, a few crates of flatbread, and crocks of honey. They're remnants from a campaign I led on Brun-Jun, just some rations I'd held as an emergency reserve."

Arcus nodded. "I, too, have a plethora of rations from various training expeditions. That's not accounting for my own meals, stowed away from restaurants I enjoyed over the years. It's probably about time I cleaned out my containers."

"Yeah," Victor grunted. "Same. I'm sure that's what Ronkerz had in mind when he volunteered us to provide the feast." As though their words had summoned them, a trio of comically mismatched inmates emerged from a cave carrying a long, surprisingly well-made wooden table. Looking at the delicate polished wood, Victor supposed that if a powerful Energy user was a craftsman outside the prison, they might still be able to work some magic with the materials in the dungeon.

As they set the table in place near the center-rear of the open "arena," one of the inmates, a short fuzzy ball of white fur, motioned at it and loudly squeaked, "Feast go here!"

"Thanks." Victor waved a hand, acknowledging the strange creature's words. In a much quieter voice, he asked, "The hell is that guy?"

"Shratling," Arcus hissed. "Native to a world one jump from Sojourn."

"Usually mischievous, but not outright criminal. I'm surprised to see one here," Arona added.

"Come on. Let's load this table up and get things moving. I'm ready to get this business done." Victor followed his own directive and began pulling casks of his cheaper wine, bushels of fruit, platters of snacks, meats, sandwiches, soups, desserts, and several other dozen dishes from his storage rings. The truth was, he was a food hoarder. Whenever he tasted something he enjoyed, he tended to buy a surplus of it and store it away. He wondered what that said about him. Conversely, he wondered what it meant that he felt a weird sense of relief cleaning all those random bits of food out of his rings.

Arona and Arcus were, likewise, piling supplies and food on and under and to the sides of the table. Victor, of course, had started with things he didn't value much, but once he'd pared it down to a few dozen platters of his favorites, he slowed, stepping back to watch his companions as they unloaded. When the entire twelve-foot table was laden with food, with baskets and crates stacked beneath it and kegs and barrels lined up to the sides, the puffball stepped out of the cave again and squealed, "Enough! You come with me! Rest before fights!"

"Ha," Victor chuckled, "looks like we're not invited to the feast."

"Not!" the weird four-foot-tall ball of dirty white hair confirmed.

"Seems inhospitable," Arona rasped, taking the lead, following the creature as it glided into the cave opening. Victor decided it must have arms and legs obscured by all that fur because it didn't exactly bounce or roll. The cave wasn't very impressive—a long, low-ceilinged gallery that stretched about a hundred feet into the cliffside. Glowing amber and white lamps on the sides revealed passages and hanging ropes, but their guide didn't take them beyond that first space. Instead, he or she or it—Victor had no idea what was appropriate—pointed to a rickety table and benches in the far corner beneath a dim amber glow lamp.

"Wait." After the pronouncement, the Shratling glided away, bobbing slightly as it moved.

Arcus, grimacing as he wrestled his tentacle, huffed and stomped over to the table to sit. Arona and Victor exchanged a glance and then followed him. Victor didn't want to reduce his size to make the bench comfortable, so he pulled one of his large-sized camp chairs out of storage and sat down to the side, facing both his companions. "Not a great situation."

His words brought a snort of amusement out of Arcus, and the man shook his head ruefully. "No, not great. If I didn't think Ronkerz would rip all our limbs off for trying, I might suggest we use the remaining recall tokens now."

Arona snorted. "Victor and I have recall tokens that take time to activate. It's interesting that Roil gave you one that fired almost instantly."

Arcus shrugged, flopping his tentacle around. "Not instantly enough."

Victor changed the subject; he already took it as a given that Roil wouldn't play fair. "Could Ronkerz really do that? Get here fast enough to interrupt the recall?"

Arona regarded him with an arched eyebrow. "Ronkerz is a veil walker. He could be standing beside you, and if he didn't want you to know, you wouldn't."

"That big a difference, huh?" Victor spat to the side and shrugged. "Go ahead and judge me; before I met Ranish Dar, I'd never spent time with a veil walker." As he said the words, he began to doubt their veracity; the more he learned about the stages beyond the "iron ranks," the more he suspected Tes had passed her test of steel and would be labeled a veil walker by the people of Sojourn. It wasn't hard for him to imagine that she could stand and observe them undetected if she so wished it.

"They call passing the test of steel a 'breakthrough' for a reason. Cultivators at that stage are on another plane, power-wise." Arcus's tone was pleasant as he explained, though punctuated with frequent grunts as he fought his tentacle.

"I know this sounds rough, Arcus, but maybe I should cut that damn thing off. If you can't control it, it might do more harm than good."

Arcus's eyes widened in horror as he sharply disagreed, "No! I can already get it to move a bit—my mind is just learning to deal with a new type of limb."

Victor raised his hands placatingly. "All right, all right. It was just a thought."

Arona watched the Pyromancer with slightly narrowed eyes, staring at the tentacle as it throbbed and pulled against the grip of Arcus's hand. "What will your father think of that new appendage?"

"Gods *damn* my father," Arcus snarled. "He and Roil both!" Arcus looked up toward the ceiling of the cave and cried, "I hope you can hear me, you shit-bred, demented, scheming lickspittles!"

His outburst brought a chuckle out of Victor and a wide-eyed stare from Arona. She leaned forward, hissing, "Don't tempt fate, fool! If Roil heard that—"

"Roil can lick my balls! I'll be dead or trapped here after tonight, and that scheming old bastard *knew*. Don't you *dare* tell me you disagree! Perhaps your masters, not being on the council, were unaware of Ronkerz's status, but I assure you, Roil knew, and I'm quite sure my father put him up to this. Money! It all comes down to money!"

"Money?" Victor was enjoying this new side of Arcus. He almost felt bad that it took having his arm ripped off and being threatened with the prospect of a new life inside a dungeon to bring it out.

Arona looked at Victor and offered a half shrug with one shoulder. "His father isn't high-tier. He's powerful due to the businesses and real estate he owns."

Arcus nodded. "Power is power, regardless of its source, and my father's well of riches runs very, very deep."

Victor frowned, reclining in his chair and crossing his left foot over his right knee. "So, let me get this straight. You think your, uh, dad and your mentor are working together to screw you over?" He couldn't keep a hint of amusement out of his voice.

"I don't *know*!" Spittle flew as Arcus pounded his fist on the table. Victor watched his tentacle writhe for a moment, waiting for him to elaborate, but it was Arona who did so.

"Your master and mine, Victor, are at odds with the current majority on the council. It's not surprising that we might be sent in here, against absurd odds, to retrieve Rasso Hine. If Arcus is correct, and the consuls know about Ronkerz being a veil walker, the only logical conclusion is that they hoped we'd get very lucky and find our target without running afoul of him. That, or they expected us to fail and never return from this place."

Victor nodded. "But your master"—he gestured to Arcus—"Lord Roil, you're sure he knows about Ronkerz?"

Again, Arcus rhythmically pounded his fist on the table as he spoke. "Roil has been in charge of this prison for millennia. I'm sure his close allies know its secrets—" His face froze momentarily as understanding seemed to flash behind his eyes. "Of course! The bastard! That's why he added me to your team!"

"What is it?" Arona leaned in close to him.

Arcus barked a short bitter laugh. "He'll avoid accusations if *his* apprentice also dies in this place."

"None of this makes any fucking sense." Victor shook his head. "Which is it? They want Rasso Hine, or they want us to die?"

"Don't be simplistic, Victor." Arcus saw Victor's glare and rapidly held up his remaining hand. "No, I didn't mean that as an insult. Think about this from my master's perspective. He has two ends in mind. One, he wants to earn points with the other consuls by bringing Rasso out of the prison. Part of that was getting someone past the blockade—you did that. Two, he wants to weaken his adversaries, Vesavo and Ranish Dar. One way to do that is to deprive them of their best students, two prodigies who embarrassed his own student." Again, Arcus laughed bitterly.

"Yeah, but you guys just said there's no way to get anything past Ronkerz . . ."

Arcus sighed heavily. "Again, Victor, please think of this from Lord Roil's perspective. If we *did* find Rasso Hine and got out with him, all would be well; Roil could scheme for vengeance in another way. If, however, we ran afoul of Ronkerz? Well, as far as he knows, that would be the end of us all. He loses a recently disgraced student—one of many in his current class, I might add—but

Vesavo loses his best apprentice, and Ranish Dar loses, if I'm not mistaken, his only one."

Victor frowned at Arcus and his feebly twitching tentacle. "I thought you were the shit, man. You telling me you're not Roil's best student?"

"No. Perhaps in his top five before the Vault of Valor debacle. Now, I can barely get him to look my way. Add to that my father's desire to be rid of me. Ha! He likely offered him a handsome sum to make it happen—"

"He wouldn't!" Arona interrupted.

"Oh, he *would*! My mother is currently waging *war* against him on our homeworld."

Victor's eyebrows shot up at that. "Jesus. What about your sister?"

"Trin? Different mother. I have *thirty-seven* siblings, Victor."

"And your dad's not a veil walker?"

Arcus scoffed, "Hardly. Level Fifty-Three the last I heard."

Victor let that sink in, processing everything Arcus had just dumped on him. In a way, he was beginning to understand his bitterness and almost felt a little sorry for him. He'd been an asshole, true, but he also had a lot of shit to contend with. Growing up, Victor had been lucky to have his *abuela*, and he might have had some problems with his cousins and even his aunties from time to time, but he couldn't imagine having a father actively trying to get rid of him. Add to that a hard-ass master willing to toss you aside to win some points against his ancient enemies, and you had a recipe for resentment with a desperate *need* to rise above your peers. It explained a lot.

"You think Vesavo and Dar will fall for this shit?" he asked Arona.

"If we all fail to return . . ." She shrugged. "I don't know."

Victor drummed his fingers on Lifedrinker's haft. "Well, I intend to return."

"As do I." Arona's voice was raspy as usual, but there was an edge to it, a hardness. Victor saw that hardness reflected in her dark eyes.

"Gods!" Arcus said, holding his hand against his eyes in dismay. "If this had happened to me before the Vault of Valor—before I'd lost . . ." He trailed off and looked at Victor, then slumped his shoulders, sliding down on the bench so he nearly reclined against the table. "I used to be more confident, but I'm not so sure I'm up to the task of fighting a steel seeker."

"They're just at a higher level, right?" Victor was half trying to encourage Arcus and half trying to confirm what he thought he understood.

"Higher level, aye, and who knows how far along with their custom class, their cultivation, their spell and skill mastery, their—"

"Arcus!" Arona reached over to grasp his shoulder. "You're among the hardest hitting casters in Sojourn, at least among the iron rankers. Take Victor's advice and think of these 'Big Ones' as nothing more than iron rankers who've leveled past One Hundred. For all we know, their training and cultivation are lacking. Vesavo has told me tales of steel seekers who were decidedly weaker than he was in his iron ranks."

"That's a good point." Victor frowned, tempted to reveal his level and describe how easily he'd vanquished some of the Tier Eight and Nine combatants in the challenge. He decided not to, though, simply because he didn't know what Arcus might do with that information once they were out of the dungeon. Instead, he said, "I've beat the shit out of some folks with dozens of levels on me. I mean, shit, these guys don't even have good food. I know high-level cultivators don't need much to eat, but think about it: How good could the training and cultivation they've been doing in this death-attuned dungeon be?"

Arona nodded. "There's something to that; the Energy is weak in the air. Their Cores may not be up to the standards we're used to."

Arcus sighed. His tentacle flexed as he stared at it, and a large goblet of wine appeared in its coiled embrace. "I did it! I pulled this from my dimensional container with my new . . . *arm*." Arona and Victor watched, holding their breath, as he stared at the goblet and ever so slowly began to raise it toward his mouth. The tentacle twitched and throbbed, but it seemed to be doing what he wanted. When he got the rim to his lip and took a shaky, slurping sip, Victor clapped his hands, and Arona laughed.

"Fuck! Nice one, man!"

"Ha!" Arcus crowed, but then the goblet tilted and poured out onto his red robes. He laughed harder as the liquid rolled onto the stone floor, leaving no hint of a stain. The sight of his pristine robes drew Victor's eye to Arcus's torn, bloody sleeve. It was utterly whole; his robe had cleaned and repaired itself. "I'll master this damned thing yet!"

Arona's black-stained lips were still curved in a broad, genuine smile, and she reached over to gently pat the Pyromancer's back. "Well done, Arcus."

"Making me thirsty." Victor summoned a bottle of honeyed mead. He'd noticed the crate of bottles from Zaafor while putting out their "feast" and marked its location in his storage ring; it was one of his favorite alcohols. As he took a long pull, he heard the faint *thump* of a drum and, close behind it, the twang of stringed instruments. "Guess they're getting their party started."

"What a miserable existence," Arona said, staring toward the distant glowing opening of the cave.

Arcus followed her gaze and somewhat wistfully said, "At least they have Ronkerz to support them. At least they have cause to celebrate."

"Were you serious about your dad?" Victor asked. "I mean, if he wanted you dead, why . . ." He'd been about to ask why the man didn't just kill him but let the words die on his tongue.

"As with anything political, it's complicated—doubly so when you consider I'm his child. A death in the line of duty, serving the greater interest of the city, however? That will aid him politically." Arcus stared at his tentacle, and while Arona and Victor looked on, he forced it to pick up his goblet and tilt the dregs of his wine into his mouth. He managed it much more quickly and steadily than the first time.

"What does it feel like?" Victor gestured to the long black appendage with its row of tiny throbbing suckers.

Arcus reached over to squeeze the tentacle with his fingers, frowning slightly. "It feels like flesh. The, um, soft, pink part is very tender and sensitive, like a hundred fingertips. At first, I thought for sure I'd seek out Yon and demand some sort of restoration, but this new arm has some potential. It's quite long if I stretch." To illustrate, Arcus grimaced in concentration, and then his tentacle extended away from him, wriggling through the air toward Arona. Victor's eyes bugged out as the narrow point began to probe toward her breasts, but she wasn't having it. She swatted it away with a pale blue flash of Energy, and Arcus winced in pain. "Bitch!"

"Please," she flatly sighed. "You're lucky you still have your new limb attached."

"I mean," Victor chuckled, "you gotta have better judgment than that, man."

"I wasn't *aiming* for your chest, woman!" Arcus growled as he rubbed the tip of his tentacle. He sucked in his breath through his teeth, grimacing. "I just got through saying they're sensitive!"

Arona ignored him, summoning a small wooden tray filled with candied fruits. "I suggest we have our own feast. It may be the last any of us will enjoy; if we lose our duels tomorrow, we'll either be dead or stripped of our gear and enslaved to Ronkerz."

Victor nodded. "I'll drink to that." He made good on his words, chugging the rest of his bottle of mead. He laughed and tossed his empty bottle to shatter against a nearby stone wall. Arona lifted one of her dark eyebrows, and Arcus chuckled. As the music grew louder and the noise of Rumble Town's celebration echoed into their stony holding cell, they all began to pull out their favorite foods—things they'd held back from the feast.

Knowing Ronkerz was probably watching them in one way or another, Victor held up a fresh bottle of mead. He didn't like their situation, and he couldn't say if he liked Ronkerz or not, but he had to admit, the giant simian demanded respect. "You know, Arona, considering your words—that this might be our last meal—how about a toast before we die? To Ronkerz!"

"Ha!" Arcus spat onto the stone floor but didn't shrink away from the toast. He held up a fresh goblet of wine. "To Ronkerz!"

Arona, grinning with half of her mouth, seemed to recognize the irony of their actions. She narrowed her eyes briefly as she concentrated, and then a delicate flute of sparkling alcohol appeared in her slender fingers. Still smiling crookedly, she clinked it against Victor's bottle and Arcus's jeweled goblet. "To Ronkerz!"

36

ALPHA STRIKE

Victor lay awake for most of the night after he and the others decided to get some rest. He wasn't worried about being on top of his game or feeling groggy; he hardly needed sleep since his body had evolved to the epic stage, and if he got a few hours now and then, he always felt fine. So, while he listened to the sounds of Arcus muttering and sometimes whimpering and the soft breaths coming from Arona, he lay on his back and thought about everything he'd seen in the dungeon. What he kept coming back to was the children.

It bothered him to no end, knowing that everyone on the council could kill him; when he returned to Sojourn, he desperately wanted to go on an ass-kicking spree. He'd been away from Earth long enough to understand how power scaled when Energy was involved, but learning about veil walkers and their seemingly exponential increase in potency rubbed him the wrong way. He'd *liked* the fact that someone being ten or twenty levels higher than another person didn't mean they could automatically dominate them. Being forced to recognize the superiority of all the people who'd passed their "tests of steel" rankled.

Nevertheless, Victor didn't see a way around it. He simply had to watch his step and rely on his alliances and the customs and laws that seemed to protect the iron rankers from the veil walkers. Even the System seemed to enforce their separation—Ronkerz should *not* be in this dungeon with all the iron rankers. In a way, Victor was comforted to see that the System wasn't without flaws. He liked that it could make mistakes; having some omnipotent, all-knowing *force* ruling over their lives was stifling. It felt good to know it wasn't perfect.

Aside from his fruitless pursuit of a solution for the children in the dungeon, he couldn't sleep because he was excited. In his mind, the whole situation was like being moved to a new, bigger school as a freshman and being expected to face off with the state champ just because he showed some talent. He chuckled at the idea; why did he still fall back on wrestling analogies? He'd fought a hell of a lot more with his axe in the last couple of years than he'd ever wrestled. He supposed it came down to formative years—memories integral to his personality.

He wondered which Big One Ronkerz would pit him against. Victor hadn't displayed many of his abilities since entering the dungeon, so he hoped Ronkerz was judging him by his appearance. He hoped he thought he was a brutish axe fighter without any finesse. Victor had quite a few tricks up his sleeve that even Arona and Arcus knew nothing about, even after watching his performance in the Vault of Valor. Thinking about that brought his mind around to how he felt his two companions would fare in their matches.

Arcus was suffering from a bruised ego, but Victor knew the mage could pack a punch. He hoped he'd pull something off and get away with a win. However, he was more interested in Arona's fight. He'd felt the depths of her power in her aura and was curious what a Death Caster like her could do in a one-on-one contest. He pictured their fights, his imagination running wild, then he drifted back to himself and began envisioning his own battle, running his moves through his mind, visualizing counters and counter-counters. The hours of the night slipped away, and though the sun never rose in the dungeon, he began to hear the sounds of people stirring outside the cave.

He was straining to hear a distant conversation when he felt a shift in Arona's soft, steady breaths, and then she whispered, "Did you sleep?"

"Nah," he whispered back, turning to look at her dim form atop a low cot between himself and Arcus. They were all lying on camping beds with blankets and sleeping bags—none of them had been willing to pull out their entire camp setups. Victor had a big tent and lots of furniture, and he was sure his setup paled compared to what the others had. Still, something had kept them modest—probably the knowledge that Ronkerz was watching them.

"You wondered if I was undead the other day," Arona said. "Now you know the truth of it—if I were, I wouldn't need to sleep."

"Ah. Never? I thought vampires slept while the sun was out."

"Vampires? Well, there are many types of undead. If I become one, I'll be more like my master—a lich." Her raspy voice took on a smoother, softer quality when she whispered, and Victor could almost imagine what she might have sounded like as a younger woman before she'd gotten involved with her death magic. She was obviously trying not to disturb Arcus because Victor had heard her whisper far more harshly near the lich-wyrm's lair.

Her mention of their earlier conversation brought a thought to Victor's mind. "Do you really hate your magic? Your master?"

"*Shh!*" she hissed. Arcus still breathed deeply, each exhalation steady and even, but Victor realized she feared the Pyromancer would hear him. "What I told you before is true, but please don't bring it up."

"All right. Sorry." Victor tried to shrug, but lying on his back, the movement didn't translate.

Arona shifted, and then her arm stretched out toward him. "Will you take this for me?" She held something dark that glinted with silver in the faint glow-lamp light. Victor reached out to grasp the object; it was about the size and shape of a socket wrench, and when his hand closed around it, he felt the deep, powerful well of cold Energy inside it. Arona let go, and he realized he was holding a dense, heavy bone. He pulled it closer, out of the shadows, to see it was dark, as if it had been charred, and was inscribed with silvery runes. It seemed familiar.

"That's one of my best summons, the one I used against the lich-wyrm. He's not yet recovered, so I can't use him in the duel and . . ." She trailed off for a moment, then started again, her voice so quiet, Victor had to lean toward her to hear. "And if I die or have to surrender, I don't want to lose him to Ronkerz. You know he'll strip us if we surrender."

"What if I lose?" Victor clutched the heavy, cold bone, wondering what creature had once walked with it as part of its skeleton.

"I have a feeling Ronkerz will make you fight last. If I win, I'll take it back from you. If I lose and you lose, the end result would be the same."

Victor sighed and put the bone into the same container he'd gotten from Dar for his cultivation items. "Well, what do I do with it? You want me to give it to your master?"

"No!" Arona's raspy whisper became a hiss. "Do not tell him you have it! If you leave this place without me, then please, just take it to Dar's estate and bury it near those lovely orchards. I'll rest easier knowing my oldest, most loyal companion made it out of this place and that he's resting peacefully in such a beautiful setting."

Victor narrowed his eyes at her. It was strange hearing words like "lovely" and "beautiful" in conjunction with burying a bone and hiding the fact from her undead master. He leaned close and whispered in a voice so low there wasn't a chance Arcus could hear him, "You really *do* hate him, don't you?"

Arona's dark eyes seemed to grow luminescent in the dim light as moisture pooled in them. "I do, Victor. I hate him with every fiber of my being."

Victor drew a breath, ready to ask her a follow-up question, wanting to know more about Vesavo and what made Arona hate him, but then thudding footsteps sounded on the stony cave ground, and Victor knew their time was just about up; Ronkerz was approaching. He heard Arona shifting, sitting up, climbing out of her blankets. Victor did the same, stowing away his blanket and comfortable sleeping platform. He'd just stood and was nudging Arcus's bed with his boot, jostling him awake, when Ronkerz's hulking form loomed into view, backlit by the glow lamps.

"Your feast was a success," the giant announced, his angular violet eyes shifting from Victor to Arona to Arcus as he stopped to assess them. "It's good that you rested rather than schemed to escape. I've set wards, and any use of those recall tokens would have ended painfully."

"We assumed you were watching," Arcus replied, stifling a yawn with his new writhing appendage.

"Excellent. I was watching and *listening*, and it seems to me that you three are, while spoiled and foolishly compliant, not exactly willing participants in your venture here. Well, perhaps that's giving some of you too much credit. Perhaps it's better to say you're somewhat unwilling pawns, hmm?"

"That's accurate." Arona shifted her staff as she spoke, placing it between herself and Ronkerz. "Does that mean you won't make us fight for our lives?"

"Ha!" Faster than Victor's eyes could track, Ronkerz lashed out and snatched Arona's staff. A flash of cold blue Energy rolled out of it, washing over the huge simian, and for a moment, Victor thought Arona had tricked the giant, that she'd somehow set a trap for him. That may have been true; it seemed the Energy was harsh and focused on the hulking figure, but he stood stoically as it poured over him. Just as suddenly as it had appeared, the Energy was gone, leaving behind a faint odor of decay, a rimed-over stone floor, and Ronkerz—utterly untouched.

"Clever but fruitless, girl." His massive forearm twitched, and with a resounding *crack*, her staff broke into splinters in his grip. Arona cried out and fell to her knees as the giant dropped the pieces of her once beautiful polished ivory staff to the frosty ground. Victor could see the tears of frustrated anger and despair in her eyes, and he wondered if her staff had been alive. How would he react if Ronkerz did something like that to Lifedrinker? Before he could envision the scene, Ronkerz grunted, "Pyromancer, you will fight first. The three of you have fifteen minutes to enter the arena."

As they all watched his lumbering form recede into the tunnel's darkness, Arona hissed, "*Bastard!*"

"I'm sorry for your loss," Arcus mumbled, awkwardly stepping close to the still-kneeling Death Caster. "I know you had him for decades and were very close."

"Him?" Victor didn't want to rub salt in the wound, but he was curious; it seemed that her staff had, indeed, been conscious.

"Ghivalt," Arona sniffed. "He was a sturdy soul and a boon companion. Many were the nights I whispered my frustrations into his ever heedful ear." With shaking hands, she gathered up the splinters of her staff, sending them into one of her dimensional containers. Watching her, comparing her staff to Lifedrinker in his mind, Victor's reluctant respect for Ronkerz began to wane.

"What an asshole."

"I wasn't trying to trap him; I simply had defensive spells primed in Ghivalt. It's a habit of mine to put him between myself and those I view as a threat. I didn't think Ronkerz would take offense." She accepted Arcus's hand and rose to her feet, suddenly holding a different staff, this one made of black-streaked gnarled wood. "Let us face today's trial."

"Right." Victor nodded and turned to Arcus. "You ready, man?"

"Not especially, but I'm resolved. Whatever champion they pit against me had best be ready." With that, Arcus's red metal rod appeared in his right hand, and the black one appeared in his tentacle's firm grasp.

"You're getting the hang of that thing."

"My sleep, though troubled with strange dreams, seems to have helped my mind come to grips with the change in my body."

"Come," Arona rasped, already walking toward the cave opening. Victor and Arcus followed, and soon they came into view of the broad, low-ceilinged opening. The sky was still dark, and Victor had to remind himself that the sun never rose in the dungeon world. When they stood in the opening, facing the stone-walled box canyon that served as Rumble Town's arena, none of them were surprised by the gathered crowds or their raucous boos and hisses.

"You'd think these assholes would be a little more grateful for the meal we laid out yesterday," he grumbled. He scanned the cliffsides, the rooftops, and the gaps between wooden buildings and figured there were something like three hundred people watching. It seemed like a lot to him, but when he considered that the dungeon had been around for thousands of years and that people were having kids inside it, the number wasn't all that high. It made him wonder at the average life expectancy inside the place. He also had to remember that he hadn't seen the other "communities" in the dungeon. For all he knew, Rumble Town housed only a fraction of the populace.

"Rumble Town!" Ronkerz boomed, his basso voice rattling the wooden structures and causing pebbles to bounce on the stone ground. Victor turned to the sound and saw the giant simian high on the cliffside in a wide cave mouth, surrounded by his Big Ones. "Today, we have *entertainment*! Three outsiders who come to us in servitude of the vile criminals who govern this world will face off against three of our Big Ones!" The crowd went wild at the announcement, though Victor couldn't help but think it was all some kind of strange pageant; the people had to know already that they were going to fight.

"Arcus! Pyromancer of the family Volpuré, step into the arena!" Ronkerz's voice was loud and shook the ground, but it was also clear, and it felt as if it were aimed right into Victor's ear. It made him wonder if the veil walker was using a voice amplification device or if Ronkerz simply had to flex his will to push his voice out on the waves of his ocean of Energy.

"Fortune be with you, Arcus." As she spoke, Arona reached out and caught ahold of Arcus's sleeve, causing him to turn toward her. "I hope you know that, despite our many contentious bouts of—"

"I know," he sighed. "I'm not always easy to get along with, but neither are you. In any case, should I perish, try to remember me as I was when we were young, crushing one dungeon after another, hmm?" The words made Victor evaluate Arcus and Arona in a new light. She'd warned him of Arcus's impending betrayal, so he'd thought they were likely enemies, but it seemed they had quite a history. It made sense, he supposed; the "gifted" students and apprentices in Sojourn seemed to be very familiar with one another. If they'd grown up at the same time, why wouldn't they have been friends, especially when they were younger and had less pressure from masters and society when their "tests of steel" were a distant proposition?

They stared at each other for a couple of seconds, then Arcus's eyes flared with bright, white-hot flames, and he turned and strode into the center of the "arena." Quietly, Victor muttered his own encouragement: "Good luck, you asshole. Burn the shit out of 'em."

As Arcus stepped away from the cave mouth and into the focus of everyone's attention, he burst into flames, a living, walking brand of white-hot fire that slowly lifted off the ground, hovering some five feet in the air as he spread his arm and tentacle, brandishing his two magical rods. The crowd seemed torn—some cheered, likely eager and excited for a fight, while others jeered and booed, clearly holding their praise for the hometown champion.

Ronkerz's voice boomed out over Rumble Town. "Fighting the mighty Pyromancer will be one of your favorite Big Ones—Fanatala the *Gasher*!" His voice rose to a heart-stopping crescendo as he howled the combatant's fighting name. The earlier noise for Arcus paled in comparison as Rumble Town began to vibrate with cheers and stomps, screams and howls. One of the shadowy figures near Ronkerz launched into the air, falling like a comet from the heights to land on the stone surface of the arena with a ground-shaking *thud*. Dust and pebbles flew into the air, and as the dust slowly cleared, Victor got his first good look at Fanatala.

She was a tall ebon-skinned woman with a high spiked white mohawk. Arcus wasn't a small man—probably Valla's size, if Victor were guessing—but Fanatala was giant-sized at nearly ten feet. She wasn't bulky like many giants, but she was powerful-looking, with arms and shoulders covered in ropy, bulging muscles. She wore a strangely shimmering green and ochre breastplate and a mask of the same metal, cast in a scowling goblinesque visage. Around her waist was a thick leather girdle, and—likely the source of her moniker—two wickedly curved swords hung from it.

Even as Ronkerz screamed, "*Fight!*" the sky above the canyon darkened and erupted with angry red and orange flashes of fire. Thunder crashed, and fiery meteors the size of compact cars howled through the darkness toward the center of the canyon. Arcus held his red rod high over his head as the flames lining his body surged upward, like a fire given too much oxygen.

"Holy shit," Victor grunted—he'd been on the receiving end of Arcus's meteor strike before, but this was on another level. It looked to him as though the whole town was going to be wiped out when they impacted the ground.

"He's dumping everything into it! His Core *and* the stored Energy he has in that rod! Is he mad? Does he seek to destroy us all?" Arona looked at Victor as though he had the answer. He just shrugged and took a step back, only to be met with an invisible wall of force. Arona had followed him, and just as the first meteor hit the ground with a cacophonous *boom*, she stumbled into the invisible barrier, too.

"Ronkerz!" She hissed and muttered something else, some curse in a language the System didn't translate, then turned back to the arena as the rest of Arcus's payload smashed down like a cataclysm. The sound was deafening, and the ground shook and jumped and lurched, forcing Victor to concentrate on keeping his balance, but even as he struggled to stay on his feet, he realized something: The fire and smoke weren't touching him. The explosion rolled out from the impact point—waves of fire, clouds of black smoke, curtains of dirt, rock shards, and rubble. Everything came up against another invisible barrier, channeled away by waves of force or magical wind.

As the fire and smoke cleared, Arona sighed and gestured up the cliffside to where Ronkerz stood, his enormous arms spread wide, his violet eyes blazing like twin stars. "He's protecting the onlookers and town."

Victor nodded; he'd figured something like that was happening. As the smoke and dust cleared, he started scanning the arena, wondering how Arcus's alpha strike had served him. The place looked as if a bomb had gone off, which he supposed made sense. What Arcus had done was the Energy-user equivalent of calling in an airstrike. The stone ground was cracked and pitted; pools of fire, red-glowing stone, and black smoke still lingered. Hovering in the center of the destruction was Arcus's fiery form.

The crowd had gotten quiet, but when Arcus slowly turned, his flaming arm and tentacle held high in triumph, a murmur broke out. Several heartbeats passed as everyone looked for Fanatala. When no one could see any sign of the champion, hushed and tentative at first, the onlookers began to cheer. The applause started near the ground, where people stood like Victor and Arona in cave mouths or between buildings, but it slowly spread until the entire canyon was roaring with it. Meanwhile, Arcus continued to rotate, basking in the praise, his body too alight for Victor to see his expression.

Ronkerz lowered his arms, but he didn't speak, and Victor began to feel a funny twinge of doubt in his gut. If Arcus had killed Fanatala, Ronkerz would know it. He would be shouting *something*—praise or anger or amusement. He wouldn't stand there on his high perch, watching Arcus intently. "He missed."

Arona looked at him sharply. "You see her?"

"No, but Ronkerz—" Just as he was about to explain his thought process, Fanatala appeared behind Arcus and drove her twin blades, not once or twice, but three times each, into Arcus's back. Arcus's flames winked out, and he fell to the ground in a crumpled heap. Fanatala held up her bloody, curved swords, and the cheers, which had abruptly stopped when she'd appeared, erupted with renewed frenzy, and the crowd took up a chant.

"Gasher! Gasher! Gasher!"

"He lives," Arona said, pointing. Sure enough, Victor saw Arcus slowly, laboriously flop onto his back, a great pool of blood blossoming out around his red-robed form. His tentacle shakily clutched a bulbous potion bottle, but Fanatala saw his movement and *blinked* away. Suddenly, she loomed over the downed Pyromancer, her boot on his tentacle, holding the potion at bay.

"Yield?" she growled, but she didn't look at Arcus. Her mask was trained upward toward Ronkerz.

Victor never heard Arcus say anything, but Ronkerz's voice boomed through the canyon, "Fanatala the Gasher has won! Her opponent yields! Welcome, Arcus the *Inferno*, to Rumble Town—our newest *Big One* in training!" While Victor and Arona absorbed those words, the town roared in a frenzy of excitement. Ronkerz let it go on for several long seconds, then held up his hands for silence. "Arona, Death Caster, student of Vesavo Bonewhisper, the Demon of Tsuva, enter the arena!"

"Damn," Victor muttered. "I think you were right. He's building an army, and I feel like we're about to be recruited."

"Yes, I'm quite certain that warrior could have killed Arcus with her strike. Teleportation skills, even short-ranged like that, are difficult to contend with." Arona looked up at Victor, her dark eyes depthless and full of secrets. "I won't be so easily conscripted." With that, she stepped into the arena as Fanatala scooped up Arcus's fallen, bloody form and simply disappeared.

Victor had to admire Arona's confidence, but he was starting to have doubts—how was he supposed to contend with someone who could blink around the battlefield? Could he kill someone he couldn't touch? "Shit, *chica,*" he muttered, hefting Lifedrinker in both of his hands as he watched the dark-robed, straight-backed Death Caster gliding through the wreckage of Arcus's meteor strike, "we might get a decent workout after all. This is gonna get good and bloody."

37

DEATH'S MAW

Ronkerz's voice roared out, vibrating the stone under Victor's feet. "Which Big One shall we choose to face this disciple of death, Rumble Town? I'll give you a choice! Will it be Zara Bloodmoon, daughter of Rex Hangar and wielder of the Midnight Scythe, or will it be Gorruk the Crusher, Wrecker of Bones, and Ravager of the Lich King?" If the crowd made any noise while Ronkerz spoke, Victor couldn't hear them, but as soon as he finished, the onlookers broke into two distinct chants. Some rhythmically yelled, "*Zara, Zara, Zara*," while others contended with "*Gorruk, Gorruk, Gorruk!*"

Victor watched Arona while the denizens of Rumble Town shouted for their favorite champions. She stood still, her twisted black staff planted in the ground before her, while cold-looking blue mist seeped out of the dirt and blasted stone, forming a hazy cloud that rose to her knees. Something moved in the cloud of vaporous air, and Victor thought he saw a faintly luminescent form lurking within it. Was she already summoning her minions? Was Ronkerz going to allow that? It seemed so, for as Victor glanced up to him, the great simian lord of the dungeon seemed to be basking in the roars of the crowd, enjoying their contest.

Before long, it became clear that the Gorruk supporters would win. Slowly but surely, more and more people stopped chanting for Zara, and the cries for Gorruk grew louder and louder. After a handful of minutes, Ronkerz stepped to the edge of his high cave and held his arms wide, silencing the crowd. "Rumble Town, you have chosen! Gorruk the Crusher, take the field!"

One of the shadowy hulking figures behind Ronkerz stepped forward and leaped off the ledge, falling to the ground with a tremendous impact that Victor felt through the stone, jarring the bones in his ankles and knees. When Gorruk stood tall, Victor winced—he was an imposing figure. The Big One was a reptilian creature that towered over Arona, easily more than ten feet tall. He wore red leather straps for armor but carried a massive metal-spiked shield and a hammer that looked fit for pounding boulders into dust. He arched his back, angled his alligator maw toward the sky, and roared.

To her credit, Arona didn't flinch, and rather than quail before his display of brute power, she flung out her hand, scattering a dozen tiny bones in a semicircle behind the Big One. Ronkerz made it clear he knew things were kicking off by shouting, "*Fight!*" Gorruk dashed forward, his spiked shield leading the way. Victor thought it was about to be over before it started, but Arona's spectral companion rose from the mist, placing itself in the giant's path. Victor's eyes widened at the sight of the specter.

The ghostly, semi-ethereal, semisolid being was skeletally gaunt, clothed in ragged, luminescent chainmail. It wore a horned helm and wielded nothing but daggerlike claws on its hands. Still, it was huge, fast, and apparently quite strong. It rose from the mist looming over Arona and was more than a match for Gorruk's rushing form as it wrapped the claws of its right hand around the edge of his shield and stepped to the side, pulling the giant with it, forcing him to stumble as he windmilled his hammer for balance.

"Take him, Shol-pan!" Arona cried. Again, the specter wailed, and he leaped after Gorruk, raking his long claws in a savage, wild frenzy, tearing long bloody grooves in the giant's flesh, ripping the straps of his armor to shreds and sending bright red blood spraying in arcs with each lightning-fast, hacking gash. Gorruk screamed his fury and pain, but Victor felt something was off. The dozens of cuts were deep and bloody, but Gorruk's scream didn't have even a hint of desperation in it. In fact, Victor recognized a kindred battle lust in that sound, and he knew Gorruk was just getting warmed up.

As the gashes mounted and Gorruk was driven farther and farther from Arona, the Death Caster began to surge with deep, cold Energy, preparing another spell. As she lifted her staff, Gorruk roared and whirled, lashing out with his spiked shield. Victor thought the specter, Shol-pan, would evade the blow, or perhaps ignore it, being less than solid flesh, but the shield struck true, and with a splash of blue-white ectoplasmic flesh, Arona's champion was thrown to the side, crumpled and deformed, tumbling over the charred stones of the arena.

Victor winced, but as he turned back to Arona, the air temperature dropped by a dozen degrees. She held her arms wide, a strained, rictus grin on her face, as a whirlwind of ghostly, ethereal blades exploded into existence, streaking toward Gorruk. The blades howled as they sliced the air, and the temperature continued to plummet as they seemed to suck the very life out of the arena, riming everything with a frigid layer of hoarfrost as they traversed the space. Gorruk had barely turned from his struggle with Shol-pan when the whirlwind struck.

He lifted his shield and roared, then bright lances of Energy exploded from the spiked surface like a starburst. Where the beams of light shone, the blades disintegrated and the frost melted. The temperature in the arena immediately began to recover as half of Arona's spectral blade storm was destroyed on impact. Still, the other half, the straggling, sputtering remnant of the whirlwind, washed over Gorruk and added to the many bleeding gashes on his hulking, green-scaled body. Even so, as his blood pooled on the stones, he stood resolute and straight when the spell faded.

Victor looked at Arona, trying to gauge her strength, but to his surprise, she'd faded from view in a new bank of ghostly fog. Gorruk strode toward it, but then, with an explosion of grave-scented Energy, like moist soil and fresh decay, the bones Arona had strewn out earlier sprang into the air. They rapidly multiplied and grew until a small army of skeletal minions surrounded the cloud of blue-tinted fog. Each of the skeletons' skulls, in all their variety, held bright, ghostly blue lights in their eye sockets, and they turned, in unison, to focus on Gorruk. The way they moved in perfect synchrony made Victor shudder as a chill ran down his spine.

Gorruk didn't wait for the skeletal monsters to act; he charged on a streak of light like a sunbeam toward the one farthest to the left and smashed it to bits with a cacophonous impact of his shield. The skeletal warrior's bones flew with a clatter, but the other skeletons leaped into action, jumping, charging, and sliding over the ground to engage Gorruk from every side. Some wielded claws, but others held gleaming weapons—hammers, axes, spears, and swords. Considering how quickly Gorruk had killed the first one, Victor thought they must not be very tough, but he was surprised to see them pushing the giant reptilian man back.

Gorruk fought with an impressive fury; he smashed his hammer in wide arcs, and it wrought destruction on any bones it touched—shattering ribs, smashing skulls, crushing shoulders, hips, and spines. The skeletons didn't die passively; they stabbed and hacked at Gorruk, carving more and more bloody rents in his scaly hide. Meanwhile, Arona didn't stand idly by. Victor didn't know what she was doing, but she floated around the melee, planting white, coldly pulsating rods into the stone as though it were clay.

Several times, Gorruk saw what she was doing and tried to intervene, charging toward her, but each time, one of her skeletal minions interceded on her behalf, taking the charge and sacrificing its life. Victor swore he saw Gorruk destroy dozens of the skeletons, yet they kept coming, and that's when he realized they weren't staying dead. No matter how badly Gorruk shattered them, the constructs slowly reformed, their bones pulling together on threads of pale-blue Energy.

He could see the Big One growing frustrated. His grunts grew more ragged and hoarse, his swings wilder and more reckless, and his blazing sunlight blasts more frequent. However, even the skeletons destroyed by that bright power didn't stay dead, and Victor felt a grin growing on his lips—Arona was going to wear him down. That's when he saw Arona's spectral champion, Shol-pan, rise from where he'd been thrown and dive into the fray, knocking aside some of his smaller allies in his eagerness to lay into Gorruk with his ten-inch spectral claws.

Arona stabbed a seventh white rod into the stone, and then she rose up, carried by her spectral mist, to look down upon the melee at the center of her formation. She clapped her hands, shouted a word that felt strange to Victor's ears, and fired a beam of strangely pulsating Energy into the nearest rod. The device absorbed the torrent of Energy and then flared with white, sickly light that made Victor's eyes water and his stomach feel queasy. The light shot forth from one rod to the next, creating a sort of luminescent netting over Gorruk and the undead minions fighting within the formation.

"Holy shit! Yes, *chica*!" Victor growled, pounding his fist into his palm as the net of sickly, ethereal Energy began to contract, passing harmlessly through the undead monsters in the ring but pressing down against Gorruk's scales with sizzling, hissing burns that brought wild, enraged screams from the reptilian's throat. As the bands of deathly Energy tightened, burning into the Big One and driving him to his knees, Arona's mist began to fade, and she slowly lowered to the stone ground.

Victor could tell she was exhausted, and it seemed she was trying to conserve some of her waning Energy because she waved her hand, and her skeletal minions collapsed in heaps of bone that crumbled to dust, leaving behind only the tiny singular enchanted bones from which they'd sprung. During the battle, Victor had thought the minions were simply exceptionally resilient, reforming and rejoining the fight over and over, but he now realized that Arona had used her own Energy to rebuild or heal them each time. She sagged against her staff, watching as Shol-pan, too, faded away into wisps of blue smoke.

Gorruk thrashed and writhed, and Victor could see the bands of Energy cutting into him deeper and deeper, driving him down, apparently helpless to resist. Arona held up her left hand and slowly, with great effort, began to clench it into a fist. Gorruk screamed in rage and pain, and just when Victor thought the fight was over, that he was done for, the scream shifted in tenor from pain and frustration to bone-deep rage.

Suddenly, Victor felt a pull on his Core, as if he stood in the presence of something massive, something profoundly powerful. Then, just as he steadied himself and focused on Gorruk—the source of that enormous surge of

Energy—he saw the reptilian man begin to change. His body swelled grotesquely, rippling as bones expanded and shifted beneath his flesh. The bloody cuts, gashes, and stab wounds spread wide, ripping and joining in long, gory furrows that rapidly filled in with glistening, iridescent green scales.

As the Big One's body expanded, Arona's trap formation fought to hold him down, to cut into him, but the Energy waves pouring out of Gorruk negated their deathly Energy, and one by one, the sickly white metallic rods *pinged* out of the rocky ground, tumbling away to clang and clatter on the arena walls. Arona fell to her knees, her pale arms shakily catching her from falling onto her face.

Victor felt the dryness in his mouth and realized he'd been holding it open. He licked his lips. "Come on, Arona! Get up!" As if she'd heard him, the Death Caster struggled to her feet, stumbling back from the still writhing, still expanding, still *roaring* Gorruk. Victor shifted his gaze to watch the gigantic reptilian form taking shape at the center of the arena.

Victor had likened the Big One's snout to that of an alligator earlier, but now he was cursing the thought—Gorruk was indeed transforming into something gigantic and crocodilian. His scales were nothing like those of an Earth-based alligator or crocodile, though; they gleamed and shimmered like metal. Worse, he'd sprouted a massive twenty-foot tail, the tip of which ended in a knobby bone-like protrusion adorned with razor-sharp spines.

As the monster thrashed back and forth, shaking off the last vestiges of his former body and armor, he whirled to aim one of his crocodilian eyes at Arona. The giant monstrosity heaved and huffed, puffing great billowing breaths out through his enormous nostrils as the eye narrowed in a hungry, almost lecherous stare. Each of Gorruk's four legs was as big as Arona's entire body, and they all ended in great black scimitar-like claws. As the monster slowly began to circle his prey, for Victor couldn't see the depleted Death Caster as anything else, Ronkerz's voice boomed out, echoing off the canyon walls.

"Arona! You may yield! Gorruk's restraint is limited with his bloodline running wild!"

Arona, holding her staff between herself and the gigantic reptile, took a shaky step back and looked up at Ronkerz's shelf, then to her right, locking eyes with Victor. What he saw in those depthless black pools didn't look like resignation or even fear. Determination was plainly written on her face, and Victor sucked in his breath when he realized she wouldn't be giving up. He almost shouted for her to concede, but something in him wouldn't let his lips form those words. Instead, he took a deep breath and bellowed, "*Kill* that fucker!"

Arona gave him a brief nod, and then, just as before, Victor felt the temperature in the arena begin to dip as faintly luminescent, blue-tinged mist began to rise from the ground. Arona raised her staff high and took a deep breath. Victor could feel her gathering Energy; the potential of her spell pulled at him, almost like the weighty nature of Gorruk's transformation. He leaned forward in anticipation, waiting to see what she would do, but the great reptile wasn't willing to be patient. With a swish of its enormous tail for impetus, Gorruk launched himself forward and closed his great jaws over Arona with a thunderous *snap*.

One second, she'd been about to work her magic, her staff held high. The next, only half her body remained to bleed out onto the blacked stone of the arena floor. It happened so quickly that she never cried out. She'd been looking at Gorruk, so Victor never saw her face, never got a chance to see if fear entered her steely gaze. He'd never know if she'd been surprised or embarrassed. He hoped not. He hoped she was too focused on her magic, too full of adrenaline and anger to see Gorruk coming. He hoped she died with that bravery in her heart and that she'd carry it with her to the spirit plane.

The ground shook as Ronkerz leaped down and hooked one of his massive arms around Gorruk's thick, scaly neck. At first, Victor thought he was congratulating him, but when he saw him squeeze, he wondered if he was angry. Would he punish the giant reptile? Would he kill him? As he squeezed Gorruk's thick neck, holding him steady, Victor saw him snake his other arm into that toothy maw and slowly extract the bloody, saliva-covered other half of Arona's body. "Too much good equipment here for you to digest, champion."

The arena broke into an uproar of cheering as Arona's upper half landed on the stone with a wet *squelch*. Her bloody, slime-covered face happened to be staring directly at Victor. Those depthless pools had glazed over. Her pretty, pale face had deep tooth grooves ripped from brow to chin, and her tongue protruded from her carefully stained black lips. Victor felt heat rising in his chest, saw his vision tinting red, and, before he realized he was doing it, he started stalking toward the corpse.

"Halt, boy!" Ronkerz roared, and once again, Victor felt the weight of the veil walker's aura pushing him back. Victor ignored him, his eyes locked on Arona's defiled corpse. One after the other, he continued to take steps. It felt like walking up a mountain through burning, oxygenless air with ten-thousand-pound chains hooked to his ankles. Still, he progressed—vessels bursting in his eyes, blood flowing from his nose and ears, and veins standing out like rivers of blood on his engorged muscles.

Ronkerz scowled, and the arena grew hushed. He took two strides to Victor and reached up with one of his enormous hands to grasp his neck, halting his forward movement. The grip felt like a band of steel, and it reminded Victor of his time as a slave in the Greatbone Mine, further fueling his rage. He opened his pathways, letting his Core unload into them, ready to cast Volcanic Fury and go for broke, but then, as suddenly as a switch being thrown, he felt the pressure of a tremendous will *pushing* his Energy back into his Core.

His mind cleared, the red in his vision faded, and Victor realized that his hands were wrapped around Ronkerz's wrist, straining to pull his grasping fingers away from his neck. Lifedrinker lay at his feet. When had he dropped her? Ronkerz must have seen the clarity enter his eyes because he nodded, then slowly relaxed his grip on Victor's throat. "That eager to do battle, eh, boy? Well, you'll get your chance, but not against me. Not yet, anyway." He glanced down at Arona's mutilated corpse. "Angry at her rough treatment? I'm not terribly pleased, either. Take heart—I'll give her a good resting place."

Once again, Ronkerz *moved*—faster and more adroitly than Victor's eyes could properly track. He tried, though, and thought he saw some blurs of motion here and there, but still, almost without any trace, Ronkerz, Arona's body, and the gigantic crocodilian champion were gone. Victor stood alone in the arena. He stooped to pick up Lifedrinker and, with her resting on one shoulder, slowly turned, soaking in the attention of the onlookers.

He sent some Energy into the runes on his armor, reactivating it, cladding himself in heavy red-black metal, scales, and leather. Lifting Lifedrinker high, he screamed—nothing articulate, no words, just a primal, bloodthirsty cry for battle, chaos, and blood. His outburst was fueled by fear and rage, but when the crowd roared their enthusiasm, the glory in his Core surged, and a mad grin twisted Victor's lips as he deeply inhaled, soaking up their enthusiasm. They wanted to see him fight, and he would give them something to remember.

38

STORMCLAW

Victor paced in a circle, Lifedrinker held over his head, shouting into the crowd's roaring enthusiasm. Ronkerz must have enjoyed the spectacle because he let it go on for quite some time before his basso voice boomed like a gong, reverberating through the canyon. He didn't try to silence Victor or the crowd; he simply allowed the power of his projected voice to overwhelm their noise as he hollered, "The last of our visitors is eager to fight, Rumble Town! Look at him! See the might of an elder bloodline, here to entertain you! Which of our Big Ones can stand against such fury?"

Ronkerz's echoing, booming voice broke through Victor's self-induced haze of anger, and he slowly lowered his axe as he listened. "Make no mistake! The man below might not be through his iron ranks, but he's a monster in his own right—a warrior with the blood of a titan in his veins, a berserker with a Core brimming with rage! You saw how he stood against my aura! Who among our champions could face such a challenger?"

The crowd, hushed by Ronkerz's thunderous voice, began to murmur in low tones—words that, disparate at first, started to coalesce into a single name that they repeated, louder and louder, until the canyon echoed with the sound: "*Stormclaw! Stormclaw! Stormclaw!*"

"My number one? My apprentice? My right hand? Lira Stormclaw? The Reaper of Bloodtide Cove? You think this challenger is worthy of *her* attention?" As he egged them on, the crowd grew more and more vociferous, howling her name and pounding their cudgels, shields, tankards, and brooms. They stomped their feet in rhythm to their frenzy, howling the Big One's name, "*Stormclaw! Stormclaw! Stormclaw!*"

Ronkerz seemed to like what he heard and saw, so he opened his massive arms, and he too shouted, "Stormclaw! Take the field!" With a flash of shining armor reflecting the moon's light, Lira Stormclaw leaped from the ledge, spreading her great gray-feathered wings and slowly spiraling down to the arena floor. Just as Victor had seen her before, she wore shiny silver chainmail, but now she also had her head encased in a gleaming polished helmet. She clutched her giant curved saber in one hand, and on her other arm, she wore a bright metallic buckler that glinted in the pale light of the moon.

Her talons crunched into the canyon floor, and Victor saw they'd cut grooves in the stone. When her hawklike gaze locked with his, she spread her wings wide and held up her sword, and the crowd went wild again. She was the biggest avian person he'd ever seen, easily nine feet tall, and her wingspan had to be more than twenty feet wide. She cut an imposing figure, especially considering her gleaming armor and the heavy, bold aura she let loose. Victor might have been intimidated if he hadn't already fought dozens of men, women, and creatures more intimidating—if he hadn't already stood up against Ronkerz's aura, which was a hundred times denser.

"Well?" Lira asked, her voice once again surprising Victor with its melodic nature. "Shall we dance?" She slashed her saber through the air between them, leaving trails of glittering light and somehow producing a crystalline ring with each cut.

Victor held Lifedrinker ready, hands loose on her haft, and began to circle the avian woman. "Ready when you are."

Lira shrieked, cracked her wings, and launched into him, her curved sword whistling as she laid about with a frenzy of lightning-fast attacks. Victor tried to answer the ferocity of her blows but found himself unable to match her speed. Still, he was a skilled axe wielder and an experienced duelist, and she didn't land any strikes clean enough to draw blood. She got past his guard a few times, but only because he saw her weapon would strike his armor and wanted to test its edge.

Once, he caught the saber on his heavy gauntlet, and though it sparked and drew a narrow, shiny scratch in the metal, he hardly felt it. His wyrm-scale vest didn't quite hold up as well, shedding a scale as she drew the blade along his ribs, but still, he was unharmed, and the armor immediately began to mend itself—the fallen scale crumbled to dust and rapidly reformed to fill the gap. It was plain that Lira was testing him, and Victor could see her shrewd, predatory gaze grow sharper as she was repeatedly rebuffed.

When she surged with Energy and began to move faster than he could track, Victor cast Inspiration of the Quinametzin. As the white-gold Energy flooded his pathways and his consciousness expanded, he began to see the greater pattern of Lira's movements, and though he still had trouble tracking her scimitar's flashing blade, he saw how she moved her feet, how her wings flexed, and where her center of gravity shifted as she went through the patterns of her attacks. He contemplated those patterns and formed responses in his mind as his armor amassed scrapes.

His grin turned savage as he predicted one of her slashes and, for the first time, stepped inside it and brought Lifedrinker down in a brutal hack against the armor on the outside of Lira's thigh. Lifedrinker, still carrying a shard of Victor's spirit, dented the shiny armor and split it just enough for her razor edge to draw a thin gash that wept blood. Lira screeched her pain and frustration and pumped her wings, hurling herself into the air, flying a dozen yards back.

Still brimming with inspiration, Victor tracked her trajectory and cast Energy Charge, flooding the spell's pattern with fear-attuned Energy. In a cloud of black and purple shadows, he ripped through the fire-blasted arena and, with Lifedrinker's edge leading the way, smashed into Lira just as she landed. She was fast, though, and put her shiny buckler in the path of Lifedrinker's edge. Victor's spell moved him like a missile, and Lifedrinker pulled and vibrated with the urgency of her hack, but even so, that shiny, platter-sized shield stopped her cold. The impact rang out like a cannonball hitting a gong, and Victor's momentum drove him past the impact point, nearly jerking the axe from his hands as Lira sidestepped his driving shoulder.

Victor's grip was mighty, and Lifedrinker loathed the idea of being taken from him; it would take the weight of a mountain to pull her from his grip, so she slid along that shiny barrier, ringing out a crystalline screech as she tore a thin groove in the metal and followed Victor as he flew past Lira. The avian warrior snapped her wings and launched herself at Victor's back, scoring two powerful blows, left and right, smashing his wyrm-scale vest in an X pattern, shattering scales, cutting the thick wyrm-hide material, and for the first time drawing blood. Victor stumbled forward but whirled, cleaving Lifedrinker in a wide, one-handed backswing.

Lira danced back, avoiding the savage blow, and then, with a surge of potent, sharp Energy that tasted like coppery blood and rust, a dozen black iron blades, each the size and shape of Lira's saber, exploded out of the ground and began to dance in the air, moving like a storm of razored metal toward Victor. Victor's monstrous vitality, bolstered by Sovereign Will, had already closed the wounds on his back, and he felt fresh, as if he'd barely begun to exert himself. His savage grin widened as he waded into the magically hacking swords and began to dance, treating each like a new opponent.

The blades wove side to side, up and down, and hacked the air with palpable *whooshes*. Even so, they were far slower and duller than Lira's gleaming saber. Victor smashed them aside with Lifedrinker and his gauntlet. Sometimes, he even ducked his head and used his helmet to catch the blades. All the while, he kept track of Lira, watching as she moved around her sword storm, timing the many swinging sabers so she could slip in and drive her much deadlier primary weapon at Victor's exposed flank or try to interfere with one of his parries.

Victor took many hits from those magical swords, but most slid harmlessly off his armor. Still, his thick lava king hide pants were beginning to show their wear and tear, and he began to bleed as the minor cuts started to mount. His right arm was the worst—no gauntlet protected his forearm, and it was repeatedly exposed as he swung Lifedrinker out to smash aside one sword or another. Even so, his natural regeneration could cope, and Victor fought the urge to scream his frustration and cast Iron Berserk. He knew Lira had more that she was holding back, and he didn't want to play his cards until he had to.

After several minutes of battle against Lira's sword storm, Victor fell into an inspiration-fueled trance, and fewer and fewer swords hit him. He'd begun to see a pattern to the whirling, weaving blades; they had to make room for each other and thus weren't truly random. If he'd had to explain the pattern, he couldn't have. He caught glimpses of it on an instinctual level and began to modify his footwork and the weaving motions of his axe to capitalize, and soon he was smashing four blades aside with each swooping swing of Lifedrinker. As he found the rhythm and fell into the new dance, he could turn most of his attention to Lira and once again frustrate her efforts to cut him.

"Gods be damned! You're good with that axe!" she grunted after a while. The words hardly registered on Victor as he wove between the slashing sabers and tried to work his way closer to the woman controlling them. As he closed the distance and began to put pressure on her despite her hacking storm of swords, Lira grunted, but it wasn't so much a frustrated sound as an excited one. The same sharp Energy filled the air, again filling Victor's mouth with the taste of rust and blood. Then, in an explosion of rock fragments, black iron plates burst from the ground and began to spin violently around Lira.

The swords crumbled to black dust, but the plates, varying in size, spun so rapidly that Victor was forced back. He ducked his head and held Lifedrinker up in defense, but Lira didn't press the attack; she was focused on her magic. The plates of magical iron wove in a whirling pattern around her body, and then one by one, they began to slam into her. At first, Victor thought she'd made an error or cast a spell she couldn't control. He soon realized what was happening, though, and growled as he watched Lira encase herself. The tall, lean warrior became a massive juggernaut of black metal.

Even her wings were covered, and though he doubted they could still be used to fly, they looked like formidable weapons in their own right. Rather than feathers, they were lined with razored blades, and as she flexed them up and down, he could see they weren't immobile. As the last of the plates slammed into place, completing her suit of dense armor, Victor roared and cast Energy Charge again, this time fueling it with rage. He didn't want to risk Lifedrinker's edge or handle being damaged before he tested that thick armor, so he led the charge with his dense gauntlet, aiming to cave in the center of Lira's plated chest.

Lira spread her arms, her saber looking small in her metal-plated fist, and seemed to welcome Victor's impact. He soon learned why. As his gauntlet impacted that thick black plate, he realized it wasn't mundane armor that coated Lira's body. The metal was rife with Energy, infused with the magic of Lira's affinity, which apparently wasn't simple iron but something far more profound, something more like the very essence of "metal."

Victor's gauntlet rebounded, the knuckles bent in by the tremendous impact. Even as his fist flew back, his body continued forward, and Victor slammed into Lira with a *boom* that cracked the stone around them. Victor's Core flared, driving rage-attuned Energy into the magical shell meant to protect him. Even without looking, he could feel the hot sun at the center of his being cool as he depleted a tremendous portion of his reserves to keep from crushing himself against the immovable density of Lira's metal-clad form.

As the waves of force washed outward, throwing stones, boulders, and clouds of debris toward the arena's edges, Lira punched her empty gauntleted fist into Victor's side. She turned with the action, putting her considerable weight behind the blow, and Victor was lifted from his feet and sent flying. As he tumbled through the air, sure he'd smash into a crowd of onlookers who stood between two buildings, he came up against the invisible force of Ronkerz's Energy. It felt like colliding with a stone wall.

"Fuck!" Victor groaned as he slid down the invisible barrier to the hard rubble-strewn ground. He struggled to take a full breath, sharp pain lancing through his torso. Coughing and wheezing, he planted his hands on the ground and clambered to his feet. He was sure some of his ribs were shattered; he could feel the bones grinding painfully as his passive regeneration worked to undo the damage. Just as he'd found his footing, he felt the ground trembling rhythmically, and that was when he realized Lira was already upon him. Victor whirled just in time to get his gauntleted left arm up and catch the descending edge of her brilliant saber.

The blow struck his gauntlet so solidly that the edge bit clean through the extremely dense, heavy metal, and he felt the saber bite a full inch into his arm, grinding into his wrist bones. Not only was Lira a great deal heavier with her armor plating, but she must have gotten some sort of strength boost; it felt as if a pneumatic hammering machine had been unleashed on him as she began to pummel, kick, and chop at him. Victor fought to deflect her blows, scrambling back, pain from a dozen new injuries spurring him away as her tremendously heavy feet stomped at him.

"*Enough!*" he roared and unleashed his Core, casting Iron Berserk. Lira swung a heavy, metal-plated boot at his knee, but Victor howled a roar of fury as his vision darkened with shades of crimson, and his body exploded with muscle. He caught her boot in one massive hand and, with a tremendous jerk of his entire body, with the muscles and tendons standing up around his neck like cords of woven steel, he threw her across the arena. Lira's wail of surprise echoed strangely from her metal-clad head as she tumbled for two dozen yards before crashing onto the arena floor with a clamor akin to a head-on truck collision.

Victor bounded after her, already bunching his legs for a leap before she even hit the ground. He soared through the air, his gigantic form outstretched, his back arched, Lifedrinker held high in one hand. She smoldered and burst into baleful flames as her own rage and battle lust rose to match Victor's. When he came down like a falling mountainside, he planted Lifedrinker firmly in Lira's metallic shoulder as she struggled to rise. With a screech of rending metal, Lifedrinker burned through the armor, flaring white-hot at her edge as she melted her way in.

Lira screamed as Lifedrinker's merciless edge bit her flesh, severing muscles and tendons and boiling away her flesh and blood as she *dug* her way deeper. Victor let his rage mount, let his will to remain lucid fall away, and with his renewed strength and much greater stature, he began to repay Lira's pummeling and then some.

He let Lifedrinker work, tugging Energy out of his opponent, and with his right hand, he grasped Lira so his left, gauntleted fist could pound her metal casing. Each blow sounded like a cannon firing, the great *bong* sound echoing through the arena, overwhelming the roars of the crowd. His gauntlet had grown with him and hadn't lost any of its density. No longer did the knuckles bend when he pounded against Lira's armor—now *she* bent. Victor jerked and punched, pounding dents into her back, her sides, her helmet, and her chest. All the while, Lifedrinker streamed black smoke from the rip in Lira's shoulder armor as she dug and burned her way into her flesh.

Lira screamed over and over. Her cries might have stopped Victor if he'd been lucid—if he'd allowed his will to keep his rage at bay—but he didn't and continued to punish her. He saw visions of Arona's torn corpse, and somewhere in his mind, they got convoluted with memories of a different face, a different woman who'd died as he watched, helpless and slow, stupidly looking on when he should have done *something*. That frustration, that remembered helplessness, drove him nearly mad with rage, and Victor didn't let up his pounding, even when Lira's screams changed.

At first, he didn't notice the difference, but slowly, even in his rage-addled mind, Victor began to register a tonal shift in Lira's screams. They went from pain-filled to angry. Still, Victor drove her to the ground, pressed his powerful knee into her lower back, and grabbed both sides of her metal-clad head, intent on either pulling off her armor or her head—he didn't care which. "*Aaaaaaaagh!*" Lira screamed, and then, like a charge in the air before a lightning strike, Victor felt her gathering that sharp, metallic Energy.

"Die!" he screamed, and with all his might, he pulled, determined to stop whatever she was doing. He might have done it. He might have killed her, but just as he felt the metal start to give, it expanded, and suddenly he was struggling to keep his grip as Lira's body grew, lifting him off the ground as his titanic form was dwarfed by *hers*. Lira's metallic body outgrew his by a third, and the rent Lifedrinker had made filled in with new metal—brighter, shinier, harder. It pushed the axe out, and Victor grabbed her haft just as Lira reached around to snag his arm and slam him to the ground.

Victor's back hit the cracked stone with a ground-shaking impact that shattered his ribs, drove the air from his lungs, and dented the back of his helm, rattling his brain and stunning him. He lay there, stars flashing in his vision, and watched the titanic form of the metal-clad avian warrior as she held up her saber. Another surge of that weird metallic Energy flooded the air, and shards of metal flew from the ground to wrap her saber, expanding it, lengthening it, until Lira stood with a monstrous sword that gleamed with iridescent, rainbow-hued metal, shining like the light of a star.

Victor grunted, trying to breathe, contemplating that amazing sword and its ten-foot blade. Lira held it above him, a metallic juggernaut poised to execute him. Victor's mind reeled, searching for a strategy, wondering if he could roll aside and avoid that deadly gleaming edge. He knew he couldn't block it with Lifedrinker. He doubted his arm would survive the attempt to block it with his gauntlet. He'd just taken his first full breath, allowing the stars to fade from his vision, when he realized why Lira hadn't struck him yet—she was waiting for him to yield. As if to confirm things, Ronkerz's voice boomed through the arena. "Yield, titan. Live to grow stronger and repay Lira for the lesson."

On his back, with a titanic blade poised to carve him in half, he felt his rage fading. Victor began to growl. It was a low, guttural sound that had little to do with his bloodline and a lot to do with his stubborn refusal to lose. If his Iron Berserk was running out and he couldn't pummel that powerful metallic shell until its occupant died, he'd try something else. Ronkerz's voice echoed through the arena again, "Do you yield?" Victor continued to growl as he poured Energy into his spell. Dark tendrils of tangible shadow began to coalesce around him, flowing out of the ground, out of the air, out of *him*.

Lira screamed and brought her blade down like a gleaming guillotine, but it was too late—a wave of palpable terror exploded out of those shadows, and Lira balked, botching the aim of her killing blow. Victor, recovered from his dazed state, felt his consciousness receding as the *other* took over. A scream that scratched his throat erupted from his lungs, and the lights around the arena flickered, their weak Energy sources overwhelmed by the darkness of his terror-fueled will.

With a crack of midnight wings, he burst from the pool of shadows into the air, circling the darkened arena. As he banked, swooping through the canyon, Terror observed the darkness and the many bright spirits surrounding him. A few were too dim to bother with, but hundreds were bright and tempting. Still, something lay between him and most of those morsels, something that, even as he watched, began to obscure them. Soon, all he could see was the single, brilliant spirit that glowed like an inferno beneath him. Gigantic, true, with a shell hard to pierce and a bright, gleaming edge that could surely cause him harm, but tempting, nonetheless.

As the spirit turned its eyes upward, spreading its broad metallic limbs and holding aloft that brilliant razor edge, Terror screamed and dove, weaving his shadows to obscure himself and confound the spirit's attempt to cut him. He had to infect his prey, had to poison that brilliant, sharp Energy with a seed of fear. As he swooped near, he screamed again, putting everything he knew of nightmares into the sound—millennia of tortured, pleading prey, conjured terrors, and lost, broken spirits.

The bright edge arced out and nearly cut him, but the shadows did their work, obscuring his true position, and Terror pulled away into the air, circling, coming around, gathering his strength for another projection of fear. This time, when he passed close, screeching his worst, most terrifying sound, the bright spirit deceived him. It feinted with its gleaming edge, but the actual attack came from those spiny metal wings. They arced upward, and the spirit spun. Terror was caught on the sharp spines and ripped from the sky to tumble onto the stony ground.

As the ground shook with the spirit's great, metallic steps, Terror tried to right himself, tried to launch back into the air, but his wings didn't work right; they were broken, and he wasn't healing quickly enough. In the back of his mind, the *other* growled, and he heard his command: *Enough. You're not right for this fight.* Terror relented; he was broken—let the *other* deal with this spirit.

As Victor came back to himself, his body still wrapped in shadow, painfully reverting to his normal form, he bunched his legs and activated Titanic Leap, narrowly escaping a devastating blow from Lira's saber. Soaring through the air, aiming for a clump of broken, scorched stones, he glanced back to see the giant metallic figure stomping toward his destination. He turned his gaze inward, saw his Core was nearly depleted, and groaned. He had to buy some time, had to give his Core a chance to regenerate some Energy. Even if he managed that, though, he wasn't sure what he'd do. Lira's armor was too dense; she was too large and strong. How was he going to beat her?

39

COLOSSAL TAKEDOWN

As he ran, leaping and dodging the brutal, weighty blows of Lira's blazing saber, Victor reached back and slung Lifedrinker into her harness. The axe had grown considerably since he'd first acquired her, but she was still only a hand axe to him in his titanic form. Against a foe like Lira, clad in her dense, magical metal skin, Lifedrinker was too small, too light. It was a problem—considering she was his favored weapon—but one that he'd have to tackle another day. For now, he had a colossus to kill.

As he leaped, landing hard in a pile of jagged broken stones where one of Arcus's meteors had torn up the arena floor, Victor took another look at his Core. Thanks to his enormous will attribute, his Energy was regenerating at a decent pace, but he still only had a third of his maximum pool to draw from. Was it enough? His Breath Core was bursting with magma-attuned Energy. Would the fiery titanic form granted by his Volcanic Fury be sufficient to stand against Lira's enormous metallic body?

Knowing he'd lose himself to the rage and likely be unable to strategize, Victor continued to stall, suffering the jeers and taunts of the crowd while he dodged another of Lira's ground-shaking charges. As she pounded past him, hacking her massive curved sword in a brilliant arc that seemed to cut the very air, Victor used Titanic Leap to launch himself to the far side of the arena. Mid-flight, he summoned the gigantic axe he'd taken from Karl the Crimson, grunting as thousands of pounds of dense black metal appeared in his hands, pulling him toward the ground.

As his feet touched down, he said, "Sorry, *chica*," and canceled his Imbue Spirit, taking his shard back from Lifedrinker. In the next heartbeat, he recast the spell, sending a shard of glory-attuned spirit into the enormous axe as he ran, dragging it behind him like a plow blade. The axe vibrated in his hands, humming with potential as the spell took hold, and Victor whirled, lifting the tremendous weapon crossways in both hands. The muscles on his shoulders and back bulged with the effort as he stared at Lira, watching her approach for the tenth time, her blazing sword held high, ready to cleave him in twain.

Karl's axe, usually dark as night and heavy as a fallen star, glowed with golden Energy, shedding sparks that sizzled and popped against the stone ground. Victor could feel its eagerness—his eagerness, considering the spirit within the weapon came from him. He smiled fiercely, watching Lira. When she'd closed the distance to just thirty yards—a few short steps for her—Victor opened both his Cores, flooding his pathways with magma and rage. Gathering that Energy up, he cast Volcanic Fury.

Lira, clad in her magical metallic form, had to weigh thousands of tons. Each of her steps crunched the stone beneath her boots, sending spiderwebs of cracks outward. When she stepped on loose rocks or even small boulders, she ground them to dust. Even so, she could *move.* She bunched her enormous legs and bounded toward Victor, perhaps hoping to interrupt his spell. It was too late, though; Victor's berserk transformations were nearly instantaneous, and by the time that blazing, star-bright saber ripped through the air at him, Victor had doubled in size, allowing him to lift Karl's axe high, as though it weighed no more than a slender reed.

Victor's parry was instinctual; he had no mind for strategy. The world had turned orange and yellow. He saw everything through a haze of heat, smoke, and flickering fire. He knew nothing but the desire to fight and kill, to destroy and demolish. When he saw the giant bearing down on him, swinging that bright curved sword, he jerked his axe upward, catching the blazing blade with the edge of his metal wedge-shaped axe-head. If he'd had the wherewithal to worry, it might have alarmed him that, following the ear-shattering *clang* of the weapons' impact, a sliver of black sparkling metal fell, steaming and glowing white-hot to the rubble-strewn ground.

Victor—faster, nimbler, and much, much stronger now that he'd embraced the wrath of his Volcanic Fury—stepped around the enormous metallic woman and swung Karl's axe in a full three-hundred-sixty-degree arc, winding it up so it *whooshed* through the air—thousands of pounds of dense, enchanted metal—and pounded it into her exposed right flank. The wedged axe-head struck her right beneath her wing, clanging against that impossibly dense, thick, metallic body with a reverberating *gong* that sent painful vibrations through the metallic haft of the axe.

The sparkling, golden glow of Victor's imbuement flared like fireworks exploding, and he felt the axe skip and slide down the woman's side. When the sparks faded, he saw the rewards for his efforts—a thin silvery scratch in the otherwise iridescent blue-black armor. Fury tinted the sepia tones of his vision toward red, and Victor roared, his mind knowing one thing—frustration. How could this obstacle stand before his wrath? How *dare* it? As renewed strength exploded through his muscles, he went truly berserk, so mad with a frenzied *need* to smash and destroy that his conscious mind was pushed deep beneath the surface as his instincts drove him into a deep madness.

With fire in his eyes, black smoke streaming from his nostrils, and a wild, crazed snarl on his face, Victor swung his hammer of an axe in great arcing blows that rang like a madman pounding on a massive bell. He pummeled Lira's metallic form, driving her back despite her enormous mass. She tried to swing her saber to intervene, and each *whooshing* slash might have ended him, might have cut limbs from his body, but Victor moved too fast in his frenzy, and his powerful blows made Lira clumsy, her slashes ugly and obvious. Victor ducked them and knocked them aside with his axe, failing to note the damage the saber inflicted as it carved grooves in the dense black metal and even slashed off bits of the axe-head.

Despite his titanic strength, despite his impossible fury, Victor's frenzy had little effect other than to push Lira around. He never dented the armor, and the superficial scrapes and gouges had little impact on its effectiveness. Meanwhile, he was draining his Cores dry; his rage-attuned Energy was drawn from the deep, powerful well of his Spirit Core, but his magma's source was far shallower. Victor's Breath Core was a tenth the size of his Spirit Core, and his Volcanic Fury required fuel from both Cores.

Unfortunately, Victor's madness didn't allow him to worry about trivialities like the source of his rage and power; he only cared that it flowed and that he could use it to destroy and kill those who stood before him. Destruction was everything, and nothing else mattered. As his frustration mounted and he failed to damage or even knock down the giant metallic warrior, almost instinctually, he pulled great torrents of Energy from both of his Cores and, with a ground-shaking stomp of his boot, cast Wake the Earth.

The effort of creating the spell drained his Breath Core of Energy, and Victor felt his reason return as his Volcanic Fury was cut short. The abrupt loss of his size and strength might have spelled his doom, as Lira was just about to hack her saber in a tremendous overhead chop, but the ground lurched violently, and she was knocked aside by a fragment of steaming stone that split the earth between them. Victor was a Herald of the Mountain's Wrath and as such felt little discomfort as the ground roiled and heaved around him. He rode the shifting stone with sturdy feet—a sailor well-accustomed to the bounding waves.

Victor's wits had returned with the loss of his fury. As he rode the heaving shelves of rock, watching as steam exploded from fissures, stones burst from the ground, and Lira was tossed about like a ship in a hurricane, he looked up to see Ronkerz standing tall, his arms wide, constraining the massive destruction of his spell to the arena. Victor's faint, half-formed hope that he might bring the canyon walls down and bury the whole damn town died before it truly had a chance to take shape.

Still, Ronkerz's efforts to force the spell to remain localized seemed to be concentrating its effects. The ground continued to buck and tilt while geysers of steam and smoke exploded from one rift after another. Shards of black, smoldering stone erupted from the already tortured surface of the arena, tilting great slabs of rock upward to grind against one another. Meanwhile, Victor found it harder and harder to maintain his balance, but nowhere near as much as poor Lira.

The gigantic metal-clad woman was tossed from one surging hunk of stone to another, and it wasn't long before her dense, blade-covered wings were bent and deformed. Victor might not have been able to impact the shape of her armored shell, but her own weight worked against her as she smashed and rolled around the cataclysmic, smoke-filled scene. Riding a slab of stone that suddenly surged beneath his feet, Victor began to laugh as he watched his colossal foe struggle.

Somewhere in the madness, he'd lost track of Karl's axe and briefly lamented the fact; it was an excellent, sturdy weapon for pounding on foes too resolute for Lifedrinker's edge. He couldn't worry long, however, because even he was beginning to struggle in the madness of the arena. The air was thick with hot black smoke, the fissures splitting the stone ground were starting to pool with actual lava, and Victor was finding less and less solid ground on which to regain his balance between tremors. He had to focus everything he had on the process.

When the ground finally stopped moving, his spell having run its course, he stood on a peak of stone created by two plates colliding near the center of the arena. Turning in a slow circle, he found himself in a miniature hellscape. Black smoke filled the air, and where there wasn't smoke, his eyes and lungs found hot, acrid steam—not surprising, considering the geysers venting near the magma-filled fissures. Where the ground was solid, it was covered in piles of jumbled, broken, blackened stone. Lira, still in her colossal form, still clad in iridescent blue-gray metal, lay with one of her legs submerged in a pool of lava. Her wings were bent like old TV antennae, and her armor was scuffed and dented—not an inch of it was pristine.

Victor hopped down, hoisting Lifedrinker from her harness. He canceled his Imbue Spirit, drawing his shard back from Karl's axe, wherever it had fallen, and then recast it on Lifedrinker, giving her back her usual shard of inspiration-attuned spirit. On nimble feet, he jumped from stone to stone, avoiding the bubbling, sulfur-scented pools of molten stone and giving a wide berth to a periodically spurting steam geyser. Lira hadn't moved, and he was hopeful that whatever spell she'd cast to encase herself in that near-impervious metallic casing would fade.

As he drew near, her giant helmet-shaped head turned toward him, and then, with a deep, hollow, echoing grunt, she lifted her gigantic leg out of the lava and let it fall to the stone with a ground-shaking *thud*. The metal glowed a soft orange-red, and magma dripped off it like oil from a hot skillet. The leg was clean of residue in seconds, and the glow faded, revealing unmarred metal. "That was a good effort," she grunted in that same hollow, echoing voice, then with a tremendous grinding of metal on stone, she began to clamber to her feet.

Victor watched her, his knuckles white where they gripped Lifedrinker's haft, and he began to despair. How deep must her reserves of Energy be to maintain that metallic shell? How was he supposed to damage her? Earlier, he'd contemplated employing his whip or even breathing magma on her, hoping it would cook her inside that shell, but she seemed immune to the heat. Lifedrinker couldn't pierce her shell. His giant axe could barely scratch it, and besides, he didn't know where it was.

As he slowly backed away from the colossus, watching her struggle to stand, her giant limbs slipping and scraping on the broken ground, Victor hastily scanned his dimensional containers, seeking a weapon that might pierce that shell. He glanced over his many spears left over from Karnice and silently cursed the fact that he'd traded the best of them away. "Not that a spear would be ideal," he grunted. No, he decided, what he really needed was an enormous maul made of something heavy enough to crack that shell—something he simply didn't have. Karl's axe had been his heaviest, densest weapon, and it hadn't worked.

Victor looked inward and saw that his Spirit Core was up to about twenty percent. It was enough to cast Iron Berserk, though not to maintain it for long. Sighing in frustration, he gripped Lifedrinker, holding her close as Lira took her first ground-jarring step toward him. Victor *wanted* to fight. He wanted to win, to break that shell and peel it off his enemy. He wanted to make Ronkerz eat his pride. Even as the last thought crossed his mind, he recognized his own wounded pride. Was he really going to lose? Was he going to kneel and accept Ronkerz's judgment?

He thought about begging his ancestors for help, but something didn't feel right about it. He was in a duel where he could yield at any moment—no one's life was on the line. Arcus and Arona had already been defeated. His people were safe back in Sojourn. Asking his ancestors to intervene felt . . . wasteful. Maybe, if he lost and took the defeat honorably, Ronkerz would work with him. Perhaps he could strike up a deal where Ronkerz would gain more by letting him leave than by keeping him around. Glancing up, he wasn't surprised to have the giant simian's angular purple eyes lock onto his. "What's your game, asshole?" Victor mouthed the words more than spoke them, but he meant them all the same.

As Lira took another step toward him, Victor nearly backed into a pool of still-bubbling magma. He glanced over his shoulder and saw that it was too large a pool to step over; the ground had split for a dozen yards in either direction, and the rift was nearly fifteen feet wide at the center, filled with hot magma that bubbled with the steam of a buried geyser. Victor stood with his back to the pool and turned to watch Lira. Growling with frustration, he slung Lifedrinker over his shoulder and let her harness snatch her into place.

"Okay, *puta madre*! Let's fucking do this!" He growled the words and took up a wrestling stance—his center of gravity low, his hands loose and ready before him. He watched the enormous metallic giant approach. She couldn't take full strides or even travel straight to him; the ground was too broken up. When she was two steps away, just seconds from being able to cleave him with that brilliant saber, Victor cast Iron Berserk, surging in size and strength. Lira didn't slow as he exploded with power, roaring as his vision tinted red.

Her enormous sword held high, Lira stepped forward and chopped down. Victor didn't stand still, however. He also stepped forward, squatting low. Now inside the arc of her sword's cleave, he slammed his chest into her metal-clad belly—she was still a good deal taller than he—and, wrapping his arms around the back of her thighs, he pulled with all his might, lifting with his quads, his glutes, and every damn muscle he could dig into. Victor's center of gravity was far lower than hers, and he stunned himself by how easily he popped her off the ground.

Everything after that was reflex, taught to his muscles through thousands of drills. He pivoted on his left foot and fell to the side, using her momentum as he'd done in a hundred wrestling and football practices. Call it a "double-leg takedown" or "wrapping up" a tackle—it didn't matter; either way, he dropped her to the ground or, in this case, into the pool of bubbling magma. Lira's arms flailed, her scimitar went flying, and then her head and shoulders splashed into the boiling, molten stone. Victor released her waist and scrambled away as she began to slide, kicking and splashing, into the crevice.

He stood and, brushing the gravel and dust off his hands, watched her slip, inch by inch, deeper into the lava. Her legs kicked at first, but she stopped, perhaps realizing she was speeding her descent by thrashing. He could see the armor turning orange-hot near the lava line, and he wondered what she was thinking. He figured she must be panicked; if she ended the armor spell, she'd be deep in the lava without protection. If she didn't, she would keep sinking, her arms too inflexible to reach up and grasp the fissure's stone edge.

Frowning, remembering how she'd held her blade back and given him a chance to yield, Victor stepped forward and grasped one of her enormous ankles under his arm, stopping her from slipping further into the lava. He looked up at Ronkerz and shouted, "Does she yield?" The crowd, recovered from the madness of his earthquake, had been screaming for his blood as Lira recovered and stood. However, a hush had fallen over the arena when Victor had thrown their champion.

Ronkerz stood and opened his arms, shouting into the canyon in his booming basso voice, "Well, Rumble Town? Who's the winner? Victor the Titan or Lira the Big One?"

As if they'd been waiting for his permission, the crowd's hushed silence disappeared as they buzzed with conversation, shouted curses, and excited cheers. In seconds, someone took up a chant, and slowly but surely, more and more voices joined in: "*Victor, Victor, Victor.*"

Ronkerz spread his arms wide and shouted, "Victor! You are the champion! Lira's life is yours." Victor locked eyes with the great simian again and knew what Ronkerz knew: He wouldn't kill his Big One. Things might have been different if she hadn't offered him mercy and if his Core wasn't empty of rage. Still, Lira wasn't the one who'd killed Arona. If he wanted to kill anyone at that moment, it was Ronkerz, and that was a fight he wasn't ready for. Victor grunted as he took a step back, heaving on Lira's enormous leg. She slid a couple of inches, grinding over the stone as more of her red-hot armor emerged from the lava.

"Come on, then, *mujer grandota.*" He chuckled, backing up another step, heaving on the leg. With great effort, he slowly backed her out of the lava until he'd dragged her entire unmoving form a dozen feet from the bubbling chasm. When he was finished and dropped the leg with a heavy, hollow *clang*, Ronkerz appeared, seemingly out of nowhere. "You could have helped," he grunted, leaning forward with his hands on his knees to suck in some deep breaths.

Ronkerz shrugged. "Better that she owes you her life cleanly." As Lira's metal casing cooled, ticking and steaming, deep heaving breaths echoed hollowly from within. "As she recovers, you should go back to your resting cave. I will repair this blasted landscape, and then you will receive your awards."

"Awards?"

Ronkerz nodded. "Rasso Hine and a treasure from Lira. Something dear enough that she remembers this lesson well."

Victor nodded, more than a little surprised that it seemed Ronkerz would stick to their bargain and then some. "Can I speak to Arcus?"

The giant simian nodded. "The man weeps, begging for an audience with you. He has something to get off his chest. I'll bring him around. I'll have words with you, too, before you quit this place." He nodded toward the cave on the far side of the smoldering canyon. "Go now. I must put this place right so my people can return to their lives."

Victor nodded, glanced at the enormous woman, still clad in her cooling armor, still lying unmoving, and turned to walk toward the cave. The crowd saw him separate from Ronkerz, saw him walking away of his own volition, and they began their chant again, hushed at first, then louder and louder until the canyon walls echoed with his name, "*Victor, Victor, Victor!*" Hearing their adulation, feeling their eyes on him, Victor's back straightened, and he lifted an arm, slowly turning from side to side, clenching his fist. He felt his Core begin to flare with renewed Energy, and something in him wanted to go berserk again, to lift his axe and scream his warcry, but he restrained himself and, with a broad smile on his lips, simply basked in the glory.

40

PRIZES

Victor sat on the stone bench where, just hours earlier, he'd been chatting quietly with Arona. Despite his victory and the still-lingering buzz of glory-fueled endorphins, images of her broken, torn body persisted in their attempts to worm their way into his mind's eye, but he pushed them away. He didn't know her all that well, so he didn't want to let himself *feel* for her the way his heart kept trying to. Was that something you could or *should* push aside? He doubted the wisdom of it, but he decided he'd try. He'd box it up until one day, when the thought of her death came around, it would be blunted by time, and he could look at it objectively. Right now, it was too fresh, too raw.

To pass the time while he waited for Ronkerz to make good on his promises, Victor pulled Lifedrinker from her harness and contemplated her edge. Despite her difficulties with Lira, she'd fought hard and managed to drain a good bit of Energy out of the "steel seeker." He could see it pulsing darkly—rivulets of metallic Energy buried in the depths of Lifedrinker's silvery metal. "I'm proud of you, *chica*. You cut her nice and deep before she grew." The axe pulsed with prideful emotion, and Victor grinned.

"You treat her well," a melodic voice said out of the dim shadows near the cave wall, and Victor looked up to see Lira approaching. She was no longer clad in armor of any kind. Rather, she wore plain rough-spun pants and a baggy sleeveless tunic that hung loosely around her feathery figure. She ruffled her wings, flexing them slightly as she approached, her talons surprisingly quiet on the stone floor.

Victor shrugged, straightening to look at Lira more directly. "She's a good companion, and she tried her best."

Lira nodded. "She's a wondrous weapon, and I hope you know how rare she is. Spirit-bonded metals are uncommon enough, but she's especially conscious. If I couldn't sense the age of her Heart Silver, I'd think she was millennia older than she is."

Victor smiled and lifted Lifedrinker over his shoulder, allowing her harness to pull her into place. "Hey, uh, thanks for not trying to finish me right away when I was down. Seems like you might have had a chance to cut me pretty good."

"Oof! That must sting your titan's ego, hmm? Well, I can say the same. You could have nudged me into that pool of lava rather than drag me out." Lira moved closer and pointed to the empty area on the stone bench where Victor sat. When he nodded, she sat down, flexing her wings to accommodate her. "You're a resilient bastard, you know that?"

"*Me?*" Victor chuckled. "Can you tell me about your affinity? I know it has to do with metal. At first, I thought it was iron—"

"Ha! You would have trounced me if it were only iron. Part of my quest for steel—in the figurative sense—has led me to refine my affinity, to broaden and strengthen it. When I was a child, I had a variant of an earth affinity, and it was, as you guessed, iron. I won't say much more simply because I don't want you to make the mistake of thinking all steel seekers go through the same sort of refinement. It would be unkind for me to lead you down a dead-end road. My affinity is, however, the reason for my visit. Ronkerz says I must give you something dear, and I understand the intention behind his lesson. That being the case, I have something very dear, indeed, for you."

"Hey"—Victor held up his hands, shaking his head with his lips quirked in half a smile—"forget about it. You put up a hell of a fight, and I don't see why I should get any—"

"No, Victor. This isn't something you can decide for me. Ronkerz made a demand, and he is my master. This gift I bear does not leave my hands grudgingly but with utmost respect for you and for Ronkerz. He is wise enough to know that I must feel loss when I consider my defeat. No battle should be entered lightly, and to walk away, defeated, from a contest such as ours, with no penalty, would upset my karmic balance."

With one hand, she dusted the stone bench between them, then gestured at the air, and suddenly, an oblong package wrapped in deep blue silk appeared on the stone. It was about the size of a football, and when Victor reached to grasp it, he found it was hard and incredibly dense. The muscles on his forearm bulged as he tried to lift it with one hand and failed. He gave up and let his palm rest on the cool silk, smiling as the object throbbed with potent Energy. "What is it?"

"Well, you have some inkling about my affinity; you saw me summoning metal from the earth to use as weapons and armor. I can *feel* metal. I can *hear* it singing to me. Not long after I learned to . . ." She trailed off and shrugged. "I won't get into the secrets of my affinity, but let's just say I learned to do something very difficult with metal. I'm sure you caught a glimpse of it in my colossus armor. That's beside the point, however. The point is that I gained a new insight into metal after that particular accomplishment—that's the important part. I began to hear different types of metal singing from the depths of the world, but I only ever heard this song once."

Lira reached out one of her feathered arms and, with polished black nails, gripped the blue silk surrounding the heavy object under Victor's hand. When she tugged, the silk slid away, and Victor lost all awareness of his surroundings as his eyes focused on the magnificent ore resting on the stone slab. The lump of lustrous metal was a deep, depthless black, but, at the same time, it was luminous, giving off an intangible glow that made Victor feel he was staring into a person's eye, almost as if he could see something in that ore, some kind of hidden intelligence or spirit.

After a while, Lira cleared her throat. "Mesmerizing, isn't it?"

Victor had to cough and lick his lips before he could respond. "Amazing. What is it?"

She shrugged. "I don't know. I've never seen it before, never read about it in any books, and none of the masters I've ever had have mentioned anything like it. Before I learned to fight, you see, I was a crafter—a metal worker. I might have gone down a different path if I'd come upon this metal back then. Anyway, I've called it soul ore simply because I feel like I'm looking into a person's soul when I stare into that depthless metal."

"Wait, you found this in this world?" Victor waved his hand around them, indicating the dungeon.

"Yes. I believe the System may have provided it as a reward for my breakthrough. Make no mistake; even with my new sense for metal, I had to explore dangerous depths in this dungeon before I heard this metal's song."

Victor stared at the metal while she spoke, and after he'd absorbed her words, he asked, "What do I do with it?" He reached out and, this time, wrapped both his hands around the lump of metal, heaving it up off the stone bench. His muscles strained with the effort; while it was a fraction of the size, he figured it weighed more than Karl's gigantic axe. Grunting, he set it back onto the stone with a dull, reverberating thud.

"Is that a serious question?" Lira cocked her head, looking at him sideways as if he were stupid. When Victor continued to stare, unblinking and unapologetic for his question, she made an irritated clicking sound in her throat. "Feed it to your axe, of course!"

"She absorbs Energy—"

"She can do much more than that!" Lira chuckled, shaking her head. "Gods! Can't you *feel* her hunger? She wants to grow, to be a match for you, but there's only so much she can do with Energy alone. You've got to feed her materials, too! Ugh!" She huffed an exasperated sigh and scratched her long pointed nails through the feathers on the side of her head. "I have to remind myself how young your axe is. Perhaps she doesn't even know what she needs. Has she not asked for ore?" When Victor slowly began to shake his head, understanding dawning in his eyes, Lira smiled and nodded. "I can see that. Trust me, Victor, this is exactly what she needs."

"How . . ." Victor trailed off, his question unfinished because he couldn't think of a way to ask how to feed metal to his axe without sounding like an idiot.

Lira smiled and leaned forward, slapping Victor's knee. "I don't mind helping. I owe you, after all, do I not? It's easier than you think; simply put the axe against the ore and leave her in peace for a while. It may take her a week or a month, but she'll slowly pull this dense metal into herself. Beware—she's going to be much more of a handful after absorbing the soul ore."

"Wait." Victor rested his hand on the ore again, enjoying the steady buzz of potential he felt tingling his flesh. "Does it really have one? A soul, I mean. I don't want Lifedrinker's personality to—"

"No! It's not alive, as much as it seems to be." She reached down to rest her hand on the stone with Victor's, her palm surprisingly warm and soft against his fingers. "There's no intelligence in there. At least not in the sense that you, Lifedrinker, and I view intelligence. If I were guessing, I'd say this ore is the stuff of the primordial universe. It has the wisdom of eons in its molecules but no real mind to use it." She shifted her hand to grasp Victor's, and after a gentle squeeze, she let go and stood up. "That's my duty done. When we meet again, I hope it won't be as foes."

"I . . ." Victor stood up, overwhelmed by how gracious Lira had been. "Thank you, Lira. I learned a lot during our fight, and now you've given me something precious. I hope you'll consider me a friend."

"I will, but that doesn't mean I won't heed Ronkerz if he says we must be foes. I hope that, when the time comes, you aren't defending the Sojourn Consulate."

"Tut, Lira," a deep basso voice rumbled from the shadowy depths of the cave. "Don't give away all of my secrets." Victor looked past Lira to see twin angular purple lights approaching—Ronkerz's eyes.

"Goodbye, Victor." Lira ducked her head, her feathers ruffling as her wings twitched, then she turned and hurried away, walking past the massive shadowy form of the simian lord.

When Ronkerz stepped into the dim light of the glow lamp, he announced, "I'll have words with you before you speak to Arcus and complete your quest." He gestured to the lump of soul ore. "Put that prize away."

Victor touched the hunk of ore and sent it into the storage device Dar had given him. He wondered how much of a strain it was for the ring to hold all the powerful items he'd put inside it. It worried him, and he decided he'd better move the ore into his vault at the earliest opportunity. Ronkerz, ignorant of his inner conversation, interrupted Victor's thoughts. "I will ask a favor of you."

That got Victor's attention. "Yeah?"

"Yes. Even in my time, your master, Ranish Dar, was often at odds with the council. Is that still so?"

Victor thought about the question and weighed his response. He didn't want to give something valuable away to the renegade veil walker, but he also didn't want to get his head crushed by one of those massive ape-like hands. "He doesn't get along with all of the, uh, consuls."

"Good! That's the way I remember him. Tell me, do you serve Sojourn, or do you serve Ranish Dar?"

"I already told you: I'm not here because I work for the council. I'm here because I owe them. It's a . . . punishment, I guess."

"Good!" Ronkerz grunted again, thumping one of his fists on the stone. "You must know something, boy. I already know how to break this dungeon and free everyone inside it. I'm waiting for some of my Big Ones to break through into their lustrous veils, and then we'll leave this place. You needn't worry about the children born here or the suffering you think you see. Their lives are hard but not desperate, and as you saw, great strength can be found here under my tutelage."

Victor frowned. "What about the people in the other settlements?"

"They'll come around to my way of thinking. As the time grows near for us to make our move, they'll join me. If they don't, they'll still be freed. I'm telling you this so that you won't return and raise any alarms with the council. I know we struck a bargain, Victor, but if you don't promise to hold your report for any but Dar's ears, then I won't let you leave."

Victor folded his arms over his chest, contemplating the warning in Ronkerz's words. "I can still tell Dar everything?"

"Yes."

"Won't the council be able to see what's happening in here? Can't they tell who's alive and who's dead?"

"They can see much, aye, but I can block and obscure just as much. At the moment, I'm quite sure they think Arcus is just as dead as Arona. They also think I'm still struggling with my ascension through the test of steel and that my Big Ones are iron rankers." He leaned forward, his knuckles grinding on the stone. "Can you do what I asked? Can you save your report for Dar's ears alone?"

Victor shrugged. "I can do that."

For the third time, Ronkerz thumped his fist on the stone and said, "Good!" Then he nodded and turned. "Arcus and Rasso Hine approach. When your erstwhile companion has said his piece, you may depart with Hine." With that, Ronkerz turned and took a lumbering step into the shadows.

Victor watched him leave, wondering if he should say something—a promise of vengeance for Arona, a threat to fight him someday, a thank you, a curse. He couldn't decide, and before he settled on how he was supposed to feel, how he was supposed to act, Ronkerz was gone. Much smaller, lighter footsteps approached, and two humanoid figures emerged from the shadows. Both Arcus and Rasso Hine wore gray rough-spun clothes. Neither held any sort of weapon, and neither wore any jewelry.

Arcus sighed and shrugged, gesturing at his much-humbled appearance, his tentacle arm twitching and writhing as it hung by his side. "I'll be a while earning some privileges back." He gestured to the clean-shaven bald man beside him. "This is the infamous Rasso Hine."

Rasso appeared to be human. Victor couldn't see anything about him that would make him stand out on Earth. Even his size was average—probably a few inches shy of six feet. He bowed somewhat stiffly. "Hello," he said in a hoarse, accented voice that sounded more like a mumble than a word.

Arcus shrugged. "I already filled him in on what the council said. He says he doesn't know anything about the invasion, but he's happy to leave this place to tell them so himself."

Victor frowned at Arcus. "You seem pretty upbeat."

"I *am*! Something about being irrevocably sprung from the grasp of my father and the demands of society—it feels good. Ronkerz is powerful, Victor, and I intend to learn a thing or two in here. If it takes a few centuries, what do I care? I've no love waiting for me. I've no family of any consequence. My father hates me, my sisters and brothers won't miss me, and my mother is busy with her wars."

Victor stepped closer, looking into Arcus's eyes, trying to gauge how much of his attitude was bravado and how much was sincere. The Pyromancer stared back at him, unflinching. Victor frowned. "Sucks about Arona, though, doesn't it?"

Those words broke Arcus's façade, and he looked down, inhaling shakily through his nose. "I can't believe she died. She was the best of us—our generation." He looked up, his eyes red and watery, the flames behind his irises mere smolders. "Please tell them I'm dead, Victor." His eyes sprang wide. "Gods! That's why I needed to speak to you!"

"What?"

"My father! He uses my sister, Trin, as a pawn. He intends to trap your friends in our family's dungeon. You have to stop them; don't let them go in."

"What?" Victor blinked, confused by the sudden turn of the conversation, but something in him understood—his heart began to thud in his chest, and his rage slowly trickled into his pathways.

"Our dungeon, it's a wave challenge, but it won't end. There's no exit provided until the dungeon is completed. Worse, it only allows Tier One iron rankers to enter, so you won't be able to go after—" Arcus's words were cut short as Victor surged forward and grabbed his shirt in his fists, lifting him so their faces were an inch apart.

"You're telling me this *now*?"

"I'm sorry! Victor, I'm *sorry*! I meant to tell you—I swear it. I'd grown to respect you—grudgingly, yes, but it was there. I've told you how I hate my father. I was *going* to help you."

Victor growled but released Arcus. "What if I'm too late? Something like two weeks have passed on the outside since we entered this dungeon!"

"My father has the dungeon control stone. He can end it. He can get them out. I'm sure that was his plan: trap them, with death looming, then *offer* to let them out for some sort of bargain—a debt owed, or perhaps a piece of property from Ranish Dar, or—"

"I'll just kill him. You said he's only Tier Five."

"Ah! He has a champion. A steel seeker. Better to have Dar confront him. But . . . he'd lose much political clout getting my father to release your friends. Do you want Dar to hold that over your head? I don't know what he's like, but I've never thought it wise to collect debts to veil walkers."

Victor growled, punching his fist into his palm and pacing back and forth as he considered his options. If Arcus was right, he needed to haul ass to wherever his family home was and make sure Edeya, Darren, and Lam weren't inside their dungeon. Frowning at the thought, he looked at Arcus. "What about your sister?"

Arcus shrugged, his face pained. "Um, different mother, but still not exactly loved by my father. She's mostly ignored by him, and I wouldn't be surprised to find her used as a sacrificial pawn; she's not exactly talented."

Victor was still struggling to wrap his head around the scheme. "I don't get it. What if Lam and the others just win? If you have to be tier one to enter the dungeon—"

"There's a reason our dungeon isn't listed in the guidebook—it's basically useless unless my father intervenes with the control stone, which strips the entrants of prizes. The only group that's ever completed the dungeon was composed of six Level Nineteen prodigies, including Arona and me. I know your friends are talented, but . . ." He let his words trail off, and Victor drew his own conclusion: Lam and Edeya were good, but they weren't *that* good. If they brought Darren, he would probably barely be at Level Ten. At the low ranks, nine levels made a big difference.

"Listen, Arcus. You need to tell me everything you know about your dad's champion. I also need detailed instructions on the fastest route to your family home." He glared at Rasso Hine. "Stand close, 'cause we're leaving in a minute, and I'm dumping you off with the council."

Arcus nodded, licking his lips. "Right, well, you need to know that he's a wizard with two powerful affinities—nature and blood. His nature affinity has allowed him to cultivate a relationship with a powerful beast—a bog lion. Besides controlling his companion, his affinity allows him to use vegetation to . . ."

Victor listened to Arcus go on and on about his father's champion, Fak Loyle, slowly building a picture of the man in his mind. Arcus described his powers, and Victor contemplated counters for them, slowly sketching a dance in his mind, one in which Fak Loyle was his partner. They moved in counterpoint to each other, Victor matching Fak's talents with those of his own, and when Arcus finished, he felt confident that he'd have a chance. "That's all I can think of. I'm sure that's everything, though—I've seen him duel a dozen times. If he has a secret, it's one he hasn't used in forty years."

"Right. Thanks, Arcus. Good luck in here." Victor punched him lightly in the chest, then reached out to grasp Hine's shoulder. "Let's go." With that, he summoned the recall token from his storage ring and channeled a trickle of Energy into it. He felt a surge of Energy, like being struck by a bolt of lightning, and the world faded in a brilliant flash of light.

41

A TIME FOR KILLING

Darren stood back and listened as Lam and Edeya chatted with Trin and her father. He thought about that, about how he deferred to Lam with her years of experience and superior abilities, and wondered if it would have made the "old" Darren resentful. Didn't he used to have to be at the center of every conversation? Didn't he used to think people would judge him if he didn't speak for whatever group he was a part of? He smiled wryly at the thought, almost as if he'd learned a secret, and maybe he had—it felt good to let other people handle things, to *not* be responsible for everything.

Trin's father was an imposing fellow. His skin was well-weathered, as though he'd spent much of his time working hard in the sun, but his manicured nails and carefully subtle makeup gave the lie to that impression. His clothes were impossibly fine—a silken suit in shades of brown and gold cut to fit him perfectly. His leather belt and boots were polished to a near-reflective sheen, and his many rings glittered with jewels. Again, Darren thought of his "old" self and how he would have envied Bohn Volpuré for his regal appearance.

"A party of four, dear Trin?" Lord Volpuré asked, arching an eyebrow. "At least I can see that you heeded my advice and sought the friends of that most competent fellow who bested your brother."

"Yes, four. You said the dungeon would open for as few as three and no more than six."

"That's right, dear. I'm just confirming a thing or two." His eyes, rather hawklike under his sharp brows, glanced over Trin's three guests, then settled on Lam. "And have you been practicing? You're familiar with one another's capabilities?"

Lam nodded. "Yes, Lord Volpuré. Just two days ago, we completed the Grotto, even the Tier One area."

Trin's father nodded, folding his arms over his chest as he leaned back in his desk chair. "Yes, yes. Very good. Well, dear Trin, I gave you the pass. Whether your party is ready or not is *your* decision." He reached toward a small gilded brass statuette made in the likeness of a young woman carrying a tray and tapped his golden signet ring against it with a tiny metallic *click-click*. "I'll have Efanie open the entrance hall for you."

"Thank you, Father!"

Edeya cleared her throat and stepped up beside Trin. "Sir, would you mind telling us how long it usually takes people to clear the dungeon? I'd like to leave a note for our friends."

Volpuré frowned and stroked his chin. "Well, it's called First Clash Coliseum for a reason. The dungeon is a series of coliseum battles, and after each battle, you're taken to a ready room, where you can rest between bouts. The arena master will permit nearly a full day of rest, but you don't have to take that long. When you're ready to fight, you simply report to the gate and strike the gong there. Conversely, if you rest too long, the monstrous gladiator handlers will force you into the arena at spear point. A word of advice: Do not attempt to battle the coliseum personnel."

"How many rounds are there?" Darren shifted and cleared his throat nervously, embarrassed by his blurted question.

"Good question, young man! The answer is that I don't know. It seems to have some random component to it. I believe the last people to clear it went through more than twenty rounds." He looked at Trin. "Do you know the answer more precisely?"

Trin looked down, her dark brows cloaking her eyes in shadow. "No, Father. I'm sorry; I don't know much more about the dungeon than what you told me when you gave me the pass."

Darren looked more closely at Bohn Volpuré, his perfect suit, refined appearance, and the all-too-familiar disingenuous glint in his eyes. This man was a political creature, and Darren's gut told him never to trust a word he said. Of course, he wasn't sure how that might apply to their present circumstance. All they were doing was paying their respects on the way to a dungeon adventure, but he resolved to be wary of Trin's father if he and his friends continued to associate with the Volpuré family. A gentle tap at the door broke him from his musings, and he turned to see a young woman in a very prim and stylish uniform standing in the open doorway.

"You called, Lord Volpuré?"

"Yes, Efanie, please guide my daughter and her companions to the family dungeon portal and unlock it for them."

"Certainly." Efanie, like all of the people Darren had seen in the Volpuré household, was a very human-looking woman, though her upturned nose, delicately pointed ears, and large amber-tinted eyes gave hints to a more exotic parentage. "Right this way, Lady Trin." She turned, took a few steps, then paused, waiting for the rest of them.

"Thank you again, Lord Volpuré," Lam said before following Efanie.

"It's my pleasure. Say, I wonder, do you suppose I might entice your comrade, Victor, to attend a celebration here upon your successful exit from the dungeon?"

Lam chuckled. "I can't speak for Victor, but I've never known him to turn down a feast."

"Excellent! My sort of fellow. I'll send him an invitation." He looked at Trin, who was already standing near the door. "Did you say he's staying at Ranish Dar's lake house?"

"I believe so—"

"Actually," Edeya's sharp voice cut through Trin's hesitant reply, "he's currently in a dungeon, doing some kind of task for the council."

"Ah, yes! Of course, of course!"

Trin narrowed her eyes and held a finger up. "Father, isn't Arcus—"

"Never mind Arcus!" Volpuré snapped, suddenly irritable. "Suffice it to say, I'm familiar with the task your companion is toiling to complete. Well," he sighed and shrugged, "we can only hope he'll make his exit from that unpleasant place in time to celebrate your victory, hmm? Off you go now, good luck!"

Darren followed the others out, sparing one last glance at Trin's father. He'd already turned to read something in a leather-bound journal—a Far Scribe book, if he were to guess. He trailed behind the four women, listening to their chatter. Trin seemed significantly more excited than anyone else, and Darren sort of felt sorry for her. He could tell she'd led a sheltered life, and seeing the pristine, rather sterile nature of their family estate, he couldn't help comparing her to the child of some of the more prominent politicians he'd worked with back on Earth.

The thought struck a chord in his mind, jarring loose a memory that had been nagging at him, and Darren hurried his steps so he could walk beside Trin. "Didn't you tell Edeya and me that you sought us out because Victor beat your brother?"

"Um, that's right, Darren."

"But your father—" he started to say, but Lam spoke over him, completing his thought.

"Said he sent you to us."

"He didn't *send* me to you! He suggested that any man who could trounce my brother so handily likely had companions worthy of note. I'm the one who figured out who you were and where to find you. Of *course,* my father wants to take credit—I can't do anything without guidance as far as he's concerned."

"Hush now, Lady Trin," Efanie said. "Don't give your guests the wrong impression."

"Efanie, why is he *like* that?"

Darren watched as the smartly dressed woman tilted her head, her ringlets of neatly coiffed hair bouncing as she considered the question. Before she spoke, she gestured to a dimly lit stairwell and started down it. "You've never shown much interest in advancement, sweet girl. Your father favors his motivated children; I believe it's as simple as that."

"What about Renny? He's still in the first tier and spends all his days lazing about, waiting for the next party to attend."

"Well, Renny's a little special, isn't he?" To Darren's surprise, Efanie looked past Trin to wink in the general direction of Lam and Edeya. "Renny's the only child from Lord Volpuré's seventh marriage."

"His *favorite* wife." Trin emphasized "favorite" like a curse.

"Well, she died very young, and I don't think your father had yet had a chance to fall out of love." Again, Efanie looked at Lam, Edeya, and Darren, this time frowning slightly. "I'm sorry, we shouldn't air our usual banter in front of guests."

Lam shrugged. "It's fine. We won't repeat any of it."

Trin waved Lam's assurances away. "Oh, don't worry about that. Sniping, sarcasm, and making judgments about others are quite the normal, expected behavior in this household. Still, Efanie's right; I shouldn't do it in front of guests."

Darren continued to listen as Efanie lamented her trouble wrangling enough staff for an upcoming feast; apparently, the head chef and his wife—the manor's head maid—were away with their four children, also employed by Volpuré, for a family reunion. "I'll have to borrow staff from Lord Arcorage at this rate!"

"I'm sorry, Efanie, but that's the price you pay for being father's favor—"

"Here we are!" Efanie announced, pointing to a large archway containing a twelve-foot-high gray metal door. She produced a metal key longer than her hand with teeth pointing in every direction, inserted it into the lock, and twisted it. With half a dozen smooth, well-lubricated clicks, the door unlocked. Pulling it wide, she gestured into the room beyond and said, "Head on through. I need a quick word with Trin."

Darren followed Lam and Edeya into the chamber but didn't miss the long look Lam gave Efanie as she pulled Trin to the side. He lost track of any unfolding drama, though, when he saw the strange room. It was spherical in nature, built from large carved stone blocks, each inlaid with a silvery sigil. At the apex of the chamber, a warm yellow light shone down on a teleportation pad, or at least that's what Darren thought the metallic circular platform was. He strode over to it, but before he could step on it, for some reason eager to hear his boots click on the dull gray metal, Edeya grabbed his elbow and hissed, "Whoa, Dare."

"Whoa?" He stumbled back a step as she continued to pull on his arm.

"Yeah, whoa! We don't know if it's all right to step on it. Wait for Trin."

"Ah, yeah. Of course." Darren turned and saw Lam walking the room's perimeter, intently studying the sigils in the stone blocks. He looked at Edeya. "Can she read those?"

"I don't think so. She's just . . . inspecting. Probably an old habit from being a military commander." She took a breath and looked as if she'd say more, but the sound of the huge metal door closing with a *clank* interrupted her.

"Well, are we ready?" Trin's smile and enthusiasm were contagious, at least to Darren, and he smiled along with her.

"I am!" he announced.

"Ready—" Edeya began, but then Lam spoke, cutting off anything else she might say.

"What did your father's chamberlain have to say?"

"Efanie?" Trin's eyes opened wide, and Darren instinctively expected a lie to come out of her lips next. That's what people who were going to lie did—repeat or clarify an obvious question before answering. He knew that because he'd often practiced the behavior; it gave a person's mind a couple of seconds to craft the lie. When Lam only nodded, Trin continued, "Well, it was a little strange, to be honest. She said I was free to use the token my father gave us but that I might want to reconsider. She said it would be safer with a party of six."

"Is that all?" Lam pressed.

"She said something else a little odd, and not once, but twice."

"Which was?" This time, Edeya was the one asking, and Darren could hear the exasperation in her voice.

"Simply that my father can end the dungeon run at any moment."

"Why would she tell you that?"

"I really don't know." Despite his earlier misgivings, Darren couldn't spot any duplicity in Trin's body language. "She was acting very strangely. I've known her a long time; I suppose I should clarify her role here at the manor. She's part of my family's personal guard. She was assigned to me as a child and later to my younger sister, Raella." She smiled and shrugged, stepping onto the teleportation pad and throwing Lam another smile. "That's why your question threw me off. My father's chamberlain is an absolute pig of an old lecher."

Edeya giggled, and Lam smiled, shrugging. "If that's all, then I'm game to give this dungeon a try despite our smaller-than-optimal party."

Darren nodded his agreement and stepped beside Trin, grinning as his boots clicked hollowly on the metal disc. Lam and Edeya were right behind him, and then Trin summoned a gilded piece of paper about the size of one of Darren's old business cards. She held it aloft, and Darren watched as a ribbon of golden Energy surged through the card. In seconds, it was gone, replaced by a cloud of glowing golden motes.

The motes danced around in the air at the center of the platform and seemed to multiply, growing in density and size. Before Darren knew it, they'd taken on an oval shape that seemed to shimmer and solidify until it looked like a pool of golden liquid hung in the air at the center of the room. "Now we just step into it," Trin announced, drawing her fancy basket-hilted rapier with a ring of metal on metal. "Ready?"

"Ready!" they all said in one way or another, and then Trin led the way, stepping through the portal with a liquid ripple. Darren looked from Lam to Edeya, nodded, and gripping his staff tightly, stepped through the portal.

When the light faded from his eyes, Victor found himself standing in the chamber from which the consuls had sent him into the prison dungeon. This time, the room was much more dimly lit, with only a single amber glow lamp pulsing down onto the teleportation pad. For some reason, he'd snatched Lifedrinker from her harness as he came through, but as he saw the two armor-clad men striding toward him from the doorway, he was glad he had. He gripped Rasso's rough cloth shirt and pulled him behind him. The man was like a child to him, easily obscured by his bulk as Victor faced down the approaching figures.

"State your name and business in this chamber!" the armored figure on the left demanded. They were both sizeable warriors—something close to eight feet tall if you counted the plumes on their shiny metal helms. The one who spoke, however, was significantly broader at the shoulders, and his growled demand had the tone Victor recognized as belonging to someone itching for a fight.

"Victor Sandoval. I'm here 'cause that's where the *pinché* recall token dumped me."

"Recall? You were in the prison?"

"But—" the second warrior—guard, Victor figured—said in a much higher, more feminine voice, only to be cut off as the first guard chopped a hand sideways.

"Silence. Fetch Watch Commander Reythis." As the woman turned and double-timed it out of the chamber, the remaining guard turned back to Victor. "Stand down. Violence will be met with a lethal response."

Victor shrugged and put Lifedrinker in her harness. Then he reached back, put a heavy hand around Rasso's thin neck, and pulled him in front of him. He had a feeling Ronkerz had been cloaking a lot more than he let on. It seemed to Victor that the council might have considered him lost. Maybe when they saw Arcus's severed arm return with a token and then registered Arona's death, they'd decided Victor would soon be dead as well. Considering the time difference, he supposed it wasn't surprising they weren't standing around in the chamber waiting for him; if he got hung up for even a week in the dungeon, it would be almost two months on the outside.

"Listen, I dunno why you weren't expecting me, but I was supposed to get this dude out of the dungeon." Victor jostled Rasso a little, and the man tried to pull away but found Victor's grip unyielding. "I don't have time to mess around. I've got places to be. Can I turn him over to you?"

"Wait for the watch commander!"

Victor sighed but shrugged, reaching into his ring to pull out the Far Scribe book he shared with Dar. Unlike many standard dungeons, the prison dungeon wouldn't allow the books to work, but now that he was out, he figured he should let some people know. He started with Dar because he thought he might need his mentor's support with the council, assuming these guards didn't let him leave. As quickly as he could, which was quite fast, given his much-improved dexterity, he scrawled out a note, letting Dar know he was out of the dungeon and had successfully secured Rasso Hine. He also said he'd be visiting the Volpuré estate for a "personal" reason.

Arcus had suggested he not tell anyone what he was going to do, and though Victor barely trusted the Pyromancer, he'd thought it was good advice. If he told Dar what he was about to do, his "master" might try to intervene, and then Victor would owe him even more. No, if Volpuré wanted to mess with Victor, then Victor would be the one to mess back. He wasn't an idiot; he wouldn't try to stand up to a veil walker, but an iron ranker with a steel seeker bodyguard? "Yeah, I'll take those odds," Victor growled, closing the book and sending it back into his ring.

The clatter of running footsteps and clanking armor made him look toward the doorway. "Sir Victor!" a new voice said as the female guard and another man, this one dressed in fine Sojourn livery, strode into the room. "Welcome back, sir. We didn't expect you so soon."

"Really?" Victor frowned. "That's strange, isn't it? I was gone for a couple of days in there."

"Verily, sir, but Lord Roil seemed to think it would be quite some time before anyone from your party might emerge. Is this the prisoner, sir?" He strode forward and stared hard at Rasso. "Are you Hine?"

"I am—"

"Come with me! I'm to bring you directly to the council hall. Victor, you should come along; the council is bound to have ques—"

"No." Victor gave Rasso a shove toward the watch commander, then started toward the door. "I've fulfilled my obligation to the City of Sojourn. Pass my regards to the council and let them know they can reach me through Lord Ranish Dar." As he spoke, Victor's voice started out clear and strident but ended in a growling snarl. His eyes had flooded with fire, and black smoke drifted from his nostrils. The guards, likely all steel seekers, backed away as he stomped through the doorway. He didn't mean for it to happen, but his mind had already gone ahead, visualizing his battle with Lord Volpuré's champion.

If he'd seen his face, if he'd seen the baleful flicker of the magmatic flames roiling behind his irises, or seen his forearms flex as he clenched his fists, or smelled the brimstone in the smoke drifting out of his lungs, or if he'd tasted the blood and murder laced through his aura, then Victor would have understood why three steel seekers backed away, casting long, searching looks into each other's eyes. Those glances seemed to ask, "Is it only me? Am I mad, or should we fear this iron ranker?"

Of course, Victor didn't see those glances. He'd dismissed the guards from his mind as he began to play out the upcoming battle in his mind. In a way, he was glad Arcus had counseled him against telling Dar about the fight, and it wasn't because he didn't want to be further in Dar's debt. The truth was that Victor didn't want anyone to stop him. If he had been willing to face that fact and understand his feelings, he might have seen that it was also why he didn't consider writing in his other Far Scribe books. He loved Valla and was eager to see her, but he didn't want to lose his focus.

"There's a time for killing and a time for loving, *chica*," he grunted, Lifedrinker once more in his hands.

"The deepest bonds of love are forged with the blood of battle. Let us kill together!" Her crystal-clear reply sounded in his mind, her voice half growl and half purr. Lifedrinker's reply almost broke him from his pre-battle focus, but rather than let it freak him out, Victor grinned and accepted the honesty of Lifedrinker's nature.

As he stomped down the steps of the Council Spire toward the busy street, people hurried out of his way, and he could understand why; he was fully limned in flame, almost as if he'd cast Volcanic Fury. Victor summoned Guapo with a surge of rage-attuned Energy. Unbidden, the spell swooped up some of the magma-attuned Energy in his pathways, and Guapo appeared from a cloud of black smoke with a wild, angry whinny, rearing high, kicking his flaming front hooves in the air. Victor leaped onto his back, and with the directions Arcus had given him firmly in mind, he raced toward the eastern edge of the city, where a few dozen miles away, the Volpuré estate awaited.

42

TRAPPED

Darren spun, scanning the platform where the enemy archers kept appearing, but it was empty. "Was that . . ." He paused to lean on his staff, catching his breath. "Was that the last one?" Lam stood over the giant, her hammer dripping gore, her shield battered and likewise decorated. She didn't answer, so Darren turned toward Trin and Edeya; they'd been fighting off the spearmen pouring out of the western portcullis. They, too, gasped for breath, and Darren saw Edeya's lips move, but he couldn't hear her over the roars of the monstrous spectators.

It didn't matter because the announcer's voice bellowed through the air, drowning out the noise: "Congratulations, challengers! You've passed your fourth wave! Return to the ready room and see to your wounds. You have one day before your next match is required!" As he finished his announcement, Darren stopped scanning the stadium, trying to guess where the announcer stood—he'd never been able to lay eyes on him.

It wasn't surprising that he couldn't single out the owner of that booming voice; the crowd was hysterical and unruly. Furry, horned, clawed, scaled, or tentacled, monstrous humanoids caroused in the stands—drinking, eating, cheering, jeering, and generally making football fans look like a children's choir. The stadium rows were ramshackle affairs of great wooden beams and pillars, and the "seating" was whatever the strange onlookers brought to sit on—backpacks, stools, buckets, furs, blankets, or . . . nothing. All in all, it was a wild, noisy, intimidating spectacle, and each time Darren had stepped into the arena, he'd wanted to back out almost immediately.

Lam clapped him on the shoulder, bringing him back to the current reality, and though she shouted, he barely heard her words as she leaned close. "Let's head out! The Energy is forming up!"

"Right!" Darren held up a bloodstained hand, offering a thumbs-up. He was a little upset to see his hand shaking, but he figured it was exhaustion or the dregs of adrenaline still in his system; the last battle hadn't been a smooth one. He started for the iron portcullis, *click-clacking* upward on its rusty chains. The team had unanimously agreed to try to be out of the main arena before the System awarded them Energy; they didn't want to risk being delayed and have to fight the next wave without a rest. As soon as they were all in the sandy tunnel, leaning against the rough stone walls, Darren looked out to see the golden Energy coalescing over the corpses of their vanquished foes.

In a rush, the Energy flowed through the air toward the four of them and split into four distinct streams. One of them slammed into Darren's chest, and he felt himself slide down the wall, nearly knocked out by the rush of warm euphoria that flooded his body and mind. He saw stars and flashes of rainbow starbursts, and as it all began to fade, he saw a System message in his vision:

*****Congratulations! You have achieved Level 13 Chaos Sorcerer. You have gained 6 intelligence, 5 will, 5 dexterity, and 5 vitality.*****

"Yes!" Darren hissed, pumping his fist as he called up his status page:

Status			
Name:	Darren Whitehorse		
Race:	Human: Base 1		
Class:	Chaos Sorcerer: Advanced		
Level:	13		
Core:	Wildarc Class: Base 2		
Energy Affinity:	Lightning 8, Chaos 7.4, Unattuned 6.1	Energy:	602/602
Strength:	6	Vitality:	47
Dexterity:	20	Agility:	5
Intelligence:	27	Will:	43

"Not bad!" He looked up to see the others also staring blankly into space; apparently, he wasn't the only one with messages from the System. His attributes were really starting to take off now that he'd gained a few levels with his advanced class—rather than five points per level as a base human, he got twenty-one. He hated seeing his pathetic strength and agility, but as the others kept telling him, no one could hope to maximize all of their attributes, and he could get items and learn spells to bolster his deficiencies. Failing that, he might refine his class to shore up his weaknesses.

"Leveled, Dare?" Edeya asked, standing with a grunt.

"Yep. Thirteen now."

"Nice, catching up fast. I just hit Fifteen, and Lammy did, too." She looked over at Trin, who was fruitlessly trying to wipe dried blood from her face with a well-used rag. "What about you, Trin?"

"Nineteen. I must be close to Twenty, though."

"Come." Lam gestured for them to follow, trudging through the thick sand into the tunnel. "We can talk in the ready room." Nobody argued, and soon they were all stomping through the deep sand—it was the same in the arena proper, probably meant to absorb blood and, as Darren had learned half a dozen times, provide for soft landings as combatants were thrown or knocked down. Not that soft landings helped all that much when people were ready to jam spears into you or crush you with massive hammers.

"Or pepper you with arrows." Darren finished his musing aloud as he rubbed at a fresh pink scar on his shoulder; he'd been struck there by an arrow two battles earlier. Nobody paid him any mind; everyone was muttering to themselves. It wasn't exactly restful in the "ready room," and they'd been staying there, between fights, for four days. Everyone was kind of tired and raw. When they stepped out of the sand onto hard flagstone and followed the smoldering torches into the square, dimly lit room, Darren groaned and sat on one of the benches lining the rough wooden table.

"Tired, Dare?" Lam asked, lightly punching his shoulder as she stepped around to sit on the other side of the table. The only other furnishings in the room were the six wooden cots and rough spun blankets folded atop them. When they'd first arrived, Lam had snorted at the cots and attempted to summon her own camping gear from a storage ring; that had been when they learned that the dungeon somehow blocked their access to dimensional containers.

"Food should be here soon." Trin peered through the peephole in the door on the far wall as she spoke. It was a stout iron-banded door through which the coliseum attendants delivered their single daily meal. Considering the chef was probably a monstrous humanoid like the spectators, Darren had to admit that he was a little surprised by how tasty and filling the meal usually was—always some variety of stew, something like grease-smeared bread, and a large tankard of surprisingly cold beer.

"How much longer can we keep this up?" Edeya asked, her sapphire wings drooping in exhaustion as she sat beside Darren.

Lam shrugged. "I'd like to try another round or two. This one was hectic, but Darren did a good job neutralizing the archers with his area spells." It was true; his Chaos Storm and Fractured Reality spells had effectively nullified the archers standing on the platforms, forcing them to flee down to the arena sands where Edeya and Trin had slaughtered them. Still, it had been a long fight.

He said what he was thinking: "It was a long battle, though. I was almost out of Energy, and if more than another wave came . . ." He trailed off, letting them use their imaginations.

"I have potions to restore Energy." Trin sighed. "I wish I'd known we couldn't use our storage devices. I can't believe my father didn't say *anything*!"

Darren shrugged. "Well, it seems like that woman, Efanie, tried to warn us off. I don't see us getting through twenty waves, especially at the rate they seem to grow in difficulty."

"Do you think . . ." Trin's words lost their impetus, and Darren could see from the unfocused nature of her eyes that she was lost in thought.

"I'm game to try another. Is there any way to retreat if we're losing, though?" Edeya asked.

"I—" Trin started to answer, but then a loud pounding on the door interrupted her. Lam jumped up and walked over to the iron-banded door, and just as she reached it, a brown furry arm pushed it open. A woman who looked more bear than person stepped in carrying a large tray laden with four enormous tankards—their evening beer. She handed it to Lam, belched loudly, and turned to leave. Behind her, another fur-covered woman, this one hunched and far less physically fit, pushed her way in.

"Coming!" Edeya fluttered her wings so she veritably floated through the room to take the tray from the small, hunched bear-woman. Darren squinted, trying to make out what their dinner would be, but all he saw were four wooden bowls and a large paper sack. The bear-woman grunted something that sounded a *little* like "thanks," then turned and followed the other woman out. They pulled the door shut with a resounding *thud*.

Lam and Edeya brought the trays over to the table, setting them near the center. Darren reached out and took his bowl. "Stew again."

Edeya sighed and shrugged. "At least it's seasoned well, and they use plenty of veggies."

"What's in the sack?" Lam asked, reaching to lift it from the tray. "Heavy!" She pulled it open, and Darren laughed at the familiar smell.

"Fries!"

"Fries?" Lam frowned and lifted out a golden wedge of fried potato. It still had the skin on it, but Darren's nose told him he was going to love the flavor. Lam tentatively took a bite, and she laughed. "Potato!"

"Yeah! Deep fried in oil or, probably, lard or tallow." Darren cupped his hands and held them out. "Can I have some?"

"Let them cool a little, or you'll burn your hands." Lam set the bag down, and they all tucked into their stew using the provided wooden spoons. Darren paused when he realized Trin hadn't taken her bowl.

"Something wrong? Not hungry?"

"I—when Edeya asked about retreating, I realized I have no idea how we're supposed to leave. I know we can ring the gong by the gate to start our next fight early, but . . ." She looked around, apparently at a loss for words. Lam and Edeya looked up from eating, Lam still chewing, but Edeya wearing a deep frown.

The younger Ghelli pushed her bowl away and glared at Trin. "Are you teasing us?"

"I wish I were—"

"Trin," Darren interrupted, "what was it your, uh, security person said to you before we entered the dungeon?"

"Efanie said—" Trin's eyes widened as things came together for her. "She said my father could stop the dungeon at any time!"

"Right, so just message him—" Edeya started to say but stopped short as her eyes widened. "We can't access our storage devices!"

"Do you think your father is monitoring us?" Darren looked across the table as he spoke, noting that Lam had yet to say anything on the topic. She was still chewing, but Darren could see the storm clouds behind her eyes. She wasn't happy.

"He may be—gods! How do I know so little? I'm an idiot!"

"You're a pawn," Lam finally said. "There's no way your father would send you in here without explaining these rules unless he meant for you to lure us inside. He knows you're not a scheming, conniving scum, so he didn't explain the dangers to you—you would have warned us, right?"

"Of course! I swear it! I'm—" Trin rapidly looked around the table. "Why? I don't understand why my father would—"

"He told you to find us." Darren groaned as everything fell into place. Trin started to object, but he held up his hand. "He planted the seed, right? Victor beat the snot out of his son, so he sent his daughter to lure some of Victor's friends into a trap."

"To what end, though?" Lam asked, nodding along as Darren spoke.

"Right. That's the million-dollar question."

"Dollar?" Edeya frowned. "Dare, speak plainly."

"I mean, we don't know if Trin's dad wants us all dead or if he just wants to hold us hostage to get something from Victor. Either way, we're trapped." Darren looked at Trin and saw she had tears pooling in her eyes, staring into space, utterly stunned by the turn of events. "Would your father be upset if you died, Trin? Be honest with yourself."

"Yes! He *loves* me!" The tears broke free from her eyes and streaked down her cheeks as she clenched her thin, pale hands into tight fights. "He buys me dresses, sends me to galas, shows me off to his friends—"

"Just you? How many brothers and sisters do you have?" Darren pressed.

Trin grew quiet, and her lips trembled as silent tears streamed down her cheeks. "Many. My mother is not on good terms . . ." Her voice fell to a near whisper as she tremulously admitted, "He has other favorites."

"Well," Lam sighed, reaching for the bag of fried potatoes, "looks like we need to win tomorrow, and we need to drag this out as long as possible, taking our full day of rest between each battle." She looked hard at Darren. "Conserve your Energy on crowds. Use one area spell or the other; don't stack them unless we're getting overwhelmed."

"Come on," Edeya said, pushing Trin's bowl toward her. "You need to stay strong. We'll eat, then you, me, and Lam can work on some coordinated attacks." Trin didn't say anything, but she took the bowl and began to eat.

Darren stared into his bowl pensively, idly turning the hunks of fatty meat and soft root vegetables with his spoon. He tried to think about Trin's father's motives objectively. What would he gain by killing his own daughter along with three strangers? Vengeance? He supposed there were some people that petty, that . . . honor-obsessed. Still, he didn't buy it. No, if Darren were a betting man, he'd say that Lord Volpuré was bargaining for their release even now. He nodded, comforted enough by the thought to bite into a crisp fried potato wedge before a panicked thought raced through his mind: Victor was in some kind of prison dungeon!

Guapo tore down the strange black crystalline road leading away from the city of Sojourn, his hooves resounding almost hollowly on the surface as it flexed with his mighty strides. Victor held Lifedrinker in one hand, and the mustang, the axe, and he himself all flickered with rage- and magma-fueled flames. Guapo's hooves thundered, and Victor hardly noticed the citizens he flew past; he moved so quickly that his vision had narrowed to a tunnel, and only Guapo's supernatural ability to manage his incredible speed kept him from colliding with other vehicles or pedestrians. After a time, perhaps frustrated with the traffic, Guapo moved to the edge of the road and pounded over the grassy berm to charge in the open space where others didn't walk.

He might have run the risk of angering some influential citizen, but that wasn't likely, not on the ground—anyone with significant means in Sojourn flew, either under their own power or in a flying vehicle. No, Victor tore past ordinary iron rankers, people who wouldn't dare challenge him for his hasty, careless passage. His aura was on full display, and even a steel seeker would pause before accosting him in the face of that potent, rage-filled weight.

Victor *was* rage-filled. He'd kept his fury simmering while he listened to Arcus. He'd held it at bay when he'd delivered Rasso Hine to the guards in the portal room. But as he'd strode through the Council Spire, it had begun to boil out of his mental containment like a pot left too long on the stove. Summoning Guapo, holding Lifedrinker, feeling and hearing their anger echo his own, Victor found his fury mounting, building to a point where, as he tore over the grasslands, he almost felt like his old self, fighting in the pits for Yund.

Even so, there was rationality left in him. He could still think. He could still objectively look at his rage and wonder why it was so stoked. He couldn't pin down a single reason; he had many. He was furious that Arcus's father was such a piece of garbage, for one. How could a man raise a son with no love, only fear, respect, and the tremendous weight of expectations? How could that same man be willing to sacrifice such a nice, *sweet* girl like Trin? Victor had only met her once, but he'd liked her! The idea that their father was so callous as to use her as a fishing lure—

Victor growled as his anger began to boil over, and flickering flames joined the black smoke escaping his lips with each heaving breath. Bohn Volpuré's failings as a father were only the tip of the iceberg of Victor's rage. The idea that two of the people he most cared about were selected as targets by that man simply because they were acquainted with Victor was enough to send him into apoplexy. Edeya! After all they'd done to save her spirit, this piece of *shit* was willing to try to use her *life* as a bargaining chip? And Lam? Lam, whom Victor had bonded with, coaxing her spirit home from a desperate crucible of the soul?

Victor lifted his head and screamed his mounting fury, and flames licked his lips as black smoke rode the soundwaves of the terrible roar. Adding to his fury was the idea that this weaseling worm of a man did all of this knowing full well that Victor couldn't legally kill him, not without first issuing a challenge, a challenge that he could accept while insisting on the use of his champion.

The laws of Sojourn were strange to Victor, but according to Arcus, there were rules about who could challenge whom in this society. An iron ranker could challenge anyone, but any iron ranker could also have a champion, and a person's champion could be any rank beneath veil walker—even a steel seeker. A steel seeker could only challenge other steel seekers or veil walkers, and veil walkers could only directly challenge other veil walkers. If someone above the iron ranks wanted to contend with an iron ranker, they had to employ an iron ranked "champion."

So, Dar could challenge Bohn Volpuré, but he'd need an iron ranked champion. Bohn could then use *his* champion to fight Dar's champion. That being the case, Victor didn't see any point in getting Dar involved and perhaps earning another debt with the master Spirit Caster. No, he'd handle Bohn's champion on his own. Of course, none of this might bear any relevance—Volpuré might have a bargain in mind, something he intended to tempt Victor with, hoping to dissuade a duel because of his formidable champion. Victor had already resolved to listen to his offer and terms, but deep in his heart, deep in his belly, full of fiery rage, Victor wanted to fight.

When he came to a fork in the road, he turned to the south, where the sign said the Venture Hills Estates lay. "Close now, *chica*. Close."

Time to cut and rend. Time to bathe in the blood of our foes.

43

CHALLENGE

When Victor crested a rise and the Volpuré estate came into view, he urged Guapo to slow to a stop. He sat there, limned in orange flames, black smoke leaking from his nostrils astride a similarly furious-looking mustang. He still clutched Lifedrinker in one hand, and she hung down beside Guapo's flank, hissing and vibrating with her eagerness to kill. Victor knew better than to ride into Volpuré's estate in such a state. If he didn't get a grip on himself, witnesses would argue that he'd begun hostilities before issuing a legal challenge.

If that were the case, Volpuré would be within his rights to have his household guard swarm him. Victor might slaughter many, but Arcus had made it clear that his father's champion wasn't the only formidable fighter in his family's employ. Reluctantly, despite his boiling blood, Victor lifted Lifedrinker over his shoulder. She just had time to send thoughts of confusion, anger, and even a hint of betrayal his way before the harness snatched her out of his hand.

"Sorry, beautiful. I have to do this with a level head." As if to reassure himself of that capability, Victor closed his eyes, inhaled deeply through his nostrils, and turned his gaze inward, staring at the beautiful balance of his Core. He'd *allowed* his rage to run rampant while he traveled. In a way, he'd been venting, and he figured riding hard and contemplating murder was a better way to vent than getting into fights or shooting his mouth off at the wrong person. Having done so, he felt some relief from the pressure of the anger that had wanted to take hold of him when Arcus first revealed his father's scheme.

Still, his pathways were brimming with magma- and rage-attuned Energy, and he needed to put their influence in check. Slowly exhaling and then inhaling again, Victor drew the rage out of his pathways and pushed it into his Core. He watched as the baleful red band around his white-gold Core pulsed brightly and began spinning a bit faster as the hot red Energy returned. Nodding, already feeling much cooled, Victor exhaled and inhaled again; this time, as his breath surged into his lungs, he pushed the magma-attuned Energy in his pathways along with it, pulling it back into his Breath Core.

"Better," he sighed, sliding off Guapo's back. "Thanks, *hermano*." He gave Guapo's shoulder a pat. "Go back to the spirit plane and charge around the meadows for a while. Burn off that anger!" He chuckled as Guapo whinnied and reared up on his hind legs, but before the stallion could argue further, Victor severed his connection to his Wild Totem spell and sent him home.

Nodding and clearing his throat, Victor reached up to smooth the front of his finely stitched gray shirt and brushed the road's dust from his thighs and knees. He didn't need to—the garments would be spotless by the time he walked to the estate gates, but it felt good; it was another way to settle his mind.

He'd long since left behind the black springy crystal roadways of Sojourn City and its nearby environs, but a few miles back, the dirt roads had transitioned to red-brown cobbles. Victor had passed by a few other estates, and he figured the wealthy lords had paid to improve the road passing through the area. Wealthy was probably an understatement. Volpuré's estate looked like a small town with a tremendous monolithic pale-gray stone keep at its center. A stone wall of similar make surrounded the outbuildings, gardens, and courtyards, but the central keep stood alone, unguarded by an inner wall, yet imposing in its towering grandeur.

As he approached the wall and the guards at the gate, Victor studied that central keep. It was probably fifty yards on a side and maybe four or five hundred feet tall. He'd seen larger buildings, certainly, but the way it stood there, like a single massive stone planted in the hillside, was impressive; he couldn't deny it.

Windows didn't mar its surface for the first third of its height, but starting there at some invisible demarcation line, stained glass and balconies peppered the smooth surface, and Victor could make out tiny people going about their lives—shaking out rugs, watering little gardens, and leaning on balcony railings as they gestured and conversed. Volpuré's household looked to be bustling and full of life. "How many kids does that *pendejo* have? Thirty-something? I guess that means a lot of grandkids and in-laws."

By then, he'd stepped into the shadow of the gatehouse, and one of the men wearing Volpuré's livery—a silver raptor on a lavender background—stepped forward. "When you stopped yonder, we'd wondered if you'd approach. What can we help you with, stranger?"

Victor, reduced to his more "human" size of something close to seven feet, smiled and hooked his thumbs onto his supple leather belt. "I need to speak to Bohn Volpuré."

"Ah! Do you have an appointment with Lord Volpuré?"

"I think he's probably expecting me. I'm Victor Sandoval. He might have some information about a few of my friends who went into the family dungeon. Something Something Coliseum. Does that ring a bell?"

The guard, a tall, stout fellow with a shock of bright red hair hanging down from the rim of his black-lacquered metal helm, stepped closer, glancing at his partner whose eyes widened. "Victor? The giant from the Vault of Valor? The one who beat Lord Arcus?"

"Ah, yeah. That's me." Victor shrugged, still standing nonchalantly.

"I'll fetch Chamberlain Potts," the second guard said, and Victor gave him a double-take because he'd never heard such a high voice. The fellow's cheeks reddened at Victor's quick glance, and then he hurried away.

"Right, well, I've instructions to bring you to the lord's parlor. I'm assuming you received his invitation?"

"I did not. I've just returned to town from a . . . quest, I guess. I heard rumors about my friends, so I came straight here."

"Well, please follow me, sir." The guard looked Victor up and down before he turned, and he seemed to want to say something, but perhaps his sense of propriety wouldn't allow it. He clamped his jaw tight and turned to lead the way through the gatehouse and into an expansive cobbled courtyard.

Fruit trees grew in circular planters along the edges, and a fountain burbled at the center, surrounded by a low stone bench. Victor smiled and inhaled the scent of citrus, and as children's laughter caught his ear, he turned to see a small boy climbing one of the trees while a pair of girls in bright dresses tried to poke him with little sticks. They all giggled, so he didn't think anything untoward was happening.

"We should make haste, sir," the guard said from several feet ahead. Victor hadn't realized he'd stopped walking, but the guard's words didn't spur him. He folded his arms and arched an eyebrow.

"Why?"

"Well, the lord's parlor is on the top floor, and we wouldn't want to keep him waiting—"

"I think I'll wait for him here. I like this courtyard fine, and the fountain pleases my weary ears. Tell your master not to hurry on my account." Victor strode over the cobbles to the fountain as he spoke, admiring the delicately carved fish that served as the water spouts.

"But, sir, I'm sure you'd be more comfortable in the manor—"

"Manor?" Victor glanced up at the imposing stone edifice. "That looks more like a keep to me. No, I've had enough of gloomy stone interiors. I'll sit here in the sun, under the stars, and listen to the fountain while I wait. Thank you for the kind invitation, however."

"As you say, sir. I'll, well, I'll let the chamberlain know. I'm sure he'll have some refreshments sent your way. I'm not sure how long it will take Lord Volpuré to make his way down to see you—"

"No worries." Victor waved him off as he sat down, leaned back against the fountain's rim, and crossed his feet at the ankles. "I'll watch the children play while I wait."

"As you say," the guard repeated, then he bowed stiffly and hurried toward the stone steps leading up to the manor's sizeable double doors. Victor watched him for a moment, then turned his gaze toward the parapets surrounding the courtyard. Just as he'd hoped, there were dozens of guards making rounds, often sending glances his way. More than that, he could see picnic tables situated in the little gardens at the edge of the courtyard and, seated at them, several finely dressed adults. Arcus had told him that the courtyard was well-populated and the perfect place to issue his challenge. He'd warned Victor not to allow himself to be sequestered away from the eyes of potential witnesses.

"I hope you were right," he muttered as he considered the objection he'd thrown at Arcus: What if Lord Volpuré instructed his kin and staff to lie about the challenge? Arcus had laughed, saying that too many people in the household had too much to gain from the lord's downfall. They wouldn't lie to the Sojourn Council for him, not about something so important as a challenge.

Victor thought it was pitiful that a man of such means held such little loyalty from his own family, but on reflection, he figured it was a simple case of "you reap what you sow." Volpuré used his family for influence and treated them like tools, so it wasn't surprising that at least *some* of them might do the same to him.

He hadn't been lying about enjoying the sun and the sound of the fountain tinkling behind him. As he leaned back, Victor closed his eyes and tilted his face toward the warmth, letting it soak through his coppery flesh into the blood coursing beneath. He could almost imagine the warmer blood spreading through spiderwebs of veins, into his larger vessels and arteries, and carrying the sun's invisible touch through his body. He sat that way for quite some time, and he might have dozed if not for the knot of worry still eating at the pit of his stomach whenever he thought about Lam, Edeya, and even Darren.

"Who are you?" a high-pitched voice asked. Victor opened one eye and peered down to see one of the children he'd been watching earlier standing by his feet. She wore a bright yellow dress with a huge grass stain near where her knees must be. As he watched, he could see the stain slowly fading as the garment's enchantments worked overtime to keep the little rascal clean.

He grunted as he uncrossed his ankles and sat up a little. "I'm Victor. Who are you?"

"Jillian."

"Jillian, huh?" Victor studied her rosy cheeks, bright yellow eyes, and golden curls. She didn't look like Arcus or Trin. Still, it was a big family. "Are you related to Arcus and Trin?"

"They're cousins. Are you one of my uncles?"

"No, I'm afraid not. Is Lord Volpuré your grandpa?"

"That's great-grandpa!"

"Ah." Victor nodded and winked at the little girl. He glanced over her head to see the others she'd been playing with lurking near the fruit tree, intently watching their conversation. "Are those your siblings or more cousins?"

"Rin is my sister, but Lop is Lord Stravian's son."

Victor rubbed his chin and nodded sagely. "Mmhmm, I see, I see. Well—"

"Sir Victor?" Victor turned toward the feminine voice to see a lithe, graceful young woman approaching. She wore the Volpuré livery, but her uniform was clearly a custom design, far better fitting than those of the guards at the gate. Her hand rested on the basket hilt of a long, slender sword, but she bore a pleasant expression as she said, "Run and play, Jillian, you nosy fetter-fetch!"

The little girl squealed a scandalized giggle and ran toward her playmates, repeating, "Fetter-fetch! She called me a fetter-fetch!"

"Apologies, sir." The woman stopped a few feet away, standing in a stiff military fashion that brought a twinge of homesick longing to Victor's heart as it reminded him of Valla. "I'm Efanie, Commander of the Volpuré household guard. I understand you're waiting for Lord Volpuré?"

"I am. Maybe you can answer a simple question. If the answer is no, I'll leave now without any trouble."

"And if it's yes?"

Victor shrugged. "Then there might be some trouble."

"Very well." Efanie broadened her stance and clasped her hands behind her back. "What is the question?"

"Does Lord Volpuré have some friends of mine trapped in the family dungeon?"

"Trapped is a strong word—"

"Don't bullshit me, lady." Victor sat up straight and leaned forward, resting an elbow on his knee.

Efanie narrowed her large almond-shaped amber eyes and glanced over her shoulder toward the closed doors of the manor. When she looked back at Victor, she offered a quick nod and whispered, "The lord will argue that they entered of their own volition and that it would be an interference to pull them out. He'll try to gain favors from you, perhaps even to force you to sign a contract of servitude in exchange for their release."

Victor regarded her while inwardly feeling quite proud of his poker face. He didn't smile, frown, or even blink; Arcus had already told him that much, so nothing was a surprise. Well, he admitted to himself, the fact that she was whispering this to him was a surprise. Did none of Bohn Volpuré's people like him? He kept his voice low and calm as he asked, "And if I refuse?"

"I'm afraid he's prepared to risk even his daughter Trin's life. He included her with purpose of forethought; the council will see her death as proof that he meant no ill will, or at least that's what his advocates will argue."

Victor smiled. "It won't come to that."

Efanie blew out a sigh, and he could see the relief behind her eyes. "So, you mean to bargain with him, then?"

"Not exactly."

Efanie looked over her shoulder again, then whispered, even more softly than before, "You must understand—Lord Volpuré holds the only control stone for the dungeon. You can't—"

"Challenge him?"

Efanie groaned and shook her head. "Of course. You're new to Sojourn." She chuckled wryly and leaned a little closer, speaking conspiratorially. "He has the means to buy the best champion, Victor. Fak Loyle has never lost a duel."

Victor nodded, leaning back against the fountain again. "Makes sense, I guess, or he'd be dead, right?"

"He's a *steel seeker*!" she hissed just as the large manor door swung wide, and a portly man in the Volpuré livery stepped to the edge of the stoop and looked down at Victor and Efanie.

"Lord Bohn Volpuré!" he bellowed, his voice echoing around the courtyard. Efanie jumped as if she'd been electrocuted and took a few steps back, standing at attention. Victor didn't want to look like a boor, so he stood from the stone bench and turned to look squarely at the doorway. A moment later, a tall swarthy man dressed in the finest suit Victor had seen outside of a movie back on Earth strode through the doorway. He was followed by a train of attendants and soldiers, but only one followed him down the steps to approach Victor—a short round fellow wearing a deeply cowled blood-red robe and carrying a gnarled, polished length of wood topped with a pulsing green crystal.

When the two stopped before him, the man in the robe stood back a few feet, and all Victor could see of his face was the bottom edge of an unkempt brown beard. Bohn Volpuré cleared his throat. "Victor, was it?"

"That's right." Victor held out a hand, and Lord Volpuré looked at it momentarily before lifting his gaze, fluttering his overlong eyelashes as he regarded Victor's face.

"How might I help you, young man?"

Victor let his hand fall to his side. Maybe once upon a time, such blatant disrespect would have gotten a rise out of him. Maybe it was the improvements he'd done with his Core, the influence of his inspiration-attuned Energy, or maybe it was just that Victor had met with enough assholes that nothing fazed him anymore. Whatever it was, the only thought that crossed his mind as Volpuré refused to shake his hand was that it would make it all the sweeter when he brought him to his knees. "You can get my friends out of your dungeon."

"Your . . . *friends*?" He affected a puzzled expression, rubbing at his chin. "My *daughter* is currently in the family dungeon, exploring it with her team. I'm afraid there must be some sort of error on your behalf."

"You think so?" Victor grinned, chuckling softly. He lifted his arms to fold them over his chest. "I'm sorry if I've challenged your wits, Bohn, but try to deduce the facts. Your daughter is in the dungeon with some friends, and I'm asking you to get *my* friends out of your dungeon. Perhaps those friends are the same people, hmm?"

"Use respect when addressing *Lord* Volpuré!" the robed man growled roughly. At the same time, he unleashed his aura, and Victor felt it hit him like a heavy thorn-filled blanket, dragging him down, scoring his flesh with psychic barbs. The pressure was immense, the aura dense and powerful, and Victor moved with it, stumbling back and even falling to one knee, ducking his head, pumping his lungs to draw breath.

"Enough, Loyle. Let the man speak." Like a switch turning off, Loyle's aura faded, and Victor took a deep breath, rising shakily to his feet. He looked around to see a crowd had gathered. The guards watched from the parapets, and dozens of finely dressed, beautiful people lined the courtyard's perimeter. Arcus hadn't been wrong.

"Will you let them out?" Victor asked, still avoiding making eye contact with Bohn.

"I'd rather not interfere, young man. My daughter's future depends on her learning to fend for herself and not to rely on the might of her family name to rescue her from predicaments. That dungeon serves a valuable purpose: exposing the entrants to the very real risk of death helps to forge their character. So, in short, no, I will not. It would take something equally as valuable as the lesson my daughter would be losing out on to entice me. Have you anything of the sort?"

"Money? A fine magical weapon?" Victor knew nothing he offered would be acceptable, so he threw those out for the witnesses to add to their gossiping.

Bohn waved his hand. "I've no need of such things. I could buy your weapons a thousand—nay, a million times. Have you nothing unique?"

"I could give your daughter lessons. I'm sure you recognize the value in learning from a stranger with some talent—"

Bohn cut him off. "Unacceptable, but you've given me an idea. If you're willing to work for my daughter, why not sign a contract with my household? I could use a man like you."

"I already owe service to Ranish Dar." Victor finally looked up, locking his eyes—bright, amber, and predatory—with Bohn Volpuré's pretty blue ones hiding behind their long dark lashes.

Bohn frowned, a crease appearing over the bridge of his nose, perhaps surprised by the angry glint in Victor's gaze. "Yet the man isn't here. Is he not your patron?"

Victor frowned, his real emotions beginning to impact his acting. "He is, but I owe him enough. I'd hoped to solve this problem on my own. I thought you might be reasoned with—"

"Watch your tone," Fak Loyle growled.

Bohn Volpuré raised a hand, holding his dog in check. "If you will not leave Ranish Dar's service nor ask him to bargain in your stead, I cannot help you."

Victor nodded and stood up straight. He looked around the courtyard, ensuring that hundreds of eyes were on the small group at the center of the square, then he cleared his throat and said, in a booming proclamation, "In that case, Lord Bohn Volpuré, I challenge you to a duel to the death. Should I emerge victorious, by right of conquest, I claim the freedom of my friends and your own daughter from your dungeon."

"Fool!" Volpuré snorted. "My champion is a steel seeker. You've only felt a taste of his power." He turned to look at the short rotund man in his silky red robes. "What say you, Loyle? Up for a bit of a display?"

"Indeed, Lord Volpuré. I'll craft you something especially handsome from this fellow's hot blood." While they spoke, Victor did his best to look like a confused idiot. He glanced from Fak to Bohn and then over to Efanie. All the while, he let his eyes bulge out and his mouth hang open.

Volpuré chuckled and held his arms wide, looking around at the many witnesses in the courtyard. "Challenge accepted! We shall feast afterward!"

44

A WALK IN THE SUNLIGHT

The onlookers didn't exactly cheer, but a definite hubbub arose at Lord Volpuré's proclamation. More of the finely dressed Fae and human-looking members of Volpuré's household had quietly begun to crowd the edges of the courtyard, and Victor started to wonder if the duel would take place right then and there. He looked up at the proud edifice of Arcus's family manor and wondered how it would weather an earthquake. As though he'd read Victor's mind, Bohn cleared his throat noisily, and the buzz of conversations died down.

"The duel shall take place atop Arkhun's Hill at sundown. Will that be amenable to you, young man?" Bohn Volpuré's smug tone was so rankling to Victor that he almost dropped all pretense. His muscles tensed, but he held himself in check, the only evidence of his rancor a small muscle twitching near his eye.

"That's fine with me. What does that give us? A couple of hours?"

Before Bohn could reply, the slender, prim woman with the golden curls stepped forward. "I'll guide him to the hilltop, Lord Volpuré. Someone should attend him while he waits."

Again, before Bohn could speak, Fak Loyle growled, "Might I suggest, generous lord, that you send a scribe along with the young challenger that he might employ his services to meticulously document his final wishes for those he holds dear. After all, one must prepare for the inevitable, no matter the bitter taste."

"An excellent and kind suggestion, Loyle. Efanie, do keep Victor company. I'll send one of Preceptor Lovus's boys out to take down his final words." Bohn turned and immediately started up the steps, Victor and everyone else apparently dismissed from his mind. The lord's smug confidence was so over the top that Victor's eyes widened with disbelief. Could a man truly be so contemptuous?

Fak Loyle watched his master disappear back into the manor, then turned to Victor. "Worry not, lad. Your name won't be forgotten. My personal historian documents each of my duels. You'll be in good company on the pages of my exploits." Victor closed his mouth and narrowed his eyes, but he didn't speak as the red-robed mage turned his back and mounted the steps.

Efanie unclasped her hands from behind her and took another step toward Victor. She didn't speak, though, watching his face as he marked the progress of the steel seeker on his way up into the keep. Maybe she saw the murder behind Victor's amber irises. Perhaps she felt the tiny flicker of his aura that slipped the firm bindings of his iron will—whatever the case, she didn't say anything until Victor exhaled noisily and turned his gaze on her. "Shall we walk, sir?"

Victor looked at her for a long moment, caught up in the bright spots of white light where the sun reflected off her emerald irises. She seemed too good, too pleasant for a place where a man like Bohn Volpuré reigned. As he had the thought, he lifted his gaze and surveyed the gathered onlookers. Not the guards who'd made a show of returning to work, but the nobility, the rich, finely dressed members of the Volpuré household. They, too, looked pleasant, for the most part. Could a detestable man raise such pleasant folks? Were they all putting on a false front? His gaze shifted back to the tree, to the children he'd watched playing earlier. No, he decided. For some reason, not all of Bohn's children were devoid of redeeming qualities.

"Sir?" Efanie prompted again.

"Hmm? Oh, right, the hilltop. How far is it?"

"A few short miles down the lane. I could call us a carriage, but unless you've something else to do, I thought a stroll might do nicely to ease your nerves."

Victor smiled. "My nerves?" He reached up and scratched the rough dark stubble along his jaw. "Yeah, I guess a walk could do me some good. I'm enjoying the sunlight." She nodded and walked to his side, and for a panicked moment, he wondered if he was supposed to offer his arm or something, but she cleared her throat and started ahead, guiding him back toward the gate.

As they approached the dark opening of the gatehouse tunnel, one of the finely dressed younger men approached, doffing his velvety maroon hat and holding it to his chest as he cleared his throat. "Ahem. Excuse me, Efanie, might I speak a moment with your charge?"

"Lord Volpuré." Efanie paused and inclined her head, taking a step back.

"Volpuré?" Victor raised an eyebrow.

"Channer Volpuré. I believe you know my brother, Arcus?"

Victor folded his arms over his chest. "Yeah, I did."

"Did? Has something befallen him?"

"Your dad didn't tell you, huh?"

"Tell—what is it, man?" Channer looked a bit older than Arcus but seemed a great deal softer, and Victor didn't feel a whiff of power leaking off him.

"Well, your brother got killed in the prison dungeon in the Council Spire. You know the one?"

"I . . ." Channer looked appropriately disturbed by the news, and Victor's frown turned more genuine. Hadn't Arcus said his siblings didn't care for him? Or had he said *most* of them? Victor honestly couldn't remember and was beginning to feel a little bad for being so blunt with the man.

"Look. Sorry to break the news to you. You should let your brothers and sisters know that he died bravely, fighting a, uh . . ." As he spun the tale of Arcus's demise, doing a favor for his Pyromancer friend, he nearly broke his promise to Ronkerz about revealing the power of the great simian and his Big Ones.

"A what, man?"

Victor shrugged. "A really dangerous criminal. I think your dad and Arcus's master underestimated that place."

Efanie cleared her throat and stepped partially between Victor and Channer. "We should keep moving, Sir Victor. It's best not to linger on the estate of a gentleman you've just challenged."

"Right." Victor grasped Channer's shoulder, engulfing it with his broad, powerful hand. "My condolences. You should probably let your family know about Arcus." He released him and turned, following Efanie out the gates. Channer tracked him with his eyes—Victor could feel them on his back—but he didn't say anything more.

Efanie turned to the left, away from the main cobbled road, and followed a narrower path of pavers on grass. After they'd gone a few dozen strides beyond the gate and away from the people living in the Volpuré manor, she turned to regard Victor through narrowed eyes. "That was rather callously done."

"Hmm?" Victor's mind had begun to wander toward his upcoming fight, and he wasn't sure what she meant.

"Telling a man his brother was dead. You could have been a bit gentler."

"Well," Victor sighed, "to tell you the truth, I didn't think that guy would feel bad about Arcus's death. He gave me the impression that he and his siblings weren't too fond of each other."

"I suppose that's a fair explanation. Arcus wasn't well-loved, but at least as many of his siblings *liked* him as hated him." Victor noted her emphasis on "liked" and chuckled.

"Not loved, though?"

"Perhaps a small handful of sisters, one brother, and some nieces and nephews. He will be missed." Again, Victor felt stupid when he caught the glint of moisture in Efanie's eyes.

"Ah, shit," he groaned. "I should have realized you probably knew him damn well. Sorry about that." He thought about telling her the truth—that Arcus was still alive—but bit his tongue; just because she was pleasant and pretty didn't mean she wouldn't report every word he said to her "lord."

Efanie looked away and shrugged. "It's understandable, you've got—"

"Nah, it's not okay. I should have thought of your feelings. You should know Arcus died like a hero, fighting off enemies who greatly outnumbered him. He saved me from more than one deadly blow. I hope you all remember him that way." It was a lie, but only because Victor had promised Arcus not to tell the truth. He wondered just how long Arcus would be in the dungeon. Would he escape relatively soon, or would new generations of nieces and nephews be living in this great house before he found his way home?

Efanie didn't look at him, her gaze firmly fixed ahead and to the left, and she reached up to rub her eyes briefly before saying, "Thank you. I, um, well, I helped raise him. I spent a lot of time training him as a boy. He wasn't the easiest person to get along with, but he had . . . a difficult road. I'm glad he made a friend out of you before he died."

Victor nodded, unwilling to add more lies to the mound he'd already dished out. They walked in silence for a while, but as they left the manor's outer wall behind and wended through a small citrus orchard to the north, he caught his first glimpse of their destination. A great grassy hill rose from the nearby farmland. At its base was a series of enormous dark gray obelisks that jutted out of the grassy soil in a faintly curved line toward the east. If Victor squinted, he could almost imagine the stone monuments were fingers and the hill a giant swollen thumb.

"Arkhun's Hill." Efanie pointed to the distant grassy slope.

"Practically a mountain," Victor grunted.

"Tell me, Sir Vict—"

"Just Victor."

Efanie inclined her head. "Tell me, Victor, why do you throw your life away this evening?"

"Hmm? The duel?" He knew he was being obtuse but was having fun, so he waited for her to answer.

"Yes. Surely you don't hope—"

Victor cut her off, squeezing his left fist until his knuckles cracked. "Well, what else can I do? Volpuré wants to teach me a lesson, and he's using—"

"Your friends and his own daughter as instruments in that lesson? Yes, I understand that, but they won't be any safer if you lose a duel—" Her eyes widened, and her mouth formed an "O" before she covered it with her hand. "If you lose, he'll have no reason to punish them."

Victor smiled and nodded. "Yeah, the duel's a win-win for them." He shrugged and stuffed his hands in his pockets, smiling into the clouds. "Besides, there wasn't another solution. I could have tried to sue the guy, you know, dragged him before the council, but that would take time, and I don't think my friends have much time, yeah?"

"You could have swallowed your pride and brought your master to intervene."

"Ah, well, that's the issue, isn't it? My pride. It's a mighty big mouthful, and I didn't feel like choking it down."

Efanie turned to him and stared while he continued to walk, almost blithely, smiling into the sunny sky, a carefree spring in his step. "Are you suicidal, then? You've no loved ones to miss you?"

"Actually, I appreciate you mentioning it. When we get up on that hill, I'd like a few minutes to write notes to my loved ones." He winked at her. "You know, just in case." He'd planned to use his Far Scribe book but found the idea of using Volpuré's scribe to send notes to his loved ones amusing. He thought about that—loved ones. He had more than a few, and it felt good to remember that.

"I'm not sure if it's bad luck," he said, chuckling as he gave voice to his thoughts. "I mean, if I write them all notes about what to do when I die, doesn't that open the door, at least subconsciously, to the thought that I won't win? Nah, I think I'll just send them notes telling 'em how much I love and appreciate them."

"Victor!" Efanie stopped and whirled, reaching out to take his wrist. "I *appreciate* that you're doing this to save your friends, and consequently a young woman that I think of almost like a daughter, but you must realize you're doomed! You couldn't even stand inside Loyle's aura! How do you propose to fight him?"

Victor smiled at her, then lifted his gaze to the hill that had grown significantly closer as they'd spoken. He thought he could make out a grassy path carved in switchbacks leading up the southern slope. "It's bigger up close."

Efanie sighed and turned to follow his gaze. "Yes, and well-watered with the blood of heroes. I've watched Loyle kill at least a dozen men on that hilltop."

Victor grunted and started walking again. As Efanie hurried to catch up to him, he looked at her. "Just Loyle? Do other people fight up there?"

"Yes. It's used by all the local lords and their families—a storied, bloody piece of land. You'll have that, at least. Your blood will mingle with that of some very great men and women."

Victor thought about it, a macabre sense of satisfaction washing over him as he pictured his spirit rising up from that hilltop, meeting some of the great spirits who'd stayed behind to haunt the place. "Yeah. Yeah, that wouldn't be a bad place to die."

Efanie gave him a sideways look, then turned back to the hill. "I don't know why I care. I don't know why I don't simply encourage you. I should be glad you're doing this. I think I'm just angry that, once again, Bohn Volpuré's greed will cost the world at least one good life."

"It's too bad, isn't it? I mean, about the dueling laws of Sojourn. It's kind of bullshit that he gets to buy his life today, you know? Even if I beat his champion, he doesn't *really* lose anything."

Efanie chuckled, shaking her head. "Oh, that's where you're wrong, Victor. If it were *possible* for you to win, then the dear lord of the Volpuré clan would lose a great deal of *face,* and to the people who rule Sojourn, face is everything. Worse, he'd lose his champion, and, once people learned of the great Fak Loyle's demise, Bohn would find dozens of challenges coming his way. Each refusal he made would reduce his standing and open him to civil suits. Inch by inch, he'd be ruined and forced to step down as the Volpuré patriarch, elevating one of his sons." She gave him a look, narrowing her eyes as she smiled ruefully. "A pretty fantasy, but still just a fantasy."

Those were details that Arcus hadn't had time to impart, and Victor found Efanie's words quite heartening. His smile must have made that apparent because she scoffed, looking away and hurrying her steps, leading from several yards ahead as they mounted the trail that climbed the hillside. He could imagine families with children and elderly parents climbing the wide, well-worn path on their way to attend a duel. Frowning, he called out, "Is that all that goes on up there? Duels?"

Efanie didn't respond at first as she continued to hike up the hill. When they reached the next switchback, though, she paused and looked down at Victor as she rounded the corner. "No. Celebrations for the seasons, for various old gods, and even events like weddings take place atop this hill."

"Huh." Victor nodded, and they resumed their climb in silence. When they reached the top, Victor looked past Efanie to see a broad grassy field, much flatter than he would have expected. Delicately carved stone pillars formed a loose circle about twenty yards from the edge. Victor counted thirty-three of the columns surrounding a space about half the size of a football field. Other than that, the top of the hill was bare of anything but ankle-high grass. "I guess we're supposed to fight in the middle?"

"The watch stones are enchanted to absorb Energy. They'll keep spectators safe from . . . misguided spells."

Victor chuckled at her choice of words. He wasn't too sure some carved stone pillars would protect people atop a hill if he used Wake the Earth, but he was hopeful they'd at least give people time to flee. Efanie walked over to one of the nearby columns and leaned against it, folding her arms and watching him. She seemed to have grown tired of his refusal to take the duel seriously and didn't have anything more to say.

Victor trudged past her into the circle, and he could feel the pressure and hum of potent Energy as he passed over the line of "watch stones." It was like stepping through a layer of dense, thick air. The depth of the power made him reconsider things; perhaps there was something far more potent buried in the hill, some Energy source that could indeed absorb his spells' power or redirect it away from the spectators. He'd only taken a few steps when a *woosh* in the air caught his attention. He turned his eyes upward to see an avian man with bright orange feathers spiraling downward.

He wore Volpuré livery and carried a well-worn leather satchel. He landed, stumbling forward, and barely caught himself before falling. "Oof! The updraft was more than I bargained for!" He turned, fluttering his wings and making clucking sounds in his throat as he straightened his uniform.

"Don't be alarmed!" Efanie called from the circle's edge. "He's one of the scribes."

"Ahem, yes." The avian fellow stepped toward Victor and held out a hand. "Tibbion at your service, sir. I've been ordered to take your last wishes down and deliver them to your family."

Victor squeezed the man's slender, downy hand in his own, careful to only apply a slight pressure. "Could you give me some stationery and envelopes? I'll write a few notes for you to deliver."

"I was told to take dictation—"

"Tibbion," Victor interrupted, "I may look like a brute, but I know how to write." With that, Victor sat down, folded his legs, and held out an empty hand. A moment later, the scribe set a stack of blank, surprisingly white uniform pages in his palm along with a fancy curlicued magical pen. As he began to write his first note, one to Ranish Dar, Victor remembered that he would be handing it off to a man who worked for Bohn Volpuré, so he decided to keep things short and amusing.

He wrote about his training and his plans to keep working on his cultivation. He said trite, meaningless things like how he was looking forward to swimming in the lake or how he hoped to have a rainstorm in the shower of his own future home. Overall, it was just a pleasant little note culminating in Victor's thanks for being such a good mentor. By the time he folded Dar's note and put it in an envelope, nearly a dozen people had arrived on the hilltop and were sitting in comfortable chairs or on blankets outside the stone circle.

Victor handed the envelope to Tibbion, then began writing quick notes to his closest friends. He wrote to Lesh, Edeya, Lam, and Darren, and then, just to be thorough, he wrote notes to Thayla, Deyni, Chandri, Chala, and even Rellia and Kethelket. When he finished, he glanced around the clearing and saw that maybe a hundred people had arrived, and the hilltop had taken on a certain festive air. As he handed the stack of envelopes to Tibbion, he asked, "How much time before the duel?"

"Nearly half an hour, sir."

Victor nodded and bent his head to the last letter he intended to write:

Valla,

I've just gotten out of the dungeon, and I know I should have written to you immediately in the Far Scribe book, but I had some business to take care of. Now I'm writing you this letter, partially to pass some time and partially because I think it's amusing that my enemy will deliver a love note for me. "Love note" is a funny phrase as I think about it, but that's what I'm writing. I just want you to know how much I appreciate you and how much you mean to me. I'm young and sometimes stupid, but I know a good thing when I see it.

Victor frowned and tapped the pen against his chin for a moment. He'd meant to write something lighthearted, something that wouldn't mean much to anyone other than that he cared about Valla, but suddenly, a dark musing passed through his mind: What if these were the last words he ever said to her? Frowning, suddenly more serious than he'd been since issuing his challenge to Volpuré, he continued to write:

If I died today, I hope you'd miss me for a while, but I also hope you'd let our love become a warm memory and that you'd find new people to love and new hopes and dreams to chase. Let your life be filled with good things, and always look for ways to enjoy the better parts of living. Don't ever dwell on vengeance or hate, on fear or envy—remember that our spirits take those things with them when we die. I want your spirit to find me in our next lives, even if it's just to say "hello."

I love you,

Victor

Victor smiled, folded the paper neatly, then slipped it into the envelope. On the outside, he wrote Valla's name and handed it to Tibbion. "Take all of those to Lord Ranish Dar's lake house."

"As you command, sir!" To Victor's surprise, the avian slipped the letters into his satchel, spread his wings, and launched himself aloft, rapidly pumping his wings as he gained altitude.

"Shit," Victor chuckled. "I didn't think he'd leave right this second." He looked around and was surprised to see hundreds of people lining the circle of stones. When he saw people's mouths moving, their hands gesturing, but didn't hear anything but a low background murmur, he realized that the magic of the stone circle must be creating a sort of bubble, a barrier that made it hard for even sound to penetrate.

With a grunt, he pushed himself to his feet and scanned the crowd for Lord Volpuré. Sure enough, he spotted him on the southern edge of the circle, sitting in an oversized throne-like chair, surrounded by finely dressed people in similarly comfortable-looking chairs. Victor looked to the east and saw the orange and red streaks in the sky that marked a Sojourn sunset. It was nearly time.

When he turned back, he saw the short round crimson figure of Fak Loyle pushing his way through the crowd and into the circle. As Loyle began striding toward Victor, Chamberlain Potts's voice boomed out, loud enough for even Victor to hear inside the magical circle, "As dusk is upon us, the duel will commence. Victor Sandoval, challenger to Lord Bohn Volpuré, are you ready?"

Victor reached over his shoulder and drew Lifedrinker from her harness. She vibrated with eager fury, not a small part of which was directed at Victor for making her wait so long. He chuckled as he sent a small surge of Energy into the runes on his clothing, instantly cladding himself in his heavy red-black wyrm-scale and lava king hide armor. From within his fearsome helm, he bellowed, "I am ready."

The hugely rotund chamberlain immediately bellowed, "Fak Loyle, champion of House Volpuré, are you ready?"

The stocky red-robed figure stopped about ten paces from Victor and lifted his twisted green-gemstone wand high. "Ready," he growled.

"Let the duel begin!" Chamberlain Potts roared.

Victor held still, watching Loyle, waiting to see what he'd do. The wizard chuckled, and, with a palpable weight, he unleashed his aura. It was so real and thick that the grass between Victor and the wizard flattened. Victor felt it touch him, slamming down like a lead blanket adorned with needle-tipped psychic thorns that sought to pierce his very spirit. This time, however, he didn't flinch, and he certainly didn't stumble back or fall to his knee. Instead, Victor relaxed his formidable will, unleashing his own aura that rippled out like a wave of murderous fire.

It was Loyle's turn to take a stumbling, hesitant step back, and he threw his hood back in disbelief. When Victor saw his blood-red eyes sunken in deep, pale flesh, he grinned, exposing his white, powerful Quinametzin teeth. "What?" he growled. "Did you think your aura was so fearsome? I've felt worse." It was true—Ronkerz's aura was a hundred times heavier than Fak Loyle's. Even Lira's had been weightier. Of course, the surprise on Loyle's face only added to Victor's enthusiasm, so his grin was something mad indeed as he canceled his Alter Self spell and surged with power. The fight was on.

45

BLOOD AND THORN

Loyle didn't stand still for Victor's first lightning-fast cleave. As Lifedrinker ripped the air, black smoke trailing in her wake, the spellcaster sank into the ground, leaving behind a pool of shimmering blood. Victor whirled, only to see Loyle reappear on the far side of the circle, springing from an identical pool. "Blood magic," Victor growled. Arcus had told him about the spell, and he'd also told Victor that Loyle couldn't perform the spell rapidly, back-to-back. Victor focused on his adversary and cast Energy Charge, fueling the spell with fear-attuned Energy.

As he streaked over the ground in a cloud of purple-black shadows, Victor heard Arcus's words in his mind: "Keep pressure on him, Victor. Anyone who ever came close to beating him never gave him a moment to rest. Be certain, though, that no matter how beaten he seems, he has another trick up his sleeve. Never let your guard down." As though the words were prophecy, just as Lifedrinker was about to split the much smaller man in half, he surged into the air, hoisted off the ground by a thorny green vine that burst out of the grassy soil, surging upward like a mythical beanstalk.

Victor collided with the thorny stalk, Lifedrinker leading the way. His armor flattened the spines that tried to pierce his flesh, and his axe gleefully ripped through the yard-thick strand of fibrous plant matter in an explosion of splinters and green juice. As he regained his senses, Victor looked up at the wildly shaking stalk, only to see it was bereft of its passenger. He whirled, looking for any sign of the mage's bright red robes. Sure enough, Loyle was on the other side of the circle again, this time dancing in a strange ritual—stomping his feet, shaking his hands, throwing his head back to cough and howl in a strange language.

Energy Charge had a short cooldown, but it wasn't yet ready, so Victor bunched his legs and used Titanic Leap to launch himself toward the wizard. As he reached the apex of his jump and started down, he saw Loyle seem to explode—blood boiled out of him like a water balloon popping in slow motion, but it didn't splash to the ground. Instead, it hung in the air like a great crimson bubble, and just as Victor began to fall toward it, the blood seemed to solidify and sprout millions of hairs. Only when Victor was about to impact the strange mass did it ripple and form into Loyle's intent—a great crimson bear.

He hacked Lifedrinker toward its enormous glowering brow, but the monstrous creature swiped madly at him with a tree-like arm tipped with crimson scythe-like claws. Victor just had time to tuck his chin and pull his limbs in close as the massive paw smashed him out of the air. The claws cut like razors as they sliced his shoulder and side, slipping through his armor as though it wasn't there, shredding his flesh and biting deep into his bones. Victor roared in pain and fury as his rage-attuned Energy exploded out of his Core. It flooded his pathways and turned his vision so deeply red that he almost lost sight of the monstrous bear as he rolled on the grass.

When he stood, Victor had more than doubled in mass; he'd been so enraged that Iron Berserk had nearly cast itself. His flesh knitted together almost instantly, and a low, angry chuckle escaped his lips as he turned toward his foe. As the bear charged him, Victor flicked out his left hand, Energy already surging into the gauntlet on his fist. A coil of sizzling, dripping magma—enlarged to match his titanic form—whipped out with a *crack*, splashing hot liquid fire over the bear's red fur and tearing a huge chunk of bloody sizzling flesh from its shoulder. The creature roared in agony but kept coming, its furious eyes a match for Victor's. Victor welcomed it, spreading his arms wide.

Just as Loyle, in his blood-bear form, leaped to try to latch his massive jaws around Victor's throat, Lifedrinker came down like a falling star, blazing and rippling with Energy as she *crunched* into the side of the monster's head, just above the ear. The bear slumped, but its momentum carried it into Victor, smashing against his chest. Victor, surging with pride for Lifedrinker's tremendous blow, turned and threw the bear to the side. Thousands of pounds of fur, blood, and bone shook the earth as the monstrous animal impacted the grassy sod, tearing a furrow twenty yards long.

Victor, remembering Arcus's words, didn't let up the pressure. He lashed out with his magma whip, hooking it around one of the bear's rear legs. As liquid fire splashed and fur and flesh sizzled, he pulled himself as he lunged, closing the distance in a mere second. Then, he began to lay into the downed bear with Lifedrinker, hacking great gaping wounds with each downward blow. As blood sprayed and drenched him in its hot, liquid embrace, Victor began to roar with wild maniacal laughter. Lifedrinker crunched through bones along with the fleshy parts of the enormous bear, and soon the beast's thrashing, clawing attempts to right itself or lash out faded, and then . . . it was gone. Victor stood, heaving for breath over a mound of mushy, coagulated blood—nothing more.

He straightened, perplexed. Had he won? A tickle at the nape of his neck, some instinctual sixth sense spurred him to dive to the side just as a hail of needle-sharp thorns ripped through the air where he'd been standing. Victor bounded to his feet, whirling to scan the circle, only to see Loyle waving his hand, hurling another torrent of magically generated thorny missiles. Victor ran diagonally, dodging the attack. As soon as he was clear, he cast Energy Charge and hurtled on waves of sparkling Glory-attuned Energy toward his enemy. Again, Loyle used his blood-pool teleportation and escaped, forcing Victor to abandon his spell as he streaked through the space where the wizard had earlier stood.

In his mind, Victor tried to calculate the timing of Loyle's teleportation cooldown. It wasn't instant, but it wasn't as long as he'd hoped. He turned, frustration mounting, rage building, and scanned for his adversary. Once again, he saw the man's portly robed figure dancing, and this time, with each awkward stomp of his feet, saplings sprang from the soil and wove together, forming an archway with the mage at its center. Victor didn't know what he was doing but meant to interrupt it.

He leaped into action, his long legs powering him across the fighting circle in just a few broad strides, and then he lashed out with his magma whip, aiming to yank Fak Loyle toward him. The wizard threw out his arm at the last second, and a tangle of saplings sprang from the ground, intercepting Victor's whip. Loyle turned and bounded away, leaving his strange archway behind. Victor stalked toward it, Lifedrinker raised high, intent on chopping it to kindling before Loyle's purpose could come to light.

Unfortunately, he'd just closed the distance when the air inside the archway shimmered with sparkling green Energy, and then a great bundle of claws and black fur exploded out of it and slammed into Victor, knocking him to the side, despite his titanic size. The creature roared, a sound that woke something primal in Victor, an instinctual desire to fight or flee. When he regained his balance and whipped Lifedrinker around, fending off the raking claws, he got his first good look at what had to be Loyle's "bog lion" companion.

The creature was close to the size of his cave bear spirit companion, but it reeked of power. Its fur was black, but its mane was tawnier, brown at the base, and much paler on the fringes. The creature had deep green eyes the color of moss, and they glinted with intelligence as the lion regarded Victor. As its massive claws dug into the turf, it growled and paced, calculated violence in those eyes.

The lion's aura was heavy and full of primal cunning and murderous intent. Victor suddenly realized he wasn't just battling with one steel seeker; this "companion" was likely as formidable as Loyle. Wasting no time, he channeled Energy into the pattern for his Wild Totem spell, summoning his coyotes with fear-attuned Energy. When he'd spoken to Arcus, his initial plan had been to summon his bear and use that powerful companion to battle with the lion. Having seen and felt the lion's power, though, he knew that would be a waste; his bear would put up a brave fight, but the lion would kill it, and it wouldn't take long.

No, this was a foe that Victor would have to deal with himself. His coyotes wouldn't be able to kill Loyle, but hopefully, they could keep the mage on the defensive, at least long enough for him to slay the mighty bog creature. His five mastiff-sized coyotes sprang from pools of shadow, their glowering purple eyes gleaming out of dark, shadowy countenances, their yips and cries haunting and strange. Victor mentally urged them to harry the mage, and they immediately spread out, crossing the circle and rapidly closing with Loyle.

Meanwhile, the lion dove at him, swiping its powerful arms. Victor knocked its grasping claws aside with Lifedrinker's smoldering edge. The beast was strong and fast, and as they began to spar in earnest, Victor enjoyed the rhythm of his battle with it. The lion was a master in the use of its natural weapons, and it had a dozen combinations of swipes and bites that kept Victor guessing. Often, it would land hits on his armor, scoring long shining dents in his wyrm-scale and rending his lava king hide. Even so, it rarely drew any blood; his armor was sufficient, and Victor was adept at minimizing damage by moving with the impacts.

He felt one of his coyotes depart the material plane, and he knew he couldn't drag out his fight, though a part of him wanted to. However much he was learning from the skilled melee combat of the lion, he couldn't allow Loyle and the beast to work together. Frowning, almost feeling guilty, he employed his magma lash. The creature could block his axe with its diamond-strong, foot-long claws, but the whip was another matter. The very first time he snapped it out, the lion, roaring and growling, swiped at it with its claws, only to have the length of molten, smoldering stone coil around its paw and foreleg. It sizzled and popped, melting through the lion's fur and flesh. The beast recoiled, yowling madly as it thrashed and bucked, trying to pull its limb free.

Victor yanked on the lash, pulling the enormous lion off-balance, and Lifedrinker was ready and waiting for the opening. He hacked her down, and her orange-hot edge bit halfway through the lion's left shoulder, severing muscle and tendon and digging deep into the bone. The lion went mad with pain and panic, roaring and screeching as it exploded in a frenzy of movement that only a feline could pull off. It ripped its right foreleg free of Victor's whip and flung itself backward, scrambling to flee. One of its forelimbs wouldn't move right, and the other was degloved, nothing but bloody bone as it tried to scamper away.

If Victor hadn't been in a fight for his life, if he hadn't been hot with rage long before the fight even started, if he hadn't been stoking his pathways with rage-attuned Energy, he might have turned his back on the creature and let it skulk away. He might have risked it recovering somehow and coming for him. As it was, Victor was seeing red, and he was aware that only two of his coyotes were still "alive." He couldn't risk that Loyle might somehow heal the beast and that it might catch him unawares while he dealt with the mage. No, Victor reasoned grimly—he had to finish it.

So, as the great, once-proud lion limped away, hobbled and broken, Victor swallowed his sympathy and cast Energy Charge. As usual, he led his charge with Lifedrinker's gleaming, hungry edge. He smashed into the monstrous beast's haunches, and his deadly axe split the great cat's spine like a master woodsman's axe felling a young oak. The *crack* rang out, and Victor's impact sent the broken, listless body of the beast flopping like a terrier's stuffed animal toward the edge of the circle.

He just had time to register the onlookers scrambling to escape being flattened by the dead or paralyzed beast before Loyle's howl of dismay caught his attention. Victor whirled in time to see the mage roiling with red bubbling Energy, surging in size as his body swelled and engorged, blowing up like an obscene doll, his white, sun-starved arms and legs sprouting from his robes, which apparently weren't enchanted to grow to match the size of their wearer. He wasn't just growing; he was *stretching*, and Victor could see the blood roiling and pulsing under his stretched-thin skin.

One of his coyotes yet remained, and it lunged in, grabbing hold of Loyle's Achilles tendon. It viciously shook its head as it tried to rip it out. Loyle reached down one of his massive swollen hands and grasped the coyote by the neck. Victor saw that weird pulsating limb contract, and then the crunch of bones signaled his totem's demise. Loyle, now something like fifteen feet tall and twice as bulky as Victor, held aloft his bulbous right hand, and blood streamed out, solidifying in the air into the shape of a scythe. Then the steel seeker stomped toward him, the ground lurching with each impact of his overlarge feet.

Victor stared, amazed by the spectacle. The man's robes were stretched tight, and the lower hem failed to cover his engorged, bouncing family jewels. It was so distracting that Victor nearly failed to react as that enormous blood-red scythe whistled through the air toward his right knee. He parried the blow just in time, his epic-level axe skills too well-honed to allow such a well-broadcast attack to hit home. As the scythe bounced away, Victor took a step back and grunted, "Arcus didn't mention *this* bullshit!"

Loyle's face was disfigured by the blood that had swelled his form; his flesh was drawn taut, his eyes bulged like pasty puffer fish, and his teeth looked tiny behind his sausage-like lips. Still, his tongue waggled in that oversized mouth, and garbled words flowed forth. "Yawl pay for *thaaah*!"

Having had enough of the freakshow, Victor scowled and launched a vicious attack, hacking Lifedrinker low and high, dancing inside the arc of that stupidly massive scythe. Her burning blade sizzled as she split Loyle's pasty flesh and released torrents of blood not once or twice but five times as Victor smoothly glided around the swollen monstrosity. Loyle teetered and wobbled with each blow, and as Victor danced away, spinning to watch his handiwork, a great pool of blood formed around the mage as he veritably deflated, gouts of blood pouring from the gashes Victor had made.

Victor wanted to put an end to the disgusting sight of Loyle's sagging, overlarge skin hanging from his emaciated form. He gathered himself for another Energy Charge, but then the blood pool bubbled and boiled, rising from the ground as though animated. The blood took on the form of a liquid serpent, and its crimson head lunged toward Victor, quick as lightning. The thing must have sprouted fangs, because he felt them pierce his thigh as it latched on. He jerked back and hacked down with Lifedrinker, but her razor-sharp, smoldering edge slid along the blood serpent's flesh as if he were trying to cut a rubber hose with a butter knife.

Suddenly, he felt a pulse, and something hot and vile entered his leg. It wasn't like venom; it was more like his earlier comparison of a hose—a great quantity of *something* was being pumped into his body through the blood serpent's bite. With each pulse, a hot, burning, dirty wave pushed into his flesh and spread further and further. He lost control of his leg, stumbled, and fell backward.

Victor scrabbled back on his hands, kicking with his good leg, but the blood serpent stretched from the pool with his movement, and another pulse of that *stuff* entered his body. Victor's vision began to tunnel, and a weird high-pitched ringing echoed through his ears. His legs, his chest, even his shoulders were numb, and they felt *wrong*, as though they weren't even his. He found it difficult to concentrate or remember what he was doing. His muscles relaxed, and he slumped back onto his elbows as the thing pulsed again, and more of the sickening sensation of having someone else *inside* his skin threatened to drive him mad.

Victor's thoughts drifted to odd places as his vision darkened further and his mind grew numb. He thought of Valla and felt relief that he'd sent her a letter. He imagined Deyni running through fields, chasing her raptor as it hunted for prey. He remembered Old Mother as she'd hugged him and said she'd see him in another life. As his limbs turned cold, and his heart's steady *thump* slowed, pausing for a dozen seconds between each sluggish beat, he remembered Tes and felt his first regret—he'd wanted to meet her again. The thought tickled something in Victor, woke some part of him that remembered who he was.

With a tremendous effort of will, he forced his wandering mind back to the present, and with his vision dark, he turned his gaze inward and regarded his Core. It was besieged, surrounded by cold red Energy. Victor turned to his Breath Core and, using the pathway he'd long ago opened when he'd learned to use his magma-attuned Energy, pulled some of that hot, burning power out, watching with glee as it burned up the cold, bloody, invading Energy. As his magma-attuned Energy burned its way to his spirit Core, Victor felt parts of himself waking up. His heart's slow *thump* became a *thump-thump*, and the magma rushed into the chamber of his Spirit Core and seared a pathway for his rage to spill forth.

As feeling returned to his chest, spreading outward from his pounding heart, Victor inhaled deeply and let magma and rage-attuned Energy mingle in his pathways. His vision came back to him, and he saw the stars in all their splendor hanging bright in the dark sky over his head. He felt the grass under his fingers, Lifedrinker's haft in his palm. He felt the blood serpent digging into his thigh, pushing its vile concoction into him, but his body was resisting now; he could feel the sickening stuff burning up in his chest, in his Core.

Unwilling to lose ground again, remembering the enormous size of Loyle's blood pool, he gathered his magma and rage and pushed them together, casting Volcanic Fury. As fire ignited in his blood, as flames flickered to life in his dim vision, Victor let his head roll back, opened his mouth, and roared his primal rage. His madness was tinged with cruel amusement as he felt Loyle's blood burn to ash in his veins.

Victor inhaled deeply and turned his gaze on the serpent, smoking and steaming as it continued to try to pump its vile concoction into his leg. He gathered his breath and exhaled a plume of magma. The liquid fire eradicated the serpent, popping and melting away its form like blood spilled into an inferno. Victor continued to blow, lifting his face toward Loyle where he stood, his sagging flesh still hanging from his much-reduced body, and doused him with the remainder of the fire in his lungs.

Loyle screamed and writhed. Perhaps instinctually, he cast his blood pool teleportation, but when he reappeared on the far side of the circle, he was still aflame and still thrashing and screaming in agony. Victor sprang to his feet, leaving a blackened, body-shaped scorch mark on the grass. His vision was tinted yellow, and it pulsed red with each beat of his heart as he approached his tortured foe. Lifedrinker no longer smoldered—she blazed. Her edge was white-hot, and she burned the very air as Victor stalked forward, trailing black smoke and leaving behind fiery footsteps that burned the damp green grass to ash.

Despite his agony, Loyle managed to get off a spell; green tendrils of vines erupted from the soil and wrapped around him, smothering the flames and, perhaps, healing him with their pulsing green sap. Victor didn't care. All he knew was his need for destruction and that this was a fool who'd tempted his rage. He blew out another stream of doubly effective magma, enhanced by his Volcanic Fury, and it splashed over those coiled green shoots, instantly bursting them as the sap within boiled to steam. Loyle screamed, and Lifedrinker answered him as she ripped through the air to cleave him in twain.

His foe undeniably vanquished, Victor arched his back, lifted his face to the stars, and roared. When he was certain all around knew of his victory, of his rage, of his hunger for destruction, he straightened and turned his gaze on those lurking outside the circle of stones. He wasn't discriminating; all were welcome to feel his fury. Victor stalked toward the first group of onlookers unlucky enough to catch his eye. He only took two burning steps, though, before a warm, malleable, but unyielding force caught him in its grasp.

A voice, familiar but unexpected, spoke into his ear: "That was well-fought, lad, but now you must cool that rage." As that weird, warm Energy pushed against him, then *into* him, driving the rage and magma Energy out of his pathways, Victor realized it was Ranish Dar. He fell to his knees as the fury left him, and he felt the draining aftereffects of his battle lust. He looked around, trying to catch sight of his mentor, but he wasn't anywhere to be seen. Could a veil walker so effortlessly subdue even a titan? He'd taken his rage away and never even revealed himself.

His titanic form had left him, along with his rage, and Victor could feel the dampness in the grass under his knees. As he grunted, pushing himself to his feet, he saw Efanie jogging toward him. "Are you well?" she asked breathlessly, her face flushed with excitement. "Gods! How—"

"Where's Bohn?" Victor asked, cutting her off.

"He's there, sulking on his throne. There are far too many people present for him to skulk off. Everyone's in shock, me included." Victor followed her pointing finger and saw that, indeed, Bohn and his retinue were sitting still, subdued and quiet. Not everyone was calm, though—a hubbub had arisen around the circle, and Victor could see that people were still wrapping their heads around what they'd witnessed.

"An iron ranker! You realize . . . I think the last iron ranker to kill a steel seeker in Sojourn was Ronkerz. He was—"

"I know who he was." Victor looked at her and then at the finely dressed nobility and their families. Did they realize how close they'd come to feeling the brunt of his fury? He hadn't wanted to use Volcanic Fury for that very reason, but had Loyle given him a choice? He'd almost overwhelmed him with that blood invasion. "Thank you, Dar," he said to the air, hoping his mentor could hear him. He took a single step toward Bohn Volpuré, but Efanie gripped his wrist.

"Your award! Gods! Look! The Energy—it's so bright!" Victor looked where she pointed, and sure enough, great balls of Energy were gathering around Loyle's corpse. They weren't golden or purple or rainbow-hued. They were like moonlight—white, ethereal, and so bright they lit up the hilltop like floodlights. Victor squinted as he watched them bubble together.

"Yeah. My awards." He grinned as he stalked toward the corpse. Not only would he take his Energy award from the System, but he had a heart and perhaps some dimensional containers to claim.

46

RESPONSIBILITY

The crowd around the circle grew hushed as the brilliant, ethereal moonlight Energy gathered. Apparently, even the jaded nobility of Sojourn didn't see a steel seeker die every day. Victor strode toward Loyle's corpse, his head high, his back straight. Watching the Energy gather, he wondered about the bog lion. Shouldn't he see two corpses bleeding out their Energy? He glanced in the direction he'd sent the beast tumbling but saw nothing. Had Loyle somehow sent his companion back from whence it came? Further questions were driven from his mind as the brilliant, potent stream of light surged into him.

He heard the crowd gasp, but that was the last input his corporeal senses provided before they were overwhelmed by his universe coming apart around him. Victor had the sensation of seeing time and space peeled apart, layer by layer, as a sound like the inside of a tornado rushed through his ears. He smelled and tasted things he couldn't name, a series of sensations that tore through his mind so rapidly as to become a single stream of incomprehensible input. As one color after another—one stratum after another—peeled away before his dumbstruck inner eye, Victor witnessed things he knew he'd never remember.

He saw beings of light and darkness, creatures too big to fully grasp, and a world so vast that Earth and all its neighboring planets might disappear into one of its continents. Voices whispered to him—cryptic messages that he immediately forgot and songs that would have made him weep if he'd had any sense of his physical body. And then it was over, and he found himself on his knees in the bloodstained grass before Loyle's broken corpse. He heard the hubbub around him; apparently, he'd put on quite a show while he absorbed the Energy. Victor ignored the voices—even Efanie's, as she hurried to his side once again. He was too focused on the System messages:

*****Congratulations! You have achieved Level 68 Herald of the Mountain's Wrath and gained 24 strength, 34 vitality, and 24 will.*****

The message only added to the euphoria he was feeling from the massive Energy infusion. He'd gained two levels by killing Loyle, and that was no small boost considering how slowly he was "supposed" to level now that he was nearing Tier Seven. He'd begun to carry some dread about gaining levels now that he was climbing well into the upper half of the iron ranks. Everyone he spoke to seemed to have a reminder about how slow it would be and how tedious it was. So far, Victor hadn't felt it, not to any significant degree, and he was hopeful he could keep proving people wrong. He continued reading:

*****Congratulations! You have learned the spell: Volcanic Fury, Improved.*****

*****Volcanic Fury, Improved. Prerequisites: Rage, Fury, or Hatred Affinity, and Magma Affinity. You channel the fury of the fiery depths. While affected by this transformation, you are immune to fire-based attacks, your magma-based abilities double in effectiveness, you recover magma-attuned Energy at a vastly improved rate, and you benefit from the effects of Berserk: double strength and speed, increased resilience, and powerful regenerative capabilities. Be cautious, for the fury of the volcano knows no bounds—reason and compassion will flee before its heat. Energy Cost: Minimum 1000, scalable. Cooldown: Long.*****

"Shit!" Victor grunted, swiping the messages away. His Herald of the Mountain's Fury class spells seemed to synergize incredibly well with his Breath Core—almost as though they were made to go with each other. Was Herald of the Mountain's Fury a dragon class? Did dragons even have classes? Whatever the case, it only made him want to improve his Breath Core all the more.

"Something's wrong?" Efanie asked.

"Nah, something's good." Victor stood and approached Loyle's corpse.

"Victor, Lord Volpuré waits for you; the crowd is eager to see him grant your demanded conquest price."

"He can wait a little longer." Victor leaned over the corpse, saw that Lifedrinker's slash had split the torso right beside the heart, and reached into the charred, bloody flesh to grasp hold of the thick, cooling organ. With a soft grunt, accompanied by the *pops* of snapping arteries, he pulled it out. Efanie recoiled, shock on her face, but Victor ignored her. He set the heart on the grass and then proceeded to strip Loyle's fingers of their rings—four in total. He picked up the heart and, with his prizes in one giant fist, dripping blood between his knuckles, strode toward Bohn Volpuré's pretentiously oversized chair.

The crowd had gravitated toward that side of the circle, and Victor could feel the hundreds of eyes on him. As he walked, Efanie babbled, "I've never seen anyone absorb that much Energy at once. Even before, when I watched Loyle duel—none of those he beat had that much; they were always high-level iron rankers or steel seekers who obviously hadn't cultivated as long as him. I think he's been a steel seeker for centuries." She glanced back at the corpse. "Or, I mean, he *was.*" Victor was halfway across the circle, and when he didn't respond, Efanie quickly asked, "How, Victor? How'd you do it?"

"You didn't watch? His affinities were a bad match for me. He put too much weight on his status—on his aura. Weight. Aura. Ha." Victor chuckled at his unintended pun.

"Why the heart?"

Again, Victor ignored her. He was before Volpuré. "Let them out," he said, his voice rumbling, almost gutturally from his gut.

"Now wait just a moment—" Bohn's rotund chamberlain began to say, but Victor's fist was around his ruffled collar in a flash. He lifted the fellow's enormous body onto his tiptoes, pulling his swollen, inflamed cheeks close to his face.

"Don't *interrupt,*" he growled, then released the man. Chamberlain Potts stumbled backward, and the crowd gasped as he almost fell. Two of the younger men standing nearby caught him, though, propping him up.

"There's no call for further violence, Victor," Bohn said, his voice smooth and calm. When Victor turned his glare on him, he cleared his throat. "Now, I understand your demands, and I'm sure we can speak about trying to come to terms, but there's the matter of the *nature* of your victory—"

"The hell are you talking about? I challenged you, you picked a champion, we fought, and I won. End of story." Victor glared around the crowd and was heartened to see quite a few of the gathered onlookers nodding along with his words.

"Well, there's some murmuring going around, Victor, that you may have had some help. Some ill-placed but well-meaning aid from a benefactor." When Bohn spoke, he affected an arch tone, and, despite Victor's height, he managed to make it seem he was looking down his nose at him as he perched there atop his throne-like chair. "Of course, I'm willing to turn a blind eye—I wouldn't want to run afoul of a *veil walker* . . ." He let his words fade as he nodded to himself, looking around the crowd knowingly, as though everyone was in on the "secret."

Victor had lost matches before. He'd dealt with cocky winners, but he'd dealt with a lot more sore losers. He'd heard the old "cheating" line of bull enough times that he didn't feel surprised when Bohn's words, fancy though they were, accused him of it. It didn't make him any less angry, however. Without thinking about it, he let his rage flood his pathways and completely relaxed his will. It felt as if he'd shrugged off an oil tanker's anchor chain as his aura rippled out around him.

Victor's aura was a hot, abysmally heavy thing—a blanket of molten burning lead. Riding that heavy, painful burden were waves of glorious, bloody battle triumphs, a thousand flavors of rage, and the deep, undeniable fear and terror of countless personal nightmares. Perhaps if the gathered people knew Victor and recognized the touch of his aura or saw him as a friend, they'd also find inspiration in those waves—some hint at the unknown or the key to a puzzle that had eluded them—but not many in the crowd around Volpuré's throne were lucky enough to feel that thin band of brightness amid the savage, brutal, painful waves that pulsed outward from his giant heaving body.

Nearly everyone stumbled back; some recovered quickly and stared with steel in their eyes at Victor's savage countenance, but most recoiled and continued to back off until they found it easier to breathe. Bohn had fallen from his throne and attempted to stand but fell again. Victor watched him crawl. He stepped forward, and a few of Bohn's sturdier relatives closed in, hands summoning weapons. Victor held up one hand, looking around as he slowly shook his head, discouraging interference. "I'll give you one chance to apologize for calling my honor into question, Bohn. One chance, otherwise, I'll accept your words for what they are—a fresh challenge."

"N-no!" Bohn rolled to his side, his hands pumping futilely as he attempted to push something invisible and intangible away from him. "I was—" he gasped, his eyes widening in horror as some imagined nightmare flitted through his field of view. "I was wrong to listen to any such rumors. Of course—" He screamed and wrapped his arms over his face, then tried again, "Of course, I don't believe them. Your honor is intact, *good* sir!"

Victor nodded, pushed the rage back into his Core, and gathered up his aura. Bohn and several other nearby people gasped in relief. He scrambled to his knees, and then some of his liveried servants ran forward to take his arms, pulling him to his feet. Once he'd recovered, Volpuré glared around, and the servants backed away. Victor knew it must have been a very long time since he'd been embarrassed like that. Centuries, perhaps. He wasn't a weak man—at Tier Five, he was stronger than most people on Fanwath. Still, he'd grown used to having a steel seeker champion; he wasn't a big fish on Sojourn.

"I'll, um, I'll head back to the keep and close the dungeon instance; it will bring your friends and my daughter out. They'll be sorry for the loss of a valuable learning—"

"Cut the bullshit, Bohn." More gasps and murmurs followed Victor's dismissive interruption, but he didn't care. He was done playing nice; hadn't Bohn and all his bootlickers thought they would watch Victor die that night? "Just go do what you promised. I'll have what's owed."

Bohn frowned, but he turned and snapped his fingers. A moment later, a pair of liveried servants ran forward, dragging a floating pavilion by gilded black cords. Bohn climbed aboard the magical conveyance, looked down at Victor and the crowd of relatives and neighbors, and said, "I'm a man of my word. Seek your comrades outside my manor's gates before the next hour chimes from the bell." With that, he banked the weird flying platform and streaked toward the tall obelisk-like keep in the distance.

Victor watched him go and, glancing away from the diminishing figure, admired the view. Beyond Bohn's manor, he could see a dozen others spread out around the nearby hills, their windows lit up against the nighttime gloom. They glowed with amber and rainbow hues as the interior illumination shone through stained glass here and there. Victor was forced to pause and step outside his righteous, rage-filled moment, admiring the beauty.

"Ahem," a man said, clearing his throat from off to Victor's left. "I say, well fought, Victor! Three cheers!" To Victor's amusement, the people around him complied.

"*Victor! Victor! Victor!*"

"Heh. Thanks!" He turned in a slow circle, meeting the gazes of people who looked genuinely starstruck. A few glowered, sure, but almost everyone was smiling, and quite a few were trying to jostle their way closer to him.

"How?" one man cried out. "Tell us how, Victor! How does an iron ranker have such an aura? How did you stand against Loyle's spells?"

Victor ignored the question, but a woman quite close, right behind Efanie, cried out, "Why the heart, Victor?"

Victor grinned, exposing his bright Quinametzin teeth. "I eat the hearts of worthy foes!" His declaration was met with gasps, retches, laughter, and even cheers. Victor joined those laughing, holding his bloody fist high. "Where's the lion?"

"It got up!" someone shouted.

Another person confirmed: "Aye! When Loyle died! It got up and ran off into the tall grass!"

"Huh." Victor rubbed his chin. "Good for that tough bastard, I guess." For some reason, his words made people cheer again, and Victor continued to chuckle, turning to the trailhead leading down the hill. "Time to go get my friends and get home." He looked around at the expectant faces and tried to tune out the buzz of conversation, questions, and adulation. He pushed his way through the crowd to the path, saying things like, "Sorry" or "I'm tired, folks" by way of excuse as he fled the festive scene. Efanie hurried behind him.

As he walked, Victor realized he was still clutching Loyle's heart and sent it into his storage ring. He contemplated the rings in his palm, then sending a trickle of Energy into his armor so it converted to his comfortable clothing, he tucked them into a pocket.

Efanie, still hurrying behind him, asked, "Would you like me to summon a coach?"

"I could ride my—" Victor cut himself off as he realized a man in a fine gray suit, wearing a pointy wide-brimmed hat and accompanied by a girl who couldn't be more than thirteen, followed close behind Efanie. They were a third of the way down the hill, and in his haste, Victor had left the rest of the crowd behind. Only Efanie and the breathless duo were with him on that particular stretch of trail. He stepped to the side, hoping they'd hurry past, but they stopped. Victor groaned inwardly as the man cleared his throat, and the girl looked at him with fierce, angry eyes and tear-streaked cheeks.

"Ahem. Sir Victor, I am Torka Vinchan, personal historian of the late Fak Loyle. This, here, is his daughter Cora Loyle—his only surviving family member. As she is of tender years and you vanquished her guardian and claimed his riches, I hereby, in full view of a member of Sojourn society in good standing"—he nodded to Efanie—"entrust her to your care. I bid you farewell, sir." He paused briefly to look at the young girl, gave her a pained smile and a nod, then turned away and started down the slope. Victor reached out to grab his shoulder.

"Hold on a minute! What the hell are you talking about?"

"The child, sir—she's without a guardian, and you've claimed her family wealth. It's only honorable that you take responsibility for her."

Victor kept a firm grip on the man's shoulder but turned to Efanie. "What the hell?"

"Um, yes, well, I believe he makes a valid point. If he's not contracted to care for the girl—"

"I am *not*," Torka said, his grim smile almost smug.

Victor's scowl deepened. "Shouldn't Loyle's employer take responsibility?"

"Volpuré?" Efanie's frown deepened, and she leaned close, her voice a near whisper. "I don't believe he'd be a kind guardian, Victor."

Victor looked from the historian to the distant manor and then down at the girl. Her eyes were dark in the dim light, and she glared at him briefly, with bloodshot, angry eyes, before looking down as she furrowed her thick eyebrows—Victor could see she'd inherited her father's unruly, wild-looking hair. Inwardly, he groaned, but he kept it contained. This girl had just lost what was apparently her only family—her father—and he'd been the one to kill him. Unable to stop himself, he voiced what was on his mind: "You can't possibly want to come with me."

The girl refused to look him in the face, but Victor saw tears leak from her eyes as she mumbled, "I'm happy to look after myself, sir." Victor reached out to grasp her chin, forcing her eyes to lock onto his. He saw anger behind her sadness, something kindred that spoke to the depths of his rage-soaked heart.

"All right." He let go of her, and she immediately averted her gaze. "I won't let you fall on Volpuré's mercy. I'll find someone to look after you."

"Sir, I must insist you unhand me. I've done my duty." Victor glanced at the historian and released his shoulder with poorly masked contempt. Torka Vinchan didn't immediately scamper off, however. He paused and held a finger to his chin. "I wouldn't mind a quote or three for the final chapter."

"Final chapter?"

"Yes sir—of Fak Loyle's biography."

Victor glared at him. A small part of him wanted to be polite and think up a quote—something interesting or even flattering about the dead duelist, mainly because his daughter was present. It was a very tiny voice, though—easily ignored. Instead, he growled, "Get out of here." Some hint of his potential for violence must have registered with the historian, because he turned and practically ran down the trail. "All right. Enough of this shit. I need to get things moving." Victor summoned Guapo using glory-attuned Energy, and the golden mustang burst from a cloud of sparkling, brilliant light, whinnying and pawing at the air with his front hooves.

Victor hoisted himself onto the great stallion's back, then held a hand down to the young girl. She wore a ruffled gray blouse over layered skirts, and she looked at Guapo with horror in her eyes. "Listen, I doubt you want anything to do with me. I'm sorry about that. Come along, though, and, like I said, I'll make sure we find a proper home or caretaker for you."

Efanie nodded. "Wisely said, Victor." She nudged Cora's narrow shoulders, pushing her closer to Victor's hand. "Go on, child. He's honorable." Cora looked up at Victor, and he could see her gather her courage before she tentatively stretched her tiny hand toward his. Victor leaned down further, snatched her wrist, and hoisted her up. She felt weightless, and he was struck by her fragility, her precarious position in a violent universe. Deyni came to mind, and he was suddenly glad she was back on Fanwath among people who cared about her. Pushing away the sudden wave of melancholy homesickness, he set the girl sideways onto Guapo's back in front of him.

"Nice meeting you, Efanie. If my friends are out of the dungeon before you get back to the manor, I'll probably be gone." Efanie looked from Victor to Cora. She didn't say anything at first, but Victor could see she had a lot on her mind. "Listen, I'm not a man like—well, like Volpuré. I'll make sure she's okay. Unless you—"

"No! No, Victor, I couldn't. My duties . . . my finances . . ." Her objections felt half-hearted to Victor, so he stretched his hand back down.

"Come on. I'll give you a ride, and you ought to think about working for someone new. If not me, I bet I can get Dar to take you on. Cora could use someone familiar around." To his amazement, Efanie nodded and snatched his hand, easily hoisting herself up behind him.

"It's good your mount is so powerful!"

"Fast, too! Hold on!" Victor put a steadying arm around the girl, and she cringed. Naturally, that made him feel like an asshole, but he couldn't help the circumstances. Was it his fault her father worked as a duelist for hire? Was Victor to blame for fighting for his life? Of course, he might see things differently from her shoes, but that was a problem for another day. At the moment, he wanted to be done with this whole ordeal, so he urged Guapo to pick up the pace, and soon Efanie was whooping and laughing as the wind whistled past and Guapo's powerful hooves ate up the distance between the hill and the manor.

When the stallion exploded out of the orchard, and the manor's wall and gates came into view, Victor said, "Whoa!" and Guapo rapidly slowed to a more sedate trot. He could see people under the glow lanterns above the gate, and as they approached, he recognized the beautiful, light-filled dragonfly wings belonging to Lam and Edeya. They turned toward him, and that's when he saw the figure on the ground between them—a human-shaped figure on a stretcher, wrapped in bloodstained rags.

47

STORIES TO TELL

As Guapo rapidly approached, Lam turned to face him, and Victor saw nothing but puzzlement on her face. When Edeya, who'd been crouching next to the prostrate figure on the ground, also looked toward the sound of clattering hooves on cobbles, she leaped into the air, her wings buzzing and throwing off motes of azure Energy. "Victor!"

Guapo came to a stop, and Victor gripped Cora around the waist and hopped down. As soon as his feet hit the ground, she began to writhe, so he let her go. She ran toward the edge of the road, and he wondered if she would keep going, but she stopped once she was a few yards away. She crossed her arms over her chest and pointedly looked away from the manor toward the very distant lights of the city, avoiding Victor's gaze.

Efanie slid off Guapo's back, and Victor sent his stallion back to the spirit plane to make space. "Who's on the stretcher?" he asked by way of greeting. He didn't wait for an answer, stomping forward, nudging past Lam to peer at the bandage-wrapped face. That's when he saw the pale wisps of steamy mist rising off the body. "Darren," he grunted.

"He was near death, but when we completed the tenth round, we were awarded racial advancement cakes. We fed him his in hopes of saving his life." She leaned over and pressed her fingers to Darren's pale forehead. "We think it's working—his wounds closed up during the first few hours."

Victor scowled, looking up from Darren's bandaged face and neck to Lam. "No potions?"

She shrugged. "The dungeon locked our dimensional containers."

Edeya walked over and grabbed onto Victor's arm, hugging it close. "It's a lucky thing Lord Volpuré rescued us when he did. We had less than an hour before the next round of comb—"

Victor's barking laugh interrupted her, but it was Efanie who spoke up. "He *rescued* you? Your friend here just fought a duel to force him to let you out."

"Truly?" Edeya's eyebrows shot up, and she squeezed Victor's arm even tighter. "Victor, we thought it was the *end*!"

"Yeah, well, unfortunately, the asshole had a champion, so he's still breathing, but if I get a good enough reason . . ." He trailed off with a glance toward Cora.

Lam scowled, eyeing the girl where she stood with her unruly hair blowing in the evening breeze, her back straight as a post as she continued to stare into the distance. "Who's this?"

"That's a . . . long story. I, uh—" A rattle sounded behind the closed manor gates, and then they began to swing open. When they'd parted enough for her to fit through, Trin—Volpuré's daughter, and the woman who'd talked his friends into entering the dungeon—slipped through. Like Lam and Edeya, she was filthy with the accumulated dirt and dried blood from many days of fighting and no baths in between. Her face looked as if she was hell-bent on committing murder. When she opened her mouth to speak, the gates crashed shut, startling her into silence.

With an angry glance over her shoulder at the imposing barrier, she tried again. "I've had it! I *denounce* my family!" Her filthy hands were balled into fists, and Victor had to admire the apparent conviction behind her angry words.

"Lady Trin—" Efanie stepped toward her, but Trin shoved her away.

"How *could* you? You *knew* what we were walking into!"

Victor raised his eyebrows; this was news to him. Efanie stammered, "I . . . Lady Trin, I didn't believe he'd leave you in there for so long. I had no knowledge of his schemes against Sir Victor. I *tried* to warn—"

"Warn me? *Warn* me? By saying it was dangerous and reminding me that my father could pull us out? How about a word of warning about storage containers? How about, 'Trin, dear girl whom I profess to love, did you know you cannot leave that dungeon without completing it?' Wouldn't *that* have been nice?"

Efanie looked stricken by Trin's rage. She drew her fancy basket-hilted rapier and held it on her palms, then knelt before her. "I failed you, Lady Trin. Please take my sword. My life is yours to claim."

"Oh, stand *up*!" Trin seethed. She brushed past Efanie and stood beside Lam. "Can I come with you for now, Lam? My father has frozen my trust, and I'll need to sell some belongings before I can afford—"

"You can come with us." Victor chuckled and nodded to Efanie. "But she's coming too."

Efanie, her cheeks crimson, stood and sheathed her sword. "Are you certain you still want me, Victor? I'm more than disgraced. I failed Lady Trin when it mattered most."

"You were under orders," Trin huffed, kicking some gravel off the cobbles. She folded her arms over her chest and scowled at the elfin woman. "And you trusted my father not to be a filicidal maniac! I'm still *terribly* angry at you, however!"

"Understood." Efanie slid her sword back into its scabbard. "Shall I arrange a carriage? I don't think we can all fit on Victor's mount—"

"I have one." Trin sighed. "I'll be sure to sell it before my father sends one of his stewards around to collect it." She unclipped a metal ball on a chain from her belt and, with a small surge of Energy, tossed it toward the cobbled road. It paused in the air before striking the stones and hovered for a moment as pink steam billowed out of it. It reminded Victor of those little smoke bombs he used to buy in Arizona for the Fourth of July—pretty much the only "fireworks" allowed in Tucson.

With a hiss and then the sudden rapid clank of metal slapping together, the ball expanded to form a floating, round, silvery vessel with a row of windows that looked like portholes. In fact, the thing reminded Victor of an antique submarine. Trin walked around it, and the others followed. Victor bent to pick up Darren, cradling him in his arms and leaving the stretcher where it lay. On the far side of the "carriage," he found a sizeable oval door standing open. "Here," he grunted, hoisting Darren into the opening so Lam could pull him inside.

Before climbing in, Victor cast Alter Self and reduced his size as much as possible, bringing him down to about six feet—much easier to climb through the opening. He turned to Cora, standing alone on the side of the road, and said, "Come on, *chica*. I know you probably hate me, but we gotta try to make the best of a shitty situation." She didn't respond, and her eyes looked as if they could melt wax if she stared long enough, but she brushed past him to climb aboard. Victor followed.

The inside of the little vehicle matched its external aesthetic; a round metallic bench lined the walls, but a single chair was built into a console before a front-facing porthole. Trin sat there, apparently intent on piloting the craft to Dar's lake house. Efanie narrowed her eyes at Victor as he turned to pull the door shut with a *clang*. "How are you so much smaller?"

Lam chuckled. "Don't bother trying to figure it out."

Victor shrugged as he sat down next to Edeya. "It's a titan thing." He found his titan bloodline an easy way to wave off questions he couldn't answer, and in a way, he wasn't lying. Hadn't Tes told him that an advanced elder bloodline was necessary to handle the spell? In an effort to change the subject, he nodded toward Darren. "Hope he doesn't fill the carriage with that steam—kinda weird to think we're breathing Darren into our lungs."

Trin made a comical gagging noise and touched something on her control panel. A moment later, the roof slid partially open, letting in the cool night air and the moonlight. "Better?"

"Much better!" Edeya sighed happily as she leaned back, resting her head on Victor's shoulder. "Sorry, Victor," she mumbled. "We didn't sleep much the last couple of nights."

"Nah, go ahead and rest. You earned it." Victor looked at Efanie and was glad to see that Cora had sat close to her. He wasn't sure what he'd do about the girl; the whole situation was awkward and honestly rather awful, but he couldn't just hand her a bag of Energy beads and send her on her way. He had to figure something out for her. He couldn't believe that a man like Loyle, someone who'd been around for centuries and likely amassed quite a fortune, didn't have a bunch of staff on retainer—a nanny or tutor or something for the girl. He wanted to question her, but he didn't want to force her to talk in front of a bunch of strangers with the guy who'd just killed her father. He had a vague hope that one of his friends or Valla could get some more information out of her.

"Is it true about Arcus?" Trin asked, looking over her shoulder at Victor.

"What did you hear?"

"That he died in the dungeon with you." She frowned and narrowed her eyes. "Did you kill him?"

Victor almost told her the truth right then and there, but his promise to Ronkerz and likewise to Arcus stalled the words in his mouth. Instead, he just said, "I can promise you that I didn't kill him. In fact, I consider him a friend. He acted honorably in there."

Trin turned back to the front-facing porthole, and everyone was quiet for a minute or two before Efanie asked, "And Arona? Is she truly dead?"

"Yeah." Victor sighed and folded his arms over his chest. "I saw it happen."

"Hard to imagine—everyone thought she was destined to be one of the youngest veil walkers ever. Such talent!"

Victor nodded. "She was something else." When everyone got quiet again, he reached into his storage ring and took out the Far Scribe book he shared with Valla. He turned to the last page and saw a new note:

Victor,

What am I to make of this macabre letter you just sent me? The courier refused to say anything about where you were or what you were doing as he delivered a fistful of letters. Lesh says his note isn't anything so gloomy and morbid—no dwelling on death and spirits and the next life! Have you done something foolhardy? If I don't hear from you soon, I'll go mad with worry!

Victor raised an eyebrow and shook his head, scratching his rough, stubble-covered jawline. "Shit," he mumbled. "*Pendejo!*" As he cursed himself, he summoned a pen and rapidly scrawled:

Valla,
All is well. On my way home. See you soon.
V

"Are you upset?" Lam asked quietly. When Victor heard her hushed tone, he looked around the carriage to see that Cora had also fallen asleep, her head resting on Efanie's shoulder.

"I, uh, might have done something stupid again. I mean, with Valla."

Lam chuckled. "You seem to do that a lot—find a way to anger the women in your life."

"Is that fair?" Victor sighed, leaning back. "I mean, most of the people in my life seem to be women. Far too man—" Victor's words were cut short by a grunt as Edeya surprised him with a jab in the ribs.

"You love it," she murmured before adjusting her position to lean more fully against his side.

Lam smiled and leaned back, and Victor could see she also intended to nap. The metal bench wasn't exactly built for comfort, though, and she grumbled something softly to herself, then summoned a pillow and blanket from a storage device and made herself a good deal more comfortable. Efanie watched her and took inspiration, conjuring a blanket and draping it over Cora. The girl partially awoke, but only long enough for Efanie to urge her to spread out on the bench and lay her head on her lap.

After a while, Efanie looked at Victor and whispered, "I've seen her around the manor, but she never spoke to anyone. Loyle kept her close; he was a very strange man."

"Yeah, well, I'm hoping—" Victor stopped short as a lightbulb went off in his head. He dug around in his pocket for the four rings he'd stripped from Loyle's dead fingers. The four rings were weighty, and Victor could see the gleam of rare materials in the moon's dim light. Most were inset with precious gemstones, but one was a simple thick silvery band. It felt weighty in Victor's palm, heavier than it should be even if it were made of gold, which it wasn't. "Let's see here," he said, and with just a tiny trickle of inspiration-attuned Energy, he attempted to bond with the ring.

As soon as he did, his mind became aware of an enormous dimensional space, larger than all his current containers combined. Moreover, the space was sturdy, and he could feel the dense weaves of Energy holding it together even more strongly than the dimensional ring Dar had given him, which held a comparatively tiny space. Victor let his mind drift over the ring's contents, and he found himself holding his breath as the treasures mounted in his awareness.

There were millions of Energy beads. He only knew that because they were kept in stacks of sturdy crates, each labeled with numerals that the System translated as 100,000. Victor counted more than fifty such crates. Beyond the beads, he found chests filled with precious gems, golden coins, and bars of rare metals. He found stacks of fine materials—from a dozen varieties of silk to refined leather to lengths of Energy-dense hardwood. Along with the riches were more mundane things—furniture, tapestries, rugs, and hundreds of finely tailored articles of clothing. Before he pulled his mind out of the space, feeling slightly overwhelmed, Victor saw two weapon racks, one lined with swords of all kinds and another with staves, rods, and wands.

He looked down at his hands. They were adorned with not one or two but five different dimensional rings. Grunting, he slid the new one over his left thumb, watching as it stretched to fit the massive digit. He figured it would be wise to sort through his other rings and pare down their number sometime soon. Looking up, he realized Efanie was staring, waiting for him to finish his sentence. He held up his fist of rings. "Hoping to find some kind of, I dunno, will or estate document."

"He may have accounts with one of the banking houses. I could go into town tomorrow to learn what I can. If—if it helps."

"Yeah. I'd appreciate that, thanks." Victor lifted another ring between his thumb and forefinger, examining the deep blue stone set in a golden band. He sent some Energy into it and was awarded with a System message:

*****Ring of Safe Harbor: The wearer of this ring is shielded from most scrying attempts and made impossible to summon against their will, regardless of any power disparity between wearer and summoner.*****

Victor grunted softly and immediately jammed the ring onto his right-hand pinky. He felt a cool breeze tickle the hairs on his forearms briefly, but other than that, he couldn't discern any difference. The next ring he inspected was also gold but was set with a black opal, or so he guessed. When he sent Energy into it, he received another System message:

*****Ring of Communion: The wearer of this ring can send mental images and messages to the wearer of its twin.*****

Victor looked up and peered over at Cora. The blanket covered her arms, but he leaned across the space and gently lifted the edge to reveal her hands where she held them tucked up near her chin. Sure enough, she had a similar but smaller ring on her right-hand ring finger. He put the larger one back into his pocket.

The final ring was made of a black, exceptionally light metal and was carved in whorls and loops with what looked like pearls set into them. He counted seven of the lustrous little orbs. As he sent some Energy into the ring, he hoped it would be mundane; the gaudy aspect wasn't his style. When he saw the System message, he almost groaned:

*****Ring of Recall: Two charges remaining. This ring will transport the wearer to their home System Stone. Beware, the effect requires several minutes to gather the requisite Energy.*****

Considering he was still a System "citizen" of the Free Marches, Victor reckoned that those two recalls could save him a fortune in visits back home. Of course, it was also nice to know he had a free teleport if he ever got stuck somewhere, and with Loyle's stash of Energy beads, he wasn't exactly hurting for money. He tucked the ring into his pocket, glad he didn't have to wear it all the time.

He zoned out for the rest of the coach ride, his mind drifting to topics that weighed heavily on him. He worried about Cora and his responsibility for the girl. It felt absurd to him that she'd been foisted onto him after he had *killed* her father. What kind of society condoned such a thing? Then there was Valla; he hoped she wasn't truly upset and that his note in the Far Scribe book would put her at ease. He wondered how Dar would treat him; the master Spirit Caster hadn't seemed bothered when he'd saved Victor from the madness of his Volcanic Fury. Thinking of that reminded Victor of his fight, and he grinned stupidly, reliving the battle in the theater of his mind.

When Trin brought the carriage down to land outside Dar's house, Victor was the first to disembark, and he let Efanie and Lam push Darren out to him. Cradling the injured, unconscious man, he said, "Lam, will you show Efanie and Cora around? Ask Mr. Ruln to find beds for them, please."

"Yes, I can do that. Then I'm going to bathe for a month."

"I'll be doing the same," Edeya sighed, hopping out of the coach with a flutter of her sapphire wings. Victor grunted and turned to the house, only to find Lesh and Valla coming outside. Almost happy to have Darren as a shield against the world, he started forward, trying to keep his face pleasant and relaxed.

"Victor!" Valla called before he'd managed a few steps. She ran toward him, her wings fluttering with the breeze of her rushing progress, and, for a moment, Victor thought she'd slam into him, regardless of his burden. She slowed, though, and when she came close enough, she grasped his shoulders and leaned down to kiss him softly. "I was worried!" Victor looked up at her, confused, then laughed; he'd forgotten to relax his Alter Self spell. She was nearly a foot taller than he.

"Sorry to worry you," he sighed as the mirth died down. "I wanted to write you a note and figured I'd make use of the scribe the asshole I challenged sent to me—"

"Asshole? Challenge?"

Victor hefted Darren. "I had to get them out of a dungeon against the, uh, owner's wishes." He gestured with Darren's body toward the house. "Come on,

Valla. Let me put him down in his bed, and then we can talk. I'll tell you all about it. How long was I gone, by the way?" He threw the last question out in an attempt to shift the focus of their conversation away from the duel.

It worked, but he knew the reprieve would be short-lived. "More than two weeks. I know it wasn't as long for you, but I was beginning to grow desperate. Only Ranish Dar's confidence and assurances kept me from pulling my hair out!"

"He was confident, huh?" Victor smiled as Valla followed him toward the house.

"Very. He seems to be quite well-informed. He assured me you were still alive, even yesterday." They came to the front door as she spoke, and Victor nodded to Lesh.

"Hey, man. Ready to get some serious training in?"

"Aye, Lord Victor. Welcome home. I was betting on your success." The way he grinned and the glint in his eye told Victor he was being literal; he'd found a way to bet on him completing the Sojourn Council's quest. Laughing softly to himself, he carried Darren into the house.

He caught sight of one of the servants. "Hey, Wensa, can you get some clean bandages for Darren? I'm betting he'll be out of it for a day or two."

"Right away!" As she scurried off, Victor looked at Valla. "Come on. Let's get him to his room. Shit, Valla, I've got some *crazy* stories to tell."

Valla nodded, and Victor was relieved to see a genuine, relaxed smile on her face. He supposed he owed Dar for that—his mentor had kept his friends from panicking about his prolonged absence, which made him wonder how much Dar already knew; could he somehow scry Victor in the dungeon? Did he already know about Ronkerz? He supposed he'd find out soon enough, but he hoped not *too* soon; he wanted to spend some time with Valla. He was eager to tell her about his time in the dungeon and about the duel, but he wasn't so anxious to explain the fallout. How would she react when he told her about Cora?

48

ADVICE

And this fellow, this 'Ronkerz,' made you fight his champions?"

Victor shrugged. "Well, only one." He hadn't said anything about Ronkerz being a veil walker or his champions being steel seekers, but it wasn't because he was trying to be dishonest with Valla; he simply felt he had to honor his vow to Ronkerz not to talk about his strength with anyone other than Ranish Dar.

Valla nodded slowly. "So they underestimated you. I suppose when your companions lost their fights, it only encouraged the prisoner king's confidence." She smiled and squeezed Victor's wrist. They were sitting together in one of Dar's smaller parlors, waiting for the lord of the house to summon Victor. As soon as he'd put Darren to bed, Dar's steward, Mr. Ruln, had told him to wait there. "A mistake too many make, hmm, love?"

Victor chuckled, perhaps a little nervously. He felt he was walking a fine line between truth and lie. "I don't know about that. The Big One he chose for me put up quite a fight. I had to get creative to find a way to harm her."

"What an odd name—'Big Ones.' It's very strange to imagine a town inside a dungeon. What were the people who lived there like?"

"Um, for the most part, desperate and dirty. I think that's part of Ronkerz's thing—the whole 'Big Ones' act and naming the place 'Rumble Town.' I think the fighting and the showmanship all have to do with his attempt to keep people motivated for his cause."

"And what is that? His cause, I mean."

"Well," Victor sighed, hating that he was hiding things from Valla, but if he were to take Dar's warnings about karmic bonds seriously, shouldn't his promise to Ronkerz have "rippled" through the universe? As Valla stared at him and a scowl began to mar her smooth complexion, he shook his head. "Listen, I don't want to make shit up, but I promised Ronkerz I wouldn't talk about his goals with anyone but Dar. He could have kept me in there, Valla. I made the promise so I wouldn't be stuck."

"So you can tell Ranish Dar but not the woman you love? The woman who spends all her time with you?" The frown line between her eyes deepened, and she leaned back in her chair. "With whom do you fear I'll share this secret?"

"No one! It's not that I think I can't trust you; it's just that, shit, Valla, *I'll* know I broke the promise. It'll bother *me*. Dar's been talking to me about karmic ties and debts and—"

"Oh, put it aside, Victor." She folded her arms over her chest and looked through the window toward the night sky and the distant but very bright moon. After a moment of awkward silence, she asked, "Are you allowed to tell me what happened when you left? Can you tell me the story behind your duel and the situation with Lam and the others? Must I be the only one who has no knowledge of your dealings?"

"Don't be like that. It's a pretty straightforward story. Arcus told me that his father was holding Lam and the others inside his dungeon, so I went there to—"

"So he made peace with you before he died?"

"Um, yeah." Victor looked down and knew he'd made a mistake when Valla snorted and stood up.

"I don't know why you're being so duplicitous, but I can't imagine this conversation will get any better. If I'm not wrong, the next thing you're about to tell me is that you challenged Lord Volpuré to a duel, then fought his steel seeker champion without first letting me know. Would it have been so hard to come here before flying off in a rage to the Volpuré estate? Would it have been hard for you to write me a plainly worded note in the Far Scribe book? I suppose I should be thankful that you remembered me at all, what with that strange note that demonstrated your willingness to die in that duel—*without seeing me*!"

"Valla, they were in trouble in that dungeon! I had to hurry—"

"They'd been in there for more than a week. I think another hour or two—"

"Maybe not! Their next battle was imminent!"

"Did you *know* that?" She didn't wait for an answer. She fled the room in a flutter of tinkling feathers, leaving Victor sitting, stunned, alone in the parlor. He didn't know what to think of her sudden anger, but he knew he felt like the bad guy again, and he was getting damn tired of feeling like the bad guy. When one of the servants, a man whose name he hadn't yet learned, cleared his throat from the doorway, Victor looked up, his growing anger and frustration instantly replaced by embarrassment.

"Terribly sorry, sir, but Lord Dar awaits you in the library."

"Oh, um, thanks." Victor stood and smoothed his shirt, then moved toward the doorway. As the servant stepped aside, he nodded and reached up to pat Victor's shoulder. He didn't say anything, but the act was definitely out of character for Dar's staff. Victor wondered if his face looked so troubled that a veritable stranger thought he needed comfort. He made a conscious effort to unfurl his brow and offered the man a nod and an anemic smile.

As he walked through the hallways of Dar's home, he fought to bring his mind back into focus, but a particular train of thought kept pushing its way to the forefront, and he couldn't help feeling some despair at it. Looking objectively at his feelings, Victor realized he felt bad about hurting Valla's feelings but was also annoyed and exhausted by the drama.

What was worse, he found his feelings of guilt weren't any different from how he might feel if Lam or Lesh—the idea made him snort a short laugh—were hurt by his actions. Shouldn't he feel despair in his heart at the thought of Valla being pissed at him? She'd made a rather good point: Shouldn't he have been desperate to see and hold her when he survived the dungeon? Shouldn't he have at least *considered* going to her before rushing off to the duel?

Altogether, the strange, conflicted feelings roiling through his mind as he walked to the library culminated in a series of questions he couldn't answer—did he *love* Valla, or did he only care about her? Was his attraction to her more physical than emotional? Was there any difference? Victor knew why he couldn't answer: He lacked experience, and the more he thought about it, *that* was a problem, too. Groaning, shaking his head in frustration, he fought to push the unquiet thoughts from his mind as he approached the library doors.

He stepped into the dimly illuminated room and was greeted by the scent of woodsy incense and the unmistakable aroma of fresh coffee. Dar sat in one of the comfortable high-backed chairs, wearing one of his usual brightly colored pajama-like ensembles, this one an eye-popping electric blue. When he saw Victor, he smiled and leaned forward, pouring some steaming black liquid into the mugs on the small table before him. He nodded at one of the empty seats and rumbled, "Have a seat, Victor. We're past midnight, and I doubt you'll sleep tonight, so have some coffee with me."

Victor did as he asked, sitting down with a sigh. "Is it that late already?"

"It is." Dar pushed the coffee to him, then without preamble jumped into the thick of things. "As you no doubt recall, I witnessed your duel with Fak Loyle. I took my leave after cooling your fury, so give me the details of what I missed before and after the fight. You may as well begin by describing what happened inside the dungeon. I can feel the weight of a bargain on your spirit. Is that why you fled the Council Spire so rapidly? Were you avoiding Roil and his lackeys?"

"You don't miss much, do you?" Victor picked up the little carafe of cream and poured a healthy splash into his cup. Dar only grunted, so Victor began to speak, pausing occasionally to sip the hot, soothing drink. "Well, first of all, that woman's bomb nearly killed me. Maybe pass along my thanks, though, because it blasted me right through one of the rune-covered pillars those ambushers were using to seal off the entrance area. Once I was out, I kicked their asses easily enough . . ."

Victor spoke for nearly an hour, going over the nature of his encounters in the prison dungeon and then talking about Ronkerz and how he'd made the three of them fight his "Big Ones." As he finished the tale, describing how Arcus revealed his father's plans for extortive vengeance, Dar chuckled and shook his head. "No wonder you raced out of the city. I'm quite pleased you didn't lose your temper before you managed to extricate yourself from the Council Spire."

Victor nodded, smiling ruefully. "It was a close thing for a minute there. Before I go into the situation with Volpuré, can you tell me what you think of Ronkerz? Don't you think it's messed up that kids are being born in that dungeon?"

"Messed up?" Dar sighed and rubbed his temples between his two stony thumbs. "We'll need to work on your vernacular before I send you to be a court champion on Ruhn. I suppose your description is apt, however. I never considered the idea that people would form rudimentary societies within a dungeon or that the System would continue to grow the place to accommodate them. I'm not too surprised to hear about Ronkerz, nor am I surprised to learn that Roil has been hiding the true nature of the situation from the rest of us—Consul Rexa would likely force him to close the place down, regardless of the lost investment with the System."

"Really? She could do that?"

"Rexa? She's more powerful than any three of us combined. Should your path cross with hers, always be deferential."

"Are you going to tell her—"

"I'll need to weigh the consequences. It seems to me that Ronkerz has made a sort of overture in that he's asked you to tell me and me alone about the situation in that dungeon." He paused to sip his coffee, then shook his head. "Let me handle the politics, Victor. You'll soon have your own schemes to manage. For now, be content knowing that I won't allow children to languish long in that dungeon. As for your debt to the council, it's clearly been paid, and now they'll need to supply a promised bonus. I take it you still wish for me to request a cultivation item for your friend's Breath Core?"

Victor nodded. "Yeah, I owe him."

"Very well. I'll meet with the council in the morning and extract what's due. Now, the duel. Were you not concerned that Bohn's champion was a steel seeker?"

"I mean, I guess so, but Arcus told me everything about the guy." Victor thought about his battle and shook his head. "Almost everything. It seemed he had one trick up his sleeve that he hadn't ever used before."

"His invasion of your blood?"

"Yeah. I forgot you watched the fight."

"Blood Mages are dangerous, and Loyle fought so much with his nature affinity that people often overlooked the true danger of his secondary aspect. I'm pleased you thought of burning the blood from your system with your magma-attuned Energy. I suspect your elder bloodline helped buy you time to think of it. Didn't you tell me that you have a feat that makes you naturally resistant to poisons?"

Like a lightbulb, the thought illuminated Victor's mind, and he nodded. "Yeah! I didn't think of that. I suppose someone else's blood in my veins could be considered a kind of poison."

"So, in the end, your victory was partly due to Loyle's affinities meeting very hard counters with your own. No doubt a man of Loyle's power was able to read a good deal from your Core despite your aura veiling. It was his folly to underestimate the strength of your Breath Core. I suppose he couldn't know that your Volcanic Fury increases the potency of the magma—on the surface, your Breath Core is less than impressive." Dar chuckled. "Not for long, if I were to wager."

"Heh, yeah. After the fight, I was thinking about how badly I need to cultivate my Breath Core. I'll work on it before I leave." The idea of leaving brought some questions to Victor's mind, but before he could ask them, Dar cleared his throat and brought up a new topic of his own.

"I noted that I have new house guests."

Victor blew out an explosive breath, then leaned back in his chair. He'd almost let Cora slip his mind, and the reminder, combined with his stress about Valla, was enough to make him reach up and vigorously scratch the short hair above his ear. "I could use your advice about that."

Dar chuckled. "So, the duelist's child was foisted upon you? I'm surprised Volpuré didn't insist on caring for the girl if only to save some face." He sipped at his second cup of coffee, then shrugged. "It was wise of you to steal away the other woman—the Fae-blood. A familiar face will do wonders to ease the girl's transition. I assume Loyle had some riches in his dimensional containers?"

"Oh yeah. Millions of beads and plenty of precious metals and gems."

"Good. You were eager to visit your home, yes? I suggest you do so. Take a week—bring the child and your new employee to your estate there; ensure her education is well-funded and she has a place to call home. I will prepare your course of study while you're gone and when you return, you will devote yourself to preparing for the trials and tribulations that await you on Ruhn. I've contacted my granddaughter—she expects you in one hundred and nineteen System-standard days."

"Seriously? Um, yeah, actually, that sounds great. I could introduce her to Thayla and her little girl. I could—"

"Yes, yes." Dar held up a hand, forestalling more of Victor's mentions of people and places he didn't know. "I suggest this not because I'm trying to be kind—I am, but that's not why. I want your head clear, and having that girl here will only distract you. Now, while I'm on the subject of distractions, do you have something else weighing on you?"

Victor frowned, feeling some heat entering his pathways. Was Dar admitting to eavesdropping on his conversation with Valla? Inhaling deeply, he pushed out the rage that had begun to trickle into his pathways and instead consciously pulled inspiration-attuned Energy out. With a clear mind, he said, "I suppose our conversation wasn't exactly quiet or private, huh? The door was open."

"Even if I hadn't heard a word, I'd know you were troubled. Victor, I know I'm not your peer, and I often express how valuable my time is, but I want you to know that you're beginning to be . . . important to me. Don't let that go to your head, but understand that I am here if you need advice. My long life has been lived in . . . phases, for lack of a better word—sometimes alone, sometimes with companionship. Though I may not seem it, I've had many romantic liaisons and many long and devoted relationships. I've also been party to many failed loves. I've witnessed and analyzed those losses, and I might have a word of wisdom for you if you but ask."

Victor nodded, slowly coming to grips with the idea that Dar had just indicated that their relationship was no longer simply contractual. He didn't want to help Victor just because he wanted to use him—he cared. Of course, Victor knew he might be manipulating him, but his words felt genuine, and he *wanted* to think Dar was sincere. As he spoke, Victor slowly began to nod, and tried to gather his thoughts, tried to think of a way to express his feelings. Finally, he leaned forward and tried to voice his fears.

"I guess it boils down to passion. When I thought about Valla before my duel, I thought about what I 'should' do, not what I wanted to do. I *wanted* to fight, but I wrote Valla a note because it felt like the right thing to do. If I really loved her, I mean *loved* her, would I have wanted to go to her more than I wanted to fight? Wouldn't I have wanted to feel her lips on mine?" Victor remembered who he was speaking to, and his face flushed with embarrassment. Still, he pushed ahead. "I mean, when I think about passion—" He shook his head, trying to find the words, afraid to say the ones on the tip of his tongue.

"Go on, Victor. What are you passionate about?"

"I don't fucking know, Dar." Victor sighed. "I love Deyni, and Thayla, and Chandri, and Edeya, and yeah, Valla fits in there, but shouldn't I feel something a lot *more* for her?"

"Putting people aside, Victor, what ignites your passion?"

"You know," Victor sighed, shrugging helplessly. "Fighting, winning—the rush of battle. I don't even know what your granddaughter is like—what her country stands for, but I'm excited to fight for her. Is there something wrong with me?"

"Not *wrong*. You are what you are. You don't pick fights, but you certainly love to win them. I can admire that trait, Victor. Perhaps love isn't something you should concern yourself with in this stage of your life—"

"But I *do* love, Dar! I feel it so deeply, so hard, sometimes that I can't think of anything else. If I love to fight, half the time it's because I think I'm protecting some*one* I love! But . . . yeah, I'm not sure how to reconcile the idea that I feel just as strongly about protecting and caring for other people in my life as I do for Valla." Victor sighed, feeling empty and defeated and utterly unresolved.

Dar chuckled. "Love is a funny thing. It can be hot and fiery or warm and comforting. It can bring tears of joy or sorrow; it can make a man or break him. I'll tell you this: Time apart from one's love can clarify things. If your heart begins to ache and you desperately want to be with your love more and more, then you might realize your love is more important than your desire to fight and your hunt for glory. If, however, you don't find yourself lying awake at night, thinking of your distant love, perhaps it might be time to be more honest with yourself and your lady."

"So, wait and see? Shit, thanks for the help, Dar." Victor laughed, and Dar chuckled.

"Yes, I began to curse myself the moment I offered advice. It's not an easy thing to figure out—the heart. Talk to Valla. Be honest. That's the best counsel I can offer. Perhaps she'll have more insight." Dar shifted in his chair, and Victor saw he was ready to be done with the subject.

"Right. I'll do that. Thank you, Dar."

"Take your week. Leave as soon as you can and bring her with you. It will be good." Dar looked ready to dismiss him, but he held up a hand and added, "On the topic of my granddaughter, you should rest assured that she is no despot. She rules with kindness, and her citizens are guaranteed certain rights and freedoms. I believe you should be proud to defend her—many nations on Ruhn are not so egalitarian."

Victor nodded. "Well, that's good to know. Yeah, I think, despite my earlier words, I would have had trouble standing up for her if she turned out to be a tyrant." He stood and smiled, and surprisingly, the expression came a lot more easily than he'd expected. Despite the lack of a resolution to his problems, he felt better having confided in someone. It was good to know he wasn't the only person in the universe feeling the way he did. "Thank you, Dar."

His mentor stood and clapped one of his stony hands against Victor's shoulder. "My pleasure. Make haste now. The sooner you're gone and back, the sooner your training can begin." His eyes opened wide, and he snapped his fingers with a *crack*. He leaned close and, in a much quieter voice, said, "I *do* have some advice for you! Dig through Loyle's belongings for something very beautiful, rare, and *expensive*, and give it to Valla. I think it might make her more receptive to your further confession."

"Confession?"

"Well, you've yet to tell her about your young ward, correct?"

"Oh, *shit*," Victor groaned.

49

HEARTS AND BONES

Victor wasn't sure where to go when he walked out of the library. He wanted to find Valla and talk to her, but at the same time, he wanted some space to think—to breathe. With that impulse taking control, he meandered back to the main parlor, dark and quiet at that hour, and then slipped out the door to the rear deck. That close to the lake, the night air was always a little chilly. Victor hadn't been there long enough to know if that changed with the seasons or if there even *were* seasons on Sojourn, but he supposed it didn't matter; he was never cold, and conversely, no amount of heat in the air seemed to make his hot blood uncomfortable.

He stepped toward the railing, found he had too much anxious energy to stand and think, and turned to walk along the house to the side deck. He caught a glimpse of Dar through a window, still sitting in the library, writing into a book on his lap. It felt strange to peer into the room after wandering through the house, as if he was purposefully being sneaky or something, so he hurriedly looked away and hustled down the steps to the pathway that wound through Dar's manicured gardens. Night birds chirped and sang, and the breeze through the trees rustled the leaves in a melancholy whisper, making it easy for Victor's mind to wander and drift.

After a while, he'd passed by the sparring ring and entered a part of the garden he hadn't explored. Night blossoms bloomed, and the cloying scent of orange and cherry filled the air. It was peaceful and relaxing, and Victor found his earlier irritation melting away. What did he have to be upset about? A woman who loved him was angry—it wasn't the end of the world. He'd accomplished something tremendous earlier that day. He, a middling iron ranker, had conquered a steel seeker! Victor grinned and, spying a small bench on the hillside, sat down to look out over the terraced gardens to the starlit lake below.

It was a beautiful view, and to his heart's relief, he found himself wishing Valla were there beside him. A tree to his left rustled, and Victor looked up to see a black feathered bird with a long fanning tail perched on one of the lower branches. A shock of bright yellow plumage atop its head drew Victor's eye, and when it felt Victor's gaze, it spread broad wings and fluttered away into the night. As it went, it uttered a trilling cry that sounded like a stuttered question, "*Wha-why, wha-why?*" Victor chuckled at the funny sound, then, as he turned back to the big tree with its drooping branches and pale birch-like bark, he remembered Arona's bone.

He reached into the storage ring Dar had given him and pulled out the thing. It was heavy and felt colder than before. Seeing it reminded Victor of when Arona had passed it to him in a cave even darker than the night where he now sat. Glancing at the moon, Victor chuckled. To his eyes, it wasn't all that dark; things were still shaded in terms of moonlight and shadow, but he could see the leaves in the trees, the tiny night creatures rustling through the undergrowth, and even the gentle waves lapping on the distant lake shore.

He rubbed his thumb along the silvery runes in the bone, noting how they shimmered, and he wondered if they'd been like that before. Had they been so bright with Energy? Arona had said her undead creature needed rest, that he wasn't "ready" for another fight. Had he recovered? "Guess we'll never know, eh, *hermano*?" Victor chuckled as he carried the bone over to the tree. "You're going to sleep until another Necromancer finds you, I guess." He thought about that word. "Is a Death Caster the same as a Necromancer?" He shook his head, smirking at his mumbled rambling, and knelt on soft turf, summoning a knife from one of his other rings.

He'd just stabbed the blade into the grass when a cold shiver ran down his spine, and a raspy voice whispered, "It would be accurate to say a Necromancer is a type of Death Caster." He recognized the voice, so he didn't respond violently, but Victor whirled around, all the same, scrabbling backward so his back rested against the tree trunk. A ghostly luminescent version of Arona hovered in the darkness near where he'd been kneeling. "You returned more quickly than I feared. I'm pleased you survived your battle, Victor." Her lips didn't move, but she seemed to sway with the words as they hissed through the night air to him.

"The hell? Are you a ghost now?"

"I suppose so. More precisely, I'm a disembodied spirit bound to that bone—my first phylactery. I prepared it as we lay in that cave 'sleeping.' Thank you for bringing it here and for not mentioning it to anyone. You didn't, did you?"

Victor shook his head. "Nah, I only just remembered it. I wouldn't have, though. I promised you."

The spirit wavered, shifting oddly in the moonlight. "You don't seem very surprised to see me."

"You're not the first Death Caster I've messed around with, and this isn't the first phylactery I've held. I should've probably guessed what you were up to. I take it you didn't explain your plan because you didn't want Ronkerz to overhear?"

"That's right. I was afraid he'd force you to give him the phylactery so that, even in death, he could bind me to his service."

Victor nodded as he grunted, climbing to his feet. He held the bone out toward the glowing, faintly translucent figure. "Well, for what it's worth, I'm glad you aren't, like, *totally* dead. Uh, what do you want me to do with this thing?"

"Thank you, Victor!" The spirit drifted back from the bone, and Victor felt a sinking sensation as he anticipated her next words. "I have another favor to ask—well, perhaps several favors." When Victor sighed and lowered the bone, a faint smile flickered over her ghostly features, and then her disembodied voice came to him again. "I asked you to bury that bone here, in Dar's gardens, because I knew that once you removed it from your storage device, my spirit would be drawn to it."

"Yeah?" Victor was waiting for the other shoe to drop.

"Yes. However, I'm still quite helpless and at the mercy of your willingness to aid me." When Victor only frowned, she continued, "I told you in the dungeon that I wasn't undead yet. That wasn't a lie. My master, whom I shall not name in the air of the world where he walks, had tried for years to get me to complete the process, to create a phylactery and perfect my undead vessel, becoming a lich like so many powerful Death Casters do. I . . . resisted because I hate him, Victor. I hate him and every other Death Caster I've ever studied under."

Victor moved over to the bench and sat down. When Arona's spirit drifted closer, he motioned for her to continue. "But?"

"Yes, well, when I saw that Ronkerz would make us fight and I knew there was a chance I wouldn't win, I devised a scheme to escape both Ronkerz and my master. Again, please don't say his name; I don't want to draw his attention." She paused, and her ghostly black eyes stared until Victor nodded. "When a Death Caster typically becomes a lich, they must spend time preparing their phylactery, then, after they've voluntarily forfeited their mortal life, an ally prepares their body to accept the undead spirit and death-attuned Energy, completing the process."

"Your body isn't exactly in one piece or, you know, *here*."

"Yes, which brings me to the favor I would beg of you. I cannot seek aid on Sojourn; my master is too well known, and he'd likely get wind of my efforts. I beg you, Victor, will you bring me to the next world you visit? The ring where you stored my phylactery is sufficiently advanced to hold my spirit without making me mad. Once I'm free of Sojourn, if we could find a Death Caster to aid us—"

"We? Us? Arona, I'm not so sure I'm up for all that. I'm not exactly fond of Death Casters—"

"Victor! I *beg* you!" Her spirit flickered as she shifted to a kneeling position while still somehow seeming to float in the air. "I'm at your mercy! I beg you not to think of me as a Death Caster but as a friend. I didn't want this, but I saw it as the only way I might free myself. My master has lived for thousands of years, and I owed him centuries of servitude. He is *not* a pleasant man."

"Well? Why did you owe him?"

"My family *sold* me to him when I was young. On my homeworld, my father is a king, and a Death Caster to boot. He bargained with . . . the man I seek to flee, and I had no say in the matter!"

Victor sighed, then gestured to the bone. "So, what? You get into the bone, I put the bone in my storage ring—the good one—and then you just ride there quietly until I take you out again?"

"Precisely! Once we're in a different world, I can help guide you to a Death Caster who may be able to help me construct a fitting vessel—"

Victor groaned and set the bone on the bench beside him. "You mean a body, right? You're going to need a body, aren't you?"

"Yes—but, Victor, people die all the time! We needn't kill anyone."

"I'm not excited by the idea, Arona, but I did think of you as a friend, and as long as you don't ask me to do anything messed up, I'm willing to help you out."

"Hear my vow, Victor: I will never act in a manner you find vile or wrong, and as soon as I have a vessel with which to turn the pages of texts, I will search for a way to rid myself of this death-attuned Energy! I hate it!"

Victor watched the specter floating before him, still in a kneeling position. The ghostly version of Arona looked very much like she had in life, only washed out and gray-tinted with faint luminescence behind her flesh that made her seem transparent. It was a trick of the light on the eye, though—when he tried to see through her, he couldn't. Curiosity got the better of him, and Victor reached out to touch her sleeve, only to find his fingers passing through what felt like cold water. When he pulled back, he found no residue on his fingertips. "Why do you hate your master?"

Arona shivered, her ghostly figure flickering with the motion. "As I said, he's vile. He counts his apprentices as his property, and he knows no boundaries of the flesh. His hands grasp and touch where he wills, and to defy him is to face confinement for years, bereft of all but the slightest trickle of Energy—a harsh lesson to mold an unruly student's behavior. Of course, his nature isn't so plain when he courts a new apprentice, and the contracts are cleverly worded. My father wouldn't have cared what it said, in any case. He convinced me, the first of his seven daughters, with lies and promises, to go along with . . . my master, to sign the document with blood and seal it with Energy. Too late did I learn . . ."

As she continued detailing the cruel practices of Vesavo Bonewhisper, Victor could hear the emotion in her voice, and it touched a nerve. He *wanted* to help her, but more than that, he wanted to remove a potentially potent Death Caster from the universe. If he could help her to find a way to convert her Core from Death Energy once she'd recovered, what sort of precedent might that set? Were there other Death Casters trapped by cruel masters? What about Dark Ember? If he went there, intent on freeing the humans of that world, wouldn't whatever he learned in his quest to aid Arona help with that goal?

He realized she'd grown quiet, and he'd utterly missed half of her tale, so lost had he been in his own thoughts. "All right, Arona. I, um, I agree; it sounds like you got a raw deal. I'll be traveling away from this world in a few months. Can you manage to wait that long?" Victor meant his trip to Ruhn—there was no way he'd unleash a Tier Nine Death Caster on Fanwath.

"I can! I wandered the spirit plane until I felt my phylactery's pull, but within that bone, I have a rudimentary home; I surreptitiously transferred many of my belongings into it before I passed it off to you. Moreover, I can pass the time by improving it as I await your summons."

"How? Wouldn't that require Energy? Can you draw Energy while in a dimensional container?"

"The ring you stored the bone in allows the flow of Energy, Victor—how else could you store powerful conscious objects within it?"

Victor realized she was right as his mind flickered to the fear geist he had stored in that ring. Did that mean he could, theoretically, put Lifedrinker in there? He slowly began to nod, then locked his eyes on Arona's. As he stared into those depthless pools, he had a shiver of doubt. With a slight scowl, he demanded, "Swear to me again. Swear that you'll never betray me. Swear it on your spirit because *I* swear, Arona, if you're somehow scheming against me, I'll rip apart what's left of you and scatter the pieces all over the spirit plane—I'll feed it to the angry spirits I find dwelling there!"

"I swear it, Victor! I swear that if you're true to me, I will always be true to you. I already owe you a great debt, and know I ask much."

Victor nodded, then held up the bone. "In you go, then. I should get back to the house."

"One more thing, Victor. Please don't mention this to anyone! If Ve—my master were to learn of my continued existence—"

"I won't tell any—" Victor started to say, but then he remembered Valla and the secrets he'd already kept from her. "I'll only tell Valla. I have too many secrets from her already." Arona began to object, but he shook his head. "You have to trust me that she'll keep your secret. I won't help you otherwise."

After a long, silent second, as her ghostly figure wavered and flickered oddly in the moonlight, Arona's raspy voice came to him again. "I agree, Victor. Thank you." With that, her image seemed to burst apart into mist and pale light that streamed directly into the bone. Victor watched the last of it disappear into the vessel. The silvery runes flared briefly, and he was sure the bone felt even heavier and colder than before. Sighing, he returned it to the storage ring with his other valuable possessions.

He sat in the resulting quiet for a few minutes, determined to find the peace and relaxation he'd felt before Arona's spirit had made her surprise appearance. After a while, as the moon dipped lower and the eastern sky began to lighten from midnight black to deep blue-gray, he felt his stomach gurgle. Victor knew he didn't have to eat—he could go weeks without food—but he liked to do it, and the idea of some breakfast sounded good. He wasn't too sure he felt up to going into the house, however. There were a lot of early risers staying in the lake house, and Victor didn't feel like talking.

As he contemplated the dwindling food supplies in his storage containers, Victor felt his mind's eye drawn toward the heart he'd pulled from Loyle. Rather than feeling repulsed by the raw, bloody organ, he felt his mouth begin to salivate. As his hunger quickened, Victor chuckled at the dominance of his savage Quinametzin greed. He withdrew the heart and held it in the palm of his large hand. "Why not?"

Victor canceled his Alter Self spell, expanding to his natural size, but he didn't cast Iron Berserk; the heart wasn't overly large. In fact, in his broad palm, it looked more like a turkey heart than something that had come out of a man. Victor lifted it to his nose and, as the coppery scent of blood generated more saliva, plopped the entire thing into his mouth. His eyes had almost been bigger than his mouth—he had to tilt his head back as he chewed to avoid juices sluicing out, and his gluttony made him laugh, further disrupting his attempts to masticate the tough meat.

Even so, Victor found the taste and texture intoxicating, and the euphoria of the Energy escaping the flesh as he began to swallow the chunks of meat his teeth tore from the organ made the morsel all the sweeter. There really wasn't anything like it—no other food, as far as Victor's Quinametzin palate was concerned, could compare to the heart of an enemy. When he swallowed the lion's share of the organ and heaved in a deep, cleansing breath, he felt the fire roiling in his belly—something was happening.

Energy, hot and roiling, spread from his stomach into his body. When he closed his eyes, he could imagine his body had been frozen, and he'd swallowed an ember that slowly thawed his flesh. Of course, that wasn't anywhere close to the situation at hand—his body was hot already, so the heat rushing through him, from his gut to his fingertips, toes, and the top of his scalp, was something different. It was alive, tingling with Energy and purpose, and unlike some other instances when Victor had consumed something potent, almost pleasant as it did whatever it was doing.

When the sensation had passed through his entire body and he began to feel normal again, he received some System messages:

*****Congratulations! You have gained a new Feat: Blood Supremacy.*****

*****Blood Supremacy: Your blood, already potent with the might of an elder species, has gained the ability to carry your aura and will. Species and individuals with the ability to infect, consume, or subvert another's blood will have to contend with your innate willpower and the effects of your aura. Moreover, those who come into contact with your blood will feel its weight until it has been cleansed. This effect would be particularly daunting to any individual who consumed your blood.*****

As he read the message, Victor couldn't help imagining a vampire drinking his blood and suffering the effects of his new feat. He laughed despite himself, especially when he pictured some of the vampyrs and wampyrs that had invaded from Dark Ember, most notably the reaver baron, Eric Gore Lust. "Yeah," he laughed, "try drinking this shit, *pendejo*!"

50

CHANGES

When Victor returned to the house, the sun was well up, and he could hear voices coming from the dining room. Peering in through the arched opening in the hallway that separated the room from the kitchen, he saw Valla sitting beside Lam, and across the table from them was Efanie. He looked further into the room, to the smaller table near the far windows, and sure enough, there sat Cora, by herself, absently picking at a plate full of food. Part of Victor wanted to retreat, to face these people later and well after he'd had a chance to speak with Valla alone, but he forced himself to step into the room. "Hey, good to see you're getting acquainted."

Valla looked at him, arching a silver-teal eyebrow. "I'm sure you were going to introduce us, but I couldn't sleep, and we ran into each other."

Victor nodded and moved to sit down. He was still his natural size, so he selected one of the larger, Dar-sized chairs, which put him beside Efanie. He saw the food on everyone's plates—bacon, eggs, grilled veggies, and thick hunks of buttery toast—and his stomach instantly began to grumble. Efanie chuckled and pushed her plate toward him; it was largely untouched.

"I'm not all that hungry—too much going on, and my nerves are shot." Hearing those words was like a splash of cold water to Victor, reminding him that he wasn't the center of the universe, regardless of how it seemed most of the time.

"Yeah, I guess last night's events kind of turned your world upside down, huh?"

Efanie nodded and gestured with her thumb toward Cora over by the windows. "Mine and Cora's both. Still," she said as she nodded to Valla and Lam, "we've been treated very kindly here, and I think we're both hopeful."

Victor nodded, trying to show understanding, but if he were totally honest with himself, he was glad Cora wasn't at the same table. How would she feel sitting in the presence of the man who'd killed her father? It was enough to make him want to get up and leave. It wasn't enough to stifle his appetite, however, so he covered his discomfort by stuffing a large hunk of buttered, honey-dipped bread into his mouth.

Valla nudged him under the table with her boot. "I was just telling Efanie how cruel life could be." She lowered her voice and continued, "I spoke with Cora briefly, Victor. She told me that she understood that our friends' lives were on the line and that her father made his living by fighting another man's battles. A very mature outlook for a girl who's just recently seen her twelfth birthday, don't you think?"

Victor swallowed—too soon—and had to fight to clear his throat before speaking. Efanie took the opportunity to voice her opinion on the matter. "She doesn't hate you, Sir Victor. She's cross but more at life and circumstances—at her father—than at you. I think I was able to make her understand that you fought for a righteous cause."

"Well—" Victor began to say, but it seemed Efanie wasn't finished.

"I hope you know that I don't expect you and your lady to be the girl's new parents. Neither does she. If you'll just give us a small allowance, enough to furnish a home and pay for a tutor, I think we'd be more than happy to move out from underfoot."

She took a breath and might have continued, but Victor was through being steamrolled. He locked eyes with Efanie and shook his head. "I'll be doing more than that. I've taken responsibility for her, and that means something to me." He nodded to Valla. "I'd like us all to take a trip back to our homeworld. I have a sizeable estate there, and I think it would be a good place for her to grow up."

"Fanwath?" Valla's eyes almost sparkled as she said the word, and Victor was reminded of all the times he'd stared into those orbs, lost in their colorful depths.

"Yeah." Victor smiled, then turned back to Efanie. "It's a lower-tier world than this, but the nation Valla and I helped to found is growing rapidly, and many opportunities abound. I have influential friends there who can see to Cora's safety and education, so if you have something binding you to Sojourn—"

"N-no! No, Victor, I would be most pleased to visit your home. What was it?" She glanced at Valla. "Fanwath?"

Valla nodded. "That's right. Victor is lord to quite an estate there, though we haven't seen his manor yet. It was just breaking ground when we came to Sojourn. You see, we'd just conquered an invasion in what was considered untamed lands."

"Ah." Efanie nodded, then turned to Victor. "Are you certain it's a good place for a young woman to come of age?"

"Yeah. As I said, it's growing quickly, and I have people there I trust and think of as family. I think it would be good for Cora to be away from this city and the . . ." Victor trailed off, wanting to say "memory of her father," but was too worried the girl could hear what they were talking about. With that in mind, he asked, "Would you talk to her about it?"

Lam cleared her throat and leaned forward, breaking her silence in a hushed voice. "I think you need to sit down with her, Victor. She must know that she wasn't given over to a monster."

Valla nodded and reached across the table to grasp Victor's wrist. "I agree. As harsh as it may seem, this is her new reality. The longer you avoid confronting the facts, the longer she'll build up whatever monstrous version of you is living in her head." Victor looked at her, a little surprised by how pleasant and supportive she was being despite their last conversation. He supposed it had something to do with the seriousness of the situation—Cora was a young girl going through a hell of a lot more than a couple's disagreement.

He glanced around the table, from Valla to Lam to Efanie, and quietly asked, "Now?"

Lam nodded, Valla squeezed his wrist again, and Efanie leaned close and whispered, "She understands your situation. Just be kind."

With a sigh and grunt, Victor pushed himself away from his plate of food and stood. As he approached Cora, he cast Alter Self, straining to get the most out of the spell. When he sat across from her, she glanced up but then quickly back down at her food—hardly touched. To his horror, Victor found himself channeling every dopey adult he'd ever spoken to as a child. "You've got to eat to keep up your strength."

She picked up a piece of potato and tucked it into her mouth. "As you say, milord."

"Ah, forget I said that—pretty stupid." Suddenly, Victor was stricken with the urge simply to be honest. "Look, I don't know what I'm doing here. I think this whole situation sucks. I know I said that before—kind of—outside Volpuré's estate, but it's true. I understand you're in a bad place right now. You're probably mad, sad, and everything in between, right? You've got every right to be. I'm sorry about your dad, but you understand I was fighting for my life, for my friends' lives, right?"

"I understand, milord." She still hadn't looked up, and all Victor could see of her face was her pale forehead beneath unruly thick curly brown hair.

Victor decided to try a different approach. "Do you like Sojourn? Do you have friends here?"

"I—" For the first time, she glanced up, and her chocolate eyes touched his for just a second before she looked back down. "I've spent most of my time at the Volpuré estate with my father. I don't have friends."

"Um, I know this is probably not a fun topic, but can you tell me a little about that? Why did your dad keep you so close? I know they told me he was your only family, but do you, um, know about your mom at all?" Her head shook from side to side, bouncing her thick curls, but she didn't speak. "All right. Well, I have an idea I'd like to run by you. I have a lot of property on another world where some very good friends live. I'd like to take you there—get you away from this place. There are children who live on my lands and people who can look after you and give you the kind of attention you deserve. I think you'll like it there." She didn't speak or look up, so Victor asked more bluntly, "What do you say?"

When she looked up this time, she stared into his eyes and didn't look away. "Do I have a choice?"

"Um—" Victor frowned, unsure of how to proceed. Finally, he settled on what he'd want to hear if he were in her shoes. "I want you to come with me and see the place. I want you to meet some of the people who live there. After that, you can decide if you want to stay or come back to Sojourn."

She glanced at the other, larger table. "Will Efanie come?"

Victor nodded. "Yeah. She's eager to go; I don't think she loves Sojourn." Cora stared at him for a moment longer, and Victor saw much in the depths of those dark eyes, but she didn't speak, only nodded, then turned back to her food, scooping up a large bite of scrambled eggs. Victor felt he'd been dismissed, so he went with it. He stood and pushed his chair in. "When I said we're going, I meant, like, today. Efanie will help you get ready." With that, he walked back over to the large table.

"Well?" Lam asked.

"She's open to the idea." Victor looked from Efanie to Valla. "I want to leave today. I know it's short notice, but Dar's only given me a week, so I want to make the most of it." They both inhaled and looked ready to ask him questions, but he turned to Lam. "I can probably afford it if you and the others want to come."

"I think—" Lam stopped and frowned, shaking her head. "I think I'll wait. I don't want to return until I've regained more of my former strength. Edeya is with Trin, watching over Darren, but I'll ask her what she thinks. I doubt Darren will wake in time to join you."

Victor nodded, once again reminded that other people had important things going on and considerations of their own. "What level are you now?"

She grinned and thumped the table with her palm. "All of us are closing in on Tier Two. Say one thing about that deathtrap of a dungeon—it provided quite a growth opportunity."

"Well, let me know if you change your mind. Tell Edeya we'll be leaving in a couple of hours if she's interested."

Efanie pushed her chair back. "So soon?"

"Yeah. I was serious about wanting to get this going. I've got a lot I want to do and only a week to squeeze it all in."

"Understood. I—" She glanced over at Cora. "I should take Cora into town for a little shopping. I have a few loose ends I'd like to tie up around here. Despite Bohn's awful nature, there are many in the Volpuré household I'd like to part with on good terms. I think a few gifts and letters sent via courier should do the trick. Would it be all right if the two of us meet you at the World Hall?"

"Yeah." Victor rubbed his chin while he thought. "I think I'm being unreasonable. Two hours isn't enough time—meet us at the ticket counter at noon. Is that fair?"

"More than fair!" She stood and started toward Cora, but Valla cleared her throat.

"Wait, Efanie!" Valla looked at Victor. "If she's going to buy things for Cora to travel with, shouldn't you give her some funds?"

"Oh, I—" Efanie started, but Victor laughed, shaking his head in chagrin.

"Yeah, sorry. I'll need to get used to this." He hadn't sorted the massive crates of beads in Loyle's ring into more convenient containers, so he lifted out a sack from his previous stash. It held nearly ten thousand beads in value—most were double or triple-attuned. He handed it to Efanie. "That should do for now. I guess you can consider anything left over as a retainer; we can negotiate a contract for you when we get to Fanwath, all right?"

"That's fair. Thank you, Sir—"

"Just Victor, Efanie."

She smiled, then curtly tilted her head and waved to the table, including Lam and Valla in the gesture. "See you soon." As she strode toward Cora's table, her voice became strident. "Up you get, young lady. We've much to do and little time in which to do it!"

Lam glanced at Victor and then Valla and pushed her chair back. "Why don't you sit back down and finish Efanie's breakfast, Victor? I'm going to go check in on Edeya and tell her what you said about returning to Fanwath."

"Um, yeah. Not a bad idea." Victor sat down again, well aware that Lam was trying to give him a chance to speak with Valla. It made him wonder if Valla had been venting, but he supposed he couldn't blame her if she had been. As she left, Lam walked behind Valla. Catching Victor's eye, she nodded and winked.

"About as subtle as a thunderak in a jewelry store." Valla chuckled.

Victor shrugged. "She's trying to help me out. Don't you agree I could use it?"

Valla sighed. "Oh, Victor! I know I wasn't exactly rational earlier, but you must admit that you don't make it easy for me. I've spent some hours thinking and a bit of time chatting with Lam, and honestly, I don't know what to say other than that. I think I need more time to think about things. Don't you?"

"I . . ." Victor frowned as he let his impulsive objection die on his tongue. Did he need more time to think? Was he sure about everything? Or, failing that, was he at least as sure as he used to be? He supposed the answer was no—there had been some changes in his feelings that bore further thought. "I guess some time to think would be nice."

"Exactly! Some time away from Sojourn is exactly what we need. Some time away from all the high stakes, the life-or-death battles, the schemes, and future plots. Let's make a promise—no talking about any of our . . . problems until the night before our scheduled return. I want to enjoy a small vacation with you and forget about all of our worries for a few days. Let's give our minds and hearts time to breathe and think. Can you agree with that?"

Victor held his hand, palm up, across the table, and Valla eagerly took it in her slender, cool fingers. "Yeah, I can agree, Valla. Honestly, it sounds great."

When Darren opened his eyes, he was swept away with almost nauseating disorientation. He saw wooden rafters overhead, but they seemed curved, as if he was looking at them through a fish-eye lens. He blinked his eyes and tried to focus, but then his world was blotted out by wood grains, splinters, and a nail head the size of a dinner plate. "Ungh," he grunted, feeling even more queasy. He closed his eyes and, as the world faded to peaceful black, began to recall strange, vivid dreams of flying through clouds, basking in the cold air of the heights and the warmth of the sun. How long had he slept?

With the question came a surge of other memories—waves of monsters, Lam and Edeya and Trin all fighting for their lives, an axe blade cleaving his clavicle and slicing deep into his chest, and worried whispers and the taste of something incomprehensibly sweet and good as it was stuffed into his mouth. He opened his eyes again, hoping to see one of his friends, but this time, instead of just the wooden ceiling, he saw a bird's head. No, he corrected himself, an avian woman's head. Black feathers adorned her crown, and a dark yellow beak sat beneath giant yellow and brown-banded irises that narrowed in contemplation as he continued to blink.

"Try to relax and let nature do its work. Your eyes are much stronger than they used to be, Darren. My name is Brimi, and I'm here because your friends were worried about you."

"Worried?" Darren asked, but his voice was strange in his ears, and it sounded garbled, more like, "Ooried?"

"That's right, love, you've been out for a few days. Try to lie still and take in everything I've got to say. It seems you ate a racial advancement cake, and it woke something up—a bloodline."

"*Uhdline?*" he asked, his voice rising toward a squawk as he tried to form the word with his strange-feeling mouth.

"An avian bloodline. That's why I'm here. I can help you to figure out how to manage the things that have changed about you."

"*Aieeen?*" Darren tried to say "avian," but, again, it sounded more like a squawk. His heart had begun to hammer, and despite Brimi's protestations, he struggled to his feet, pleased that his arms, hands, and legs were responding normally. He looked around, frowning at the strange perspective. Was he taller than before? The avian woman held out her arms, trying to steady or restrain him; he couldn't tell. She was much shorter than he, and as he looked around, his vision kept zooming in on every little detail.

He almost fell several times as he stumbled to his bathroom and finally managed to fight his way through the door to peer at himself in the mirror. "What the hell?" he cried, though, again, it came out like, "*Aaah-kah-ell!*" Darren had, indeed, changed. He was easily a foot taller than before, looming over the sink, stark naked, save for a pair of tight underwear.

His body didn't look all that different, but there were a few disturbing changes. His head was covered in lustrous brown, mottled feathers, his eyes were enormous angular things like you might see on an eagle, the irises golden and beautiful, and his nose and mouth had been replaced by a long hooked beak.

Darren, too stressed and frankly panicked to speak, turned to look at his back and saw faint lumps along his spine just beneath his shoulder blades. "No wings?" he tried to ask, too distracted to worry about what the words came out sounding like.

"You've just barely awoken your bloodline, but, as is usual when something like this occurs, the first changes are to your sensory organs—your eyes, mouth, nose, and ears. As you advance your bloodline . . ." She kept speaking, but Darren couldn't hear her over the pounding of his heart, the roaring of his thoughts. He mentally called up his status sheet and scanned what he saw:

Status	
Name:	Darren Whitehorse
Race:	Human: Base 5, Thunderbird Bloodline
Class:	Chaos Sorcerer: Advanced
Level:	18
Core:	Wildarc Class: Base 2

Energy Affinity:	Lightning 8, Chaos 7.4, Unattuned 6.1		Energy:	1445/1445
Strength:	6	Vitality:	72	
Dexterity:	45	Agility:	5	
Intelligence:	57	Will:	68	
Points Available:	0			
Titles & Feats:	-			
Skills:				
System Language Integration			Not Upgradeable	
Wildarc Cultivation Drill			Basic	
Staff Mastery			Basic	
Sense Chaos			Basic	
Spells:				
Arclight Wisp			Basic	
Shocking Arms			Basic	
Fractured Reality			Basic	
Chaos Storm			Basic	

"*Ut thah uuuuck!*" he screeched, clapping his hands to his head.

"Hush, Darren! Really!" Brimi scolded. "You should be thrilled. You realize that if you keep advancing your bloodline, you'll be able to fly, yes? A predator avian, too! What handsome eyes you have! And those feathers! Goodness, but you're going to be something, given time. Now, regarding your attempts at speaking—Darren, you must try to form the words further back in your throat. We intelligent avian species have a very advanced syrinx in our throats. It takes a little practice, but you'll soon learn to enunciate properly . . ."

She continued to babble on, but Darren couldn't focus on her. He was staring at the backs of his hands where fine, downy feathers seemed to have replaced the hair that used to grow there. He looked at the tips of his fingers and saw that his nails were dark black, pointed, and hard as iron. Frowning, he looked at his status sheet and, with enormous concentration, tried to form the word in the back of his throat, "*Thunderbird*."

51

GOING HOME

Victor looked around his cultivation chamber, deep beneath Dar's home, and slowly nodded to himself. This would be a good place for Lifedrinker to consume the treasure Lira had given him in the Iron Prison. He'd thought about keeping her in his vault, keeping her locked safely away and concealed around his neck, but when he mentioned the idea to Dar, his master had vehemently discouraged the plan. He said that such an evolution would require the ebb and flow of Energy and that Lifedrinker's spirit might feel stifled in such an environment. He feared such containment might lessen the potential of her evolution.

So Victor had agreed to leave her behind to slowly consume the enormously dense "soul ore." Dar had vowed to keep the axe safe and sound, so Victor wasn't worried about her. He knew he'd feel a little naked without her, though, and that was probably why he hesitated to set her on the ground. "You know why I'm leaving you, yeah, *chica*?"

"I must feast! I must grow more powerful to better fight at your side! I do not fear the solitude."

"Heh, okay, okay." Victor pressed the side of her blade against his forehead and basked in the warmth of trust and love, then he knelt and gently laid her on the stone ground. A moment later, he summoned the absurdly heavy lump of ore from his storage container, and it slipped through his fingers to the ground with a resounding *clunk*. Victor's eyes widened as he saw hairline cracks in the solid stone spreading out from the edges of the ore. "Okay, beautiful. I'm gonna put your blade on this stone. Take your time and do it right."

Victor had no idea what he was talking about. Was it possible for Lifedrinker to *not* take her time? Could she do something wrong when it came to incorporating this new powerful metal? He didn't know, but she didn't correct him. She was silent and only emanated eagerness as he picked her up and gently propped her at an angle with her metallic axe-head resting atop the ingot.

Victor sat back and watched for a moment, and at first, he didn't think anything was happening. Then he saw it.

Where her metal touched the ore, a hazy gray cloud was forming, and as he peered more closely, Victor could see tiny sparks of electricity, almost like static, dancing in the hazy barrier between the two metals. Victor put his hand over the glow lamp he'd brought with him. As the room plunged into darkness, he saw the real light show. Lifedrinker was aglow—not just her metallic head, but her haft as well. More than that, she danced with tiny sparks, and the space between her and the ore was like a miniature hurricane as the weird reaction continued to build.

Victor stood, looked at his wonderful axe, his steadfast companion, one more time, and nodded. "Okay, then. See you soon." Then he left, rapidly climbing through the tunnels to Dar's home. He was late; he and Valla had been heading to the coach when Victor had remembered the ore and decided he should get Lifedrinker started on it.

Feeling rushed, knowing Cora and Efanie were probably waiting for them, he jogged through the house, then outside to where Mr. Qwor had pulled the coach. It hovered above the ground, door open, but it wasn't alone; Trin's coach was there, and to Victor's surprise, Edeya burst through the front door and hurried past him, aiming for the little submarine-shaped vehicle without sparing him a glance.

"Hey," he called. Edeya froze and turned to look at him, and Victor was sure it was surprise he saw in her eyes as she took him in.

"Oh, Victor! Sorry, we're in a rush!"

"Where to?"

"Um, to pick up a friend of Trin's. An avian woman—" She frowned and shook her head, then in a jumble of hurried words, tried to explain, "We think Darren's waking up a bloodline. He's, um, growing a, uh . . ." She threw up her hands and blurted, "He's growing a beak, Victor!"

"Oh? Shit . . ." Victor wasn't sure how to respond to that. "Should I stay? Should we postpone our trip?"

"No! No, you go. We can handle this. Lam's with him now, in case he wakes, but Trin has an avian friend who should be able to explain things to him better."

"All right. Keep me posted. I'll check the Far Scribe book when we get to Fanwath."

"Have a good trip!" Edeya waved and then jumped into the vehicle, which, with a weird burbling, buzzing sound, drifted away toward the city.

Shaking his head, Victor climbed into Mr. Qwor's coach. He pulled the door closed with a *thud*, then collapsed into the cushioned seat beside Valla. He tapped on the panel with his knuckles, and Qwor launched them into the air. "Sorry for the delay," he sighed, stretching his legs out toward the opposite seat.

Valla, shaking her head but wearing a wry smile, took ahold of his hand. "You got your axe situated?"

"Yep. She's all set." Victor leaned back and sighed. "You should have come with me. That ore is so wild—I think you would have enjoyed seeing it before Lifedrinker eats it. I couldn't hold it up with only one hand. It fell to the cave floor and *cracked* it!"

"I hope it's not too much for your lady axe to handle." Her tone was light, but Victor still felt a twinge of worry. He hoped so, too.

In an attempt to not dwell on his anxiety for Lifedrinker, he changed the subject. "Did you hear about Darren?"

"Yes. I suppose it's a lucky thing that the winged people of my origin world didn't have beaks—seems such a thing would make kissing difficult."

Victor frowned. "Yeah, I hadn't thought about that. I guess the universe is big and full of variety, huh?" He still wasn't sure about where he stood with Valla, but he took the fact that she was holding his hand as a good sign. Almost tentatively, he leaned toward her, but she was quick to take the hint and closed in for a kiss. He smiled as they parted. "I'm *damn* glad you don't have a beak."

Less than an hour later, they exited the coach and approached the row of token vendors at the World Hall; sure enough, Efanie and Cora were standing there waiting. Efanie had shed her Volpuré livery, and both she and Cora were dressed similarly in rather formal-looking layered skirts and blouses. They looked nice, and Valla said so as they approached, taking a minute to lean forward and fuss with the frilly fabric around Cora's collar. Victor watched, and he could see that Cora was starstruck by Valla, staring into her eyes with the first expression he'd seen on her that wasn't tinted by sadness or anger.

When Victor had come to Sojourn, the System had charged him a toll of nearly a hundred thousand beads. With that in mind, he was a little surprised when the attendant, after looking up Fanwath on her elegant crystalline tablet, quoted him a price of only two hundred thousand beads for four "transport tokens." He didn't complain, but it puzzled him enough to bring it up with Valla as they walked toward their designated transport circle.

"Perhaps it has something to do with the level of Sojourn's System Stone."

"Undoubtedly," Efanie chimed in. "I paid a hefty fee when I left my world, which has a much less advanced stone."

As they worked their way through the crowd, through the enormous chamber with its many support pillars, arched ceilings, and decorative mosaics, Victor saw that Cora's eyes were wide with wonder as she looked around. It puzzled him slightly, considering she'd been the only child of a very wealthy, powerful man, and, before he could think better of the question, he nudged her shoulder. "Hey, have you been away from Sojourn before? Were you born here?"

"I've never been to the World Hall, milord. I went with my father to visit my homeworld once when I was nine, but he used a portal created by a great magus from Lord Volpuré's household." She almost stopped speaking, but then she seemed to remember the rest of Victor's question and added, "I was born on Avendus, but my father brought me to Sojourn when I was three—a-after my mother died. I have no memory of that trip."

"Ah." Victor cleared his throat. "I see." The more he learned about the girl, the more he realized his own sob stories were certainly less than unique. Inwardly cringing, afraid he was about to pull open a fresh wound, he asked, "And you have no other family on, uh—what was it? Avendus?"

"That's right, milord. When we visited, my father was settling old business. I spent the time in a hotel room." She spoke flatly, with little expression, and Victor decided to let it rest. He caught Valla looking sideways at him as if judging his reaction, and he offered her a tiny shrug, ensuring Cora couldn't see the gesture. Valla squeezed his hand, and they continued in silence.

Soon enough, they came to their transport circle—a smaller one in an alcove set off from the main hall, and when they'd all moved to stand at its center, Victor nodded to Efanie and Cora. "You two first. I'll follow as soon as I see you're safely away."

"As you say, Victor." Efanie placed one of the travel tokens in Cora's upturned palm. "Channel a little Energy into this." Cora nodded, and then, with a flicker of light and a tinge of ozone-scented air, she was gone. A bare second later, Efanie disappeared. Victor looked at Valla, locked eyes with her, and they both channeled Energy into their tokens. As before, the world vanished in a flash of light, and then, almost instantly, Victor found himself standing in the dimly lit, quiet portal room beneath the Colony Stone of the Free Marches.

The space, while large enough to hold dozens of people comfortably, was tiny in comparison to the World Hall, which added to some of the disorientation common with teleportation. Cora was kneeling in her skirts, Efanie leaning over her, gently stroking her thick curly hair. Before Victor could see if she was all right, stomping feet alerted him, and he spun to see several guards in Rellia's household livery approaching from the stairwell. They had weapons drawn, but when they caught sight of Victor, they relaxed, and expressions of excitement replaced their alarm.

"Lord Victor!" one of the guards—a former member of the Ninth, if Victor wasn't mistaken—shouted. His eyes scanned the rest of their party and widened noticeably when he saw Valla. "Lady Valla! Welcome!" He turned to one of his comrades. "Run! Alert the seneschal! Lady Rellia will want to know about—"

"Easy, man!" Victor laughed. "We'll be here a while, no need to have a meltdown." Despite his words, one of the guards had already sprinted for the stairs, and Victor could hear her feet pounding on the steps as she ascended. He chuckled, then turned to Cora. She was already up on her feet, and though she was a little pale, she seemed all right. He looked at Valla. "Ready to see your mom?"

She folded her hands before her, fidgeting a little, and gave him a surprisingly easy smile. "I actually *did* miss her. Yes, it'll be nice to visit."

Victor inhaled deeply, feeling some nebulous satisfaction. He turned to Efanie. "Let's head up. You two all right?"

"Fine, um, Lord Victor." Victor groaned inwardly but didn't bother trying to correct her; they were about to be surrounded by guards and attendants who would refuse to be casual with him. He led the way up the stairs, and when he came out on the platform surrounding the City Stone, his eyes widened as he took in the changes to the budding capital of the Free Marches.

In the time they'd been away, the walls that used to surround the Colony Stone had been much reduced, and Rellia's keep moved back nearly half a mile. Huge cobbled boulevards led away from the central hill—one toward the sea, one in the opposite direction toward Rellia's ever-expanding fortress, and then another that ran north-south. All along those wide avenues were buildings, almost exclusively built from pale stone. It certainly didn't look like a frontier town any longer.

Massive city walls loomed in the distance, though the area inside them was less than crowded, and Victor could see plenty of places for expansion. Aside from Rellia's keep and the enormous observatory jutting up from the shore, only a few buildings were taller than two stories. More than the changes in architecture, the increase in population drove home to Victor how much the town was growing. He judged it was still early morning based on the sun, but he saw throngs of people milling about outside stores, at restaurants and taverns, and bustling to and fro.

"Lovely," Efanie said, and Victor turned to see her staring toward the Silver Sea. The waters were tinted orange and yellow by the rising sun but shimmered to reflect their namesake as the waves rolled toward shore.

"Yeah, it's pretty country."

"Lord, Lady, will you follow me to the keep? I'm sure Lady Rellia is eager to greet you."

Victor looked to the guard who'd followed them up and nodded. "Yeah, we'll say hello." Victor had already written a note in his Far Scribe book tied to Gorro ap'Dommic, his governor, so he doubted Rellia was really going to be surprised to see him and Valla. As he thought about it, he looked at Valla. "Didn't you message Rellia?"

She shook her head. "I wanted to surprise her." She took his hand and pulled him down the steps toward the roadway leading east to the keep and its tall pale walls. The guard hurried to lead the way. He was a Shadeni and decently well built, but he had to veritably scurry to keep ahead of Valla's and Victor's long strides. Recognizing that, Victor looked over his shoulder to see Efanie and Cora falling behind, so he slowed a little, tugging Valla's hand.

She realized what he was doing and laughed. "I really *am* eager, aren't I?" She turned back to the keep, and Victor followed her gaze. The gates were the same as before—huge and metal, prepared long before the Free Marches were conquered and transported from Gelica. They stood open, and the gap between them was already filling with soldiers forming on either side, creating an honor guard for Rellia and her "noble" visitors.

The street was lined with what seemed to be governmental buildings. Victor saw a library, a courthouse, and even a constable's office and jail. He lost track of the other sights as Rellia appeared, flanked by her more important advisors and courtiers. She walked between her row of impressively armored and armed soldiers.

She looked different—taller, more regal, and certainly more finely dressed than he remembered. She wore a high-collared purple cape and a form-fitting black gown, ribbed and tooled to accentuate her tall, lean posture. Her rapier hung at her side, and her lustrous curly red hair was pinned back and held down by a glittering diamond-studded tiara. Despite the finery and the show of regal bearing, her face looked the same as ever. Rellia's crimson eyes glittered in the morning sun, her red-painted lips spread in an enormous smile, and she broke away from her guards and hurried toward Valla, lifting her skirts to keep from tripping.

Valla's feathers rustled as she softly fluttered her wings, boosting her forward to smash into her mother. She caught her in an embrace, lifting her off her feet and spinning around once. Victor laughed and slowed, giving them a little space, holding out his hand to signal Efanie and Cora to stop. He looked at them and said, behind one hand, "That's Valla's mom."

Cora's eyes widened. "Her mother rules these lands?"

Victor shrugged. "Kind of. Really, it's a republic of sorts, with landholders having the voting power. I, uh, have a lot of votes." As Valla and Rellia finally separated, Victor stepped forward and couldn't help but smile in response to Rellia's genuine enthusiasm for seeing him. She held out her arms, and Victor scooped her up in a hug.

"It's good to see you, Victor! Are you always this big now?"

"Nah, I can make myself smaller. This is my normal size, though." As he set her down, she took one of his hands and pulled him toward Valla. Victor resisted and said, "Let me introduce Efanie and Cora."

Rellia paused and turned to the two smaller women, one who looked like a human child and the other who looked very much like an elfin Fae. "Companions of yours?"

"Cora," Victor said as he pointed at the girl who looked down nervously, "is my ward. Efanie is looking after her." Efanie tugged on Cora's sleeve as he spoke, and the two performed remarkably graceful curtsies.

Rellia raised an eyebrow at Victor. "Welcome to the Free Marches. As Victor's ward, Cora, you're a member of his household, and, as a member of his household, anything you ever need, I will endeavor to provide."

"Thank you, Lady." Cora curtsied again. Some weird, primal part of Victor felt proud of her in that moment.

"Come," Rellia said, tugging his hand again as she reached out with the other to take Valla's. "We have much to discuss, and something tells me you're eager to see your own lands. I think you'll be pleased when you do! First, though, I must insist that you and my daughter join me for an early brunch." She turned to Cora and Efanie. "You'll both attend, of course."

As they nodded, Victor allowed himself to be led toward the keep, uncomfortably emotional by the sensations washing over him. Was this what it felt like to come "home"? Was Rellia so much like family to him? Had he forgotten his real home? Tucson felt like a distant dream, his cousins, aunts, even his *abuelita*, ghostly and faint in his mind's eye. He supposed he'd given up on ever seeing them. He'd accepted that his grandmother was gone for good, at least in this lifetime, and hadn't thought about that part of his life at all.

As they stepped into the shadows of the gatehouse, he felt a similar shadow in his heart—a melancholy acceptance rearing its head, reminding him that, despite all he'd gained, he'd certainly lost plenty, too. The thought had a strange effect on him, and he turned to look over his shoulder at Cora. Her eyes were wide as she looked around at the guards and regal décor. At that moment, he vowed that she wouldn't experience any more loss, at least not until she was well and truly grown and no longer his responsibility. She was still young—hopefully, young enough to build enough joy atop her own melancholy experiences to help her avoid the kind of ephemeral despair that had chosen such an odd time to grip his heart.

52

NOTHING BETTER

Victor rode Guapo at a sedate pace alongside the carriage Rellia had provided for Cora and Efanie. He glanced up, shading his eyes to see if he could spot Valla, but she'd flown too far off, eager to survey the landscape. She wanted to spy out the things that had changed on Victor's land, promising to stop and alert Thayla to his impending arrival before rejoining Victor at his estate. He was jealous, of course, but also understood; she'd felt stifled around Sojourn, nervous about flying with so many other vehicles and powerful beings populating those skies.

As the carriage's wheels rumbled and bounced on the cobbles, Victor once again found himself impressed by the fact that there *were* cobbles; Rellia and Borrius had made it a priority to establish "highways" between their lands and the various keeps and strongholds in the Free Marches. Such an endeavor might have taken decades on medieval Earth or even years with modern technology, but with Earth Casters and stoneworker artisans, the job had taken mere weeks—at least the initial broad single-lane paths like the one Victor and his companions currently traversed.

They'd passed quite a few burgeoning villas and farms as they went through Rellia's holdings, but as they crossed into Victor's lands, traffic had fallen off considerably, and they'd not passed a single dwelling, signpost, or farm in hours. He wasn't too surprised. Most of the lands he'd granted early on were further south and east, on the way to the Shadeni and Naghelli holdings. He didn't even know where his "hermitage" was, trusting Rellia's assertion that this road would lead him right to it.

The carriage was open on the front and sides, with a black fabric roof that could be rolled back. Efanie had left the roof up because the sun was hot—much warmer than Sojourn's—and despite her dark brown hair, Cora had very pale skin. Victor urged Guapo closer to the vehicle, drawn by two hearty-looking roladii, and leaned close so Efanie could hear him. "I think we're getting close. Maybe another hour or two."

"Good! This carriage was a nice gesture, but it's not a smooth ride!"

"Yeah, Fanwath could use some advances in magical vehicles, that's for sure."

"Perhaps you could send one home!"

"Yeah, maybe, but if I'm not wrong, I bet Deyni and Chala will be teaching Cora to ride soon. You might as well get in on the action."

"Oh, I can ride!" Efanie laughed. "We've quite a few swift beasts on my homeworld."

Victor nodded. "Should have guessed that." He clicked his tongue, and Guapo slowed, allowing the carriage to pull ahead. Then he rode up to the other side so he could speak more easily to Cora. "What do you think?"

"What about, milord?" She shaded her eyes to peer out at him.

"Fanwath!"

"I thought Lady Rellia was beautiful, and her home was quite lovely. I enjoyed the meal. However, this carriage is rather rough, and those beasts do smell a bit foul."

"Yeah, but what about the world?" Victor waved one arm expansively, indicating the fields of blue-green grass, brilliant red and orange wildflowers, and the distant mountains under the deep blue sky.

"It's enormous! I was awestruck when I saw the sea, but then we rode into these grasslands, and it seems they are just as vast and far more colorful! I saw a pack of brightly furred hounds racing beside us for a while. What are they called?"

"Those are boyii hounds, and they're dangerous for a girl all alone, but they wouldn't dare approach while I'm here."

"Wild beasts? Is the land so untamed?"

"Yeah," Victor chuckled. "I guess it is. That's why there aren't any people or houses around; these lands were uninhabited by people for a very long time. I'm glad you liked the sea—my house is supposed to have a view of it."

"Supposed to? You haven't seen it?"

"No! I had to hurry to Sojourn to help a friend after we conquered the invaders here. I hired a governor for my estate and gave him instructions to build my home."

"I see." Cora had let her gaze drift to the countryside, but she looked back at Victor, her eyes touching his for the first time since coming to Fanwath. "You help your friends often, don't you, milord?"

"I try to, Cora, but I'm not a saint. I'm selfish in ways, too. I let my temper get the best of me, and I like to fight too much. I try to make sure I'm on the right side of things, but sometimes, it's not always black and white. Do you know what that means? Black and white?"

"Yes, milord. My father taught me about shades of gray. He said his service to Volpuré was shaded in gray. He used the 'black and white' argument more than once to explain to me why he wouldn't leave. Why he wouldn't stop fighting."

Victor nodded as Cora looked down, and it seemed this was a good spot to end the conversation. It felt as though he'd made some progress, and he didn't want to push things. They traveled in silence for a while, though Victor pointed out some wildlife a few times—large colorful birds, another pack of boyii hounds, and a herd of wild deer-like huldii. Eventually, the road, which meandered mainly to the south, veered west and began to climb a steep slope. When they reached the crest of the hill, Victor stopped Guapo, and Efanie pulled the reins so they could take in the view.

From the ridgeline where they sat, the road wended down a grassy slope into a vast basin bordered by hills and mountains to the south and east and the Silver Sea to the west. Craning his neck, Victor saw nothing but grasslands and small copses of trees to the north for as far as his eye could see. The road curved south, though, and passed through a patchwork of small fields neatly planted with a variety of crops. Farmhouses dotted the landscape, and just at the edge of his vision, far to the south, Victor could see the walls of a small village that butted up against the slopes of a prominent hill. He wasn't sure, but he suspected the structure on that hill was his new home.

"What a beautiful place!" Efanie cried. "Isn't it wondrous, Cora? Such lands would be impossible to find on Sojourn!"

"Does it remind you of your home, Miss Efanie?" Cora's voice was hushed and, if Victor were any judge, wonderstruck.

"A bit, love, but the weather is more pleasant here, and where we had trees, I see meadows and flowers."

"There are forests here, Efanie. I'll have Nia assign someone to show you around and introduce you to the other factions nearby; I don't want you stumbling into the Naghelli lands before they know who you are."

"Naghelli?"

Victor chuckled. "I'll explain, but first, let's get moving; I want to see my home!" He nudged Guapo forward, and Efanie clicked her tongue, flicking her reins. That final leg of their journey went by quickly as Victor's interest was piqued the entire time. He watched the farmhouses go by, waved at the folks working in the fields, and more often than not had to stop and exchange greetings with former soldiers who recognized him. It seemed that most of the people living in that wide coastal valley were former members of the Ninth, and Victor couldn't have been happier to learn it.

"You're quite well liked," Efanie remarked as they finally passed through the little village—a tavern, a general store, a tailor and bootmaker, and a broad market square—and approached the steep cobbled road that led up the hill where Victor could see stone-block walls surrounding what he suspected was the courtyard of his home.

He nodded. "We fought for these lands together, so yeah, we respect each other." A single guard stood ready with a spear near the open gates, so Victor slid off Guapo's back and sent the steed back to the spirit realm before he approached. He'd only made it to within twenty yards before the guard stiffened, slammed the butt of his spear into the ground, and shouted, "Lord Victor approaches!" Victor chuckled, shaking his head. He supposed it wasn't hard for folks to recognize him; compared to the Shadeni and Ardeni, who made up the majority of the population, he was a giant.

He waved a hand in greeting. "At ease."

"Welcome home, Lord Victor!"

"Thank you." Victor turned and waited for Efanie to pull up in the coach, then moved around to help her down. When he held out a hand for Cora, and she took it without hesitating, he smiled with genuine pleasure. She took the steps in a single bound, and with everyone on the ground, they started for the gate. Several groomsmen hurried past, aiming for the carriage and the roladii, and Victor called after them, "Arrange for that coach to be sent back to Lady ap'Yensha."

"Will do, milord!"

Victor nodded and led the way into the courtyard of his new home. It was evident that the outer wall, courtyard pavers, and house's first-story walls were all built from the same stone—pale and smooth but slightly porous. It contrasted nicely with the dark polished wood of the trim, doors, and second-story walls. The windows were made of tinted crystalline glass that obscured his attempts to peek inside, and the steeply slanted roof and gables were covered in bronze-colored metallic shingles.

The home wasn't massive, but it was artfully built of materials that were clearly uncommon. It had a grand central entrance, with ten-foot-high doors made of finely tooled, dark mahogany—Victor knew this from having inspected the ingredients in the "hermitage" container—and branching out from that central structure were long wings where, he knew from studying the plans, he'd find bedrooms, a "trophy" room, more than one parlor, a dining room, a library, and even an "exercise hall." The central structure before him would hold the entry hall, the kitchens, and a great room complete with a grand fireplace. From the outside, Victor was pleased with how it all came together.

"Welcome home, Lord Victor," a familiar deep gruff voice said, and Victor looked down from his perusal of the house to see Gorro ap'Dommic, his governor. He stood on the hardwood decking that ran the length of the central building, just outside the broad double doors.

"Gorro! I see you got the place cleaned up for my visit." Victor chuckled and stepped forward, holding out a hand. Gorro took it, though it was more accurate to say Victor's hand engulfed Gorro's as he gave it a solid squeeze.

"Just so, Lord Victor! We just finished washing away the remnants of last night's debauchery."

They both had a chuckle, and then Victor let go of Gorro's hand and looked around, surprised to see no one else in the courtyard to greet him—not that he really missed the attention, but he'd expected it. "Kind of quiet."

"The kitchen staff are busy working on your welcoming feast, the grooms are seeing to your carriage, and the cleaning staff are busily finishing off their preparations for your return—airing the lord's suite and guest rooms, dusting, bringing in the house plants and all of that fine work. I'm sorry, milord, but the house has largely been unused since we finished construction, as I only require my small room, the map room and study, and a single place setting at the dining table."

"And what about Nia and the guards?"

"She's just on the eastern edge of town. We've begun construction of a guard barracks, courthouse, and jail, and I thought it wise for her to oversee the work."

"Ah, fair enough." Victor nodded, looking around. Then Efanie shifted, and he remembered her and Cora. "Oh! Gorro, this young woman is Cora Loyle, the ward I wrote to you about. Efanie is her . . ." Victor trailed off, unsure of the proper term for Efanie and her role with Cora.

Efanie opened her mouth, but when she failed to speak immediately, Gorro cleared his throat. "Based on what you wrote, milord, I believe the term you're searching for is 'governess.' Yes, I believe that would be appropriate. We've prepared rooms for both of them overlooking the garden." He smiled and sketched a short bow toward Cora and Efanie. "I believe you'll be pleased, ladies." He turned back to Victor. "The kitchen staff is anticipating a large party—Sir Tellen and Lady Thayla with their family. Do you have any confirmation regarding their attendance?"

"Not yet, but I'll be surprised if at least Thayla and Deyni don't come. We'll know soon; Valla flew out there to ask." Victor gestured to Efanie and Cora. "Why don't you show them their rooms, Gorro? I'm sure they want to unwind a little before all the company arrives."

"Yes, of course, Victor—it is still all right if I address you so?"

"Yeah, absolutely."

"Very good. Victor, I was hoping I might speak to you about the estate's balance sheet while you're here. Will we have time to sit down and go over the lease and tax income? We should review a list of employees and—"

Victor waved his hand, chuckling, and clapped the older man on the shoulder, careful not to knock him over. "I'll sit down with you, don't worry." He nodded to Efanie. "Go on now. I'm going to take a walk around before anyone else arrives."

"Your rooms are—"

"Up the stairs and all the way to the end of the east wing." During the campaign, when he'd been idly passing the time before sleep, Victor had often studied the building's plans, imagining the finished product.

Gorro nodded and waved toward the doors. "This way, ladies."

Several hours later, Victor sat in the gardens behind his home with Efanie, Thayla, and Valla. He'd spent time wandering around the town, reuniting with Nia and several members of his "household guard," who were all former soldiers in the Ninth, and then Valla had arrived with Thayla, Deyni, and Chala.

They'd hugged and made small talk, catching up on all the news they had already shared via Far Scribe book, but Victor enjoyed seeing their faces again and feeling Deyni's little arms wrapped around his neck. After a while, they'd eaten a delicious dinner featuring roast game hens and a pie that reminded him of dates and cinnamon. Now they watched Deyni demonstrate how her latest pet—a feline that resembled a bobcat save for its lustrous blue fur and short white tail—could perform a variety of tricks.

Cora sat on the cobbles near Deyni and her cat, and Victor couldn't get over the fact that Deyni was nearly the same size as the other girl despite being three years her junior. He didn't know if Cora was just small, a late bloomer, or if Deyni was ahead of the curve. Considering the question, he realized he was thinking in human terms, and despite her very human appearance, he had no idea what Cora's species was.

Did she seem human-like because of a common Fae ancestry like so many of the people he'd seen on Sojourn? Whatever the case, they seemed to be getting along well, and he was pleased to imagine Cora taking up with Deyni and her older stepsister. He frowned at the thought. "Where's Chala?"

"She's napping." Thayla gestured toward the house. "Last night, she didn't sleep—she set a snare in the field near our village, hoping to capture a lone boyii pup that's been coming around, raiding the feyris pens." Thalya laughed, shaking her head. "She stayed up watching the snare in the hopes of taming the little beast and adding it to the girls' menagerie."

Valla chuckled and gently stroked Victor's arm as she leaned against him, speaking almost wistfully, "Did she succeed?"

"No! He never showed his little thieving face! Now Chala's worried he met with the wrong pack and was killed by an alpha."

Victor sighed, too, and shifted, trying to get comfortable on the little stone bench. He'd come to the amusing realization that his home wasn't built for a man his size; he'd had to reduce himself drastically to enjoy the furniture and accommodate the door frames. He looked beyond the little square where the girls sat and saw the final rays of the sun on the glimmering waters of the Silver Sea. The view was even more spectacular from the windows and balcony of his suite in the house.

"God," he said wistfully, putting an arm over Thayla's shoulders and pulling her to his side. "It's so nice to be here. Look at that view!"

"It's beautiful," Thayla agreed. "You've got to come and see the village, Victor! There are so many little details I want to share with you! Ancient trees, mystical little hollows, burbling springs with water so pure and clear that you'll never want to drink anything else—I could go on and on. Everyone's so happy to be here!"

"It is a wondrous piece of land," Valla agreed. "I saw so many animals! Herd after herd of huldii and great flocks of ranevii. It seems the wildlife had fled the undead, and now they've made their way home. The forests are alive with colorful songbirds, and the fish in the streams are so thick, their scales shimmer and reflect the sun as I fly over."

"Ancestors!" Thayla chuckled. "I'd love to see the land from the air. What a thought! I never considered how such a perspective could color things."

Efanie cleared her throat—she'd been quiet, probably nervous to be in the company of people who were so close and affectionate. "I'm delighted that we'll be staying here."

Thayla's eyes widened, and she nodded. "That's right! This must be a very big change for you! Are you nervous?"

"Only in that I don't know anyone. I know how to take care of myself otherwise." She winked, and Victor laughed.

"She's Tier Eight, Thayla."

"*Eight*?"

"Well, I stopped pushing myself decades ago." Efanie sounded almost defensive as she added, "I grew busy with my career as a weapons instructor and guardian for the Volpuré girls, and then—"

"I was impressed!" Thayla held up a hand to protest. "I wasn't being critical!"

"Oh!" Efanie blushed crimson.

"Things are different on Sojourn," Victor added. "Anyway, I think it will be nice having her around, but her priority will be Cora."

"Of course!" Thayla smiled at Efanie. "As for not knowing anyone, you can rest easy—you know me now, and I'll show you around the neighborhood. Have you told her about the Naghelli, Victor? I think Kethelket would be quite interested in sparring . . ."

As she launched into a description of the Naghelli village and the wonders of their architecture, Victor smiled and leaned back against the wrought iron garden fence. He was pleased to have Thayla close again, even if it was just for a few days. More than that, Valla had been so affectionate that he could almost forget they were putting off a more serious discussion until after they'd spent some time relaxing on "vacation."

As the conversation drifted from topic to topic, he found his mind wandering, watching Cora pet Deyni's cat, giggling as it rumbled a fierce purr that Victor could hear from a half dozen yards away. He had a lot on his mind, or more precisely, a lot he'd buried away in his mind, but at that moment, things were good, and he was happy. Valla let go of his arm to lean closer to Efanie as she described the flowers of her homeworld and how they differed from those growing around Victor's garden.

"I'll be right back," he murmured, standing up. Valla smiled at him, and Efanie nodded, continuing her description. He stepped away from the bench and onto the patio with Cora and Deyni, pausing to squat down beside them for a moment. "Hey, Deyni, what do you think? Could you help Cora tame a pet like this?"

"Um, maybe not like Ziff, not at first, but we could find her a boyii cub! Oh!" Her magenta eyes sprang wide. "Victor! Chala almost caught one last night! Could Cora come over? We could help!"

"Not tonight, but soon, for sure. Does that sound fun, Cora?"

Busily stroking the cat's smooth fur, Cora didn't look up. "It does, milord."

"'Milord?'" Deyni giggled. "You can call him Victor."

"Is—" Cora looked like she wanted to ask permission, so Victor finished the thought for her.

"It's perfectly all right. I prefer it, actually, but you can call me whatever you want." He looked back at Deyni. "I was glad to see you and Chala, but I noticed Chandri's not around. Is she back at the village?"

"Oh, no." Deyni shrugged, reaching to tickle the spot above the cat's fluffy white tail with her nails; the creature's purr intensified. "She's exploring. She took a boat onto the Silver Sea."

"Really?" Victor's grin grew wider. "She wanted to do that. I'm glad she went through with it."

"She formed an exploration group with soldiers and a, um, what's it called when someone makes maps?"

"Cartographer?"

"Right!"

Victor nodded, pursing his lips in thought. "Do you girls want to see the beach? There's supposed to be a path that leads down from the garden."

"There is!" Deyni laughed. "I've seen it."

"Can we?" Cora asked, looking around the garden and over at the other adults.

"You can. This is your home now if you want it to be, Cora. Go explore."

"Come on!" Deyni grabbed Cora's hand and snatched up the delicate silken leash for her cat. Its purr turned into a grumble as it stood, arched its back in a massive stretch, and followed the girls down the path. Victor, a permanent-seeming grin stuck to his face, trailed behind. He watched as their walk turned into a run, and then they were gone, slipping through a wrought iron gate and dipping out of sight as they descended the hill toward the shore.

The only thing he could think about was how much he would have loved growing up in a place like this, with people like Thayla and her family around. He felt some heaviness lift off his heart at the thought, realizing Cora had a good chance of finding real happiness again.

When he reached the fence and leaned against it, looking down the hill to see the two diminishing figures as they hurried down the path, he turned his gaze toward the water and imagined Chandri out there on a ship, sailing toward distant shores, finding new "untamed" lands. He almost envied her, but he had his own adventures ahead, and he couldn't find it in him to be jealous. Soon, he'd be learning how to travel, physically, through the spirit plane, and he'd be visiting another world with strange customs and people descended from the likes of Ranish Dar.

His purpose for travel was different than Chandri's. He wasn't an explorer, but that didn't mean everything wouldn't be new to him. "Besides," he sighed, reaching up to touch Lifedrinker before remembering she wasn't with him. Folding his empty, grasping fingers into a fist, he gently thumped it against the fence. "I might not be going to explore, but I'll be going to fight. What's better than that? Nothing."

Status			
Name:	Victor Sandoval		
Race:	Quinametzin Bloodline: Epic 2		
Class:	Herald of the Mountain's Wrath: Legendary		
Level:	68		
Breath Core:	Elder Class: Improved 3		
Core:	Spirit Class: Epic 1		
Breath Core Affinity:	Magma: 9	Breath Core Energy:	2200/2200
Energy Affinity:	Fear 9.4, Rage 9.1, Glory 8.6, Inspiration 7.4, Unattuned 3.1	Energy:	34045/34045

Strength:	466	Vitality:	611 (672)
Dexterity:	190	Agility:	213
Intelligence:	172	Will:	649
Points Available:	0		
Titles & Feats:	Titanic Rage, Ancestral Bond, Flame-Touched, Greater Titanic Constitution, Titanic Presence, Desperate Grace, Challenger, Elder Magic, Born of Terror, Battlefield Awareness, Battlefield Presence, Aura of Command, Epic Quinametzin, Mountain's Resilience, Behemoth's Regeneration, Blood Supremacy		

Skills:	
System Language Integration	Not Upgradeable
Spirit Core Cultivation Drill	Advanced
Breath Core Cultivation Drill	Advanced
Cooking	Basic
Animal Taming	Basic
Unarmed Combat	Basic
Knife Mastery	Basic
Spear Mastery	Basic
Bludgeon Mastery	Improved
Axe Mastery	Epic
Grappling	Advanced
Sovereign Will	Advanced
Titanic Leap	Improved
Aura Veil	Basic
Spells:	
Iron Berserk	Epic
Inspiration of the Quinametzin	Epic
Channel Spirit	Improved
Enraging Orb	Basic

Globe of Insight	Improved
Project Spirit	Improved
Dauntless Radiance	Basic
Heroic Heart	Basic
Spirit Walk	Basic
Tether Spirit	Basic
Harsh Light of Justice	Improved
The Inevitable Huntsman	Improved
Aspect of Terror	Advanced
Imbue Spirit	Improved
Honor the Spirits	Improved
Alter Self	Improved
Energy Charge	Basic
Banner of the Champion	Basic
Wild Totem	Advanced
Impart Nightmare	Improved
Guard Ally	Basic
Volcanic Fury	Improved
Wake the Earth	Basic
Roots of the Mountain	Basic
Greater Spirit Binding	Advanced

ABOUT THE AUTHOR

Plum Parrot is the pen name of author Miles Gallup, who grew up in Southern Arizona and spent much of his youth wandering around the Sonoran Desert, hunting imaginary monsters and building forts. He studied creative writing at the University of Arizona and, for a number of years, attempted to teach middle schoolers to love literature and write their own stories. If he's not spending time with his dog, you can find Gallup writing, reading his favorite authors, or playing *D&D* with friends and family.